C000063015

AIRSHIP 27 PRODUCTIONS

Six-Gun Terrors Volume 2
© 2015 Fred Adams Jr.

Published by Airship 27 Productions
www.airship27.com
www.airship27hangar.com

Cover and interior illustrations © 2015 Zachary Brunner

Editor: Ron Fortier
Associate Editor: Gordon Dymowski
Marketing and Promotions Manager: Michael Vance
Production and design by Rob Davis.

ISBN-13: 978-0692479780 (Airship 27)
ISBN-10: 0692479783

Printed in the United States of America

10 9 8 7 6 5 4 3 2 1

VOLUME TWO
FRED ADAMS JR.

FANG AND CLAW

FANG AND CLAW

Who trusted God was love indeed
And love Creation's final law–
Tho' Nature, red in tooth and claw
With ravine, shriek'd against his creed–
- Tennyson, "In Memoriam"

I

CAPLOCK MOUNTAIN, NEVADA: OCTOBER, 1871

orporal Jamie McDiffett leaned back, carbine across his thighs, against an outcrop, one of those big domes that push like knuckles through Nevada's skin. He was appreciating the last bit of the sun's warmth trapped in the granite. Sunset came later atop Caplock's spiny ridge than it did to the lowlands, but once the sun went down, the temperature quickly followed suit in the rarified air of the High Sierras. From his aerie, McDiffett could see the whole valley below him before the sun fell below the horizon, and would see it again as soon as the moon rose.

Thirty feet behind him in a clearing among the tall pines, the rest of his patrol was slurping down salt pork and beans. He hoped they'd leave him enough for a decent supper. The patrol had been camped here for four days watching the valley for any movement of hostiles, but so far none had shown a face.

Hostiles. Jamie snorted to himself. What a fifty-cent word for redskins, he thought. Call them what they are: savages. Animals. He'd stayed on with the Army after the war, and ended up in the Indian campaigns. Suits me fine, he thought. I'd as soon shoot one of them as a coyote. Ain't no difference between the two.

Behind him someone said something he couldn't hear and there was laughter. Everyone laughed again, and Jamie turned his ear to catch what everyone found so funny. Because he was listening hard, he heard a faint scrape on the rocks to his right. He twisted, bringing the Winchester around and working the lever, jacking a shell into the chamber. He held his breath as he eased to a standing position, straining his eyes in the darkness.

A low rumbling growl came from below. He swung the rifle in the direction of the sound and heard another snarl to his left. He saw a pair of glowing green eyes rise from the rocks until they were as high as his own. At that moment, the moon cleared the ridge and Jamie saw what owned the eyes. He screamed and as life fled him, he heard gunshots, and the screams of his companions let him know he wasn't dying alone.

II

A pink dawn spread across the big sky behind Durken and McAfee as they lay prone on a bluff watching eight men gathered around a campfire eating breakfast and drinking coffee. The pair had been tracking the rustlers for two days since they stole thirty head of cattle from the north pasture of the Triple Six Ranch.

Beyond the fire, a water hole lay, and the cattle were milling around it, sharing with the gang's horses what little grass the hard scrubland terrain provided. Durken worked a quid of tobacco in his cheek as he studied the herd through a pair of binoculars, a gift from William Tecumseh Sherman when Durken and McAfee served him as scouts in the March to the Sea and Durken was sent to hunt down the notorious sniper The Angel. He said under his breath, "I can't see the brands in this light, but I see that steer with the broken horn from our herd. Those are our cows for sure."

McAfee looked over his shoulder. "In a few minutes the sun'll rise behind us. That'll give us an advantage we need, what with eight of them and only four of us." Smeck and Jones, two of the Triple Six's hands were waiting a hundred yards back with the horses. "Of course we could send Smeck back for the sheriff."

Durken grunted. "By the time he brought a posse here, those boys'd be halfway to Mexico. No, we have to take them now." He studied the men again. "Oh, hell."

"What's the matter?"

Durken passed the binoculars to McAfee. "Third man from the left. I'd know those sideburns anywhere." Below, a tall, heavy set man sporting a thick head of auburn hair and mutton chop sideburns was pouring coffee from a campfire pot.

"That's Bob Henry."

"Yep."

"He's a long way from the Twenty-third regiment. That complicates matters."

"No it doesn't. He's thrown in with bad people, and we have to deal with him the same as the others."

The pair crept back from their covert and stood out of sight from below. Durken and McAfee were every inch cowboys. Both were tall and rangy, though Durken had a few inches on McAfee, and both were lean and sinewy, as if their bones were connected with jerky. Durken's salt and pepper mustache arched over either corner of his mouth and drooped around his stubbled chin like the top bar of an ox yoke. McAfee had tried a mustache once, but it stuck straight out like a pair of brooms and he abandoned the project. When they spoke, both cowboys dropped the "g" from nearly every "ing" word but bring, swing and thing.

Smeck and Jones were waiting astride their horses and holding the reins of Sweetheart, Durken's Appaloosa and McAfee's big roan Thunder.

"We count eight of them," said McAfee. "And they definitely have our cattle."

Smeck said, "How do we take them?"

"McAfee and I'll come at them head on with the sun behind us. You two circle around south and get into position to shoot between them and the herd so we come at them from right angles and don't end up shooting each other. Sun'll be up pretty soon. Let's go."

Smeck and Jones rode quietly away and Durken checked the rounds in his revolver.

"Too bad about Henry," said McAfee. "We saw a lot of action together."

Durken holstered his Colt and shouldered his Winchester. "A man makes choices; he lives with them, or dies from them."

McAfee and Durken returned to their hiding place. The sun had risen behind them, but the camp below would still be in shadow for another minute or two. "Once we have the sun, I'll call them out," said Durken, "and they'll do one thing or the other."

"Yeah, they could throw down their guns and throw up their hands."

"Or they could die."

Durken watched the shadow erode from the camp until the morning sun was full in the rustlers' eyes. "It's time." Durken fired a shot with his rifle that blew the coffee pot apart.

"Put down your guns. You're surrounded," he shouted. But before he finished the sentence, the rustlers sprang to their feet, grabbing for pistols and rifles.

Some of them panicked and shot wildly into the sun. Durken and McAfee opened fire and three of the men fell in the first two seconds. Two threw up their hands in surrender. Two ran for cover among the bawling steers. Henry ran for the horses.

"Damn it all," said McAfee and whistled sharply. Thunder came at a trot and before the roan could stop, McAfee had a hand on the saddle horn and a foot in the stirrup. He vaulted onto Thunder's back and rode straight down the bluff and through the camp, scattering the embers of the fire.

Bob Henry had slipped a bridle on a grey mare and was riding her bareback at a gallop, reins in one hand and a rifle in the other. He turned his head and saw McAfee riding full tilt after him and brought his horse up short.

Henry swung around and snapped off a shot that grazed McAfee's ear. McAfee kept coming.

Bob's mistake was standing still. Before he could lever another round into the chamber, McAfee rode Thunder straight into the mare, the roan's thick chest catching her broadside and bowling the other horse over as if she'd been hit by a locomotive. Bob spilled and rolled and dropped his rifle.

Before he could get to his feet, McAfee was on the ground, his Winchester pointed at Henry's head. "Steady now, Bob. Don't be a fool."

Henry squinted into the sun and blinked as much with surprise as anything else. "Clarence? Clarence McAfee? Is that you?"

"Sure enough."

"Well, I'll be damned."

"That's a foregone conclusion, Bob. Now stand up. Slow."

Henry rose to a crouch. The wind ruffled his thick red hair. His eyes twitched side to side as he thought quickly and then fixed on McAfee. "You and me, we fought a lot of battles together, Clarence."

"That we did."

Henry grinned. "And we both saved each other's ass more times than we could keep track."

"That's so." McAfee touched his ear and his fingers came back bloody. "But you shot me, Bob."

He laughed. "Hell, I didn't know it was you." A long pause. "I don't suppose you could see your way clear to letting me get back on that horse and ride out of here."

"Can't do it, Bob. We messed in your business and killed a bunch of your friends. I let you go, it'll never be over for either of us. I don't want to spend the rest of my days looking over my shoulder and wondering when you might suddenly show up."

Henry's grin faded. His dark eyes widened. "Come on, McAfee, you don't have to do this. All I want is a chance."

McAfee thought it over for a moment and laid down his rifle. "All right, Bob. I'll give you a chance." His hand hovered over his holster. "Stand up like a man."

Henry hesitated and finally straightened. "Ain't much of a chance, Clarence."

"Nope, but it's all the chance you get."

The gunfire from the camp had stopped. The steers had settled down. The only sound was the desert wind in McAfee's ears. Henry's hand jerked for his gun. For Henry's single shot McAfee fired two bullets, both hitting their mark. Henry fell forward and lay face down in the sand. McAfee was still standing over him when Durken rode up on Sweetheart.

"Smeck and Jones have three of them back at the camp," said Durken. "One's shot up pretty bad; probably won't make it back to Bacon Rock." He looked down at the corpse and clucked his tongue. "Damned shame about Bob."

"I hated to do it," said McAfee.

"If not you, it would've been me or somebody else tomorrow, or next week, or next year. It's the choice he made." Durken turned Sweetheart and was about to ride away when he said, "We do have one problem, though."

"What's that?"

"In all that gunplay, two of Eldridge's cattle were killed. He's gonna be mad as hell."

Durken and McAfee rode with the rustlers; their horses roped together, some in their saddles and the rest over them to Bacon Rock to turn them over to the sheriff. Durken rode rear guard with a rifle in his hand and McAfee rode point with a double-barreled shotgun over his saddle. Smeck and Jones herded the cows back to the ranch.

It was the next morning when they finally entered the town's main street and tied up at the jail. Elmer Bennet, the town sheriff came out to greet them. Bennet was a big man with a red face and iron grey hair showing below his hat. "What's all this, McAfee?"

"Rustlers, Sheriff. Took thirty Triple Six cattle off the ranch. We chased them for two days and brought them back for you."

Bennet eyed the dead men. "You took these men, just the two of you?"

Durken shook his head. "Nope. We had help. Smeck and Jones were with us. They're seeing to the cattle."

"Well, get the live ones down. I got an empty cell inside."

One of the rustlers shouted, "They bushwhacked us, Sheriff."

Bennet said, "Is that so?" He looked to McAfee and turned back to the rustler and said, "Seems as if gunfire went both ways from the looks of his ear." He shouted through the door. "Shub."

Shub Carter, Bennet's portly deputy came out. "Get accommodations ready for these two." Then to McAfee, "Take the dead ones to the Doc's place, and get him to look at that ear. In the meantime, I'll find out whether there's paper out on any of these fellows. You boys may be in for a reward on one or two of them."

Durken and McAfee took the bodies to Doc Chambers, the town physician, dentist, coroner and undertaker where they laid them out in the shed behind his combination house and office. McAfee sat in a chair while Chambers poured raw whiskey over his ear. "Damn, that stings, Doc," McAfee grumbled.

"There's a cure for that too," he said, handing McAfee the bottle. McAfee took a long pull of the whiskey while Chambers finished dressing the wound. "No sense me putting a bandage on it, 'cause you'll just pull it off anyway. Keep the damned thing clean or it'll get infected and probably rot off."

McAfee handed Durken the bottle. He was about to take a drink when Chambers said, "Hold it right there, Durken, unless you're shot someplace I can't see. Medicinal purposes only."

"Well," said Durken, handing back the bottle, "if you're done with McAfee, I guess he and I'll go across the street to the Silver Dollar and we'll continue the healing process."

In the Silver Dollar Saloon, Liam, the owner was wiping down the bar with a rag, something that had become as unconscious a habit as breathing when he had nothing else to do with his hands. The saloon was deserted in the mid-morning. Liam's customers were either busy at their jobs or sleeping off last night's drunk. Liam, an Irishman, was born and raised in Nevada, but he still spoke with the Irish lilt of his immigrant parents, as if he were born with it like his red hair.

"Well, look at this, now. Durken and McAfee." He grinned. "A bit early in the day for a drink ain't it?"

"Depends on your point of view, Liam," said Durken. "Your work day's just starting out. Ours is about done."

Liam eyed McAfee's ear. "And it looks as if you boys were hard at it." He reached under the bar and set out two shot glasses. He took a bottle of whiskey from the shelf behind him and as an afterthought set out a third glass. He poured the drinks and raised his glass. "Here's to living another day."

Durken and McAfee knocked back their shots straightaway, but Liam didn't dump his drink down his throat. He poured it slowly over his tongue, tasting every drop. "Ahh, that's the stuff." He poured another round for Durken and McAfee and turned his glass upside down on the bar. "I'm guessing you need a little food with your breakfast. I'll see what's in the kitchen. In the meantime, enjoy the bottle."

Liam went into the back and a few minutes later came out with plates of beef and potatoes. Now tell me, boyo, who nicked your ear?"

McAfee and Durken were most of the way through the story when the doors of the saloon swung open and a man in uniform strode in. He wasn't particularly tall, but his erect military carriage made him seem so. He was lean and hard; his wind burned face and squint testified to tough years in the saddle, though his uniform was immaculate and his boots shone through a thin film of dust. He wore a broad-brimmed hat with crossed sabers and braid that identified him as cavalry and captain's bars on his shoulders. He looked as if he'd earned them the hard way. A flap-over holster held his pistol at his waist.

He stood for a moment, his eyes adjusting to the dim light of the saloon, then he stepped up to the bar and looked Durken and McAfee over. They returned the favor. "I'm looking for McAfee and Durken. Would that be you two?"

Durken grinned affably and said, "I'm Durken and this is McAfee. And who might you be, Captain?"

"I'm Captain Nathan Harper. I was sent to find you and deliver this message." He reached into his tunic and pulled out a sheet of paper. Durken unfolded it and McAfee edged around to read it with him. Liam craned his neck to see the message and Harper said, "Excuse me, sir, but the message is for their eyes only." Liam frowned, miffed, but backed away. He pointed to the bottle, but Harper shook his head.

Durken folded the paper and looked to McAfee before speaking. "Can you tell us what this is all about?"

"All I can say is that you men are to come with me. I don't have the authority to say more."

"I guess we'll have to sleep later," said McAfee. He took two silver dollars out of his vest pocket and laid them on the bar. "I'll have to finish the story some other time, Liam."

"That's all right, McAfee; I figure I'll hear it six times over when Smeck and Jones get to town."

Durken said to Harper, "Our horses are pretty tired, and so are we."

"We don't have far to go, and your horses will be seen to."

Durken nodded and turned to McAfee. "Then let's don't keep the General waiting."

Sweetheart and Thunder were still tied to the hitching rail at the jail. Harper's horse was at the livery. As they walked down the street, McAfee said, "That was the General's signature; no doubt about it."

Durken nodded. "Yep. What I don't understand is why he'd send anybody higher than a private or maybe a corporal as a messenger boy."

"Must be pretty important. I guess we'll find out soon enough."

They joined Harper and rode north away from Bacon Rock. Durken and McAfee were too tired to talk much, and Harper had nothing to say. He was considerate enough to not hurry them and push the horses, so the ride took almost an hour before the party reached its destination.

Ahead they saw the telegraph line paralleling the Union Pacific Railroad that cut across Nevada and linked it to the East and the West. They followed the tracks for a few miles to a kickout siding where an engine with a small train of cars stood beside a water tower. The engine bore the insignia of the U. S. Army on its cab and coal tender. The black iron beast looked like a faithful horse waiting for its master, every so often chuffing to let off steam as it idled at the ready. Beyond the short line of rail cars, four canvas tents stood in a field camp arrangement.

Harper led them to the second car past the coal tender, a Pullman coach painted a bright yellow with dark green trim like a circus wagon. Most of its windows were covered, and twin stovepipes poked through the roof near the front of the car. There Harper dismounted. Two soldiers guarded the car's small railed vestibule. Both snapped to attention as he approached. He and the cowboys tethered their horses to the vestibule's railing.

"This way, men," said Harper, climbing the iron step stairs. He tapped at the door. A voice grunted from inside and Harper opened the door and went in. Durken and McAfee looked at each other like two men about to dive down a pitch-dark well, shrugged, and followed Harper into the car. And there they found the General.

IV

General William Tecumseh Sherman sat behind an ornate desk in what looked for all the world like a Boston parlor with oriental rugs on the floor, delicate furniture, and a gilded fireplace with a finely carved mantle. Damask draperies hung from the rail car's windows to give the illusion of floor length dimension, and the chamber was softly lit by oil lamps in filigreed wall sconces.

Sherman, famous for sleeping in the same fly tents as his infantrymen looked as out of place as a blue thistle in a bowl of roses. If anything, he looked even more unkempt and haggard than he had when Durken and McAfee served him as scouts during the March to the Sea. He sat at the desk in suspenders and shirtsleeves. His grizzled whiskers hadn't seen a razor for days and his hair hadn't been brushed or combed for at least a week.

Harper snapped to attention and his sharp salute was answered with an offhand wave from the General's forehead. He looked up from a pile of papers he'd been poring over when they came in. A bottle of whiskey stood at a corner of the desk, and beside it a half-filled cut glass tumbler.

"At ease, Captain." He chewed the stub of an unlit cigar as he looked the cowboys up and down. "Durken and McAfee," he said.

"It's been a few years, General," McAfee said.

"You can't imagine how glad I am that you're here." He gestured to the dainty parlor chairs. "Pull 'em up and have a seat." Sherman frowned in disgust. "There's not a substantial stick of furniture in this whole rolling whorehouse. This car was fitted for the taste and comfort of the esteemed William Belknap. Is the name familiar?"

McAfee spoke up. "President Grant's Secretary of State in charge of War, as I recall."

"For the moment. The corrupt son of a bitch is sucking every illegal teat west of the Mississippi. Sooner or later it'll catch up with him, but for the moment he and his hoity-toity wife live like French royalty. Witness this coach. The only reason the bastard isn't in jail now is that the rest of Washington's just as corrupt as he is. And Grant lets him crack the whip on me. Politics." Sherman spat the last word like a curse.

"I requisitioned a rail car to make this trip," he swept an arm around the room, "and this is what those miscreants in the War Department gave me. Must have thought it was quite a joke. Frankly I'd rather sleep on the ground than in that canopy bed in the next room."

"Well, sir," said Durken, "I'm happy to see that your surroundings haven't altered your disposition."

Sherman snorted. "You know why I'm out in this million acre wasteland? Because Grant knows damned well that if he leaves an old war horse like me in Washington with no war to fight, I'll end up starting one for him on the lawn of the Capitol. I'm happy to be here instead, handling the Indian situation."

"Must have brought you to some difficult decisions," said McAfee.

"Bozeman Pass made up my mind for me and Washington's too," Sherman said. "The combined tribes butchered eighty soldiers wholesale, and that took care of most of the decision making. There are two objectives that must be met to win any war: first, defeat the foe in battle and second, crush the enemy's will to fight. We have achieved the former but it appears we have a long way to go to achieve the latter. What I'm about to tell you and what you're about to see is classified information. You remember what that means?"

Durken and McAfee nodded assent. Sherman reached under a pile of papers in the middle of his desk and pulled out a tintype photograph. "What do you make of that?"

The stark black and grey picture showed the corpse of a dead soldier. He lay on his back beside the ashes of a camp fire, his limbs splayed outward, a pistol in his hand, and his head turned toward the camera. His face, or what remained of it, was in bloody tatters, an eye hanging from its socket. His throat was ravaged, and his uniform tunic was torn open. A hole gaped in his chest where his heart had been ripped out.

The pair studied the photograph for a moment. "Where was this picture taken, General?" McAfee asked.

"About a hundred miles from here at Caplock Mountain, ten days ago."

"The Sierras. Been there once," said McAfee. "Scouted elk for our boss Homer Eldridge on a hunting trip. Pretty rough country."

Durken pointed at the photograph. "The man wasn't shot, beaten, tomahawked or skewered with arrows. He's been clawed, mauled, bitten. It doesn't look like Indians. It looks more like some animal got him," then to McAfee, "Wolves?"

"I don't know," McAfee replied. "Could be, or maybe a bear or a catamount; enough of them up there. But it looks wrong. Except for his face and chest, it seems he's pretty much intact. He hasn't been eaten."

"That's a bad way to die," said Durken.

"I agree," said Sherman. "Now look at this picture."

The second tintype showed the dead soldier in the foreground and behind him, the mauled corpses of six other cavalrymen. Rifles, pistols, and sabers lay scattered among the dead.

Sherman handed a large hand glass to Durken. "Look closely at the ground around those men."

McAfee and Durken peered through the lens. Durken grunted then said, "Shell casings, and plenty of them."

"Some of those Winchesters were empty when another patrol found this massacre. These weren't greenhorns. They were battle hardened troops; some of them rode with us through Georgia. There was one hell of a fight took place here, and all of those men are dead. And what don't you see?"

McAfee continued to study the photograph. "Enemy casualties; none of their dead are in sight."

"And nowhere nearby either. The patrols scoured the perimeter for a mile around. No sign of them." Sherman turned his cigar between his thumb and finger. "The likeliest culprit is Red Hawk."

"The Tonnewa chief?" said Durken. "I thought their tribe was in Ohio near where I grew up."

"They were 'relocated,' as the white population expanded," said the General. "First to Minnesota, then to Nevada. I have tacit cooperation from the other tribes in the area, but Red Hawk swore his people would never be uprooted again. Silver was found in their assigned territory recently, and you can guess what that means to Washington. It's time for the Tonnewa to be relocated again, and we can't find them. Does the term *guerilla* warfare mean anything to you?"

McAfee spoke up. "That's Spanish, isn't it? Means 'little war?'"

"Close enough; small bands engaging in ambush and hit-and-run raids on isolated locations. The Indians have been doing it since the French and Indian War, and maybe before that, but never anything like this. This is something new."

Durken was studying the picture. "Something else is missing, General: horses. Whoever killed these men took the horses."

"No, we found them scattered nearby. Apparently they were run off before or during the attack so the soldiers couldn't get away."

"And they left the guns and food," said McAfee. "None of these men appears to be scalped either. If the Tonnewa, or any Indians did this, it makes no sense. I count seven bodies. It's hard to tell from the picture; were the hearts missing from others?"

"Eight" said Sherman. "There was a dead sentry nearby. All eight had their hearts taken. And you've hit on the core of the matter, McAfee: *If* Indians did this. If they didn't do it, then who did?" He paused a moment as if weighing his next words carefully, "Or what?"

"You say 'what'" said Durken. "Do you have an idea?"

Sherman relit his cigar, and blew out a cloud of blue smoke. "A theory has emerged. It's pretty far-fetched. The attack may have been made by animals. It's too rocky for tracks, so we don't know for sure what species they might be, if that's the case. Maybe the Tonnewa have figured out a way to train them to attack in packs, like lions in Africa or wolves here."

"There may be something to that," said McAfee. "I've read that some of the tribes claim special relationships with animals; see them as protectors."

"I'm inclined to think that's a lot of medicine man hokum," said the General, "but at this point, we have to look at every possibility. That's why I'm bringing in an expert; man's name is Rupert Hollister. He's a world-renowned zoologist from England. It so happens he's visiting the West to study what he calls its 'indigenous fauna.' He knows as much about predatory animals as any man alive."

"There might be something else," Durken said, scratching his chin. "What if it's humans pretending to be animals?"

"Yeah," said McAfee, "I recall reading in some book about tribes of savages who wore animal skins, heads and all and used weapons kinda like maces or battle axes made with claws and teeth to do the same damage and look like the animals did the killing."

"That's a possibility I hadn't considered," said Sherman, "and that's why I've called you here, to give me a fresh perspective. But if so, how could they kill a patrol of eight armed men with nothing but hand weapons and leave no trace? Whatever the cause, we have to stop it and fast. I've kept this business quiet so far to prevent panic and unwarranted reprisals against the cooperative tribes. If word gets out, who knows what will happen?" Sherman turned in his chair, took a long breath and slowly let it out. "It's almost as if the enemy's turning the tables on me, using terror to sap the will of my men. I need this stopped and now."

Loyalty to cause and country often defies logic, but some commanders inspire it naturally by their nature and their actions. Durken and McAfee were silent for a moment, and finally looked to each other and nodded at some unspoken agreement. Durken said, "What can we do to help you, General?"

For the first time since they'd entered the car, Sherman, ever so faintly, smiled. "You two served me well as scouts in the Georgia campaign, and I haven't forgotten how you brought down the Angel, Durken. If ever I was on the run, you two would be the last men I'd want chasing my bony ass. I want you to go to Caplock Mountain and root out what did this to my men."

McAfee spoke up. "General, with all due respect, our boss Mister Eldridge won't be too receptive to us going off on a mission like this on such short notice."

Sherman grunted. "I've had the dubious pleasure of Homer Eldridge's acquaintance during the war when he sold arms to the Union Army. Harper."

The Captain, who had been standing silently all this time snapped to attention. "Yes, sir."

Sherman said around his cigar, "Have Corporal Barlow draft a dispatch to Mister Homer Eldridge in Bacon Rock. Tell him that the United States Government is requisitioning the services of his ranch hands Durken and McAfee for an indefinite period on a matter concerning national security. And that they are to be restored to their jobs on their return without prejudice. And that if he wants to continue selling beef to the U. S. Army, he'll cooperate. Finally, tell him that if he has any objections, he can stuff them up his pompous derriere. Bring it for my signature. He'll know my hand. He's seen it on enough requisition forms."

Harper saluted and left the car. McAfee looked toward Durken and both grinned. Sherman frowned. "Homer Eldridge got rich selling me arms and ammunition; it's about time he paid his country back a little. Now, men, raise your right hands; you're about to re-enlist."

"And once we're back in, as I understand the word 'classified,' that means we can't tell anyone where we're going or why, right, General?" said Durken.

"That is correct, now or in the future."

Durken grinned again. "Mister Eldridge is gonna love that, sir."

This time Sherman grinned too, in spite of himself.

V

"God damn it!" Homer Eldridge pounded his fist on his desk. "I can't spare both of you. We have a cattle drive to Reno in two weeks. How long would you be gone?" He chewed an unlit cigar in agitation.

McAfee said, "As the General states," he pointed to the letter in front of his red-faced boss, "for an indefinite period."

Durken and McAfee stood in their boss's office, McAfee hat in hand, and Durken hat on head. One wall of the high ceilinged room was covered with paintings collected by the late Mrs. Eldridge, and another an arsenal of exotic firearms on display, a reminder of Eldridge's previous profession: arms dealer (some said to both sides of the War of Secession). Trophy heads of elk, bighorn rams and antlered deer were gradually replacing paintings on a third wall and surrounded the window behind his desk.

"You read this message?"

"No, sir," McAfee replied, "I did not. But we were right there when he dictated it; heard every word."

Durken chuckled. "Especially the part about your objections."

Eldridge glared at Durken. The short, chunky owner of the Triple Six Ranch ran an agitated hand over his bald head then through his beard. He was dressed, as always, like a San Francisco banker as he thought befit his station as a "gentleman rancher." Though they'd never say it to his face, the locals all saw him as an overdressed pretender who never did an honest day's work. For as long as he'd owned the Triple Six, Eldridge had never roped a calf, branded a steer, or even so much as repaired a fence.

"The General had one other thing to say to you, Mister Eldridge," said McAfee.

"What's that?"

"He said, 'Don't make me come down there.'"

Eldridge fumed. "Who does that man think he is pulling a stunt like this?"

"Don't have to think," said Durken. "Seems to me he already knows."

"Well you tell him I ..." Durken and McAfee leaned in, eyebrows raised, all ears. "Oh, hell, never mind. Go find Smeck and Royster and send them over here. They won't do a worse job running things than any of the other idiots on my payroll."

As they strolled past the kitchen, Durken and McAfee looked in on Maggie, the plump, red-haired cook for the Mansion (as Eldridge called his oversized house). She was cutting carrots over a kettle of stew. She looked up as they stopped in the doorway. "And what trouble are you two in today?" she said, laying the knife on the mantel and wiping her brow with her red gingham apron.

"Oh, no trouble," said Durken with a grin. McAfee and I are just going away for a spell."

"And where might that be?"

"Ain't allowed to say." Durken's eyes looked to the side as he absently brushed his mustache away from his upper lip.

Maggie cocked a fist against her hip and a skeptical frown creased her forehead. "Is that so? And what'll you be doing at this unknown destination?"

"Ain't allowed to say that neither," Durken replied.

Maggie's eyes darkened. "If that stuffed shirt Eldridge sends you riding into danger again, I'll grind glass in his soup." Maggie and Durken's affection for each other was a long gone secret.

"Wasn't Eldridge gave the order, Maggie," McAfee said.

"And who might that be then, or can't you tell me that either?"

Durken shook his head. "'Fraid not. But don't worry, Maggie. Don't I always come back?"

"Aye, with a bullet hole, or a knife cut sewn up like a gunny sack or a bone or two broke." She turned to wag a finger at McAfee. "And you; if this one don't come back and you do, McAfee, you'd best watch your skinny arse 'cause you didn't watch out for his."

"Aw, Maggie, I'll be okay," Durken said, taking her hand in his, his face softening. "I promise you I'll come back alive." McAfee diplomatically turned and walked out the back door to leave the pair a moment alone.

As McAfee crossed the yard toward the bunkhouse a voice called out to him. "Clarence?" It was Eldridge's daughter Sarah, Miss Sarah to the hands in general. Like Maggie and Durken, Sarah and McAfee were also

"you'd best watch your skinny arse..."

fond of each other—maybe enamored would paint a truer picture—much to the irritation of Eldridge and the disappointment of many local beaus who dreamed of someday owning the Triple Six.

Sarah Eldridge was five feet two inches of blue eyes, blonde curls and feminine charm. Today she was wearing a green dress with ruffles at the hem of her skirt and the cameo brooch that McAfee bought for her in Reno. Instead of her usual smile, Sarah wore an anxious face, her pretty mouth pouting.

"Father just told me you and Durken are going away and you won't say where or why."

McAfee took off his hat and turned it by the brim in his fingers. "Yep, that's true, except for the 'won't.' I guess it's more like 'can't'."

"But when will you come back?"

"I can't tell you that because I don't know myself."

"It's dangerous, isn't it?" Tears welled in her eyes.

"Could be, but I'll have Durken along. He won't let anything bad happen to me."

Sarah noticed his ear. She reached up and touched it tenderly. "And you're hurt. Oh, Clarence," Sarah sobbed, and collapsed weeping into his arms. McAfee tucked a finger under Sarah's chin and lifted her face for a kiss that gave more promise than words could ever muster.

VI

After supper Durken and McAfee were packing their gear in the bunkhouse when Charlie Ming came in. Charlie, a former railroad cook Eldridge hired after the Union Pacific finished laying track in Nevada, was a good example of adaptation and survival, straddling two cultures. His appearance bore witness. He wore patched overalls and a shirt sewn from an old striped mattress tick, but a long queue hung from beneath his little brimless hat. From the neck down he was in the U. S. of A., but his head still aimed at his birthplace.

"Hey, Charlie," said Durken. "That was some good ham soup you brewed up tonight. Strong enough to climb out of the bowl and do a fandango all on its own steam."

Charlie grinned at the joke then his smile faded. "I hear talk you two go away; Smeck say nobody, not even the boss knows where."

McAfee nodded. "That's a fact." He stuffed his extra Henley shirt into his knapsack.

"Danger, no?"

"Maybe so," said Durken. "But I reckon we'll get by all right." He underscored the statement by pushing bullets into a few empty loops on his gun belt.

"I make sure you do." Charlie reached into the pocket of his overalls and pulled out something small. He handed it to McAfee, who turned it over between his thumb and forefinger. It looked like a coin, round, tarnished copper, about the size of a half dollar. Chinese characters encircled a square hole in its center.

Durken cocked his head to the side and squinted at it. "What is that, Charlie?"

"Good luck charm. It kept me safe all the years I am in America. Those symbols are the Five Poisons; Scorpion, Toad, Spider, Centipede, and Snake. You carry their poison to fight others' poison."

"Kinda like fighting fire with fire, huh Charlie?" said McAfee.

"Yes, fire with fire. Take it now. Be safe, my friends, and bring it back. I may need luck again someday."

Durken took the charm from McAfee and looked at it thoughtfully. He held it up to his eye and framed Charlie in the square hole. "We'll see that we do."

The sun was low when Captain Harper arrived at the ranch. Thunder and Sweetheart were saddled and ready, and after quick goodbyes, Durken and McAfee mounted up and rode away from the Triple Six without looking back.

"Are we going to the General's siding now?" McAfee asked.

"No, we have to make a stop in Bacon Rock to pick up another member of the party."

"You mean that animal fella what'd the General call him, McAfee?"

"Zoologist."

"Yeah, him."

"No," Harper interjected. "He's at the train now being briefed by the General. We located another man who might be an asset. He just got into town. Ever hear of Jack Butler?"

"The buffalo hunter? Yeah, I've heard of him," McAfee said. "Claims he's a cousin to Wild Bill Hickock and drinks a pint of whiskey with his breakfast every morning. I read in some book he shot more buffalo one year than Bill Cody."

"Oh that's dime novel bull, McAfee," Durken snorted.

"Actually, it's true," said Harper. "Cody was always pretty much a plainsman. So's Butler, but he's a mountain man in the bargain. As to who's the better shot, it's a tossup. The reason Butler shot more buffalo that year is that he spent more time shooting and less time posing for photographs and telling tall stories to nickel novelists. Butler's personality is closer to a grizzly bear than anything else, but he tracks and kills with efficiency."

They rode in silence for a while in the deepening twilight. Durken finally spoke. "Not to talk out of turn, Captain, but why'd the General bring Butler to this party?"

"Four heads are better than three," said McAfee.

Harper's voice took on a somber tone. "You saw the photographs. Those were good men, experienced Indian fighters, and someone or something took them down with no apparent casualties. I suppose the General figured that if he sent four hard cases on the mission, at least one of them would report back."

"Four?" said Durken, "Is that zoo fellow a hunter too?"

"No, he's just a scientist. I'm going as well." Durken and McAfee both looked at him with mild surprise. "I rode with the force that ran down Quantrill in Kentucky. The General mentioned *guerilla* warfare. That's how I'd describe Quantrill's tactics. The General thinks my familiarity with it will be an asset."

Durken whistled. "I bet you have some stories."

"None that I'm particularly fond of recounting. There was a job to be done. We did it. That's all."

Durken nodded. "That I understand."

Soon the lights of Bacon Rock came into view and in a few moments the three were riding up the main street of the town. The store fronts were mostly dark, but the glow of lamplight from the windows of houses dimly lit the dusty thoroughfare.

"So," said McAfee, "where do we look for Butler?"

At that moment, they heard a shout and a crash. A man came hurtling through the front window of the Silver Dollar still holding a chair by its legs. Harper said, "I think we just found him."

From what Durken and McAfee learned later from Liam, the brawl started when one of the local cowboys started baiting Butler about his bearskin hat, comparing it to a lady's nether regions. Butler endured the first two jibes, but at the third, he stood up, towering over the jokester, who was no midget himself. Butler jammed his fur hat over the cowboy's head, picked the man up bodily and threw him headfirst into the piano, interrupting Keever, the house musician's rendition of "Beautiful Dreamer." And the fight was on.

The cowboys found out quickly that drinking nearly a fifth of whiskey didn't slow Butler one bit. One punch from him was enough to put any of them on the floor. But there were plenty of cowboys. They swarmed over him like ants on a stick of penny candy. At one point, Butler had four men hanging from his arms, legs and neck but they couldn't pull the giant down.

In the midst of battle the little pianist picked himself up, righted the piano bench, set his derby back on his head, and followed the protocol of most saloons when a fight breaks out: keep playing and play loud.

Butler roared and charged into the nearest wall, slamming the cowboy hanging from his neck into the lath and plaster. The cowboy collapsed in a heap on the floor. Butler pried a second fellow's fingers loose and threw him over the bar. The man with the chair ran at Butler, and Butler caught him by the shoulders and spun, hurling him, chair and all, through the window.

Harper, Durken and McAfee ran through the swinging doors just in time to see Liam run over a tabletop and lay a club across the back of Butler's head with a two-handed blow fit to fell an ox. Butler staggered forward, shaking his shaggy head like a wet dog. He turned with a snarl and probably would have pulled Liam's arms from his shoulders if a bullet hadn't kicked up the sawdust on the floor in front of his feet. Harper cocked his revolver for a second shot. That brought Butler up short. "Quit it now, or the next one goes in your knee, Butler, and the one after that in your head."

Butler stared hard at Harper for a second then burst out in a hearty laugh. "Just having fun, Harper." He grinned and Durken and McAfee saw that his teeth were red with blood that dripped from his mouth into the coarse black spade of his beard and onto the front of his buckskin shirt.

"You know him?" McAfee said.

"We've met," said the Captain, never taking his eyes or his pistol off Butler.

The saloon doors swung in just then and Bennet and Shub ran into the Silver Dollar. "What the hell's going on in here?"

Liam pointed to Butler and shouted. "Sheriff, that animal started a fight and tore up the place."

Bennet looked around the room, noting a few broken chairs and five or six ranch hands sprawled in various degrees of unconsciousness. Finally he looked at Butler. "You started it?"

Butler grinned again. "Well, Sheriff, that depends on your point of view. That little weasel there," he pointed to the cowboy with the fur hat still over his head lying beside the piano, "made a few disparaging remarks about my headgear. You could say he started it. As for the first blow, that would be me."

"Who are you anyway?" Bennet started to ask over the jangling piano. Keever had switched to "Red River Valley." Bennet turned and shouted, "Stop that goddamned music, Keever, or I'll throw you in a cell for being a nuisance." The piano stopped in mid-measure. "Now, mister, tell me who you are and what you're doing in Bacon Rock."

Butler put on an expression of mock piety. "I'm just a citizen here in the service of my country, Sheriff. I . . ."

Harper cut him off. "This man's name is Jack Butler."

"The buffalo hunter?" Bennet frowned. "Well he won't be hunting any in my jail."

Harper held up a hand. "Sheriff, he has been conscripted by the United States Army. He's in my charge."

"Is that so?" said Bennet. "Well as of right now, I figure he's in my charge."

"I must insist that you release him into my custody." The Captain handed a paper to Bennet who studied it carefully then passed it over to Shub. "Those are his orders. I'm sure you recognize the signature."

Bennet turned to Durken and McAfee. "What's your part in this?"

McAfee spoke up. "We weren't in on the fight, Sheriff. We got here just before you did, but what the Captain here says is true. He's Army and they need him."

Bennet thought for a moment, considering the potential difficulty of wrestling Butler into a cell. The Sheriff figured he'd have to kill him first and chose discretion as the better part of valor. "All right, Captain, I'll turn this man over to you, but you take him far away from here, and if he ever sets foot in Bacon Rock again, I'll throw him in jail 'til he's as grey as my grandmother."

Liam spoke up. "What about all the damage to my place? I have plenty of chairs, but who's going to pay for that window?"

"Hell, Liam," said Durken with a chuckle. "It ain't no more than you get in here most Saturday nights."

Harper rolled his eyes, an exasperated look on his face. "Write up a statement of damages and costs and give it to the Sheriff. He can forward it to me and I'll see that the Army makes full restitution."

"That means they'll pay up," McAfee said to Durken from the corner of his mouth.

Durken nodded. "I figured as much, but thanks for nailing it down for me."

On the ride to the siding, no one spoke for a while, and then, as if he couldn't tolerate the silence for another second, Butler burst out in a bawdy song about an Indian squaw and a deer in rut. What his singing lacked in quality, he compensated in volume.

"For God's sake, Butler," said Harper, "will you quit that caterwauling?"

Butler finished his verse before turning to the Captain and saying, "What's the matter, Cap, don't you like music?"

"What I can't figure," said Durken, "is how you managed to kill so many buffalo. Seems to me if you sung like that, they'd hear it and stampede a mile before you could get them in your sights."

"It's because I know when I can sing and when I can't. Ain't that right, Cap?" he quipped to Harper. And he launched into another bellowing verse followed by a third that lasted almost to Sherman's train.

Harper said, "Butler, you come with me." He told one of the guards, a lanky sergeant missing most of his right ear, "Take these men to quarters and see to their horses."

"Yes, sir." The guard saluted and turned to McAfee and Durken. "This way, men."

The sergeant walked ahead with their horses. As they followed, Durken said to McAfee, "I'd give four bits to see the show in that rail car right now."

McAfee chuckled, "I'm guessing it'd rival Moses and the Pharoah."

"Yeah, but the General usually has things his way in the end."

"I suspect they understand each other already. Could be they've done business before. Harper seems to know Butler well enough."

"And no love lost between the two. Harper brought him to heel pretty quick, though."

Durken stopped to roll a cigarette and McAfee hung back with him, letting the sergeant walk out of earshot. "That tells me Harper's no Sunday school teacher, and Butler knows it. Butler rides the Captain, but he only gets as close as the end of Harper's tether. I get the feeling there's quite a history between those two." Durken lit his cigarette and resumed walking. "I'd also bet neither one of them sleeps while the other's awake."

Beyond the rail cars were canvas tents the size and shape of the old command tents officers used in the war. From one to the left came the soft nickering of horses. From one to the right came the soft music of a flute.

The sergeant pointed to the right. "You men will quarter there." He turned and led Thunder and Sweetheart into the tent to the left.

"All business, ain't he?" said McAfee.

"You didn't recognize him? That's Jim McKenna, one of the General's personal guard from the Georgia campaign."

"Don't recall I ever met him."

"You'd remember if you did. That man could put his fork down, shoot you in the head and go back to his breakfast without missing a bite. He's one of the coldest killers I've ever known."

"Well," said McAfee, "I guess the General knows what he needs."

"Yep," said Durken, grinding his cigarette under the heel of his boot. "But what does that make us?"

"I reckon we'll find out."

They pulled the tent flap away and stepped inside toward the sound of the flute.

In a corner of the tent, a lean man with steel-rimmed spectacles, sandy hair and a trim mustache sat on an army cot playing a silver flute. He was dressed in checked tweed trousers that ended just below his knees, canvas puttees, and red gauloises over a collarless white shirt. His head turned as they entered and he nodded acknowledgment of their presence and continued to play. In a moment the piece ended and the man set the flute on the cot and stood. He was tall and muscular in the way of a gymnast or an athlete.

"That's a piece by Mouret, isn't it?" said McAfee.

"Yes, indeed," the man said. He held out his hand. "I'm Rupert Hollister."

McAfee shook his hand and found the man had a grip as strong as his own. "I'm McAfee. This is Durken."

Hollister shook Durken's hand as well. "I'm pleased to meet you. General Sherman speaks very highly of you both." Durken and McAfee had met Englishmen once before when two of them, actors with a traveling Shakespeare troupe spent a week as Eldridge's guests at the Triple Six. Hollister's accent was similar, but less pronounced than theirs, as if traveling all over the world and speaking its other tongues wore down its edges a little.

"The General had some good things to say about you too," said McAfee. "He says you're an expert on dangerous animals."

Hollister chuckled. "I hold with the wag who says that an expert is no more than 'a man far away from home giving advice.'"

"I guess you qualify on that score," said Durken. "England's a pretty far piece."

"Oh, I'm not from England, though I was educated there. I was born in British Guiana – South America – my father was the overseer on a coffee plantation there. I grew up right on the edge of the jungle and that's where I first learned about what Tennyson calls 'nature red in tooth and claw.' And you gentlemen, where are your origins?"

"I'm from East Ohio," said Durken. "No jungles, just lots of cows."

"I'm from Providence, Rhode Island," said McAfee. "Fewer cows, more dogs and cats.

"Yet each has his story, unique in the world." He eyed them up and down. "So, first names?"

"We don't use them much," said Durken. "After a few years in the Army, we both got to thinking our first name was 'Corporal.'"

"And there's nobody else around here named McAfee, or Durken either," McAfee added. "Keeps things simple."

Hollister nodded once emphatically. "Well then Durken and McAfee it is. I was about to have a nightcap. Won't you join me?" He reached into a leather rollup and pulled out a dark, long-necked bottle. Another dip into the bag procured shot glasses. Hollister pulled the cork from the bottle with his teeth and poured rim high shots of a rich amber liquid.

"A word of advice, gentlemen, sip it first and enjoy the flavor a moment instead of just bolting it down."

McAfee sniffed his drink. "This is whiskey, isn't it?" he said, emphasis on "is."

Hollister grinned. "That's Scotland you smell, my friend. Single-malt and sixteen years aging in an oaken cask. That bottle's been around the world with me."

Durken sipped his whiskey, rolled it on his tongue for a second and nodded. "I see what you mean. That doesn't taste anything like the sheep dip they pour at the Silver Dollar. Usually need to drink a beer afterward."

McAfee sipped at his. "It's like drinking smoke."

"That's an astute description," said Hollister. "Now drink a little more."

"Got a kick to it," said Durken.

"Yes indeed," said Hollister. "And now, bottoms up." He held his glass high. "To adventure." He upended his shot and the cowboys followed suit. The whiskey burned the whole way down.

"That's some good liquor," said Durken.

"I save it for special occasions."

"Well, don't let Jack Butler see it, or he'll pour you a shot and put the rest in his canteen."

"Or just gulp down the bottle and leave you the stopper," Durken added.

Hollister nodded, corking the whiskey and slipping the bottle and glasses back into his rollup. "Yes, the buffalo hunter. The General had a few things to say about him as well. Working with him will likely be its own challenge."

"I can see where he might pose a problem now and again." Durken started rolling a cigarette.

"My fear is that he'll shoot to pieces anything that moves before I have a chance to identify it."

"I understand your point," said McAfee, "But from what I've seen in the photographs, it might be smarter to shoot first so you're alive to identify it later."

That remark pretty well shut down the conversation, so Durken and McAfee each took a cot, stowing their gear underneath. McAfee propped himself on one arm and opened his copy of *Tristram Shandy* to read by the yellow lamplight. Durken stretched out on his cot and closed his eyes. "If I snore, shoot me."

"I won't have to bother," said McAfee. "I expect Butler'll do it for me if you wake him up."

At that moment, Captain Harper pulled back the tent flap and stepped inside. His expression was grave. "Come with me, men," he said. "There's been another incident. This time it's civilians."

IX

Durken, McAfee, and Hollister followed Harper to the General's car. Harper rapped on the door and without waiting for a response, stepped inside. Sherman sat behind his desk, a look of agitation on his face. Butler, uncharacteristically quiet, spilled over the seat of one of the delicate chairs to the right. A weary young private, dusty from a hard ride, stood to the left, his hat in his hand.

Sherman turned to the private. "All right, everybody's here. Men, this is Private Willet. Now, Private, the whole story, in detail from the beginning."

"Sir, General, I . . ." Willet stammered.

Sherman turned his head to Harper. "Get this man a chair and pour him a drink."

Harper poured three fingers of whiskey into a glass and handed it to the Private, who lost no time in gulping it down. He sat in the offered chair and began his story.

"We were on patrol between Manson's Pass and Caplock Mountain yesterday afternoon, and as we always do, we swung past a silver claim just beyond the pass. The Mingott Brothers, Seth, Byram, and Aubrey have a mine there. They work it hard; they've tunneled deep into the hillside. I guess it's a lean vein and they do get some silver from it, but I'd bet they don't get far past breaking even.

"Anyway, it was about half past three when we got to the near end of the pass, and that's when we saw the vultures circling. I've seen plenty of dead people, but my Lord . . ." Willet began trembling, his face ashen.

"Easy, son," said Sherman patiently. "Just tell us what you saw."

"There were five of them at the camp, all dead; the Mingott Brothers, at least I think that's who they were. Their faces were mauled something awful, so it was hard to be sure. They and two colored men who worked for them were all near the fire pit in the middle of the tents. They were torn to shreds. And all five had their hearts ripped right out of their chests."

"Were there guns out? Did it look like a fight?" Harper asked.

Willet swallowed hard and went on. "Two of them had revolvers in their hands. One of the coloreds had a ten gauge shotgun. Looked as if he fired both barrels. The other one had a hatchet in his hands."

"Were there tracks?" said Hollister, eagerness in his voice.

"The ground was packed pretty hard in the middle of the camp, as you'd expect, but behind one of the tents, we found paw prints."

"Describe them to me." Hollister had produced a small leather bound notebook and a pencil.

The Private shook his head from side to side. "I don't know. They were animal tracks for sure; paw prints about the size of my hand."

"With your fingers open or closed? I'm trying to get an idea of size."

Willet held up his hand and spread his thumb and fingers. "About this big."

"And how many toes?"

"To be honest, I was so shook up I didn't bother to count them. My God, I've never seen anything the like of this. Those bodies . . ."

Hollister scribbled a quick drawing on the page of his notebook and held it for Willet to see. "Did they look like this?"

"I can't say for sure. I didn't look at them too much. I was more concerned about the dead men."

"You said it was a silver mine," said McAfee. "Could you tell if any silver was taken from the camp, maybe a robbery?"

"There was no way to know. We didn't find any in their tents. They may have had their cache buried someplace nearby or hidden inside the tunnel."

Harper said, "Has the site been disturbed since?"

Willet shook his head. "No, sir. Some of the men wanted to bury the bodies, but we'd all heard the order that came out after the Caplock Mountain incident to leave things as they were. We covered the bodies with blankets and drew straws to see who would ride to the outpost and who would stay there and stand guard. We were all spooked, and I'm not ashamed to tell you, I was glad to ride away from that place. The Lieutenant tried to send a telegram to you, but the wires were down someplace in between, so they sent me on horseback with the message."

Sherman turned to Harper. "I want you to go to Manson's Pass immediately. I want you to get on the trail before it runs cold. Leave my car here and take the train. You can ride it as far as the depot at Lickskillet and take the horses from there. Find out what happened and who's responsible."

"Yes, sir."

Sherman turned to Willet. "And you, Private, get some rest. You've done your duty. There's a cot waiting for you in the billet tent. Dismissed."

Visibly relieved that he didn't have to go back to the scene of the slaughter, Willet rose wearily to his feet and saluted. "Thank you, sir."

Willet stepped out of the car and closed the door behind him.

Durken broke the silence. "So, General, do you still think it might be the Tonnewa tribe killing these people?

Sherman stared at his desk for a moment and looked up. "At this point I don't know what to think. I'm counting on you men to find out, and quickly. You saw what this has done to Willet. If it keeps up, it'll terrorize troops and civilians alike, and that I cannot have. Do what you have to." The room was silent. He picked up a sheaf of papers from his desk, looked at them for a few seconds then as an afterthought looked up and said, "Dismissed."

X

The gear and horses were loaded into a box car and the men into a troop coach. Within a half hour, the engine was chugging its way north across the darkened desert. Butler snored at the far end of the car. Hollister sat writing in his notebook. Harper rode forward with the engineer. Durken and McAfee slumped in seats on opposite sides of the aisle as the car rocked gently from side to side.

"Thought occurred to me," said Durken.

"What's that?"

"We might be riding the wrong direction to find answers."

"You mean Seven Stars?"

"He'd be someone to talk to. He knows more about more than anybody I ever met."

Seven Stars, the blind chief of the Monatai tribe—neighbors of the Triple Six ranch, had been educated as a boy by Jesuit missionaries and served as a secretary to Father Leonardo, a former Vatican expert on early civilizations and pagan religions. Seven Stars knew of realities that other people scarcely dared to dream.

McAfee nodded. "Let's see what we learn at Manson's Pass. No sense giving him half a picture."

Durken nodded. "Makes sense to me." He pulled the brim of his hat below his eyes and ended the conversation. McAfee continued for a long while staring through his dim reflection in the window glass into the darkness beyond and wondering just what the hell was out there.

XI

The train pulled into the Lickskillet depot early the next morning and as they climbed down the steps from the vestibule, they saw Harper climb down from the cab of the locomotive. He wasn't alone. Jim McKenna was right behind him.

Durken spat tobacco juice in the dust at his feet. "Guess the General decided to send five killers instead of four."

Before McAfee could answer, Butler came swaying down from the train behind them. "Good morning, Cap," he called to Harper. "Good day to shoot something. Where can a man get a drink in this town?" Harper opened his mouth to say something and thought better of it.

McKenna's cold blue stare fixed itself on Butler, and Butler stared back at him for a long moment then slapped his thigh. McKenna's pistol was half out of its holster when Butler burst out laughing. McKenna relaxed and turned on his heel to follow Harper who had already begun walking away.

Harper was still laughing when Durken stepped into his circle, almost nose to nose. Butler stopped laughing.

"Let's understand each other. I don't know what's between you and Harper, Butler, and I don't give a hog's ass about it. But between you and me, don't go playing pranks with Jim McKenna when I'm in the line of fire."

Butler's eyes twitched sidewise like he thinking something over. McAfee's fingers brushed the handle of his Colt. Something woke up just then in the back of Butler's head, maybe common sense. He grinned at Durken. "Just having fun, Durken."

"I've seen your idea of fun twice now, Jack. Don't show me a third." He turned and walked away from the grinning Butler, and McAfee waited until Durken was two steps out of Butler's reach before he turned the same direction.

"Something wrong with that man," said Durken.

"Maybe he's come to believe too much of his own myth."

"What do you mean?"

"Man like that has nothing else in his life but his reputation, and that gets bigger and more outlandish every time some new dime novel comes out. I think he's got so he believes it all and if he doesn't live up to it every day he won't exist anymore."

Durken pondered this for a bit then said, "I think he's just a drunken son of a bitch. And for the life of me, I can't understand why the General put him in the same sack with Harper and McKenna, what with the hard feelings between them."

"Like the Captain said, Butler tracks and kills with efficiency."

"And we don't?"

McAfee stopped and faced Durken head on. "You saw that picture. Eight armed men, soldiers, all killed the same way. I'm guessing whatever happened it wasn't one attacker, or two or even three. There were plenty of hands in this, and at best you or I can only shoot one bullet at a time, and only in one direction at once. And if he sent a whole troop up here, word would get out pretty quick what was going on."

Durken shook his head. "Well, if the General wants to keep this business quiet, Butler's about the least quiet person he could send."

Hollister stepped up to them. He was dressed in his knee pants and puttees and had added a matching tweed jacket cut like a suit coat and belted at the waist. He also sported a short brimmed grey hat like a banker's Stetson. "Chilly this morning," he said, rubbing his hands together. "Where we might we get some breakfast?"

Lickskillet had only one hotel, and its dining room served as a general meeting place for the community every morning. The décor was anything but elaborate, but the coffee was hot, the slabs of ham were thick, and the eggs were fresh. As the three walked in, they found Harper and McKenna already at a table and pulled up chairs to join them. An aproned waiter took their orders and in a few minutes, the five of them were digging into breakfast.

A few minutes into the meal, the Sheriff, a tall, red faced man with the spidery veins of alcoholism netting his cheeks and nose, came over, his mug of coffee steaming in his hand. He looked them over and spoke directly to the Captain. "You're Harper?" Harper nodded. "I'm Ben Stafford, the Sheriff." He didn't offer a hand to shake and neither did Harper. "I got word from the Governor's people that you were coming and I'm to give you whatever help you may need."

Harper smiled thinly, "Right now, we don't really need anything Sheriff. We'll be moving out as soon as we've eaten."

Stafford said, "Just the same, before you go, stop over the jail. I think we should talk."

Harper nodded. "I can do that. I'll come over as soon as I finish my coffee."

Stafford nodded and turned to McAfee, Durken, and Hollister. "You three ain't soldiers."

"Actually, we are," said Durken, "at least me and him." He pointed to McAfee. "You might say we reenlisted."

Stafford mulled this over, nodded again, and left.

Harper and McKenna drank the last of their coffee and left for the jail while McAfee, Durken, and Hollister finished eating. As they walked away from the table, a tall cowboy in a leather vest over a faded flannel shirt yelled across the room, "Hey, short pants."

Durken and McAfee stopped but Hollister kept walking.

"Hey sonny, I'm talking to you. Don't you walk away from me."

Hollister stopped, turned, and smiled. "Were you addressing me, sir?"

The cowboy laughed and said to his friends, "Did you hear that? He don't just dress funny, he talks funny too." The friends guffawed. The cowboy stood up and walked all around Hollister, and McAfee realized that Hollister had kept walking to give himself space. Hollister turned on the balls of his feet as the cowboy swaggered around him, the Englishman still smiling and never losing eye contact. He was as tall as the cowboy, but fifty pounds lighter.

"You know, boy, I don't like you."

"The feeling is mutual."

The hotel's owner, a short heavy man in a vest and a collarless shirt came around the counter. "That's enough, Roy, leave the man alone."

"Shut up, Thompson," said one of Roy's companions, pointedly running his thumb over the hammer of his pistol.

Roy continued his pacing as Hollister continued to turn, moving but seeming not to move. McAfee started forward, but Durken put a hand on his arm to stop him. "Let it play out a while."

The cowboy looked him up and down. "I don't see no iron on you. You better run, boy, while you can."

Hollister maintained his smile. "I don't need a gun to deal with the likes of you, cowboy. I just have to hold my nose."

Roy's eyes went from mean to angry and he hauled off and threw a roundhouse punch at Hollister's head. Hollister caught Roy's forearm and twisted it using the bigger man's momentum to throw him forward into a somersault that landed him flat on his back. Still holding Roy's forearm, Hollister planted his foot in Roy's armpit and twisted the arm a few degrees the wrong way. Roy bellowed in pain.

"You're really stupid, you know?" said Hollister, still wearing his hat and smiling. "You swung at me with your gun hand, and your holster's out of reach from the other." He kept Roy's arm twisted with his left hand and with his right plucked the pistol from its holster and sent it spinning across the floor. Two of Roy's friends started out of their chairs and Durken's Colt was out while they were still in a crouch. "Stay put."

Roy twisted his torso and tried to kick at Hollister, who let go of Roy's arm and caught his foot. Another two handed maneuver and Roy was face down on the floor. He struggled but had no more success than an insect impaled on a hatpin. "Now, cowboy, do you still think I'm funny?" The good humor was gone from Hollister's voice. He twisted the foot and Roy grunted in pain. "Or would you like to be my friend?" He twisted the foot again, a little bit harder.

"You know, boy, I don't like you."

"Yeah! Yeah!" Roy shouted. "I want to be your friend."

"Good. That's it then." Hollister let go of the foot and Roy rolled over on his back and sat up, glaring at the Englishman, who offered his right hand to pull him up. When Roy took it, he tried to yank Hollister off his feet, and Hollister hit him with a left hook that laid him out cold on the floor.

"When he wakes up," said Hollister to Thompson, "tell him he may want to be my friend, but I don't care to be his."

As they crossed the street headed back to the train, McAfee said, "That was some fancy fighting, Hollister."

"When you travel to other places, you learn things if you pay attention."

Durken said. "I've seen Charlie Ming, our cook at the ranch, fight a little like that once."

"Well," said Hollister, "He sounds like an interesting fellow. I hope I get to meet him some day."

McAfee nodded. "I expect you two'd get along just fine."

Hollister stretched and took in a deep breath. "So where do we go now?"

McAfee pointed northwest to a mountain range, blue in the morning haze with white capped peaks as if a stray wave from the ocean had wandered inland. "There."

Back at the train, they found their horses waiting to be saddled. Two pack horses were already laden with equipment and provisions. Butler and Harper were arguing again.

"There's no place to carry a case of whiskey, Butler, and even if there were, I wouldn't allow it. That's all there is to it."

"Come, on Cap; be reasonable," said Butler, his foot on a small wooden crate. His gruff voice was creeping from joviality to anger as the dispute continued. "I can't start the day without a good stiff drink, nor end it neither."

"I'm in charge of this mission, and I say no. Your drinking problem is just that, Butler," Harper said, the tension rising in his voice, "Yours."

Durken wasn't watching Butler and Harper. He was watching McKenna, who had stepped a few feet behind the mountain man to his left. Butler was too absorbed in the argument to watch two doors at once. "Now you listen here, Cap," said Butler, a little louder, poking a finger at Harper's chest.

Before there was anything to listen to, McKenna, in a blur of motion, drew his Cavalry Colt and fanned a flurry of shots into the box. Splinters flew, glass shattered, and as the smoke from the gunfire drifted away, whiskey poured through holes in the wood and disappeared into the sand. Butler stood openmouthed and stared first at the ruined box, then at Harper, and then at Mckenna, who stood two paces away with his pistol at arm's length aimed at Butler's head. Butler snarled and bared his teeth. McKenna cocked the hammer.

"I'm going to give you the benefit of the doubt and assume that you can count, Butler," said Harper. "Six rounds in the pistol; five went in the box. Where the last one goes is up to you."

This time, Butler didn't laugh. His eyes slowly moved first to one side then to the other. He turned without a word and lumbered away from the siding. McKenna held his pose, following Butler with his gunsight until he disappeared around a corner, presumably in search of an open saloon.

"Captain," said McAfee, "With all due respect, I think it's time you explained to us what's gone between you and Butler, and why he's even here."

Harper turned to McKenna. "Go to the telegraph office and see whether there's any new word from the General and then see to the horses." The sergeant saluted and walked away.

Harper stood for a full minute before speaking. "Yes, I think you should know, since this mission has put us all together. What I tell you stays with you. Durken, McAfee, that's a given, but, Hollister, I need your word that the story goes no further.

Hollister nodded. "I understand, Captain. I agree."

"Let's go in the coach where we can sit comfortably. It may be a long time before we can do that again." They followed Harper into the coach where they all sat. Harper lit a short cigar. Durken and McAfee rolled cigarettes. Hollister pulled a briar pipe from his pocket and stuffed it with tobacco.

And Harper began his story.

"You know that Butler is close kin to a fifty-cent whore. He'll serve anyone who pays him. But he's also a bully and a coward for all his size and bluster. I first met him when he was working as a scout for the Union Army."

He turned to Hollister. "Durken and McAfee know about Quantrill's Raiders. Are they familiar to you?"

Hollister nodded. "Pro-Confederate irregulars who finally were conscripted into the Southern Army. They pretty much burned Lawrence, Kansas to the ground and in one afternoon killed a hundred and sixty people to avenge the deaths of some of their wives who were held hostages against them and died in captivity. They were the horseback equivalent of pirates, or if you prefer, privateers once they were brought under the aegis of the Confederacy. From what I learned from reading about them they honed guerilla tactics to a sharp edge."

"There's that word again," said Durken.

Harper continued, "My command went after Quantrill and we brought him to ground in Kentucky. Butler scouted for a squad that chased down Bloody Bill Anderson. The war ended, but some people wouldn't quit. Bill Anderson's chief lieutenant Archie Clement, 'little Archie the bushwhacker' they called him, kept a gang of the Raiders together and raised holy hell in Missouri right after the war."

"We heard tales of him clear down in Georgia," said McAfee. "It seems he had a habit of scalping his kills. They called him 'Bloody Bill's head devil.'"

Harper nodded. "He and his men killed twenty-two Union soldiers in a train ambush in sixty-four. They scalped and otherwise mutilated all the corpses. After the war, they terrorized Missouri, disrupting elections and generally robbing and pillaging. Butler was part of a group of four scouts who tracked Clement, trying to find his hideout. Clement's boys got the drop on them and took all four of them prisoner.

"Clement knew who Butler was. Apparently his reputation preceded him, and Archie thought Butler would be a valuable asset, or maybe a bit of prestige to have under his thumb. Clement offered a deal to Butler: join the Raiders and he'd let him live. As I said, Butler was a coward and would likely sell his own mother to keep himself alive. He agreed. Then Archie told what the price was for his initiation into the gang. He had to kill his three companions, but first he had to scalp them and give their scalps to Clement."

Harper was silent for a moment. Durken said, "Since he's still walking around, I'm guessing that's what he did."

"Yes, the animal killed three good men after he scalped them alive to save his worthless neck. Apparently Butler's loyalty swung with the pendulum of victory. He was savvy enough to see that Clement and his men couldn't last, so the first chance he got, he ran away and turned himself in to the Army giving them a tall tale about how he infiltrated the Raiders and could tell them all about their whereabouts and operations. Killing his comrades came out later when Clement's men were captured and Clement was shot off his horse in Lexington. The feisty little bastard was lying on the ground and still trying to cock his pistol with his teeth when he died.

"Clement's men had plenty of stories to tell about the three months that Butler rode with them. I figure most of it to be lies, trying to get back at Butler for selling them out, but if half of what they told is true he was near as bad as Archie Clement himself.

"A warrant was issued for Butler, and I served it myself. Someone like him is never hard to find. But before he could be tried and hanged for murder, desertion, treason and other charges, he was pardoned. Apparently he had some friends in high places. Washington was chaotic after the war, and plenty of things happened that never should have. Butler's pardon was one of them."

"I get the impression," said Hollister, "that your feelings toward Butler are more than frustration that someone you arrested has gone free."

Harper drew a long breath. "One of the captives Butler scalped and killed was Andrew Harper, my brother."

No one spoke for a moment, then McAfee said, "And the General knows this?" Harper nodded. "Then why put the two of you together like cats in a sack?"

"As I said earlier, Butler is good at what he does, and the General wants the job done quickly."

"But there's more."

"There's always more. The longer I'm a soldier, the more I hate politicians. It seems Butler's pardon has become something of an embarrassment to certain people in Washington. It would be convenient for them if he went on a dangerous mission and never came back."

"That explains McKenna," said Durken.

"Not exactly. In some ways the General is doing me a kindness, putting me in a position to avenge my brother. The mission comes first, but Sherman always has an eye on tactics. McKenna is a threat to keep Butler in line, but his real role in this business is first target."

Durken said, "Things boil over, Butler sees McKenna as the bigger danger and goes for him first instead of you, and he never gets the chance to fire at the second target before it fires at him."

"Yes." Said Harper, "and now you know."

The coach door opened and McKenna stepped in and saluted. "Sir, the horses are ready. Butler hasn't returned. Shall I fetch him?"

"Yes, Sergeant. Try to bring him back breathing."

McKenna returned in a few minutes with Butler over his horse. Durken and McAfee were afraid McKenna had shot him, but it turned out that he was dead drunk. Unable to take whiskey with him, Butler decided to drink as much as possible before he left. The team saddled up and soon was riding away from Lickskillet and heading for Manson's Pass.

XIV

The party rode for more than an hour and experienced the unsettling feeling a great level plain creates. They could see the blue mountain range ahead in the distance, and if they looked back, they could see the dim outline of Lickskillet melting into the horizon, but the mountains seemed no closer.

"If you don't mind me asking, Captain," said McAfee, "What did the sheriff have to say?"

"Like most lawmen, he resents the Army moving on his territory and leaving him out of the conversation. You could give him the benefit of the doubt and say he's looking out for the people who pay for his badge, but he was mighty pushy about wanting to know what's going on. In fact the discussion got pretty loud near the end. All sorts of rumors have sprung up and people are getting edgy."

"Seems like a reasonable reaction," said Durken, "knowing what we do."

"Until the General says different, the orders stand. We can't tell a soul."

They passed through mile after mile of sand and scrub seeing nothing alive but an occasional skittering lizard or a snake weaving a tortuous path from one spot of shade to another.

"Fascinating that anything at all lives out here," said Hollister. "I hope we pass this way on our return. I'd like to take a little time to study the reptiles, perhaps collect a few specimens."

"First things first, Hollister," said Harper. "The General said maybe the Indians found a way to train wild animals to attack in a group. I know wolves do, and I've heard that lions hunt in packs."

"Prides, Captain," said Hollister with no condescension in his voice. "A group of lions is called a pride, and it's only the females that hunt in the group. As far as has been observed, besides lions and wolves, only hyenas and wild dogs hunt in packs, but science learns new things all the time."

"And you've seen all of these creatures?"

Hollister nodded. "I've been fortunate enough to have observed them all in the wild."

"What about training them?" Durken said. "I saw a circus once where a man had two lions in a cage with him and he made them sit, stand, and roll over just like a dog might."

"Although I've never seen them firsthand, I have heard of tigers being trained as circus animals, and the chief of one of the native tribes near my father's plantation kept a full grown jaguar on a leash as a pet. But training them to hunt in a group would be difficult if not impossible. Cats are generally solitary animals. Dogs, however are often trained to hunt in a pack, like those trained to hunt foxes in England. Wolves are unlikely candidates because before they could be trained, they would have to be domesticated, perhaps raised in captivity from birth."

"But getting a gang of lions or tigers or hyenas out here is unlikely," said McAfee. What about bears?"

"Bears are familial, not social creatures and don't usually share in a hunt. Of course the key word is 'usually.' Nature has its aberrations. I'll reserve judgment until I see the kills."

It was about this time that Butler woke from his stupor and hollered and bellowed, demanding to be untied from his undignified position over his saddle. In a few minutes, the bleary-eyed mountain man was upright, both feet in the stirrups and reins in his hand, but if Durken or McAfee had to bet, they'd put their chips on the horse doing the steering.

A lone rider approached from the direction of the mountains. At a distance McAfee could make out his cavalry hat, and as he came closer, saw his corporal's chevrons. He pulled up beside Harper and saluted.

"Captain Harper?" Harper nodded. "I'm Corporal Travis. The telegraph lines are working again. General Sherman sent word you were coming. Major Denning sent me to meet you and conduct you to the site."

"Carry on, Corporal."

Travis wheeled his horse and set off at trot. "Guess we won't be stopping any time soon," Durken said and nudged Sweetheart in the ribs.

"Rough as the terrain is up there, I'd just as soon ride in the light of day," McAfee said and flicked his reins, setting Thunder after them.

The rock-strewn scrub soon gave way to grassy slopes with a few stunted trees and shrubs. The trail was hard ground and as they climbed the mountainside, the way grew steeper and the trail was crisscrossed with roots belonging to the pines and the larch trees that looked like petrified snakes or tendons standing out on a straining arm. The higher they went, the denser and taller the pines grew, their upper branches blocking the sun and creating a green twilight in the middle of the afternoon.

Further along, the trail devolved into a series of switchbacks zig-zagging across the mountain's face, compensating for its steepness. McAfee looked back at Hollister, who seemed to be looking at everything but the path.

"Remarkable," he said. "First growth trees; a forest primeval if ever I've seen one. Your country fascinates me. It seems to have a little of everything in its geography and its seasons. Will we go as high as the snow line?"

"Doubtful," said McAfee.

Butler, who rode in sullen silence to this point, spoke up. "You been here before, McAfee. Any towns close by where a man might get a drink?"

"Only Pisspenny, far as I remember, and that's about a day's ride to the south."

"What an odd name for a town," said Hollister. "Why is it called that?"

"The place started out as just a trading post and a few other buildings, but when people started coming this way looking for silver, a man named Roy Jenkins, who owned the trading post and the saloon decided to make it official and name the town Urgent, his way of saying 'argent'."

"From the Latin *argentum*, meaning silver," Hollister chimed in.

"Right. Anyway, as the town grew and the need emerged, Jenkins built a long row of outhouses and decided to charge a penny to use one. So, now most people just call it Pisspenny."

Butler snorted. "Why didn't folks just go behind a building?"

"Because Jenkins was also the mayor of the town and he put up an ordinance against it. So if you were caught and found guilty, it wasn't Pisspenny anymore, it was Pissdollar."

Hollister stared incredulously at McAfee and then burst out laughing, realizing McAfee was pulling his leg. Butler joined in, but Durken remained silent. Hollister turned to him. You didn't find that funny Durken?"

"Yeah, the first time I heard the story. That was about six occasions ago."

They reached a shelf-like plateau in the mountainside that looked as if someone had run a saw through the top of the mountain and pushed it back fifty feet. The trail widened and in places gaps in the trees provided a panorama of the desert below. "How much further, Corporal?" said Harper. "Another mile, give or take, sir. Not far past the bend you see ahead."

XV

As they rode into the camp, Durken was the first to spot the sentry perched on a high outcrop of granite, rifle at the ready. He relaxed when he saw Travis and whistled to his friends. The Mingott brothers' camp was a horseshoe of tents clustered around a fire pit, the open end of the horseshoe facing the mouth of the mine. The trees had been cleared nearby and the trunks cut up for posts and lintels to support the roof of the tunnel that gaped in the face of the near vertical rock.

Blankets covered five mounds around the campfire. A boot stuck out from one blanket and part of an arm and its hand from another. Blackflies buzzed around the mounds, frustrated by the woolen covers. Two days' decay had filled the clearing with the stench of death.

The men dismounted and Travis said, "We've left things as we found them." He took the corner of one of the blankets gingerly between his thumb and forefinger. "I have to warn you, sir, it's not pretty."

Harper said, "We've all seen enough dead men in our day, Corporal."

"Yes, sir, but not like these. This one's Byram." He pulled at a corner of the dark-stained blanket, revealing the body underneath. It came away with a sticky tearing sound from the congealed blood that had soaked through it and glued it to the corpse. A hand stuck to the blanket as if holding on to it, modestly trying to keep the dead man's privacy, then fell away, bouncing on the hard ground.

Byram Mingott's face was twisted into a mask of pain and terror. The rent skin was turning from grey to a bluish green and the eyes that stared from retreating lids looked like boiled eggs going soft with rot. The jaw was wide open in a silent scream over a ragged gash in the body's throat that looked like a second screaming mouth.

He wore canvas work pants and leather suspenders over grimy long underwear. The placket of the Union suit was torn away exposing a crater scooped in Byram's chest and clotted with gore. No one spoke.

Hollister stood a moment, scribbling in his notebook, then, oblivious to the odor of putrefying flesh, dropped into a crouch and pulled a cloth tape measure from his pocket. He sketched the wounds and carefully recorded their dimensions and those of the claw marks, especially the spread from one claw to another.

"What do you think, Hollister?" said Harper.

"I can't really say until I've seen the other four bodies. I need to determine whether the same animal or a number of them killed all five of these men." He paused. "That's odd."

"What is?" said Harper.

"I see plenty of claw marks but none from fangs." He scribbled a notation in his notebook. "It doesn't look as if this man has been bitten at all. That is inconsistent with what was found on the bodies at Caplock. I've never seen anything quite like this." He went back to his examination.

Harper turned to Travis. "What about the mine tunnel?"

"It goes about four hundred feet into the mountain and dead ends. We found nothing unusual inside it."

McAfee said to Travis, "That messenger, Private Willet, said there were tracks. Could you show us?"

Travis looked to Harper, who nodded. "Yes, they're back here in some soft ground." Durken joined McAfee and followed Travis beyond the circle of the tents.

"A few of the tracks were stepped in before we knew what we had here, but some are still sharp." He pointed behind a large rock. "There." Harper called to him and Travis walked away.

Durken and McAfee crouched to get a good look at three paw prints in the soft earth. "That's odd," said McAfee. "The heel pad looks like a catamount's; the teardrop shape of the toe pads says catamount too, and there's no claw marks like you'd find with a dog or a wolf, but I count five toes not four."

"Yep, and there's something else. Based on the prints I'd say the cat was creeping up on the camp, not running or leaping. And look at the heel pads and the toes. You can tell right and left paws in those tracks by the toes, but look close. In all five prints the edges of the heel pad curve in. They're all hind paw tracks. What kind of cat walks only on its hind legs?"

"I'm hoping Hollister can answer that question."

Hollister was crouched over the third of the bodies, a short stocky black man whose work-gnarled hands clutched a .10 gauge shotgun by its barrel like a bludgeon. His dark skin, mottled with decay, made his wounds look even more grotesque. The black man's lower jaw hung to one side, ripped away by a savage blow. Hollister took his time, meticulously measuring and recording the wounds.

"Both hammers are down on the shotgun," said Butler. "Looks as if he fired both barrels then used the gun as a club."

"You're probably right," said Travis. "Look at that tent. He pointed to a flap in the canvas that was pocked with dark holes. "That accounts for one shot."

"So he missed with one barrel. What did he hit with the other?"

"Maybe he fell and fired in the air."

Hollister knelt beside the fourth body and pulled the blanket away. It was the second black man. He lay face down and Hollister carefully rolled him over. His dead fist curled around a camp hatchet. "That's Hobie," said Travis.

Harper pointed to the shredded ruin of the face and said, "His own mother wouldn't know him. How can you tell?"

"Because the other darkie's Abner. Couldn't be anybody else."

Durken eyed Travis coldly. "Didn't learn much from the war, did you?"

Hollister spoke up. "Same as the others; this man was clawed but not bitten." He pulled a magnifying glass from his jacket and looked close-eyed at the blued blade of the hatchet. "There's hair stuck on the edge." Hollister set down the glass and tore a small piece of paper from his pocket. Carefully he plucked the tuft of hair from the hatchet and folded the paper around it. He scribbled a notation on it and slid the paper into his pocket. Then he resumed measuring and taking notes.

"Well, what was it? Animal hair? Human hair?"

Hollister stopped writing and looked up at Harper. "Captain, I won't know until I examine it thoroughly. I can't examine it thoroughly until I'm done with the bodies. If you interrupt me, it will only take longer." He turned back to his work.

Butler snickered. "That's right, Cap, let the man do his job. Then once we know what we're after, I'll do mine."

While Hollister examined the body with the same exacting care, Harper pulled Durken and McAfee aside. "While he's at it, I want you men to scout the perimeter and see whether you can pick up any trace of what may have done this."

"So it's 'what' now, not 'who'?" Durken said.

Harper shrugged. "The photographs from Caplock Mountain are nothing compared to seeing this carnage firsthand. If men did this, I don't know how."

"How much did the patrol search?" said McAfee.

"Not much at all. The men you see here guarding the site found this mess. They've been on watch ever since. I don't think any of them has even had a chance to sleep, and I don't think they could have anyway. I know I couldn't. Besides, these men are horse soldiers not trackers."

"We taking Butler with us?" said Durken.

"I thought you might. For all the trouble he causes, he knows what he's doing, and as good a shot as he is, he might come in handy if you find something moving."

McAfee pointed behind the boulder. "When Hollister finishes with the bodies, bring him back here to look at those prints. They're peculiar. They look like catamount tracks but at the same time they don't. I'm curious what he thinks about them."

They walked back into the circle of the tents where Hollister was setting up a tripod for a camera. "I have to take pictures now before what light there is gets dimmer. I'll be using a flash to help the exposure, so you may want to move the horses beyond the tents."

The uncovered dead made a grotesque tableau. Beyond them the mine tunnel gaped like the shadowy mouth of Hell, waiting to swallow them. Butler was sitting on a flour barrel dozing. Harper kicked the barrel and Butler's eyes slowly opened. "Go with Durken and McAfee to scout the perimeter."

"I'll do that, Cap," Butler said. "And if I find anything feisty out there, I'll bring it back alive so's you can deal with it *mano y mano*. Maybe read it the riot act, eh?" He turned to McKenna. "See you later, Jimmy boy." He picked up his Winchester, which had been propped against a nearby tree, slung over his shoulder and saluted as he strode away.

XVI

The three began a parallel sweep in a broad circle with the camp as its center. McAfee was the closest to the camp with Durken in the middle and Butler on the outside. Fifty feet from the camp, Butler became a different person. A light, almost noiseless step replaced his heavy swaggering tread. Despite his size he stalked like a ghost through the heavy brush, barely disturbing the branches and foliage as he passed through them. He carried his rifle delicately in both hands. He was in his element.

They moved through the twilit forest without speaking for nearly a half

hour before Butler whistled sharply, one note. Durken and McAfee froze
in their tracks. Through the trees they could see Butler beckoning to them
without looking up from the ground.

Durken and McAfee peered around Butler from either side. "If that ain't
dried blood, I'm a Mason," he said pointing to a broad leaf. A brownish
stain the size of a half dollar spotted the leaf. "And just beyond, if you look
close, you'll see the grass pushed down where something either lay down
or fell."

"You got sharp eyes, Butler," said Durken."

"Kept me in business this long." He turned a full circle peering through
the trunks of the pines. "Stands to reason whatever was bleeding was
leaving the camp, not creeping up on it."

"So we draw a line from the camp through where we're standing past
that laydown and that's a good bet which way they went."

"No," said Butler. "That shows which way one of them went." He pulled
a long bladed hunting knife from his belt and blazed the closest tree to the
blood spot. "Let's circle some more and see what else we might find." As
Durken and McAfee walked away, Butler said, "One good thing." Both
looked back. Butler grinned. "If it bleeds, it ain't no ghost."

McAfee found the next sign. He smelled it before he saw it; fresh
resin oozed from parallel gashes in the trunk of a thick pine as if some
animal had used it to sharpen its claws. Other claw marks showed where
it climbed the tree to a limb a dozen feet off the ground. McAfee signaled
the others and as they approached, he hooked his boot on the lowest
limb of an adjacent tree and hoisted himself upward. By the time Butler
and Durken came to the spot, McAfee was up the tree craning his neck,
peering toward the camp.

He scrambled back down. "Claw marks look as if something big
climbed this tree to that limb. From the tree next to it, at that height I can
see straight into the camp."

Butler said. "Narrows it down a little. Wolves don't climb; cats do."

Durken studied the limb overhead. "You figure that limb would hold
your weight?"

"Mine for sure, but not Butler's. What are you getting at?"

"Gives us an idea of size. As big as you or me, but less than Jack."

"A catamount?"

"Could be. What do you think, Butler?"

"I've seen them climb trees before. And some of them go six feet or
more nose to tail and a hundred fifty pounds easy."

"We have to get Hollister out here to look at this." Said McAfee.

"He'll be a while with his camera," said Durken. "Let's search a little more."

Two hours later they had nearly circled the camp when Butler whistled again. This time instead of looking at the ground, he turned left to right in a three quarter arc and back again, his rifle at the ready. "Looks like somebody dropped something," he said.

At his feet was a lump of flesh roughly torn from its source. The putrefying heart lay nestled in the gnarled roots of a tree. Ants busily moved over it, systematically stripping it of nourishment. "I don't know whose that is," said Butler. "But we can narrow it down to five prospects."

Butler led the way back into the camp, walking through the brush with the same silent grace he'd exhibited earlier, but now slowly swiveling his head from side as he pressed forward, watching and listening.

"What do you make of all this?" Durken said.

"It's worrisome," said McAfee. "Looks as if the killers came from different directions and left in different directions too. Looks as if they scouted the camp in advance and planned their attack. If they're animals, they're a far sight smarter than any I ever saw."

"Ever read about anything like this in some book?"

"Nope."

"Damn."

"Yep."

At the camp, the soldiers were digging graves for the dead. Hollister was taking his last few pictures. McAfee sauntered over. "I've had my picture taken a few times in the war and once after. I never saw a camera quite like that one." The camera had an expandable face that opened like an accordion.

Hollister put his head under the camera's hood and made a few adjustments. "It's a new type. I had to be taught how to use it." He poured a grey powder into a tray with a foot long handle. "Likewise this material: it's called magnesium."

"I never heard of it before."

"Nor did I. It seems your military intelligence is first in line for anything new before the rest of us even know it exists. You might want to look away." Hollister held the tray over his head and squeezed a rubber bulb. A flash as bright as lightning lit the scene, and Hobie's agony was captured forever.

"We found a few things I think you need to see. And you might want to bring that camera with you."

#

Night came quickly to the pine shrouded mountainside. Near sunset the party had lowered the miners, rolled in their blankets into the newly dug graves. Harper said a few words, and the soldiers quickly shoveled the dirt over the corpses as if to bury the horror of their deaths with them.

The miners' camp had plenty of supplies in the tents, and one of the soldiers set to boiling a pot of beans with a chunk of ham thrown in. Potatoes cooked in a Dutch oven in the fire pit. The men huddled around the fire like primitives who believed that its glow would hold back not only the darkness but whatever prowled under its cover.

"Where's Hollister?" said Durken.

"He's in the mine shaft," said McAfee. "Said he needed it dark to work on his pictures."

Durken spat and his tobacco juice sizzled in the fire. "I'd say it's darker out here than it is in there." He looked up. "I don't see one star."

"That means no moon either. Not that it would shine much through the trees."

They ate their supper in silence. Some were too tired to talk, and some were too hungry.

Durken turned to Harper, who sat brooding, hands wrapped around a tin cup of steaming coffee. "Captain, these boys haven't slept for two days. How about if McAfee and I take their watch tonight?"

"That's generous of you. I'll need one more man. McKenna?"

Before the sergeant could answer, Butler spoke up. "I slept most of the ride out here, Cap. Let me take it. Unless of course, you'd rather not sleep while I'm up and around." He stood up and stretched like a bear fresh from hibernation.

Harper hesitated, thinking then nodded his head. "All right, Butler. You can take the trail. McAfee, you and Durken decide between you who watches which end of the camp. The rest of you turn in."

Hollister came out of the cave wiping his hands on a rag. "The chemicals are drying, Captain. You can see the photographs shortly."

"No hurry for me. I've already seen the real thing."

Hollister scooped a cupful of ham and beans onto a tin plate. He ate his meal with great relish, as if all he'd seen that day were shown to someone else.

"So, Hollister, you ever see tracks like we found today?" McAfee held a stick into the fire pit and pulled it out to light his cigarette from its yellow flame.

"No, I can't say that I have," Hollister replied around a mouthful of food. "But Nature is full of oddities; mutations we call them. Sometimes creatures are born that are well, different from the rest of their species. Sometimes these differences die with the animal. Sometimes they are passed on to further generations. When that happens, we call that a mutation."

"We had a two-headed calf born at the ranch once," said Durken. "Poor critter didn't live too long."

"If it had lived and bred another like itself, that would be a mutation, otherwise, it's just an anomaly, as I said, an oddity." He chewed his food for a moment and went on. "The prints I saw are consistent with some of the slash marks on the bodies; five toed paws. There's nothing definitive yet, but it seems as if, based on measurement, that more than one animal was involved in the attack. And more than one of them has five toed paws."

"How many?" said Harper.

"I can't say for sure; possibly three, maybe more." The others stared at him as Hollister scooped another cup of beans onto his plate as if he'd just commented on the weather. "Of course that's only those that attacked the camp."

One by one, the soldiers left the fire and went to their beds. Between Hollister's speculation and the thought of sleeping on a dead man's cot, no one, no matter how weary would sleep much that night. Durken, McAfee, and Harper stayed by the fire while Hollister finished his supper.

"I don't mean to nag you, Hollister," said Harper, "but what do you make of this?"

Hollister set down his plate and wiped his mouth with the back of his hand. The firelight turned the lenses of his spectacles into golden discs. "To be honest, Captain, I don't know what to make of it. What we have here is unique to my experience. We appear to have predators that attack but do not eat, except possibly the hearts of their prey. These predators have bitten and clawed their prey in one instance yet only clawed them to death in another. Although they may not be impervious to weapons, those weapons are not sufficient to bring them down.

"The paw prints indicate that we may be dealing with either a mutation or perhaps even a new species. Except for occasional nomadic tribes, this area has been largely uninhabited for as much as a thousand years. It is possible that something we've never seen before has survived here all this time, and westward expansion has pushed us into its bailiwick.

"So, Hollister, you ever see tracks like we found today?"

"What troubles me are the indications that we are dealing with something beyond feral cunning here. These predators exhibit a rudimentary sense of strategy. They attacked at the camp from different directions, blocking any path of retreat and seem to have struck in a coordinated effort."

Hollister was silent for a moment. "Something troubles me even more; the heart Butler found on the path."

"What about it?" said McAfee.

"It was not eaten but carried away, which suggests conscious purpose. There is no indication that any of the hearts was eaten here. Why would an animal tear out a heart and take it with him? I am making a leap here, but it almost suggests some sort of ceremonial use, and there we cross the lines between beast and man, a fusion of animal consciousness with human."

"I read about some warriors in old times that ate the hearts of the men they killed to take on their power," said McAfee.

"Many of your native tribes here in America have practiced ritual cannibalism until recent times.I know that some of the tribes in South America still do."

"So you don't think they're a pack of trained animals?" said Durken.

"I can't set that possibility aside completely. If we are dealing with a heretofore unknown species, there is no way to know if they could be trainable and to what degree."

"So what do we do now?" said Harper.

"I've been thinking about the heart. When you scouted the area, did you find any trace of wolves, bears, other predators?"

McAfee shook his head. "Now that you mention it, no."

"You'd think a prize morsel like that heart would attract a wolf, a coyote or maybe a bear, but except for the ants, it was untouched. The absence of predators suggests that they were driven away, frightened perhaps, or simply survival savvy."

"When we hunted in this area two years ago, there were bears, wolves, and coyotes among other meat eaters."

"And none of them touched the heart after the predator dropped it. If it was intended for some purpose and is important enough, whatever took it may come back for it. Since we had no way to know whose heart it was, I persuaded the Captain to not bury it with the victims."

"You mean bait," said Durken.

"Indeed," said Hollister. "I have an idea, if you all agree."

The sky cleared later and the moon rose over the pointed tops of the pines like a cautious face peering over the pickets of a fence. Durken and McAfee sat silently in the heavy brush a few yards from the tree where Butler had found the heart. Durken held his Winchester at the ready, and McAfee held Abner's .10 gauge. Butler and McKenna were still guarding the camp.

Hollister set up his camera beside the trail with a clear view of the heart nestled in the tree roots. He sat behind the camera, his flash at the ready. Harper waited beside him.

Hollister's plan was simple. Return the heart to the place where it was dropped and when someone or something returned for it, take its picture. Then they would know their enemy. "When the flash goes off, I'm counting on the surprise and shock to give us an advantage," he said earlier. "Unless we're attacked directly, don't shoot. I'm hoping we'll see which way it goes and be able to follow it, or at least its trail. I also expect that the flash will blind whatever comes for a few seconds."

"Won't that flash blind us too?" said Durken.

"There's a trick that cave explorers use when they go into a tunnel from daylight. They shut one eye until they move into darkness, and when they light their lamps open that eye so that they can see well until the other adjusts. The flash is only an instant, then we'll be in the dark again, but if you don't keep one eye shut when the flash goes off, you'll be as blind in both."

So they waited unspeaking as the moon rose higher and bits and pieces of ragged light filtered through the dense upper branches of the pines. Two hours passed with no sound but their breathing. Then a scuffling, furtive noise made them all stiffen.

Closer. Another noise, a soft padding on the trail. Durken's practiced ears recognized a two-foot tread.

Closer. A quick glimpse of a dark shape in the dim moonlight.

Closer. He raised his rifle, aimed it as near to the source of the sound as he could reckon, and shut his right eye, straining with his left for any mote of light in the tree shrouded forest.

Hollister's flash erupted like lightning and the image burned onto Durken's retina was that of a man caught in his stealth an instant before surprise and panic set in. He was dark-skinned, dark-haired and bare-chested. He wore buckskin breeches and feathers that projected down and to the right of his head.

Durken squeezed his left eye shut and opened his right. He heard the thud of retreating footsteps and a panicked crashing through brush as the intruder raced from what he must have thought was the wrath of one of the gods. Hollister cried out, "He's running. Don't..."

A gun roared behind Durken and McAfee. The shot echoed from the cliffs to their right.

"Damn it, hold your fire!" Harper shouted. He struck a match and lit a lantern. His eyes were ablaze with anger in the yellow light. "Durken, McAfee, why did you shoot?"

"Wasn't them, Cap." Butler stepped from the darkness. "And I'll bet you five bucks I put him on the ground."

Hollister snatched the lantern from Harper's hand ran through the trees in the direction of the Indian's flight.

"Hollister, wait," shouted McAfee. "There may be others."

Hollister stopped suddenly. "Oh, you damned fool," he said. "You've killed him."

"Just doing my job," Butler said, working the Winchester's lever and jacking a fresh round into the chamber.

"Your job is guarding the camp, Butler. I should have you shot for deserting your post."

"You could do that, Cap, but I figure that wouldn't rest your soul too easy now, would it?" He strolled toward Hollister whistling "Sweet Betsy from Pike" through his teeth as he glided easily through the brush.

"Damn," said McAfee under his breath. "He came up right behind us and I never heard him. How long do you think he was standing there?"

"I don't know," said Durken. "We're good, but Butler's damned good, and that worries me."

"Durken, McAfee, come here." Harper had joined Hollister and Butler and was standing over the dead man.

In the glow of the lantern, the brave lay face down. Butler's rifle left a hole you could put your thumb into between his shoulder blades. Hollister rolled the body over. The bullet blew a hole in his chest you could almost put your fist into as it passed through him.

"Tonnewa?" said Butler.

Harper nodded. "That's how they wear their feathers. We might have asked him if you hadn't killed him."

"One of the feathers is broken," said Hollister. "Does that have any significance?"

"He fell face down," said Durken, "so I doubt the feather broke when he fell. Like a lot of the tribes, the Tonnewa braves earn feathers by counting coup, touching their enemies in battle. A broken feather means disgrace or failure."

"So he failed to bring back the heart of his victim and was trying to redeem himself?"

"Could be," said Durken.

"What's that?" said McAfee, pushing back the shock of hair that spilled over the brave's throat. A rawhide thong circled his neck like a lady's choker and on it, a white amulet the size of an arrowhead. McAfee pulled it off and held it up to the light. The pendant was carved from bone and formed a rough triangle. On the thong, the amulet hung point down with the flat of the triangle on top. Small points projected from its top, and when McAfee turned it over he saw what was crudely carved on its reverse: slanted eyes, a muzzle and fangs; a cat.

"What's he wearing around his waist?" Harper said, pointing to a sort of tawny sash or belt.

Hollister squinted through his spectacles. "It's a pelt of some kind. Thick, close hairs. I'd say it's from some sort of animal, possibly a lynx or a mountain lion." He seemed to have completely set aside his anger with Butler and was studying the dead brave as if he were examining some specimen in a laboratory.

"Let's get the body back to camp," said Harper.

"I have a better idea," said Butler. "Maybe we ought to leave him here, but take his heart out first. When his friends find him they might think twice about coming back."

"That would make us no better than them," Harper spat.

"You think you and I are better than them, Cap? I wish I could dig up Quantrill and ask his opinion. I'm going back to my post before somebody shoots me." Butler turned and started walking back to the camp, whistling as he glided through the brush.

Back at the camp, McAfee, Durken, Hollister, and Harper sat by the campfire.

Harper broke the silence. "So what does all this mean?"

"I don't know," said McAfee, "but Durken and I know somebody who might. Ever hear of Seven Stars?"

"The Monatai chief? He's been a thorn in the paw of the Indian Affairs

Bureau for a long time. He's educated and uses the white man's law against itself. But at least he doesn't advocate violence like Red Hawk."

"Seven Stars was educated by Jesuit missionaries when he was a boy." McAfee went on. "He learned under an old priest named Father Leonardo, an expert on ancient religions and the supernatural for the Vatican. When Father Leonardo's sight failed him, Seven Stars became his eyes, reading to him from his books and from his correspondence with the Vatican. Because of that, Seven Stars knows one hell of a lot most people never heard of. That plus the fact that he's an Indian himself tells me he might give us some answers."

Harper shook his head. "This is an Indian situation, and the General wants it kept under a rock. You can't go telling some third party, especially an Indian, what's going on here. That's totally unacceptable."

Durken broke in. "Captain, Seven Stars is our friend and he's honorable. If we tell him it's classified and he's not to discuss it, he won't. And if you think he'd use this situation for leverage, you're wrong. He might know ways to deal with this nightmare that we won't find out otherwise 'til after a lot more people are dead, maybe us included."

"You trust him," Harper said.

"Like Durken and I trust each other," McAfee said.

Harper didn't speak for nearly a minute, and neither did anyone else. "All right, McAfee, go see what Seven Stars may know about all this. I'm trusting your judgment."

McAfee held up his hand. "I'm not worried about him, Captain, and you shouldn't be either. Durken and I will set out tomorrow at sunup."

"No," said Harper. "Not Durken. I need his eyes and his gun here. You ride back to Lickskillet with one of my men and take the train to Bacon Rock. Talk with Seven Stars and get back here as fast as you can."

McAfee nodded. "Yes, sir. I'll leave in the morning."

Hollister spoke up. "Captain, might I go with McAfee? I may add a different perspective to the knowledge."

Harper rubbed his chin. "I suppose there's not much more you can do here. Go ahead. And McAfee, I'm going to draft a message to the General. As soon as you get to Lickskillet, send it to him."

XIX

The sound of singing rang through the night from the little log church. "Faith of our Fathers" was a Catholic hymn, and some of the congregation questioned using the song in worship, but the lyrics' sentiment expressed a joy in the faith and a love of God that transcended sect and tradition. Jan Belsen was late for the Wednesday prayer meeting, but the Lord would forgive him the few minutes it took him to rescue one of his sheep from a narrow ravine where it had stumbled and fallen and surely He would understand why he came in his boots and overalls.

The Holy Brethren, a Protestant religious commune near Lickskillet had prospered this season; the harvest would be rich and they would put back more than enough food to last them through the harsh Nevada winter. The rising moon shone on the church and the little cemetery beside it, cold light in contrast to the warmth that poured through the church windows.

Belsen was about to open the church door when he heard a low growl behind him. He turned and saw a dark shape crouching in the shadow of the steeple. It stepped into the moonlight and stood erect, and what he saw paralyzed him with fear. A flat head with pointed ears framed glowing green eyes and a muzzle with a whiskered nose and fangs like icicles. The head was surrounded by the thick, cruel muscle of hunched shoulders that sloped downward to furred forearms and hands tipped with claws.

Belsen tried to cry out but the scream froze in his throat. His eyes darted back and forth seeking escape and he saw more of the hideous things creeping through the trees and among the headstones in the churchyard like the dead rising from the graves. In a blur, claws lashed out and caught Belsen under his bearded chin. Blood spurted as he fell, his last conscious thought: if only I came to the church on time, the Devil would not have overtaken me.

XX

The night passed without incident in the camp, and at dawn, McAfee and Hollister saddled their horses and rode across the desert toward Lickskillet. Durken's relief from the night watch came as the riders were shrinking into the distance. It was cold enough that when Durken blew out a long breath it steamed in the morning air. Corporal Beckley brought Durken a cup of coffee along with his own and sat beside him. Durken was tired, but he figured if the boy wanted to talk, it wouldn't hurt him to be sociable.

"The Captain says you and your partner were scouts for Sherman." He pushed back his cap and a shock of hay-colored hair spilled from under it.

"Yep." Durken sipped his coffee. It was strong and hot as a red horseshoe.

"I served under Meade at Gettysburg," Beckley said proudly.

"McAfee and I missed that one. His regiment, Third Rhode Island went north but the General kept us on with him. You seem kinda young for the war, Beckley."

He chuckled. "I was only fourteen. I lied about my age, but I think they would have taken me anyway."

"From what I hear, if ever there was a hell on earth, Gettysburg was it."

Beckley wrapped his hands around his cup. "I wouldn't argue that. What'd Jesus say, 'Satan has desired you that he may sift you as wheat?' That's a pretty fair picture of how it went. I brought back a souvenir myself." Beckley pulled up the front of his tunic and showed Durken a jagged scar just above his belt buckle. "Piece of artillery shrapnel got me, but I lived to tell the story."

"Plenty of good men didn't, on both sides." Durken drank his coffee to the last swirl of grounds, and as he always did, flicked the last swallow away. "We both lived this long; let's hope we survive to see the end of this venture. Thanks for the coffee, Beckley." Durken stood up and as he walked away, he looked back to see Beckley already scanning the horizon. He's a good soldier, Durken thought, and like any good soldier he's marching straight into the jaws of death all over again.

As Durken entered the camp, Harper saw him coming and called him over. "Now that it's light, maybe you and Butler can pick up a trail from last night. But I'd guess you need some sleep first."

Durken took a long breath and let it out between his teeth. "As tempting as that sounds, Captain, I'd just as soon get a look at things before the trail goes cold. Where's Butler?"

"Sleeping over in the far tent. I told him to sleep like the others in the tunnel, but he said he doesn't like being closed in. I didn't argue with him."

As Durken got closer to the tent, he could hear Butler's stertorous snores. Durken drew back the flap of the tent. Butler was sprawled face down on a cot, his arms spilling over its sides. A moth-eaten blanket covered his legs and torso. Durken kicked a leg of the cot and said, "Wake up, Butler." Durken repeated himself and the snoring continued.

Durken shrugged and stepped back out of the tent. He kicked the front pole and the tent collapsed. A bulge reared up in the middle of the grey canvas. Butler threw off the tent, pluttering and cursing, knife in hand, to find Durken staring him in the face. "Time to go to work, Jack."

Butler stared at him for a moment as if waiting for his thoughts to focus along with his eyes. "You're lucky I like you, Durken."

Durken's expression didn't change. "I guess so, for both our sakes. Let's get to it."

Butler stared at Durken for a few seconds then laughed and crawled back under the fallen tent to retrieve his hat and his rifle.

McAfee took advantage of the train ride to catch up on the sleep he missed the night before. When he woke, Hollister stopped writing in his notebook. The carriage swayed from side to side as the train rattled down the tracks.

"There is so much I don't know about catamounts, and up to now that's the closest I can come to a culprit in these attacks. I've seen a few mounted in collections or museums but only one alive in the wild, and that was at a distance. What can you tell me about them?"

"Maybe you ought to ask Butler."

"I did," said Hollister, his brow creasing. "All I got was some long-winded adventure story."

McAfee grinned. "How do you know I won't give you the same?"

"Because you're not Jack Butler."

"Maybe we could start with what you know about them so what I say doesn't overlap."

Hollister took a deep breath as if he were about to sing an opera and McAfee almost regretted his suggestion. "What you know as a catamount is also called a cougar, mountain lion, puma, panther, or painter. The word catamount is a shortening of 'cat-of-the-mountain' and is a sort of catch-all phrase for a large wild feline native to North America. Zoologists call them *puma concolor*, a member of the *Felidae* family."

"You missed one name," McAfee said. "Out here folks call them 'Indian Devils'."

Hollister jotted this bit of information in his notebook. "They are part of the same family as the common house cat according to some authorities, although that is still subject to some debate. The *puma concolor* can grow to a length over six feet and weigh as much as one hundred seventy pounds, about the size of a grown man. They are nocturnal animals, as well as crepuscular."

"I know 'nocturnal'; you'll have to explain the other word."

"'Crepuscular' means they are active in twilight, often even more so than in full night. They are, like their cousin the cheetah in Africa very swift and in the open can run as fast, or perhaps faster, than a horse. They are what we call 'obligate carnivores,' which means they survive strictly by eating meat, and they are usually solitary animals. Only mothers and kittens live in groups with adults meeting only to mate, which makes their attacking in a pack an unlikely occurrence."

Hollister stopped speaking and looked expectantly at McAfee, waiting him to pick up the thread of the conversation. "That's pretty comprehensive. A few years ago, I scouted for a hunting party. My boss Homer Eldridge brought some of his friends up from San Francisco to hunt elk. We crossed the same range as Caplock Mountain, but a little bit further south. The third day in, I was following spoor and I heard a commotion ahead. I crept up and saw a catamount attacking a full grown bull elk. The cat had either bitten or clawed – it was hard to tell which—through the tendons of one the elk's hind legs so it couldn't run or maneuver too good.

"The cat was full grown too, tawny with that spike of hair over the ears. Or maybe I should say ear. This one had been in a few fights in its career; its left one was missing. It would run in from the elk's injured side and either slash or bite the elk's legs or flank or belly, making it bleed, weakening it, then dart out of reach of its antlers just to run in and rip him again. The elk fetched that cat one kick that would've stoved in its skull if it caught him in the head instead of its shoulder. The cat rolled over two or three times, shook itself off and jumped right back into the fight.

"Finally it sprung. The cat leapt on the elk's back and dug in all its claws. The woods were all torn up at that spot, brush trampled, duff dug up by the hooves. Just imagine a thousand pounds of desperate animal wheeling, bucking, trying to throw Death off its back, like a bronc in a rodeo, the elk bawling in anger or fear, or both.

"Finally, the elk wore itself out and sank down on those big knuckled knees, and that's when the cat tore open its throat. The slash wounds looked pretty much the same as those we saw on the miners, but the flesh was more torn up because the cat bit big chunks out of him, some while he was still bleeding out. I backed away from the clearing and as I did, the catamount realized I was there. It raised its bloody maw and looked me square in the face and snarled at me, a sound like a drawn out cough, as if to say, 'This is my meat. Go kill your own.'"

"And you didn't shoot it?"

"What right did I have to interfere? We were both hunters and he found the elk before I did. That cat was doing nothing different from what I was doing, and probably had more right to it because what he did was by instinct. And for that matter, it was his preserve, not mine. I never told Eldridge about it either, because that fool would have insisted on hunting it down and bringing the catamount's hide home to hang over his fireplace. There were plenty of elk on the mountain and Eldridge got what he came for. I figured that was enough."

"And you didn't see that catamount again?"

"Once near the end of the trip. I was alone again, and I was passing under an outcrop. I looked up and saw nothing there then looked again and saw the critter perched on its haunches like a housecat looking down at me. I knew it was him because of that missing ear. My rifle was at the ready, but I didn't shoot. We eyed each other for a long minute and he turned, gave me a twitch of his tail, and disappeared. He could've pounced on me, probably would have killed me in the bargain, but for some reason he didn't."

"Professional courtesy," said Hollister.

"I guess so. That or a favor returned. That's as much as I can tell you."

"It is amazing, isn't it?" said Hollister. "Nature red in tooth and claw. It's frightening and awe-inspiring at the same time. Once in Africa on the Serengeti Plain I saw a cheetah chase a gazelle. I've never seen two creatures move so fast. It was like a contest between grace and power, but they were both outrunning death; the gazelle from being eaten and the cheetah from starvation."

"Who won?"

"The cheetah; unfortunate for the gazelle, but that is the way of Nature. There are many more gazelle than there are cheetahs, or soon there would be no more gazelle."

"And then there would be no more cheetahs."

"Quite so. Either that or the cheetah would adapt and find different prey."

"Seems to me Nature provides and leaves a place for all the animals in the scheme of things."

"How does the old Anglican hymn go?" Hollister hummed a few notes.

"All things bright and beautiful; all creatures great and small; all things wise and wonderful, the Lord God made them all."

"On the other hand, said McAfee, 'Did He who made the Lamb make thee?'"

The corner of Hollister's mouth quirked up in a crooked grin. "Blake's Tyger; an apropos sentiment, McAfee. But we're not dealing with tigers here, I'm certain."

McAfee reached into his vest pocket and drew out the cat's head amulet. He turned it over in his fingers, studying it from different angles. "And I suspect that whoever made the Lamb had nothing to do with whatever killed those miners."

Hollister closed his notebook. He took out his pipe and made a great ceremony of packing it with tobacco. In a moment, his face was wreathed in aromatic smoke, and his eyes gazed unseeing through the window. McAfee reached into another pocket and drew out Charlie's good luck charm. He ran his finger around the edge of the copper medallion and wished he had left it in Manson's Pass with Durken.

Durken and Butler moved quietly on foot through the forest, leading their horses. Durken wore his duster against the chill, and Butler wore a dark bearskin cape that matched his hat and made him look more like quarry than hunter. Durken let Butler lead, partly because Butler was more experienced at tracking in the mountainous country and partly because he didn't want to turn his back on him. They started at the site where Butler shot the Tonnewa brave and moved westward across the ridge. The pair walked without speaking, listening intently for any sound out of place. Occasionally Butler would stop and hunker down, peer at something on the ground or in the bushes, and then stand and motion for Durken to follow.

An hour into the trail, the sunlight faded. The sky, which started the day a brilliant blue had turned pearl grey. The forest greens took on a somber cast. Butler stopped and stared at the ground. "Somebody tethered a horse here." Durken saw several hoof prints all in a tight area.

"No shoes on the hooves. An Indian."

"And look there," Butler said, pointing to the sparse grass. "The horse was tied up long enough to browse."

"Do you figure it was the brave from last night rode him here then went to the camp on foot?"

"Looks likely. But if it was him, where's the horse now?"

"He sure as hell didn't ride it away. Looks as if someone followed him here, maybe waited for him, and when he didn't come back took his horse and high-tailed it."

Butler did the slow turn Durken had seen him do before, eyes piercing the dense forest. "Or they're out there right now watching us. At least we know we're going the right direction. Let's keep moving."

The trail widened as it wound around the mountainside and the slope became steeper, rising sharply to their right and dropping as sharply to their left. The men rode now in single file, rifles across their saddles. Butler led, staring at the ground and the edges of the trail for any sign of their quarry. Durken rode behind watching through the thick veil of foliage for a trap or an ambush. He'd ridden hundreds of scouting missions during the war, yet never one that made him so edgy. He reminded himself that these were men they were tracking, only men, but he still felt as if he were tracking something much more dangerous.

A half hour later Butler said quietly. "Do you feel it?"

"Eyes on us?"

"Don't look. Uphill about two hundred feet. I got wind of them a few minutes ago. Maybe there's a parallel trail up above. Either that or they're damned good stalkers. They can't shoot, rifles or arrows, for the same reason we can't. Too many trees; no visibility."

"So what do we do?"

"How good you train your horse?"

"Pretty thorough."

"He do a buck and wheel?"

"Yep."

"We'll keep moving 'til I think I have a clear shot. When I tell you, yell like there's a rattler on the trail and set your horse to it. I'm hoping I can get a drop on them while they're looking at you. Once I start you shoot downhill or back of us at anything that moves."

Durken nodded. "Just say the word."

They rode on, the horses picking their way among the rocks and roots. Ahead a small stream coursed down the mountainside and flowed across the trail. Its path left a narrow opening in the wall of trees like a crevasse in a glacier. "Get ready," Butler said as calmly as if he were asking the time of day. They entered the gap. "Now."

Durken whistled two sharp notes and tugged at Sweetheart's mane. The big Appaloosa reared and whirled in a tight circle. "Snake," shouted Durken. "Snake!"

Butler slid off his horse and landed flat-footed, aiming his Winchester over his saddle. As Durken dropped to the ground behind Sweetheart, Butler opened fire, pumping the lever of his rifle as fast as he could work it. Durken crouched and spun in a half circle, watching for attack from below or behind. As quickly as it began, the gunfire stopped. The boom of the last shot echoed three times around the peaks and then silence.

Butler stared intently over his saddle into the trees. "Anything behind or below?"

"Not that I can see."

"We're lucky there were only two of them and not a half dozen." Butler stepped around his horse. "I'm pretty sure I got one of them. Let's go see." The climb was steep and in a few minutes Durken was winded. Butler pushed on, moving gracefully in spite of his bulk and breathing as if he were strolling down a sidewalk. Near the top of the ridge he stopped and waited for Durken to catch up. Butler pointed to a dead brave slumped against the trunk of a larch. "Got him." A bow and arrow lay beside the brave where he fell, a wound in his chest. Three feathers pointed downward and away from the top of his head.

"Same feathers as the other one. He's a Tonnewa," said Durken.

"We're lucky they didn't have rifles." Butler bent over the body and grabbed a handful of long dark hair, pulling the head back. He reached to his belt and pulled out his knife.

"You ain't gonna scalp him, Butler?"

Butler gave Durken a look one might reserve for a foolish child and slid the blade between the dead man's throat and the rawhide thong that encircled it. A flick of the knife and the thong fell away. Butler picked it up and held it in his palm for Durken to see. The thong had the same triangular cat's head they'd found on the other Tonnewa. "Let's get out of here. The one that got away'll be back with his friends, and they likely won't be bringing bows and arrows."

The train pulled into Bacon Rock early in the afternoon. McAfee and Hollister found a soldier waiting with saddled horses at the livery stable and they rode north toward the Monatai reservation.

"Tell me more about this fellow Seven Stars," Hollister said. He was riding a grey gelding with the ease of someone who has been in the saddle since he could walk.

"There's a lot to tell, I suppose," McAfee said, arching his back to stretch. "When he was a boy, two Jesuit missionaries, Father Leonardo and Father Giacomo, came to his village. They recognized the intelligence and the promise Seven Stars had and they took him with them to educate him and I suppose to make him one of them."

"I take it they didn't succeed."

"Oh, they educated him all right, and they might have made him a priest like themselves, but things didn't work out that way. Father Leonardo came here straight from the Vatican. He'd held some high seat there and ran afoul of their politics. They punished him by sending him out here, if that's a punishment, taking him away from that nest of vipers. I've read about the Borgias; their story makes the Vatican look like the halls of Congress."

Hollister chuckled. "I agree. I've read Niccolo Machiavelli's *The Prince*. So if they educated the boy, why didn't he enter the ministry?"

"Father Leonardo was a scholar, an expert on old religions and such. Sometimes the Vatican still consulted him on the subject. He taught Seven Stars to read, in a couple of languages in fact, and when Father Leonardo's eyesight began to fail, Seven Stars became his secretary. The old priest would have Seven Stars read to him from his books, a lot of them about sorcery and witchcraft and pagan tribes. He was too proud to tell the Vatican he'd lost his sight and a message came from the Vatican for Father Leonardo only, and he gave it to the boy to read to him and write his response. That violated Papal secrecy, but before the Vatican could act against Father Leonardo, he died.

"Seven Stars was banished from the church, but he could read and write, so he turned from religion to law. As chief of the Monatai, he uses the courts to fight his tribe's battles, and more often than not, he wins. He's never forgotten the lessons he learned at Father Leonardo's knee. He's blind now himself, but he still knows a lot more than most people."

"How did he become blind?"

"He lost one eye to a bobcat when he was a boy. He lost the other in a battle." McAfee didn't elaborate on the incident in which Seven Stars saved his life and Miss Sarah's fighting the Starry Wisdom Sect. That was a story for another time.

"I look forward to meeting him. He sounds as if he's worthy of a book all his own."

"No argument there," McAfee said. "See that mesa up ahead? The Monatai village is just on the other side."

The village was tucked into a hollow behind a high mesa, shielded from the wind and the harsher afternoon sun. As they approached, McAfee raised a hand in greeting to a brave with a rifle sitting on the mesa's ledge, letting him know they were approaching as friends.

"I thought the Monatai were friendly," said Hollister.

"They are," McAfee replied, "but at the moment, things are a little taut between the tribes and the government. When the chiefs give their word, they keep it, and they expect the same in return. For some reason, Washington doesn't feel quite the same way about it. They uproot a tribe, give them land, and then revoke the treaty when it suits them. It's an insult to the chiefs' integrity, and if they resist, they're met with force."

"And retaliation breeds harsher retaliation. I've seen the same pattern among natives in the colonies in India, Africa, and Australia."

"Then you understand why it's important to stop these massacres as fast as we can before white people start shooting anybody with a red skin."

They entered the cluster of teepees and McAfee held up a hand. "Don't dismount until we're welcomed."

"Protocol; yes, I understand."

Two Monatai braves came forward and took the reins of their horses. One of them, a tall man with graying hair in long braids spoke in halting English. "Welcome McAfee, enter as friend."

McAfee removed his hat. "Thanks, Blue Knife," said McAfee. "This is my friend Hollister. We come to see your chief."

"Welcome, Hollister, enter as friend." Hollister followed McAfee's example. "I thank you. I am pleased to meet you."

They dismounted and the other brave led their horses away. Blue Knife said, "Come with me. Seven Stars is in his lodge."

"Blue Knife is Seven Stars' uncle," McAfee explained.

Hollister observed everyone he saw with polite curiosity, and the villagers did the same to him. McAfee chuckled. "I guess you're as novel to

As they approached, McAfee raised a hand in greeting...

them as they are to you. They see people dressed like me every day around here, but your outfit's something new."

"Every tribe has its distinctive dress, like the feathers on birds. Even yours and mine."

"I never thought of my duds that way, but now that you say so, I see how that could be true."

Seven Stars' lodge lay at the far end of the village. Animal hides covered a framework of thin, straight poles to form a conical tent about ten feet in diameter at the bottom. The outside of the lodge was decorated with native symbols and to the side of the entrance, words in carefully rendered script.

Hollister read aloud, "*Et ipsa scientia potestas est.* And knowledge is power."

"And that is truth," came a voice from inside the lodge. A tall, regal man in tribal buckskins stepped through the open flap. His long dark hair hung loose to his shoulders unlike the braids favored by his fellow Monatai. Across his empty eyes he wore a simple band of tanned leather. He held a bulky book in his hands.

"Hello, Seven Stars."

"McAfee, my friend." Seven stars smiled, showing teeth as white as bleached bone. "And you have brought another with you. Who is your companion who reads Latin so well?"

"This is Rupert Hollister," said McAfee, "a scholar like yourself."

"I am honored to meet you, Rupert Hollister," said Seven Stars, extending a hand in greeting.

"And I to meet you, Chief."

"Please come in from the sun and tell me what brings you to our village."

They sat in the tent and McAfee said, "What kind of book is that?"

Seven Stars handed the large, heavy book to McAfee. It was bound between thin slabs of polished wood and its pages were thick. He opened it and found the pages were covered with tiny raised bumps instead of printed words.

"Is that Braille?" said Hollister. "I've heard of Braille books but I've never seen one."

"Yes," said Seven Stars. "It is the New Testament."

McAfee ran his fingers over the bumps. "These are letters? Looks like Morse Code."

"Yes, it is a code of sorts. I read the letters with my fingers. An irony, isn't it; a book I can read and you cannot."

"If I may ask, how did you get this?" said Hollister. "I'd imagine Braille books are rare."

"A favor returned," said Seven Stars with a cryptic smile, then to McAfee. How is our friend Durken?"

"He's well, but occupied elsewhere."

"And that occupation is the reason for your visit?"

"Seven Stars, your knowledge has been a great help in times of trouble before, and we're hoping it will be so again." McAfee took Seven Stars' wrist and placed the cat's head amulet in his palm.

Seven Stars turned the amulet over in his fingers, feeling every curve and point. "It is as I feared," he said. "Tell me how you came by this."

McAfee recounted the story of the attacks and the mysterious assailants with Hollister filling in details of his findings. Seven Stars listened intently, his brow furrowing more deeply as the tale continued. When they were finished, Seven Stars sat silent for a long moment then he sighed deeply as a man would when he has reached a difficult decision.

"I am torn. Although I bear no ill will to you, McAfee, nor to you, Hollister, I have no affection for your General. While he has never raised a hand against the Monatai, I fear that given a reason or an order, he would do so as easily and with the same dispatch that he has toward other tribes. He gives orders, yet he follows them as well. Expediency, not his conscience, often guides his hand.

"Yet I am a practical man. I realize the danger this uprising presents to all the tribes, and for that reason, there are two things I will relate to you." And Seven Stars began his story.

XXIV

"Within the last two seasons, the chiefs of all the tribes in this territory met in council, among them Red Hawk of the Tonnewa. Many chiefs spoke of their grievances against the white man, tales of treachery, of deceit and of brute force exacted against them, most at the hands of the Cavalry.

"Many of us spoke of peaceful solutions, but others, like impatient children, were not satisfied. When it was Red Hawk's turn to speak, he demanded retribution against the whites and especially against the armies that persecuted our people. 'We must drive them off our land,' he said. And when others argued that we could not possibly defeat the blue coats in battle, he laid out his plan.

"'The white devils are a belly that will never be filled,' he said. 'They give with one hand and take with the other. They drive us from place to place because they want what we have after they have given it to us. We must make them not want it, and the weapon we must use is fear.'

"Having no eyes, I could not see what Red Hawk was doing, but as he spoke, he dipped his fingers into his pouch and drew them out covered with paint. As he spewed his venom, he marked his face for war.

"'In the past,' he said, "we were feared because of our numbers when men fought as men, knife in hand, not as the whites do with pistols and rifles and cannons. Now we must make them fear us because our vengeance is so terrible that even their fiercest warriors will hesitate to trespass on our lands. We must become something so dreadful that they will stay away in fear for their lives.'

"All of us opposed Red Hawk's plan, seeing little good to come of it, I perhaps the most forceful, and in anger, he left the council, saying, 'When I am through with the white devils, I will return for those who have opposed me.'

"Having heard your story, I realize what Red Hawk has done, and now I will tell you a story of my people from the founding of this world.

"When First Father brought our ancestors from the Third World to this one, they found an untamed wilderness. The animals held dominion and at first did not welcome the newcomers and killed many because the people had no defense. First Father persuaded the animals to allow my people to live and grow corn in one valley and there they would stay. The animals agreed that so long as the people stayed in their valley, they would be left in peace.

"But when our numbers grew, the valley became crowded and it became more difficult to feed everyone. One day Tonako the white fox found the man Grey Cloud scratching at the ground with a hickory branch, trying to till the unyielding earth. 'Tell me brother,' he said to Grey Cloud, 'why do you labor so in this rocky soil when just beyond this hill is ground so fertile you need only drop a seed and it will sprout?'

"'Because the land beyond this valley belongs to your kind, and if we leave this valley they will surely kill us.'

"Tonako said, 'I too am pursued by the bear, the wolf, and the cougar, and if I were not so swift and sly, I would surely be eaten. They are strong and feared because they have fangs and claws and they kill and eat the smaller creatures of the wild. You have neither fangs nor claws, but I can make you their equal.' So he showed Grey Cloud how to fashion a knife from flint and with it to carve a bow from the branch of a hickory tree and taught him how to shoot the arrows he made.

"'Go now,' said Tonako, 'and when you kill a creature, eat its heart, for that is the secret of the strength of the bear, the wolf and the cougar. You will gain the swiftness of the deer, the vision of the hawk, and the fierceness of the badger. Become great as the bear, the wolf, and the cougar are great, and you will no longer have to fear them.'

"Grey Cloud set out armed with his bow and his knife, and the first creatures he saw were two cubs, the children of Kinchaka the cougar. The cubs had wandered from their den while their mother slept, and having never seen a human before, did not run from him. Grey Cloud fired one arrow that pierced them both and with his knife he cut the hearts from the cubs and ate them greedily. 'Now I will have the strength and the skill of two cougars,' Grey Cloud said.

"But Matinka the eagle saw what Grey Cloud had done and flew to Kinchaka's den and told her what had befallen her cubs. Kinchaka first raged, hot with anger. She wished to find Grey Cloud and rend him to pieces. Then her rage became cold and she devised a better way to punish him and all humankind as well.

"Kinchaka went to Witch Woman who put a spell upon Grey Cloud. To replace her lost cubs, Grey Cloud would become a cougar when the moon rose, and as he had killed her cubs, so would he kill his own kind and eat their hearts. And for a time, Grey Cloud was human by day and a beast by night, killing man, woman and child, becoming ever stronger and more terrible.

"The people prayed to First Father, and he came in a white mist from the mountainside. The people told him of their peril. He searched the hearts of one and all and found fear in every heart but Grey Cloud's. That night, when the moon rose, Grey Cloud became the beast again. First Father lay in wait for him and seized the monster, binding him with a rope of braided sliver and hurling him over the precipice at the Fourth World's edge.

"'And you,' First Father said to Tonako, 'for your treachery and your meddling will no longer wear your fine white coat. Your pelt will remind all of the blood that was shed because of you,' and he struck the fox with his hand, and Tanako's coat turned red.

"'What has been done cannot be undone,' First Father said to Kinchaka, 'You lost two cubs but caused the deaths of many men because you turned to dark magic. If I had not come, all my children would soon be dead. Men now know arms and will use them. They will now leave this valley and wander as your equals, and fear you no more.'"

Seven Stars was silent for a time, as if he were debating whether to go on. "There are legends of my people and others of warriors who followed Grey Cloud's path. They ate the hearts of their prey, man and beast alike and became beasts themselves, Cat Warriors after Kinchaka's curse. And this I believe is what Red Hawk has done. He has used dark magic to bring the spirit of Grey Cloud into himself and he has seduced others to follow him."

Hollister broke the silence that followed. "You're talking about shapeshifting."

"Yes. Such legends are not unique to my people. Every land has its tales of men who become beasts."

"You mean like werewolves?" McAfee said. "I've read some stories about them."

"Lycaon in greek myth, and weretigers in India," said Hollister, "and werebears in Russia, and the dominant predator in the region of any story. I heard tales about men who became jaguars when I grew up in Guiana."

"And silver works against them?" McAfee asked.

"So the legend says." Seven Stars turned up one palm then the other. "Gold to represent the sun; silver the moon."

"Yes," Hollister said, his voice rising in excitement. "That would explain why the bodies at the mine were clawed but not bitten. Those men were covered with grit from the mine; silver dust. It was in their clothes, on their skin."

"And the slashes on the tree; they weren't sharpening their claws, they were cleaning them."

"And why the miners were attacked," said Seven Stars, "because they were taking silver from the ground that could be used against the beasts."

"We have to get back there as quickly as possible," Hollister said. Those men are in more danger than they realize. Can we get a message to them?"

"We can try to send a telegram from Bacon Rock before we get on the train."

"Then we should leave right now."

McAfee stood. "Seven Stars, thank you."

The Chief stood. "I hope the knowledge will help you to end this threat to us all and that you and Durken will both return from the battle." He turned to Hollister. "And you, Rupert Hollister, are welcome here again. I believe we have many things to discuss."

"It will be my honor, Chief."

A few miles from the village McAfee and Hollister came to a fork in the trail. "Where does that lead?"

"To the Triple Six Ranch," said McAfee, "the place where Durken and

I work as overseers." As they took the fork toward Bacon Rock, McAfee paused to look back toward the other trail. There was nothing that he wanted more than to ride to the ranch and to see Sarah, to hold her in his arms, but he knew that once there, he might not leave again. He nudged his horse and set off at a trot to catch up with Hollister.

"So what do we tell the General?" said McAfee.

"We tell him the story."

"You know what he'll say."

"What was his word? Hokum?"

"Yep. That's the word."

"Myths are often based on fact; they begin as real historical incidents, are retold and embellished into legends, and finally become instructive fables."

McAfee pondered this for a moment. "So sometime in the past, someone really became a werecat?"

"Or simply killed a number of people in a savage manner and made it look as if a wild animal had done it to cover his tracks. Then the story grew into legend and myth."

"But you don't think so."

"Science and magic. When superstition can be proven true through the scientific method, it ceases to be magic and becomes science. Two hundred years ago men would have been burned alive for using technology they accept as an everyday occurrence today. 'There are more things in Heaven and Earth, Horatio, than are dreamt of in your philosophy.'"

"Shakespeare, right?"

"*Hamlet*. I believe in evidence, and the more I see, more I agree with him."

"But it's still going to be a hard sell to the General."

XXV

McAfee and Hollister arrived at the General's coach an hour later. A half dozen of the General's staff and guard were at the site but the General and his adjutant Corporal Barlow were gone. "The General was called away," said one of the soldiers.

"Will he be back any time soon?" McAfee said.

"I can't say," the corporal told him. "I just stand here and wait. Nobody tells me anything."

"Well, what do we do?" said Hollister.

"We sure as hell don't wait," McAfee replied. "Those men are in danger."

"Could we get a message to them?"

"We could try to telegraph Lickskillet and have one of the soldiers at the train ride out with the message. That might be the best idea."

"Let's do that, then," said Hollister. "With luck, we'll get back to Manson's Pass before dark."

"If we push it," said McAfee. "Let's go."

Durken, Harper, McKenna and Travis sat in a tent at the mine site. A light rain had begun a few hours earlier and pattered on the canvas.

"Now we know for sure the Tonnewa are responsible for the massacres. What we don't know is where they are and how many of them there are." Harper scratched a match on the sole of his boot and lit the stub of a cigar.

"They're likely a day's ride away from us or the brave Butler killed last night would have come on foot. That and we saw tracks of other unshod horses nearby."

"But the braves who followed you yesterday were on foot."

"Just because we didn't see horses didn't mean they didn't hide them somewhere close by."

McKenna spoke for the first time that day. "How many Tonnewa are in this territory?" McKenna's familiarity with Harper suggested greater authority than his rank afforded.

Travis said, "I can answer that, or at least give an estimate. The last official count reported about two hundred total, but I don't know how many of them are men, women, or children. When the latest relocation order came out, we went to their last village and found the site abandoned. They just vanished, but that's easy enough to do in this wilderness, especially if they split up into smaller groups."

"We'd need at least a battalion to comb through these mountains," said Harper, "and that's exactly what the General wants to avoid. There's no way we could bring that many troops in without attracting a lot of attention. Officially, we aren't even here."

"But you're assuming the whole Tonnewa tribe is in on this business," said Durken. Both of the Tonnewa we've killed wore the cat's head symbol.

Maybe it's just a small group of raiders attacking while the rest of the tribe is in hiding. Or maybe Red Hawk's operating on his own with a few followers."

"That's an even tinier needle in the haystack," said Harper.

"And logistically a smaller force could hit and run and stay hidden in these hills forever." McKenna pared his thumbnail with a pocket knife. "It would be almost sheer luck to find them."

"Speaking of luck," said Durken, "it's too bad the rain started up. That'll make it harder for us to pick up their trail again."

"You should have pushed on," said Harper. "Maybe you two would have found their camp."

"And maybe we wouldn't, Captain. The rain started soon after we turned back, and it would have washed away what little of their trail we could follow. If Butler and I'd pressed on just the two of us and found a gang of them, we might not have made it back here and you wouldn't know what little you do now. And if they're moving all the time, who's to say they'd still be in the same place when we came back with reinforcements." Durken ground out his cigarette. "But they know where we are. We've killed two of their braves now and they'll want revenge. Maybe they'll come to us, and if they do, we can be ready for them."

Harper pondered the thought. "Up to now they've struck at night, but since we've seen them move in the daytime, there's no guarantee that we're safe before dark. The tunnel seems easy enough to defend. We can't be surrounded in there. If we pull down these tents, there'll be no cover for attackers once they leave the trees. Set the men to it, Travis."

"Yes, sir." Travis saluted and left the tent.

"I didn't want to say this in front of Travis," said Harper, "but tomorrow we abandon this site and move to the outpost at Dixon. This situation calls for a lot more men than I have here, and I can't give the order for reinforcements. That has to come from the General."

"We could leave now," said McKenna. "We still have a few hours' daylight left."

"Unless the weather clears night will fall early. Between the rain and the darkness, we'd have one hell of a time getting off this mountain. And I don't want to chance a twilight ambush either. We ride tomorrow."

McAfee watched the landscape sliding past the window of the train. Before they left he'd sent a brief telegram to be delivered to the soldiers waiting at Lickskillet. It read simply: Consulted Seven Stars. Have information. Be on guard. General unavailable for report or orders. Arriving tonight.

The shadows were long when the train pulled into Lickskillet. A private named Welton met them with their horses and the three set off toward the camp. The closer the sun sank toward the horizon, the more McAfee turned the word over in his mind: crepuscular.

McAfee and Hollister agreed before they left the train that what Seven Stars had told them was for the Captain's ears and Durken's only. The horse soldiers were spooked enough already, and neither wanted wild rumors to make things worse, so they limited their conversation to the weather and the landscape.

Two miles from Lickskillet, they saw riders coming from the southwest, eight men, and as they got closer, McAfee recognized Sheriff Ben Stafford in the lead. McAfee and his companions halted their horses and waited for the sheriff to approach.

As they got closer, McAfee could see the badges on the chests of the men with Stafford. Eight deputies; way too many for a town Lickskillet's size. This was a posse drafted for the occasion. McAfee saw the look of anger in Stafford's face, and something else, fear. The sheriff pulled his horse up short and said, "You men come with us."

"Sheriff, we have to meet up with Captain Harper," McAfee said.

"Harper can wait," Stafford said. "You're coming with us and I mean now."

Welton spoke up. "Sheriff, I have orders to take these men directly to the Captain."

"I don't give a damn about your orders, boy. You can go to Harper or go to the Devil if you want, but these two are coming with me."

Welton's hand moved over the flap of his holster, and McAfee said, "Don't be foolish, Welton. There's way too many of them for you to be a hero." Emotions were running way too high for rash actions. He held his hands up, palms forward, in a gesture of submission. "All right, Sheriff, we'll go with you. Welton, you ride on to the Captain and let him know we'll be along later." Welton's eyes darted from McAfee to the sheriff and to his men, and he finally nodded and without another word nudged his horse and rode away.

"Where are you taking us, Sheriff?" said Hollister.

"Not too far. There's something I want you to see." He wheeled his horse and his men followed suit. They rode in a group with McAfee and Hollister in the middle of the pack, surrounded by grim faced deputies.

"This can't be good," said Hollister to McAfee.

"No, it can't, but I figure the quicker we get this over with, the quicker we'll be on our way to the Captain."

The group rode in silence for several miles until a cluster of buildings came into view, houses, barns, and a church. Stafford turned to McAfee and Hollister. "That farm belongs to a group of Protestants call themselves The Holy Brethren. They call it a 'commune' where they all work and live together and share everything. Or I should say they did."

"What do you mean, Sheriff?" said McAfee.

"You'll see," he said, turning away.

They passed through fields of mounded hayricks, neatly ranked and uniform in size and shape, like yellow gumdrops on a store counter. A field of corn shocks testified to a good harvest. Beyond the corn field they saw a stream, narrow now, that would swell again in the spring runoff from the mountain snows to give the crops their water.

The church stood apart from the houses and barns on a small hillock dotted with trees and brush. It was built of rough hewn logs and like the houses looked as if nothing short of a stick of dynamite could dislodge it from its foundation. The church door stood ajar, and in the packed earth near the entrance McAfee saw a huddled shape covered by a blanket.

They tied their horses to a rail outside the church and Stafford led them through the door. "This is what I want you to see," he said, sweeping his arm in a gesture that took in the whole of the church's interior.

The tableau that McAfee and Hollister saw was a slaughterhouse.

Bodies were strewn around the church pews like discarded dolls, throats bitten through, limbs torn from their torsos, in some cases bodies all but decapitated by savage blows. Every chest was torn open. There seemed to be no surface in the church that escaped the bloody spattering.

Near the altar a dead woman lay on her back, an infant torn in two clutched half in one hand and half in the other. It was all McAfee could do not to vomit at the scene. He'd seen plenty of corpses in the war and after, but the sight of the dead mother and child was more than he could manage. He knew it would haunt him for the rest of his days.

Hollister stood silent. He had respectfully removed his hat and McAfee was relieved he didn't take out his notebook and tape measure.

"Twenty-three people," said Stafford, his voice rising, "twenty-three unarmed peaceful people worshipping in their church. Dead. Massacred." His big hands closed into knotty fists. "You two don't even look surprised. Who did this?" he hissed through clenched teeth, "You know, don't you? Tell me!"

"Can't, Sheriff," said McAfee. "We're under orders. I agree you ought to know, but neither of us has the authority to tell you. We can take you to somebody who does."

Stafford stared at them for a long moment, took a look around the gore spattered church and shoved his fists into his pockets. "Then let's ride."

A t twilight, a mist rose from the plain below and crept up the mountainside like a thief. The moon would be up soon, and everyone in the camp was edgy. The guard around the camp was doubled and Durken was posted on the hillside over the mine entrance. A hundred feet to his right was McKenna and Beckley to his left. Below, Butler sat alone at the fire pit, wrapped in his bearskin cloak, slumped as if he were dozing, but Durken knew full well he was wide awake and had all his senses attuned to the gathering darkness. Butler volunteered for the post and nobody argued. He'd set aside his Winchester in favor of an old style .52 caliber Sharps buffalo gun. "Whatever I hit with this," he boasted, "stays down."

The horses had been moved into the mine tunnel to prevent them from being run off and leaving the group stranded. "They didn't attack last night," Harper had said, "and maybe they've moved on, but maybe they haven't. We have to behave as if they're still out there. If they don't attack tonight, we'll move out in the morning and get off this damned mountain."

So they waited and they watched and they listened. The forest at night is never silent; there is always the call of a nocturnal bird, the snap of a branch, or the swish of some creature or another passing through the dense brush, but this night, there was no sound, as if the mist were a shroud over a corpse.

Below in the mine tunnel, Travis and his men were crouched just inside the entrance, rifles at the ready. If the Tonnewa raid us tonight, thought Durken, we'll give as good as we get. Like Butler said, they bleed the same as we do.

At the fire pit, Butler thumbed back the hammer of his rifle. His sharp ears had picked up just the faintest movement beyond the circle of the firelight. He raised an eyelid barely enough to make out a dim shape the size of a man in the mist. Come and get it, you bastard, he thought. I got one with your name on it.

The shape inched a step closer, and Butler ever so slightly turned the barrel of the Sharps toward the approaching target. Get him full in the chest, he thought.

At that moment, a night breeze sent the mist swirling away for a second, and Butler stared into the raw face of horror. It was a man, or what had once been a man, but its face was furred and angular, fanged like a cougar, and its sinewy arms ended in five fingered hands that hooked into claws. The beast gave a coughing snarl, and charged.

The Sharps roared, and the beast tumbled backward, knocked down by the shot. Butler jumped to his feet and jacked another shell into the chamber, swinging the muzzle to one side then the other looking for more attackers. And that was when he saw the creature he had shot rise to its feet again. He fired a second shot into its chest and the beast fell again, but by this time, Butler had other things to worry about. At least twenty of them came charging through the trees into the camp.

Behind him, rifles roared, but had little effect. The catman that Butler had shot sprung at him but found the bearskin cape as effective as a chain mail shirt in deflecting its claws. The fanged head snapped at Butler's throat, but he pushed the jaws away before they could close on him. He dropped the Sharps and closed his hands around the furred throat, put his thumbs under the catman's chin and pushed upward, snapping its neck with a sharp crack.

A second beast jumped onto Butler's back and would have killed him for sure if a blast from the miners' .10 gauge shotgun hadn't taken its head off at the neck. Butler turned and saw Harper clutching the smoking gun. A catman pounced on Harper, knocking away the gun and ripping at the Captain's leg. With a feral roar Butler grabbed the creature with both hands by the scruff of its neck and swung it around, hurling it into the fire pit.

The beast rose in the pit its fur aflame, clawing at its face and making a sound that mixed the yowl of a panther with a human scream. It fell back into the fire and didn't rise again.

Durken fired three quick shots into another of the catmen but with no more effect than a hornet's sting. McKenna had scrambled down from his position and was dragging the Captain to the tunnel entrance when one of the creatures struck the back of the sergeant's neck with a blow that swiveled his head like a broken doll's.

Butler tackled the beast and wrapped his arms around it, holding it face to face. By this time, Durken and Beckley had dropped into the clearing. "Get him in the tunnel!" Butler shouted, squeezing the monster in a death grip as it sunk its fangs into his shoulder. Butler bellowed with pain and with a heave jerked the catman upward then down snapping its spine. The creature screeched and Butler dropped it to the ground where it flopped helpless like a landed trout.

But Butler's victory was short lived. Three of the catmen leapt on him and brought him down. Durken pulled his Bowie knife from its sheath and plunged it between the shoulders of one of the beasts. It yowled and tried desperately to claw the knife free, but its hunched shoulders wouldn't let it reach the handle.

Two more of the catmen charged at Durken, and he drew his Colt and fired two shots point blank into the face of the nearest one, knocking it backward into its companion. He cast a quick look at the pair ravaging Butler and realized that he was done. Durken spun and dashed toward the tunnel's mouth, the monsters closing on him.

XXIX

McAfee heard the first shots at a distance and cursed the mist that kept their pace at a slow walk. He flicked the reins and Thunder sped up to a trot. "Come on," he shouted to the others.

"Are you crazy?" said Stafford. "I can't see six feet in this fog."

"Trust the horses." He spurred Thunder and soon he and Hollister were far ahead of Stafford and his deputy.

The shots continued ahead. "I don't know what's going on, but it's got to be trouble. Do you have a gun?" McAfee called back to Hollister.

"There's a carbine in a scabbard in the saddle."

"That'll do."

The rising moon made the fog iridescent and cast an eerie glow over the landscape where the silvery light broke through the cover of the trees. McAfee strained his eyes and spotted a dark mound in the middle of the trail. He reined Thunder back and stopped, Hollister almost colliding with him.

McAfee pulled his pistol and hopped down from the saddle. He nudged at the shape with the toe of his boot. "Oh, damn."

"What is it?"

"It's Welton, or what's left of him." He swung back into the saddle. "Lord knows what's happening at the camp. Come on."

McAfee broke from the trees into the clearing and saw three of the catmen chasing Durken as he ran toward the mouth of the tunnel. Without a second's hesitation, he spurred Thunder who jumped the fire pit and plowed into the beasts headlong, knocking two aside and trampling one underfoot. One of them scrambled to its feet and came at Thunder, arms spread and claws dripping blood.

A shot from behind put the catman on the ground, and Hollister rode past McAfee into the mouth of the mine. McAfee followed and dismounted, ready to fight the charge that he was sure was coming. The catmen loped to the opening and suddenly stopped. They snarled and raged, slashing the air with their paws in frustration. The fiends whirled like dervishes in a berserker fury, outraged that their prey was only a few feet away but they couldn't reach them.

"It's the silver in the rock," said Hollister. "They can't tolerate the silver."

Horses. Stafford and his deputy rode into the firelight totally unprepared for what they saw. The catmen whirled and charged them *en masse*. In a moment both were pulled from their mounts and disappeared under a writhing heap of tawny bodies.

Beckley started out of the tunnel, a carbine in his hands. Durken grabbed him from behind and threw him to the ground. "We've got to help them," Beckley cried.

Durken held him down and tried to settle him. "Son, this ain't Gettysburg. They're past helping. And that rifle won't do you no good."

Hollister had gone back into the tunnel and returned with a half dozen small stones in his hand.

"What's that?" McAfee said.

"Maybe a weapon."

Outside in the firelight they could see McKenna's body lying in a heap, his head cocked at an unnatural angle, his unseeing eyes staring at them. The catmen had left Stafford and his deputy and one of them half crawled to McKenna's body. The feral attack was set aside now, and the creature moved with purpose. It rolled the sergeant face up and ripped away his tunic. With a powerful slash, it tore open McKenna's chest then reached in and pulled out a gory lump of flesh.

The creature, still in a crouch, turned slowly to face the men watching from the tunnel. It held the dripping heart high like a trophy and snarled in triumph.

Something whistled across the clearing and the creature shrieked in pain, dropped the heart, and clutched at its eye. Hollister stepped out of the tunnel, whirling his handkerchief as a sling. He released a second stone that struck the beast in its muzzle, and it sprung away howling and clawing at its face. It dashed into the forest and the others followed. In seconds the clearing was empty and the only sounds they heard were the crackle of the fire in the pit and the piteous mewling of the broken-backed creature beside it.

"That was some trick, Hollister," said Durken. "What did you throw?"

A grim smile played across Hollister's face. "Silver nuggets. You learn things if you pay attention."

Holister stepped warily into the clearing. He looked in every direction before he approached the crippled catman. He circled the creature slowly, studying it from every angle. The beast followed him with hateful eyes, its cries becoming snarls of rage.

Hollister leaned in for a closer look, and when he did, the hideous head snapped at him and its paw swiped through the air and hooking in his canvas puttees. The monster pulled itself toward him and sank its fangs in his calf.

A flash of steel in the moonlight, and a saber separated the beast's head from its shoulders. Light glowed in the slanted eyes for a second then was gone. Durken wiped the blade on its fur. "Damn it, Hollister, curiosity's supposed to kill the cat."

"I'll be all right; it barely broke the skin. These puttees are made to stop snakebite."

"Now maybe you can tell us just what the hell we're up against."

"**W**e have a real dilemma here," Durken said, sitting on a stump cut beside the fire. It had blazed all night, lighting the clearing to the dense dark trees, and Durken had sat watch the whole time. "There's too much we just don't know."

"We have Seven Stars' story," said McAfee, "and based on what we saw last night, I'd give it some credence."

It held the dripping heart high like a trophy...

"What's Hollister have to say about it?"

"Nothing much. Just like you and me, he wants to know more. He's back in the tunnel now with the bones of that thing that fell in the fire." McAfee gestured to the dead werecats covered by a tarpaulin. "I guess he'll take a look at them next, take pictures and all"

"We know they can die," said Durken, "and that's a useful fact."

"Something else to mull over, they left dead behind this time, maybe they took the bodies from Caplock and the raid on the Mingotts to make it look like they couldn't be hurt or killed."

"That or so nobody would know what they were."

McAfee nodded agreement. "And what Seven Stars told us about silver seems to be right. You saw what happened when Hollister caught that catman in the eye with a nugget."

"Fire doesn't do them much good either." Durken fished a plug of tobacco out of his vest pocket. He bit off a chew and sat a while, his jaw working. "How many of those things would you say attacked us last night?"

"Two dozen easy." McAfee stared into the fire. "I've been thinking about Seven Stars' story. If they are men in the daytime and these catmen at night, then they can hit us either time. Harper said there were at least two hundred Tonnewa. All of them can't be those monsters, but that's still a lot of force to contend with. That trail's the only way we know out of here, and this is their mountain. They could circle around us and ambush us with guns or just with bows and arrows if we try to ride out of here today. Do we take that chance?"

"We don't know where they are or how many of them there are, but they sure as hell know where we are."

Travis came out of the tunnel and sat by the fire with them. "How's the Captain?" said McAfee.

"Pretty bad. We gave him morphine from the medical kit, and he's been asleep for a while."

"He's in no shape to command, and with McKenna dead, I believe that makes you the ranking officer, Travis."

The corporal shook his head. "You're right, but I wish you weren't. I don't have any more idea how to deal with this mess than the Man in the Moon."

"We have to see to the Captain," said McAfee. "When you say pretty bad, how bad is he?"

"We bandaged him up as well as we could. The wounds already look infected, and if gangrene sets in, he could lose that leg or maybe even die. We have to get him to a doctor."

"Hauling him down this mountain's gonna be tough enough without having to fight our way past a few hundred Tonnewa the whole trip, let alone those animal men," Durken said. "We know what we're fighting now and how to hurt them. The way I see it, they can't afford to let us off this mountain alive, but if we can find some means to keep them off our ass long enough, maybe we can get away."

"We can't get word out for reinforcements," McAfee said. "Besides, I wouldn't feel right bringing men in here who don't know what they're fighting."

"One thing I don't understand," said Travis.

"What's that?"

"How you two can just sit here calmly and talk about this like it's just another battle."

"Because that's what it is," said Durken. "Besides, we've seen worse."

Travis stared at him, waiting for the answer that would never come to an unspoken question.

Durken looked up at McAfee who had risen to his feet. "Where you going?"

"To talk to Hollister. I have an idea."

XXXI

McAfee followed the tunnel into the mountain. The ceiling was higher than he could reach, and two men, arms extended could barely touch the walls. The rough stone and hand-hewn beams testified to backbreaking labor for little reward. Near the end of the tunnel Hollister crouched over the skeleton, which he had carefully arranged on a blanket. He looked up as McAfee approached and stood, wiping his hands on his trousers.

"It's fascinating," Hollister said. "The bone structure is essentially *homo sapiens*, but with variations in shape that suggest mutation. The elongated skull and the fangs are definitely feline, but the ribcage and hips, for example, are distinctly human. These creatures seem to be an entirely new species. It's a puzzle."

"Yeah, that's interesting, but we're in a tight spot. Harper will die soon if we don't get him to a doctor, and likely so will we if we stay here. I need to know what you can tell me about these things."

Hollister packed his pipe as he spoke. "Well, they are material beings, and as such the laws of physics apply to them."

"What do you mean?"

"You hit them with enough force and they move. You proved that when you rode them down with your horse. Durken decapitated one with a saber." He gestured toward the bones. "Fire burns them, fatally in this case. Gunshots may injure them, but not as they would you or me. Their Achilles heel seems to be silver; it has an almost poisonous effect."

"Yeah, I remember Seven Stars talking about Grey Cloud being trussed up with silver then thrown off the edge of the world."

"Exactly. I took the chance last night of throwing a piece of silver and it worked. They can't come into the mine tunnel because of the silver in the rock and the dust everywhere. And look at this." Hollister took a pinch of dust from the floor of the tunnel and sprinkled it on one of the thigh bones. A faint wisp of smoke rose from the dust. "It seems to be corrosive to them. I don't know why; it defies all logic."

"Like you said, 'more things in heaven and earth'. It doesn't matter why. I say if it works, how do we use it?"

"Silver bullets may be lethal."

"We'll go through the miners' equipment and see whether they have loading gear, that and we need to find the Mingott Brothers' cache of nuggets. If silver works against these things, we'll need all we can get our hands on."

"Something else to think about: The hair on these creatures seems to match the hairs I found on the hatchet. That means that the ones who attacked the Mingotts were the same species, if not the exact ones that attacked us tonight."

"I have to ask you something; that flash powder of yours."

"The magnesium?"

"How much of it do you have?"

"Almost two pounds; I've used a lot but we brought plenty."

"If you mix it with blasting powder, how will it burn in the open?"

"Literally like Guy Fawkes Day. Fireworks manufacturers started using Magnesium in the mid sixties. It accelerates the ignition of the gunpowder."

"The miners have three kegs of blasting powder in their supplies, and they have a near full barrel of lamp oil."

"What do you have in mind?"

"A way to maybe end this business here and now."

Hollister stared at the bones on the blanket. "I'd hate to think that we're destroying evidence of a monumental scientific discovery."

"I'd hate to think of another church full of dead bodies."

Hollister nodded resignedly. "Quite right."

The miners did not have equipment for casting slugs and loading ammunition, but McAfee found a box of shells for the .10 gauge shotgun and set about replacing the shot with chunks of silver ore dug from the walls of the tunnel. The men had searched the camp thoroughly but had not found the Mingott Brothers' stash of silver.

Durken grunted as he swung his pick into the wall of the tunnel. "If we don't have enough silver dust, this plan could get pretty dicey."

"Yep. But it's the best we've got." McAfee hefted a pick of his own and started in on the wall.

Travis and Beckley came down the tunnel shoving another soldier ahead of him, a private named Felix. "Go on," said Travis, "tell them."

McAfee and Durken set down their picks. "Tell us what?"

Beckley spoke up. "When we were searching the camp, Felix here made it a point to stay close to the fire pit. I smelled a rat, and I was right. Tell them, Felix."

The private avoided their eyes. "I found the silver. It's under a couple of the stones around the pit."

"So you figured you'd come back later and get it for yourself. Greedy bastard," spat Beckley, cuffing him on the back of the head. "We ought to shoot you right now."

"How much?" said McAfee. "A little or a lot?"

"Moosehide sacks, three or four that I saw." Felix stammered.

"Nuggets or dust?"

"I don't know. I didn't pick any of them up. I just put the rocks back in place."

"Show us."

The Mingott Brothers' mine had been more successful than they had let on. Under the fire pit stones were four leather sacks of silver nuggets and six of silver dust. Durken hefted one of the sacks of dust and said, "What do you think?"

McAfee said, "It'll do." He looked up at the grey sky. "Let's just hope the weather holds."

XXXIII

An hour before sunset, soldiers stood guard a half mile from the camp while Durken, McAfee, and Hollister set about laying what they hoped would be a lethal trap along the trail. Using a mix of Hollister's magnesium and the Mingotts' black powder, they laid a rough oval about 100 feet long bisected by the trail. Brush was heaped in mounds across the path at either end. Lamp oil was splashed on the branches and trunks of the pines and the brush piles. The plan was simple: lure the Cat Warriors into the oval and ignite the magnesium-powder mix, the resin-rich pines would burn like matchwood, and the blaze would trap them inside an instant inferno.

A lighted lantern in the brush pile at the camp end of the road would be broken with a gunshot and the flaming oil would spring the trap. Simple.

What was dangerous was the means of luring the creatures into the oval: human bait.

"We have to get them to chase us," said McAfee.

"Shouldn't be too hard," said Durken, "seeing as how they seem to want to kill every human they see."

"We just need to lead them into the trap and get out of it ourselves."

"That may be easier said than done. The horses are fast, but we don't know how fast those critters can run. What'd Hollister say? As fast as a horse or faster?"

"He was talking about a regular catamount running on four legs. These are hybrids running on two."

They had picked a spot on the trail to lay the trap where their horses could run almost flat out, but so could the catmen. "It'll be close."

McAfee looked back into the trees. "I expect it will."

To give themselves an extra edge, Durken and McAfee had poured sacks of the silver dust over themselves and rubbed it onto every surface of their horses' hides. Riding out of the camp in the twilight, they looked like grey ghosts. If Hollister was right, the silver would keep the catmen from biting them, but there were still the claws to worry over.

"This is the most expensive suit of clothes I ever wore. We look like those lead soldiers my brother Russell and I used to play with when we were kids," said McAfee.

"Maybe the catmen'll see us and fall down laughing, do you suppose?"

"I doubt it."

"Me too." Durken pointed to the shotgun. "I feel the best about having that little beauty with us." Beckley spent the afternoon with a file sawing through the long barrel and leaving a wicked short gun that would spray a wide pattern of silver nuggets. Since Durken was the better shot of the two, they agreed that he would shoot the lantern and McAfee would handle the scatter gun.

"I'm hoping one shot'll snuff out the whole gang of them," McAfee said, "and if not the first round, then the second. I don't expect I'll have a chance to reload."

As they rode out of the camp in the deepening twilight, no one spoke. Wishing them good luck was a given. They'd need more than their share to pull this off.

As they rode down the trail, McAfee said, "Durken."

"Yeah?"

"If for some reason I don't survive this, give my regards to Miss Sarah."

"I'll do that, and you do the same for me to Maggie."

"Are you kidding? If I come back and you don't, she'll kill me herself."

They rode through the gathering gloom of the forest beyond the fire trap, every sense alert. "You know," said Durken, "I hate to say this, but I wish we had Butler with us."

McAfee nodded. "He was a good hand in the woods, no matter what else he may have been; sure could have used his eyes and ears."

"Yep. And he redeemed himself in some ways when he saved Harper."

"And Harper saved him, at least in the short run. Funny how a common enemy shifts the balance between men."

"Sh." Sweetheart's ears pricked up. Durken leaned forward in the saddle, listening. He gently reined his horse around and McAfee did the same. They strained their eyes into the darkness beyond the trail but could see nothing in the shadows. Furtive sounds came from the brush. Durken said quietly, "Get ready. They're here."

McAfee cocked the hammers of the shotgun.

Durken nudged Sweetheart in the ribs and both horses set out at a slow walk back toward the camp. Thunder nickered and twitched nervously. McAfee tightened his grip on the reins with one hand and the stock of the shotgun with the other.

Something crashed through the brush to the left and Durken shouted, "Go!"

The horses took off and behind them, the trail filled with snarling furred horrors. One that lay in ambush sprung at Sweetheart, narrowly missing the horse's flank with its claws and falling to the path to be trampled under Thunder's hooves.

Another leapt from the brush and clamped its jaws on Durken's forearm, knocking him from the saddle. The beast let go at once, howling and swiping at its muzzle with its paws. McAfee wheeled Thunder and bowled over three of the catmen. He reached down and grabbed Durken's arm, yanking him into the saddle. With his other hand he swung the shotgun and fired a blast into the charging swarm. He didn't look back to see how effective the shot had been, but he heard a caterwauling chorus that chilled his blood.

Sweetheart ran ahead, riderless. "Bolt!" Durken shouted at the horse, which broke into a dead run. Then to McAfee, "Let him go. We don't have time to get me back in the saddle. Ride for the trap."

McAfee spurred Thunder and the horse surged ahead, the pack of howling monsters close behind. "We're close," he shouted over his shoulder. "Be ready."

Durken reached for his Colt. It had fallen from his holster when he fell from his horse. "Lost my gun," he shouted in McAfee's ear. "I'm taking yours." He pulled McAfee's revolver from its holster and cocked the hammer.

Ahead, they could see the dim flicker of the lantern. "Almost there. Hang on."

Durken dug his fingers into the ridge of Thunder's saddle. They were running along the open part of the trail now and Thunder was galloping. The horse jumped the first brush pile and landed inside the oval. Behind them the pack sprung over the barricade.

Thunder jumped the second brush pile and as a handful of the pack leapt over it Durken spun in the saddle and fired a spray of shots. The lantern shattered and the magnesium-gunpowder mix erupted in a white hot flare, catching two of the catmen in midleap and setting their pelts aflame. They rolled on the ground howling as the blaze whooshed around the oval and rose instantly into the oil-soaked trees, trapping most of the pack inside a towering wall of fire where their wailing voices rose in a hellish chorus.

McAfee hauled up on Thunder's reins and fired the second shell. The catmen who escaped the flames fell to the ground. He dug frantically in the pocket of his duster for more shells with one hand as he broke open the breech of the shotgun with the other.

One of the creatures rose slowly to its feet, snarling, and then a second. They moved more slowly now, arms outstretched, their clawed hands silhouetted by the crackling blaze behind them. The others lay where they fell. McAfee snapped the gun shut and cocked the hammers as the first one sprang.

The shot caught it in mid-air but its momentum carried it forward enough that the beast's claws raked Durken's chaps and Thunder's ribs. The horse reared and McAfee went over backward, taking Durken with him. McAfee went one way and the shotgun the other.

The second catman sprung and McAfee found himself wrestling with the wrath of an angry god. Claws sunk into his shoulders through his duster. He held the snapping jaws back with a forearm and thrust a silver-coated thumb into one of the monster's glowing green eyes. The effect was immediate. The beast-man's head jerked back and the creature yowled in agony. Wisps of smoke puffed from the socket of its ruined eye.

The creature pushed itself away and raised its arm to deliver a death blow. The shotgun roared and the blast knocked the catman sideways, rolling it three times side over side before it came to rest and lay still.

"Give me some shells, quick," said Durken. There may be more of those things coming."

The howls rose in pitch and volume as the flames closed in on the Cat Warriors. Two of them tried to rush through the wall of fire and emerged on the other side aflame from top to bottom. One, Durken dispatched with the shotgun. The other ran blindly, shrieking into the forest, crashing headlong into a tree and falling on its back a few yards into the brush.

"Let's get out of here," said McAfee.

"Shouldn't we wait to make sure we got them all?"

"The fire may spread. There's no wind now, but that can change in a hurry. If we didn't kill them all, we killed enough of them."

"You all right?" said Durken.

"I'll live," said McAfee. "But I'll be digging nuggets out of my hide for a week. You got some of that spray on me when you shot the cat."

"That sawed-off ain't exactly a precision instrument." Durken whistled, then after a pause whistled again. Sweetheart trotted into the firelight. He patted the horse's shoulder. "Good boy."

Durken and McAfee saddled up and rode for the camp.

Behind them in the trees, a single green eye, glowing with malevolent hatred, watched them ride away.

XXXIV

At dawn the patrol left the Mingott Brothers' camp with Harper on a travois pulled by his horse. He became feverish overnight and ranted in a delirium about death, revenge and justice.

Hollister reluctantly packed his camera equipment and in a tow sack the bones of the immolated catman and the head of the decapitated one packed in salt. Hollister buried the rest of the remains inside the tunnel in the hope that he could return for them later.

"There's so much to learn from all this," he'd said, but even his scientific curiosity was overridden by common sense. Maybe the catmen were finished, and maybe not. Besides them, the other Tonnewa were still hidden somewhere in the mountains, maybe over the next rise, and what good was discovery if one didn't live to tell about it?

Durken and McAfee scouted ahead while Travis and the remaining soldiers from his patrol rode with Harper. Hollister caught up with them just before they reached the scene of the fire from the night before.

They stopped at the entrance to the trap and stared at the desolation. The fire had burned itself out overnight, and in the pale dawn the oval looked like a patch of Winter in the midst of Autumn. The ground was white with ash and the charred trunks and limbs of trees stood stark and bare. Smoke hung in the air and in the shadows an orange glow showed where the fire still smoldered in the duff, ready to flare again with the right puff of wind.

Hollister stared at the scene and said almost reverently, "'Bare ruined choirs where late the sweet birds sang.'"

"We're lucky it rained the day before," said McAfee. "Otherwise this whole mountain'd be a bare ruined choir."

"And we'd've likely smothered in that mine," said Durken.

Hollister jumped down from his horse and started into the oval. He swiveled his head from side to side. "You said there were at least a dozen of the creatures trapped in the fire."

"I didn't take the time to count," Durken replied. "Things were a little hectic."

"Where are their bones?"

Durken and McAfee looked at each other. "Come to think of it," said McAfee, there should be a few bodies out here where we shot them."

Durken turned his head from side to side, peering into the trees. "That means trouble."

"Looks to me as if the Tonnewa are still taking away any trace of their warriors. Stands to reason; people fear what they can't see, and what Seven Stars said goes right along. They want to scare people away from here. "

"Damn."

"Yep."

Hollister, who couldn't hear the exchange, stood in the midst of the ashes, his disappointment evident. Durken shook his head. "Hollister, it looks as if there's still somebody or something prowling around out there, and if you want to live to tell the world about it, you'd better get on that horse and ride away from here now." He turned to McAfee. "Do you want to go back and tell Travis, or do you want me to do it?"

"I'll do it." McAfee nudged Thunder in the ribs and headed back the way they came.

Hollister rummaged through the ashes with the toe of his boot. "What's this?" He bent down and picked up a small object. He held it up for Durken to see. "It's one of those cat head amulets."

"Glad you didn't come away empty-handed," Durken said. "Now let's ride."

Hollister tucked the amulet into his vest pocket and climbed back into the saddle. He and Durken rode away, Durken's Winchester now across his thighs.

McAfee caught up with them soon after and the three riders carefully picked their way down the treacherous path off the mountain. When they reached the scrubland below, Hollister said," Are we waiting for Travis?"

"No," McAfee replied. "We have to get into Lickskillet as fast as we can and send a telegram to the General. We need a lot more men than a patrol to go after the Tonnewa."

"You're going back?" Hollister said, with sudden enthusiasm.

"Yep," said McAfee. "We have to find the tribe and see to it this problem doesn't continue."

"I want to go with you."

"That'll be up to the General to decide," said Durken.

"Something else we have to do," said McAfee, "is tell the town that Stafford and his deputy won't be coming back."

XXXV

As it turned out, Lickskillet had two doctors, one who doubled as a veterinarian and one who also served as the town dentist. They left Harper with one and Hollister and McAfee went to the other, figuring Harper would keep the first doctor busy enough.

Doctor Tyler, who took care of Harper, was young and fresh from the East. Doctor Shadwell, the vet, who saw to McAfee and Hollister's injuries, was old and cranky with a thick head of coal black hair and a drooping mustache whose color belied his wrinkled cheeks and forehead.

Shadwell pulled his spectacles down the bridge of his nose and squinted at Hollister's calf. "What bit you son?" he said. "I've dealt with just about everything a man or a horse can have from chillblains to the clap to a broken neck, but I've never had to treat bite marks quite like these." Hollister and McAfee looked to each other and said nothing. "I'd guess a wildcat, but the jaw line's wrong, and it sure ain't a wolf did this."

"I'm not certain," Hollister said. "It was dark, and I couldn't really see what it was. I thought it was a big cat of some kind."

"Mmm-hm," Shadwell said, unconvinced. He swabbed at the bites with a wad of gauze steeped in hydrogen peroxide. "Good thing you got in here quick. You could've gotten lockjaw if infection set in." He wound a bandage around the wounds and ripped a foot of it longways to tie it off field dressing style.

"You an Army sawbones?" said McAfee, recognizing the technique.

"For six years I was the post surgeon at Fort Laramie. I tended men and horses alike, but I left the Army before the war started and I settled out here." He said to Hollister. "Keep that leg clean unless you want to come back and see me again." Then to McAfee, "Sit down." Shadwell nudged a chair forward with his foot. "What's your complaint?"

"Got some scratches on my back." McAfee said, pulling his suspenders off his shoulders.

"So I'm guessing you were Army too. Which side did you serve?"

"I was in Third Rhode Island; scouted for Sherman in Georgia." McAfee unbuttoned his shirt.

Shadwell pursed his lips. "Sherman. I hear he's around here these days, in charge of the 'Indian situation.' You boys aren't working for him, are you?"

Again, McAfee and Hollister exchanged glances. "That's all right," Shadwell said. "You don't have to say. I was in the Army; I know how it is." He looked over the claw marks on McAfee's shoulders. "You get these from the same source as him?"

"Yep."

Shadwell was silent as he scrubbed out the claw marks with peroxide. McAfee flinched as the disinfectant stung its way under his skin. "Put on a clean undershirt if you have one. Those wounds are in a place I can't bandage them very well. Same goes for you about keeping the site clean."

He washed his hands as McAfee buttoned his shirt. "I don't know what's going on around here, fellows, and maybe I don't want to know. But Stafford left here yesterday with a posse that came back to town without him all looking like they'd been to the gates of Hell."

"Two of them took me to that Brethren Camp out by Stoner's Creek. I hope you or the posse finds the sons of bitches that slaughtered those people. Killing them isn't near good enough justice, but it'll have to do."

"What about the posse?" said McAfee.

"Yeah," said Shadwell. "They regrouped, rounded up some more men and some more guns, and rode back out of here about an hour before you arrived."

McAfee threw a five dollar gold piece on the doctor's desk. "Come on," he said to Hollister and they hurried out the door.

Durken was waiting with Harper while Travis was at the telegraph office sending his messages to Sherman and to Major Denning at Fort Dixon. He was sitting on the porch of Tyler's office smoking a cigarette under a hanging wooden sign in the shape of a molar.

"We got a problem," said McAfee.

Durken stood up and flipped the butt of his cigarette into the street. "Tell it to get in line."

"That posse of Stafford's gathered up more men and they're on the hunt for anything with feathers."

Durken shook his head. "We can't leave before we get orders and reinforcements. You know that."

"Well the horse is out of the barn now," said McAfee. "The whole town will know what happened by sundown, and in a week the whole territory will know."

"But they still think it's natives they're after," said Hollister.

"And that's what bothers me most," said McAfee. "Those men won't know what they're riding after until they find it."

A little past sundown the posse returned cold, tired, and frustrated. They had found no trace of the killers and were smart enough to get off the mountain before dark.

In the meantime, Travis received word from Fort Dixon that a platoon would arrive the next morning to pursue the Tonnewa. Sherman's adjutant Barlow sent a message from the General telling Durken and McAfee to accompany the troops, to use all resources necessary in pursuit of the tribe, and to "take no prisoners."

"Don't leave much room for interpretation, does it?" said Durken.

"Not much."

"What about me? Did he say whether I can go with you?"

Durken scratched his chin. "Read me the part again about resources."

"It says to 'use all resources,'" McAfee read.

"Reckon that includes experts?"

McAfee nodded. "I guess there's some room for interpretation after all."

"I think we need to do one more thing today."

"What's that?"

"Find somebody who can turn that silver we brought back with us into .45 caliber slugs."

XXXVI

Hollister, McAfee, and Durken spent the night slumped on the hard benches of the rail coach to avoid confronting the locals. They were wakened in the morning by Travis. He stuck his head into the car and said, "Platoon's here."

Outside, twenty men had dismounted and were warming themselves around a fire. Travis brought them over and then saluted as a young lieutenant standing apart from the group turned toward them. "This is Durken, and this is McAfee, sir," he said to the lieutenant, and this man is Hollister, the animal expert."

The lieutenant sized them up for a moment before speaking. "I'm Lieutenant Robert Pomeroy," he said. "So you served under Uncle Billy, eh?"

Durken said, "Truth be told, Lieutenant, I never referred to the General that way; thought it was disrespectful."

Pomeroy's eyes narrowed at the subtle reproach. "Is that so?"

"Durken? Is that you?" A beefy sergeant stood and ambled over. "And McAfee; I'll be damned. They didn't tell us it was you we was meeting."

Pomeroy opened his mouth to reprimand the sergeant for interrupting, but before he could speak, the sergeant said, "Carson, Jones, look at what we got here."

Two of the soldiers rose to their feet, and in a moment, McAfee and Durken were in the middle of a handshaking, backslapping reunion.

Wilkins, the sergeant, smiled a foot wide and said to Pomeroy, "We rode with these boys in Georgia, sir," then to McAfee and Durken. "Damn, Durken, you got old."

Durken grinned. "You don't look no younger, Pike, but that just means nobody shot you yet."

"Or hanged you, boy."

Pomeroy said coldly, "If you don't mind, Sergeant, we have business to conduct here."

Wilkins' smile faded. He snapped to attention. "Yes, sir. Sorry, sir." He saluted and he and the others turned back to the fire. Over the lieutenant's shoulder Wilkins winked.

"According to my orders from General Sherman through Major Denning we are to accompany you men in pursuit of the Tonnewa tribe and to deal with them as necessary."

"Yes, sir, said McAfee, that's what the General told us to do."

"You've been in direct communication with General Sherman?" Pomeroy seemed miffed that they had a direct line to the General and he didn't.

"Yep," said Durken. He paused to light his cigarette. "We've been under his direct orders from the start of this adventure."

Pomeroy eyed Hollister. "And this man, why is an animal expert necessary?"

"Lieutenant, I suspect that your Major Denning didn't tell you every detail of this situation, maybe because he wasn't told himself. As far as we know, the information's still a secret," said McAfee.

"Yes," said Pomeroy. "This operation is classified."

McAfee gestured to the rail coach. "Part of the problem is that things have happened that will likely let the cat out of the bag, so to speak. I'd suggest that we sit down a while and talk this over, let us give you the particulars. And if you don't mind, we just woke up and could sure use a cup of that coffee they're brewing."

Getting the coffee took a little longer than expected because Pike, Jones, and Carson insisted on introducing Durken and McAfee to every man at the campfire. Pomeroy stood by fuming at the delay but held his peace. In the car, Durken and McAfee told the story of the raids on the patrol, the mining camp, and the church. When they got to their battles with the Cat Warriors, Pomeroy raised a hand.

He laughed. "That's preposterous. Catmen?"

"That's why we have Hollister with us," said McAfee. "Tell him what you know."

"What I've found is evidence that we may be dealing with a new species, a hybrid cross between animal and human characteristics. They appear to have some intelligence and they may have been trained – I wouldn't say domesticated – but somehow brought to bear against what the Tonnewa consider interlopers on their land."

"And these animals attack in a group."

"Yes," said Hollister. "They exhibit coordinated behavior as you might find among lions, hyenas, or wolves."

"We thought these assaults may have been made by Tonnewa warriors dressed in animal skins and using weapons made of catamount fangs and claws, that is, until we saw these creatures firsthand." McAfee opened his knapsack and pulled out the picture of the Caplock Mountain massacre. He handed it to Pomeroy and said, "This is what they did to an armed party of experienced soldiers."

Pomeroy stared at the tintype and said nothing.

Durken said, "The platoon is under your command, Lieutenant, and it's not my place to step over your decisions as to how you run them. I do say, though, with all due respect, that they ought to know what they may have to face on that mountain. We'll leave that up to you."

Pomeroy stared at the Caplock picture. "You say you killed most of them."

"Seems so," said McAfee, "although we can't be sure they're all dead. If you doubt our word, you can ask Corporal Travis; he was there. I don't want to see good men die for nothing, Lieutenant. I'd suggest you tell them what we told you."

Pomeroy snorted. "I can't have my men spooked with fairy tales and ghost stories. Besides, you said most of them are already dead. You'll keep those stories to yourselves. They'll be given information as they need to know it. We have Indians to find, and we'll find them and we'll rout them by the book."

He stood and pointed at Hollister. "And he stays here. You two are Army and I need you to scout for me, but he's a civilian and I don't want him along scaring my men and getting in the way." Pomeroy strode out of the car and closed the door behind him a little harder than necessary.

"Why is an animal expert necessary?"

Hollister broke the silence that followed. "Headstrong and foolish."

"Yep." Durken said. "That man's leading us into a bear trap with his eyes shut."

"Like an ostrich." Hollister started packing his pipe.

"What's that?" said Durken.

"A big bird that, according to common belief, buries its head in the sand when danger approaches in the hope that what it doesn't see can't see it or hurt it."

"Sounds like Pomeroy to me," said McAfee.

"I've seen them in the wild, and they don't really do that, you know, but I thought the image suited him. I assume 'by the book' means by standard operating procedure?"

"Yep," said Durken looking out the window. "But I reckon the book for this fight ain't been written yet."

McAfee and Durken left Hollister in the car. As they walked away, McAfee said, "Maybe we could telegraph the General and tell him we need Hollister with us."

"I don't want to get into a pissing contest with Pomeroy that'll make him an adversary. He's a young dog and flexing his muscles to show his authority."

"It's too bad Harper's still out of commission. He outranks Pomeroy and could order him around."

"Last word on Harper, he's still delirious. We're better to stand up to Pomeroy over something big, not something small, if and when it's necessary. Besides Wilkins and his men ain't greenhorns, and I figure we can fill them in when the time comes."

"And it will."

XXXVII

The party set out an hour later, riding toward the distant blue mountains. Besides Hollister, Pomeroy ordered Travis and his men to stay behind. Durken rode at the rear of the group and as he expected, Pike Wilkins soon dropped back and fell in beside him.

"Your lieutenant seems seldom right but never in doubt."

"This is his first command," said the sergeant.

"He a West Pointer?"

"Nope, The Citadel."

"The Citadel? He doesn't talk like a southern boy."

"He ain't. He's from Massachussetts. His uncle's some political bigwig; got him into West Point right after the war, but the boy got kicked out his first year over some scandal or another. So they sent him to the Citadel then swung him a post out here to keep him out of their hair. He's not really too happy to be out here. But The Citadel trained him up good enough, I guess. He knows all about logistics and tactics; he's just short on horse sense."

"That's why he's got you."

Wilkins chuckled. "That's what Major Denning said, pretty much. 'Try to keep him aimed in the right direction.'"

"Good luck with that."

"He'll learn," Wilkins said, "if he lives long enough."

"That's the trick, ain't it?"

By late afternoon the party had reached the foot of the mountain. Pomeroy wanted to press on to set up a bivouac at the mining camp. "It's only a few more miles," he argued.

"Yes, sir," said McAfee. "I'd estimate about six and a half. But they're some of the toughest miles you'll ever ride. You may want to camp here and start fresh at first light. Sunset's about six o'clock this time of year and it gets dark in those trees mighty fast." In the back of his mind, McAfee was turning over Hollister's word again, "crepuscular."

"What you might do, Lieutenant," said Durken, "is send one or two of your men up the trail a ways and let them take a look and tell you how the land lays. Once you get past those meadows and up into the tree line, it's a tough go."

Pomeroy thought about it for a minute and called Wilkins over. "Sergeant, take two of the men and ride up the mountain. Scout the terrain and come back. I need to know whether we should push on or wait until morning."

"Yes, sir," said Wilkins who saluted and reined his horse around. "Beckwith, Jones, come with me." They rode off while the rest of the platoon dismounted and let their horses browse in the scant foliage.

"That was clever," said McAfee to Durken when they were out of Pomeroy's earshot. "You let him make the decision based on what one of his own men tells him."

"That way, it ain't you or me bucking his authority. I figure he'd listen to Wilkins easier than us, and I'll bet Wilkins comes back and says to stay put."

It was a bet Durken would have won if McAfee had taken it.

Wilkins returned in an hour with the word that the trail was too dangerous for twilight riding. "Based on what I saw, sir," he told Pomeroy, "we'd have to all but crawl along that path, especially in dim light, and I doubt we could make it to the camp before dark."

Pomeroy waited a full minute before delivering his decision, although he'd likely reached it in the first two seconds. "Very well, Sergeant. Have the men set up camp here and we'll move out in the morning."

That night by the fire, one of the soldiers, a young private named Dickerson said to Durken, "Sarge says you brought down the Angel. Is that right?" The infamous Confederate sharpshooter harried Sherman's forces through most of the Georgia campaign, killing key officers and specialists and became almost legendary among the Union soldiers.

Durken stared into the fire and didn't answer for a while. Finally he turned his head to look Dickerson in the eye and said, "Son, how many men have you killed?"

"Some," he said. "You can't really count in a battle. You just keep shooting 'til nothing's moving anymore."

"You ever stalk a man while he stalks you, and he's gonna kill you if you don't kill him first?"

Dickerson shook his head. "Can't say I have."

"It's a whole different contest." Durken looked back into the fire. "I suspect if Wilkins told you the story, he also told you I fired the luckiest shot in the war."

"But you fired it and the Angel didn't."

"That's true, but there was no glory in killing him. A lot of men died in Atlanta that night on both sides. He was one of them, I wasn't. You follow orders, you do your job. That's about all there is to it."

Silence fell on the group and for a while, they watched the sparks sail upward and vanish in the starlit sky. "What can you tell us about these Indians we're chasing?" one of the soldiers said.

"They're some of the fiercest and the deadliest fighters either of us have ever faced," said McAfee. "They've killed armed, experienced soldiers. They give no quarter, and neither should you. Best I can tell you is to keep your eyes open and your rifles cocked." He turned to Wilkins. "Pike, you haven't said squat about what you've done since the war."

Wilkins shrugged. "Most of what I've done these boys did with me or heard the stories after the fact."

"Well, Durken and I haven't heard them yet. Suppose you start with Appomattox, and don't spare the details."

In the morning the platoon rode out with McAfee and Durken in the lead. The climb proved no easier the second time than it was the first. It was past noon when they finally reached the ledge around the mountain. Durken and McAfee, wise in the way of bosses and commanding officers refrained from saying "I told you so."

They rode through the burnt oval where Durken and McAfee trapped the Cat Warriors. A light rain had fallen, washing much of the ash away, and McAfee had no doubt that after a healing winter, the death trap would turn the same verdant green as the rest of the forest around it.

The Mingott Brothers' camp appeared to be as they left it, for which McAfee and Durken were both relieved. The miners' graves were undisturbed, but why would they not be. Their hearts weren't buried with them.

Pomeroy left four men at the mine to establish a base camp and immediately set out on the trail of the Tonnewa. Durken led them along the path he and Butler had followed a few days before, past the spot where the dead brave had tethered his horse.

"Beyond here's where the Tonnewa began stalking us, so be watchful," he told the soldiers." It's a tossup whether they'll find us more vulnerable on horseback or leading the horses on foot on narrower parts of the trail. It's half and half as far as I can see. When we're walking the horses, don't all walk on the same side so's they can shoot at us from one direction."

Durken looked to Pomeroy. "Anything you'd care to add, Lieutenant?"

"That about covers it," then to the party at large, "You heard Durken. Stay sharp. Let's move out." The sky showed grey through the gaps in the trees as they plodded single file through the brush, but the threat of rain was unfulfilled until late afternoon.

McAfee rode behind Durken watching the flanks while Durken studied the trail. After two miles of narrow, difficult path, it joined a second trail that came down the mountainside at an oblique angle and the conjoined path widened a little. Durken slipped down from Sweetheart's saddle and crouched, studying the ground.

"It's more packed down here, but I don't see anything recent. I'd guess nobody's ridden through here since the last rain."

"But a wider trail means it's more used. Could be we're getting closer to their camp."

"Could be." He stood. "Lieutenant, we may be getting close, but that means we also may be riding into an ambush. McAfee and I could scout ahead, or we could all ride together. Pomeroy again made a show of thinking it over. "We'll ride *en masse*."

Durken climbed back into Sweetheart's saddle and they moved down the trail.

"So we ride *en masse*," said McAfee.

"I let him call the shot at this point," Durken replied. "I'd guess if the Tonnewa are still around here, they know we're on the way. It's difficult for eighteen men to be stealthy all at once."

When the rain began it was a light drizzle but it soon advanced to a steady fall, big fat droplets spattering on the trees, the horses, and the men. The trail became slick and treacherous, and the steep slope that fell away to their left promised a bad fall for a misstep. Pomeroy had donned an India rubber waterproof cloak that covered him from head to foot and draped over his saddle and arms.

"Must've been all the fashion at the Citadel," muttered Durken, "but I'd like to see him try to pull his revolver or his saber from under that rig."

"A good commanding officer never fires a shot; that's what enlisted men are for." McAfee chuckled. But I must say I liked the idea of those Roman officers riding out front swinging a sword."

"I'm sure it inspired the troops." Durken suddenly put up his hand. "Look through the tops of the trees. There's a clearing up ahead. Let's move on but go slow."

"Arms at the ready, men," said Pomeroy.

They found the Tonnewa camp. The trees opened into a large, flat clearing. A rain-swollen stream cascaded from above and ran through it in a steady flow. Tribal teepees stood in a rough circle. A fire pit sat black and cold in its center. There was neither movement nor sound.

"I count sixteen teepees," said McAfee. "What do you think?"

"Could be as many as a hundred people, but I don't see hide nor hair of them." Durken dismounted, warily looking around. Behind him, the cavalrymen formed up across the clearing in a zig-zag line. Durken looked back at Wilkins, who gave a curt nod.

Rifle at the ready, Durken strode to the nearest teepee, McAfee behind, covering him. He held the Winchester in his right hand, a good grip on the stock and his finger on the trigger while he reached for the flap with his left. He took a long breath and let it out before he yanked the flap aside. Empty.

The village was deserted although there was evidence of recent activity. Hides were stretched, curing. A slab of venison hung from a tree branch out of reach of bears and wolves. Cooking pots and bowls lay around the fire pit. It appeared that the Tonnewa had simply vanished, leaving possessions, food, tools, everything they owned.

The rain tapered to a drizzle while the men searched the village, then it stopped altogether. Wilkins strolled over to Durken and McAfee. "Well, boys, I guess we keep looking." He pulled the stub of a cigar out of his tunic and was about to scratch a match on his belt buckle when McAfee caught his hand.

"Wait." McAfee wrinkled his nose. "Don't light up yet," and to Durken, "You smell that?"

Durken sniffed the air. "Something dead." He turned to the soldiers. "Follow me, men." The cavalrymen went after Durken past the edge of the camp into the trees. In a smaller clearing, they found the Tonnewa.

Bodies, dozens of them in varying states of decomposition lay in a heap. The stench was overwhelming. Arms and legs in Indian buckskins projected from the pile and the faces they could see wore expressions of agony. Most of the bodies were in tatters. At the top of the mound, a flock of turkey buzzards were tearing at the corpses with the diligence of laborers digging a canal. Below them a pack of coyotes, their meal interrupted, turned and snarled at the intruders.

Pomeroy stared, speechless with shock. One of the cavalrymen gagged and vomited. Another simply said, "Holy Mother of God." Beckwith impulsively raised his rifle and shot one of the coyotes. Startled by the sharp noise, the buzzards took wing and retreated into the trees patiently waiting for the interruption to end. The report echoed among the stony peaks.

Beckwith was jacking another shell into the chamber when Wilkins grabbed the rifle out of the private's hands and for a second looked as if he was going to club him with it." "You fool," he snarled. "If any redskin on this mountain didn't know we were here already, they sure as hell do now."

"I'll bet my pay not one of those bodies has a heart in it," said McAfee.

And at that moment, a different sound came from beyond the trees that made the hair rise on their necks.

A keening moan, a banshee chorus rang from the trees beyond the clearing. The group crept forward. Thirty yards from the charnel mound was a pit. It was twelve feet across and fifteen feet deep with sheer sides. At its bottom seethed a mass of writhing, wailing bodies.

The cavalrymen pointed their carbines into the pit.

"Back off, boys," said Durken. "If they were a threat to anybody, they wouldn't be down there."

McAfee turned to Pomeroy. "Well, Lieutenant, I guess you've found the Tonnewa."

XXXIX

The soldiers threw ropes into the pit and those who were able climbed out, but most had to be hauled up in improvised harnesses pulled by the horses. Twenty-seven people, the larger number of them women, children and the elderly, were brought out alive. A greater horror in a day filled with them lay below, another dozen or so corpses rotted at the bottom of the hole dead from starvation, exhaustion, and exposure.

The Tonnewa huddled, shivering in a mass beside the pit.

McAfee said to them, "Any of you know white talk?"

A wizened man stepped forward from the throng. He spoke haltingly. "I know some."

"Ask him what happened here," Pomeroy insisted. Near frenzy, he grabbed the front of the old brave's jerkin and shook his fist as the white haired man shrank back. "Tell me!" he snarled. "Where are the warriors?"

"Easy, Pomeroy," Durken said, pulling him away. "Let McAfee handle this."

To the old man, McAfee held up his hand, palm forward and said, "No one will hurt you. What is your name?"

"I am called Long Bear."

"Long Bear, I am called McAfee." He gestured to the soldiers. "These men seek Red Hawk. Can you tell me where he can be found?"

Long Bear's voice quavered as he spoke. "Red Hawk has gone, and the Cat Warriors with him. When we heard your sound, we feared it was Red Hawk returning to kill more of us."

"We have seen what Red Hawk has done to white men. What has he done to your tribe?"

"As his hatred for the white man has filled him, it has eaten his love for his own people. He keeps us like cattle, and he kills us to take our hearts to make him strong."

"When was Red Hawk last here?"

"Four days. He was never away so long, and we hoped that he was dead."

"How long have you been in that pit?"

"Seven, eight days."

"Ask him how many men were with him," Pomeroy said.

"How many warriors ride with Red Hawk?"

Long Bear opened and closed both hands twice. "Four hands, maybe more."

"That would account for the gang that attacked us at the Mingott camp," said Durken.

"And Red Hawk's down quite a few now," McAfee said.

Long Bear gestured to the Tonnewa behind him. "McAfee, my people are cold and tired and hungry. Let us go to our tents now."

McAfee looked back to Pomeroy who shook his head. "No." He turned to Wilkins. "Sergeant, line these savages up. You may as well stand them on the edge of the pit."

Durken stared at Pomeroy. "You're going to shoot these people?"

"They're part of a hostile tribe that has killed both civilians and soldiers. I can't take the chance of leaving them to regroup and attack again." Then more quietly, "And as for your catmen, what if these people know how to control them or breed them or whatever?"

"I don't see any Cat Warrior medallions on any of these people."

Pomeroy's eyes widened. "Uncle Billy's orders were specific: take no prisoners."

Wilkins spoke up. "These people haven't killed anybody, Lieutenant, and they're not going to. I can't abide murdering women and children just to put a medal on your chest."

Pomeroy's eyes blazed with anger. "Are you defying my orders, Sergeant?"

In a blur, Durken pulled his Colt and thumbed back the hammer, aiming the pistol at Pomeroy's head. "You give the order to fire, and I'll obey it."

Pomeroy's eyes twitched wildly. "Shoot this man! He's threatening your commanding officer!"

The soldiers looked to each other, unsure what to do. McAfee levered his rifle and brought it around to bear on them.

The ratchet of another rifle. "You boys do that, and you'll have to shoot me too." Wilkins stepped away from the men nearest him. "I'm a soldier not a butcher." Carson and Jones cocked their rifles. "We're with you, Sarge," Said Carson.

The other soldiers were frozen, caught between orders and survival and many on the edge of hysteria. McAfee saw Pomeroy's hand slip under his waterproof groping for his holster and realized that one shot would set off a gunfight that would kill them all. He shifted his grip on the rifle and swung it two-handed across the back of Pomeroy's head with a sound like an axe hitting a locust tree. The lieutenant fell face down in the mud.

"Sergeant Wilkins," McAfee said in as authoritative voice as he could muster, "Lieutenant Pomeroy appears to be indisposed and unsuitable for command. I think that leaves you as ranking officer. What are your orders?"

The soldiers looked to Wilkins, who let out a long breath. "You men," he pointed to a pair of privates. "Pick up the lieutenant before he suffocates and put him over his horse. The rest of you help these people back to their village."

"You know, Pike," Durken said, "The General's orders said 'take no prisoners.' That's open to interpretation. If you let them go they ain't prisoners any more than they'd be if you'd shoot them."

Wilkins' brow furrowed. "If I let them go, Pomeroy's going to be mad as hell when he wakes up."

"He's gonna be mad as hell when he wakes up anyway."

"I'll probably end up in front of a firing squad."

"Not after we explain things to the General. Pomeroy was unhinged by it all; he was shaky to begin with, but what we found here broke him. Let these people bury their dead."

McAfee reached under Pomeroy's cloak and took his pistol from its holster. He handed it butt first to Wilkins. "Give this back to him when he gets control of himself." McAfee started toward the tribesmen. "I need to talk with Long Bear some more. I got some questions need answered."

Pomeroy came to that evening back at the Mingott camp. He came boiling out of the mine tunnel snarling and raging to find everyone seated quietly around the fire, which made him even angrier.

"Lieutenant Pomeroy," said McAfee jovially. Glad to see you're awake. Come have some coffee."

Pomeroy's eyes bulged. "You and you; all of you, I'll have you all up on charges. This is mutiny. I'll have you all shot."

McAfee grinned. "You know, you suffered quite a blow on the head in your encounter with the Tonnewa, Lieutenant. Sergeant Wilkins had to relieve you of command and take charge of the situation in your place."

Durken jumped in. "And the Indian situation being as a touchy as it is, I figure he did the right thing letting those people go. After all, how do you suppose the other tribes would act after the Army shot a bunch of defenseless women and children? I figure there'll be commendations all around."

Pomeroy seethed. "I'll see you all hanged for this."

"We'll see what the General has to say about it." Durken pointed to the pot of potatoes and beans. "In the meantime, sit down, have some supper."

Pomeroy grabbed a rifle leaning against a stump and levered a shell into the chamber. "I'll eat your liver for supper, Durken."

Before anyone could move, there was a hiss and an arrow exploded out of Pomeroy's chest. He dropped the rifle and wrapped his fingers around the shaft, eyes filled with surprise and mouth gaping. He stared into Durken's eyes for a second then pitched forward.

Before he hit the ground the men were on their feet, guns pointing in every direction, expecting an attack, but no more arrows flew. No one breathed. In a few minutes the sounds of the forest resumed as if nothing had happened.

Later, Durken and McAfee stood outside the tunnel. "No markings on that arrow," said Durken. "What do you think?"

"I think Long Bear understood English a whole lot better than he let on. Before we left the Tonnewa camp he said, 'Your leader and Red Hawk are brothers under the skin.' I thought maybe he meant the General, but this puts a whole different light on the comment. Whoever shot that arrow could've done it at any time, but he saved his shot for Pomeroy. I'm betting on Long Bear."

"He could've shot any one of us."

"And he didn't shoot 'til Pomeroy was ready to shoot you. Like I said, Long Bear understood all too well what went on today. I'd say he was repaying a debt."

Durken said, "What's Wilkins want to do about it?"

"He wants to go back to the Tonnewa camp in the morning, but I'd guess they'll be far away by the time we get there. He agrees with me that Red Hawk could be anywhere on this mountain, and that he's not part of the Tonnewa tribe anymore, so they aren't the issue."

"But he's still out there."

"Likely so, and I suspect we haven't seen the last of him."

"What'd Long Bear tell you?"

"He said that Red Hawk came back from the council of chiefs mad as a scalded bobcat. He told his tribe that if the others wouldn't join him in fighting the white man, they would do it alone. Long Bear said that plenty of the braves were in favor of the idea 'til they learned how Red Hawk planned to do it."

"Cat Warriors. Magic."

"Long Bear's words were 'evil medicine.'" He shrugged. "At least it ain't the Old Ones."

"I'm starting to think it's all of a piece."

"Anyway, Red Hawk won over enough braves, most of them the younger more impulsive ones to follow him, and the first thing they did was kill the men who opposed the idea."

"And ate their hearts?"

"Yep," said McAfee. "And Long Bear said they made the rest of the tribe dig that pit we found and put them all in it. He said the night they went into the pit, they heard drums and chanting, some kind of ritual or ceremony going on, a lot of howling and caterwauling then nothing 'til the next day.

"Red Hawk's braves shot arrows into the pit and killed a few to make the others cooperate. Long Bear said they took the youngest and strongest first. There was a lot of screaming and then at dusk the drums and chanting again."

"And the dead ones at the bottom of the pit?"

"A lot of the old people and the braves who were injured fighting Red Hawk didn't last long jammed into that hole. They had to stand on the dead bodies because there wasn't room enough for them to lie down or maybe even sit. They fell asleep on their feet. As they got hungrier, Long Bear was afraid they'd start eating the corpses, but we got them out of there before it got that far."

"I'm starting to think maybe we were wrong to spare them. I remember something the General said to me once, 'Sometimes good men have to do terrible things to show mercy.' I can't imagine living every day with that memory."

"Look at all we've been through, and you and I are still thinking straight. Just like that burn patch in the forest'll heal, so does the human heart."

"You read that in some book?"

"Nope, made that one up all by myself."

"Make sure you write it down. I'd hate for you to forget it."

The next dawn found the Tonnewa village as deserted as it had been the day before, but this time as much as the small band of tribesmen could carry was removed from the site. Soon after, the platoon was on its way down the mountain with Pomeroy's body over his saddle. Durken, McAfee, and Wilkins agreed on the story that the platoon had found the Tonnewa camp with no one in it who posed a threat. A rogue group of tribesmen under Red Hawk had broken away from the Tonnewa and was responsible for the massacres and for the death of Lieutenant Pomeroy in an attack on their camp.

"What about your men?" Durken asked.

"They've been with me for a lot longer than they've been with Pomeroy, and there's no love lost there. In fact, I think some of them are relieved that he's gone."

"He didn't belong in the saddle." Durken snorted. "Pomeroy belonged in a field tent with maps and reports and adjutants saluting every time he farted."

McAfee said, "He might have adapted to the life, if he left room for other people."

"Maybe so," said Wilkins, "but I figure a lot of men would have died along the way."

Once they reached the flatlands, Wilkins and the platoon went north toward Dixon and McAfee and Durken rode for Lickskillet. When they arrived, they found Hollister arguing with a tall man with a tawny moustache in a striped grey suit and a derby hat. Three others dressed in similar outfits stood close behind him.

"Those things represent evidence of important scientific discoveries. You can't just take them away. They need to be catalogued, to be studied."

"Professor Hollister, I understand your position, but I have my orders." The tall man's face showed absolutely no emotion. It was as if Hollister were talking to a statue. "We are to take all evidence related to this case with us to New York as a matter of national security, and that includes all photographs, artifacts, and notes on the case."

As Durken and McAfee approached, Derby man's friends slowly turned away from the argument and toward them, their stares flat and cold. Durken and McAfee stopped five feet away and waited for the conversation to finish.

"I'm not giving you my journal," Hollister sputtered. "That's my personal property. It has much more in it than just the past few days. It has the entire record of my observations in this country."

"Let me remind you, sir that you are a foreign citizen here on the sufferance of our government. If you fail to cooperate, you are subject to arrest, possible imprisonment, and likely deportation as a threat to national security. Choose your next words wisely."

He turned and looked Durken and McAfee up and down. "And you men are?"

"I'm McAfee and this is Durken. And you are?"

"I'm Special Agent Willis Tate of the United States Secret Service." He pulled back the lapel of his jacket revealing a gold badge pinned to his vest. "I need to speak with you two as soon as I'm finished here."

Durken ignored him. "What's going on here, Hollister?"

"They want to take my research notes, my specimens, everything concerning the Cat Warriors."

"I'd advise you not to say those words together again, Professor." He turned to Durken. "As I understand it, you men are currently active members of the United States Army. We are acting on authority way over your heads, and I'd advise you to not interfere."

"He's got us there," said McAfee to Durken. "Agent Tate, we're going to see to our horses and then go over to the hotel for something to eat. Then we'll be coming back here. We'll be available to talk whenever it suits you." And to Hollister, "And we'll talk with you later too."

As they walked away, Durken said, "What do you suppose that's all about?"

"My guess is that the government wants to keep as tight a rein on this business as it possibly can. I figure Tate'll give us an earful on the subject."

"Those men with him look like a hard lot too. Dressed that way they look like Pinkertons, and I'd put them in the same bag with Jim McKenna."

"I agree. Whoever sent these fellows isn't fooling around."

Tate caught up with Durken and McAfee at the hotel. The waiter was just serving plates of beef stew and coffee when he pulled up a chair. One of his henchmen stood a few feet away, thumbs in his belt. "What'll you have?" the waiter said and Tate ordered coffee.

"Your friend Hollister isn't very cooperative," Tate said, resting his forearms on the table. "He was told when he signed on the mission that it was classified and confidential."

Neither McAfee nor Durken spoke.

"What about you two? Do you have any reservations about keeping the matter quiet?"

"The General said 'classified' and as far as we're concerned, that's all there is to it," said McAfee.

"I had hoped you'd see it that way. I read your dossiers. You were both good soldiers, and I hope you continue that way."

"Us keeping quiet is one thing, but what about that church full of people who got killed?" McAfee said. "A whole posse saw that mess."

Tate looked away for a moment then back again and said, "The Brethren. Yes, that was unfortunate. Seems there was a fire and they were trapped in the church; no one escaped."

McAfee eyed Tate coldly but let the matter drop.

Durken spoke up. "But it is too bad that Hollister can't make some good from all of this. Without him we likely wouldn't have done as well as we did against those creatures."

"I'd rather you not refer to the 'enemy' in those terms. The official position is that the attacks were made by a rogue group of hostile natives and that the situation is now under control."

Durken nodded. "And that's how it stays?"

"Yes. As the General has told you." Tate stopped while the waiter set a mug of steaming coffee before him then resumed when he went away. "The object here is to prevent panic and overreaction on the part of the civilians."

"What that really amounts to is saving face," McAfee cut in.

"There is some element of that," Tate conceded, "but the larger issue is the potential persecution of the tribes who are cooperating with relocation. We don't want all the tribes to suffer because of a few renegades. There are elements in Washington who believe extermination of the natives wholesale is an acceptable solution and advocate that position."

Durken took a swallow of his coffee and set down his mug. "What you're saying is if the story of the 'enemy' as you put it is kept under the blanket, it'll mean a better shake for the tribes as a whole."

"That's about the size of it."

"If you don't mind my asking," said McAfee, "how is it that you're involved in this business? I thought the Secret Service was set up to guard the President and to work for the Treasury Department."

"In recent years, our duties have expanded. At the President's discretion, we handle matters involving national security."

"Something that happens on a mountain in the middle of nowhere involves national security?"

Tate took a long breath before answering. "The country is still reeling from the war, and there are elements, foreign and domestic, that see an opportunity to exploit that vulnerability. The White House wants as much of the land settled and stable as quickly as possible. Continued trouble with the Indians will hamper that object, and persecution of the tribes wholesale will only fan the flames."

"So what we have here is utilitarianism at work."

The first smile they'd seen twitched across Tate's lips. "The most good for the most people. You've read Bentham?"

"Yep. We weren't always saddle tramps, Tate. Durken and I can read and write, and if we're hard put, we can cipher too. I guess our dossiers didn't mention that fact."

"I didn't mean any insult. I was just surprised to hear the word in this setting. And as for the General, he has nothing but praise for both of you."

"What's going to happen to all of Hollister's notes and the things he brought back from Manson's pass? Will they just be destroyed?"

"My guess is that they'll be studied by experts, most likely at the Smithsonian Institution in Washington."

"That's all well and good," said Durken, "but I wonder if there might be some way Hollister could have his papers back, minus the ones that tell about this incident."

"Or better yet," said McAfee, "have Hollister invited to the party. I figure as well-known a scientist as he is, the folks in Washington would be glad to have him on board. After all, he can give a first-hand account."

Tate nodded slowly. "That's a reasonable request. I'll see what I can do." His eyes said otherwise.

"The object here is to prevent panic and overreaction..."

"There's one more thing you didn't mention." Durken stirred his coffee idly. "Once you've figured out the what and the how of this business, what will you do with it?"

"That is a decision way past my reach," said Tate. "Of course apart from scientific curiosity and an eye for dealing with such occurrences in the future, the information would be examined for its potential military uses."

McAfee's head snapped up. "Potential military uses?" His eyes blazed and his voice rose. "You mean make more of those things and turn them loose to win some battle someplace?" His knuckles whitened as he gripped the table.

Tate's sidekick took a step forward and his hand slid into his coat. Tate made a restraining gesture. "Don't be naïve. Everything that we encounter is examined for military use. This will be no exception."

"You didn't see what those things do."

"I've seen the photographs."

"Seeing pictures and being there are two different animals," said Durken, putting a hand on McAfee's wrist. "Come on, partner. Time for us to go." He stood and dropped a dollar on the table. It spun and landed tails up. Durken pointed at the coin. "I used to think that eagle stood for something worth fighting for. Now I'm not so sure."

Outside, Durken and McAfee walked toward the train. In the distance, clouds had settled over the peaks of the mountains but the late autumn sun shone warm on the Lickskillet streets as if to underscore the completely different worlds each represented.

"We've been in a war together and we've killed a lot of people between us then and since," said McAfee, "but I'd never even think about what these people are planning to do; turn people, human beings into those monsters on purpose."

"Like Charlie's Five Poisons," said Durken. "Fight fire with fire. Red Hawk uses it against them, they use it against him."

"More like 'we' use it, don't you mean? We're on the same side as 'they.'"

"When you put it that way, it makes it all the worse."

"And who's to say once the renegades are stopped that 'they' won't use this weapon against other enemies? An army of monsters that lays waste to towns, villages to do just what Red Hawk proposed: use fear as a weapon."

"That's a troubling thought, but I don't see much we can do about it."

"Me either, but if I think of something, I'll see it through."

"If you do, let me know. I'll be right beside you."

"Another consideration: seems that Tate knew all about the Cat Warriors before he ever got here. That means maybe somebody was onto this before we ever left Bacon Rock."

"You think the General knew? Or Harper?"

"Harper didn't know; the whole attack at Manson's Pass caught him by surprise. Maybe the General knew and maybe he didn't. Maybe he was told to keep everybody in the dark. We all take our orders from somebody, him included."

"Might be something we want to ask him."

"I'd wait 'til we're civilians again before we do that."

Suddenly one of the Secret Service agents burst from an alley and ran in the opposite direction. Ignoring Durken and McAfee, he sprinted up the street to the hotel.

The pair looked at each other and said in unison, "Hollister," and set off for the train at a dead run. As they rounded the corner of the livery stable, they saw smoke rising from the coach. Flames blazed through open windows, licking at the roof of the car. A lone figure was riding away on horseback.

Gunfire. The Secret Service agents emptied their pistols at the retreating figure, but Hollister was too far away for them to fire with any accuracy. A moment after Durken and McAfee arrived, Tate came running, flanked by his men. "Get horses!" he snapped at the agents. "Get after him." The agents ran for the livery.

He turned to Durken and McAfee. "And you, help us. That man is a fugitive from the United States government."

"Sure, Tate," Durken said. "As soon as we get our orders from the General."

Tate's stare went from hot to cold. "You men are in the service of the American government, and I'm ordering you get on your horses and get after that man."

"You're right, Tate, we're Army. And as I recall, we can't be used to enforce the law. What's that called, McAfee?"

"*Posse comitatus.* My Latin's a little bit rusty, but the drift of it all is that members of the military can't enforce law and order on non federal land. Nevada's a state, not a federal territory, so by law, we can't help you."

Tate's eyes blazed with anger. "Since you like to quote the law, McAfee, let me quote one for you: the Third Enforcement Act. It passed not too long ago and it gives the President the authority to suspend *habeus corpus*. I'm his direct agent. I could lock you two up right now and you'd never see daylight again."

"But to do that," Durken said, gently brushing his duster behind his holster, "you'd have to arrest us first. That could be difficult, particularly since your boys are all busy grabbing horses at the moment."

By the look on Tate's face, they knew they had him. "Fine. Stay here, or go home, or go to Hell, or whatever your general," he snarled the word, "tells you to do. I'll deal with you later." Tate turned away but Durken's response stopped him cold.

"Based on his direction, Tate, I figure Hollister's headed for those mountains. I hope your city boys are good in the saddle, 'cause if you don't catch him before he gets to the treeline, you'll have the Devil's own time finding him up there."

Tate glared at them and spun on his heel, heading toward the livery.

The story that came out later had it that Hollister insisted on making an inventory of his artifacts and notes before he turned them over, and that he had things spread out in the coach cataloguing them under the watchful eye of two of the agents. Their attention flagged as the job proceeded, and Hollister lifted the lid from a tin of his flash powder. He lit his pipe, and before the match went out, he closed one eye and said, "In the country of the blind, the one-eyed is king," and threw the match into the open tin.

Blinded by the flash and stunned by the explosion, the agents were helpless to stop Hollister from grabbing an armload of his notes and his bottle of single malt whiskey and running out of the coach, but not before he smashed a kerosene lamp on the floor starting a blaze between himself and the agents. In seconds the whole car was afire and Hollister was swinging his leg over a horse that was tethered near the siding.

Durken and McAfee didn't wait to ride back on the train. They saddled up before Tate could pull some stunt to enlist them in the pursuit and were soon on their way back to Bacon Rock. "Have to give Hollister credit," said McAfee, "he's a plucky son of a bitch."

"Yep, and I hope he makes the treeline before Tate's people catch up with him. He knows the trail and the lay of the land and they don't. Besides, I figure he has other reasons for going back."

"The remains he buried in the cave? I thought of that, but even if he does dig them up, he'll have a tough time getting them away from here. He doesn't have supplies, not even a gun unless there was one on the saddle. What do you figure his chances are?"

"Hollister's no tenderfoot, and he's used to living in the wild. I figure he'll survive, but those Secret Service boys'll give it their best to catch him. Tate doesn't look like the sort who takes being a made a fool of lightly."

"You're right about that," McAfee said, "but even more important to him, the people who give Tate his orders are going to come down hard on him if Hollister gets away."

"Wouldn't that be a shame?"

The ride to Bacon Rock took a little longer than the train trip and it was the middle of the next day when the town came into view.

"So, do we go to the ranch first or report to the General?"

Durken thought it over. "I guess we'd better see the General first. I'd hate to go back to the ranch and get yanked away again once I got settled."

"Yeah, you're right. Let's go face the music."

General Sherman sat, as before, behind the fancy desk in the fancy rail car with an even greater mound of papers before him. He looked as if he'd never left the spot.

"Butler dead, McKenna dead, Pomeroy dead, Harper out of commission, Hollister a fugitive, and the Secret Service yelling for your heads on a pike. What the hell went on out there?"

"Well, sir," said McAfee, "it's a long story, and if you don't mind, we'd be more comfortable to sit down to tell it."

For the next hour McAfee and Durken recounted everything that happened since they left the General a week before.

When they finished, Sherman stubbed out his cigar on the desk. "That's some story, and I'd find it hard to believe if it came from anybody but you two. Jesus." He turned his head aside as if he were studying something far away.

"I'm not comfortable with the idea that Red Hawk may still be out there, but you did what you could. I may have a bigger problem with the Secret Service than the Indians. I'll do what I can to keep you two out of the stockade or the penitentiary, partly because of how well you've served me in the past, partly because I put you in this situation, and mostly because I don't appreciate the god damned Secret Service snapping its fingers at me like I'm some liveried servant.

"When you came here and I was gone, I was in Denver on President Grant's orders. I had to sit there and listen to that upstart Tate tell me do this, don't do that. Those people have Grant's ear, like too damned many people in Washington, and they're using that edge to pursue an agenda.

"New York," Sherman snorted. "Why's the Secret Service headquartered in New York now when their job is to protect the President?" He slammed his fist on the desk and his bottle and glass jumped. "To get them away from the scrutiny of Congress, that's why. And to put them in the lap of the Robber Barons. That's what they call them now, the wealthy men who pull the strings on Grant and for that matter, half the government."

"Maybe you should've run for president yourself," said Durken. "Nobody'd likely push you around."

Sherman hesitated before answering then turned to look Durken in eye. "Because they'd have me shot faster than Abe Lincoln."

"So what do we do now, General?" McAfee said.

Sherman heaved a sigh. "You do what I'd like to do but can't: go home. Go back to your lives."

"You mustering us out?" Durken asked.

"No," he said quickly. I won't do that because if I did that bastard Tate would be on you like a duck on a June bug. As long as you're Army, I can protect you. Let's just say I'm putting you on indefinite leave."

"Thank you, General," Durken said, standing. McAfee echoed the sentiment.

Sherman raised his head wearily and said, "And thank you, both. I mean that sincerely. Dismissed."

XLVI

The shadows were long when Durken and McAfee rode through the main gate to the Triple Six. The sun was near setting and the sky was that shade of dusky rose you see only in the fall in Nevada. The clouds had dark violet shadows tucked among the roses.

"Good to be back," said Durken.

"Yep," McAfee said. "Nowhere near as much excitement as scouting, but it has its attractions."

"And there's one of them." Maggie had come out onto the front porch of the mansion, wiping her hands on her apron. When she saw them riding in, she hopped off the porch and ran three steps, then remembered herself and stopped, waiting for Durken to come to her. He rode Sweetheart up to the hitching rail in front of the house and climbed down. "Hullo, Maggie."

She put on a mock frown and stood, arms akimbo, fists on her ample hips. "And it's about time you rascals came back here."

"Durken grinned, "Aw, Maggie, it's only been a week."

"Eight days," she said, shaking a finger. "Eight days you've been gone and me not knowing whether you're alive or dead."

"Told you we'd be back, and I didn't even get a hangnail."

She eyed his chaps. "And what might that be?" She pointed to the row of slashes.

"That would be the reason why I wear chaps." Durken put his arms around Maggie and lifted her off her feet. He turned around and playfully spun her, feet in the air. She beat at his chest with her fists and said, "Put me down you scalawag."

"See," Durken laughed, "strong as ever."

The front door opened and Homer Eldridge filled the doorway. "Well, I see you've decided to grace us with your presence again. Are you back for good, or is this just a stopover?"

"Back for good as far as we know, Mister Eldridge," McAfee said, taking off his hat and smiling, not for his boss but for Miss Sarah who stood behind her father craning her neck for a look at him.

"Well, as soon as you tend to your horses, come to my office." He turned around, almost colliding with Sarah and shut the door before she could step onto the porch.

Maggie, who had been caught in Durken's embrace the whole time pushed herself away in a spluttering show of unconvincing indignation. "Let go of me, you baboon. I'll be lucky if I still have a job after that display."

McAfee laughed, "Unless you've taught Miss Sarah everything you know about the kitchen while we were gone, I think your job's safe."

"I think he'd fire her as daughter before he'd fire you as cook, Maggie." Durken put a finger to the brim of his hat. "If you'll excuse us, we'd better see to the horses. You heard the boss."

"Hmmph," Maggie snorted and turned to the mansion. Over her shoulder, she said, "And you two clean those boots before you come tromping through my kitchen. I just mopped the floor."

"Yes, ma'am." McAfee looked up and saw Sarah framed in a second floor window. She smiled, blew him a kiss, and disappeared.

"It is good to be back, ain't it?" Durken said.

"Yep, if you can overlook Eldridge."

A half hour later, Durken and McAfee entered Eldridge's study where he was polishing a long-barreled Colt revolver. "Look at that beauty," he said, turning it so that the gold filigree on the handle caught the lamplight. "Made especially for me by the factory. For every gram of gold in that handle, some of the frame's been filed away under the grips to keep it balanced." He spun the cylinder with a ratcheting click. "Perfect."

Durken tilted his head back and studied the pistol out of the bottom of one eye. "How's it shoot?"

Eldridge looked up, suddenly irritated. "I haven't fired it." He added, "Yet." And he probably would never fire the gun; like so many that decorated the walls in his study, it was probably just a showpiece, not a workingman's firearm. Eldridge kept the rifles, shotguns and other weapons for everyday use in a rack in the back hallway near the kitchen.

Eldridge set the pistol on a cloth and folded it over. "It's a good thing you two are back. You'll be heading the drive to Reno in six days."

"That'll disappoint Smeck," said McAfee. "He was looking forward to the extra pay."

"Smeck couldn't find Reno if he followed the railroad tracks. I need you two in charge."

"How many head?" Durken said, sitting in one of the leather guest chairs without being invited. McAfee followed suit a second later.

Eldridge looked ready to say something about it but changed his mind. "Six hundred head. They're going to the Union Pacific depot and you'll be paid for them on delivery."

"If there isn't anything else, Mister Eldridge," said McAfee, "we're tired and hungry."

Eldridge frowned. "You can't tell me anything about where you've been or what you've done for the last week?"

"Nope, and it's too bad too because it's quite a story," Durken teased, "but orders is orders."

"And we're still in the Army until the General tells us otherwise."

Eldridge swiveled his chair to look out the window, turning his back on McAfee and Durken. "Get out of here."

"Yes, sir."

As they crossed the yard toward the bunkhouse, Durken said, "That was almost fun."

"Yep, but dealing with Eldridge likely won't be much fun for the next few days."

"Probably not, but he'll get over it. Let's go see what Charlie's cooking up."

"Best idea you've had all day."

They found Charile bent over a kettle in his kitchen off the bunkhouse stirring a thick stew with a big wooden paddle that looked like a sawed off oar.

"Hey Charlie," said McAfee, "What's in the pot?"

"Chicken stew," he said with a grin. "You lucky you come back now. None left later." He jerked his head toward the dining area. "They all eat like hogs."

"A compliment to your cooking, Charlie," Durken said, pouring coffee for himself and McAfee from the old tin pot on the cookstove.

McAfee dug in his pocket and pulled out Charlie's good luck charm. "I want to give this back to you before I forget," he said.

Charlie took the coin and rubbed it between his thumb and forefinger. "It gave you luck?"

"I guess so, said Durken. "We're here and in one piece, ain't we?"

Charlie's grin faded. "Bad trouble?"

They looked at each other. "Yeah," said Durken, "pretty bad. So, how soon'll that stew be ready?"

Hollister entered the Mingott camp cautiously as the shadows closed over the mountainside. Nothing stirred. The graves of the miners were still undisturbed, and he saw no fresh tracks in or around the clearing. He stole from the brush into the tunnel, his head swiveling from side to side, expecting an attack at any second, but none came.

He shivered, not from fear but from the high altitude cold. Hollister couldn't see his breath in the air yet, but he might later. He'd run from Tate and his agents wearing only his walking suit. His woolen Inverness cape was likely burned to a cinder in the rail car. A slit for his head in a blanket he found near the tunnel entrance made a good improvised poncho.

A lantern hung from a spike driven into one of the timbers. He lit it and strode through the tunnel to its end where he had dug a shallow grave to bury the Cat Warrior remains he had to leave behind. Hollister pulled away the mound of rocks he'd piled on the grave to keep out scavenger animals and eagerly thrust the blade of a shovel into the packed earth. He quickly reached the burlap sacking he'd used to wrap the flesh and bones and pulled out the sack. It seemed far too light.

He pulled away the burlap and when he saw the remains, he cried. "No. No. Bloody hell!" Hollister clapped his hands to his head. "How could I have been so damned stupid?" At his feet lay catman flesh and bone eroded, dissolved into a shapeless mass by the corrosive effect of the silver in the soil.

"I'll get my proof," he said. He reached into his vest pocket and drew out the cat's head amulet. He turned it over in his fingers, studying it from all angles. "One way or another," he muttered, "I'll get my proof."

McAfee and Durken spent the next three days in the saddle rounding up steers for the drive. Word had it that General Sherman's Pullman was gone from the siding, and neither Durken nor McAfee had heard from him or Tate or for that matter from Hollister.

"Sometimes I think these cows have it best," McAfee said as they rode across the north range. "They pretty much eat when they want, sleep when they want, shit when they want, and none of the others really care one way or the other. Not a worry in the world."

"Not 'til we drive them down the chute into a rail car and they roll off to the slaughterhouse." Durken was silent for a moment then said, "You're still stewing about Tate and the Secret Service's plans for the Cat Warriors, aren't you?"

"Yep. That idea just gnaws at me and won't let go."

"Well, we can take some comfort that Hollister grabbed his notes and skedaddled and the rest of it burned up. I figure he took the best part of it all. Tate and his boys won't learn much from the ashes in that rail car."

"I suppose you're right, but I have a feeling the people who pull Tate's strings won't be satisfied until they have what they want. That means Tate won't give it up because he can't. I keep thinking about Red Hawk too. The thought that he might still be on the loose bothers me."

"Well," Durken said, "we haven't heard a word from the General, and if Red Hawk or any of the Cat Warriors were back at it, I imagine, he'd've called us in."

"You're right."

"If Red Hawk's dead, amen to that. If he isn't, we'll know when we know. Meanwhile, let's see to these carefree cows." Durken nudged Sweetheart in the ribs and started after a steer that was straying from the herd. McAfee watched him ride away, envying Durken's calm. It was as if he could put any problem in his pocket and forget about it, just set it aside until it was time to deal with it. Equanimity, thought McAfee. That's the word. I wish I had Durken's equanimity.

Blue knife sat cross-legged as the sun rose over the mesa that overlooked the Monatai village to one side and the open range to the other. From a distance he heard an eerie sound, strange music. He stood and strained his eyes to see a lone rider approaching. The man wore a dun colored poncho that draped over his thighs and saddle, and if he had known the word, Blue Knife would have said that he also wore a sort of turban wrapped around his head.

The horseman halted below the mesa and held up both hands in a peaceful gesture. One held a silver flute. "Greetings, Blue Knife. I am McAfee's friend Hollister. I wish to speak with your chief Seven Stars. May I enter your village?"

The drive was uneventful all the way to Reno. The cows behaved, the men behaved, and if there were any hostile Indians operating in Nevada, they were all somewhere far from the trail.

"Every time we come this way it reminds me of the drive when we met that Dayak wagon train coming the other direction," McAfee said, wiping sweat from his brow with his bandanna.

"Yeah, if ever there were human rats, that bunch answered the description," Durken replied, "them and that preacher Penrod. I still wake up in the middle of the night once in a while and think about them."

"You'd never know it by me," McAfee said. "Far's I can tell, you snore from the time you close your eyes 'til sunup."

"Speaking about thinking, I wonder if we'll see Abner Hague this trip. Do you ever reconsider his offer to give you a job?" The wealthy cattleman once tried to lure McAfee away from Eldridge after McAfee backed his play in a saloon fight.

"Once in a while I wonder how that might have turned out, but I never get past leaving the Triple Six."

"Yeah, Miss Sarah's a powerful reason to stay put."

"I don't see you looking off to some far horizon, either."

Durken laughed. "Guilty as charged. Who knows? Play your cards right, and maybe someday you'll be running the Triple Six and I'll be working for you."

"Knowing Eldridge, he'll likely have a ten-year plan in his will so he can give orders from beyond the grave."

"If he ain't too busy in hell." Durken spat tobacco juice from the corner of his mouth. "On another topic, I can't wait to get to Reno." He shook dust from his coat. "I need a bath worse than I need a drink."

McAfee nodded. "Can't disagree on that point either."

The heart of the dying fire painted Red Hawk's face the color of rage. Under a crude leather patch his eye socket ached from the cold where the white devil had struck him with silver. From five hands of Cat Warriors all gone but six men, and now those were half afraid because they had tasted defeat at the hands of the soldiers and the men the soldiers brought with them. They sat with him by the campfire, one foot on his path and one on the path of desertion and retreat.

The Tonnewa Chief knew the legends well and knew that silver was the bane of the Cat Warrior from the time of First Father, but even Red Hawk was shocked by its effectiveness. He had promised his followers glorious victory as their numbers grew, but their losses at the hands of the two cowboys made his words ring hollow. The freeing of the Tonnewa and thus the loss of his source of hearts for the transformation ceremony had driven him to desperate measures.

Red Hawk took a bundle wrapped in deerskin from his pouch and set it on the ground. He then removed his feather band, his jerkin and his breeches and squatted naked before the fire. He tied a strip of animal pelt around his waist and he removed the patch from his raw eye socket. Red Hawk nodded to the brave with the drum. He let the beat enter him and matched its rhythm with his heart.

Behind him the three remaining braves began to chant and he joined in, fingering the cat's head amulet at his throat. He unwrapped the deerskin and took the heart of Two Arrows in his hands. It hurt him to lose a warrior and comrade, but great deeds required great sacrifices. Red Hawk needed the heart to harvest more. The drum beat and the chanting intensified. As it hit a crescendo, Red Hawk held the heart over his head in offering then with frenzied force, sank his teeth into its flesh.

Reno was bustling as always; the city never seemed to quite shut down. The streets were filled with people all day and most of the night. Before the war, the place was little more than a crossing over the Tuckee River, just a bridge and a hotel, but by 1870, the coming of the railroad made Reno a major transit point for the Comstock Lode with silver and cattle going out and goods and passengers coming in. Earlier that year, the Nevada Legislature made Reno the county seat of Washoe County, and the city showed no sign of slowing down.

By suppertime the cattle were in a holding pen for the night, and Durken and McAfee were standing at the bar in the Silver Angel, Reno's most popular saloon, raucous, smoky, and loud. At one end of the cavernous room, a gas lit stage featured a small orchestra and the Thede Sisters, a pair of painted women who sang bawdy songs in delightful two-part harmony.

Somewhere into their third drink, Durken looked into the mirror behind the bar and saw that he and McAfee were bookended by two men in suits and derby hats. Before he could say anything to McAfee, Tate's head appeared between their shoulders. Behind him were two more agents. "Durken and McAfee. What a surprise to find you two here."

Durken and McAfee turned slowly from the bar to face Tate, and as they did, the agents on either side of them turned toward them, like mechanical figures on a Swiss clock. "You here for the whiskey or the floor show, Tate?"

"Neither. We're in Reno on official business. I heard you were in town and decided to look you up."

"Well, now that you've done that, maybe you and your boys could step away. You're blocking our view of the stage."

Tate's mouth opened in a humorless grin, showing a few teeth under his neat moustache. "Your friend Hollister's still out there. And we're going to get him; count on that. He could be hung for a horse thief by any lawman in Nevada, but that's not punishment enough. All I can say for you two is you're damned lucky you didn't help him escape. Otherwise, you'd be breaking rocks on Alcatraz Island right now. You're also lucky we're busy tonight. Enjoy your freedom while it lasts." He turned and like a covey of quail following its lead bird, the agents with him turned as one and followed him across the floor and out the swinging doors.

"That man's a plague." Durken poured another shot from the bottle.

"No," said McAfee, "Tate's a crusader, and that's worse. Plagues don't discriminate, hold grudges or follow orders."

At that moment, a roar from the crowd caught their attention. One of the Thede sisters was making a show of modestly pushing down the hem of her hoop skirt while a cowboy at a front table held up a pair of pink bloomers like a trophy. Another cowboy tried to snatch them away from him and punches flew. Soon the whole front section of the Silver Angel was one big brawl.

Durken picked up the bottle. "This might be a good time to get back to the corral."

McAfee downed his drink. "Yeah, I'd rather not be here when Jack Pyne shows up." Jack Pyne, the legendary Reno sheriff, seldom carried a gun but kept order in the city by the sheer force of his will, that and the coterie of shotgun-toting deputies who followed him around.

They shouldered through the crowd that pressed in gawking at the melee and stepped out onto the boardwalk in front of the saloon. Halfway down the block, McAfee said, "And here he comes." A short, compact man in a black vested suit and banker's Stetson strode toward them followed by a half dozen armed men.

Jack Pyne stopped as he reached Durken, pulled open his coat to reveal a shiny badge, and said, "You keep that bottle corked on the street, cowboy. Drink it someplace else."

Durken nodded. "Yes, sir. I'll do that."

Pyne turned to McAfee and looked him up and down as if he recognized him then did it again. The Sheriff seemed ready to ask his identity when down the street, the fight spilled out of the Silver Angel and into the thoroughfare, knocking down passersby and stopping wagons and carriages. "Damn it," Pyne muttered. "Come on, men." And they followed him at the same unhurried pace toward the brawl.

"Hope none of our boys are in the middle of that mess," said McAfee.

"You know what Eldridge said, if they land in jail, leave them there."

"Yep. He's the milk of human compassion."

"Who do you figure's the toughest? Pinkertons, Secret Service, or Pyne's gang?"

"I'd say it's a tossup."

"Maybe we could put them all in an arena like ancient Rome and let them battle it out."

"If we're lucky, won't be any of them left, and the world could be a better place for it."

LIII

The cattle buyers came early and the deal was done before breakfast. The bank draft was signed in payment and McAfee walked from the train yard to the telegraph office to send a message to Eldridge that he had the payment in hand. As he approached, he saw two of Tate's men standing outside the door, one to either side, as if they were guarding it. He hesitated a moment, then decided he wasn't going to let them intimidate him.

In the office, Tate stood at the counter, a message in his hand. He turned to the operator and said, "This is one of them. This is McAfee." The operator nodded and pulled a message slip from a pigeonhole over the telegraph keys. He offered it to McAfee.

The telegram was addressed to him and Durken and was sent by Corporal Amos Barlow, the General's adjutant. McAfee read the terse message: Red Hawk incident. Report Bacon Rock immediately.

McAfee folded the slip and tucked it into his pocket. "Seems we've both gotten the same message," Tate said.

"That so? You read other people's letters too, Tate?"

Ignoring the jibe, Tate said, "We're leaving for Bacon Rock in a half hour. We've got a private train waiting for us at the station. You and Durken can ride with us and bring your horses in the boxcar. It'll save a lot of time."

McAfee nodded. "Sounds sensible, but I can only speak for myself. As soon as I send a message to my boss, I'll go discuss it with Durken."

"Don't take too long," Tate said. "The General did say 'immediately.'"

Outside, Durken said, "How do we know it was a real message? What if it's something Tate cooked up to lure us away and lock us up or worse?"

"We don't know for sure," McAfee replied, "but we can't take the chance that it is real and we not go. I know you want to take down Red Hawk as much as I do, and if this is real, we'll have a chance to do that. I say we go with our eyes open and our guns loaded. And there's another reason we can't ignore it."

"What's that?"

"The telegram says report to Bacon Rock, not Lickskillet. Sounds as if Red Hawk's in our backyard now."

Durken nodded. "You're right. Let's go talk to Smeck. I guess he got his wish after all, or at least half of it."

McAfee gave Smeck instructions for the trip back. "So, since I'm in charge now, do I get foreman's pay for the run?"

"For Pete's sake, Smeck, if Eldridge doesn't pay you for it, I will," said McAfee.

At the cook wagon, Charlie packed them a sack of food for the train ride. "Bad trouble again?"

"Could be, Charlie," said Durken. He took a swallow of coffee. "Won't know 'til we find it."

Charlie took his good luck charm from a pocket of his overalls and rubbed the coin in his palm in a circle five times and held it out to Durken. "You take it for now. "I rub off enough luck on me for a while."

"Okay, Charlie." Durken raised his cup in salute. "Much obliged."

As they rode to the station, McAfee said, "Should we send Eldridge another telegram to let him know we're not coming back with the crew?"

"No, I figure we should just let it be a surprise. Who knows? Maybe he'll be happy if we bring him his payment early."

"Think so?"

"Nope."

"You're probably right. Let's just give it to Smeck."

At the station, the boxcar for the horses was waiting, its sliding door open and a ramp propped against the car. They led Thunder and Sweetheart into the car and saw five horses already tethered by their bridles to rings in the car's walls.

"I figure the trip'll take til tomorrow afternoon, so we'd best unsaddle the horses."

"What's that?" McAfee pointed to a large, square object under a tarpaulin nestled in a dark corner of the car. He walked over to it and pulled the canvas away. It was a cage, large enough for one, maybe two catamounts, or maybe two men.

"Looks like Tate plans to bring something back alive" he said.

"Unless that's for us," Durken said.

"Not unless you give me a good reason." Tate stood in the doorway of the boxcar.

"You figure on catching one of those catmen?" Durken shook his head. "If you do, you're crazy, or whoever gave you the order is crazier. The only

"How do we know it was a real message?"

way you'll bring one of those things back is dead over a horse." He added,
"If you can kill him."

"We'll see about that. Secure your mounts. We're leaving in five minutes."

The train ride was tense. Durken and McAfee rode at one end of a coach
while Tate and his men rode at the other. The Secret Service men took
turns staring at the cowboys as if they were under surveillance. The
cowboys ignored them and took turns sleeping.

Finally, Tate crossed the divide and sat on a seat directly across from
them. His men watched from their end of the car but couldn't hear what
was said because of the clatter of the wheels on the rails.

"Maybe I was a little bit heavy-handed last night. But we have to work
together today, and what useful purpose does it serve to be antagonistic
with each other? None that I can see."

After a long silence, Durken said, "Tate, I don't like you. I don't like your
agents. And I especially don't like what you're trying to do." He added, "Of
course I'm speaking just for myself when I say that. McAfee here's entitled
to his own opinion. "

McAfee shrugged. "I don't much care for you either," looking Tate
square in the eye. "We're here because the General said to be here. Let's
understand each other. Don't expect me to jump when you say jump. I'll
leave that to your trained monkeys. I take my orders from the General."

"And if he orders you to obey my orders?"

"Ain't gonna happen," said Durken, "because he doesn't like you any
more than we do."

"We'll see about that."

"Yep, I suppose we will. Don't get your hopes up." Durken pulled his hat
over his eyes and ended the conversation.

Late afternoon the next day the train arrived at the siding outside Bacon
Rock. Durken and McAfee decided to leave the horses where they were
in case they had to ride the train to another destination. They and Tate
climbed the steps to the vestibule of the green and yellow Pullman and

one of the guards opened the door. Durken and McAfee strode through, but when Tate tried to enter, the guard stepped into the doorway, rifle at port arms.

"Let me by," Tate said.

The soldier shook his head eyes fixed on a spot just north of Tate's forehead. "No, sir. General's orders. Durken and McAfee only."

Tate glared over the man's shoulder at Durken, who smiled, gave him a single emphatic nod, and closed the door.

Corporal Barlow, the General's adjutant sat in a chair just inside the door and Sherman was standing in front of the ornate hearth warming his hands. "Can't even get a decent fire going in this toy fireplace. When will it start snowing around here?"

"Another week or two," said McAfee. "It can start as early as September, or as late as December. Of course it comes sooner in the mountains."

"I hope I'm out of here long before then." He crossed to his desk and sat down. "What has Tate told you?"

"Nothing," Durken said. "We weren't really conversational on the trip back here. What was his word, McAfee?"

"Antagonistic."

"Yeah, that's the word. We were antagonistic."

Sherman snorted. "That miserable bastard pulled some strings and roped all three of us into this snipe hunt." He relit his cigar and puffed out a blue haze. "On one hand, he demanded you two because you're the best people for the job. On the other hand, he likely takes some delight in having you two under his thumb, since you stood up to him with Hollister.

"But I have a few strings of my own to pull. I agreed to put you in the party, but I demanded that you operate independently of Tate's control. The Secretary agreed, so you're going with him, but you take no orders from him. Kind of an armed truce. Does that sit all right with you?"

Both nodded. "McAfee and I were wondering why you called us here instead of Lickskillet or someplace closer to Caplock Mountain."

"There's been another incident, not far from here. You know the Diamond T ranch?"

"Jasper Petty's spread. That's only a half-day's ride from here." Durken started rolling a cigarette and looked up at the General, who nodded permission. "Was it another attack?"

Sherman took a paper from the nearest stack. "It was small scale, and we almost missed it."

"But the hearts were missing," McAfee finished for him. "And Tate knew about it but didn't tell us."

Sherman nodded. "Correct."

"How many people?" Durken asked.

"Only two this time, a pair of ranch hands out riding the fence line. They didn't come back at dusk and the next morning Petty sent men out looking for them and found the bodies."

"Were they torn up like others we've seen?"

"The bodies were gnawed, apparently by coyotes, but they weren't clawed like we've seen before. Their throats were cut with a sharp blade, likely in their sleep. The ranch hands found one of them lying by the fence. The other was close by, probably dragged by the scavengers. If it is Red Hawk, he's picking on smaller numbers. That tells me you boys pretty well depleted his force. Two hearts, two Cat Warriors and he had to kill them in a conventional way to get them."

"Why would he head this way?" Durken said. "He could hide 'til the Second Coming in those mountains."

"That's what I'm hoping you can tell me."

All were silent then finally McAfee spoke. "He vowed vengeance against the chiefs from the tribal council who opposed him. Based on how he handled his own tribe, maybe he's here to settle some scores with them."

"Or with us," Durken said. "That's why Tate wants us here, isn't it? To draw out Red Hawk."

Sherman nodded. "Could be. It makes sense. And so does what you said about revenge."

"Maybe somebody ought to warn the chiefs."

Sherman rolled his cigar from one corner of his mouth to the other. "You're right." He nodded. "We have a reasonable relationship with most of them. Having them killed off one by one while they're supposed to be under our protection would be disastrous."

"How can we help?" Durken asked.

"Go with Tate and his men and see whether you can pick up a trace of Red Hawk. Find the son of a bitch and kill him."

McAfee broke in. "I don't think that's exactly what Tate has in mind, General." He told Sherman about the cage in the boxcar and Sherman's face darkened with anger. He turned to Barlow. "Tell Tate to come in here."

Barlow opened the door and spoke to the guard who was still blocking the doorway. The guard stepped aside, and followed Barlow unto the room. Barlow sat in his chair, leaving Tate to stand like a school boy in the headmaster's office. Tate and Sherman eyed each other coldly, and finally Sherman broke the silence.

"Tate, I received a telegram yesterday requesting that I cooperate with you in the pursuit of Red Hawk and any other renegade Tonnewa."

Tate nodded. "Yes, general, I received the same message, more or less."

"Request denied."

Tate's face looked impassive, but his eyes betrayed his anger. "You have direct orders . . ."

"I do not have orders," Sherman said, in the command voice that could snap a brigade to attention at a hundred paces. "I have a request. I also received this telegram." He held it in front of him dangling it between his thumb and forefinger. "It's from the Secretary of War in response to a request of my own. Agent Tate, you are free to conduct your investigations in my theater of operations under the sufferance of the United States Army, so long as it does not interfere with my prosecution of the Indian situation. As for help, let alone cooperation, I don't have to do squat.

"Further, I am sending sergeants," Durken and McAfee looked to each other with raised eyebrows. "Durken and McAfee with you while you are on this mission, not to assist you so much as to supervise you to ensure that you do nothing contrary to the Army's interests. If you should do so, you will find that you are not the only one with highly placed friends. Cross me, Tate, and you'll find yourself in that cage you have in the boxcar on your way to Federal prison."

Sherman put his head down and busied himself with some papers on his desk then looked past Tate to his adjutant. "Corporal Barlow, will you please show Agent Tate out?"

Tate stared at Sherman with a look of pure venom. Without another word, he turned and stormed out of the coach.

Sherman relit his cigar. "Damned foolishness."

Durken said, "Exactly what do you want us to do, general?"

"I want you to find Red Hawk and bring him to ground."

"Tate may be a more a hindrance than a help."

"You're right, but I have to accommodate Washington. Tate's here, and he wants to catch Red Hawk too. He'll cooperate up to a point. If he gets in your way, warn him once."

McAfee spoke up. "One other thing, sir."

"What's that?"

"It's almost dark now. Tate won't be ready to leave before sunup. I'd like to ride to the Monatai village and speak with Seven Stars. If we let him know that Red Hawk's around here, he can be on the watch himself and warn the other tribes."

Sherman nodded. "Do that." Durken and McAfee stood. "And, men..."

"Yes, sir?"

"Congratulations on your promotions. Dismissed."

LV

They saddled their horses, and before climbing into the saddle Durken paused. He took his Colt from its holster and flipped out the cylinder. As McAfee watched, he clicked through it and emptied the bullets into his palm. He reached behind him and took six grey-tipped bullets from his belt loops. The silver slugs they'd loaded in them in Lickskillet had dulled over the past few weeks. Durken rubbed one against the sleeve of his duster and burnished its tip to a bright shine. McAfee waited, knowing better than to empty his gun at the same time.

One by one, Durken loaded the silver bullets into his revolver then locked the cylinder in place, turned it a click or two to ensure the mechanism was working freely, and then slid it back into the holster. "Never hurts to be safe," he said. "Your turn."

As McAfee loaded the silver bullets into his pistol, Tate and his men came out of a tent a few yards away. They stared at the cowboys. "What do you think you are doing?" Tate said.

Durken swung a leg over Sweetheart and settled into his saddle. "I think we're following orders, Tate. We'll see you at sunup. Be ready to ride." That said, Durken flicked Sweetheart's reins and he and McAfee rode from the camp.

The stars were showing in the chill night air when Durken and McAfee reached the Monatai village. The moon would rise soon. To let the watchmen know they were not sneaking up on the village, McAfee whistled a verse or two of "Old Folks at Home."

They found Seven Stars in his lodge sitting before a small fire. He sat cross legged, a blanket around his shoulders. He was punching a short awl through a piece of coarse paper. Before they could speak, he said, "McAfee and Durken. Welcome, my friends."

"Evening, Seven Stars," said Durken. "What's that you're doing?"

"I am writing in Braille, the language of the blind," the chief said with a broad smile. "It pleases me no end to do one more thing I thought lost with my eyes."

Durken ran a finger over the bumps on the paper. "You can read this?"

"As easily as you read a newspaper or a handbill." His smile flattened. "I hear worry in your voices. Tell me what has happened."

"Good news and bad news, Chief," said McAfee. "You were right about Red Hawk, but we put a considerable crimp in his plans." For the next hour Durken and McAfee told the story of their encounter with the Cat Warriors at Manson's Pass, their discovery of the Tonnewa in the pit near their camp, and the news of a nearby attack. Seven Stars raised his head as if he were looking through the chimney hole in the teepee at the stars. He sat that way for a long time before he spoke.

"It may be Red Hawk, or if he is dead, it may be his followers. It is good you have come to me. I will send word to the other chiefs of the Council and warn them of the danger. Red Hawk's forces may be small, but like a plague that begins with one victim and grows to wrap a whole tribe in pestilence, he may begin with two or three warriors and infect many to spread his evil."

From a distance McAfee and Durken heard the soft music of a flute. "That's Beethoven," said McAfee. "Is Hollister here?"

Seven Stars nodded. "He came here seeking asylum, and he is welcome with us. He wishes to learn our life and our ways."

"That may be a problem for you if the Secret Service people find out he's been hiding here," said Durken. "They want him pretty bad."

"If they turn their eyes here, they will not see him. He lives in the desert beyond the mesa. Hollister says that he does not wish to place us in jeopardy."

"They may not see him," said Durken, but if they hear that flute, the hunt's over."

Seven Stars laughed. "You have too little faith in your friends and too much in your enemies."

"No offense meant, Seven Stars, but sometimes that's the safest policy."

The night wind blew a chill over Hollister as he stirred the small fire he'd built in the desert miles from the Monatai village. He didn't want his experiment to jeopardize the people who had protected and befriended him. From stories told him by the tribal shaman and other accounts of shape shifting Seven Stars had shared with him in their many discussions, Hollister had pieced together an idea of how the transformation rite should be practiced and what was needed for its execution.

Tate and the other fools wanted the knowledge for venal reasons, and that was why Hollister had taken it from them. He served a higher purpose, the advancement of science. His material proof was gone, destroyed, but he could still use what he had learned to make evidence of himself.

He chuckled. Imagine how the stuffed shirts of the Royal Society in London will react when I make my presentation and after they scoff and demand proof, I become that very proof as they watch, what the scientific method calls "reproducible results." But first, he thought, I must learn to induce and to control the manifestation. And there is but one way to do that.

Hollister opened his knapsack and took out a lump of flesh. He regretted killing the ranch hands but great advancements require great sacrifices. Hollister deduced from the accounts he had heard from Seven Stars and from the shaman that the core of the transformation was a self-induced trance of the type he'd learned among Yogis in India and witch doctors in the African bush.

Red Hawk and his minions had not become simply mindless animals, he thought. They used strategy, coordination, purpose. So then could he.

Hollister jotted some final sentences in his notebook and set it beside him. The pale moon edged over the distant mountains. It was time. He stripped off his clothing and folded each item, placing it in a neat pile. He tied a sash fashioned from a catamount pelt around his waist then he tied the cat's head amulet around his throat. Did he imagine a spreading heat, a vibration from the artifact, or was it simply his pulse, heightened at his excitement?

He turned his silver flute in his hands, watching how it caught the firelight. Who knew what would happen next? What to play? Hollister on a whim chose *Eine Kleine Nachtmusik*. Yes, he thought, a little night music was apropos. When the piece was finished, Hollister pulled the cork from his bottle of whiskey and took a mouthful, savoring the taste, and swallowed, feeling it burn the whole way to his stomach. Then he knelt facing the glowing embers and took the last contemplative breath that precedes a dangerous leap.

Instead of a drum, Hollister beat at his thighs with the heels of his hands in a steady pulsing rhythm, willing his heart beat and his breathing to match it. He rocked back and forward, slowly. Everything in Hollister's mind and body were attuned to that rhythm as he stared across the fire into the darkness.

As he rocked, he reached forward and took the heart in both hands and raised it to his mouth. Hollister bit into it and found the muscle thick and tough. He clenched his teeth and shook his head like a terrier with a rat and tore off a gobbet of flesh, then another and another.

Time ceased to exist. A rush of wind filled his ears. Hollister blinked. On the other side of the fire pit, a catamount sat on its haunches studying him. It gave a coughing snarl and tossed its head.

Hollister may have said the words aloud or only in his mind, but he heard them echo around the mesas. "I am your vessel. Enter me."

The catamount sprung over the fire and entered Hollister's body as if it had dived into a pool of water. And the change began.

Hollister quivered then shook violently as the spirit seized him. His skin began to itch, and tawny fur sprouted at the crown of his head and flowed down his body as if he'd been anointed. His forehead flattened and his jaws extended forward into a muzzle as his nose turned black. Blood dripped from his mouth as fangs broke through his gums. Claws erupted from the ends of his fingers and toes, and his shoulders bulged, pushing his head forward and forcing him into a crouch.

Hollister's thoughts were a crimson swirl. He rose from his kneeling position and spread his arms full span. He tried to shout in exhilaration but all that came out was a coughing snarl. Then the mind of the beast took over and he ran and he ran and he ran through the moonlit night.

He fought with the beast for control of his mind, and gradually felt the alien presence ebbing. He slowed to a walk, and finally sat on a boulder under the moonlight. Breathe slowly, he thought. Hollister watched the hot breaths steam out of his muzzle in white plumes. Think. Reason: Who am I? What am I doing?

He rose full height and stared into the white eye of the night. I am Rupert Hollister, he thought, and I am in possession of myself. An experiment must have a witness. Seven Stars. He turned and started back the way he came, running now at a comfortable lope, not the dead run of mania.

The Secret Service men were pushing their horses, despite the hazard of one of them stepping in a chuck hole or stumbling in the gritty sand. Around them, dark clumps of sage brush dotted the moonlit desert.

Tate frowned, straining his eyes at the dim landscape. They'd lost the cowboys' trail in the dark. Orders. He snorted. Whatever Durken and

McAfee were up to, they weren't going to get away with it on his watch. He fumed at the thought of Sherman trumping him and rubbing his nose in it. The only thing in this direction was the Monatai village. Seven Stars, that meddling Indian was mixed up in this somehow, and Tate was determined to find it out.

Carver scouted ahead while Tate and the other three gave their horses a rest. "What do you think Durken and McAfee are doing out here?" It was Billings, the youngest of the agents, and the newest of Tate's team.

"Nothing in the national interest," Tate replied. "I'm going to see those range rats at the end of a rope before this is all over."

"From what I've heard about those two, you'll have to shoot them first. They won't go down easy."

"Don't let loose talk and gossip worry you. They may be good, but we're better, all of us. Remember who we are."

Gunshots. Tate reined his horse around and listened for more. No more gunplay. From the dark came a hideous scream of pain and terror. "It's Carver," said Tate. "Come on." They set out, but within a hundred yards, Carver's riderless horse ran past them in the other direction at a full gallop.

They rode into a rough circle of brush, pistols in their hands, and found a dark form lying in the center. The horses began to skitter and whinny, and before the agents could dismount, black shapes hidden in the brush came alive and swarmed into the moonlight. Tate had found the object of his quest.

The gunshots were distant, but traveled far enough across the desert that Durken and McAfee heard them. Without hesitation they spurred their horses and rode toward the sound. Moments later, they heard more gunfire, closer now, and plenty of it.

In the circle of brush, the Cat Warriors who had ambushed Carver attacked Tate and his crew with a vicious frenzy. One of them sprang at Billings and knocked him from his saddle. Billings hit the ground and rolled, still holding his pistol. He fired three shots point blank into the catman's face, and rolled away from it in time to fire at a second creature raking its claws down the flank of Tate's horse as it tried to climb its back to get at the agent.

Behind Billings, the Cat Warrior that he had shot rose slowly to its feet, shook its head violently, and dove onto Billings' back, wrapping its legs around his torso and burying its fangs into his neck. Hot blood sprayed black on the sand in the pale light and Billings fell.

Moore and Sullivan's horses reared in panic. Both stayed in the saddle but it did them little good. One of the catmen dove at the right rear leg of Moore's horse, clamping its jaws on it. The mount stumbled and fell sideways, pinning Moore's leg under its bulk. The catman leapt over the horse's body and swept its claws across Moore's face, tearing away his right cheek. Moore screamed in pain and the Cat Warrior screamed in triumph as it dug its other paw into Moore's throat and ripped it open.

Two of the creatures tugged at Tate, trying to pull him from his saddle. One of them sank its fangs into his leg as a shot rang from outside the circle. The catman sprang backward, swiping at its face with its paws. It whirled wildly, shrieking until it fell to the ground and lay still.

In the meantime, Durken and McAfee rode full tilt into the clearing, guns blazing. The silver bullets were effective. The Cat Warriors fell quickly, most of them dead in seconds. McAfee jumped from Thunder and dispatched the last one still writhing on the ground with a shot to the heart.

Durken whirled full circle, looking for more attackers, but none were left. Three of Tate's agents lay in the sand, one disemboweled, the other two mauled beyond recognition. Tate sat on the ground as the last of his agents wrapped a strip of cloth around his thigh to stanch the flow of blood.

McAfee grabbed Tate by his lapels and hauled him to his feet. He screamed in Tate's face. "This is what you were after, Tate! Look at it! This is what you want to turn loose on the world!"

Tate's agent reached for his gun where he'd set it down. He stopped at the click of the hammer of Durken's Colt. "I wouldn't do that, boy." The agent turned and looked straight into the pistol's muzzle. " A silver bullet'll do you as good as those catmen."

Tate looked McAfee in the eye. "Just following orders, McAfee. The same as you are."

McAfee snarled in disgust and threw Tate to the ground. "Come on, Durken. These may not be the only ones running loose. Seven Stars may need help."

Durken flipped the cylinder out of his Colt and shook loose a bullet. He dropped it in Tate's lap. Just in case one of those things wakes up."

As they mounted the horses, McAfee said, "How many silver bullets do you have left?"

"Two. You"

"The same. Let's hope Red Hawk doesn't have too many friends with him."

Blue Knife sat at his post on the mesa. He heard what sounded like gunshots, but faint with distance. His attention diverted, he didn't hear the stealthy tread of the one-eyed catman as it crept up behind him. Red Hawk reached from behind and wrapped his paws around the brave's throat and before he could cry out the monster dug its claws into his flesh. With a wrench of his thick shoulders, Red Hawk ripped Blue Knife's head from his neck. The headless body fell backward, its hot blood pooling on the ground.

Red Hawk stood and warily crawled to the edge of the mesa to study the Monatai village below. Where are you, Seven Stars? Where are you? And then he saw him; at the far end of the lodges. Seven Stars stepped from his tent and carrying a lighted lamp began walking toward the foot of the mesa. Why does a blind man carry a lamp? Red Hawk thought.

But before he could contemplate the question, he was tackled with the force of a bull.

Hollister had seen the Cat Warrior climbing the mesa minutes before. He was too late to prevent the creature from killing Blue Knife, but Red Hawk would have to kill him before he killed Seven Stars.

Red Hawk, bowled over by the collision, rolled to his left and sprung to his feet. Another Cat Warrior! Not one of his own. Hollister leapt at him with a vicious swipe at his face, which Red Hawk barely dodged as the claws whistled past his eyes. He lunged at Hollister, but Hollister sidestepped the rush and dug his claws into Red Hawk's arm, throwing him in a somersault that nearly put him over the rim of the mesa.

Before Red Hawk could right himself, Hollister was on him again, clawing the warrior's back and ripping wide gashes in his fur. Red Hawk shrieked in pain and surprise. He never thought he would have to fight another like himself.

The battle was terrible and furious, slashing and biting, rending flesh and breaking bone. Both soon bled from a dozen wounds, each worse than the one before. They circled each other now, chests heaving, snarling and spitting. Red Hawk had the disadvantage; the noise they made would surely alert the village and Seven Stars with it.

Red Hawk charged, and Hollister sidestepped with a sideways kick that caught the catman just above his hip. Pain exploded in Red Hawk's side as the kick spun him. He howled in frustration as he swiped with both paws, nails raking the empty air. The pair leapt at each other and locked in a furious dance of death. They hit the ground and rolled, snapping at each other's throats.

Hollister's jaws clamped on Red Hawk's muzzle, and the Cat Warrior's blood ran into his mouth. They rolled over and over, and suddenly there was no ground beneath them. They had gone over the rim of the mesa.

The fall was long and the cliff sheer. By nothing more than fortune, Hollister landed with Red Hawk's full weight on top of him on a boulder that snapped his spine with a wet crack. Red Hawk, dazed by the fall, staggered to his feet. He raised his paw to deliver the *coup de grace* and stopped. He heard chanting in a strange tongue and knew the voice: Seven Stars.

Red Hawk turned toward the foot of the mesa and saw the dark hole in the rock. A cave; there he would meet his opposer and tear out his pulsing, dripping life. He looked down at Hollister's broken body. The light was already dimming in the enemy's eyes. He could be dealt with later.

Where were the other Monatai? Surely they had heard the sounds of the fight between him and the unknown catman. Red Hawk snarled in derision. They were likely cowering in their tents, women all. He stood upright and strode boldly to the cave.

As he peered into the entrance, he saw a faint glow from deep inside. He edged through the entrance and followed the light and the sound of Seven Stars' voice. The tunnel rounded a corner and Red Hawk found a chamber perhaps three strides across with no other exit. Seven Stars sat cross-legged on the cave floor. The lamp Red Hawk had seen beside the chief lit the room and painted the rocky walls a deep yellow. Seven Stars' shadow loomed behind him, dancing in the flickering light.

"So you have come, Red Hawk." Seven Stars stood slowly and as he did, his black shadow filled the wall behind him. His voice echoed eerily in the cave.

"I come to kill you, traitor to your kind." Red Hawk's words came as a hissing snarl.

"Kill me, and then what will you do? You cannot win this foolish war you have begun."

"I will have satisfaction." The catman took a step closer.

Seven Stars turned his head slowly from one side to the other, listening. "Will it satisfy you when First Father throws you over the edge of the world?"

"Wives' tales," Red Hawk hissed.

"Like the wives' tale of the Cat Warrior? If one is true, surely the other must be."

"No matter. It will be joy enough to tear you to pieces." Red Hawk crouched to spring.

Seven Stars took a knife from his belt. "If you can." The long tapered blade flashed in the lamplight. "My knife is silver, Red Hawk. Let us see if that too is a wives' tale."

Red Hawk felt his empty eye socket. "If you can find me to stab me, blind man."

Seven Stars smiled. His foot raised a few inches and came down gently on the lamp, snuffing its flame and pitching the cave into blackness. "Now we are both blind, monster."

Red Hawk roared and leapt where Seven Stars stood, hungry for the Monatai's flesh. His claws found empty air and he crashed headlong into the wall of the cave.

"Here."

The voice seemed to come from every direction in the cave. Red Hawk whirled, claws slashing. He found flesh and heard a grunt of pain, then felt a fiery agony as the silver dagger ripped his shoulder. Red Hawk screeched and stumbled backward against the cave wall. He lashed out and his claws tore the Monatai's skin, but before Red hawk could get a firm hold, Seven Stars was out of reach again.

"Here."

Red Hawk turned and as he did, the silver blade cut a burning slash across his forehead. Blood ran down his face and he felt the venomous sting of the silver.

"Here."

Red Hawk staggered madly around the darkened room, swiping aimlessly at an enemy that deftly dodged his blows. He heard a shuffling sound in front of him and swung both arms around Seven Stars' torso, digging his claws deep as he tried to pull him close enough to bite his throat. The Cat warrior shrieked as the silver blade drove deep into his chest, setting his body aflame with torment.

Durken and McAfee rode into the Monatai village unchallenged. As they rounded the mesa, McAfee saw the body sprawled on the granite boulder in the moonlight. He and Durken dismounted and ran to the outcrop.

They saw a Cat Warrior, torn and bloody, lying still. McAfee climbed the rock and inched cautiously toward the creature.

"Watch out. He may not be dead," Durken said, drawing his pistol.

McAfee already had his gun in hand. He cocked the hammer and pointed it at the still form. Its eyes opened. McAfee started back and then he heard what sounded like human speech, faint, distorted but words nonetheless. He leaned closer and barely made out the words, "More things, McAfee,..more things." The eyes closed and the catman was gone.

Durken climbed the rock and crouched beside McAfee. "Hollister," said McAfee. "It's Hollister."

A sound behind them made them both swivel and aim their pistols. Seven Stars staggered from the mouth of the cave at the foot of the mesa. He bled from wounds all over his body, and in his right hand he carried a silver knife. The fingers of his left gripped the fur of Red Hawk's severed head.

"*Il fait accompit*," said Seven Stars, sinking to his knees.

"What'd he say?" said Durken.

"I'm not sure, but I think he means it's over."

For two days Seven Stars lay in a delirium from his injuries. For the safety of the Monatai, the chief had sent them all into hiding, except for Blue Knife who refused to leave his nephew and stayed as watchman over the village. McAfee and Durken sat in a vigil by his pallet until the medicine man arrived to minister to the chief's body and soul.

McAfee dozed for a time and when he awoke, he saw Durken knotting a strand of Seven Stars' hair.

"What are you doing?"

Durken held up the long dark lock of hair. At its end a copper coin was fastened through its center. "Charlie's good luck charm. I figure if anybody needs luck now he does."

"Can't hurt."

They sat outside the teepee for the better part of two days as drums beat, voices chanted, and smoke like incense came from the tent. Neither even suggested leaving the village to report to the General. At one point McAfee asked Durken, "Do you think we ought to go for the doc?"

Durken shook his head. "We've both seen men hurt that bad before. They either live or they die no matter what we do. It all depends on the strength of the man."

The tribe returned on the second day. The same day two of the braves found Hollister's clothing, his notebook, and a human heart. They brought these things to Durken and McAfee and as the cowboys waited outside Seven Stars' teepee, they read Hollister's account of his quest to become a Cat Warrior as evidence of his discovery, the murder of the Diamond T hands and his plunge into dark magic.

On the third day Seven Stars awoke.

Respecting the ceremony, the cowboys waited until the medicine man and his entourage left the tent before they entered. The air was still thick with the bittersweet scent of burning herbs mixed with sweat and infection. Seven Stars lay on his pallet covered by a rough-woven blanket. His forehead was shiny with ointment and a wrinkled squaw sat beside him tending the bowl that served as a censer.

The leather band that covered Seven Stars' empty eyes had been removed but the eyelids fluttered over the vacant sockets. Seven Stars' chin lifted and his head turned in that deliberate way unique to the blind, a listening counterpart to the sighted taking a look around. He reached a hand from beneath the blanket and reached out. He touched Durken's wrist. Durken saw the parallel slashes healing in his forearm, pinned shut with cactus needles.

Seven Stars said something in Monatai to the old woman and she rose and shuffled out of the lodge.

"Durken," Seven Stars said.

"Yep."

"And McAfee?"

"Right here, Chief."

"It is so good to have friends."

"That it is," Durken said.

"And our friend Hollister?"

"Dead."

"I feared so." Seven Stars did not speak for a few breaths. "He stayed with us and strove to learn our ways, but I knew his reasons from the start."

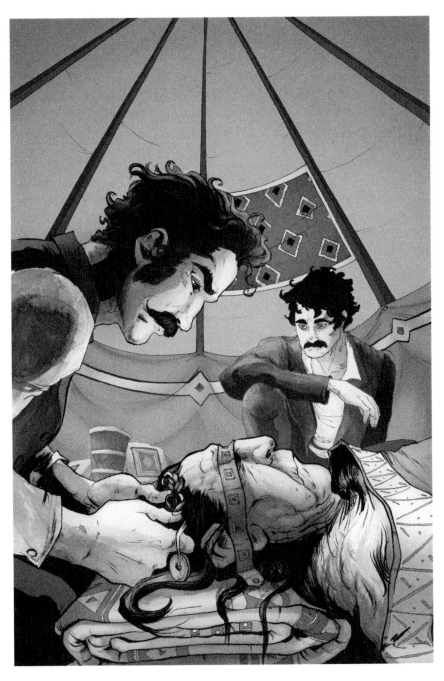

"Charlie's good luck charm. I figure if anybody needs luck now he does."

Mc Afee leaned in. "You knew he wanted to make himself a catman?"

"He asked questions that circled his object like the eyes of a hawk on its prey."

"And you didn't try to stop him?"

Seven Stars sighed. "I of all people understand too well the quest for knowledge. If he did not learn the truth he sought from me, he would have sought it elsewhere. A boulder in a stream only forces water to seek another path to the same end."

"And it didn't hurt to have him handy when Red Hawk came to your village."

Seven Stars chuckled and his mirth turned to a spasm of wet coughing. "A good chief must take all measures to protect his people."

"Fight fire with fire," said Durken.

"Yes, Durken, fire with fire."

McAfee said, "Seven Stars, we have a lot of things to talk about, but right now, you need to rest and get better."

The chief nodded and said. "Yes, things to talk about and decisions to be made."

"Plenty of time for that," said Durken. "I suspect you'll be here when we come back tomorrow."

"I believe so." Seven Stars smiled. "It is good to have friends."

LXII

Late that afternoon Durken and McAfee arrived at the General's siding. The train was still there, but the tents were gone. They tethered the horses and as they climbed the iron stairs of the ornate Pullman car, the door opened and Corporal Barlow came out holding a sheaf of papers.

"Durken, McAfee, the General's been waiting for you."

Sherman had pulled the chair from his desk in front of the gilded fireplace and sat, feet propped on the andirons, reading a thick sheaf of papers in his hands.

His head turned when they came in and he stood. "All I can say, is you two better have a damned good story as to why I haven't heard from you."

"Oh, it's a good one, General." McAfee said. "The big news is that you don't have to worry about Red Hawk anymore."

"And the Cat Warriors?"

"Done for now. Maybe for good."

Sherman nodded and crossed to his desk. He poured whiskey in his glass. "Now tell me why."

As Sherman sipped his whiskey and puffed at his cigar, McAfee and Durken set out the story of their visit to the Monatai village, the attack on Tate and his men and Seven Stars' battle with Red Hawk.

Sherman sat chewing his cigar for a time then said, "And Hollister? What about him?"

"When the tribe left, he stayed at the Monatai village with Seven Stars and was killed when Red Hawk attacked." McAfee stopped short of telling Sherman exactly how Hollister died.

"Damned fool. Scientific curiosity gets a man killed same as any other kind. I get the impression you're not telling me quite everything about the matter." Sherman's sharp eyes pierced Durken and McAfee in turn. "But I guess you've told me enough."

"What about Tate?" Durken asked.

"Tate's gone back to New York to Secret Service headquarters. I guess his bosses are pretty angry with him because Hollister got away and he lost all of Hollister's notes and specimens."

"What about the Cat Warriors we killed out in the desert. Didn't he bring them back here?"

"Oh, those bodies." Sherman looked down and smiled grimly. "He had some bodies wrapped in blankets, requisitioned a lot of salt to preserve them. He had them secured in that cage in the boxcar. Barlow asked him why dead bodies needed to be locked up and Tate wouldn't answer him. Said it was 'top secret.' You can imagine how disappointed Tate was when the boxcar caught fire the night before he left. Burned everything but the wheel trucks and the padlock on the cage."

McAfee grinned. "With all due respect, sir, I get the impression you're not telling us quite everything about the matter. But you've told us enough."

Sherman looked them in the eye. "And let that be the end of the matter, and let's hope we never have to deal with anything like this again."

"Yes, sir."

"I'll have Barlow take your statements, although by the time the government's done with them, you probably won't recognize the story. You've served me and your country well, men. I'm headed to Colorado next. Before I discharge you, I have to ask, would you consider staying on with me. There's plenty to be done out here. I could use your help."

McAfee shook his head. "I'm flattered by the offer, General, but there's a lot to be said for an everyday life."

Durken nodded agreement. "I've fought enough Indians, human and otherwise for a while too. But I think I speak for us both when I say that if you need us again, you know where we'll be."

"I respect your decision. Who knows, maybe I'll go somewhere else and see how other people live. I've sure had a belly full of America." Durken and McAfee stood and Sherman did too. He snapped to attention and saluted them. "Dismissed. And thank you."

As they rode away from the train, Durken said, "You did the right thing by Hollister."

"Let him be remembered for the good not the bad," said McAfee. "I figured that as things stand, this business is over. Let him be remembered as a scientist, not a monster and a killer."

"I guess we can look people in the eye and say that the man who murdered those hands from the Diamond T is dead, because it is the truth."

"That's how I see it."

"Now we have another issue to deal with."

"What's that?"

Durken chuckled. "If everything's 'classified,' how do we explain to Old Man Eldridge how we got back a day ahead of the drovers?"

"Maybe we can sneak in without him seeing us."

"Best idea you've had all day."

Once they got the horses settled, the first order for Durken and McAfee was getting a bath and a shave. As Durken put it, "The women won't want hug us if we smell like the hogs."

"Or kiss us if our chins feel like porcupines."

They boiled water in Charlie's big copper kettle and took turns carrying buckets of it to pour into the old galvanized wash tub where first McAfee then Durken scrubbed off a week's worth of the trail with a bar of lye soap. Durken was toweling himself off with a flour sack and McAfee was shaving when Smedley, one of the hands who stayed behind when the drive left came into the bunkhouse.

"Eldridge wants to see you two in his office right away."

Durken poked a leg in his Union suit. "Who told him we were back?"

"Dunno." Smedley chuckled. "Maybe he smelled you when you rode in. I know I could."

McAfee set down his razor and wiped the shaving soap from his jaw. "Well, we almost made it, Durken. I guess Maggie'll just have to put up with your stubble."

Durken rubbed a thumb across his chin. "No worse than usual, I guess." He buttoned his shirt and pulled his suspenders over his shoulders. "Let's go listen to the old man bellow."

As they crossed the yard, Duken raised his head and turned it one way then the other. He took in a breath of air as if tasting it. Cold and damp. It'll be snowing any day now."

"Yep, but I bet it won't be cold and damp in the boss's office."

"Hotter than Hell, most likely, at least where we're sitting."

"I'll ask you the obvious question. What are you doing here a day ahead of the drive? And where's my bank draft for the herd?"

"Smeck has the payment, Mr. Eldridge," McAfee said. "He should be here with the rest of the gang sometime tomorrow."

"As for why we're here," said Durken, "we were called away on some important military business."

Eldridge opened his mouth to launch a diatribe, but McAfee headed him off. "But, you'll be happy to hear that the Army's through with us. We're just civilians again."

Eldridge frowned. "Well don't expect me to pay you two foreman's wages for the trip."

"Only half." Durken grinned. "You can give the other half to Smeck."

Eldridge shook his head. "If it wasn't for my Army contract, I'd fire you both. And don't expect to pull a stunt like this again. Close the door behind you."

"Yes, sir," said McAfee. He and Durken stepped into the hallway and pulled the door shut.

"Now," Durken said, "since Charlie ain't back yet, let's go see if Maggie can rustle up something for us in the kitchen."

McAfee hesitated. "You know, there's one thing we haven't talked about. Hollister's notebook. It's still in Seven Stars' tent. We don't want Tate to get his hands on it."

"That's true. But since Tate's back east for now, I figure it'll keep until Seven Stars is well enough we can talk it through and make some decisions.

I reckon Seven Stars will handle it right. He always has in the past. In the meantime, I don't know about you, but I'm starved."

The drovers returned the next morning and life returned to normal for two days. Then on the third day just after breakfast Smeck came into the bunkhouse. "Hey Durken, McAfee, there's an Indian outside says he has a message for you."

"Must be from Seven Stars," McAfee said. He and Durken strode outside to find Laughing Wolf waiting in the yard sitting astride his paint, wrapped in a bright blanket against the chill air.

"Hello, Laughing Wolf," said Durken. "Is your chief well?"

Laughing Wolf nodded, unsmiling. "He walks."

"Smeck said you have a message for us, is it from Seven Stars?"

"Yes," said Laughing Wolf. "Seven Stars says that you should come to our village to say farewell to your friend Hollister."

"Now?"

"Yes. Now." Laughing Wolf wheeled his horse and trotted through the yard toward the gate.

"I get the impression this is no light occasion," McAfee said.

"Seems that way."

Durken went back inside to tell Smeck he and McAfee had business to attend to. "If anybody asks, tell them we had to ride to the Monatai village and we should be back by dark. He headed for the stable to saddle Sweetheart and found McAfee slipping the bridle over Thunder's ears.

The weather had turned colder over the last two days, and a few stray flakes of snow spun from the grey clouds. A thin scrim of ice topped the water in the trough in the mornings, and the cowboys could see their breath in the air.

The scrubland showed patches of white as the snow fell a little steadier. "Good thing we drove the herd to Reno when we did. We lucked out."

"Yeah, said Durken. "Three days on the trail and we could be up to our ass in snow. Remember that drive two years ago? We were both chipping ice out of the cows' noses just so they could breathe."

"You know, I figured the Monatai would have buried Hollister by now, that they'd want to be rid of him and Red Hawk too."

"Hollister wasn't one of the tribe. Maybe there's some special ritual they follow."

"Anyway, Seven Stars wouldn't ask us to come if he didn't have a good reason."

"Nope." Durken pulled his hat lower on his brow and McAfee shut up.

LXVI

As they approached the mesa, Durken and McAfee raised their empty hands to the sentry. Recognizing them he motioned them on into the village.In a few minutes, they were inside Seven Stars' lodge.

"It is good that you have come," Seven Stars said. His wounds were healing, but he walked stiffly and had some difficulty when he rose to greet them. "If you please, follow me."

Seven Stars limped from the tent and led them to a sheltered nook around the mesa. There they found a wooden pallet raised into the air on lodge poles and covered with a blanket. A fire burned nearby. The medicine man chanted and danced around it with a bouncing step, shaking a rattle made from a decorated gourd. His face was painted yellow and red stripes coursed across his cheeks from his ears to his nose.

"I thought you buried the dead," said McAfee.

"The human dead. Wide Sky dances around the body now, keeping the evil spirit trapped inside until its vessel is destroyed so it cannot escape and enter another host." Seven Stars pulled away the blanket.

Hollister lay in repose, clawed hands folded across his chest. His feline features seemed almost peaceful. He wore his tweed walking suit and puttees and looked like the pet of a spoiled rich child dressed in doll clothing for a whimsical photograph. His shoes, unable to fit over his paw-like feet, sat beside his head. Under one of the furred hands, McAfee saw Hollister's flute. Under the other he saw the leather binding of the zoologist's notebook. Beside the corpse was a bundle wrapped in deer hide, the heart of the second cowboy.

"It is time." Seven Stars took a brand from the fire and lit the straw under the body. The straw was damp from the snow, but it soon caught and the fire spread to engulf the pallet in bright orange flames. Wide Sky continued to dance as the smoke rose to blend with the grey clouds.

"I thought you would want this." Seven Stars reached under his robe and pulled out a long bottle. He handed it to Durken.

"Hollister's scotch whiskey." He looked to McAfee and raised his eyebrows. McAfee nodded in agreement. Durken pulled the cork from the bottle. "You have your rituals, and we have ours."

"Of course," Seven Stars said.

Durken raised the bottle in salute and tipped it back, taking a long swallow. He handed it to McAfee. "So long, Hollister." He drank from the bottle and as an afterthought offered it to Seven Stars. The chief hesitated and then raised the bottle to his lips.

The three passed the bottle and kept their vigil until the pyre burned to ash.

"What about Red Hawk?" McAfee asked as they walked back to Seven Stars' tent.

"He too will have his ceremony. We must ensure that his evil dies with him."

Seven Stars' tone told Durken and McAfee that their visit was over. "Well, we thank you for honoring our friend and for allowing us to be present."

"Much obliged, Seven Stars," said Durken.

The chief held out his hand. In it was Charlie's copper coin. "This is yours?"

"No, actually it belongs to Charlie Ming. I figured at the moment you needed all the luck you could get, no matter the source."

"I thank you." Seven Stars nodded gratefully and the pair left his lodge, maintaining a contemplative silence as they mounted their horses and rode away.

One of the tribal elders entered Seven Stars' tent. "Your friends have left the village."

Seven Stars rose painfully from his pallet. "Let us do what must be done." As Seven Stars left the cluster of tents, the tribe followed, man, woman and child through the gauzy snowfall.

Beyond the mesa hidden from view was another raised pallet. On it Red Hawk's corpse lay furred, fanged and naked. His one-eyed head sat on his chest, gazing at his distended feet. The tribe gathered around and as Wide Sky chanted, the villagers joined in. The medicine man danced around the pallet shaking his rattle. He slashed at the air with Seven Stars' silver knife. The chant intensified and the Monatai swayed with its rhythm as Seven Stars lit the straw on the pallet.

Instead of rising from the blaze, the smoke gathered above the pallet and roiled. A keening wail came from the dark cloud and as the villagers continued to chant, the smoke took the shifting form of the dead Cat Warrior, whirling, slashing with its claws, unable to find escape.

A harsh wind began to blow and as the villagers watched, a great white cloud in the shape of an ancient man holding a thick silvery rope swooped down from the sky, wrapped the rope's coils around the wailing spirit and bore it away to the edge of the Fourth World.

A good inch of snow covered the ground by the time Durken and McAfee rode through the gate of the Triple Six.

McAfee stared through the pale curtain to the lights of the mansion where he thought he caught a fleeting glimpse of Miss Sarah at her window. "I must say it'll be good to get back to everyday life again."

"Yep," said Durken. "'Til the next time."

T he young boy was named Long Eyes. Seven Stars selected him from the youth of the tribe for his intelligence and his quickness to learn. The boy now sat cross legged on the floor of Seven Stars' lodge, reading from a sheet of paper by the firelight.

"T-h-e," the boy sounded out letter by letter. Seven Stars had taught him the English alphabet, drawing the letters from memory in the packed earth of his lodge with a stick, but he did not teach him to read. That may come later, but for the time being it was best he not understand the words whose letters he read one by one and be burdened by the knowledge they imparted as Seven Stars had once been.

As a scholar, Seven Stars believed in his heart that to lose Hollister's knowledge would be a disgraceful waste of the man's life. Before Hollister's funeral, he instructed Long Eyes to tear out all of the pages of Hollister's notebook that had writing on them. The notebook that burned on the pallet held only blank pages.

As the boy read the letters, Seven Stars plied the short awl he used to write in Braille and punched out the letters one at a time between the lines of his Braille Bible. As a page of the notebook was completed, it was fed into the fire lest other eyes discover its secrets. The transcription was a slow, painful process, but the winter promised to be long and snow laden, plenty of time for the work at hand.

"L-y-c-a-n-t-h-r-o-p-e."

One less mystery in the world.

One less thing undreamt.

Except in nightmares.

THE END

HÎNQÛMEMEN

Closing time was creeping up on the Silver Dollar. It was Saturday night, bleeding into Sunday morning when a lot of people cork their bottles and reach for their Bibles. The night had been what Liam the owner called a quiet one; nobody was shot and only three fist fights broke out.

Durken and McAfee sat at a table away from Keever's jangling piano, sharing a bottle with Smeck and Royster, two of the hands from the Triple Six. The only other people in the place were a half dozen cowboys at the bar and a stranger who sat brooding over his whiskey at a nearby table. The stranger sat hunched over his drink staring into it as if he would find the answer to some great question in the bottom of the glass.

One of the barflies, a grizzled old man in a ragged pair of canvas pants and a faded flannel shirt that had seen better days ambled over to the table. His watery blue eyes gazed at the bottle of whiskey. "Would you fellows buy a poor man down on his luck a drink? Buy me a drink and I'll tell you a story you ain't heard before."

"Why not," said Durken, who loved a good story.

"What's your name, old fella?" McAfee said. Looking closely, McAfee realized the man wasn't what he seemed. His unkempt shock of white hair and his haggard appearance made him look much older than his true age.

"My name's Jack Creasy." At the next table, the stranger's head snapped up and his dark eyes fixed on the old man.

Durken reached for the bottle and poured a drink which the old man gulped down as if he were dying of thirst. 'Now that you've had your drink, Jack Creasy, tell us the story."

"It was in fifty-nine. I was riding with Billy Joe Walton's gang. We were on a spree that would have made us bigger than the James Gang or the Younger Brothers if Billy Joe hadn't got killed, but I'm getting ahead of myself.

"We robbed the bank in Wynn Gap, right on the California-Nevada border, and in those days Tom McLaughlin was the sheriff."

"I've heard of him," said McAfee. "He was one tough son of a bitch. Had a reputation for never letting a man get away."

"Well, he's gone too, got stabbed in the heart breaking up a saloon fight over some dance hall gal. Anyway, he was the sheriff. He got wind of the bank job from the little weasel at the livery stable that was to watch our horses and have them ready for us to ride. We come out of the bank and ran straight into gunfire. Tom McLaughlin and his deputies were laying in wait for us.

"They got Billy Joe and Mitchell Long right off, and the three of us who were left put down two of his men on our way to the livery. We had to grab what horses we could, because ours were nowhere to be found. We rode out of town as fast as those nags could carry us, and as we went past, we saw that livery boy sitting on a hitching rail laughing at us and flipping a fifty cent piece. Red Cammon pulled his horse up short and shot the little bastard right off the rail like a crow off a fence post.

"We rode for hours, and every time we looked over our shoulders, we saw the dust cloud behind us; never any closer, but never any further back either. Based on the size of the cloud, we figured there were six of them at least, and if they caught us, we were done. There was nothing ahead of us but desert, and we had no choice but to just keep riding."

Creasy paused and eyed the bottle, raising his eyebrows. Durken nodded and poured another drink for him. "We figured the chase was just about over. The horses were whipped and so were we. The sun was as hot as iron in a forge, and we had no water. And they'd've caught us for sure if it hadn't been for the sandstorm."

"Sandstorm?" Smeck said.

Creasy spread his hands and his voice rose. The second drink brought out the performer in him. "It was the biggest I ever seen," he said. "Late in the day it came out of the North like a big brown wall and hit us broadside. The sand blacked out the sun and it scrubbed at us 'til I thought my skin was gone. We just covered our faces with our bandannas and rode on. And then as fast as it came, it quit. The wind died down and the sand settled as if it never happened.

"But when we looked back, the posse was gone. I guess McLaughlin and his men thought it was too dangerous to ride through it and turned back. We were rid of them, but we were in a fix anyway. Here we were, in the middle of the desert with no water and the nearest town at least a day's ride.

"It was near sunset when we rounded a dune and we saw a lake. We thought it was a mirage at first; we all seen them before. But when we got closer, we saw that it was real; the deepest blue I've ever seen. Frank Tenner jumped off his horse and ran right up to the edge. He dipped his hat in the lake and scooped out some water, took a drink, and poured the rest over his head. He was laughing and saying, 'It's real! It's real!' when his horse put its head down to drink.

"I thought I was seeing things. The water kinda rose up in a big ball in front of the horse, and before it could move, the water surrounded it head to toe like it was in a ball of glass. I couldn't hear it, because it was sealed up inside but it was struggling something awful. While we watched, it just sort of faded; at least that was what it looked like at first, but I saw soon enough, the poor animal's meat was disappearing right off its bones until there was nothing left but the skeleton.

"The water globe dropped the bones and started for Frank, who was just standing there too startled to think, let alone move. He turned to run but stumbled in the sand and the water caught him by his lower leg. He screamed something awful. The globe was kind of attached to the lake by a trunk of water. Red rode in to help Frank, and when he rode through that trunk, something broke and the water fell flat on the sand.

"Frank was crawling away and Red rode in his direction to pull him onto the horse when the water regrouped and the big ball got Red. I was too scared to move. I just sat there and watched as Red and his horse disappeared in that ball of water like Frank's horse did. The ball dropped the bones and started after me. I spurred that horse, but I didn't really have to. It seemed to know by instinct that this was life and death."

Creasy's eyes widened. "I looked back and saw the whole damned lake rise out of that basin to chase me. I seen the ocean before, and that's what it looked like, like them huge waves. It would gather itself up like a big hand with a loud hiss and crash down on the sand and drag itself forward. Those waves were tall. Once after dark when the moon was rising behind it I looked back and while I watched, one of those big waves rose up and blotted out the light like a big dark shadow then it fell again.

"The horse was tired and dry before we found that lake. By sunrise, he was pretty well played out, but I lived this long, and I wasn't going to lay down and give up. When the horse fell, I took off on foot. The water stopped long enough to make a bone pile out of my nag and then it started after me again. But I noticed it wasn't quite so tall when it rose up, and it wasn't moving quite so fast.

"The sun was getting high now, and it was drying up. The water was slowing down, but so was I. I floundered in the deeper sand and struggled to stay ahead of it, and just about the time I thought I was going to collapse, it stopped moving. It wasn't a big body of water now, but more like a big flat puddle in the sand. It tried to gather itself to move again, but it couldn't.

"And then I made a mistake. I suppose I was addled by the heat and the shock of it all, but I'd out run Tom McLaughlin and this lake from Hell too, and I just had to crow. I got close to it and I started to laugh, crazy-like and dance around. "Ha ha! Got you, you son of a bitch! Ain't so tough now, are you?

"And that cursed water gathered itself one last time and shot out a finger like a striking rattler and caught me by the ear. I struggled and struggled with it but it wouldn't let go. Then my ear come off. I fell backward in the sand, and that finger of water fell flat and just dried up." He brushed away the hair that hung in snarled hanks over the side of his face. "And that's how I lost that ear."

On the side of Creasy's head was a mass of scar tissue where his ear had once been, a glossy patch looking like someone cauterized the wound with a hot knife.

There was silence around the table for a few seconds then Smeck and Royster looked at each burst out laughing. Creasy's face fell. "You don't believe me?" He stood up and shouted. "It's true! It's true! I swear it's true."

"You old buzzard," said Royster. "Tell us a story like that and expect us to believe you? I have half a mind to turn you upside down and squeeze those drinks you cadged from us out of your simple head."

"I ain't lying! I ain't!" Creasy began flapping his arms and jumping up and down in a tantrum. Liam came from behind the bar and grabbed him under the arms from behind and shoved him through the swinging doors into the street. He shook his head and without another word went back to wiping down the bar.

"What a crazy old coot," Smeck said. "Did you ever hear such horseshit in your life?"

"It's true." The gravelly voice surprised the cowboys. They turned to the stranger seated nearby and found him staring at them. "What he said is true. I take it you've never been in Inuit country up north." No one spoke and the stranger went on. "The Inuit tell stories about what they call Hînqûmemen, 'The Engulfer.' It's a killer lake that chases and eats people who take its water. Jack Creasy speaks the truth, and I'll draw on any man here who calls me a liar."

"Easy, friend," said Durken. "Nobody's calling you a liar, but I have to ask, how is it you know he's telling the truth?"

The stranger stood. His dark eyes glared at them. "Because I'm Frank Tenner." He turned and strode out of the Silver Dollar every other step thumping the floor with the end of his wooden leg.

THE END

ABOUT OUR CREATORS

AUTHOR

FRED ADAMS - is a western Pennsylvania native who has enjoyed a lifelong love affair with horror, fantasy, and science fiction literature and films. He holds a Ph.D. in American Literature from Duquesne University and recently retired from teaching writing and literature in the English Department of Penn State University.

He has published over 50 short stories in amateur, and professional magazines as well as hundreds of news features as a staff writer and sportswriter for the now Pittsburgh Tribune-Review. In the 1970s Fred published the fanzine *Spoor* and its companion *The Spoor Anthology*. *Hitwolf, Six-Gun Terror* and *Dead Man's Melody* were his three first books for Airship 27 is his first, and his nonfiction book, Edith Wharton's *American Gothic: Gods, Ghosts, and Vampires* will be published by Borgo Press in 2014.

ARTIST

ZACHARY BRUNNER – graduated from the School of Arts with a degree in filmmaking. Upon gradution, he realized that he would rather pursue a career in illustration, needing a more creative job than the high-stress environment of film production. He began working with comic writer Jim Krueger on two graphic novels, *The High Cost of Happily Ever After*, and *Runner*. "High Cost" is currently available at Amazon, "Runner," is expected out later this year.

While studying at SVA, Zachary worked as a concept artist on an animated film called *Brother*, directed by Sari Rodrig. The short film went on to win countless awards all over the world, having been shown at festivals such as Cannes and the Student Emmys. Zach currently is working on Sari's second short animated film, *Essence*.

For the past year, he has also worked as a storyboard artist for Torque Creative, the in-house advertising agency for Mercedes-Benz. He is also currently working on several storyboards for short independence films.

Other print projects included *Christopher Rising, Penny Dreadful, The Poisonberry Fortune* and *Foot Soldiers, Volume 1*. He plans on furthering a career in concept art and in the comic book industry.

HOWL OF THE WOLF

It is 1969; Newark, N.J. Former Green Beret Jim Slate comes home from Vietnam to live a quiet, peaceful life. His wish is cruelly denied him when he is kidnapped by Michael Monzo, a local gang boss who wants to rule the entire city. To do this he must bring down his rivals.

Monzo recruits an occult practiner who can turn an ordinary man into a vicious werewolf and then control his actions by the use of a magic amulet. But to carry out this heinous plan, he needs a subject. And so Jim Slate is snatched and turned into a "Hitwolf."

But Slate is no one's puppet and, despite the curse put on him, he will not be controlled. After he manages to escape his master, Slate disappears into the thousands of acres of New Jersey woodlands known as the Pine Barrens. But Monzo has no intentions of losing his pet killing machine. Now the manhunt begins to capture Jim Slate...dead or alive!

YOU CAN'T STOP THE
SUN FROM SHINING

Sonny Bill Williams (SBW) is a once in a hundred-year athlete with immense sporting talent. He has been a national and international champion across Rugby Union, Rugby League and Boxing.

Williams began his career in Rugby League and has played in the Australian NRL with the Canterbury-Bankstown Bulldogs and the Sydney Roosters. He has played for the Toronto Wolfpack in Super League and has played Rugby Union for Toulon in France, Canterbury, Counties Manukau, the Crusaders, the Chiefs and the Blues in New Zealand and the Panasonic Wild Knights in Japan. He has won 58 caps for the New Zealand All Blacks and was a member of the teams that won the 2011 and 2015 Rugby Union World Cups. He has also played Rugby Sevens for New Zealand, competing in the 2015-16 World Rugby Sevens Series and the 2016 Olympics.

Williams has boxed professionally seven times, winning all of his heavyweight bouts. He was the New Zealand Professional Boxing Association (NZPBA) Heavyweight Champion and World Boxing Association (WBA) International Heavyweight Champion. Away from sport, Sonny Bill Williams focuses on his family, his Islamic faith and is very involved in charity work and promoting social justice.

YOU CAN'T STOP THE SUN FROM SHINING

SONNY BILL WILLIAMS

WILLIAMS

WITH ALAN DUFF

HODDER

First published in Great Britain in 2021 by Hodder & Stoughton
An Hachette UK company

This paperback edition published in 2022

1

Picture section design by Christabella Designs
All images courtesy of Sonny Bill Williams unless otherwise credited

A CIP catalogue record for this title is available from the British Library

Paperback ISBN 9781529387889
eBook ISBN 9781529387865

Printed and bound in Great Britain by Clays Ltd, Elcograf S.p.A.

Hodder & Stoughton policy is to use papers that are natural, renewable
and recyclable products and made from wood grown in sustainable forests.
The logging and manufacturing processes are expected to conform
to the environmental regulations of the country of origin.

Hodder & Stoughton Ltd
Carmelite House
50 Victoria Embankment
London EC4Y 0DZ

This book is dedicated to my mum and dad

CONTENTS

Introduction

by Alan Duff

I might be the last person you'd expect to find working with Sonny Bill on his autobiography. I've written eleven novels, two adapted to feature films, and three non-fiction books, and I'm a former syndicated newspaper columnist, now writing for television. I'm not a professional sports writer.

But, like most Kiwis, I love rugby – even though I played my last game almost thirty-two years ago, and at a low level. My meagre claim to representative success is playing for the Canterbury under-15s a long, long time ago. I had a season of rugby league as a young man, so I know first-hand what a tough game it is. And I have loved boxing since I fell in love with Cassius Clay, who later changed his name to Muhammad Ali to reflect his new religion, Islam. Of course, sporting colossus Sonny Bill is also a Muslim convert, and more than a few pundits have compared the two athletes. This pundit happens to believe that they share more than just unique athletic ability; they are both known for being exceptionally decent human beings, doing good for the wider community. As Tom Humphries observed in the *Irish Times* in 2010:

> Every now and then a sport gets gifted a character who seems destined to transcend its boundaries and become something more broadly iconic. An Ali. A George Best. A Babe Ruth. A Joe Namath. Rugby has found one such. Sonny Bill Williams . . . Even to the untrained eye he is something special.

Like many, I was onto the phenomenon of Sonny Bill from the time of his incredible NRL debut for the Canterbury Bulldogs at the supposed-to-be-tender age of just eighteen. I say 'supposed to be' because he was as far from physically and mentally tender as it gets. Humphries described him as 'granite'.

I met Sonny Bill for the first time in Paris at the end of 2017, when he was touring with the All Blacks and I was preparing to return home to New Zealand after almost a decade of self-exile. He was accompanied by his inimitable manager, Khoder Nasser, and it was then that a collaboration between us was first discussed. Khoder suggested that being 'outsiders' gave the three of us a certain affinity. And so it has proved: we all feel we're a good match when it comes to getting Sonny's story on these pages.

Sonny Bill is considered a sports superstar throughout the rugby and league world. Throw in New Zealand heavyweight boxing champion and All Blacks Sevens Olympian and there you have it: a sporting hero like no other before him. But as Sonny Bill shared his life story with me, other qualities emerged. I learned of his humility and extreme modesty – indeed, shyness. I would discover a courage that went beyond that found on rugby fields and in the boxing ring. He is strong-minded, a man of unwavering principles. And EMPATHY has to be in capital letters because he has it by the bucketload.

Many of Sonny's personal qualities can be attributed to his religion. To become a Muslim – or start the process of conversion, at least – only a few years after 9/11, when most of the Western world considered Islam and terrorism to be inextricably linked, takes more than courage. That decision not only put his stellar sporting reputation at risk, it exposed him to the odium of the prejudiced and the ignorant, and not a few otherwise rational people whose minds had been turned by those horrific attacks. Sonny will tell you he was no different: he once conflated Islam with terrorism, as I did myself. But through its teachings, Sonny discovered a deep inner healing and peace. He is living proof that the basic tenets of Islam preach goodness, charity, humility and a love of Allah. No, he has not converted me, and he never attempted to, but he has taught me to be more open-minded.

With Sonny living in Sydney and me in Auckland, we were forced by Covid-19 to conduct our exchanges on Zoom, but we quickly warmed to each other. Sonny Bill would begin each two-hour session by asking: 'How are you, Alan? How's your family? You all good?' He is a listener, not someone who is tripping over himself to talk about Sonny Bill the big sports star. Far from it. The more we talked, the more I would gently push him to go deeper. Although Sonny is modest and without ego, he is not secretive, and he didn't shy away from discussing personal issues. This book is about getting to know the real Sonny Bill Williams, who at a young age went from obscurity to becoming the subject of headlines and media-hyped controversies.

Some of the negative media coverage of Sonny over the years really bothered me, and I'll admit I wanted payback, but Sonny is bigger than that. He has no interest in naming names or throwing anyone under the bus. And in any case, Sonny Bill's actions speak louder than their words. Watch a replay of what happened after the Rugby World Cup 2015, when young fan Charlie Line was tackled by a security officer as he ran onto the ground during the triumphant All Blacks team victory walk. Observe Sonny's body language, how he helps Charlie up and walks him back to his parents before taking off his gold medal and putting it around the kid's neck, hugging him. Instead of losing his head in all that joyful clamour around him, he put this young kid's welfare first. You are probably aware of that incident, but you're probably not aware that he stayed in contact with Charlie and his parents, just as you do not know of Sonny Bill's countless other acts of kindness and empathy.

That trait came through in every talk session we have had. 'Bro' and 'my bro' he uses frequently. It has got to the point where he's got this old codger saying the same, not just to him and Khoder, but to my mates as well! His desire to use his profile to help lift Pacific Islanders and Māori was declared from the start. To my mind, he grew another 6 feet 4, standing there like a rigid sentinel willing to die to protect/inspire his/our Polynesian people. He made sure the photographer who took the photo for the cover of this book was of Pasifika background, and ensured one of the editorial staff was too.

You hear that a few times and you start to realise that this project – being this guy – is bigger than this ardent admirer realised. Sonny Bill tells of being heavily influenced by Malcolm X. This reminded me that I read

Malcolm X's book years back and now at least can refer to YouTube video interviews with this extraordinary African American, a reformed ex-inmate from the ghetto who discovered Islam and dared to tell white America that their appalling abuse of black Americans made them no less than 'devils'. An accusation that obviously did not go down well with white America.

Sonny is not for one moment echoing those same thoughts. But an awful lot of what Malcolm X had to say on white racism rings bells with him, as they still do with me. Listening to Malcolm X talk brings on a series of 'hey, of course!' moments. Like I experienced decades ago while going through my Muhammad Ali adoration period, my astonishment at Malcolm X's utterances are echoed by Ali. But both men's legacies continue to echo down the ages and inspire younger men of colour to stand taller.

When you're a younger adult still forming your views on life, some incredible insights get slowly consumed by your own maturity. But those notions that are still sticking forty years later? Well, that's wisdom and righteousness resonating down the generations.

I have found in Sonny Bill a whole bunch of righteous notions, going from faint to thundering down the years as he became more self-aware thanks to his conversion to Islam. The man who wanted so much to become a better person is well on the way to achieving that.

He is determined to do what he can to help lift brown people – Polynesians, including we Māori who came from the Pacific islands around 1250. To be an example to youngsters so they might aim for his heights, in sports, in business, professional careers – anything but menial employment forever doomed to live on Struggle Street. And to remind them not to ignore their own moral compass as they find their way. His desire just to be a decent human being is the motivation behind much of what he does now.

He donated a large sum of money to the Christchurch earthquake fund because he was there, playing for the Canterbury Crusaders, when that shattering event occurred in 2011. He went back to Christchurch in 2019 to comfort his fellow Muslims after fifty-one people were slaughtered by a madman while praying in their mosques.

When I speak of Sonny Bill's greatness, I don't just mean it in terms of his sporting genius, in the sense of him being 'biggest', 'fastest', 'strongest' or 'cleverest'. I mean it in the sense of the largeness of his heart for the wider world.

Every writer working with sporting heroes will claim to be privileged and humbled by the opportunity. Well, I'm no different: I am both. But I'll go further than that and say that being involved in this story is a gift. The last thing Sonny wants is for me to sprinkle these pages with praise. 'Water off a duck's back, bro,' is how he handles the adulation. 'I just strive to be a better person. A better husband, father, friend, citizen.' He insists that he is ordinary, but Sonny Bill is far from that. He is truly extraordinary, not just as a sportsman but as a man, as this book will show.

And with that, I will hand you over to Sonny.

Alan Duff
2021

CHAPTER 1

Sleeping with my boots on

I was around seven years old, lying awake on a Friday night while my parents partied in the lounge room. But it wasn't their singing that was keeping me up; it was excitement – because Saturday was footy day. So even though I was in bed, I was fully dressed for the game in my club jersey, shorts, long socks . . . even my footy boots.

I thought about footy constantly. Thanks to my brother, Johnny, I already knew the names of some of the famous rugby league players in the NRL. Johnny, who is two years older, was a very good player. Our old man had been a top player too, but, as he said himself, he'd blown his chance to make the big time because he wasn't focused enough. He later coached age-group teams for years, and every one of his teams won their championship.

I lived for winter Saturdays and played footy at lunchtime and after school, while at home I passed, kicked, tackled and discussed the game endlessly with Johnny. I ignored bad weather; I just wanted to play. When there weren't enough numbers to make up teams, a few of us kids would still get together and practise. That's where my offloads were born.

My entire family was obsessed with the NRL, so it's no surprise I was too. Rugby league was always part of what we did and what we talked about. And it didn't just come from my old man's Sāmoan side of the family; my white half-Australian mum's family was into it too. Mum's father, William 'Bill' Woolsey, had been a top league player as well as a boxer and bar-room brawler. His reputation was fierce, on and off the field. So rugby league was in my genes, and I guess I was lucky enough to be born with sporting talent.

* * *

Fast-forward about eleven years to 2004 and a dream was on the verge of coming true. I was in Sydney, in the Canterbury Bulldogs changing room, about to make my NRL debut at age eighteen against the Parramatta Eels. And guess what? I'd forgotten my boots! I must have been that nervous packing my stuff. Seven-year-old me would have been shocked. At that moment, I wished I'd slept in them.

A team talk started but I couldn't concentrate properly; all I could think was, *What do I do, I don't have any boots?* I was panicking. Without a word to anyone, I slipped outside to look for my brother in the crowd. Johnny saw me and waved, and I ran over and told him the problem. I asked him if he could drive home fast and get my boots, but he said he didn't need to: he had a new pair in his car that I'd given him when they'd issued us players with heaps of free gear. Phew!

After that, I remember warming up. It was a surreal feeling, the same feeling I would experience some years later playing my first game for the All Blacks. Thinking, *Is this really happening?* But at least I knew the Bulldogs players; I'd been hanging around the club the last two years as a young guy on a league scholarship, and even the most feared senior players had been kind and encouraging. I'd practised with them and guys like giant Willie Mason and Matt Utai had inspired me. So many of them went out of their way to make me feel welcome and treat me like I was one of them, even before I took the field alongside them. But I still felt like an outsider and was aware I had a lot to prove.

Hearing the crowd coming into Telstra Stadium, I knew that this was it. All those years of watching NRL and playing with my mates back home, all the practising and training were about to pay off . . . I hoped. The noise and excitement of the fans emphasised the significance of the moment. In a few minutes, my career was about to start. It was really, really daunting.

There were others having their debut in that game too, like Willie Tonga, Reni Maitua and Hutch Maiava – and though future Hall of Famer Johnathan Thurston had made his debut two years earlier playing first grade for the Bulldogs, I know he was as nervous and fired up as I was that day. Us novices got on well, so we all looked out for each other, but really, with any debut, you are on your own. It is up to you to put in the effort and play a good game.

The whistle blew and it was on. Starting off with a big shoulder-charge hit put an end to my nerves. And before I knew it, the game was over! We'd won 48–14, and after the final whistle I heard my name being chanted by the crowd. How could that be?

Afterwards, the team went out drinking and celebrating. Many in that Bulldogs team trained hard, played hard and partied hard. I had proved I could match them on the field, but there was no way I could match them off it. At that point, I didn't even want to try. I didn't drink and I was still the shy new fella, not comfortable in a social setting with guys who seemed full of self-confidence and knew so much more than I did. If there were more than two people in a room, I struggled to speak up. So, after one of the biggest moments of my life to date, I went home to my old man's place with Johnny. Dad had moved to Australia by then. I can remember us in my old man's lounge room rewatching the game together. I was sitting there and I was spinning. I'd look at Johnny and it was like, *Bro, did that just happen? Did I really just play NRL?* And he'd look at me and he's asking the same thing. After the colour, noise and frenetic activity of the game, I was pinching myself. It all felt like a dream. My old man, being the typical Islander father that he was, kept standing up and walking around, laughing and saying out loud to no-one but us, 'That's my son. That's my son.'

I'd paid for Johnny to come over and join me in Sydney six months before that debut. Even though Dad was here, I was missing family and Johnny had been getting into some serious trouble back home, so it seemed like a great opportunity for a fresh start. I found a dope pipe in his trouser pocket not long after he arrived; that's the state he was in at the time. He knew he was on a bad path, and it was one he didn't want me to follow. Johnny had been adamant that I accept the offer to go to the Bulldogs in Sydney as a teenager because he didn't want me to end up like him, in trouble with the law, selling weed, drinking, fighting, running with the wrong crowd. I was a mama's boy and wanted to stay home, but Johnny said, 'Bro, you've got to go or you're going to end up where I am.'

John Arthur – Johnny – was a talented footballer but everyone thought of him as the 'bad' brother. He was never a bad brother to me. (As far as our mum was concerned, if she answered the phone and someone asked for either Johnny or Sonny, she'd say no-one of that name lives here. We have a John Senior, a John Arthur and a Sonny Bill.) I credit Johnny with so much of my success because he's always had my back. He'd practise with me, gee me up when my confidence was low – he made me want to do better on the field to impress him. Johnny would deal with bullies who hassled me. When he was around, I felt safe. I didn't have to be anyone but myself with him. When I played well, he felt as if he'd played well with me. If I struggled with a personal problem, he struggled with me. My big uso (brother) was always there for me, ready to listen and keep me company.

My old man – John Senior – was pretty hard on us growing up. It wasn't like he didn't praise us, but often a compliment came with a longer critical assessment of what we'd done as well. Sometimes that was difficult for my brother and me to cop. Nowadays, he is a very different man. He often tells me how proud he is of me and says, 'I love you, son.' But back then – like a lot of Kiwi rugby and rugby league dads, so it's not just a Sāmoan thing – his attitude was that you don't praise a kid too much or it'll soften him. It made for a tough environment, especially when he was often our footy coach.

I'm not blaming my father. He was just a product of his environment, of a brutal childhood and growing up suffering racism from mainstream New Zealand at a time when every Islander was called or thought of as an 'overstayer' and there were often police raids targeting Pacific Islanders. So I do understand that my old man comes from a different era and grew up in very different home circumstances. He didn't know any other way. But when you're young, growing up with an old man hardened by his own life experiences means there can be some tough moments and harsh words to bear. It is difficult to reconcile the wonderful grandad my father is to all his grandkids with the father he was when I was young. He was the father his own childhood made him. I thank my Islamic teachings for gaining that understanding about my dad, and it shows me people can change and grow.

* * *

The magic moment that first lifted me out of my neighbourhood was when the Bulldogs scout John Ackland and another scout, Mark Hughes, were watching my good mate Filinga Filiga play in a provincial league competition. I was playing in the same tournament and they liked what they saw and told me they were keen on signing me to the Bulldogs. I was fourteen.

At the time, I thought this guy was just doing me a favour because he knew my grandfather, Bill Woolsey. Pops had a big reputation. (Legend has it he was once injured and needed thirty stitches to a head wound but pushed aside the teammate who was sent on to replace him and refused to leave the game.) I was standing there, listening to this man say that he wanted me to sign with an Australian rugby league team and I was genuinely thinking it had nothing to do with me being a good player and that he was just doing it for my family. Looking back on it, I had shot up that year. Though I was still skinny as a tadpole, I reckon he looked at my big frame and could see it filled out and packing muscle one day. He was right. I went from 85 kilograms to starting my first NRL game weighing 102 kilograms.

I was in a state of disbelief after the offer, thinking I didn't really deserve to be singled out, even though I'd been chosen for the New Zealand under-16s when I was only fourteen. We went to Australia (I'm pretty sure my beautiful Nan paid my fare) and played a few games up in Queensland, where I was named Player of the Tournament. But I still thought these dudes were doing my family a favour!

Later, because Dad was working out of town, I went with my mum in her Honda Civic to go sign the Bulldogs' contract. My brother and I used to tease Mum about that car, and when she drove us to school we'd ask to be dropped off down the street so no-one would see it. Mum would do a burnout as she left to let us know what she thought of our embarrassment and to remind us we should be grateful for the lift! We quickly learned never to ask for an early drop-off.

I signed the contract on the bonnet of Mum's car. It was for a year initially and came with four payments of $250 each, so $1000 in total. It meant that the Bulldogs had the option to sign me up down the track and I was firmly on their radar. It was a lot to a fourteen-year-old! Mum and Dad said the money was supposed to go towards my schooling. Yeah, right. I drew some money out and bought a pair of Chuck Taylors. Thought I was the man walking around the neighbourhood in those. I wore them everywhere, including to school even though I wasn't supposed to.

But it wasn't just money. When you sign with an NRL club you're sent a care package, so I got a parcel full of footy boots and Bulldogs training gear. At the time, a few young guys in the area were getting picked up as NRL trainees and they'd get their packages and then walk around wearing clothing from whatever club had picked them – Parramatta, say – and other kids would see them in the club colours and ask, 'Who does this guy think he is?' I didn't want to do the wrong thing or have people think I was full of myself and boasting about my footy, so I never went outside in my Bulldogs gear. Wearing the Chuck Taylors was cool; wearing NRL colours felt boastful. Yet once on the field, my attitude was: *I'm gonna show you!*

About twelve months later, I was offered another scholarship, but with the option of either going to Sydney or staying in New Zealand till I was eighteen. Going to Sydney meant I would be training with the club and would be closer to my dream of playing first-grade NRL. In the period between the first offer and the second, a lot had changed in my game experience: I went from playing against fourteen and sixteen-year-olds to playing in the under-21s team my dad coached for the Marist Rugby League Club in Mount Albert. Johnny had been playing up in grades too, but then he'd gotten into some trouble and had to appear in court. He was sentenced to periodic detention and couldn't play footy on weekends, so it looked like Dad's team would be short. The old man asked if I wanted to play because I'd trained with them and knew them all growing up. Though I was anxious, I couldn't say yes quickly enough.

That experience of playing against men in Dad's under-21s side proved invaluable in preparing me for the big time. I matched their physicality and never showed fear on the field. I had the fitness and the ferocity to back myself every game.

One of the first times I played with the under-21s, we were up against Mount Albert, and they had some big boys in their team. Dad put me on the wing to start so I wouldn't get mangled in the forwards. This big guy runs at me and I was like, *Here we go.* I lined him up and did a massive shoulder charge. *YES!* Sure, I'd been scared playing against the men, but having the older boys in the team around me gave me the confidence not to hold back.

At half-time, Johnny rocked up as a spectator, and I spotted him on the sideline. By now, Dad had moved me in from the wing. I was in the middle, trying to mix it with the big boys, and this dude ran at me and I shoulder-charged him. Even though my arm went dead, he went flying. My brother yelled, 'Yo! That's my little brother! You just got smashed by a fifteen-year-old!'

After that game, I knew I really could mix it with the adults and that I just might have what it took to go far in this game. We ended up in the final that year and Dad picked me to start over an older player in the team, who naturally got upset at being on the bench while this skinny teenager was chosen ahead of him. I played really well and we won the competition. I might have only been fifteen and playing against men but from that moment I knew I belonged.

When he heard the options the Bulldogs had offered me, Johnny told me I should move to Sydney. I was excited by the opportunity, but I was scared of leaving my family behind. I had low self-confidence off the footy field and it always held me back and made me wary of big-noting myself. I'd never even told any of my mates that I'd been picked as a future Bulldogs player. It was that push from my brother, who I had always looked up to, that made me go. I only told a couple of my best mates I was going a day or so before I left New Zealand. One of them was Thomas Leuluai, a future Kiwi great, like his old man James Leuluai. Thomas is the only player younger than myself to play for the Kiwis. Filinga Filiga, who'd been picked up before me, injured his knee, so I travelled to Australia with Edwin Asotasi, Roy's younger brother.

***

I look back and I feel like I was on the edge between two worlds. On one side, I had low self-esteem – what I think of as an Islander mentality – which came from all I'd ever seen, all my father had ever seen. It was the drag that comes with the expectation of only ever filling low-income jobs, resigned to manual labour like digging holes or house painting, like my dad did. You're not supposed to ask questions; you're supposed to just shut your mouth and do as you're told. It is a fact that Māori and Pasifika kids have a higher rate of youth suicide. If you are dealing with a lack of self-belief, and that is exacerbated by the education system, higher levels of poverty and systemic racism against people of colour, then your outlook can be a negative one.

I got my right arm tattooed when I was fourteen, Sāmoan-cum-freestyle. It was to identify as Sāmoan, but it had a deeper meaning too: it was to show my individuality. But my need for that said a lot about my insecurities, my sense of not feeling good enough, even though from the outside looking in, people were perhaps thinking: *He's a cool cat. Look at him leading the way with his outrageous shoulder charges, the offloads, the running – and now he's got his own version of a traditional Sāmoan tattoo*. But, really, it was more about putting that mask on, a plaster over the internal bleeding of not truly loving myself. In class, I kept my shirt sleeve rolled down over the tatt, but outside the classroom I rolled up my sleeve and proudly showed it off.

In my family, there had always been a sense of being kept down, which must have fed from when they brought Sāmoans over to New Zealand in the 1960s to do all the shitty jobs: the mind-numbing factory work; the low-paid night shifts as cleaners. They lost their connection to land and mostly lived in urban areas. I had to wrestle against that in-built mentality in order to believe I could do and be anything. I didn't think I could do anything except sport. On the rugby field, I was the boss. I had to tell myself I had the best job, not the shittiest. I was smashing guys four to six years older than me, and I could actually shine.

Before I was offered the chance to move to Australia, my mate and I set up a homemade gym with discards from his older brother but we had no idea what we were doing. I look back now, laughing. We used old breeze blocks as weights to bench press and we'd take turns holding the bricks in place so they didn't fall off while the other worked out. It was a mad buzz and we'd pump hard thinking we were Ronnie Coleman, who was crowned Mr Olympia eight years running. We were trying to improve ourselves. I'd go for road runs, not knowing why except that it helped feed my confidence – I knew that was necessary if I was to really succeed. When I was a young kid I was good at athletics, but by about ten or eleven I would watch NRL on television and think, *If I can play footy on TV it means I am successful.* From then on, footy seemed a pathway to success for me, and the symbol of that success was being able to buy my mum a house.

I grew up living in state housing in Mount Albert, a working-class suburb of Auckland. A lot of the houses had been built in the fifties and sixties and many were double-storey, packed side by side. You could almost always hear what was happening in the neighbours' houses. My parents were paying low or subsidised rent, but it meant the house was never truly ours. My mum and dad lived pay cheque to pay cheque so could never get ahead, but I knew Mum dreamed of owning her own home one day. The house we lived in was run-down and there were places where you could see there had, at one time, been wallpaper on the walls but it had been stripped off. There were remnants here and there that showed what had been. I had this thought fixed in my mind: *I'm going to buy Mum a house one day – a house with fancy wallpaper.* I couldn't see that happening through education. I knew that school was not for me. *Stuff school, what has it ever done for my family?* So, sport was the only way.

I'd get out there and do shoulder charges and make spectacular offloads, all this amazing stuff on the paddock, and I'd slap down my low self-esteem for a while. At the same time, I held back when we weren't playing, in the club house or sheds or at training, because I didn't want to step on anyone's toes or say or do the wrong thing. If anyone of higher social status or in a position of authority spoke to me, I was like, 'Yes, sir.'

If I was asked to say a few words after a match, my mouth would go dry. I didn't feel like my voice counted or that I had the knowledge to speak up. I was this fair-skinned Sāmoan and never felt like I owned my own space or place in the world.

I sometimes struggle even now, despite all the success in four different sports. For so long I'd thought, *Who needs education to succeed?* I didn't see a pathway for my family or myself through education, and I saw how the system let down those who didn't have money or status. But that has changed. Through my experiences in life, I have learned the value and power that comes from knowledge and I have experienced the naivety one can have without it. From my own growth, and to show my kids sport isn't the only avenue for success, I went back to school and enrolled in a Bachelor of Applied Management through Capable New Zealand, a school within Otago Polytechnic. That was a big thing for me, but I've learned that you can find empowerment through understanding history. Knowing your people's history can give you the confidence to go to any level of society, to enter any room and be articulate, talk your talk and stand up for what you believe in instead of being held back by the expectation that the Pacific Islander or Māori is either meant to stay silent or make people laugh.

* * *

When I went over to Sydney, I was still the young bloke who mostly kept his thoughts to himself, worried I would say the wrong thing or show I didn't understand something. A guy named Garry Carden trained all the young Bulldogs guys at Belmore. Garry was at the club for thirty-seven years all up, before leaving in 2020. He looked after so many of us and made sure we trained hard. His conditioning helped me put on that seventeen kilos. His dedication and expertise definitely prepared me to step up and shaped my career in the important early days.

> I've been lucky enough to train the two best players that have played for Canterbury in the modern era in Sonny Bill Williams and Johnathan Thurston. Sonny is the best athlete I've ever trained. He was just a big, tall, skinny kid when he arrived. But he used to do a lot of things that other kids never did. He was always doing stuff on a balance beam and the rest is history, of course. People see Sonny's work ethic now, but we give them that work ethic when they come to the Dogs. – Garry Carden

Training and working out in the gym was easy. I knew exactly what I had to do by then and did it. It was the other stuff that was harder to navigate. I was supposed to enrol in a high school, but I wanted to work, because I thought that was the quickest way to make it into the team. On that first visit, I worked and trained for eight weeks and then went home for two weeks. Once back in Auckland, I didn't want to return to Australia because I knew I'd miss my family too much. I loved being back home with them, my mates and especially my mum. I didn't want to leave. But I knew deep down that the only way I could make something of myself and buy Mum that house with fancy wallpaper was to go back to the big smoke in Australia. My old man kicked my arse, but I was pretty driven to try to make it for my family on my own, because we didn't have much. Still, leaving them for the second time was even worse than the first. It was such a massive thing for a fifteen-year-old to do. I was going back to a place without family or close mates. It was really tough. I trained hard in Sydney, but I had no-one to confide in, no-one I felt I could tell how lonely I was. I was too shy to admit how homesick I felt. I would lie in bed, staring at the ceiling, unable to sleep because I felt so homesick. The only thing I knew I could do to distract myself was train hard and push myself physically, so by the time night came I was hopefully too tired to feel. It didn't always work and so I would stare at the ceiling and wait for the sun to come up again. It was a really trying time.

Back in Sydney, I again had the choice of work or school, but I found out going to school would delay my NRL debut, so I got a job labouring on a building site, digging holes and carrying stuff. I went from training twice a week and playing touch footy with my mates back home to working full-time as a labourer and training professionally. I'd leave the house in the dark and get back in the dark. Along with nine other scholarship boys, I lived with a couple named Mary and Peter Durose in what was called the 'Bulldogs House', but as much as they looked out for us all, it wasn't home.

I did that labouring for a while and then I got a job in an embroidery factory, where I was the storeman out the back, while dreaming only of running out onto the field with the premier NRL Canterbury Bulldogs team. But while that wouldn't happen for a couple of years, I did at least manage to graduate from the storeman job to something more linked to footy.

As far as my playing went, I was really starting to hit my straps and made the Canterbury-Bankstown under-18s SG Ball Cup team, competing against all the major NRL clubs, barring Queensland. It was a real big deal. I was now training like a full-time professional and being part of that set-up took my game to another level. That improvement would see me named Player of the Tournament. For a shy fella a long way from home, this was a huge boost to my self-esteem. It also led to the Bulldogs bringing me closer to their home ground by giving me a job doing all sorts of tasks at the club. As soon as I'd finished my work, I could go sit in the grandstand and watch the guys train. It was heaven! Watching stars like Matt Utai, Hazem El Masri, Mark O'Meley, the Hughes brothers, Steve Price, Brent Sherwin, Nigel Vagana and Willie Mason right there in front of me, showing me how to train and play hard. I knew one day soon my turn was coming.

Matty, Nigel and Willie asked me, the kid, how I was, did I need anything? Man, it is something else to get acknowledgement from guys like that when you are a young fella. These guys really made me feel special. I have taken this lesson with me, and I always try to make sure the young guys are heard and seen.

I first met Sonny just after I signed with the Bulldogs. I remember going to training on my day off and driving through the car park at Belmore and seeing two young fellas sitting on the ground on the edge of the car park near the fire exit. As I drove past, I gave the Kiwi wave . . . two eyebrows up, and they both returned the wave. I then noticed a tattoo on the forearm of one of the guys and so recognised them as Island boys.

I got out of the car and walked over to them. They were two young brothers who looked lost. I asked what they were up to.

'Just waiting for training,' the one without the tattoo said.

'What time's training?'

'Six pm.'

I looked at my watch and saw it was 4 pm. 'Man, you guys are early. You from New Zealand?'

'Yeah, bro, Auckland. I'm from South, he's from Central.'

'Ah, sweet. I'm from Central too. I'm Nigel.'

'Oh, hey. I'm Edwin [Asotasi].'

'I'm Sonny.'

'You guys Sāmoan?' I asked.

'Yep.'

Sonny came across as quiet. Street smart, tough, didn't say much, but what he said he meant. I would come to learn that, above all, he was loyal. Would stay and fight to the end with you. He always wanted to protect . . . a trait I still see in him today. When I walked over from the car, I thought about what it felt like when I arrived in Sydney as a twenty-five-year-old. I knew how these guys might be feeling. All I wanted to do was check that the young brothers were okay and let them know if they needed anything, I was there for them. – Nigel Vagana

I used to make sure I got through everything I was supposed to do in the morning so I could then spend time watching the guys in my position, see what they did. Even though a lot of it was new, I just soaked up everything. The cool thing was I got on really well with the gear steward; he was Italian and his name was Fred Ciraldo.

Freddie had been with the club for years and he looked after me, taught me the ins and outs of the club. Freddie would often tell his boss he needed me to help him out, so I'd be there helping him on the field and then one day Steve Folkes, the coach, came over and said a couple of guys had injuries. 'Can you come and stand in?' he asked me. You bet I could!

That session turned into invites to train with the first-grade team, even if I was just holding the tackle bags. I loved it. Two years before, I'd been playing with my brother in teams my dad coached, and now here I was at sixteen in the company of these illustrious footy stars. The first-grade players were kind to me. There were no big egos, no 'I'm too busy and important to interact with the rookie' stuff. I thought they were all lovely guys, really good dudes who were always happy to chat to me. They could have said to me, 'Take my dirty laundry home and wash it and bring it back neatly folded' and I would have been happy to oblige.

* * *

Being on the edge of the team like that meant I was laying the foundations for my debut game. I would see what they were doing and go away and work on my skills. I'd train with them in the morning, then train either alone or with my age-group peers in the late afternoon and into the evening. The one thing I didn't imitate or copy was their drinking. I didn't touch alcohol. The other scholarship boys all drank hard; I was the only one who didn't indulge. Yet no-one, not one person, ever pressured me to drink.

Growing up, there was a lot of love in the house, but my old man drank quite a bit and it made things pretty volatile, which put me off alcohol. I now understand my father was drinking and gambling, trying to bury the pain from a tough upbringing with extremely violent uncles after his mother abandoned him at the age of ten. He didn't talk about it when I was young, so I didn't know much about what he'd been through. I remember the old man and his mates drinking at the club. It was like that *Once Were Warriors* boozing scene. I remember him actually belting a man for slapping his partner in the club rooms. That violence was normal to him. It was what he knew. Though he never laid a hand on Mum, us kids often walked on eggshells in case he lost his temper with us – Johnny especially.

Even though Dad's brothers were bikies, they were a close family. When they came round to our home, their boots would all be lined up out on the front doorstep and all these big, fierce dudes would be sitting quietly and respectfully inside while my little Pākehā mum,

Lee, cooked them a big feed. Stereotypes are made to be broken!

We had a real stroppy redneck neighbour who the old man had a row with one time because our dog was barking. Dad was trying to talk to him and the neighbour told him he was a black coconut and that he should shut the dog up before he did. Dad was smart enough not to jump the fence and have it out with him, as he'd be the one arrested for trespass with violent intent, or whatever the charge is. But Mum called my bikie uncles, who didn't care about the consequences of jumping over some redneck's fence. Luckily, the guy took off at seeing these hulking Sāmoan gangies turn up.

If I hadn't become a professional sportsman, I could have easily wound up selling drugs, hustling, maybe ended up in prison. Sport has saved many like me.

* * *

Instead of starting me in the under-20s season when I was seventeen, the Bulldogs put me straight into reserve grade, playing against men – hard, experienced, fully grown men, some of them ready to knock my block off. I more than held my own and was playing really well and made the New South Wales under-19s side – but then injury struck. I was scoring a try and popped my shoulder out. I tried to play on but I knew I had done something bad. I had to have a shoulder reconstruction and was out for the rest of the year. This was my first real experience of injury impacting my career, but I managed to keep focused and not let the depression overwhelm me too much. I just had to get it sorted.

Mark Hughes picked me up from the Bulldog House and took me for my surgery. On the way home after the op, he said to me, 'I've got some good news. You've been picked in the top twenty-five for next year.'

That knowledge took my mind off my shoulder! For a start, it meant I'd go from earning ten grand a year to forty-five grand. I would be rich! I could buy my mum that house! I was so ecstatic, it actually got me through my misery at being out with injury for so long and I worked hard on my fitness and rehab to make sure I made that team.

My shoulder had healed by the time the 2004 preseason training started. I was still very shy, but because I'd been working at the club for a year and knew some of the guys, it was not such a massive step up physically. However, mentally it saw me struggling with the two sides of myself – the confidence I displayed on the field was the complete opposite once I stepped off the ground.

That pre-season training was as I expected: really, really hard. But I loved almost every moment. When the coach told me he was starting me at centre for the trials, straight away I put on the bravado. *Yo, I'm sweet.* Inside, I was in turmoil. The self-doubt is always there and I started to doubt myself and ask myself if I was really ready. When I was training or playing I was okay, but at night I would lie there worrying, scared I'd blow it. Make a fool of myself or, worse than that, let down my teammates. I was constantly wrestling with myself and that internal conflict can be pretty exhausting. In the end, I would learn to drown out the negative feelings and focus on the positive, but it didn't mean the doubts left me. I just prepared hard so I could walk with them.

Who was I marking in that first game? In the first half I was up against the Australian centre, Mark Gasnier. The second half I marked Matt Cooper. Yet again, I held my own. I stood up Cooper one time. I stood him up and did an outside-in. Gasnier didn't get around me at all and he was the best attacking centre at the time. Although it was only a trial, as a now eighteen-year-old holding his own against the best in the world, it gave me huge confidence.

I remember as a kid watching my dad play and here I was doing the same thing, real aggressive; I almost had a fight with Matt Cooper. After that game I knew for sure that I definitely had what it took to play in this league.

Two weeks later I was named in the starting Bulldogs side at centre for the season's first game. I was so excited, so nervous. Remember, I'm only eighteen. But on the day, my only thought was to make my family proud. Pity about the forgotten boots! Well, that was the only blemish on the most unforgettable day of my young life.

Waking up the next morning and seeing my performance written about and spoken of in the media in the most complimentary terms was overwhelming. In the back of my mind I was thinking, *If only they knew how shy I am, what low self-esteem I have.* That massive outpouring of praise was a lot to deal with.

Four games after that and my name was read out as a New Zealand international in the Kiwis team. I still remember the phone call. What a feeling! I was to become the second youngest to represent New Zealand behind my good mate Tommy Leuluai. That is big! Us boys from the same hood, who went to the same school and who grew up together, both achieving a feat like that was really special.

I played pretty well in my first Test against Australia. The next Bulldogs game was against Souths, and I came off the bench only to be injured and was out for ten weeks. Injury rendered me helpless and, to my mind, my life kind of meaningless. That's the first time I experienced a serious depression I found hard to shake, for what was I – *who* was I – if I couldn't play footy?

After the time out, and putting my effort into rehab, I was put into reserve grade. I played really well, and the coach called me back into the premier team, and I then had a great run of playing every game well.

People talk a lot about my talent, but my success on the field only comes about from hard work beforehand. I've always been a dedicated trainer who takes no shortcuts; in fact, I'm more likely to do the opposite, taking on extra training, doubling up on repetition exercises and hard aerobics, trying new things and always pushing myself. Maybe my low self-esteem, my never thinking I was good enough, pushed me to train that much harder. I know they say practice makes perfect, but does it really? Personally, I have never been able to visit that room of perfection. I guess I know I'll never be able to, but the inspiration I get from striving to be my best is what I love. My best as a player, sure, but it is more than that. I strive to be a better person both on and off the field. So as far as footy goes, I did everything asked of me and then some.

The offloads are a perfect example. It started when I was young, maybe ten or eleven, trying flash things in the backyard with Johnny, or with my mates, or on the school oval, then putting them to the test in a game. To see one come off for the first time only makes you work harder at perfecting the pass

In the backyard I started off trying big hits with my brother, my mates and even my little twin sisters, Niall and Denise! Although I held back a bit with my sisters, the practice might have done them a good turn; Niall ended up captain of the New Zealand touch team and won Olympic silver with the New Zealand rugby sevens.

> Growing up with two older brothers – Sonny is three years older and Johnny five years – I looked up to them, wanted to hang out with them and do whatever they were doing. Older siblings are often too cool for the younger ones, but they were both good to me and my sister Denise. They let us join in their footy games and backyard cricket. One of them would come racing down the driveway and bowl me out then do the same to Denise. The penalty for being bowled out was we had to feed them, like slaves, for hours. 'Niall, get me this.' 'Denise, can you get me . . .' We'd play footy in the lounge room; our brothers would go down on their knees and we had to score a try past them. We got smashed, absolutely smashed. But we loved it. – Niall Williams

For me, it was about proving myself by smashing the big guys (never my sisters!). That's how the shoulder charge came about. Remember, I had a point to prove to other Islanders: that even though I was a fair-skinned Sāmoan, I was still one of them and this was how I'd prove it.

* * *

37

It is strange. When we started working on this book, Alan asked me to recall my childhood. At first I couldn't think of anything significant – not until my wife reminded me of an event so significant it helped define my life. After I told her about it, I must have blanked it out, again parking the memory in some dark corner of my mind.

In New Zealand, there's an organisation called the Plunket Society which offers services to promote the health and wellbeing of kids under five. Registered nurses known as 'Plunket nurses' would come round to help mothers feed and care for babies. Given that Mum had twin girls to look after as well as two older boys also needing attention, a Plunket nurse suggested Mum drop one of us off at Barnardos – a charity dedicated to providing care and support for children and families in need – to give her a break. Lee Williams was a very protective mum, and when she took the nurse's advice and sent me there at four years old, she trusted that I would be looked after. I was in the backyard of the Barnados residence playing with the kid of the woman who ran the place. Two teenagers were in the kitchen cooking chips when the fat erupted in flames. One of them ran outside with the pot and, depending on who you ask, either threw it without watching where it was going or it exploded.

Whatever happened, the result was I ended up with boiling fat down the backs of my legs. I guess one reason

I've blanked it out all this time is the pain. It's a kind of pain only someone who's been severely burnt can understand. The other kid only got a few drops of hot fat on him, yet his mother scooped him up, ran inside and put him into the bath, which she filled with cold water. In the meantime, yours truly was left outside alone, screaming his head off. Luckily, the neighbours were washing their car and, hearing the commotion, jumped over the fence and hosed me down. Without their quick thinking, the result would have been catastrophic.

I spent six to eight months, maybe longer, in the intensive burns unit at Auckland City Hospital. When my parents came to visit, the doctors forbade them to touch me because the skin grafts were so fragile, and they needed to stretch and become elastic. Mum still cries when she tells this story, even thirty years later.

When we went to see Sonny Bill at the hospital, they would get him to walk to us but when he tried he'd fall to the ground and start screaming for us to pick him up. I would go to help him but his dad would have to pull me away because we'd been told to leave him. He would be crawling and looking at us. It was the most horrific thing to look at your kid in that much agony, crawling along the ground and just saying, 'Why aren't you helping me?' They said if we picked him up and carried him, the skin wouldn't stretch and he wouldn't be able to walk.

When he came home, my wee boy, just four years old, was in a wheelchair, a sight to break any mother's heart. We had to give him baths and his skin kept coming off and we had to do the bathing as part of the healing process. Oh, how that child suffered, and his parents with him. – Lee Williams

Mum put on a brave face but she was dying inside and bawled her eyes out after every visit. I do have memories of incredible pain. The healing process took several more months, during which time Mum had to unbandage me and rub a special cream on my legs.

When I had finally healed, I started school, where a different kind of pain was waiting.

Because of my scars, the kids there called me 'Kentucky Fried Chicken legs' or 'SBL' (Sonny Burnt Legs), and that stuck with me my whole life. It shaped my childhood a lot. I was always really self-conscious, and I reckon it just added to my poor self-esteem. It was a very, very tough time.

It was worse at intermediate school, because as I got older I became more worried about what other people thought, and of course the self-consciousness got worse. My first day there, I was wearing shorts and I remember everyone staring at my legs. It was bad enough being half-Sāmoan and having a pale complexion without the stares as well.

From then on, I wore long pants, even on boiling-hot days. On weekends, playing footy, I had to wear shorts and my legs were so white – and scarred – it felt like they glowed. I remember one time I put fake tan on them; I was running around with legs the colour of Donald Trump's face!

I think the burns had a huge psychological effect on me. Growing up, I had a lot of demons from that. But I think I turned that on its head, too; I was determined to make those skinny white legs muscly. Maybe it made me train harder? I do sometimes think about the effect of those burns on the person I became. When I talked about it with Alan Duff for this book, he suggested that the experience took me to the edge of the pain barrier, which means I can push myself harder at training than others can. He may have a point; even if the memory is buried, the knowledge is there.

Later, aged twenty-one and playing for the Bulldogs, I got the whole back of my right leg tattooed. (My left leg wasn't as scarred.) Later, I'd run into young guys – white guys, Anglos – who had the exact same tattoo, copied from shots of my tatt. I've heard getting tattooed over scar tissue is particularly painful. I'd have to agree with that. My leg was so sore, and I had it done in one eight-hour sitting. But I was so excited at finally being able to wear shorts and not feel bad that I was prepared to cop the pain.

* * *

Before the tatts, before I started making a name for myself in footy, I was down at our primary school playing on the monkey bars one Sunday, just for something to do. There's an Islander church next to the school and some big Island kids came over and slapped me around. I went back home and told Mum what happened.

As I said, my mum is very protective, and she goes, 'Right. Let's go!'

We marched down to the church, and I stood in the doorway hanging back as she walked in.

I marched in and these Islanders are thinking, *Who is this crazy Palangi woman interrupting our church service?*

They tell me, 'Excuse me, but the pastor is speaking. Are you okay, lady?'

'No. I'm not okay. My kid was playing at the school and some big, older kids came and gave him a hiding. Now, I don't know what kind of God you believe in, but to me that's not what God teaches, giving smaller kids a hiding.'

This is in the middle of the sermon and everyone stops.

'I'm coming back here next Sunday, and I want you to find out who did this and make them apologise to my son.'

At home, later, my husband John is going off at me. How dare I, a white woman, walk into an Islander church like that? But I didn't care. When I'm in the right, nothing stops me.

> The next Sunday, John drives me, John Arthur and Sonny
> Bill to the church. But even though he's a tough Sāmoan who
> doesn't take shit, John ain't going into that church and nor is
> John junior.
>
> I did. And I came out with the guilty kids, who apologised to
> Sonny Bill. – Lee Williams

This white, red-haired, freckled lady who believed in doing the right thing no matter the consequences taught me a lot. I hope that, like her, I will never budge, not even for an army, when it comes to my principles. A classic example of this is when I left the Bulldogs in 2008. Maybe if, at the time, I had more confidence to speak out and discuss the issues I was wrestling with, things would have been different. But I didn't know how. There was so much speculation about why I walked out and none of it comes close to the real reason. It wasn't about contract dramas or money or playing another code. The truth was, I was losing my sense of self and had lost sight of that fire my old lady gave to me. I know what is right and what is wrong, but I was losing the ability to only walk towards the good. Physically I was okay but mentally my head was in a bad place. I thought running away was my only option. At the time, I didn't realise you can't run away from the man in the mirror, and nothing I did was going to stop a confrontation with him, with myself. But right then, I had to do something or else I truly believed I'd be lost – to alcohol or to drugs or to a dangerous situation I couldn't handle or survive.

CHAPTER 2

Dressing a deep wound with sticking plaster

In our house, no-one could have loved us more than our mum. She stuck up for her kids and made us feel good about ourselves. Dad loved us in his way, but he didn't show it like Mum. I'm not judging my father; he'd had a tough life and he'd had to adapt just to survive. He took a big interest in our sports, and we knew we made him proud, but he'd never been taught to love unconditionally.

When I got older, I could see where Mum's love came from: her mum, our wonderful Nan, a woman I miss greatly. Such a beautiful lady. She was a little woman whose Australian sense of humour we found a bit weird till we got to know her style. She was always singing, laughing and teasing us and she loved having us around. Her house was often the meeting place for our family;

she was a welcoming, loving woman who loved a chat. Pop, on the other hand, was this gruff, unapproachable man of few words; we'd heard he was a real tough guy who would punch other men out. We never got to know him because he didn't want to know us. He ignored us kids and we didn't dare upset him. He and Nan were chalk and cheese.

Neither of our houses had much by way of food – unless Dad had a good win on the horses – but Nan always had a few lollies or some ice cream for us kids. The first thing we did when we got to her place was check out the fridge for treats. There'd be chocolate broken into small pieces to make it last longer. Our favourite lollies. To us it meant everything, as we hardly got sweet treats at home.

As kids, Sonny Bill was the one with the self-control. While the rest of us scoffed our ice cream or iceblock as soon as we got it, he put his in the freezer box then would pull it out later and eat it in front of us really slowly, laughing at our envy. I think he might have felt sorry for us, though, because he always gave us a lick or two. – Niall Williams

I can confirm what Niall said about Sonny having self-control. But while I remember watching him eat his saved iceblock, I have no memory of him giving me so much as a single lousy lick! – Denise Williams

On the weekends, either my twin sisters or me and my older brother Johnny would stay on at Nan's after the family visit. There'd be some pretty heavy sadness if you were the one who had to ride home in Mum's Honda Civic, because those who stayed could look forward to a day and night of luxury. It might mean going into town with Nan on the bus, playing *Space Invaders*, going to a movie and having ice creams before heading home to more sweet treats. Man, that was like gold for us. At bedtime she would rub Vicks VapoRub into our chests and then turn on the electric blanket. That was the height of luxury!

I was lucky to have such fiercely loving women in my life. And they would both stick up for us kids in an instant. Like I said, Dad was different. Mum's got some strong thoughts about Dad's family and why he struggled as a parent:

For a few years, some of John's family didn't like me – I guess because I was white. My mum and dad didn't give two hoots that he was Sāmoan, just as long as he looked after me and I was happy. That's all my mum cared about: that he took care of me like she had.

When they had a funeral in his large family, everyone was expected to give money and quite a lot. John's mum was pretty demanding. I'd tell her we couldn't afford it; we had our own little kids to look after. I'd say, 'The person we're giving the money to is a relation of a relation of a relation I don't even know.' Money to feed the mourners and leave nothing to feed my own kids? To hell with that. It had nothing to do with me being white. I was just making sure I looked after our children first. So many Islanders get into financial trouble trying to meet this social obligation. They worry about what other family members will think if they don't contribute. Not this little white lady! I look after my own kids first.

Was I intimidated by them? No way! I didn't care if there was a hundred of them; I'd take them all on if I knew I was right. I wasn't just a little Pākehā girl you could walk all over.

If you are doing something right, you always know it is right. If I'm doing something good and fair dinkum about it, I'll keep going all the way to the end. But when you know you're doing something wrong, you get a bit hesitant, a bit lost, and think, *Yeah, maybe I am in the wrong here.* I told my kids: 'If you do something wrong, then just admit it. It's not the end of the world.'

Because of suicide and all that, I used to say to them, 'I just want you to know that I don't give two hoots if you've done the worst thing in the whole wide world. I want you always to know the door's still wide open, and we might not be able to fix it, but we will talk about it and try to make it as good as we can. You will be getting a kick up the backside and not getting away with it, but never think you can't come home, because nothing is ever that bad that your own home is closed to you.'

My mum [Sonny Bill's Nan] was unbelievably nice. One of those real Aussies, just cracking jokes and always finding the brighter side to life. She used to live in Paddington, in Sydney, back when it was a rough area, not posh and expensive like it is now. Six kids living in a two-bedroom terrace house. Her dad, my grandad, went up the road one day to get a loaf of bread and never came back. Left Gran with six kids having to top and tail in beds. I suppose that's where Mum got her humour from. You have to look on the bright side of life, even when it's pitch-black and miserable. She gave me that outlook and I tried to pass it on to my kids. I think they all turned out pretty damn good.

Mum met my Kiwi dad while he was playing league in Sydney. They moved to Auckland in 1957 and lived in a flat they said was terrible. I wasn't born yet. They asked Housing Corp for a house to rent. When they said they didn't have any available, my dad went, 'Righto, we're leaving our kids here with you. We are not taking them back to that scummy flat we're living in.' The Housing Corp people scurried around and next thing we knew, we were living in a very nice house reserved for their senior managers right near the beach in Westmere – another suburb that's now flash, where houses sell for a couple of million and more.

I met John down at my father's club, City Newton Rugby League, when I was still at high school. He sat behind me and when I got up, I accidentally moved my chair onto his foot. We got talking and we liked each other straight away. He later told me other people had said, '*Do you know whose daughter that is? Bill Woolsey's.*' John didn't care.

John Arthur and Sonny Bill were born before John and I married. — Lee Williams

* * *

I can't remember the exact moment the thought formed of buying Mum a house one day. Maybe it was knowing her and Nan's histories. And because I wanted to see her live in a place with fancy wallpaper that was all her own. All I really know is, the older I got, and with my sport improving all the time, that dream got stronger. I could make it happen when I was only a young man playing NRL, and it felt so good.

I would encourage young Pacific Islanders and Māori to get hold of a dream like that and never let it go. Because dreams can and do come true. And sporting success is not the only way; there are all kinds of businesses and professional careers and trades you can get into. There's nothing to stop you from claiming one of those career choices and just going for it.

I wish I had a magic wand to wave self-belief into our Pasifika and Māori youngsters, since we have the most catching up to do. I see now so much untapped potential;

it's like a human diamond mine waiting to be discovered – by ourselves.

Everyone can have dreams beyond your own little world. And dreams evolve depending on what stage of life you are at. My dreams as a young bloke were to play in the NRL and to buy my mum a house. Then they changed into playing with the All Blacks. Each time you achieve a dream, it is important to reflect and create a new goal. Now my dreams are to be the best husband and best father and family man I can be. I want to be a spokesperson for my people and to give a voice to those who can't speak up for themselves. If you had told me twenty years ago I would be standing up for refugees and trying to speak with the Australian prime minister about asylum-seeker policy, I would have laughed at you. But I have evolved, learned and kept trying to honour the spark my mum ignited in me.

Life really does boil down to an attitude. And succeeding isn't measured by money or status; it can be doing something well. Being the best you can be. My attitude to sport helped me achieve because I recognised the importance of training hard all the time with no let-up. When I least felt like training, that was all the more reason to get out there and do it. Sleeping in was not an option. Being really fit allows you to do more in a game, because your lungs are not gasping for air, your brain is clearer. A very fit player can compensate for having less talent than a lazy one. I was lucky I carried that attitude my whole life. However it may have looked from the outside, I always valued hard work and never tried to coast on talent alone.

It's funny how my flamboyant style of play made me look to some like a self-confident extrovert. I definitely was not that when off the field; you could hardly get boo out of me. That perceived flamboyance in my early days and right up to my mid-twenties did not go down well in rugby union and rugby league circles. The two codes had a conventional attitude, a set of fixed game plans that coaches sternly instructed players to follow. As I got older, I'd always question things and say what I thought I could do better or what the coach could do better. For some reason, when it came to rugby league, I wasn't scared to express my opinions. But it took years for me to get to that point and only came when I let myself believe I knew what I was talking about.

I did write everything down and try to stick to the coach's game plan. But I did best when I just went out there and played. I worked so hard training, put so much effort into every game, and I would stick to the structures as best I could. I prided myself on making the two-tackles double, getting up and reloading fast, doing the grind work. That was the glue that held everything together –

doing your job and a little bit more. Then could come the flavour, the specialness.

When it comes to coaches, you can have great ones and you can have less than great ones. But no matter how good a coach might be, if they don't have talent to work with, they ain't got nothing. I think we get too caught up in this idea that the coach is more important than the players. In reality, it's the players who bring the majority of what you need to win a game, and then the consistency – and attitude – to win a competition. A true coach is more of a people manager; he (or she) understands the different backgrounds of individual players, understands how to get the best out of each one, how to bring them together as a team. Yes, structure is needed. But the coach is only one element in a team of players and reserves. And remember, it's the players, not the coach, who actually go out and play. If I mess up, it's not my coach's fault. A good coach can bring out magic, and I have had some amazing coaches do that; I'll introduce you to a few of them later in the book. Game plans and tactics are important, but you've got to have the skills to draw on.

Thinking about my parents and talking about structure makes me realise something. I think my dad's problem is he had no structure to his life. Brought up by his grandmother and his uncles, he'd never been given that. He was a very hard worker, a real good player in his day, and a stand-out coach throughout the age groups. Like I said, Dad grew up in a brutal environment of countless beatings from uncles who were all boxers. To see him now as the most loving, consistent grandad is to understand that you can outgrow a rough childhood. But you can't know what you don't know; everyone understands that. I think lumping everyone into one group and expecting them to react the same way is not realistic. We are all different and react differently. To be a good coach, you have to understand the individuals on your team and help to bring out the best in them in a tailored way.

* * *

The burns I suffered as a four-year-old were just the beginning. On the injury count, Mum tells me I was dropped on my head as a baby by one of my teenage cousins and fractured my skull. Dad saw my head swelling and raced me to hospital, breaking every speed limit ever invented.

So it is possible that my experience of spills, burns, breaks and infections may have given me the means to endure all my league and rugby injuries. Another painful memory was when I was nine years old and got tackled. Then several of the opposition boys were punching me in the back. I just got up and kept playing. The next day, my back really hurt. Mum took me to hospital and next minute, I was in intensive care getting a needle in my spine and the blood drained from a big sac that had formed on my lower back. I'd got infected where they punched me, and it was so bad I could have died. Poor Mum ground her teeth for years over that one, wishing she'd been at the game so she could have given my assailants a slap around the ears!

I hadn't played more than twenty games with the Bulldogs before I got injured and had a long stint on the sidelines. Although the injury would heal, the dark place I'd find myself in would not be as easily fixed.

I was defined by the game of rugby league and for a young fella from Auckland who had dreamed of playing NRL, the thought of this dream evaporating was devastating. The season before I had been named the Rugby League International Federation (RLIF) Rookie of the Year and the same in the Rugby League Players Association (RLPA) awards. And I had earned the respect of some people I really admire, like Graham Lowe, who was the Kiwis coach from 1983 to 1986 as well as the coach of numerous international clubs. He was quoted in the *NZ Herald*:

During my coaching career I was fortunate enough to have guided three of the best of all time – Mark Graham, Ellery Hanley and

Wally Lewis. I don't say it lightly, but I think Williams will turn out to be better than each of them.

Williams, who has just turned nineteen, has already received numerous accolades. Canberra Raiders great Laurie Daley has been really impressed by his talent and is in no doubt he will be New Zealand's greatest.

But none of that mattered if I couldn't play. I have no memory of being complimented by the great man himself at the time. I'm flattered and humbled, but if people could have seen into my mind, they'd have been aware how unprepared I was for all that acclaim and how much I struggled to deal with the setbacks of injury. Just about every person who finds success young goes through the same thing: your immature mind is not equipped to deal with that fame and those stresses.

I could feel a nagging inner pain that I couldn't put my finger on. In fact, I looked the other way. I truly believed I was a better person because I was a good footy player. Turning nineteen and getting paid a truckload of money and being showered in praise by the media and rugby league commentators, including former great players and coaches. You'd think it was every young man's dream – till it happens to you.

Don't get me wrong. It didn't go to my head straight away; I was still shy. But in the back of my mind I could sense something major changing. Winning and starring in an NRL grand final might have been a highlight, but I was only four years away from a personal crisis – not as a player, but as a human being. I was being praised to the skies, but those words didn't heal my inner self. Inside, I was deeply unhappy.

* * *

That first season was also my first experience with alcohol. To begin with, I hated the taste – and I hated the hangover even more. Going out with the boys to pubs, I couldn't really handle people coming up and telling me how great I was, buying me drinks. *Who, me?* Suddenly, the shy Islander boy standing outside the nightclub was getting called to the front of the queue. People would be shaking my hand, patting me on the back. It messed with me.

My first time in a nightclub, I went to the bar to buy a round of drinks and I had no idea what to do. I ordered bourbon and Cokes for my teammates, two each. A beautiful woman introduced herself while I was at the bar. She said, 'I saw you interviewed on television and saw how shy you are. I find that really appealing.' I kind of stumbled my way through the conversation.

We talked for a while and then she said, 'Aren't you going to invite me home?' As a naive teenager, that was my introduction to the world of women.

The league culture was train hard and play hard – and then party hard. When it came to alcohol, I was a very late starter. I'd seen the damage it could do. But it didn't stop me.

* * *

One day, not all that long before I moved to Australia, Mum took me aside to say she and Dad had split up. Niall, Denise and Johnny were staying with Mum, but I chose to stay with Dad because I didn't like the idea of him living alone.

Six months later, Johnny was living with his girlfriend and selling drugs out of his rented house. It is strange even saying that, because it is so far away from the man he is today. Johnny is now a Muslim, the proud dad of six kids, happily married, and he doesn't touch drugs or alcohol. But back then, things weren't good.

Funny thing, when I got offered the Dogs scholarship, my old man stopped treating me like a boy and started treating me like a man he respected. He had a second run-around car that he let me drive. I didn't even have a licence! Dad's cousin, who we called Uncle Ben even though technically he was our second cousin, came to stay with us and he was on the dole. In the mornings, I'd put on my school uniform so my father could see me heading off to school, drive around the block and wait until Dad left for work, and then come back and be on PlayStation all day with Ben. Then I'd put my school uniform back on for when Dad came home so he thought I was a good lad. But Dad was much harder on Johnny and never made it easy for him.

My brother was my hero growing up. He had a reputation for being one of the hardest players on a footy field and he didn't mind a fight. I was more withdrawn and wasn't really into fighting as a youngster. I didn't get into many fights throughout my long career in the three footy codes either. It might seem a bit ironic then that I became a boxer.

I stopped going to school because I knew I had the Dogs scholarship coming up. Like I said earlier, school had never really interested me. I think I said in one interview that I was no rocket scientist. I also had that chip on my shoulder about getting an education. For me, it was all about footy.

I had a bad feeling when I stopped seeing my brother Johnny at school. I remember an incident while he was still at school; we were at a bus stop and Johnny went off to a petrol station to buy some smokes for himself, and this kid across the street, walking along with two girls, gave me the evils. I didn't even know him. Next thing I knew, he came over to confront me. I was really scared about what he would do.

Then Johnny arrived and flew at the dude and they got into it. After Johnny dropped the guy a third time, he got up and pointed a finger at us both then walked off. I won't name names, but this guy would end up becoming a professional boxer.

I had a feeling he would come back with some dudes and was thinking, *Hurry up, bus*.

Sure enough, a carload of older guys cruises slowly past and they're all staring at us. I'm saying, 'Bro, let's ring Mum to come pick us up.' Johnny's acting all hard, the only way he knows. But he agrees and we head to the petrol station and I use their phone to call Mum. I'm begging, 'Please, Mum, you've got to come get us', just as we see the older guys' car pull up.

They march in and punch Johnny a few times; they must've thought I was too young and skinny to bother with. The staff have just pulled us into the back room when Mum rocks up. She goes off her head at seeing Johnny with a cut above his eye. Good old protective Mum.

Johnny was my other protector. One time at school, a big boy hit me with a cricket bat and Johnny came sprinting over – he was on detention or something – and beats the guy up. Even now when people are saying, 'Oh, Sonny, you made it, you've done real good,' I think of my steadfast brother and inwardly thank him for taking care of me while I developed – and, of course, for warning me not to follow his path when I was fourteen. I truly believe I might not have made it if not for my big brother's love, and I will always be grateful for that. Obviously, we are super close.

Sonny Bill's older brother, John Arthur, would never let anyone hurt his brother. If you wanted a bodyguard, you couldn't get any better than him. He has a sense of humour too.

One day, he and Sonny Bill were leaving a Bulldogs game in separate cars, John Arthur's car in front. This was when Sonny Bill was too shy to say who he was and didn't think he was that good, even though the media and the fans were singing his praises.

John Arthur tells his driver to wait up, gets out and points at Sonny Bill's car. 'Hey! Look who's in that car – it's Sonny Bill!' And as everyone started running over to get a look at Sonny Bill, John Arthur's got back in his car, laughing at the fans mobbing his little bro!

If Sonny Bill was worried about something, John Arthur would bring out his dry sense of humour just to lighten Sonny Bill up. Those two are so close. John Arthur doesn't tell his brother he's played like a star if Sonny Bill's game wasn't quite up to his high standard. He is always straight up with him, which is exactly

Johnny and I have talked about where his own playing career might have gone, but he has no regrets along those lines and only wishes the best for me and our little sister Niall, also a national representative in two rugby codes. I'm proud of Niall, but just as proud of my other sister, Denise, and of Johnny.

I do wonder, too, if Johnny and I might have had an easier road if Dad had been a better role model. Dad will admit he was a hard man. I went through a phase where I did not look up to him, because he was a man of few words and some of those words could have been kinder. Once I learned what his childhood was like, I began to understand him better, but there have been times when I could have used some paternal wisdom and support.

When I was in my last two years at the Bulldogs, I was in the headlines for being blind drunk in public or being with a woman in a bar. I wasn't proud of this, but it wasn't enough to make me change things. I was caught up in it all. Johnny was in Australia with me, but because we were living in that moment we didn't see the immediate danger. I needed someone to talk things through with me, talk some sense into me, but there wasn't anyone doing that, least of all my old man. And, to be fair, my parents weren't really in a position to help me navigate the world of professional sports, because it was a million miles away from what they knew. I would have to work it out as I went, and at that point I wasn't doing it well.

Sonny Bill was good at phoning or doing FaceTime when he was overseas – not just with me but with all his family. When he first appeared in the newspapers as the eighteen-year-old league star in Sydney, my mum and I would go up the road to buy the papers and then sit down and read every word. It just felt unbelievable, the things they were saying about him being a superstar and all that. We just couldn't believe our boy was all over the newspapers.

After a few years of this, we'd got used to it; we could have built our own library with the amount of stuff written about him. I did take it to heart when negative things were said about him, as any mother would. Then I took the attitude, *They'll say anything to sell newspapers*. One time I read that I was in Australia, when I was sitting here in Auckland with my mum.

You wake up to the media with a son like Sonny Bill. How they use a headline mentioning him just to get your attention, then you read the piece and it's hardly about him at all. They'll use his picture, so naturally you read what they have to say, only to find it's more about someone else, like a teammate who did something silly. To the media, it seems that just playing in the same team is enough to drag you into something.

Of course, if they love you, then you're fine. You're the teacher's pet who can do no wrong, even when everyone knows you are doing wrong. But if they get dirty on someone and start attacking them, they can ruin the person's career, destroy his or her self-confidence.

Does any player like reading harsh criticism about how they played? How would a journalist like it if after every second piece they wrote, their boss wrote a scathing review naming them? But there are good journalists who are fair. I'm just dirty on those who maybe don't think about the consequences for the person they're writing about. Maybe they could take a breath and ask themselves what effect their article will have on the player. — Lee Williams

In later years, I've come to understand I got some of my loving qualities from Dad. He might not have been able to express his love through words, but it was there in his actions. He was always playing cricket with us, and he coached my brother's footy team. Sure, he had a gambling habit, and we all know a gambler loses more than he wins, but if he had money, he'd give it to us. But as a husband? Let's say he was far from Husband of the Year. When one person is drinking and gambling and the other is home looking after four kids, tensions rise. No child ever really knows what goes on between their mother and father. That's just the nature of relationships: sometimes they work, sometimes they don't. You can't change your past, only how you react to it. You can't erase bad memories or bad deeds, or correct poor decisions. You can only learn from them and face the future with a positive mindset.

So, I was a late starter to alcohol, and I might've let it get the better of me a bit, but one thing I can say is I was almost always a lovey-dovey drunk.

* * *

At the start of 2005, I was on seventy grand a year, which to me was a lot of money. I mean a *lot*. I was going to get Mum that house with nice wallpaper, buy Dad a car, look after my brother and twin sisters. Little did I know the player-manager sharks had smelled blood. Dad had moved to Sydney with his new partner, and I just let him choose who would be my manager. Neither of us knew anything about money, so we trusted others to tell us what to do. As it turned out, it wasn't smart to remove ourselves from financial decisions.

I was not making many good decisions at all around that time. One night, I was at this club in Kings Cross drinking with the boys, and these two guys were walking around staring at everyone. It was late and I'd had a few, so I was full of swagger. Thinking I was the man, I deliberately stepped back into one of them.

'Yo, what you doing, bro?!'

He stood his ground. 'Come outside and I'll shoot you in the leg – see how your footy career goes after that.'

I sobered up pretty quickly and had more than second thoughts: I was out of there!

The guy walked off to talk to his mates on the other side of the bar – or maybe to get his gun – and I took my chance and scooted out through the kitchen and hailed a cab. My legs have always been my best asset!

The Doggies would end up barring players from drinking in the Cross. The ban was put in place because of a big fight between a bouncer and one of the boys, but I am sure there were lots of other incidents that no-one ever heard of. Like that one.

This was at a time when I was playing my best footy, and I wasn't able to step back and look at my life. I wasn't mature enough to appreciate the privileged position I was in and see that obligations come with that. People look up to you, kids idolise you, many of them want to become the next Sonny Bill, and I was not taking on the responsibilities that came with that fame.

My natural bent is to overthink things. But I wasn't thinking at all. I wasn't in a good space – or, rather, I felt all that was required of me was to train hard and play hard and, yes, party hard. It's funny; we Islanders often excel physically but ignore the mental side of things. We avoid going a bit deeper and asking ourselves why we behave in certain ways. Yet our Polynesian ancestors were strong and fierce and must have been strong mentally too. Though, admittedly, they did not have a modern lifestyle full of temptations to deal with.

I feel from my own experiences that I'm a good person, but I know now if I'm not held accountable for my actions by something greater than myself, I can lose my way.

Around this time, I knew I was going astray and, like my mum, I wanted to do what was right. I'd met this guy, Khoder Nasser, who was a fight promoter, and I started hanging out with him, intrigued by what he had to say about life in general. He knew everyone and everyone respected him, not only because he was a promoter, but for who he was, his character. It seemed to me they liked him because he was a good man.

Before I started talking to Khoder, I was caught in a spiral of play hard, party hard and I wasn't making good decisions about who I was hanging out with. In a footy club, there are party boys, there are family men, there are guys with good morals and guys with bad morals. And then there are the hangers-on, who are only there for the free booze or drugs and to have a good time. They don't care about you, but you kid yourself they are your mates. I wasn't judging or caring; I was just partying and whoever wanted to join me was the friend I'd spend time with. Thankfully, I came out the other side of this but for a while there it was not good. I've come to realise that to understand someone's character, you can often look at who their five closest friends are. At that time, the people I was hanging with were not known for their good character.

I was looking for something but it took me a while to realise I wouldn't find deeper meaning in a shot glass. I had to walk away from temptations. And that is much harder to do than say. It is something I would struggle with for years, because those temptations are always there.

Khoder had integrity and was a man of his word. When I talked to Khoder about his life, he started telling me a bit about his faith and what being a Muslim meant to him. Gradually, some part of me seized on that. This was something greater than myself.

I was yearning for a deeper meaning to my life. I think a good part of the aching inside was a spiritual need. I'd got through that dark frame of mind when I was first injured, but all this drinking, partying and womanising made me realise I was dressing a deep wound with sticking plaster. I'd always dismissed the wound as low self-esteem, but I was starting to understand that it was more than that. I was heading for a reckoning – with myself.

CHAPTER 3

A curve ball straight to the head

I'm often asked if I had any personal rivalries in league and rugby. I don't think I ever approached a game with the idea of getting the better of any particular individual. I did want to mark out my territory and once on the field, my shyness and low self-esteem ceased to exist. I only wanted to stamp my mark on the game. To be like an animal in the wild, establish my territory. I would want to get the better of any opponent who stood in my way.

It was a massive buzz playing against Gorden Tallis and the Broncos in my first year of NRL and seeing the fearsome man charging at me. No disrespect to Gordie, because we are mates these days, but it was a huge boost for me and the other young Islander boys in the team to see our teammate Roy Asotasi run through him and score a try. It was like announcing a changing of

69

the guard. Us young boys were coming. Tonie Carroll, Shane Webcke and Petero Civoniceva from the Broncos were other players I liked to go up against. It was never overwhelming for me; it was more like excitement mixed with adrenaline. Same when I went to play rugby: I loved playing against the biggest names.

Playing against other Islanders or Kiwis was also a big buzz because we play a physical style of game. We're all big and brutal and can do the physicality thing all day long. I remember playing for the New Zealand Test side after only a few NRL games for the Bulldogs. Man, playing for my country at only eighteen – against Australia, the best team in the world – was a big moment.

I came on in the forwards and ended up playing some big minutes. I remember being very physical with every man headed my way. I loved it! That was my mentality back then: I was the young guy trying to prove himself, to show that I belonged out there, playing with and against the big boys. I'd attempt to smash the biggest or strongest guy on the field, even though I was still in a boy's body. Unfortunately, we lost that game to Australia 37–10.

At the end of that year, I'd be named in the New Zealand team for the Tri-Nations Test and would line up against Australia in Auckland. Being on the big stage back in my home town was a thrill and I managed to carry on my form from the Dogs season and won the Man of the

Match award in front of my family and friends. It was a huge accomplishment for a nineteen-year-old.

I was playing for New Zealand, playing for the Bulldogs and it was all happening. I didn't care who I was going up against. I was there to play. But I did love playing against the Polynesian/Māori-stacked Warriors. We all try to give back what we receive!

As a youngster, before I left New Zealand, a few of us in the New Zealand under-16s team were invited to train with the Warriors and their development team. In that team, there was one particular player who went on to carve out a magnificent career (I am not going to name him). My best mate's older brother grew up with him. They had been friends since they were kids. We're in the gym on the bikes, and this guy walks in and I'm like, 'Hey, bro!', then calling him by his first name. I was excited at seeing someone from my hood. I said my best mate's older brother's name and told him he said to say hello.

This guy gets on the bike beside me, looks me up and down, and doesn't say a word. Just turns away and starts biking. I was so embarrassed. Some years later, he and I were playing in the same team and I never said a word to him about the incident, though I never forgot that snub. It gave me the motivation to play my best footy whenever we met the Warriors. And to always respect and give the young boys coming through my time.

A couple of years later, in my next encounter with the Warriors, Stacey Jones was still playing for them and the game was a big deal. I got forty or fifty tickets for my family and friends. Their old guys were typical Kiwi boys out to put shots on you. Fine. Bring it. This was my element.

I remember Clinton Toopi targeted me early on. To be honest, I was a little flattered that he knew who I was. But this type of thing on the footy field didn't phase me at all. I was actually quite used to it. It took me back to the games I used to play against South Auckland footy teams like Māngere East or Ōtāhuhu, playing against massive Islanders putting it on you. And to survive, I had to give them a taste of a fierce shoulder charge.

In this game, Clinton ran the ball from dummy half and in I went with the biggest shoulder charge – bang! Down he went. I also tackled Stacey Jones and ripped the ball off him. I remember thinking, *I've just done that to none other than Stacey Jones.*

During that game, I managed to make a break from inside our half and then put our fullback under the posts for a try. Doing all this in front of my friends and family in New Zealand was something I will never forget.

Later that year, we played the Panthers in the first preliminary final at the Sydney Football Stadium. They had a massive pack like us, led by two of the best Islander players at the time – Tony Puletua and Joe Galuvao. They were called the 'hair bears'. Man, they were playing some exciting footy. In that same game, Steve Price, our captain, went down injured. Coach Steve Folkes called me over and said, 'I'm going to need you to play prop. Are you up for it?' I said sweet, even though on the inside I had moments of fear, most of all of letting my teammates down.

But I kept it simple, a formula I'd bank on for years to come. Stay in the game, work hard, do all the little things my teammates respect and the magic will come. Follow a good deed with a good deed and a bad one with a good one. Thankfully, I ended up playing well and we won. We were off to the grand final.

In the 2004 final against the Sydney Roosters, their feared English enforcer, Adrian Morley, put a hit on me. I just thought, *That wasn't so bad. Is that all you got?* Like Ali said to George Foreman in their Rumble in the Jungle in Zaire in 1974: 'That all you got, George? I thought you hit harder than that!' It was the biggest upset win in heavyweight boxing history – and at the end of that grand final thirty years later, we upset a fair few when we held up the premiership trophy.

In that grand final, as soon as I entered the field I put a massive shoulder charge on, and the crowd went crazy. I knew I was ready for the biggest game of my young career. To be honest, it was nothing new to my 2004 'Dogs of War' teammates. Hits like that is what we did to each other at training, with hardened players like Mark O'Meley, Willie Mason, Reni Maitua, Hutch Maiava, Roy Asotasi, Adam Perry and Steve Price flying into each other and me. Our whole Dogs team did it and that was only practice. We took that into game day and we were ahead of the pack from practising for real. We had the flash in the backs of Willie Tonga, Johnathan Thurston, Matt Utai, Hazem El Masri, Braith Anasta and Brent Sherwin. Our forward pack was big and ruthless. I mean *ruthless*.

But I fitted that mould, and the coach and guys I was playing with had helped me become that ruthless player. I'm proud that in those last two games of the 2004 season I showed I could do the tough stuff as well as the flash stuff. At the end of that game, we were crowned the NRL champions of 2004.

But here's the thing: if I've played well, I feel like I'm part of the team and I deserve to be there. If I had a bad game, it's the opposite: I feel so down on myself, like I don't belong and only ever will as long as I keep having good games.

That's how a lot of the players feel, as if the game and only the game defines who and what they are. That's why lots of us fall apart when we retire, turn into boozers, get hooked on drugs, become the pub bore living in the past and often die way too young from poor health issues. Falling from the top of sport to forgotten, and becoming a shadow of your former magnificent physical self on the way down, has to be so hard to accept. I was starting to understand how complicated a player's life can become when either the physical or mental starts to suffer. I distinctly remember straight after that 2004 grand final being overwhelmed by an intense joy. It fuelled the celebrations. But then, a few days later, that was gone and I was left with an aching feeling of emptiness. The thought, *Is that it?* went through my mind. I know now how important it is to have gratitude for everything that happens to you and to always reset and give yourself a new dream to chase.

A contact sports career doesn't usually last longer than ten to twelve years, and many players are only at their peak for six or seven years and then are dropped, never to be heard of again. Luckily, my career extended many years beyond that, and the fact that I got to play four different sports – if boxing can be called 'play'! – is a privilege I appreciate more as I get older. But I have also learned that I need more than sport in my life to feel right and live well. I have carried a knee injury since I was twenty. At the time, a surgeon told me I might have only two years left of playing. No way was I accepting that. I deliberately targeted that knee area in training by building strength around it. I feel for players whose careers suddenly end at, say, age twenty-seven or twenty-eight. To go from big star to forgotten is a long way to plummet. And some of the fans demand so much of their heroes, yet as soon as they drop in form, it's out of sight, out of mind.

Even after that incredible year of my first premier season, things started to feel out of whack because all I was focused on was sport. I knew where I stood when I was playing, but the party hard after-game culture was starting to throw me off balance. And throughout most of that year, the whole team had had to deal with a harsh media spotlight after rape allegations were made against unnamed players after a pre-season trial match. The lead detective later came out and said the allegations didn't stack up, but every member of the team had to visit police headquarters in Sydney for questioning and to submit a DNA sample. I was a young bloke with my family in New Zealand, so I didn't have much to say, but others in the team spoke out about how that impacted them and their families. Everywhere the team went, there were cameras on us. Our every facial expression was discussed and even what we wore was commented on. Each one of us was under suspicion until the police declared that no player would be charged and there was no evidence to pursue. That was my first experience of how something can be amplified before the evidence is examined, and how judgements can be made by the media and the public without anyone knowing the full story.

That's the thing with elite sport. There are many, many benefits that come your way, but there are things that can be difficult to handle, especially if you are a young bloke living away from family and friends and suddenly in a bubble that removes you in some ways from everyday life. You have to work hard not to lose touch with your own moral compass.

And I get it: with fame comes expectations, especially in the sporting world. I think being a boy with such low self-esteem didn't help me either. I never felt like I belonged with all those big stars. So the idea that I was not only a star, but a role model, was hard to come to terms with. It made me feel unsettled and unsure of myself. Nowadays, being a role model is something I am proud to be and take very seriously.

***

Let's fast-forward to 2012. I was coming off a successful 2011 World Cup campaign and also a Crusaders Super Rugby season and I was starting to feel at ease in the fifteen-man game. To be closer to Mum, I signed with the Hamilton-based Chiefs. I still felt like I had a lot to prove as a union man and joining a club that wasn't considered a title contender was the best place to do it. And what a season it turned out to be!

Unknown to me and my new teammates at the time, that year would see the start of a fierce rivalry between my old club and my new one. Although there was no expectation on us from fans, media and the like – we were labelled one of the least likely teams to win the 2012 Super Rugby title – that didn't stop our squad from working hard during the off-season to be ready for the ambush we intended to unleash on the rest of the Super Rugby franchises.

After twelve weeks of boxing preparation, which resulted in me winning the New Zealand Professional Boxing Association (NZPBA) Heavyweight Championship belt, I came into the pre-season team training a lot later than most of the others. I was mentally fresh and in the best physical shape I'd ever been in, but I was quickly made aware that so too were my teammates. That mentality of striving to get better as an athlete but also now as a Chiefs' team member was expected not just of me but all of us.

Like me, Dave Rennie was also in his first year at the club. He may have been the captain of the ship, but below the deck Liam Messam was also laying the foundations for us to thrive as a team. We had started pretty well in the competition but I'd say most people didn't take us seriously until we went up against my old teammates at the Crusaders. From that game's first whistle, the battle began and a fierce rivalry ignited that is still alight today.

There was lots of niggle between All Blacks teammates, and lots of lead changes saw a tough, uncompromising game end with a Chiefs' 24–19 victory. Performances like that don't just happen overnight, a lot of hard work and prep go into them. As a team, we still had many mountains to climb, but it was a great feeling beating the competition favourite and starting to see the fruits of our labour. We had just put everyone on notice that the Chiefs of 2012 were no longer the easybeats of the competition.

Questions were still being asked about us by some: 'Can they keep this form up?', 'Can they deal with the expectation of fans?', 'Can they sustain this effort for the whole season?' and 'Do they have what it takes?'

The answer to them all was an emphatic, 'YES!'

Our season, off the back of hard mahi (work) on the field and great camaraderie driven by everyone loving being in each other's company off field, had me feeling completely at ease. Crudz, Liam, and many other of my Chiefs teammates and I were having world-class seasons to remember as players and it was all focused on one goal. A goal we were edging closer to. Deep down, though we never spoke about it, we all knew which team we'd have to beat if our franchise was to win our first-ever championship: the Crusaders. Even though we'd beaten them in the early stages of the season, that hadn't stopped many people believing they would win the comp. With over 90 per cent of their starting team having played for the All Blacks, it would have been hard not to think they would finish at the top of the ladder. But we put paid to that when we topped the leader board at the end of the regular round and earned ourselves a home semi-final against them.

I've played in World Cup finals and big pressure games, but there's something about playing against some of your good mates in a huge contest that makes it that much more special. Maybe it is the pride of not wanting someone you know so well to get one over you, or maybe it is wanting to make your close ones proud on home soil – like I used to try to do all those years ago by putting on massive shoulder charges to get the praise of my big brother. Either way, my teammates rose to the challenge. This game is one of my favourite games of my sporting career across all codes.

We won the game 20–17. Against my former teammates and a Crusaders' side stacked with current All Blacks, we all had a night to remember. I had a hand in the first three tries and was a physical presence everywhere on the field.

In the first lineout of the game, my man Benny Tameifuna pushed their captain and leader out of the way. It was a very unexpected play, and some say it is the memory of that, and other actions that night, that still keeps the flames of that fierce rivalry going. I know that act had me thinking that reputation meant nothing out there that night. It was our time.

The next week, we played the Sharks in the final and we won 37–6. I scored a late try and then jumped into the crowd as a sign of my appreciation to the Chiefs' faithful. We were the Super Rugby 2012 Champions. I still get goosebumps remembering that night. Who would have thought?

***

Of course, it's not just the rivalries that inspire you to lift your game. It's the guys in your own team who you want to excel for. When I played with Aaron Cruden in the 2012 Chiefs team, we developed an almost spiritual connection, like we could read each other, feel one another's presence. I think we were two players with something to prove and that connection shone bright in every game.

> I think our playing styles complemented each other really well.
> We were both keen and eager to improve and grow as players.

We would talk about different situations that might occur on the field and what we needed to do to create a positive outcome for the team. Sometimes you just have automatic synergy with another player and that was the case between Sonny and me. He certainly made my job easier and enjoyable with his X-factor play-making ability. Sonny's work ethic was always top shelf and it became infectious for others around him. I remember a contact training we had, the boys were ripping into each other, as they do. Then Sonny stepped forward to put one of his trademark big hits on Ben Tameifuna, who weighed a healthy 135 kilograms. The collision was brutal with both players giving 110 per cent, neither player backed down from the challenge. The rest of the team just stopped, looked at each other and there was a collective feeling that we all needed to bring more intensity into our sessions if we wanted to be successful. That moment really set the tone and the standard for the rest of the season. These types of moments happened regularly around Sonny. He was someone who was completely dedicated to his craft, he was never satisfied and always pushed boundaries. This mindset contributed to his greatness. And it was a pleasure to get the chance to play alongside him. – Aaron Cruden

When the Chiefs' opportunity came up for me, they were ranked thirteenth out of fifteen Super teams, but that didn't bother me. In fact, I relished the challenge. When Dave Rennie asked if I wanted to come on board, I was in.

It was one of the best decisions I ever made. I am forever grateful to the franchise and to the people of Hamilton who helped me fall in love with the game of rugby.

I had a lot to prove. I wanted to show that I was one of the best players in my position and I deserved to be there at the highest level. That goal lit a ferocious fire in me and I was driven to show what I could do.

Liam Messam was there, and we became like brothers, really close. My cousin Tim Nanai-Williams, Aaron Cruden, Liam and I all had something to prove. People were saying we were a team of supposed deadbeats who'd lost too many games. They were wrong. What I found when I signed with the Chiefs was a bunch of guys totally committed to each other and determined to turn things around. We were all burning with that desire.

Aaron and I played together in every game and it gave us a deep understanding of each other's styles. Liam and my cousin were in the same zone. It seemed like we'd been playing together our whole careers. The special plays we were all coming up with out on the field were a reflection of how tight we all were and the natural flair we had. The future stars in our team of nobodies – guys like Brodie Retallick, Robbie Robinson at fullback, Lelia Masaga on the wing, hooker Hika Elliot, Sam Cane, Tim Nanai-Williams, Augustine Pulu, Tawera Kerr-Barlow, Richard Kahui, Tanerau Latimer and Ben Tameifuna – were ready.

Everyone in that team had an awesome connection. It didn't matter what colour you were, or where you were from, everyone's feet were firmly on the ground.

Our careers kind of went hand-in-hand, playing together in the Chiefs, in international Tests. We had the same spots on the team bus. I remember one time on the bus, Sonny asked to hotspot my phone. I asked how come he had no data.

'I forget to pay my phone bills, bro.' He then admitted his power got cut off quite often because he forgot to pay his power bill.

The buzz in the team at hearing he was joining the Chiefs was unreal. His performances in 2012 were outstanding. He got Player of the Year. Absolutely deserved because of his influence on all of us, but especially as a role model for the Polynesian players. He lifted their level of professionalism and we all took inspiration from his incredible training routine.

I remember one end of year with the All Blacks, we finished up in Cardiff. Sonny had this cool necklace, which he offered to me to wear that night. Luckily, I put it in my room.

In the morning, everyone woke with sore heads, and we went out to the bus taking us to the airport. Sonny asked for his necklace. I couldn't remember where I'd left it. He said it cost him five grand! I was near pooping myself, scrambling through my gear bag looking for it, thinking I'd have to pay him $5000. Thank God I'd thrown it in my bag.

Over the years of playing in the All Blacks together, he opened up with those of us close to him. We still tracked each other for the number of Tests we played. We'd have chats about different Tests and Dane Coles and I were league fans, so we'd drill him about different games and players.

We knew from his time in the Chiefs he was big on family. He shared his vulnerabilities with us, which we appreciated. As rugby players, we are supposed to be tough dudes with no vulnerabilities. Give me the vulnerable Sonny Bill. The honest man, the good man. — Sam Cane

Sammy is a man I'd follow into battle any day. When I was out there on the field, I'd love looking up and seeing Sam next to me. I'd know it was time to go hunting.

Dave Rennie, of Rarotongan extraction, was a shrewd coach with the kind of street skills that had him change tactics depending on who we played. He took away the opposition's strengths and played to ours. He allowed us to play a freer game and helped us hit the opposition with surprises. That's where the offloads really came to the fore. And as much as I admire Dave, he would be the first to agree that a team needs talented, quality players with a determined attitude and a total team commitment to win consistently. Players who refuse to be dominated by, let alone lie down for, an opposition with a far bigger forward pack, a swifter backline. The Chiefs were a team that fitted perfectly with my work ethic and, man, they sure worked hard at every moment of every practice, and anyone who slackened off found someone eager to take his place.

We were all expressing ourselves on the field and my offloads became the norm and what most of the team did. We connected on the field and that was reflected off the field as well. On trips away, the likes of Hika Elliot on guitar had us all expressing ourselves with our singing voices. Though Hika sang enough for everyone! I know I've talked before about us Polynesians and Māori being naturally shy around others. I think that comes from growing up in a culture that demands strict respect for older people. But we can change that and pull the personality out of each other when we get together because we know each of us is vulnerable, a bit socially hesitant, just with that bro-talk, the laughter, the classic eyebrow-lift in greeting, the 'You all right, bro?', the 'Chur, bro', the knowing looks followed by a giggle, a sly mirrored grin. There were plenty of funny characters in that team to get us laughing, and we were always in stitches at funny jokes or word plays – but only off the field. On the field, it was pure focus and a passion to win. Those guys, that team, created the perfect environment to bring out the best in me, on the field and off.

It was the Chiefs' first championship win in the seventeen-year history of the competition. I think the ESPN report on the game says it all: 'The Chiefs won this game not because of one big-name match-winner, but because they have forged an unrivalled team spirit – they would not be beaten.'

Some people get caught up in that world of, 'What's in it for me?' But the age-old adage that in giving you receive is what it is all about, as I was coming to understand. It's not about wanting, wanting, wanting everything for me, myself and I. Rather, it's about giving of your whole self to another, giving your time, your aroha, your sympathetic ear. That's what it means to be not just a great sportsman, but a decent human being. I feel like at the Chiefs we all learned that it isn't about star players, it is about playing as a team and *for* the team, watching out for each other and leaving it all on the field, because that is what teamwork means.

* * *

Being a decent human being and talking about the choices that lead you there is way more important to me than talking about my offloads, but I do know rugby and league heads want to know every detail about them. And I obviously enjoy doing them!

When I first came to All Blacks rugby in 2010, I brought my offloads with me, but I soon picked up the coaches' attitude to them: *It's not how we play rugby.*

I think the action was a bit before its time in 2010. But I'd faced the same attitude in rugby league in my earlier days. The coaches couldn't get their minds around it, despite the obvious advantages. I didn't understand why they couldn't see this. In the 2011 World Cup semi-final against Australia, I remember assistant coach Steve Hansen saying, 'Whatever you do, don't offload.'

Fast-forward to the 2015 Rugby World Cup and it was a different story. The same man would agree that one of the biggest weapons in my arsenal was my second-play-creating offload. It even had a name: 'KBA' – keeping the ball alive. I offloaded in the final on the biggest stage with my first two touches of the ball. It resulted in Ma'a Nonu scoring to give us a handy lead. I think now if I hadn't backed myself and pushed the boundaries, would I still have achieved what I did? Would I still have played with the All Blacks?

In my younger days playing rugby league, I'd had a coach sub me off for offloading. Another time, I was pulled off the field for picking up the ball with one hand and spilling it.

The thing about the offload is it's such a vital part of the game, especially when done correctly. With that

Mum, Dad, Johnny and me. Back then, Mum
and Dad's mixed relationship would have
raised a few eyebrows.

Family and sport were what
mattered to me when I was young.
Mum kept this clipping of me at
age eleven from the local paper.
I dreamed of playing professional
rugby league and of representing
New Zealand in the Olympics.

Mum, Johnny, me, Denise and Niall.

Sports
One giant leaper

BY DARREL MAGER

Mt Albert youngster Sonny-Bill Williams (above) has been selected to jump the Tasman early next year, and it's little wonder.

In a leap he nearly clears the long jump pit at Owairaka District Primary School. He's also an outstanding high jumper and sprinter.

Auckland want him as a representative at January's Transtasman Games athletics tournament in New South Wales.

Making the team adds to the 11-year-old's long list of achievements, which include:

● Captaining the school's winning under 56kg team in the Auckland Rugby League competition, and scoring an abundance of tries.

● Repeating the feat for the school's rugby team.

● First in high jump at the North Island Colgate Games.

● Picking up a swag of medals at this year's Auckland athletics championships (high jump 1, long jump 3, 100m 3, 200m 3).

Sonny-Bill is excited at the prospect of competing in Australia.

But to get there he needs to do what most overseas competitors do regularly — hunt for sponsors. He needs more than $1000.

"I really want to go. I've been training every day, going for runs and biking," he says.

He hopes the games are part of a larger step towards representing his country in the future at the Olympic or Commonwealth Games.

"That's the dream. I'd like to play rugby league too."

There were five in the bed (the four of us, and our
mate Toby) . . . And no wallpaper on the walls.

At fourteen, I was training hard to play in the NRL.

Nan always had my back.
And she paid for my very first
sporting trip to Australia.

Mum and me at my graduation.

Me and Denise.

My big bro.

Me and my old man, John Senior.

Me and Nan – I miss her.

Johnny, Niall, Denise and me.

Johnny, Mum and me.

Making my debut with the Canterbury
Bulldogs in 2004 was a dream come true,
and winning the premiership that year was
awesome. But, off field, I was about to
head into some dark times.

Reni Maitua, Willie Tonga and me with the 2004 premiership trophy.

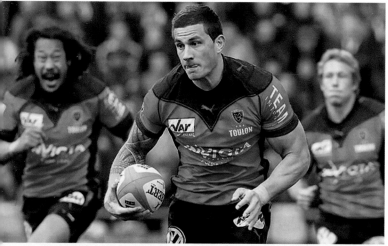

Tana Umaga, me and Jonny Wilkinson: I was taught rugby union by the best.

Me and my Toulon teammates.

Moise, Karem and me.

Me and Khoder Nasser.

Training with Tony Mundine.

With my NZPBA Heavyweight Championship belt.

Fighting Francois Botha.

Anthony Mundine, me and Quade Cooper and the WBA International belt.

Referee Lance Revill calling an end to my fight against Clarence Tillman for the NZPBA Heavyweight Championship.

Going back to New Zealand, I had my sights set on one goal: to play rugby with the All Blacks. I played a great season with the Crusaders and then I joined the Chiefs, where I had one of the best experiences of my sporting life. With the mighty Kieran Read (above left), and my mid-field partner at the Crusaders, Robbie Fruean (above right).

The winning Super Rugby Chiefs side.

The support I got from all around the world was awesome. The fans in Cape Town (above) were among the best.

Greg Inglis bumping me off to score the first try of our big game in 2013.

In 2013, I came back to Australia to play for the Sydney Roosters. That year would see me play in another premiership-winning team and Nick Politis would present me with the Roosters Players' Player award.

glass-half-full on-field mentality coming naturally, I've always been one to test the boundaries and go for the offload when no-one expects it. Big plays in big matches change the course of the game.

I love seeing young guys playing without fear and just expressing themselves, doing things coaches can't coach, just like they would have done as youngsters out in the backyard. I think that's the difference between New Zealand teams and the teams in a lot of other countries. Nowadays in New Zealand, you are taught to back yourself on the field because that's when the magic happens. Another example of this is the Fiji rugby sevens: they are so hard to defend against because you don't know what will happen next. They are the Harlem Globetrotters of sevens rugby and it resulted in them winning the first ever Olympic gold medal for their country. What a special sight that was! And they backed that up in Tokyo in 2021 with another gold medal.

In the 2013 NRL grand final, if I hadn't stayed on the opposite side of the field from where I was supposed to be to attack a gap I'd seen, I wouldn't have got that short ball off Sam Moa and put a flying James Maloney away to take the lead in the biggest game of the year.

In the 2015 Rugby World Cup Final against Australia, I went out and made a statement with two offloads. Out on the biggest stage, I shook off my off-field insecurities and backed myself with the mentality: *You gotta play, Sonny. Play. Be in the game. When you get the ball, you know what to do with it.* Out there, I backed myself, I trusted my skills and preparation, and I did what I always do: followed my instincts.

If players don't trust their instincts and push the boundaries, there is no growth. Sure, we need to stick to the majority of the game plan, but the game plan needs to have the space built in so that players can express themselves and have the freedom to find the magic. Polynesians and Māoris have a lot of that natural flair and if it wasn't for coaches like Todd Blackadder, Steve Folkes and Dave Rennie pushing me to express myself on the field, who knows, I might not have overcome my lack of confidence off the field and allowed that and my inner critic to affect the way I played. I may not have trusted myself enough to fully step into that space and I may never have reached my full potential and stood up in those big games. When you do and it is all going right, nothing feels better.

Those are the good times. But sometimes it's a double-edged sword. The red card in the Lions series, for example. I truly believed I was going to give my brothers a psychological advantage, smoke the guy, demonstrate physical dominance having come off a personally very good performance in the first Test. I told myself:

Be aggressive, Sonny. Be physical. What happens? The guy ducks and my shoulder slams into his head. I am making history as only the second All Black to receive a red card. At the time, I felt so ashamed for letting down not just my team but my country.

Looking back on it now, I know I was just doing my best. The truth is, you can't win 'em all. There are going to be times when you get clipped in the boxing ring, spill a ball, drop a pass. But the *I'm not good enough* Islander mentality could really weigh me down sometimes, and no amount of media praise for the vast majority of my playing career could change it. I've had some incredible press and I might have this big name, I've heard Keven Mealamu and Jerome Kaino – two of the All Blacks greats – complimenting me, but I don't hold on to any of that. I have struggles like everyone else. The struggle doesn't stop, and even when you think you've got life sussed, got it all figured out, there's that curve ball coming straight for your head.

CHAPTER 4

You can't run from the man in the mirror

Injuries are part of an athlete's life. We all carry them, and you just have to hope that with good luck and good management they won't end your career too early, before you've had a chance to prove what you can do. I've seen some heartbreaking injuries stop great players in their tracks. I've got a list of dodgy body parts. At the top of that list is the curve ball I've known about for some time: my crook knee. I must have had close to fifteen knee operations on the same knee; I've got no cartilage there now, which pretty much means it is bone on bone. It is crazy to think I have stayed a sportsman for so long. Maybe without the knee issue, I could have gone on another two years, because of my training and the drive I've always had. My knee was a daily struggle that

I just had to fit into my routine, the daily maintenance of recovering.

But let me rewind back to the start. My first big operation was when I was seventeen and had a major ligament reattached in my shoulder. Once I was back playing, I forgot all about it. But my knee injury was so severe they took out all the cartilage on my meniscus, and I had bone bruising and a bit of bone chipped off.

The doctor at the Dogs at the time – he's now passed away – was a good fella by the name of Hugh Hazard. He was this old Aussie dude who was always smoking. He told me I had to be careful, or within a couple of years I wouldn't be able to play anymore. I heard this and thought, *Really? My career could be over by twenty-three?*

That situation shaped a lot of my life for the next fourteen years. I spent so much time taking care of my knee: rehab, stretching, building the muscle around it, going to the pool, using an ice machine not just after a game but after every training session. Sometimes nothing could stop it swelling up but that just steeled me, prepared me better for going hard in the latter years. That good doctor had planted a seed in my head, and I was determined that I'd be around longer than two years. I'd last another five years at least. That's the number I carried around in my head. *Five years. Five years, Sonny.*

Injuries dogged my career, like they do a lot of sportspeople. I suffered a slipped disc in my back. Did my Achilles in the first game of the Olympics rugby sevens. But, then, I reckon a lot of good came from this knee, because it changed my mental attitude to sport. It was never just a matter of training and playing hard, but preparing as well as I possibly could and doing all those little one-percenters that might not sound much but which, added up, can make the difference between winning and losing. I used an ice machine for a good ten years and I don't think any opposition knew about the knee or they would have targeted it, big time.

I was taking painkillers and anti-inflammatories almost daily and always before a game in the last five years of playing just to get on the field. There's this product you can inject into the knee that acts like a buffer, but that's not enough; if I don't keep up my rehab routine it starts to really ache, because I've got mad arthritis. That's why boxing is such a good sport for me: less stressful on the joints, the knees, it's more about upper body effort and moving.

And it's not just my knee that is dodgy. One thing about the shoulder charge: if you get the timing slightly wrong, you'll come off second best. My left shoulder has given me quite a lot of grief over the years. That carries over to boxing and throwing a left hook, most orthodox boxers' favourite shot. Think David Tua. I have to adjust to get the little left shoulder muscles firing so I can throw the shot.

My body carries the memories of every game and every fight. But I was taught how to look after my body. The teams had doctors and physios and whoever or whatever else you needed to help get your body right. I may not have valued school enough to pay attention, but I was attentive and diligent to everything I was taught in regards to my knee. But it was my mind that really got messed up in the early years. And there was nobody watching out for that, or showing me how to fix things.

In 2004, I was on top of the world. I had more than any young man could wish for, especially one coming from my background. Right? Wrong. I was just a young man trying to come to grips with who I was, what I wanted to be and how to achieve it.

But where was the book on that? Who did I go to? I didn't have any authority figure or role model to talk with, to ask for guidance. There was no-one to steer me onto the right path. You see, in sport, if you excel at it, everyone considers you The Man. You can do no wrong, even when it's obvious you are doing just that. I'm not saying I was ever a bad person; I never lost the manners taught to me by Mum and by Nan, and it is in my nature to be polite. I was still shy, hardly said boo to anyone off the field. But I was a slave to my lusts and desires. I made bad choices and didn't do myself or my family proud.

The fact is, I was struggling with who I was on the inside. On one hand, I was this supposed star, this big-time sportsman who had it all. Yet inside I had nothing. That's what I went through in stage one of my rugby league career, aged eighteen to twenty-one.

The plaster kept getting put over the wound, but, as I discovered, you can't hide from yourself. Injuries and alcohol fuelled some bad behaviour and I made mistakes. I am not going to justify them. They were my doing. But having my mum see the headlines when I was caught peeing in an alleyway was not great. And that was the tip of the iceberg.

In those years, I had my share of women; some might say I was promiscuous. But I was a young guy and that's what all the guys around me were doing. I was just following the group, not questioning whether it was right or wrong. What young man turns down a beautiful woman? The society I moved in condoned and even lauded that behaviour. I actually had my own internal moral code, which is why I always felt really bad whenever I ditched a woman and moved on to the next. Inside, I knew it was wrong, and when you're a shy, polite person like I've always been, that inner turmoil is a wild storm. But feeling bad is not the same as knowing how to do something about it.

That wasn't the full extent of my bad choices. There is no excuse for the drink-driving, for which I deserved the media avalanche. I had stayed at a friend's place after a night out and was headed home early the next morning, not thinking for a moment I was over the limit. But I was on my P plates and so I shouldn't have had any alcohol in my system at all. In hindsight, I can see our Bulldogs CEO was managing a situation, but in doing that he ignored what was happening to me. If he really cared about my wellbeing, he wouldn't have put me in front of a hungry media pack while I was in such a vulnerable state. Yes, I had been binge drinking, but it was symptomatic of a greater battle that needed to be confronted, and I wasn't strong enough or confident enough to do that on my own. I didn't have the words to tell people that I was feeling overwhelmed or depressed, and no-one saw my behaviour as a red flag or something to ask about. There was no conversation from anyone about my wellbeing at all. I was told to admit publicly I had a drinking problem and sent on a course for problem drinkers. The drinking was a symptom of a much bigger issue that was never once addressed and nobody paid any attention to that. I did need help, but a short course like the one I was signed up for wasn't the medicine I needed for the deep wound I was carrying.

I'm not making excuses; I'm ashamed of the things I did back then and they clash with who I know I am. It might sound strange, but I can't say I'd change anything if I could because without all the things that I went through I might not have had the knowledge and personal insight to have found the biggest blessing of my life – Islam. As brother Malcolm X said: 'Only from the depths of darkness can one reach the greatest of lights.' So, despite my shame, I had to hit my personal rock bottom to finally confront the man I saw when I looked in the mirror.

There were other moments when, caught up in the party-hard culture after a game, I drank too much, took drugs and let myself down. And then there was an incident in a nightclub in 2007, when I fooled around with a woman in a toilet stall. Both she and I will have to live with that mistake for the rest of our lives. It made headlines around a good part of the world. It was embarrassing, and not just for myself. There's the woman involved, of course, though she was a single adult woman and so it really was no-one else's business what she did. But I had a girlfriend at home who was publicly humiliated as well as suffering the pain of being cheated on. She surely did not deserve to be at the centre of a media storm.

I understood the reason I was struggling. The party culture, the money, the access to drugs and alcohol. I was wrestling with it but I wasn't saying no. I was selfish and I had no-one to answer to. Like so many young people in today's society, I had no boundaries and I was struggling to put some up on my own. It was up to me, but I didn't know what to do about it or how to do that. Gradually, it became clear to me I had to change everything. Once I became a committed Muslim and adopted a totally different lifestyle, the fog started to clear. But believe me, it took quite a while for conversion to happen, for me to reject what felt like an enjoyable lifestyle as a party boy. All humans are resistant to changing their ways. And temptations are always there so it is easy to slip back.

This was part of the change that saw me leave the Bulldogs. I was starting to learn more about Islam and the Muslim faith, and my friendships with people like Anthony Mundine and Khoder Nasser were being noticed and commented on. I turned up to training one day and the coach said to me, 'You aren't turning Muslim, are you?'

I tried to laugh it off, but then comments were made about my friends, and that made me very uncomfortable and angry. No-one had paid attention to my private life before then; no-one cared when I was drinking or partying hard as long as I was doing what they needed on the field and it didn't make the press. And even then, it was all about damage control, not about my wellbeing. Yet now, when I was trying to get myself right, suddenly my private life was a concern because of religion.

It all came to a head in 2008. I thought, *I've got to get out of here. Make a complete break, start afresh somewhere else.* I asked Khoder, who had taken over as my manager by then, to look into the possibility of a contract with a Super League club.

That was when Tana Umaga, the first Sāmoan to captain the All Blacks, called me out of the blue from Toulon in the South of France. 'Would you like to consider changing codes to rugby union and play with the team I'm coaching here?' he asked.

A Sāmoan superstar wanted me to switch codes and play in a foreign country just as I'm heading into a personal crisis and wanting out from the Bulldogs, out from Australia, and an opportunity just to reset everything?

I was wrestling with it all but I couldn't see how I could stay. I was scared what would happen. As I said, people were starting to talk about the fact that I was keeping company with Muslims, asking why I was hanging out with 'those kind of people' – 'those' as in Muslims. This just brought out the steel in me and raised my hackles. Like my mum, I will not be told who I can mix with, not by anyone. Choosing my company is my right, as it is yours. If only I could have understood earlier that I needed to change for my own happiness, contentment and to find inner peace rather than blotting out all that need in the noise of partying. I was well aware my sudden departure from the Bulldogs would not go down well with my teammates and fans. I don't blame them for being angry. Or for the wider community declaring they hated me. But no-one knew what was going through my mind and why I felt I had no alternative but to run away.

At the time, though, I could hardly make a press statement explaining the dark place I was in and how I could see no way out. I was overwhelmed but didn't even understand myself why I had lost my way so badly, so had no idea how to explain it to the media, the faithful Bulldogs fans, the coaches and team support staff. If I had known how, maybe things would have been different, but I wasn't able to open up like that. It wasn't something I was doing lightly; I wrestled with it and knew I wasn't just disrupting my own life – it was going to impact my teammates, my family and what people thought of me, something that I had always cared a great deal about. Normally I was so worried about doing the wrong thing or upsetting people that I did nothing and bottled up my feelings. Finally I understood the problem was me and I had to do something to heal myself.

Once I'd decided I would take up Tana Umaga's offer, he said I needed a Sāmoan passport, as apparently there would be fewer visa problems than if I was travelling on my New Zealand passport. So, off to Sāmoa we went, Khoder and myself. I'd been in touch with one of my cousins and we went to his village. They gave me a big welcome, and someone knew someone who knew – you know how it goes.

Tuila'epa Sa'ilele Malielegaoi, the Prime Minister of Sāmoa? Yep. Second day in Apia and there I am sitting having a cup of tea with the PM. He said, 'Are you going to play for Sāmoa? Because if you are, I can get you the passport right now.' I managed a few words in Sāmoan. He called on his driver, who took me down to the passport office, where they were expecting me and knew who had sent me. *No problem, Sonny Bill.* Someone even asked if I wanted a bus driver's licence too! With the passport all sorted, I returned to Sydney. Khoder was promoting Anthony Mundine's next fight, which was to take place in five days' time, so he arranged for his brother, Ahmed, who we call Honks, to travel with me to France via Singapore and London. I'd thrown my phone away, but even before we left, Honks' phone started going off. 'The news is out, bro!' Someone had called a radio station to say they'd seen me at the airport. It was like some weird action movie . . . almost!

At immigration, the guy at the counter calls me over and asks gruffly, 'Where are you going?'

'France.'

'Why are you going there?'

'Um, for a holiday.'

I am a bad liar and didn't sound convincing.

I couldn't wait to get on the plane. When we finally boarded, it felt like an eternity before the doors closed. I was praying that we would take off before the police could board and drag me off the plane. I was so relieved when we were finally airborne, but then I just had my thoughts to worry about.

When we landed in Singapore, Khoder called and told Honks that the Bulldogs administration were trying to subpoena me for breach of contract. I found out later I was the only player in Australian rugby league history to have his club take such action against him. The NRL was also looking to take legal action. The media were waiting for me at Changi Airport with a heap of questions.

Finally, we were on the plane again, but our troubles still weren't over. Going through immigration at London's Heathrow, the guy at the counter looked at my passport and asked, 'What is this?'

'A Sāmoan passport, sir.'

I had to get a map and show him where Sāmoa was.

He told me, 'You can't enter France with this passport. You can enter Britain only.'

I had no clue why this would be the case, but I wasn't up for arguing. I spent two days hiding out in London while the passport problem was sorted. The media were trying to find me, the guy with the subpoena was supposedly looking for me. The manager we signed the contract with was Tana's guy, so we stayed with him, holed up in the attic of a house in Wimbledon, not daring to go out. I spent a lot of time thinking, not really talking to anyone. Every morning I was there, I woke up with a migraine and the thought kept going through my head, *Did I do the right thing?* I was so grateful Honks was with me. He knew the magnitude of the situation and he also knew how to lighten the mood. I love my brother Honks. Finally, we were told I had to go to a consulate somewhere near Hyde Park to get a visa. Honks gets a car, drives me to the visa office and I run in while he parks nearby. I got things sorted and then sprinted out with my visa, convinced I was moments away from being arrested and sent to jail – for breaching a footy contract! That's how naive I was back then.

To avoid the media certain to be waiting for me at Toulon, we flew to Biarritz on the western coast of France. There, I went to a local gym in Pau to work out, and someone recognised me. So I rushed back to the hotel, where the manager – a Frenchman – told me and Honks to pack our things because the media were on to us. This was at about 6 pm. They put me in the car boot and covered me with blankets. Talk about living like a fugitive in a spy drama.

Honks and I drove about eight hours to Tana's house, where I found out that because of legal problems with the contract, I couldn't start playing straight away. The NRL hired lawyers in France, that's how badly they wanted me back. Then I ended up having a big blow-up with Khoder because, back in Australia, Labor powerbroker Graham Richardson had negotiated a settlement down from the asking price of $1.5 million to $750,000 plus $200,000 legal fees and another €70,000 for the French lawyers. Lawyer Mark O'Brien was helping me with the details. I didn't have that kind of money, so Anthony Mundine and some close friends paid it between them. I will never forget their generosity. Half a million each is big bucks to throw at a mate. Now I was in debt big time, and I still didn't know if I was definitely going to be able to play.

But, on the bright side, I was now free to reinvent myself. It was time to address the problems I had and have a long hard discussion with that man in the mirror. I didn't know what would happen. All I knew at that moment was things had to change.

CHAPTER 5

Finding a good space

The perception that I walked out on the Doggies, in breach of my contract, just for money and to try out another rugby code isn't the true story. There are grains of truth in that version, but not the whole salt mine. After I left, I was horrified to be told that, according to *Zoo Weekly*, I was the most hated person in Australia, placed ahead of the Bali Bomber. But just like you can't stop the sun from shining, life goes on and so has mine. I had a lot of turmoil still to go through but years later, after I retired, some really humbling words were said about me. I guess it shows how I conducted myself on and off the field made a positive impact on some people.

Sonny would be the best athlete I've coached from a pure athlete sense . . . As he has got older, he has matured. His training habits and his off-field habits are world class now. He will be a good role model for the young fellas in the club. – Steve Hansen

He's been a great role model for both codes. Especially for young kids growing up in New Zealand, who don't feel like they get the opportunities everyone else gets. What he's shown is that with hard work and determination, you can do whatever you want. You've got to give him full credit, not only for what he's done on the field, but what he's done off the field for the people of New Zealand as well. – Benji Marshall

I know most kids ran around the backyard and even on the professional footy field imitating and commentating 'SBW' as we offloaded. Any big hit was labelled SBW too. He set the trends on the field with style, flair and success, but the trends he sets now are what makes SBW truly great. Trends like being a great father, great husband, great leader in the community and so much more. What he taught me was that above all, always, Alhamdulillah. – Quade Cooper

If you've got a Williams in your side, you just have to follow him. He will show you the way. It's almost biblical. He may be the best player ever to come out of New Zealand. Everyone wants to watch him play, people idolise him. I love to watch him play. – Ray Warren

Sonny Bill inspired a generation and will continue to inspire.
Grateful for the lessons and our friendship. Proud to have him as
a brother. – Liam Messam

I am grateful that playing sport at the highest level, even with its hardships, has brought such joy to my close ones. And when it comes to compliments, although they are nice to hear, I am always aware of the dangers of taking them to heart. One day's compliments can be the next day's criticisms. But I do care about giving back and doing the right thing. Sport has enabled me to make a difference, and I will keep doing that. The money that came with being an elite sportsperson enabled me to look after my family.

But all that was still in the future . . .

Singapore. London. Biarritz. A long drive to Toulon. A million bucks owed for breach of contract. Playing for Toulon would give me breathing space, and some good people wanted me there and played a big part in my switch to rugby union.

Tana Umaga was one of those good people. Philippe Saint-André, coach of Toulon and future coach of Les Bleus, the French rugby team, and Jonny Wilkinson, England and Lions great and arguably the finest fly half to play the game, were two others.

So, my rugby education started with Tana having the foresight to ring Khoder and say he was serious about offering me a role with Toulon. It had never crossed my mind to play rugby. There had been a little bit of noise in New Zealand about that possibility, but to hear from Tana was mind-blowing. For a man like him to have faith in me really helped settle my nerves and made me seriously consider it.

We spoke on the phone and he said, 'Not only will you make it in rugby, you are going to thrive.' These words gave me such a lift and I could see a way to give myself a break from the dark place I was in. I didn't know who or what I was, only that I was trying to be a better person. Leaving Australia and going to France was the circuit-breaker I needed. In reality, I was running away from myself, but I now know sometimes that is what you need to do to sort out what is important.

Tana offered me a way out of an intolerable situation, and I was so grateful to him for believing in me.

I was a fan of Sonny's from his Bulldog days as a mere eighteen-year-old in that hardest of contact sports playing with and against the hardest of men. I'd heard word of his wanting to leave the Dogs but I wondered if he was serious. I knew of his exceptional talent and could see his work ethic in how he ranged wide and did as much with the little things as he did coming up with big plays, as often as not game-changing.

He didn't just come from nowhere; this Sāmoan boy had everything an athlete could want. Our club owner had never heard of him so I showed him videos and he was immediately interested. But could I get him to switch to rugby union? Seems I did that all right. – Tana Umaga

At a critical time in my life, when I desperately needed someone to look up to and mentor me, Tana Umaga was there. As a man, he is all substance, completely authentic – and of course he has a sporting track record like few others. An Islander, a fellow Sāmoan, an All Blacks captain, he opened the door for me – and I came with massive complications, what with the personal stuff, the code switch, the Bulldogs management after me over my breach of contract. Tana not only believed in me, but he had also told his boss, Mourad Boudjellal, a mega-rich comic-book publisher and the owner of Toulon Rugby Club, that there was this rugby league player who had all the qualities to become a rugby union superstar. (Tana didn't mention this to me at the time; I only found out years later. The eccentric Mourad has since sold Toulon – hailing Tana as his best signing in a side stacked with international stars – and switched from rugby to soccer.) Tana's foresight changed my life. Who knows where I might have ended up if he hadn't called when he did?

Looking back on it, my rugby tutelage in France was second to none. Even though that first year was tough, I flourished, and I played some of the best footy I've ever played, just in a different code. Okay, getting a yellow card in my first game for a shoulder charge was not great. That was just me wanting to impose my physicality. A few games later, though, I got Man of the Match.

The great Jonny Wilkinson was not just my teammate but my tutor, teaching me a new code. A man selfless with his time and, by the way, shy like me – maybe even more so. To me and many others, the best fly half ever to play the game, and he's so shy? Well, what a coincidence. And how lucky was I to fall on my feet like this? My work ethic matched his, and I gladly followed the example he set. With hindsight, I can say quite a few of the international players saw playing in France as the equivalent of a very well-paid holiday, but not me and Jonny. To give you an example, after one of our first training sessions as a team, we had all showered and I had even had some physio. To my amazement, when I was leaving the stadium, Jonny was still out on the field, practising his skills. My admiration for him really started on that day.

Moving from England to play for French team Toulon at the age of thirty was a very big decision for me. I needed a change. I loved how passionate and rugby-loving the club and region were but, above all else, there were a few guys playing there that I couldn't ignore. Sonny Bill Williams was a major one of these. Playing alongside him was a once-in-a-lifetime type of opportunity. So I went and even though we only shared one season, it was well worth it and more.

Our first few pre-season training sessions unfortunately involved me having to row on a machine and sprint up hills next to him. He absolutely destroyed me on both. I remember thinking that this was perhaps the most physically gifted individual I had ever seen. He was built for this sport.

His incredible coordination, power, agility and speed, not to mention his immense level of skill, were obvious to see from the first few games we played together. He just soared above the best the league had to offer in so many ways. He was going to be the future of the game, there was no doubt about it.

What I valued most about our relationship came from getting to know him off the field. I could sense that he was so keen to challenge himself and see what he was capable of. He had an unquenchable thirst for stepping up and giving things a go.

What made it work for me, though, was that he was never afraid to show his vulnerability. By doing so, he expressed total humility and humanity. I knew right then and there that he was going to lead the game into a brilliant new space and that rugby, whatever the code or format, was in very big and exceptionally good hands. — Jonny Wilkinson

I feel like Allah put me in that place to learn from one of the true greats, and he was a great teacher. He was encouraging, and I learned the value of honing my skills and continuously working on them. He's the one who taught me the simple catch and pass that can make the big moments second nature to you. If you put in the training and the preparation, you have the skill set to step up in those big moments in a game. He demonstrated that. Perfect the basics. He practised every kicking skill for hours and hours.

Jonny instilled confidence in me – and remember, at this point I'd still never played a single game of rugby in my life. He used positive language to build me up, and in every game he expressed his faith in me, trying to get the ball into my hands and involving me as much as possible. Then, after a game, he would sit down with me and go through every facet of what had just happened. Our field position meant a different tactic for each situation, rather than my usual 'just play harder' approach. He'd say, 'Sonny, when we get down to their end of the field, we do such-and-such. If we go between our forty and their forty-metre mark and have gone six phases, well, we look for space behind.' I'd go home and write everything down.

The guidelines Jonny gave me stuck throughout my rugby career, that's how good he was, how generous he was – a true great of the game, playing out his last season in Toulon and sharing his knowledge with a rugby novice. He always wanted me with the ball: 'Sonny, go there, it's coming your way.' 'Sonny, step into first-five while I organise out the back.' 'Sonny, head that way!' Next instant, the ball lands in my hands and I have clear space, or just one or two tacklers to beat, with mates running off either shoulder. I couldn't help thinking, *This is unbelievable*. The English and Lions great has so much faith in this shy boy? That's what you call empowerment. And his approach was so simple: trust, have faith, believe in the player outside you.

Philippe was the same. 'Just do your thing, Sonny. One of your biggest attributes is physicality. Use it when and how you like.' That type of buzz. *Okay, how about this?* Shooting out and smashing a guy. Jonny was a mean tackler himself, punched way above his weight – figuratively, I mean, not literally. He was the fairest player; a real English gentleman. But he would try to make even bigger hits than me. He'd do a hit and I'd say, 'That was all right, Jonny.' He would be laughing at me and we would have battles to see who could go hardest. We all know who won that, but it was more a private contest between mates.

As I have said before, when I'm not talking about or playing footy, I'm a man of few words. Footy is business.

Social interaction is a lot harder. Back then, asking someone to go for coffee was just not something I could do.

I'd be thinking, *This is Jonny Wilkinson!* And he was a quiet guy too. Plus, Jonny was always in demand; all his teammates wanted to tap into his knowledge. I would have to wait in line behind five other guys. That is why I say he was such a selfless individual and not for one second up himself. He'd give the rest of us whatever help we asked of him, then go off and hone his own skills. I so appreciated his time and friendship.

One of my fears when I first joined Toulon was that the other players would lack respect for me because I was a rugby union novice, but that proved unfounded. And I mean completely unfounded. They were the opposite; they gave me mad respect. As Tana had predicted, I was thriving in this new game, and the more I played, the better I got. Fast-forward to the last game I played for Toulon – in the losing final against Cardiff – I got Man of the Match.

As soon as Sonny Bill started training with us, I knew my gut feel was right. I saw the traits, how he thinks around issues, his work ethic of not just doing as asked but always doing that bit extra. Not to shine, just for the team. This boy loved being around teammates and was the perfect team man with no big ego, not temperamental.

I remember we had a return-to-play protocol, where you have to observe a set training routine before the season officially starts. His family were visiting and so he missed this routine. What does he do?

There was a median strip near where he lived. It was dark, and he got his father to park his car and turn the headlights on while he ran up and down this median strip. I know now this was a reflection of his dedication to training.

He was well loved and supported by everyone in the Toulon team. And the fans quickly came to love him. They'd not seen a player quite like him. Off the field, he kept pretty much to himself, other than a couple of Muslim mates, one of whom was in our team.

The great Jonny Wilkinson and Sonny Bill were very much alike. Both shy, both extremely hard trainers. They spent hours and hours more than anyone else training, perfecting. JW was a good teacher and his pupil Sonny soaked up everything, both from JW, myself and others he respected. This young man was determined not to just learn a new code but to excel at it. He was always going to be a great. The great players all show the same qualities of determination and being open to learning, not thinking they're better than everyone else. What made him even more special is that he wanted to be a better person. Which is kind of rare in a rugby player of his stature; most feel they don't have to be anything but great on the field.

We had a terrific group of internationals from many countries at Toulon, many of them greats in their own right. But I don't think they'll mind me saying that Sonny Bill stood out as one of a kind. – Tana Umaga

Philippe came and sat beside me on the team bus to ask me to stay on. He promised he would select me to play for France as he would soon be the French coach. Jonny and Tana were also telling me I had what it took to play at international level.

It was such a boost and made me feel it was possible. While in Toulon I had played against international players and certainly felt I got the better of them. But if I was going to play at that level, then I knew I could only ever play for one country: New Zealand.

***

There were a lot of good things happening professionally in that year in France, but on a personal level there was more darkness than light. I wanted to succeed so badly. In the early days, the pit of depression was at its worst. I would wake up with migraines and I now know why: everything was about me. I had decided to commit to becoming a Muslim, but that didn't mean I was transformed into a new person overnight. There was still an inner voice saying,

Me, me, me. Everything I was doing was still all about me, not something bigger than myself. I was grateful for what was happening to me with those three legends right behind me. But even a professional player has more private time to themselves to think, often brood on things.

After the first French season ended, I went back to Australia and spent six weeks in boxing camp – not just with Khoder, but with other Muslim brothers. We'd go for walks, do our prayers. I was starting to understand how necessary it is to be in a positive environment. So, when I returned to France in 2009 for my second season, I had a different mindset. I was no longer all about me. While of course I always wanted to succeed and continually improve, I was realising the importance of gratitude, being grateful for everything that comes my way and recognising something bigger than myself.

I loved it over there in Toulon; loved playing with international legends. One of the surprises was how the Toulon fans embraced me. And the more and better I played, the more they loved me. It was humbling and uplifting at the same time. And, of course, the people loved us Top 14 rugby players like we were their own sons. Toulon people love their rugby so much they have a statue of a rugby ball! I'm embarrassed to say this, but in Toulon there is one of those 'Bring Back Buck' things, but with my name. (For those who don't know, it's a New

Zealand thing; when the great All Blacks captain Wayne 'Buck' Shelford was dropped by selectors in 1990, fans started turning up to games with signs reading BRING BACK BUCK.) My first year after playing for the All Blacks, I visited Toulon and went to a match. The club got me to walk the ball out for kick-off and the crowd went crazy. It's a special place, Toulon, especially for the rugby community.

I wasn't just thriving on the field; I was starting to blossom socially, too. I love the French people, but I gravitated to the North Africans and Africans. Toulon is in the south of France, so we were near the tip of North Africa and I met people from Morocco, Algeria, Tunisia. There were people from all over. I'd brought my brother Johnny over, and we became good friends with a Tunisian family.

In that second year, I became even closer to that Tunisian family, who I'm still in contact with today. They helped me to become a better Muslim just through the example of the selfless way they lived and the kindness they shared with so many. I played with a Muslim guy, too: Olivier Missoup. We became really close and roomed together, said our prayers together. He understood my struggles, too. It was really cool to have a kind of soulmate. We went to the mosque together and talked at length. I am also still very close to him today.

The forming of these relationships really helped in my off-field life.

I don't need to tell you about the quality of this rugby player. He was physically impressive and technically incredible. A player like this you want to share more time with. It is nice to discover you share something in common and, for us, that was a religion about values of respect and sharing.

Sonny came to spend the end-of-year break with me and my family in Paris. This was the first time we were able to be together outside of Toulon.

Sonny met my mother and my family cocoon. I also took pleasure in showing him around my hometown of Paris. We also shared prayers in different mosques in Toulon.

Most of all, I met a friend of rare humility who has great respect for people and who takes time to learn about the history of the people he meets. This is a rare quality these days and not what you would expect of a sports superstar.

Sonny can find himself in a large villa or a small studio. It makes no difference to him. He has the values of sharing and does not give importance to material things. Once I stopped by his hotel where the All Blacks were staying and he gave me some training gear. This is typical Sonny.

In our younger days we were both a bit, shall we say, restless. Today, we're both dads of three and four. Sonny has been important in my personal and spiritual development, and his influence continues to this day and into the rest of my life. May Allah protect my brother and his family. – Olivier Missoup

I only had two drinking episodes the whole time in France, so it wasn't like I was mixing – as in, wining and dining – with your typical French people. But living there did broaden my horizons. Family visited me, including my dad and his new wife who came to stay with me for a while, which was great.

I was worried when Sonny left the Bulldogs, and I had talked to him about it. But I knew what was happening, and that he was struggling. I knew from when he was a young age that Sonny had what it took to play in the NRL and I was so proud every time I saw him play because he put everything into the game. He's always been like that. When I was coaching his brother's team, Sonny would turn up to train with the older boys because he wanted to push himself harder. I was confident that one day he'd play rugby league for New Zealand. But when he told me he was leaving league to play rugby union, I was surprised. And then when he made the All Blacks team, I was shocked, but I shouldn't have been. Sonny has big cojones and a big heart, and he backs himself when it matters. All his effort and his strong work ethic paid off. The first game he played with the All Blacks was in England and I watched on the TV back home in Australia with my wife. When he ran out on the field, I cried. I was so proud and happy for him.

I went over to visit Sonny in France and I could see the change since he'd left Australia. He'd got himself into a good space with good friends around him and I knew he was going to be okay. I didn't know at the time that he would become the sporting star he would, and end up representing New Zealand in rugby league, rugby union, rugby sevens and make an Olympic team, but I was proud of him even without those achievements. All I want is for my kids to be happy and thrive. — John Senior

Dad was right, I was happy. Travelling to other cities, I saw how people in different parts of the country lived, how proudly different from each other they were. I loved the restaurants, which were all about friendship and conviviality, community.

I travelled around, too. I went down to Barcelona, flew to Morocco, London. Travel opened up my mind even further. All these new people and new experiences helped to take the focus off myself and I learned there was more to life than just sport – unlike in Australia, where rugby league is all-encompassing. There, I was sucked into the big footy machine, whereas in Europe, rugby is big but not massive. They're just about all mad soccer fans.

I was living a whole new life, and it was changing me.

* * *

One time, I was travelling to Marrakesh with Khoder and the plane hit the worst turbulence I had ever experienced. It was like in the movies when the plane suddenly drops, people get thrown around and hit their heads and people cry out and start praying loudly in desperation. Like my mum, I had a fear of flying but unlike her, I had learned to manage the terror most of the time. That day, the terror was overwhelming. I was sure we were about to die. I looked over at Khoder and he was so composed and calm and when he saw my face he started laughing. I couldn't believe it. I asked him why he wasn't scared and he told me: 'My trust in Allah.' His faith meant he wasn't afraid.

Two months later, Olivier and I were with the team travelling to a game in a private plane and we again hit really bad turbulence. The plane was juddering and falling before climbing back up to a higher altitude and then falling again. People were screaming and the boys were terrified. Something happened in that moment, and I felt this incredible calm settle over me. I wasn't scared and I just thought, *If it is my time, then it is my time*. I started to silently thank Allah and gave thanks for my life, what is called making Dua in the Islamic faith. I looked over at Olivier as our teammates wrestled with their fear and he was like me, calmly accepting whatever happened. We looked at each other and had this mad connection as we realised we both were unafraid. I have never been scared of flying since then. I put my trust in Allah.

Everything had changed for me and I was so grateful to be learning and experiencing things outside what I had known up until then. Everything was new and different, even the old buildings were unlike anything we have in New Zealand and Australia. My favourite place to eat was an Algerian restaurant, run by a Muslim brother, and I could tell he was struggling because all the busy restaurants were on a strip down by the beach. I'd always go there and have my couscous and a bit of lamb, and sometimes it would be just me and the owner. We'd talk, he in his broken English, about his life and his kids and family and I would share with him stories about my life in New Zealand. I just felt this connection, like I did with the Tunisian family I mentioned. I'd often choose to sleep on the floor of their cramped house rather than sleep in my big mansion up in the hills with fantastic views.

One of the sons of the Tunisian couple, Moise, had become a good friend of mine. I had met him at a club during my first year in Toulon: he was working in the cloakroom at the time, taking people's jackets and coats. I wasn't drinking but I still had that attachment to the party life. We were both wanting to be better people and I'd go into the club with the boys, then hang out with Moise in the cloakroom. We'd sit there and have mad yarns and talk about life, our struggles, while my teammates were having a rip-roaring time on the booze next door. We became very close.

Then in my second year, 2009, when my mentality had done a 180-degree turn and my focus was just on playing good footy, I ended up spending a lot of time with Moise's family. His mum would feed me to bursting. Cholesterol levels in that house would have been through the roof! They lived in a one-bedroom place: Mum, Dad and five kids. Materialistically, they didn't have much, yet they were so grateful to Allah for what they had and happily shared food with me, a foreigner. Just their specialness as a family drew me in. And as they became more important to me, I introduced them to my friends. I wanted to share my life and the people who meant a lot to me. It is what we all do. And a beautiful thing happened from that. A close Australian friend's sister ended up marrying Moise's younger brother, Karem. They now have a lovely family of their own and live in Brisbane. We are still very close. I kind of opened the pathway for that brother to have a different life.

I consider Sonny like a brother from another mother, not just a friend. Sonny is a better human than he is an athlete. Simple and humble.

He was looking for balance when he got here to Toulon. He found it in faith and family. Life is made of chance meetings, as happened to us.

Sonny was up for helping all the time. He'd take my mum shopping or just come and visit the kids in the centre I worked for and play basketball and PlayStation with them.

I live in a tough area but that was not important to him. He would come down from his beautiful villa with its magnificent view of the city to join me and my family.

After I started staying with him, when I read articles about him, it was as if the person the articles were talking about did not exist. He has never changed, he has always been the same; he really is that person, true to himself, to his principles, to his faith.

His parents gave him principles and that is what brought us together. His whole family is like that, brother Johnny and his twin sisters. Those of us lucky enough to know him feel privileged. – Moise

Once it got out that I was now Muslim, the word spread like wildfire in the Muslim community. 'Sonny Bill is a Muslim and he's playing for Toulon.' Not that I'd made a statement about it; they'd just noticed me at the mosque every week. I actually wasn't ready to go public at that stage; I was still fighting a few demons. But the seeds were planted in my soul, ready for the most beautiful flowers to grow.

One improvement was that I wasn't drinking in my second year. That didn't affect my relationship with Tana or the boys in any way. I knew my path. I was in a really good space and didn't touch alcohol. I would still go out with the boys. I didn't say to them, 'I'm not drinking because I've become a Muslim.' But it was probably pretty obvious, seeing as I was hanging out a lot with Olivier, the other Muslim guy in our team. Tana never said a word to indicate he was aware of the path I was on. I know he respected my work ethic and my constant drive to be a better player, and that was what mattered.

It was tough telling Philippe at the end of my contract in 2010 that I wouldn't be taking up his offer to play for France, even though I could name my price. I was sorry to say goodbye to Tana, but I know he understood. When I left Toulon to head back home to pursue an All Blacks jersey, he took me aside and said, 'Here is my last Test jersey – now go and get yours.'

The lessons I learned from Tana Umaga in those two years have stayed with me. As a coach, Tana always kept it simple. For instance, with defence, I kept looking for the perfect answer. But I was overthinking it. When looking at the opposition's attacking set-up, Tana explained, just step back and ask the guy who is on the inside of you and the guy on the outside of you who they are going to tackle, and then take the one left. Simple, but very effective. It allowed me to be very physical and to play without hesitation. Throughout the rest of my career, I stuck with that approach, simplifying things. It sometimes seemed to me that the higher I went in rugby, the more overcomplicated the coaches would make it. But I've always felt that keeping it simple works best. It ain't a chess game out there. To this day, when I'm helping out coaching youngsters, I really try to implement that mindset: simplicity, simplicity, simplicity. Times three, just in case you missed it!

The other thing Tana really encouraged was my physicality. That's an Islander thing. Don't suppress your natural instincts. Philippe and Jonny Wilkinson gave me the same message.

Giving me his Test jersey says it all about how Tana regarded me. That gesture is still one of my best memories.

* * *

I mentioned briefly above that I dragged my brother Johnny over to France with me. You'll probably have noticed by now how important Johnny's support has always been to me. When we were working together on this book, Alan Duff talked to him about how he felt about supporting me and about his own footy career potential. Johnny knew he was a good player. But he also knew there were heaps of guys in his team just as good. He lacked the will that I had shown from a young age. That's why I'd play in my age group then go and play another game in his age group – the experience of playing older, bigger, meaner guys really helped prepare me for the big league – whereas he and his mates would play a game and then look ahead to where they'd party. They drank and smoked weed. I wasn't blind to their off-field behaviour, and I am not making moral judgements, but I knew that lifestyle wasn't for me, and it never was until I played NRL and discovered the party life.

I saw a lot of fights growing up, between other kids and between adults, and Johnny was one hell of a scrapper. I was the younger brother and could very well have followed in his footsteps, but I vowed to myself I wouldn't be like that. Even as a teenager, I was determined to stay focused on my rigid training routines and keep that dream alive of one day buying Mum a house. Throughout the age groups, I'd always get the boys on the team to do extra training. That kind of enthusiasm is something you're born with. Keeping it up is the hard part.

I've been lucky that, through all the ups and downs, I've had my brother there to support me. First he joined me in Sydney, then in France. When I left Toulon for New Zealand and moved on to Christchurch to play for Canterbury, he came too. And he's joined me in other ways. He watched my conversion to Islam and one day in France asked to come with me to a mosque. He's converted now, too, so we're still on a shared journey and he has my back always. That was such a special moment when my uso asked to come to masjid with me and made his sha'hada (became a Muslim).

That kind of support is so important – and, equally, a lack of support from those around you can have devastating consequences, as I discovered in my early years in Sydney. I had to make some huge changes to my life to get to the good place I found myself in after a couple of years in Toulon. Back in 2007, I was in the opposite space, in what's called the party life but should be called the toxic life. Cocaine, painkillers, prescriptions, women, alcohol. I was dabbling in it all while learning about the media, how it can both build you up and knock you down, and you have no control over which way it'll go. Though, to be fair, we sportspeople can be silly or unwary enough to feed them fuel to set the fire alight.

The reactions of the clubs often increase the damage done to players rather than supporting them. Often, when their players are caught doing something stupid (I am not talking criminal here), the club apologises and dumps the blame on the player, when in many cases we're talking about an unsupported or misguided youth in a bad culture rather than someone who's inherently bad. There are plenty of examples of players getting drunk and doing things that are stupid, yes, but not violent or abusive or harmful to anyone else – and yet it becomes a black mark against their name. I think of my own DUI charge. That was foolish and dangerous. But a player in a tipsy running race or falling asleep in a club or a cab shouldn't be front-page news and doesn't really warrant an apology, does it?

This is not to say that club administrators are uncaring and self-serving, nor that the media are all wrong and bad. But they are part of the world any young sportsperson has to navigate and you make a misstep at your peril. You have all this fame and money that's supposed to be making you feel so cool and on top of the world. People – especially the media – expect you to be a role model. But how can you be if acclaim comes at the age of eighteen or nineteen? Neuroscientists say the brain isn't even fully developed yet at that age. I am not making excuses for violence or assault; that is different. You know that is wrong early. But behaviour that hurts no-one should not be treated as a major crime.

The bad behaviour that is so often pilloried can be more than just youthful stupidity; it can be a sign of deeper problems. Is a 'role model' allowed to feel depressed? Have mad moments of ecstasy followed by dark despair? This is not how the success script is written. I know

I struggled with the attention. When I was eighteen, I'd be out in public and people would want a photo with me, ask me to sign their footy shirts; they'd say nice things to me, call me to the front of the club and restaurant queues. Suddenly I was a public figure – how is a shy boy supposed to cope with that? That's not in the script either, and I had no-one to guide me. So I found my own ways to deal with it. By having a smoke before I went out or a couple of sleeping tablets to relax me, I was trying to take the fear away. I didn't think about the consequences – that it can make you drowsy and lead to you doing stupid stuff, like finding yourself asleep on the floor at some stranger's pad. And that's just small stuff; the consequences can be a whole lot worse. One time, I went on a bender that lasted from Friday night to Monday morning. The only reason I came home is I knew I had a surgery appointment at 11 am. I don't remember anything about the operation except waking up and finding my girlfriend crying next to the bed as the doc really gave it to me, telling me I had so many drugs in my system I could have died.

It is not easy for me to open up like this. But I feel it is important to be honest, and I hope younger people take notice of my mistakes and avoid making the same ones themselves.

At the end of 2007, playing with the Dogs, I had a moment of clarity; I knew I could not continue down this road. I decided I couldn't go on living like this, feeling like I couldn't control my desires or break out of the vicious circle I was stuck in. Depression was just one of the feelings I would carry every morning-after. Yet even as I was deteriorating mentally, my footy form had got better; it had not suffered in any way. We were going into the semi-final against the Eels and I felt full of confidence, determined to make this a good game for me.

In the first five minutes I get involved, make a couple of statement tackles, go looking for the ball, make a break, do a mad offload to our fullback, who sets up Willie Tonga, who runs, trips, pops up a beautiful ball to Matt Utai, who scores in the corner. You see how I'm not the troubled, lost guy on the field?

Two minutes later, the Eels' Nathan Hindmarsh, who everyone had been talking up before the match, decides to run the ball up. Okay, I'm gonna smash him, but he's a smart old hand, and as I swing my arm at him, he ducks his head, right on my forearm. My arm goes dead.

I get up, thinking, *Something is wrong here*, but I keep trying to play . . . No, I can't. I've broken my arm. I tried to come back in the second half, said to the team helpers, 'Just bandage me up, I'm going back out.' My first run with the ball, I couldn't even move my arm. I get tackled, feel something else click, or snap, in my wrist. I get up, walk across the field and know it's bad. The depression hits before I even leave the ground. I'm a man who is defined by his game and it has been taken away from me. I am worthless. I feel empty. There's one way I know of to banish that feeling: I start drinking, kidding myself I am still The Man, even though inside, deep down, I'm feeling a huge sense of loss. I know the serious injury means I'm out – again.

In those days, taking alcohol and drugs was how I dealt with the dark times; it was the only way I knew. I go back to my first major injury in 2005, only my second year in NRL, when I did my knee and was out for the rest of the year. I was living with another injured player, Willie Tonga, and we just partied. Every day of the week except Mondays. Willie never touched drugs, but I did. I touched everything going that was supposed to give bodily pleasure.

Come Monday, it's 6 am and Willie and I were sitting in the car with training due to start in a few hours, asking ourselves what had we done, where had we been? Who were these women in the car with us? At least Willie had his Christian faith, so he'd say a little prayer then off we'd go to training. But because of that psychology of mine, I never felt like I belonged to the team if I was out injured. I have to believe I am contributing in order to feel like I belong. I didn't think about being on full pay during that time. I can't remember feeling guilty about that. I guess it was just my contract. I am sure the club knew I was partying all the time; they just didn't say anything. It seems the clubs only get worried when something goes public and the media get a hold of it.

When Willie and I flatted together, we'd go partying, and yet I remember going past his room and he'd be sitting there reading the Bible. I don't know what it was, but I felt this connection to God when I saw the calming effect his Christianity had on him. That was probably a faint signal trying to awaken my own spirituality. I never once made fun of his religious belief, not even as a joke between mates. It felt too big and important to make light of it.

By the time I headed home from France, though, I had come a long way, in my footy and in my life. Khoder Nasser was a major influence; he really helped me to get my head right. He talked straight to me, did not hold back on criticising my off-field behaviour or pointing out the odd mistake on the field. If I messed up off-field, he'd ask, 'What are you doing, mate? Seriously, Sonny, pull your head in.'

No-one else had ever pulled me up like that. When I was in the company of Khoder and the people he surrounded himself with, I saw it was a healthy way to live: no drugs, no alcohol, no women, yet lots of laughs. He was someone I could bounce ideas off, someone I could talk to about things I didn't share with anyone else. He became a close confidant, with his blunt honesty, sincerity, loyalty and integrity. I feel lucky that when I needed it, he helped to show me a better path. I am grateful I had the courage and the strength in myself to listen to the message from the One God when I most needed it. I realised I needed boundaries and discipline to be a better man and I found that in my faith. Sometimes I wonder where I'd be if I hadn't been supported by the strength of Islam and turned my life around.

CHAPTER 6

You are just a caretaker

I have been talking about myself for too long now, so I'm going to take a break and let my big bro, Johnny, share his thoughts about his little brother – though I reserve the right to dispute any of it!

***

Sonny and I competed with each other back in the day. I'd ask: 'How many tries did you score, Sonny?' 'Two.' 'Well, I scored three.' Or it would be vice-versa. We were a real competitive family, Dad and us four kids.

Sonny was pretty driven from day dot; he had the speed and that little sidestep. Bit of a cheeky little fella, and we could never catch him because he just sidestepped away, kind of like this taunting way of staying just out of your reach. He had style even at a young age.

Knowing him like I do, and seeing him play at the top for nearly twenty years, he never got scared of it that I could see. He loves the big occasions, and the bigger it is, the more he rises to it. I remember him as a kid playing and, honestly, it was like a man against boys. He just stood out as he went through the grades. He even stood out when cadging a game with us older kids, which we didn't mind because he was a hell of a player.

Then he went to first grade and I thought, *Here we go, this is the real big league, his Bulldogs debut.* His first or second touch he makes a big break, sets up a try, scores one himself. His name was all over the papers and on television the next day. A 'new star is born' kind of thing. Yet despite his amazing fame, the rest of the family and I still see the same old Sonny we've always known. Humble, loving, down to earth, great sense of humour and loves to tease or be teased.

He's my little brother, and I had our mother's protective streak as far as he was concerned. At our primary school once, someone came running up to tell me one of the tough boys at the school had given Sonny a hiding. At lunchtime I gave that boy a hiding in return. I still have that protective instinct today. When I've watched or read what some of the media have had to say about him over the years, naturally I'd get mad. Because their comments do *not* match the countless videos I've watched of him over and over. My bro was never a player 'past his best', 'over the hill' or 'chalky'; he was never 'Money Bill'. My brother is a freak of nature like none ever seen before.

Only a handful had it in for him, but that doesn't make it any less hurtful and infuriating. I think they're resentful because he's always done things his way, like the back-and-forth code switches, and has triumphed each time. They don't like his total independence. Some may even hate that with every code switch, he hits the top. Not the middle and never the bottom. The *top*.

One journo said he shouldn't be picked for the Rugby World Cup because in his last Test his form was poor. How could he say that when it just wasn't true? I sometimes wonder if him being a Muslim might be a problem for his Caucasian Kiwi critics. I've watched footy all my life and, listening to the commentators, you'd think you were watching two different games when you hear what they say about him. I'd heard of how 'Super' Sid Going, playing back in the 1960s and 70s, used to say that as a Māori he had to play twice as good to get selected in the All Blacks. Maybe it's the same mindset with Sonny being Muslim: *You better prove yourself to us, boy.*

I know Sonny changing from league to union upset more than a few people, especially when he proved a big star at the new code. Sonny changed both codes forever, with his offloads adopted all over the world.

We're a pretty private family and that includes Sonny. He loves our family environment and never, I mean *never*, boasts about his on-field exploits; doesn't say a word about it unless to laugh at something he did. I've heard people talk about him and I never said I was his brother. Just had a laugh even when they criticised him. I don't want people talking to me just because I'm Sonny Bill's brother. I want them to talk to me for who I am, not someone with a famous brother.

Do I have any regrets not making more of my league career? Not really. In our team of seventeen-year-olds, there were eleven guys just as good as each other. Sonny was way better, and he was two years younger than us. We all had talent, but who of us had Sonny's drive?

I got into trouble as a teenager. Sonny never did. I got a six-month suspension for whacking someone in a game when I was sixteen. I broke the jaw of this big Island boy who wanted a fight with me. I was banned from all contact sports, and once that happened it was the end of league for me and I went down the wrong track. But at least I knew enough to warn Sonny off following my path.

I was in New York playing rugby for about eighteen months, then came home and hurt my neck in a car crash. So, I was a bit down over that when Sonny called to see if I wanted to join him in Toulon. I loved it over there. My older daughter speaks fluent French now.

On my dad, I'll only say he had a tough life that hardened him. To see him now, the alcohol is gone and he's a cool grandad; my kids, Sonny's and our sisters' kids all love him to bits. I'm a bit soft with my kids, more of a friend than a father, and I let them get away with too much. I don't need to hit them; I just raise my voice and that's enough. Like with my teenage daughter, she's at that point where she wants to try things out. I'd rather she felt free to come and say, 'Dad, I've done something wrong' than be too scared to approach me. I want my kids in that frame of mind where they think they can tell their dad anything and it'll be okay. She might get a telling-off, but she'll have a loving, understanding ear.

I remember Sonny from a young age would train with his team then run to catch the end of our training. It could be hosing down, he didn't care, he just wanted to get stuck into more training. Same on Saturday game days: my little bro was so greedy for game time he was prepared to play boys two years older, and at that age there is a difference in strength and maturity. No problem to him; he could hold his own. I think us being half-caste, we weren't fully accepted either by the full Sāmoans or by the whites. So we had to go twice as hard to prove ourselves. That's how I learned to fight. I was the whitest Sāmoan among all my cousins, and they used to tease us. I just went up the road and learned from a boxing trainer how to throw a punch and started whacking them. The teasing stopped.

Sonny had the same attitude, except he did it with hard tackles, shoulder charges. Always the next level up, always dominated. He can play like a Mack Truck or like a Ferrari. Even though he's my brother, I know my sport well enough to recognise greatness, the player who can do it all: sidestep, a weaving run, draw them in, a big arm reaches out and — boom. There's the offload he made uniquely his own, the tackling, turnovers, so many moves seen and unseen that change a game.

He goes from top of the rugby league tree to rugby union in Toulon, back to New Zealand to play for Canterbury and, without playing a single Super Rugby game, goes straight into the All Blacks. Wins a Rugby World Cup in 2011, the following year joins the Chiefs and they win the title. Who's their stand-out player? Him, of course. Shall I go on?

Okay, 2013, back to league for the Sydney Roosters and they win the grand final, and again he was the stand-out player. You need any more convincing? Okay, same year, 2013, he plays rugby league for the Kiwis against England. Man of the Match. Back to rugby 2014, back in the All Blacks, in 2015 he's in the World Cup squad, wins a gold medal with a series of offloads and match-winning moves. Gives his medal to a kid. One commentator said he did it to bring all the attention on himself. This is my shy brother, the bro with so much empathy, and that's what is said about him?

I think everyone knows that sports commentators have got their favourites. Meaning, they can't see anyone else, even if someone is doing amazing things in the same game or off the field. One of the many things I learned is to be fair with people. If you're fair with them, then you can stand your ground knowing you've done the right thing.

* * *

Thanks, bro. I'll take it from here and pick up in France.

In my second year at Toulon, everything had changed. The self-indulgent stuff was all behind me. Clean. Free. Unburdened. That desire to be in the All Blacks was even stronger, and not from the traditional base of dreaming of it since I was a little kid. (You already know what my dream was: to buy Mum a house with fancy wallpaper, which I did, and it is the home she still lives in today.) Until I moved to Toulon, I had never given rugby union a thought. League was my one and only game. To tell the truth, I'd had the attitude that union was a softer game, while league was for real hard men. But I discovered otherwise. Like with every sport I've been involved in, I see it as a challenge first and foremost.

I ended my time with Toulon on a high. We were in the European Cup grand final and I scored and the crowd went crazy. It was such a buzz, and being in a much better state of mind in life generally made it all the more enjoyable. I remember getting the ball about thirty metres out, banging off my left foot, right foot, going straight through and scoring the try. I threw the ball into the crowd for joy. Tana was on the bench, and he was jumping up and down. I ran over and gave him a hug and all the bench boys came and hugged me. Even though we lost that last match against Cardiff, it was the same feeling that I would have for the Chiefs in the 2012 Super

Rugby final. In that game, I'd score the try that would seal the win, and then jump up into the stand with the fans as my way of saying thanks for your loyal support, my way of conveying, *We won this for you.*

That was my last game for Toulon. After that, I headed home to see if I could make the All Blacks. Back in New Zealand, Johnny and I visited Mum and our sisters and spent some time with them, then it was off to Christchurch. My first match there was for a local club, Belfast, where I met Bill Bush, the legendary Māori prop and All Blacks enforcer. He was so welcoming to me. My presence drew a massive crowd for a club match; I think around 4000 people. Stats show I made thirteen offloads, twenty-one carries and scored a try in my fifty-minute appearance. It was nice to be back among ordinary folk, where I feel most comfortable.

I played five National Provisional Championship (NPC) games for Canterbury, then was selected for the All Blacks. That was huge. I might not have been a loudly nationalistic type of guy, but that did not mean I valued the jersey any less. I saw it as a question of playing with the best. The All Blacks are the best sporting team in the history of all team sports. So, you have to represent with mana, play at your highest level, because of the All Blacks' history. If you're playing with the All Blacks, you can say you're among the best in your position in the world.

I knew All Blacks status meant a lot for my family, but for me, it meant I was one of the best. So there was big pressure in that sense, but I took great pride in stepping up to that.

They have this saying in the All Blacks: 'You are just a caretaker. Leave the jersey better than you found it.' That is a really humbling way to play. You are forging a path for those to come and honouring all those in whose footsteps you are following. As I played with no sense of self-preservation, I knew it wasn't hard for me to leave everything out on the field. Even if I started on the bench, when I came on, I gave it my all.

I realise that seeing me go from the NPC to the All Blacks must have been a bit strange for my All Blacks teammates. I came with a massive reputation as the party boy who was all about money, someone who did not honour his contracts, was a code- and club-hopper, that sort of thing. I felt I had to remove that stigma, and the best way to do that was play well.

But I also could have an attitude of, *If I've shown you that I can play rugby at a high level and been vulnerable enough to reach out to you, yet you still put that stigma on me, then my levels of respect for you would evaporate.* I've had that mentality since I was a youngster. Maybe it's just self-protection. What I did know was I had come prepared through rigorous training, and from not touching alcohol or putting any other toxic substance in my body.

I've still got that training mindset. Just this year, I wasn't satisfied with my boxing sparring. I didn't get dusted up, yet that's what my mind told me. Three o'clock the next morning, I'm wide awake thinking about that 'failure'. By four, I was back in the gym training. That day I did three sessions.

I had that mindset going into the All Blacks. I remember that first game, at Twickenham against England, running out there and standing in a huddle and looking up to see Jerome Kaino watching me, smiling and nodding. He's smiling at me, like saying, *You're here, bro. I'm right here with you.* I was getting mad energy from him seeming pleased that I was there, and it was just as mad a vibe for me being there with him.

Sonny was the ultimate professional, from how hard he trained to what he ate. It was a huge privilege to see him operate in that space. For me and the other players, watching him was inspiring.

For me, Sonny single-handedly changed the game from how teams defended against the offload. But also in how players wanted to play the game. It all came from him setting the example, with totally original thinking and execution.

But my fondest memories of Sonny aren't on the pitch, it's how giving he was with his time to anything: family, community and those in need. Being a superstar in demand, he would always be willing to give his time to my kids.

As a brother, I not only admire him for what he's done for sport, but for how inspiring he has been through his Muslim faith and being a genuinely great person/leader/father/husband/brother. The man is a true legend. – Jerome Kaino

Thank you, uso! But it was me who was inspired by my teammates. Look to one side and there's Ma'a Nonu. Over there, Joe Rokocoko, the flying Fijian-born winger. The steady hand of Keven Mealamu. It was such a proud moment because I was remembering how determined I'd been to take up the challenge to make the All Blacks. And suddenly there I was; it was happening for real. On the way to Britain, I'd watched the All Blacks game against the Wallabies in Hong Kong. It was the first time I'd ever seen them play live. The year before, when I was in Toulon, a bunch of us players went to watch them play France in Marseilles. But when we got there, one of the guys had forgotten the tickets! He'd brought a power bill instead of the tickets Tana had got for us. So we stood outside the stadium and listened to the haka, then drove home.

Now, here I was, with not even one Super game behind me, and I was one of them: an All Black. It was a great achievement.

The game went well. I did a few offloads, did my defensive job. Then I hit half a hole and go down real late, look up and there's big Jerome right there to give a mad offload to and he draws an England defender and then passes to Hosea Gear, who scores in the corner. JK runs up and gives me a big hug and I'm so pumped because I belong.

After the game, Ma'a Nonu gave me a tie as a debut player. To think, only two years before I had walked away from rugby league and made the switch to union. Now I was back in Europe, and I'd just had my debut for the All Blacks. It was a special time because I had achieved a goal I had set myself.

I loved the All Blacks' environment, playing with the very best, hearing their thoughts on the game, each of us free to let our voice be heard. Because of my Islamic faith, I am not comfortable supporting alcohol, gambling or bank-based businesses. They are part of my no-go zone when it comes to wearing a sponsor's logo, and the All Blacks totally respected my position.

In the team structure, there are always individuals who stand out for different reasons. Extroverts, funny guys, musical talents, serious dudes, quiet men, loud fellas. I used to love being alone sometimes, just by myself, happy in my own company. But I also enjoyed chilling with the boys and, I have to say, us brown boys naturally gravitate towards each other. It's just how it is with us Islanders and Māori.

* * *

Making the All Blacks' 2011 Rugby World Cup team was another goal achieved and I am really proud of the way I played throughout that whole tournament. I was so happy for my country and my teammates as we achieved something special, beating France 8–7 in the final. I would like to give a special mention to France's captain, Thierry Dusautoir – what a player he was. He almost got them home single-handed. Being awarded the Man of the Match award in a beaten side in a World Cup final was a special feat in itself.

2011 Rugby World Cup Squad

Forwards: Kieran Read, Adam Thomson, Jerome Kaino, Victor Vito, John Afoa, Brad Thorn, Sam Whitelock, Ali Williams, Anthony Boric, Keven Mealamu, Andrew Hore, Corey Flynn, Tony Woodcock, Owen Franks, Ben Franks, Richie McCaw (c.)

Backs: Mils Muliaina, Israel Dagg, Isaia Toeava, Cory Jane, Zac Guildford, Conrad Smith, Ma'a Nonu, Sonny Bill Williams, Richard Kahui, Daniel Carter, Colin Slade, Jimmy Cowan, Piri Weepu, Andy Ellis

Fast-forward four years and I was to achieve another goal, making the All Blacks 2015 Rugby World Cup team. Every time I was given an opportunity, I played exceptionally well. Among my All Blacks teammates, I was thriving on the biggest stage.

2015 Rugby World Cup Squad

Forwards: Kieran Read, Sam Cane, Victor Vito, Jerome Kaino, Liam Messam, Brodie Retallick, Sam Whitelock, Luke Romano, Ben Franks, Owen Franks, Charlie Faumuina, Wyatt Crockett, Joe Moody, Dane Coles, Keven Mealamu, Codie Taylor, Tony Woodcock, Richie McCaw (c.)

Backs: Ben Smith, Julian Savea, Nehe Milner-Skudder, Waisake Naholo, Ma'a Nonu, Conrad Smith, Malakai Fekitoa, Sonny Bill Williams, Daniel Carter, Beauden Barrett, Colin Slade, Aaron Smith, TJ Perenara, Tawera Kerr-Barlow

To beat the Wallabies 34–17 in the final was the first time in World Cup history a team had won back-to-back and retained the Webb Ellis Cup. I'll never forget that game.

Half-time comes and Steve says, 'You ready?'

'Yeah, sure I'm ready.'

I was more than ready – I was pumped! I'm supposed to run out with the team, but I go out early and then the boys come out. 'Bro, you pretty much missed the team talk!' To me, the time for talking was long over. It was time for action.

My second touch was an inside offload to Ma'a for a try. It put us in a commanding lead and, to be honest,

I just wanted to contribute. *Give me the ball, give me the ball*, I remember thinking. Nugget (Aaron Smith) must have been sick of hearing my voice. Allah blessed me to be involved in such a special team. In my opinion, that side will go down as one of the greatest rugby teams in history.

I was rooming with Ma'a for the final week on that tour and we got hold of the trophy and slept with it in our room. We changed into our lavalavas and just floated on a cloud. Ma'a was one of the cleanest guys you could ever meet; he would have everything spick-and-span, and nice scents everywhere. So there's us two Sāmoans in traditional lavalavas, sitting in a room that smelt like a flower garden. And there's the Webb Ellis Cup sitting there gleaming – beaming, it felt like – at us! *We've done it again, bro!* Although there was always a competitiveness between us, I never felt it got in the way of our friendship. I consider Ma'a a close friend for life and I wish we could have partnered up more. I feel like we would have been an unstoppable combination.

* * *

Growing up in a household with little money gave Sonny a special affinity with those less fortunate. That's why he advocates for refugees; he really connects with people whom life has not treated kindly. Part of this concern for others can be seen in the respect he shows his opponents. After the All Blacks beat the Springboks in the 2015 semi-final, Sonny's opposite, Jesse Kriel, was sitting under the goalposts completely dejected. They'd come to that game convinced they'd beat the All Blacks and it had all come crashing down. At that low point, he felt a hand on his shoulder and then Sonny was crouching down beside him, telling him he'd get over this. Sonny embraced his enemy of only minutes before, helped him up. Kriel later said Sonny had every right to be over with his teammates celebrating their victory, yet instead he had stopped to console him, embracing him. That just shows the type of player Sonny is, the calibre of the man. – Khoder Nasser

Sport can bring out the best in people. It can forge bonds and create an understanding, and I have learned a lot from my teammates and from my opponents. I do respect my opponents, and the better they are, the more I respect them. I don't think openly showing that respect is anything to be ashamed of. If anything, it's the opposite. It's part of our Polynesian/Māori culture. Show respect. Though maybe not on the field! My brother Israel Dagg has something to say about that.

Sonny and I were similar in being family oriented. Growing up in big households with all our brothers and sisters meant we loved to have company around us. Me being Māori and him Sāmoan in a predominantly white Canterbury environment definitely drew us closer.

In Cape Town in 2011, playing for the Crusaders against the Stormers, we had a hell of a win. But it came at a cost: I tore the quad of my hip that turned into five months out of action. But typical Daggy, I thought I might as well hit the town and drink myself stupid all night.

A team meeting was called. It turns out I'd been spotted in the lobby, kicking up chaos, and had given us all away. We go into the meeting room and the coaches reveal what they know. I was under the pump, everyone coming at me, left, right and centre. The only thing is, I hadn't been the only one out that night. But I took it on the chin and didn't say a word.

I've got quite emotional by this time. Next minute, Sonny comes and stands alongside me. 'I was out, too,' he told the coach. He stood up and had my back. He didn't have to. I made the dumb decision to be an idiot in the lobby and ruin it for everyone. But Sonny stood up for a brother. No-one else did.

I realised then this guy is a genuine brother, to take some of my heat. Like when I missed selection for the 2015 Rugby World Cup, he came around and sat with me for ages, telling me stuff like, 'This game does not define you.'

What rugby player says that kind of thing? He was right there as a brother, and you never forget times like that. People only get the media version of Sonny. Not the caring and genuine man I know. In fact, the most caring man I've ever met.

Back home in Christchurch, I'm on crutches and Sonny turns up. 'Come on, let's go for a ride.' He'll never forget his friends and family. Always asks after someone's family. A lot of media people portray him as something he is so far from being, you'd think they invented a story and just run with it. They have no idea who the real Sonny is.

The Sonny I know treats everybody the same. Big rugby stars. The cleaner. Ordinary people. He doesn't care. You — all of us — are the same in his eyes.

Playing with him, every time he got the ball, I knew to hang off his shoulder, knowing I'd get the offload. Against Tonga in the Rugby World Cup, I scored from one of his offloads. So many games he set me up for tries.

Playing *against* him when he moved to the Chiefs was another story. Daunting to see the big fella ready to put a monster hit on you.

Wherever he goes he takes people with him; he doesn't say much but we players see his micro-skills, how he is 100 per cent a team man. No secret to his success. He trains like no-one else I've ever seen. Take a look at his 900 abs.

Sonny is a big part of my life. I want people to know the real Sonny. Love you, my brother. — Israel Dagg

Love you too, my uso. Words like this and those connections with my teammates mean a lot, but just like with the 2012 Super Rugby semi-final against Izzy's

Crusaders . . . respect? That can wait until after the game! I tried to smash Israel every chance I got. He is one of the finest players New Zealand has produced, and we're mates from Canterbury and Crusaders and All Blacks days. Izzy can pull a laugh out of anything. But on the field? In the heat of battle, there was no time for laughs – that was always my mindset when I played.

That reminds me of something that happened in my first rugby league season in Australia in 2003. I was actually quite shocked when I got there to find there was such a thing as Aussie Islanders (how naive I was). And I was even more shocked to find they didn't seem like us Kiwi Islanders. We showed respect by running hard or smashing each other, but it only went so far, and afterwards, at least in my experience, it was all about love between us Islander players. But on this occasion in 2003, this brother wanted to fight and bring the niggle.

It was different to my norm, but I thought, *Okay, if they're the rules over here, I will have to adapt.* I get tackled by him and I guess he wants to show who is boss, he keeps pushing my head down. I got up and pushed him. So then he tested me with fists up. I have a mad thing about wanting to take down bullies. He was psycho; his eyes were bulging and he'd clearly lost it, but I wasn't going to back down. I had a fleeting thought that maybe I'd bitten off more than I could chew, but that thought never lasts long, not out there in the arena. *Get in first*, I told myself. Which I did, with some good accurate shots. His face was bleeding and his rage had got worse. He wanted to keep fighting. But the ref sent us both off.

I was walking off, thinking it was over now. I didn't want to fight anymore; I was leaving it on the field. Then I heard voices screaming, 'Sonny! Turn around, he's coming!'

I turned and saw this enraged monster coming at me as he stripped off his jersey to reveal a body packed with muscle. Man.

He runs up and I catch him with a perfectly timed left hook – this is before I ever thought of being a boxer. Down he goes and everyone's going mad. The guy's bench jumps up and joins in. One king-hits me, I chase him and reply with a left hook. Johnny was in the melee somewhere, our bench has joined in, spectator fans from both sides are in. Unbelievable.

There was an aftermath long after that and Johnny was not so lucky. He was in this bar one time and these guys were giving him lip because they knew he's my brother. He followed one to the toilet and dropped him. But then my crazy bro comes back to the bar and carries on drinking for an hour or so. When he walked outside there were five guys waiting for him. But at least it was fists, not guns and knives like nowadays.

But that's not how we do it where I come from. For us, Islanders and Māoris playing against each other, especially at the highest levels, is a special buzz. Many of us come from the exact same background. Playing against each other is special because we know it's going to be hard, but it's only our way of showing respect to one another. If we play Sāmoa or Tonga, our reputation doesn't mean a thing. I've played some of my toughest games against those teams.

And my teammates and their respect mean the world to me. Over the years, I have forged friendships that will last for life. I won't attempt to name them all, out of fear of missing someone out, but Sammy Whitelock was one. Although I struggled socially down south, he had a way of making me feel at home. A family man who will definitely go down as one of the great, if not the greatest, locks to have played the game (even if I will always be stronger than him in the gym).

2010 was my first year with the Canterbury squad. I knew who Sonny Bill was and had heard of his Bulldogs and Kiwis credentials and his switch to rugby in France. He came up and introduced himself and we hit it off from there. I have a memory of a Ranfurly Shield match and us up 20–10 but we could not get out of our own half. Sonny did that, single-handedly.

I soon learned he was something special – we all did. He had the ability to change a game. In any team sport there are just a handful of people with that ability, with that X-factor. He had the skill to break a game open.

Both of us were keen to achieve our long-term goals. We started our first Test match together. We played for Canterbury, the Crusaders and the All Blacks together and became close. In our sport, we're competitive. Yet Sonny's training still stood out and a lot of players followed his example.

He understood what he had to do off the field; he was approachable and loved to discuss everything about the game. Yet he was so modest and humble. Just not in the gym! Where he compared himself to everyone in weights and aerobics, whatever. And when he got the better of someone he joked and teased and took the mickey. Sonny Bill Williams is a very special man, both as a player and a person. – Sam Whitelock

Another close brother, Liam Messam, I'm sure won't mind me saying that one of the reasons we connected was I could see through his front, see the frailties behind the tough facade. He was our leader in the 2012 Chiefs, the man we all looked up to, who led by example. And he put aside his personal issues for his team brothers. We went from being a bunch of misfits to competition champions in one season. Recently, Hunga spoke publicly about the mental struggles he faced, how he was trying to be that quintessential Māori warrior while inside he was in great pain. If someone like Hunga can be honest about his struggles, then I am not ashamed of admitting my own.

* * *

I would go on to play with the All Blacks until 2019. That last tour was a whirlwind and I am so grateful for it all.

When I look back at who has influenced me and who helped me become who I am, I always think of Johnny. If I didn't have my brother's support, I definitely would not be where I am today.

He was no angel, but he is a good man, especially with his kids. Okay, if they make him mad he'll call me, and though we don't talk about the actual situation, we're on the phone kind of exchanging feelings by mental telepathy. He asks for advice without asking for advice, if you get my drift.

I've heard him say to his son, 'Don't worry about that missed tackle. You did ten massive hits today. Son, as long as you're happy, as long as you understand who gave you your skills – it wasn't me. It was Allah. Be happy when you play no matter what.'

You might be thinking, what has this got to do with rugby? Well, I think it's who a person is behind the player image that is most important. If I wrote this book and did not acknowledge those who helped lift me up, then forget my reputation as a player. That would make me a selfish, egotistical man all about me, myself and I, and not worthy of anyone's respect.

CHAPTER 7

A memory buried in a shallow grave

When I was in France, I'd had the feeling that I could compete against the very best and that's when I started to believe in myself as a rugby player and yearn for more competition. Which led me to New Zealand, of course. Then to make the All Blacks and play well obviously felt good. But inside I was still carrying that same old desire to keep improving.

In those years, I was living a really clean life, studying the game, learning, but still retaining my Islander physicality and flair, and it was all starting to come together. We had a weighted ball at home in Christchurch. Johnny was living with me and every night we would do fifty catch and passes each side just to give me confidence throwing a long ball. But I got an injury called osteitis pubis, which caused pain low in the stomach and groin, from over-training.

So what do I do? Train, and then go home and train some more. My dedication levels were extremely high; I'd do extra video sessions, soaking up everything. And my faithful bro, Johnny, he was there with me all the way.

***

On 4 September 2010, Johnny and I were at home in our unit in Christchurch – it was the day after I'd played my first game for Canterbury. At about 4.30 am, I was woken by this terrible roar. I hit the light and saw the whole room was rocking from side to side.

My door swung open and there's my brother standing there in his undies; I remember watching his stomach going from side to side with the room. We were both in shock. Being woken abruptly in the middle of the night to find the world shaking and shuddering is a pretty full-on experience. We were upstairs and my brain, realising an earthquake had struck, was assessing if it was safer up here or out on the street – if we could even walk downstairs.

When it kept going, we decided the street was a safer place to be and made our way outside (once Johnny found some pants!). It was scary and there was a lot of damage to the building. We learned later it was a 7.1 magnitude earthquake and that two people were injured and one person died from a heart attack. Later, there were aftershocks, but things got back to normal pretty fast for me. And then, five months later, it happened again – but worse.

On 22 February 2011, at 12.51 pm, I was doing recovery in the pool with teammate Tu Umaga-Marshall in central Christchurch, just down from the apartment hotel I was staying in because my unit had been rendered uninhabitable by the September 2010 earthquake. Suddenly, the whole place started going off. I mean, *off!*

Our hot pool was going from side to side, and someone shouted at us to stay in the pool. Don't ask me why. The shaking was so violent I swear our brains were sloshing madly in our skulls. Who can think in a situation like that? One guy jumped out of the pool and tried to run, but he was staggering like he was on drugs or something.

The big pool was full of aqua-joggers and the water had turned to waves. It was overlooked by big glass windows, and I was waiting for them to shatter and come down onto the heads of the aqua-joggers. Man, it was more than surreal. You couldn't make a movie of it. As soon as it stopped, I knew I was in a state of shock, as was everyone else. To this day I can still feel how it affected me. It's something you can't explain unless you've been in a major earthquake. It's like a memory buried in a shallow grave.

Tu jumped out and ran to his phone because his kids were at the movies at the other end of town. He was trying to call his wife, but he couldn't get through. We didn't know then that the phone towers were either down or so badly damaged they weren't working.

We got changed and ran outside to witness destruction everywhere. Tu was already worried sick for his kids' safety and in an even worse state when we saw the devastation. We were just walking around in a state of total shock. On the street, a whole row of verandahs had come crashing down and we could see a leg sticking out of a pile of rubble, a hand. It was just awful. And my mate was just beside himself with worry for his family. Eventually, we got the good news that they were unharmed.

It was as if the whole world had been turned upside down then thrown from a great height. It was pure mayhem. We saw what looked like a tablecloth laid over someone who was obviously dead. I heard crying, screaming, groaning; it was like a scene out of some horrific nightmare.

About twenty people were gathered around a truck, trying to listen to the radio. The ground had turned to liquid in some places. Homes, schools, shops and office buildings were destroyed and roads, bridges, power and phone lines badly damaged. I could go on a lot more about what I saw, but the event has been covered enough in the media, by writers and historians, and I find the horror hard to describe.

At first, I was really worried because my sister Niall was in town. But because all the phones were down, I couldn't reach her. That kind of sick anxiety is something you don't ever want to feel. Some people had that same feeling, but it didn't come right for them. They never got to see their friends and family again. It turned out Niall and Johnny and everyone I knew was okay, but we would soon learn that 185 people had died and nearly 200 were seriously injured. So many people were left homeless, businesses had been destroyed. I know we all felt so helpless and the fear of another quake was very real.

I wanted to help in some way, and not long after an idea occurred to me: I could hold a boxing match to raise money to help with the recovery. Though it took a while to organise, eventually we made it happen. It was held in West Auckland on 5 June 2011, on a weekend when Canterbury had a bye. I fought Tongan heavyweight Alipate Liava'a. I won that fight after six rounds, but more importantly I was able to personally donate $100,000 to the Christchurch Earthquake Appeal.

Looking back on it, I feel proud to have contributed. It's a way of sharing pain others have gone through and for us lucky, unscathed people to be grateful. After the earthquake, our rugby ground – the famous Lancaster Park – was no longer usable, and having to play games away from home meant seeing less of my mum. She was terrified to fly but now she had something else to fear. Many people, including Mum, were scared of another earthquake. And with our schedule completely changed, there just wasn't the time between games and training to get to her place. I did manage to see her briefly, though, which I think Mum appreciated!

Funny, when John Arthur and Sonny Bill got back from France, I thought at least my children were closer and safe. Then that massive earthquake happens.

I had to leave work that day because I couldn't stop crying with worry; three of my four kids were in Christchurch. I was so upset – terrified, actually – and I'd had no contact from them. Eventually we spoke on the phone and Niall said she was training on a footy field when the ground just started rolling like a green sea.

John Arthur and Sonny Bill were staying in a hotel and they said it was like a war zone, with fires in the building and the staircase cracked. They ran around making sure people got out. When John Arthur called me on video, I said, 'Is that flames behind you?' He said, 'That's the next-door building on fire.' I so wanted my kids out of there.

Not long after, Sonny Bill was contracted to appear in an ad. Some bigwig in the ad company sent a helicopter to get him from Christchurch.

That day, I get a phone call from Sonny Bill.

'Where are you, Mum?'

'I'm sitting at Nan's having a chat.'

'Go outside,' Sonny Bill says.

So out we go.

'Look up, Mum.'

I looked up and saw a helicopter hovering quite low.

'Can you see me waving?'

He must have asked the pilot to open the door and tip the chopper towards us so we could see him – waving!

'Oh my god! It's Sonny Bill!'

It was such an unexpected bit of humour after the terrible things that happened in the earthquake. He circled a couple of times, waving, then he was off.

I told my friends, and they didn't believe me. Sonny Bill's always been a character, that boy. Has that prankster, joker thing. That's what his family know him best for. – Lee Williams

As far as rugby went, playing with the Crusaders in 2011 made for another great year, though obviously we were all affected by the earthquake. The city was full of broken streets, with thousands of houses destroyed or red-zoned as too dangerous to enter. There's no question we had the Crusader fans in mind every time we ran out onto a field. Playing-wise, it felt I could hardly put a foot wrong. Even when we were up against the tougher South African sides on their home soil – the Stormers, the Cheetahs, the Sharks – me and my Crusader teammates were in the zone, and I was doing crazy offloads, having an absolute ball.

Something else was crazy whenever I played in South Africa. The local fans cheered more for me than their own players. It was embarrassing, actually, and I remember running on with the team for the first time, and Kieran Read looking at me puzzled and smiling. *Am I hearing what I think I am? Is that my name they are chanting?* I guess it was because of the offloads and my particular style of playing; South African players love physicality. And I loved South Africa and its people right back. I even vowed to marry a South African one day – which did actually happen! Cape Town will always hold a special place in my heart because of the hospitality and kindness the locals showed me.

Towards the end of the season, and with the World Cup to come, we eventually succumbed to the fatigue that came from all the long-distance travel to South Africa and Australia, and we lost the final to the Queensland Reds, who had my good mate Quade Cooper playing for them. But it was still a massive year.

I really saw the power of sport during that time, how people depend on their home side to go out and perform for them. With virtually every person in Christchurch affected to some degree by the February earthquake, the city was going through a lot of hardship. The massive clean-up and the start of a long, slow rebuild took its toll, so I think rugby was more important than ever. The people of Christchurch looked forward to us Crusaders playing every week. I've been told many times that we lifted their spirits, especially if we won – and even more so if it was a nail-biting win. Sports fans love the drama, too.

In the days after the quake, I ended up moving into a mate's house because our hotel was deemed unsafe. Johnny and I needed some clothes and it wasn't as if we could go to a menswear store and buy some. The entire city centre was off-limits and suburban shopping malls had been damaged. Niall had been staying with us with her husband, and so together we went into the city to try to get back into our room and retrieve some of our things.

At the time, there was a lot of looting going on. It is a despicable act at any time, but particularly when people's lives have been so devastated. We got to our hotel, and Johnny and I each went to our own apartments. We snuck in and I remember the stairwell and the stairs were all cracked and broken, so that one stair is here while another was over there. Crazy sight. I got into my apartment and gathered up my clothes while my sis kept watch outside.

I heard something and looked out the window and my sister was calling up to me. Cops. Damn. We went down and showed the cops our ID, so they knew we weren't looters, and they recognised me. But they did say they assumed we were up to no good until we explained who we were. It was a weird time.

The only thing that was normal was playing rugby. Although we fell one game short, with everything going on in Christchurch off the field, it was amazing the feats we were achieving on it. Me and the fearsome uso Robbie Fruean were making a lot of noise as a fierce midfield partnership, and a lot of people in the media and the public were calling for higher honours for Robbie. Unknown to many, Robbie had a heart problem from rheumatic fever, something a lot of Islanders have due to poor healthcare growing up. It is just another struggle my community has to face. Despite this, Robbie still managed to carve out a successful career and it is rugby's loss that his heart condition meant he was not able to reach his full fitness potential and play at the highest level. The uso would have looked great in black!

Still, there were games when the old mind starts playing up, letting negative thoughts start dancing around. No-one had any idea of my internal struggles, because I had worked out ways to overcome them by being really physical in a tackle, leading with my shoulder but making it legal by having my arms outstretched, or running hard and often breaking through one or even several defenders. That's how I deal with negativity: try to knock it over!

Like I've said, I approach my sport with a simplistic mindset. Follow a mistake with a positive. A positive with another positive. Reset. Reset. Reset, even when you're stuffed. *Work ethic, Sonny. Work ethic.* And generally, when I kept at it like that, I knew I would play well. If I made a less-than-ferocious tackle, I'd come down hard on myself. *You can do better than that, bro!* None of this two-minded tackle or two-minded carry. Make your mind up and go full-on. All game and every game.

I hope youngsters reading this, or having it read aloud to them, heed what I'm saying. Train better than hard and never let up. Keep it simple and play like every game is your last. You might not get acknowledgement from outsiders straightaway but, more importantly, your teammates will see your efforts. Eventually, you will see the fruits of your labour, maybe not through natural ability but through hard work, discipline and a positive attitude.

CHAPTER 8

Pushing the boundaries

So, what about this boxing caper?

Even though I have an exceptional love of playing sport, never in my wildest dreams did I envisage myself a boxer. It came from necessity, to get myself out of debt. Remember, Anthony Mundine and some other close brothers had helped me get myself out of a hole by putting up a million dollars to buy out my contract with the Bulldogs, and I was determined to pay them back as soon as I could.

I was in a bad way at the time: I had walked out on the Bulldogs, and both the club and the NRL were chasing me. I'd gone from having the highest reputation as a player in Australia to being the most hated. I was injured again, and I was a million dollars in debt with no idea how to make that right. They were dark times and desperate times. It was a deep hole and I didn't know how to pull myself out of it. I was doubting myself. Had I made the right decision, leaving the Doggies? Yes – I knew that was one thing I'd done right. If I hadn't walked away, who knows where I would have ended up. I had to go to save myself from myself. If I hadn't found the courage to confront my demons and insecurities, I don't know where I would have ended up, but I know that it wouldn't have been a good place. I thank God that Islam gave me the strength to confront myself. There are a lot of people who never manage to do that and they, and all those around them, suffer.

No-one can change your ways to get yourself out of danger but yourself. It's like smoking or any other addiction: only you can change it. After a year in Toulon learning a new footy code, I was stronger, more focused and looking to secure my financial future, so I was back in Australia learning yet another new sport that might help me do that: boxing.

I spent six weeks in a camp in Brisbane, training, and it turned out to be a really special time in my life. When I came over from France, I was still fighting my demons to some degree; trying to find out who I really was and who I wanted to be. But after six weeks in Brisbane, training, praying and keeping company with Khoder and other knowledgeable Muslim brothers, I could feel the change happening.

One of the Islamic teachings is that to be content with what you have, you have to be in the moment and understand that whatever comes along is a blessing. Even adversity gives us something, teaching us what to be grateful for. Being content with what I have is a life lesson I was finally learning and I was more at peace with myself.

Being in good company and giving my time to charity events made me feel particularly happy, as if one of my yearnings, secret even from myself, had been revealed. I wanted to give back; it just felt so natural and it fitted my empathetic nature. When you're in a good environment with the brothers and all the talk is not about you, the self-centred individual, things become clearer. You can focus on more important things, like gratitude to Allah, understanding moral principles, appreciating nature's beauty.

Allah was constantly on my mind and I was starting to realise that that was why I loved this environment. That's what made it all so special, not the boxing. But the boxing was good too! The first of the seven fights I participated in between 2009 and 2015 knocked a significant sum off my debt. It was 27 May 2009 and I was up against Gary Gurr; he wasn't a boxer, just a bar brawler out for a payday, like me. Jumping in the ring, I was a bit nervous, but as soon as the fight started, my old footy personality kicked in. I was out to dominate. *It's either you or me.* He didn't last long.

When I went back to Toulon, I took with me a stronger commitment to Islam. Moise picked me up from the airport and started to talk about going out to meet girls and I told him I was leaving that life behind. I knew that I wanted to live more for my Creator, wanted to be a better man and a better Muslim. We talked and sounded each other out about our troubles and from then on we both walked that path.

Well, that second year in France turned out to be amazing in terms of growth as a rugby player and, more importantly, growth as a person. It was all thanks to the Islamic faith that I had found my true self. And I'd enjoyed the preparation for that fight with Gurr so much I started to think more about boxing as a sporting challenge.

My second fight took place when I returned to New Zealand in 2010 with the goal of making the All Blacks. I didn't have much prep for that bout, but the guy I was up against couldn't really fight. He lasted two minutes and thirty seconds. Yes, it was a rubbish fight, but at that time, it was more about decreasing my debt than boxing.

In 2011, I had two more fights. The first was back in Australia, against Scott Lewis, who'd knocked out Carl Webb. Webb was a former Australian Golden gloves champ and rugby league enforcer turned boxer who was very good at both sports – till Lewis surprised everyone and knocked him out. Webb got fatigued, which in any sport invites danger, but in boxing the consequences are lights out. It's a cruel sport. For me, it was the same old story in the ring. I went from really nervous and uncertain to achieving something special purely from hard work and determination. I wasn't a boxer – far from it – but that didn't stop me from getting in there and having a go.

For my first four fights, I'd been my own trainer. I didn't know any technique, didn't know anything. I just relied on my athlete's instincts to move around and throw jabs. That can only take you so far, as I found out against Lewis. That fight went the whole six rounds and I won on points but I realised if I wanted to step up and fight better opponents, my approach would have to change.

In Australia, I reached out to Anthony's dad, Tony Mundine. Tony was a former British Commonwealth middleweight champion who everyone thought might go all the way to world champion. But then he went up against undisputed world champion Carlos Monzón of Argentina, and he got beaten. Interestingly, Monzón's life ended in tragedy: he was sentenced to eleven years in prison for killing his partner and then was killed in a car crash while on weekend furlough leave. Life lessons like that remind us all that triumph can go hand in hand with disaster.

The fifth fight was the one I held to raise money for the Christchurch Earthquake Appeal, and it gave me the same feeling I'd had when involved in charity events back in Brisbane.

My next chance to box came after the 2011 Rugby World Cup win: a win the country had waited twenty-four years for. We played in front of 60,000 people at home – it was awesome to be part of rugby union history and an unforgettable climax to a really good year. I'd been a part of the Canterbury ITM-winning team, played a part in the Crusader Super Rugby grand final. Now I was a World Cup winner with the All Blacks. I definitely surpassed all my own personal expectations in that first year back home in New Zealand. As a rookie rugby player in the fiercest, most competitive rugby environment in the world, I was holding my own and then some. What a year!

Then, in February 2012, I had a chance to win the New Zealand boxing heavyweight title. I used my training for this fight as a way of getting fit for my first season with the Chiefs in the Super Rugby competition. I'm thinking how cool it would be to look back at my sporting career and have New Zealand heavyweight boxing champion listed among my accomplishments. Of course, making my family proud was another goal for me, because my grandad had fought for the New Zealand cruiserweight title and lost.

I was originally slated to go up against Richard Tutaki, but he ran into some troubles, so US-born, New Zealand-based Clarence Tillman III stood up instead. We asked Tillman why he wanted to fight me; he would have seen my last fights and thought, *Who is this mug? He can't fight, this guy's a joke – a dual-code rugby player right out of his league.* He disrespected me from the start. I can understand where he was coming from, thinking I'd had only four fights against easybeats, none of them real boxers. He was probably saying to himself: *Guy can't even throw a proper punch.* And he was right: I didn't really know how to throw a punch. But Allah has blessed me to be a fast learner when it comes to sport. I had my first actual professional boxing camp and I was sparring with good boxers and holding my own. I improved so much over those twelve weeks. Yes, I had Mount Everest to climb because of my inexperience, but I was feeling better about myself every day. Training is my forte and, man, did I train for this fight.

By the eighth week, I had sparred eleven to twelve rounds with four different boxers, one of them former world champion and my good mate Anthony Mundine. I held my own against all of them. I had the mindset, and it was about dedication, just waking up every day and getting into my regime without let-up. On the pads with Tony, I felt comfortable for the first time, like I belonged there; slip, catch, feint.

After a gruelling eight weeks in Sydney, I had four more weeks in Hamilton. I was really, really fit, though still had a bit to learn technique-wise. My main sparring partner in New Zealand was young Joseph Parker. He hadn't turned professional yet, but the quality was there. You learn so much from sparring, especially with someone like Parker. I had some good sessions with him, copped some good punches and gave a few of my own back. Sparring is the next best thing to the actual fight. Watching back the videos of my sparring with Joseph, a future heavyweight champ, even I was surprised by how much progress I'd made. I guess being Pop's grandson meant fighting was always in my genes.

My fight with Tillman started before the first bell was even rung, with my opponent shoving then punching me at the weigh-in – a punch I felt. Walking in for our weigh-in and press conference, you could feel the atmosphere; it was almost like Tillman hated me, and for no good reason other than contempt, I guess, for my daring to hop into the ring with him, an African American guy from New Orleans. Boxing is a gladiator sport and it attracts all types.

As soon as we rocked in, Tillman locked eyes with me. Yet I was looking at him thinking he wasn't so huge after all. He started the trash talk, like he was disgusted at being in the same ring as me. I'm feeling confident because of all the work I've done. I'd fought good fighters and held my own. So, I had nothing to be scared about. We go face to face and he really starts mouthing off. And I transform into the man I am on the footy field: I stand my ground.

I'm giving some lip back, then he shoved me and king-hit me with a hook. But even though I was a little rattled, I was that fit that I thought he had just pushed me. My boys went off. My brother tried to get to Tillman, Liam Messam piled in, Choc, old Tony, they were all trying to get a shot in. Because you don't do what Tillman did.

The media narrative was that it was just another Sonny Bill circus. Watching the video, I saw he really hooked me a beauty. I'm a little bit rocked by this, naturally, because I know the real-deal punches are coming soon. I have to admit, I later went to my room and lay down thinking about how hard that guy punched. Lay there looking at the ceiling thinking, *If he rocked me with that punch, what's going to happen in the fight?*

The next day was fight day. Tana Umaga came to my house before the fight, and I remember the look on his face, like he was really worried for me. Gave me a kiss on the head and said, 'Good luck, Uso.' From that look, I realised everyone must have thought I was going to get smashed.

So, I rock up to the stadium and I'm pretty nervous. In the ring, Tillman's walking towards me, trying to stare me down. Immediately, my old self steps up. That white

Sāmoan kid the big Islanders tried to bully and smash, to step over. It was just like that, having that moment to think, *You think you're going to put it on me? All right, let's see what you've got.*

The first-round bell goes and I'm moving, trying to get a feel for it, and I feel like I'm faster than him. I throw once at the body, then he comes in and tries to throw, but they're wild punches and I evade them easily. I throw a hook that just misses him.

I step back and then I hear Choc: 'Check hook, Sonny! Check hook!' His favourite move, where he pretends to throw a jab and then throws a hook. You have those little moments in the ring where you can hear the voice of someone you know. I threw a hard jab, another to the body, before I went into that pretend jab then threw the hook. Bam! Right on the button.

Tillman stumbled around and I went into jungle mode, like I was having a fight at school. No technique, I just started swinging. Next thing, the ref, Lance Revill, stops the fight. I've won! I'm the New Zealand national heavyweight champion! To this day, it was one of the best feelings of any sporting event in my life – I think because of where I came from, with no boxing experience, the stuff I'd been through. And here I am, the official heavyweight boxing champion of New Zealand. Yeah, it was some buzz.

My next biggie, my sixth fight, was a year later, in February 2013, against South African heavyweight Francois Botha. He'd fought heavyweight legends Evander Holyfield, Mike Tyson, Lennox Lewis, and the tough-as-teak Shannon Briggs. Sure, Botha was in his forties when we fought, but he came with forty-eight wins, eight losses, three draws.

I was playing rugby in Japan, doing boxing training as well. I did my pec in a game, tore it. I was out for ten weeks and I thought we'd have to call the fight off. Our date was already set but I needed an operation. I talked about it with Khoder and I decided, *Yeah, this is an old guy, I only need three weeks' training.* But in the back of my mind I was thinking about the greats he'd fought. Still, I told myself I'd be able to move and dance and tire the old guy out. I flew a physio over from Australia to work on my pec day and night, and then we only had two and a half weeks before the fight. Sure, I had the injury, but I was in pretty good condition otherwise and thought I'd just dance for the ten rounds.

Fight night comes around before you know it. I'm looking across at my opponent, who has fought all these top names; okay, he didn't beat any, but he was no pushover either.

The first round went well. The second, even better; I was finding my target. But when I sat down at the end of round two, I felt buggered. And there was Botha, ignoring his stool, standing up. I knew then it was gonna be a long night. He got some good shots in and in the last minute of the ninth he landed a punch that shook me. I don't remember much about the details because of the concussion I carried after but the controversy around the length of the fight is hard to forget. But that fight was always going to be ten rounds, though others started saying it was cut short. It is easy to watch the replay on YouTube. In my corner at the end of the second round, I either spat or took out my mouthguard. My corner was talking, but I wasn't listening. I looked at my brother, Johnny, and he was looking at me with this real scared expression. His face was saying to me, *I know you're gassed. Your bro knows you better than anyone.* And I looked at him and did a silent, *Yeah.*

Yet I went out and fought Botha, and even though I remember feeling gassed, it doesn't look like that in the replay. All I know is, fitness and prep are everything, and my two and a half weeks of prep was not enough. It was my core fitness that got me there.

In those last four minutes, starting when Botha clipped me in the ninth with a minute to go, inner nature, animal instincts, took over. I just had to hang on, survive the onslaught. I don't remember those two little flurries in the last. I was in the survival zone.

Training with Tony Mundine, he doesn't really do the technical; his objective is to work on fitness first, then the best teacher: sparring. In preparing for Botha, I did no sparring, so it was a mad learning experience both for myself – to do sparring for real – and learning the sport. It ain't play. It's coming up against a full-grown hulky man of vast experience who's intent on knocking you out. Like any heavyweight, when he connects, you feel it down to your toes. Other than a gunfight, this is the ultimate arena.

It was a learning experience for Khoder, too, in seeing that fitness allowed me to box those ten rounds, moving around, firing off shots. Learning that few sports are as deadly serious, carrying potentially terrible consequences if you drop your guard, lose concentration for a second or two. With a guy like this, a mistake means lights out.

It was a close call for me because Botha took me to a place of fatigue I had never experienced before. In hindsight, as a novice fighting ten rounds with only three weeks' prep, I am proud I was able to hang on and win that match-up. From a technical point of view, Botha covered my jab by coming over it. I didn't really know what he was doing. I didn't have that repetition learning in my head: jab, feint, jab, move to your left and throw the right cross, next step in and throw the left hook, whatever. I was just going by instinct. I won that one,

187

but it could have gone either way. I took away the title and a concussion.

I only had one more fight, against Chauncy Welliver in 2015, the year of the Rugby World Cup. I prepped really well, and the eight-round fight reflected that: I won easily.

Now that I've retired from footy, I have decided to dedicate my final last sporting flourish to boxing. Boxing is a way to transition out of sport. Though maybe I'll do some coaching of either footy code. The fighter of now is not the same one who fought Botha. There is so much growth left to do, so much learning, it makes each day exciting because of the challenge. It's that mad training mindset again.

But boxing is a tough sport. You are always one moment away from disaster, and you are completely on your own with no teammates to support you and back you up. The struggle I have in getting better as a boxer and learning more about what works and what doesn't is that I can't just fight anonymously to get experience. I don't have the luxury of making mistakes without anyone watching and analysing. But the challenge to overcome fear, to become a better fighter, drives me. It is always the challenge that pushes me forwards. Overcoming fear. Going into an uncomfortable situation. That takes courage.

Now I'm out of league and rugby union and have taken on being a television rugby union and rugby league commentator, I'm as uncomfortable as I've ever been. But I am doing it. I am driven by that desire to be better at something. And also, to stand up as a man of colour and be broadcast into lounge rooms around the country, that is a huge deal. That is something bigger than me, so despite my fear, I am taking that opportunity. If I took the soft option, I would never have come back to New Zealand after Toulon. I could have stayed there and played for France. The money they pay the top players in France is really good. But I wouldn't have been true to myself. I wanted to be an All Black.

And look how it turned out: I played fifty-eight Tests for the All Blacks, won a lot of respect and even won over some of my detractors.

Taking yourself right out of your comfort zone pays big dividends, and not just in overcoming the challenge. For too long I was also fighting my low self-esteem. Truth is, I still am. Being live on television? Me, the shy Sāmoan boy who knows he'll never defeat all his demons?

Yes. Me, the half-caste Sāmoan – take out shy; it doesn't matter if I'm shy or not. Me, the league and union player, on the small screen, speaking to an audience around the world. That's what I mean.

I would love it if every brown-skinned youngster – if youngsters of any ethnic origin – heeded these words and said to themselves: *If Sonny Bill can do it, then so can I.*

Kids, if you already have doubts in your mind, or demons you wrestle with each and every day, please be gentle with yourself. But also understand that you are not alone in that. So many of us carry internal struggles that no-one can see. We all have deficiencies, no-one is perfect. Believe me about that. In my time as a sportsman, I have learned that even the people I've admired and thought had it all figured out have their struggles. No matter who you are or how strong someone may appear, everyone has difficulties they need to overcome. No-one is perfect. If I could, I'd put my arm over all of your shoulders and let you know, yes, life might be a struggle sometimes, but with discipline, hard work and patience you can make it better. You might have to learn to live with your inner demons like I have, but you will make it. So don't give up on it. Things can always get better.

I was talking with a young athlete recently who wanted advice. I told him he needed to sacrifice if he really wanted to succeed. You can't lose yourself in social media. You can't watch TV or chill on your phone all day and expect to make progress. Training or doing something positive – rather than wasting your time, and your life, staring at a screen – is the only way to make things happen. It is up to you to define what you want and then work for it. I have always had that focused work ethic but now the daily structure and discipline that Islam has given me has sharpened that.

It has allowed me to stay on top of my demons for the most part; praying five times a day, for example, allows me to step back every day and see the big picture. It gives me the headspace to reflect and to be grateful for the things in life that matter to me – my children, my loving wife, my loving family, my beautiful house with fancy wallpaper. In a world that is so fast-paced and that puts too much value on fleeting things that only gratify for the briefest of times, it's easy to get lost and caught up in valuing things of no substance. I did that and I am very proud that my faith helped me refocus on what truly matters. I found the peace I was searching for, and it has allowed me to thrive in all areas of life, especially mentally, taught me the importance of gratitude and to follow an empathic heart. So whatever path you end up on, it needs to be one that gives you a positive attitude and a driven mindset because a kid with this is a kid who's going places.

I need to stress that I can still get negative thoughts saying, *You're worthless. Who do you think you are to go and commentate? Who are you to have your own gym with the aim of going as far as you can in boxing?* Even those close to me don't get why I feel like this. To be honest, sometimes I don't. But it's a daily struggle. For all my achievements, for all the praise, the acclaim, the million compliments, I know I'm in for a daily fight with my biggest opponent: myself.

CHAPTER 9

Insha Allah
(God willing)

Faith is an intimate connection between a person and their Creator and for me, faith has brought great comfort and self-knowledge. I realise that the One God doesn't need me at all but I, on the other hand, can't live without the One God. One of the reasons I connect with Islam so strongly is because I believe faith should put you on a path to be the best version of yourself and Islam has definitely done this for me. With my faith, I believe in the afterlife and that when I die I will end up in Jannah (paradise) or Jahannam (hellfire), depending on my actions in this dunya (world). My belief in the One God makes me accountable and I strive constantly to better myself. I know that Allah sees all that I do and more importantly what is in my heart, that knowledge and the discipline of Islam helps focus me to keep myself on the straight path daily. I have learned that a life with no boundaries is one I get lost in. The Prophet Muhammad (Peace Be Upon Him) said there will come a time when holding onto your religion will be like holding onto a hot coal. I strive to hold that hot coal daily. I have also learned that the best Muslim is the one who has the best character, someone who keeps the Oneness of God at the front of their mind, while being well-mannered and respectful of family and the wider community. Someone who is honest, kind and shows courage when needing to speak up for the voiceless and fight against injustice will reach Paradise. This is what I strive to do. It strengthens my faith in Allah to know that unjust, corrupt and inhumane people will have to answer to the Knower of All one day. To be honest, I don't even wish to entertain the thought of hell for one second. May the Most High keep me and those I love away from hellfire.

Islam is a way of life and it is obligatory for a Muslim to strive to pray five times a day, give to charity, fast, visit the sick and think about the less fortunate. It is a religion based on five pillars of belief and practice:

Shahada (faith)

Muslims believe the only God is Allah and that the Prophet Muhammad (Peace Be Upon Him) is the final messenger of God.

Salat (prayer)

Islam suggests worship five times a day: at Fajr (dawn), Dhuhr (noon), Asr (late afternoon), Maghrib (sunset) and Isha (night). A person must wash (hands, mouth, nose, face, arms and feet) before prayer, but if you can't, you can still pray. You can pray alone or in a congregation at the masjid, where you get the most reward. For me, the beauty of praying five times a day is that it gives me a connection with my Creator all throughout the business of the day. It protects me against temptations and keeps me focused on what is important for me in this life, my family, my wife and being a good man, so it gives me a contentment in my heart. Jumah (Friday noon prayer) is special to Muslims and is done in a masjid if possible. Muslims face in the direction of Mecca, in Saudi Arabia, when they pray. In eastern Australia, that means facing in an easterly direction and in New Zealand in a south-westerly direction.

Zakat (alms)

Islam requires that charity, known as zakat, be given to the poor or needy. In addition to this, Muslims are encouraged to give as much as they can in voluntary charity. (This is not just monetary; it can be volunteering or other acts of kindness and generosity.) You don't have to give if you have nothing to give. Islam directs you to look after those close to you – your family, your friends. It encourages you to help those in your inner circle who need it first.

Sawm (fasting)

During the month of Ramadan, the ninth month of the lunar calendar, Muslims fast from dawn to sunset and gather in the evenings to break their fast. While fasting, Muslims are required to abstain from food and drink, including water. But the fast goes beyond this; you are also required to abstain from sex and you must strive for purity of thought. Muslims are required to start fasting when they reach puberty, although some younger children may want to fast and they are permitted to do this. My eldest daughter, Imaan, did a few days of fasting with me this year. It was a beautiful thing to eat our Surhur, a meal before first prayer at sunrise, with her. I was so grateful to sit with her to eat our porridge and in the calm and peace of those moments I felt such a deep connection to Allah and to my daughter. Eid al-Fitr is one of the major holidays in Islam and is a three-day celebration marking the end of the Ramadan fast. The date is determined by the sight of the new moon. Eid is a celebration that includes family gatherings, prayers, feasts and gift-giving. One of the most beneficial things you can do for your body is to intermittently fast. Not only does that month of fasting benefit me physically but I can feel the benefits mentally as well. It always seems to humble me and give me gratitude for the simple things, like being able to eat and drink. Ramadan always seems to come at just the right time for me.

Hajj (pilgrimage)

Every Muslim is required to make the pilgrimage to Mecca once in their life if they are financially and physically able to do so. All outward symbols of rank and wealth are erased during the pilgrimage, as Muslims from every part of the globe come together for the purpose of worshipping God. Muslims who have made the pilgrimage are referred to as hajji and are celebrated and respected when they get home. I have visited Mecca on an umrah pilgrimage, which means visiting at a time of the year other than during the hajj. It was an awesome experience to pay respect, strengthen my faith, pray and learn. Though I have done umrah myself, I can't wait to perform the hajj with my family. Insha Allah, soon.

* * *

For me, Islam has lit the way through the darkness. It's given me a sense of empowerment of the deepest kind. It gave me the strength to turn away from self-indulgence and the world of alcohol, drugs and superficial relationships, and I can honestly say that without that strength I would have been lost. Islam has bettered every part of my life. I know without question Islam has made me happy, content and given me solace. But with Islam, as with everything in life worth doing, discipline is all-important. You have to commit. I did.

That discipline has given me a freedom to go wherever I want in life. It has helped to heal the unsure, shy and self-conscious young man I was and enabled me to strive to be better all the time.

Discipline and prayer have given me natural highs that no amount of alcohol or drugs could ever give. Those things might feel good at the time, but the day after, the week after, you feel something toxic inside you. In Islam, we get up early to perform our first prayer of the day. I then usually read some of the Quran and then wake up my wife, trying not to wake up one or two of the kids, who have often snuck into our bed in the night. It's such a beautiful beginning to the day because your heart knows you've started the morning doing the right thing.

For me, the beauty of these prayers is like protection against a world that is all about being on the go and accumulating. Being able to step back and see the big picture and be grateful for what I have been blessed with is an important thing.

I think Islam has helped me to understand that rather than accumulating material things, one should accumulate values; it has given me a moral code to live by. Simple things like giving your time visiting the sick or helping a charity out is another form of zakat. I challenge anyone to go see a kid with cancer or to witness an adult suffering terrible pain, and not feel grateful for your own good health.

Yes, I can still get caught up in the worldly rat-race and put value on things that in the long run won't bring me the happiness my soul yearns for. But that doesn't happen so much anymore now I have grown and learned so much from the teachings of the Prophet Muhammad (Peace Be Upon Him) and from reading the holy Quran. If I do have moments of discontent, I know how to get back on track. Having a content and happy heart is one of the most precious things you can strive for. This is how my soul loves to feel. I've been lucky to achieve a lot but what means the most is to have reached a point in my life where I feel content and happy. To me, this is a small slice of what paradise must feel like. I am so grateful to Allah for the blessings I have.

I say his faith is the most important thing to happen to Sonny Bill. Finding something he believed in so much, that changed his mental attitude. As his mother, I knew he had a special goodness from a young age. The kid who saved his pretty skinny pocket money to buy his mum fudge? What kid even thinks of that?

Sonny Bill cares deeply about others and he'll stick up for people being treated badly, no matter the consequences to himself. He has compassion and empathy, qualities you don't often find in exceptional sportspeople, as they're usually so focused they zone others out.

Sonny Bill has gone from being a boy of few words to a good talker. When he's explaining his religion, he does it in such clear terms that even I can understand. He's so honest in what he says and talks from the heart. Yes, he's definitely got better at talking as he's got older and had more and more diverse experiences. Actually, I feel so blessed that all my four kids are good people.

I've become a Muslim too. I follow the basic things, like being good to people, helping others, being careful what you say about others so you don't hurt their feelings. The lessons of Islam are about being a good person, just like my mum taught me. – Lee Williams

Like so many people, I was horrified when I heard the news of what happened in Christchurch in March 2019. Even now, I struggle to put into words how deeply this affected me. The horrific attack on two Christchurch mosques, when fifty-one worshippers were killed and over forty injured at Friday prayers, devastated those communities and horrified people right around the world. That vile act showed me that good people will always support one another and that bad and evil exists and we should always speak out against that. Later, I found out that the murderer had also scoped out mosques in Ponsonby and Hamilton. My daughter and I often go to mosque together after I pick her up from school on a Friday and we could just as easily have been caught up in this murderous rampage.

It is at times like this that fame can help make things a little easier for people or provide comfort. A lot of my Muslim brothers and sisters reached out to see what they could do to help. Anthony Mundine, Hazem El Masri, Bachar Houli and Ofa Tu'ungafasi are just some who came together to visit Christchurch and to speak with those who'd been injured and those who had lost loved ones. That is a strong message in Islam, to look out for each other. Fighting against racism and hate speech was an important thing for me to do after what happened and I will continue to support my brothers and sisters who have been affected by those murders.

I owe a lot to my Islamic faith and I will always try to give back when I can.

* * *

One of the first players to fly the Muslim flag in the NRL was Anthony Mundine, who made his first-grade debut in 1993 for the St George Dragons. Another player proud of his Islamic faith is Hazem El Masri, a Bulldogs player who made his first-grade debut in 1996 and who I played with at the club. Hazem represented New South Wales and Australia, and was one of the best kickers in the game. Choc and Hazem are both incredible sportsmen and very good men, and I admire them both.

When you look at it from a pure sporting perspective, Choc's career is really amazing and almost second to none. He is definitely one of the best sportsmen to ever come out of Australia. He was at the height of his sporting powers when he switched from footy to boxing, following in the footsteps of his legendary old man (and my current boxing trainer) Tony, who my children know as Uncle Cowboy. Choc would then dominate boxing for many years in Australia and go on to become a three-time world champion. Choc's sporting talent in rugby league and boxing is often overshadowed because he is outspoken in his personal views, especially for his people. He can rub some up the wrong way and sections of the media have been harsh, but to me he will always be a man with a loving heart who passionately speaks up for what he believes in. When I was at my lowest ebb, he was there to help me, both financially and spiritually. I will forever be grateful.

Hazem and I were close at the Dogs and although we never spoke of faith back then, I always respected the way he carried himself. At the time, I was blind to that type of faith as my religion then was the game of rugby league. One of the regrets I have about when I left the Bulldogs was the fact I didn't show our friendship more respect and tell Hazem how I was struggling and why I was leaving the game. The boy I was back then didn't have the words, but I know Hazem was hurt and took it personally that I didn't speak to him about it all. With my head in turmoil, that just wasn't on my radar, but the beauty of Islam is that we are taught to forgive one another. I'm glad that we have become close again over the years.

When I played footy with Hazem, I had no understanding of what Ramadan meant for an elite athlete. But the one thing I am sure all Muslim athletes get asked about is how they combine training and playing with fasting during Ramadan. I often get questions about how it impacts on my training and how I play in a game.

As I said earlier, Ramadan is a very special time and part of my connection with my Creator. It is about focusing on being grateful for the things we have and concentrating on being a better person, so it is a time I look forward to. But the first week of fasting can mean your energy flags, until you start to get used to it, so Muslim athletes have to modify some of what they do. When it comes to the mechanics of training, I find fasting easiest with footy-based training, and so I push back any weight training until I break the fast at night.

When I first started fasting, I was very scientific about the process. I'd work out when I should eat carbs and what other types of food would help. But the whole fasting and playing sport is not an issue when you believe in what you are doing and are committed to it. More recently, I have stopped trying to manage it all so tightly and just trust the process.

Islam has helped me in so many ways and embracing all the pillars of Islam is important to me.

CHAPTER 10

You do better when you know better

What a special year 2013 would be, not only for what Allah allowed me to achieve on the field but, even more so, for what happened off it.

While I was playing Super Rugby for the Chiefs in 2012, these guys from the Panasonic Wild Knights flew over from Japan to offer me a rugby contract. I told them I had already committed to going back to league and playing for the Sydney Roosters and I couldn't break my word. I had made that commitment to Roosters Chairman Nick Politis years before. But these guys were really keen to have me, so their offer went from a minimum twelve-month deal to a twelve-game, four-month offer. I appreciated the respect they showed, flying all the way over to New Zealand just to talk for a couple of hours, and I liked their enthusiasm and the challenge their offer presented me, so after clearing it with the Roosters, I said yes.

I arrived in Japan in August 2012, right after winning the Bledisloe Cup with the All Blacks, and put my head down learning the plays so I could give my all to the team. I made my debut in round two of the competition. We narrowly lost that game, but I played the full eighty minutes and felt good. The next week we won, and I was getting a feel for the Japanese rugby ways. But it all fell apart in round eight, when I was injured. I left the field and went straight to the hospital for an MRI scan. At first it didn't seem too bad, but further tests showed a serious pectoral tear which required an operation, and that meant I would need time to recover. I was disappointed I couldn't be there for my Wild Knights teammates and help them reach the heights they aspired to, and for the Panasonic fans, who showed me a lot of faith and love. Although where we were living wasn't known as a tourist destination, I loved my time playing in the Japanese comp. The fast pace and high level of skill the Japanese play with was a surprise but I can see why the Cherry Blossoms are pushing some of the top teams in the world these days.

It was a daunting time as I had to have an operation, have the scheduled fight against Francois Botha and be fit to start with the Sydney Roosters for the 2013 NRL season, so there was a lot of pressure. But the truth was, I was getting used to that. And now I had Allah in my corner I could deal with that pressure head-on. But I was about to find out that 2013 had more in store for me than I had ever imagined.

***

I was shopping in the city, in Sydney, and that day I spotted the woman who would become my future wife, working in a clothing store. I was with Johnny, and I don't know what gave me the bravado – my wife would tell you it was her beauty, so let's go with that. I saw this beautiful woman and so asked Johnny to look at some clothes and I walked up to her and started chatting. Her name was Alana and after we'd talked for a while, I asked for her phone number and said I wanted to take her out to dinner.

She declined and wouldn't give me her number – in fact, she asked how many other women I'd approached that day. The audacity! This was a woman who wasn't afraid to stand up for herself or call me out, and I guess that only made me want to get to know her more. Later, I found out Alana had South African heritage and that South African fire was on display to me immediately. (That fire is something I see nowadays in our children, especially little Aisha. I can picture her now with her arms folded, her face with her eyebrows in a bunch telling me off. Alhamdulillah, the blessings of children. Insha Allah, that fire is only used by my kids positively when they get older or I am in trouble.)

I left my phone number with Alana's colleague and I didn't hear anything for a couple of weeks. Then she finally messaged me and we talked. Alana told me that she knew I was a footy player and had been wary. Understandable, when you consider my past reputation. We talked for a while and she explained that she'd talked to her cousins, who told her I was now a Muslim, and that that was the reason she had decided to meet me, but she didn't tell me she was Muslim herself.

After we chatted, we arranged to meet up where Alana was living, at her aunty's house. On the way, I stopped at a service station to get petrol and texted to ask if she wanted anything. Her message came back: 'Yes, please. Eight ice creams.' *Eight? Damn, that is one sweet tooth,* I remember thinking. I bought eight ice creams and rocked up to the address Alana had given me.

A man, who was her uncle, answered the door and he greeted me in the Muslim way: 'Assalamu alaikum.' I was invited inside and in the hallway there was all this Quranic writing and Islamic art on the walls and then there was her family, who the eight ice creams were for. Before that,

I'd had no idea that Alana was Muslim. Obviously family meant a lot to her and I had a good chat with them all, and then Alana and I spoke for about an hour. Our shared faith and other shared interests got me wanting a stronger connection with her. I left there knowing this was a sign from my Creator. I wasn't partying or even drinking at the time, and was definitely not living that toxic lifestyle I had been the last time I played NRL but nor was I in a place where I could say I was at complete peace with my Creator.

Driving home, I gave myself a real hard inner talking-to. I was living back in Sydney, playing for the Roosters, and I admit it would have been so easy to slip back into the bad behaviour that had got me in trouble in the past. But I didn't want that; I knew I had been blessed with so much, and I didn't want to go back to those dark days. I had to be a better Muslim, and I just had a feeling Alana was key to that. I told myself my meeting Alana was a sign. It was time for me to really be a man. Time to stop being selfish and time to step closer to Allah.

* * *

I was halfway through the season with the Roosters. When I joined in 2013, they were near the bottom of the ladder. But now we were being talked about as potential finalists and I was playing really good footy. It was a big decision to come back to the NRL because I was aware that one day I would come up against my old Bulldogs teammates and I knew some of them and some of the fans did not think of me kindly. There was still a lot of anger at me because of what had happened. But I was not the young man they used to know; I didn't drink, and there'd be no more raucous pub and club sessions. I had made peace with myself and my past behaviour.

It didn't feel like I'd been away from the game for five years. I guess muscle memory kicked back in. I was living in the fancy Eastern Suburbs and Alana's first impression of me was right: I had been seeing a few girls casually, which I knew as a Muslim was wrong. Yet none of them were touching my soul. I say that without wanting to be disrespectful to these women at all. The issue was with myself, about who and what I truly wanted to be and what I wanted in my life. To any young man involved in sport at a high level, the dream is supposed to be what I had on a silver – or gold – platter. But it wasn't making me happy. I felt lonely and disconnected. I truly believe that without boundaries in your life you will eventually follow only your own desires and it will lead you into poor decisions and selfish behaviour. I may have changed many of my ways but I was still selfish in my desires when it came to the biggest test of all – women. May Allah forgive me.

Alana was beautiful, but she was different from the other girls I knew. Not so conscious of my image. When we talked, I felt like it meant something. When her uncle opened her door that day and greeted me, it was a reminder of where I needed to be, of where my mind should be – a reminder that this wasn't just another woman I was chasing. I knew I had to step up and be better.

The day after seeing Alana and meeting her family, I changed my phone number and deleted my contacts. Four weeks later, we were married. Eight years later, we have four little blessings in our life. Some would say, that's crazy, there is no way you could possibly get it right in four weeks. I say to them, I married my beautiful fiery wife for Allah's sake and not only has she helped me become a better version of myself, we have been blessed with so much happiness and four children also.

> When I met Sonny, it so happened that we were at the same point of wanting more spiritual meaning in our lives. We met at the right time and grew together and kind of learned along the way. And though we had our moments, we stuck with it and came to a point of strength because we'd started at the same sort of uncertain place. – Alana Williams

Islamic courtship is very different from what others may experience. When Alana said yes to me, that was the start of our journey together. We both wanted to grow. I wanted to keep being a better person. Faith, family, my wife are what matters to me. To be honest, when we first got married, I know we didn't love each other, but we definitely respected each other and we knew if we worked at it and valued each other, love would come. We always strive to be the best person we can be for each other.

We are learning. We've definitely had our fair share of arguments and the last thing I want to paint is a picture-perfect household, because it definitely isn't that. With time, patience, effort, understanding, respect and connection to Allah, I can humbly say we are in a great place together. As Muslims, we believe that marriage is half your religion because of the protection it gives you. It protects you from temptation, and you focus instead on the relationship with your husband or wife, and the close friendship that grows between you.

I love my wife and appreciate all she does for myself and our children. I guess, like life, marriage is a work in progress. I'd say the key for us as a couple has been the growth, whether that be in improving our knowledge of Islam or just understanding each other better. I think any family juggling four kids and the demands of life knows that the struggles are constant, they never stop. But there are also very happy times.

Alana and I both want the same things for our children. We want our house to be a peaceful place and to bring our children up to have strong morals and ethics and also to give them the confidence and strength to be proud of who they are. I don't want them ever to be afraid to voice their opinion or speak up for themselves. It is scary because we live in an age where there are often no healthy boundaries. The rates of addiction to alcohol, drugs and gambling are high. Suicide is an issue in our young and depression and anxiety are growing diseases. I know from my experiences in my late teens and early twenties, I could have ended up in a much darker place. I know people I mixed with back then are still struggling and fighting with their demons. Alana and I will do everything we can to help keep our children from having negative experiences like that. With Allah helping us, we will guide them and protect them and I will pray that my Creator helps keep my children and my wife safe always.

It's the old story: you do better when you know better. I know so much better now. I thank Allah for all of it.

* * *

By 2013, I knew a lot better but the decision to come back to Sydney and play for the Roosters meant I would again have to confront the demons that had seen me leave the Bulldogs almost five years before. And it also meant I could make peace with my leaving once and for all with most of my former teammates. I was happy to see many of them personally and talk through what had happened. I had coffee with the old skipper Andrew Ryan and it was good to chat to him and others. I was able to convey that I was grateful for the opportunities that the Bulldogs had given me and I now had the confidence to face this situation and move forwards in life without any animosity or any ill feelings around the club.

My relationship with the Canterbury fans was more complicated. Many of them were very generous and whenever I ran into them in the street they were always quick to remind me that although they were Dogs fans and had been upset when I'd left the club, they still supported me. I felt good talking to them and always walked away feeling better. But then there were others who would never let me forget that I walked out on the Dogs. They were still angry and didn't think that the NRL should have let me back into the game or that Nick Politis should ever have been allowed to sign me up. Players, coaches and board members leave clubs all the time, some by choice and others not. The business of elite sport is brutal but the loyalties of many still hark back to the spirit of club rugby, something I understood. These fans fuelled their anger by hurling abuse at me and saying the most hideous things about me and my family, yelling from the sidelines when I was on the field and occasionally saying things in public. Some of this was hard to cop, but I realised to still feel this strongly they must have, at one time, felt a lot of admiration for me and felt let down. I'll say to these fans, Canterbury Bulldogs was the football club that gave me an opportunity to realise a dream and become a professional sportsman in the NRL. We won a premiership together, and no-one can ever take the joy of that away. The man I am today is not the man I was back then, but because of that journey I confronted my issues, worked on my mental health and found the strength and boundaries I needed within Islam. I am proud of who I am now. And back in 2013, I was ready to play NRL.

***

That year was a rollercoaster of emotions. Behind any chance of success was a lot of struggling and hard work, both physical and mental. It had been five years since I'd stepped out on a footy field to play the game I grew up loving – rugby league. I had just hit my straps in the international game with the All Blacks and I had been playing with ease in union so it might have been easier to stay in New Zealand. But I had to step up and deal with any unfinished emotional business. And I wanted to keep my word, which I had given to Nick Politis and David Gyngell, who I had talked to years earlier and promised that one day I would pull on a Roosters jersey. That time was now.

I could definitely feel the pressure and excitement leading up to that first game. I was determined to prove to my teammates that all the fuss about my return was warranted and that I could still play in the NRL and add value to their team. I never thought it would be a walk in the park, but I also hadn't counted on coming up against two of the best straight off the bat. I don't know why I hadn't; I knew the calibre of players in the NRL. And then it was on. Big Sam Burgess came at me off a goalline dropout and ran straight over the top of me before Greg Inglis ran riot. It was the dose of reality I needed. That game not only fired me up and gave me more of a motivation to show my worth, it made me realise a couple of other things. I needed to be stronger in the gym and I needed to be really mentally tough to offset the young warriors who wanted to mark their territory and come after me. I was a target and I had to be greater than them.

With these thoughts in my mind, I started meeting our strength and conditioning coach Keegan Smith first thing in the morning for extra weight and strength sessions before our scheduled training. And I started using visualisations to sharpen my mind. Each week I would visualise what could happen on the field against various opponents. I'd done this a little bit with the All Blacks so it wasn't entirely new to me, and it worked. Before that first game, I had never really understood how individual rivalries could elevate your efforts but when Sammy Burgess and Greg Inglis smashed me in the face, it hit me! I will always be thankful to them, the fans and the media too. They loved what they saw that night in that game and never let me forget it. All that helped me play harder and eventually took my game to another level.

The Roosters had finished near the bottom of the ladder in 2012 and that proved the catalyst for the hunger in the squad I stepped into. The team connection and culture at the Roosters was impressive and I was living clean and going above and beyond in training. I saw that second effort in my teammates; it was embedded in everyone and so it was the norm. There were a lot of similarities between this Rooster side and the Chiefs team of 2012 and that felt good. There were a lot of hungry young guys like Jared Waerea-Hargreaves, Roger Tuivasa-Sheck, Sam Moa, Mitchell Aubusson, Mitchell Pearce, Frank-Paul Nu'uausala and a young future NSW and Australian captain Boyd Cordner, alongside Anthony Minichiello, James Maloney, Michael Jennings, Daniel Tupou, Shaun Kenny-Dowall and Jake Friend to name just a few.

But even with all that talent, we still needed to believe in ourselves as a team. With the coaches' demands for the perfect game defensively and our natural flair on attack, we started getting a feel for our style of play and found that self-belief in ourselves and in each other. Being really successful means doing those one per cent things you don't see on TV. Every week we reviewed everything, and earning your teammates' respect in those sessions translated to putting in the effort in the game.

As the season went on, we could feel something special brewing, but through all that we felt the same happening at Souths – both our sides were having seasons to remember. I couldn't shake the thought that Russell Crowe's team was waiting to pounce and I believed we'd be the teams in the grand final together. I didn't watch many other games that year but I made sure I watched every Rabbitohs game to keep tabs on what they were up to. If we were going to do the impossible and win the trophy, I knew we had to beat this team to do it. But I had a deep sense of belief in the Roosters players and our team energy, and that belief never wavered no matter the scoreline.

Rusty Crowe is like Nick Politis, he is the lynchpin of the club behind the scenes and, just like with Nick, I had real respect for him. He seems the kind of guy you want to play for and every week Greg Inglis and Sammy

Burgess would come out and play their hearts out for the team, the fans and for Russell.

The Roosters and Souths headed into round twenty-six, the last round of that year before finals footy, in first and second place on the table. Whover won this game would not only go into the finals as a slight favourite but they'd go in with the confidence of knowing that they had just beaten their main rival and be crowned the minor premiers.

This was one of my favourite games of the year. It had everything – pressure, aggression, skill, brute force and two teams determined to win. And it all unfolded in front of a crowd of more than 60,000 fans at ANZ Stadium.

Souths and the Roosters are rugby league foundation clubs and that night the two teams put on a show that I was blessed to be a part of. Trent Robinson put me in the centres to defend as Shaun Kenny-Dowall was out injured. It was a massive task, because the majority of their tries had been scored down their left edge, with Greg Inglis their chief attacker. I had spent years playing centre in rugby so I was up for the job. It's simple, right? Stop GI, stop them.

Well, stopping Greg Inglis is not so easy! Their first assault was on our twenty-metre line. I saw Greg Inglis screaming around the back, nothing I didn't know was coming considering the amount of footage I'd studied of him and Souths. One of the big Burgess boys sets the play because of his size and it is usually a fast one, and then the ball goes through Adam Reynolds' hands out back to Inglis, who then has plenty of space to work his magic.

I have spoken about the mental warfare that happens on the field – well, this time it was my turn to make a statement. The ball left Reynolds' hands and I timed it beautifully and set out to make a massive shot on Inglis, their best player, to set the tone from then on. Well, I definitely made a statement . . . that Greg Inglis is bloody hard to tackle! He bumped me off and ran through another would-be defender on his way to score the game's first points. It wasn't the best way to start the game. I was under the post and Minichiello was talking to me, but I was in my own world. I remember thinking, *Far out, that is definitely making the highlights reel but not in my favour*, but then I told myself there was still seventy minutes left to play. I had to make some of my own plays to offset Inglis. I can't remember GI coming down outside too many times for the rest of the game because every time I could see a play unfolding where he'd look like getting the ball, I was there ahead of our defence line, screaming at him to let him know he might bump me off again but he better be ready for it because I was coming. Alhamdulillah, he didn't, because I don't think I could have lived with the embarrassment of getting bumped off twice in one game.

At the end of that game, the highlights reel was full of remarkable moments from both teams and I was pleased that I had made some positive impacts. But winning that game was only the beginning, our eyes were on the real prize – holding up the Provan-Summons Trophy at the end of the grand final.

The next game was a hard-fought game of attrition against Manly and we won that 4–0. Young gun Roger Tuivasa-Sheck scored the game's only try. I always knew he was destined for greatness as he has freakish skills topped off with a humble head on his young shoulders. I look forward to seeing him take his talents over to the fifteen-man game of rugby because the world deserves to see talent like his.

We had the week off and then we were going up against my old Bulldogs teammate Willie Mason's Newcastle Knights. But during that week, I went out to dinner and ate some seafood that didn't sit right at the time and then got worse. I ended up not being able to hold anything down. Food poisoning was not the prep I needed, and I couldn't train because I was so sick. I wasn't sure I would be able to suit up, but I made it to the game and although I had the utmost faith in our side I knew I couldn't miss it for the boys. I struggled through warm-up and by kick-off I was hoping I'd have enough energy to make it through.

Early in the game, a young player from Newcastle tried to put it on me to fight. I don't know if it was a tactic, because it didn't really happen to me very often. I always tried to play hard and fair but his provocation failed to do what he might have hoped. I wasn't intimidated; I fired up and suddenly had the energy and motivation to play with more determination. We won that game and I was lucky enough to get the Man of the Match award. We were off to the big dance!

To my and many others' surprise, twenty-four hours later, in the other major semi-final, Souths got beaten by Manly in a massive upset. This meant we were playing a grand final against the Sea Eagles and we'd already beaten them three times that year, so we went in deserving favourites.

Deep down I was confident we could get it done. And the truth was, because it was Manly, I wasn't as nervous as I would have been if we were going head to head with South Sydney. I made a silly error early, which led to them scoring the opening try. But that's the luxury of playing a team sport and something you don't get in the ring. If I am in a fight and I do something silly, I can be dropped in the opening round. But on the footy field, with your teammates around you, you can redeem yourself and collectively work your way back into the contest. We had a great side led by Sam Moa and Jared Waerea-Hargreaves in the forwards and though Manly dominated physically in the first half, thanks to some James Maloney and Daniel Tupou brilliance, we went into the half-time break 8–6 up. I had slowly worked my way back into the game and could feel my involvement increasing. During the break, the coach and a few players were talking but I was in my own head again.

I remember it as if it was yesterday; there was so much emotion in the sheds and I was sitting there talking to myself, saying, *Still forty minutes to go, follow a bad deed with a good deed, back yourself, be in the play and always say Alhamdulillah.*

We hit out in the second half but everything seemed to go Manly's way and they shot out to a ten-point lead. Usually it's impossible to come back from a scoreline like that in such a big game, but this Roosters team wasn't made up of the usual players following the usual script. That game with that awesome group of men will always hold a special place in my sporting memories because of the courage we showed in sticking to our style of play. The way the team held tight and pushed the boundaries despite what looked like insurmountable adversity was incredible. Not only did we come back to win the game 26–18, we did it with the style that only players who dared to dream could. When the final whistle blew, I dropped to the ground into sujūd to thank my Creator for making yet another dream come true.

The year of 2013 was by far the most daunting year in my sporting career, even more so than when I'd been a rookie stepping into first-grade NRL. After five years out of the game, I was about to face up to the club, teammates and fans I had walked out on. The pressure of expectations, my own and others', along with the very vocal wish of some for me to fail, meant there was a lot to deal with. But my deep sense of drive and dedication, along with the support of my teammates and people like Nick Politis and David Gyngell saw me enjoy one of my most successful years, both on and off the field. As a sportsman, I was part of an NRL premiership-winning team and I was named the Roosters Players' Player, something very special to me. I was also named the International Player of the Year. That year also saw me meet the future mother of my children and I would come through the season with no major injuries. Alhamdulillah.

CHAPTER 11

The coaches

Over the years, I have played under a fair few coaches and sussed out what works well for me. People always ask who was the best, and the truth is I learned something from them all – even if it was what didn't work. I've mentioned some of them earlier, but here are my thoughts on some of the coaches who made an impact (in no particular order).

Steve Hansen (All Blacks coach, 2012–2019)

Steve is a very good people person. I don't think he taught me anything new from a skill perspective; his strength is his ability to motivate players, to compel them to be at their best, and he did that with me.

I learned from him that, along with the skills and the mindset, getting the player to be at their greatest is hugely important. The All Blacks environment is a blessed one, with the best players in the world and an amazing array of talents. One guy can jump in a lineout twice his height; one can sidestep twenty men; another is a kicker; and yet another is someone who nails everyone in a tackle.

The depth in the All Blacks team is unbelievable, and I think most rugby heads would agree that New Zealand, boiled down to the wider squad of thirty-two All Blacks and then again to the twenty-three Test-playing squad, has the most depth of talent of any rugby-playing nation. That's why if you get injured in the All Blacks there's someone ready to take your place, and they will be determined to keep that spot and not want to hand it back. He might be your best mate. Doesn't matter. This is business. The business of elite-level sport.

So, besides a solid game plan and being able to push the limits of each player, a good coach knows that every player has a unique personality and each will respond to a coach's talk in a different way. Steve knew that and he was an unbelievable motivator, always the one guy in the room who could get the best out of me.

I really admire Steve because of his persistence in the face of failure. He didn't let defeat stop him and with this persistence he went from his struggles with Wales and then came back to the All Blacks. After losing that 2007 quarter-final to France, he didn't give up on his dream of becoming senior coach. The All Blacks would end up winning two World Cups with him as coach and he would go on to become the greatest international rugby coach of all time. The statistics of his reign back that up. I will always respect that resilience and the journey he went on. The only thing that bothered me after a while was that Steve didn't always hold himself to the same accountability and honesty that he placed on me and others.

The only thing I would have loved Steve to have done during his tenure as All Blacks coach would have been to bring in an assistant coach of Māori or Pacific Island heritage to mentor and teach his coaching knowledge and skill set to. Instead, that opportunity was lost. That is my only criticism of his reign.

One more word on Steve 'Shag' Hansen: he's married to a Māori. I don't know how he got her, because she's beautiful. But he could talk underwater, Shag, and I think that was the winning way of him. He spoke from the heart.

Dave Rennie (Chiefs coach, 2012–2017)

The Chiefs won back-to-back Super titles in 2012 and 2013. Dave Rennie is a very strong-minded individual, and that 2012 season was awesome. Dave is huge on culture; he had to blend and bond a group of guys mostly from outside of the Hamilton–Waikato region and he did that well.

His focus was that simple game: forwards lay the foundation, backs get involved whenever we see fit. The thing I loved about Rens is that he backed me as a leader and he stressed what I could do for the boys, especially the younger players. I knew what to do, but I needed someone to empower me to do it. I didn't do all that tough stuff with the youngies; they need encouragement and they need to be instilled with confidence. That's what inspires them to go out and play well.

Rens expected my leadership role to continue off the field too. He involved me in everything, and naturally I felt an extra obligation to live up to his expectations. Maybe he deliberately planned this? Whatever. It worked.

I remember our semi-final against the Crusaders in 2012 was like a final. That game. Man, I bet it is etched in every Chiefs player's memory.

My combo with Aaron Cruden was perfect. We could read each other's minds. Brodie Retallick was just a youngster then. But he showed why he was destined to be an All Blacks lock great. That young man had everything, including no shortage of the necessary mongrel his position requires. Tim Nanai-Williams (my cousin) was on the wing (and just like his older brother, was very unlucky not to play for the All Blacks – I would love to have seen him on the world stage in that black jersey). Sam Cane, future All Blacks captain and a real nice guy, was there.

And Liam 'Hunga' Messam was there – he had been in and out of the All Blacks, and I don't think deserved that treatment. He never gave less than 100 per cent every game he played. Maybe some of the coaches didn't like his flair, his unpredictability, but it wins more matches than it loses. Rens rated him, though, and New Zealand rugby sevens coach Gordon Tietjens includes Liam Messam in his greatest rugby sevens team of all time. Hunga and I were inseparable off the field. Brothers. I think having a coach of colour really helped bond us. We are still very close, like all those Chiefs boys are to this day.

Trent Robinson (Roosters coach, 2013–present day)

Trent Robinson was only thirty-six and in his first year coaching NRL when I met him. Robbo was on his way back from England to take up the Roosters gig, and he came via Japan to see me as I was contracted to return to league. Robbo's strength was his humility and his approachable personality. His door was always open, and I felt I could have a yarn with him anytime.

We really connected at that meeting in Japan. I appreciated his holistic approach to footy. In one sense he was old school, yet he was new school in some of his thinking. I loved that he came and watched me play rugby in Japan, where I was doing little grubber kicks, throwing outrageous offloads. I knew going back to league was going to mean a different structure, but he always wanted me to play my own game, which means playing with my eyes up and looking for opportunities, or creating them.

I also got on well with our attack coach, Jason Taylor, who would say to me, 'What were you doing there?' and 'Why did you do that?'. I'd tell him, 'I saw this, so I did that,' sort of thing. He said, 'You've got to get back to position because we need to run this line.' So, we had a few awkward conversations, but I consider them conversations of growth.

I brought my rugby mindset to league as a back rower: always scoping, always watching where the play was heading, looking for where the gaps were. If I had to go from one side of the field to the other, then I would. It didn't matter to me if it wasn't in the league playbook. The objective was and always is to win.

What I loved about Robbo was that as long as I was doing those little one-percenters on defence, getting back in position, breaking out then getting back, he supported me. If I was doing all those little hard-yard things – the things the people at home don't see on the television screen – then he left it up to me what I did on attack. Robbo never said, 'This is the way it's done and always been done and it's going to stay that way.' I have so much respect for him for that.

Wayne Bennett

I have a lot of respect for Wayne Bennett. He is one of the best motivators I've ever had. He only coached me once, with the Kiwis against his own Australian Kangaroos. As soon as he got to our camp he said, 'Come with me, Sonny. We're going for a coffee.' I'm thinking, *Wow. This is none other than* the *Wayne Bennett.* I was peaking at the time, on fire with the Doggies, and had been injured a bit in the previous two tests against the Aussies.

He said, 'You think you've done your Kiwi jersey proud? Well, have another think about it.' He was saying that I had to step it up again. He would come down the back of the bus and sit and yarn with the players. We loved him. I ended up playing one of my best games in the black jersey after that chat.

Because we represent so much out there in the field, coaches who understand the connection between Māori, Aboriginal and Polynesian boys are usually the most successful ones. Wayne respected and understood them.

Apparently he reached out to me when I left the Doggies. Unfortunately the message never reached me. If there was one man who could have changed my mind, or who might have understood what I was doing, it was Wayne Bennett.

Steve Folkes (Canterbury-Bankstown coach, 1998–2008)

There's my Bulldogs coach, Steve Folkes – he passed away in 2018, sadly. He believed in me from the start, this eighteen-year-old kid from New Zealand. He was the first coach to let me play a roving position. Even if I wore the number 11 jersey – which is the right-back edge, and you're supposed to stay there – he'd expect me to get the ball on both sides. He figured the more often I got the ball in my hands, the better the chance to break the line with my unconventional play. He just let me go out and play my game.

Shortly after the news broke that I'd been caught drink-driving, we had to go to a charity event, or maybe it was a club promotion. Steve came to tell me that the media were waiting outside the club and I should come in his car. When we arrived at the event, the cameras were clicking, the microphones were at the ready, but Steve just walked me past them all into the club. Not much was said, but his support at that time meant a lot to me.

My relationship with Folkesy ended with my abrupt departure from the Bulldogs. I wasn't at war with him or the club. Things happened that I didn't like, but I didn't have the maturity to talk it out or speak up.

I was such a fan of Steve's and now he's gone I can't ever sit down and talk with him man to man about it all. I am sad about that.

© CAMERON SPENCER/GETTY

Alana and I with our little blessings. God willing, we are blessed with more one day.

Some of my All Blacks teammates in Paris.

With Springboks captain Siya Kolisi, South Africa's first black captain.

© SIMON WILKINSON/PHOTOSPORT

A Kiwi and an Englishman: always a battle, always respect, no matter what the code.

The final siren – me and Jerome Kaino celebrating the 2011 World Cup victory.

Offloading to Nehe Milner-Skudder in the 2015 World Cup final.

Showing support to Jesse Kriel after the All Blacks defeated South Africa in the 2015 World Cup semi-final.

Winners! Me and Ma'a Nonu with the Rugby World Cup.

I always tried to play with passion and physicality, especially at the highest level. But sometimes you get it wrong, as I did on this night. I became only the second All Blacks player in history to be red carded. It was a big game versus the Lions in 2017, and it was tough knowing I had let my teammates down.

With Charlie Line – he is wearing my medal.

A special night playing for the Auckland Blues, with Tana Umaga as coach. Here I am offloading to Ihaia West for the match-winner against the Lions at Eden Park in 2017

Ofa Tu'ungafasi and I giving thanks during the 2019 Rugby World Cup.

Sevens rugby was fast – this photo is from the 2016 Wellington tournament.

Niall, Mum and me.

With the great Usain Bolt.

It was time for a new challenge and a new dream – representing my country at the 2016 Rio Olympics in the rugby sevens. I was so proud that I made that team and so did my sister Niall. My dream was shattered by injury but Niall brought a medal home.

© DAN MULLAN – WORLD RUGBY/GETTY

In Christchurch, alongside some of the Pacific region's most well-known Muslim athlet – Hazem El Masri, Ofa Tu'ungafasi, Willis Meehan and Bachar Houli – who came to giv support and respect to the brothers and sisters who had been shot in the horrific attack

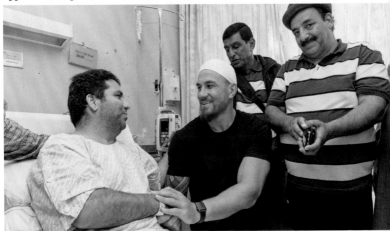

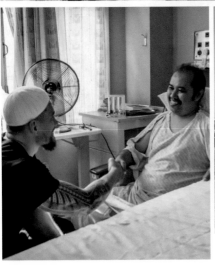

In Lebanon visiting a Syrian refugee camp.

The 2011 and 2015 victorious All Blacks World Cup teams. Grateful to have worn the jersey fifty-eight times and to have shared some special memories with some good men. Always Alhamdulillah.

The end of my time with the All Blacks. Standing alongside these men was an honour: Ben Smith, Ryan Crotty, Kieran Read and Matt Todd.

If my story shows
anything, it is that
hard work and
focus can make a
difference. I hope
can encourage other
to back themselves
and be brave enough
to chase their dream
What matters most
to me now is faith
family, friends and
helping to point out
injustice in the world
I have been given
gift and a profile, an
I have to use them
make a difference
And I still love my
sport! Rugby union
rugby league, rugby
sevens, boxing –
love them all.

Todd Blackadder (Crusaders coach, 2008–2016)

I loved Todd Blackadder's coaching at the Crusaders. He was another coach who just let me play. That 2011 season was a tough one, especially in light of the dramatic effect the February earthquake had on both the citizens of Christchurch and us players. I know I was unsettled by the quakes and the horror we saw. The team fell at the last hurdle, against the Queensland Reds.

Playing for the Reds was my close buddy, a brother, Quade Cooper. Funnily enough, our friendship started about this time. He is like a younger brother (though he looks older than me!). Although I couldn't see it then, as I am so competitive, I look back at that night with happiness because although we lost, my brother won, so essentially I won too.

Even though I made lifetime friends with people like Ben and Owen Franks, Sam Whitelock, Kieran Read and Izzy Dagg, to name a few, while at the Crusaders, I wasn't enjoying the long periods away from my mum and the family. Todd understood this and yet he always had confidence in my ability, which I appreciated. He didn't try to bog me down; he just told me to play my natural game, be aggressive and, yes, offload, but be smart about it.

When I arrived, he helped me believe in myself. The hardest thing about leaving the Crusaders was telling

Todd, because we had such a good relationship. I give thanks to my Creator for blessing me with such a good coach and a good man.

Seeing his son, Ethan, reach the heights he has in New Zealand rugby and make the All Blacks team is no surprise to me. Growing up in that household and carrying the genes of his old man made it inevitable.

Tana Umaga (Toulon coach, 2008–2009)

Tana is a man I had a lot of respect for even before I met him. His support and belief in my ability to play rugby brought out the best in me, on and off the field. He is a former All Blacks captain and I got to know him well when he threw me a lifeline after I started to self-destruct at the Bulldogs. Without his faith in me, I am not sure where I would be now. I was heading for burnout and on a bad path when he reached out and made me believe I could make the switch from league to union.

Tana's strength is his loyalty to the boys. He always puts the team members first, and with his experience being the first Islander captain for the All Blacks, he understands the pressures young Islanders face and the struggles we have with everything that comes with it. I consider Tana a friend for life and I'm grateful for my time learning from him.

Philippe Saint-André (Toulon coach, 2009–2011)

At a time when I was so caught up in trying to learn every little detail and every new rule in a game I'd never played, Philippe taught me, or reminded me, of something special: to simply step back, take a breath and remember your strengths. He never wanted me to overthink the game and always pushed me to play with my instincts and back myself.

I guess when you have the likes of Jonny Wilkinson inside and Tana outside, you don't need to think, just listen, watch and you'll be okay. As I was. Philippe has had a lot of success and if it wasn't for my desire to play for the All Blacks, maybe things could have been a lot different. Who knows what might have happened? The country of France could have ended up being called home.

Brian McDermott (Toronto Wolfpack coach, 2019–2020)

It's not every day you get to work with a coach who has headed up five Super League premiership-winning teams. Brian is the most successful Super League coach in history and it was apparent to me straight away why he was so successful – because he is always thinking of ways to improve our side by understanding our strengths and the opposition's weaknesses. He is a realist who understood we lacked a bit of depth in our team, but that didn't stop him from coming up with ways for us to not only compete but win games. Although we didn't have the luxury of a big squad or younger players to pick from, I went into each game with the sense that we could compete. Brian is a very good man who always had all players in the locker room fully committed. I am disappointed that I only got to play for him on a few occasions. I think if the circumstances had been different, with a bit of time and a few more resources, Brian could have led that Toronto team somewhere special. He was looking after the team in a really tough period and the disruption of Covid was a challenge but he was always supportive and honest with all of us foreigners. I look forward to seeing him as a head coach of another club, maybe even in the NRL, soon.

Gordon Tietjens (New Zealand All Blacks rugby sevens coach)

Going to the Olympic Games was a dream I never thought would be possible. But then one day, I set my sights on making it happen. To succeed, I needed to know all that was required to make the cut and understand the demands of the game. Who better to ask than the most respected coach in rugby sevens history? Gordon 'Titch' Tietjens has led the New Zealand team to the most tournament wins in the history of the game. When I spoke to Gordon, he was very clear on what I had to do and although I knew it would be a massive challenge, with his guidance and support, I knew I had the best chance possible of making the Olympic rugby sevens team. Without his belief and backing, I don't think I would have made it to the standard needed. Achieving that goal is something I am very proud of. Yes, injury meant my Olympic dream ended badly, but I will always be able to say I was coached by the best coach in that field. For twenty-two years, he guided the New Zealand rugby sevens and in that time they won twelve World Series titles, four Commonwealth Games gold medals and two World Cups.

Craig Bellamy (Melbourne Storm coach, 2003–present day)

The only coach I've never been coached by who I strongly admire is Craig Bellamy. After fifteen years at the Melbourne Storm, his record of winning premierships is impressive. But the aspect I admire most about Craig is his ability to give fringe players and players other clubs have given up on a second chance. Not only does he bring out the best in these players, he helps guide them on the path to become world class. A coach who can do that is one who understands that every player is different and coaches them accordingly to unite a team.

***

I think the key takeaway about coaching for me – and I have said it earlier – is that the best coach is one who understands that a team is made up of a range of personalities, and what works for one person won't necessarily work for another. You have to be a true people person and understand how to get the best out of each individual player. But you can't just use the same formula and the same tactic every time. Doesn't matter if it is an under-16s team or the All Blacks, you need to know your players so you can maximise their strengths and help them to overcome any weaknesses. You need to listen, observe and understand each player so you can work out how to unite them to play as a fierce, competitive team. And that is a winning combination.

CHAPTER 12

Going for gold

You know by now that sport has been my focus since I was a kid. At first, athletics and rugby were equally as important. Me, Johnny and my sisters Niall and Denise were all members of Roskill South Athletics Club. I was a sprinter and high jumper. I think I still hold the club high-jump record for ten-year-olds at 1.43 metres. But when I was about twelve it became all about playing rugby league in the NRL, followed by the challenge of rugby union and making the All Blacks team. Then, in 2015, a new challenge worked its way into my brain: the Olympics!

You could say I am a very driven individual. I have found one of the keys to my happiness and self-development is to set goals for myself. Whether it is aiming for the Olympics or being with my kids, I always take the same approach – full steam ahead and leave no stone unturned in order to achieve that goal.

As youngsters, most of us get excited about the Olympics; I know I did. It is the mega sports event that stops most of the world. So when it was announced that rugby sevens would be included in Rio 2016, I thought first of the challenge and then the buzz of being there as an athlete. And it was special to know my sister was on the same journey.

People see Sonny for the amazing athlete he is – the two Rugby World Cups, playing for the Kiwis, winning NRL titles for two different clubs, a New Zealand Super Rugby title with the Chiefs, being crowned the New Zealand heavyweight boxing champion. As a sports fanatic myself, I couldn't have asked for a better role model than my own brother. I guess I kind of lived my journey alongside his in getting to represent New Zealand in two different sports. But I'm not saying I'm the female Sonny Bill!

He is the best of the best when it comes to New Zealand athletes, and I admire everything he's done on the field. But it's off the field that I admire him most: the good person he is, the kind, caring, giving, humorous personality that only those close to him know.

Speaking about him I get quite emotional, because he holds such a special place in my heart. I remember when I was nineteen and did my ACL joint. I always made the national touch squad, and coming back from that injury was the first time I missed out. I was absolutely heartbroken, having lost the only thing I was madly passionate about. I wasn't great at school. Sport was my passion. What was I supposed to do now?

Sonny, who was playing for the Crusaders, told me and my partner, Tama, to come down to Christchurch and stay with him. He said, 'You can work for me part-time,' and he got me a personal trainer. So I looked after the household and I trained. My trainer got me into the best shape I'd ever been. When I went back to touch rugby I was the fastest, fittest, strongest in the team and got my spot back.

Now, no-one knows about this, but Sonny paid for me and my partner to go on this trip around Europe with the New Zealand Academy team and we went to Spain, Italy, England, Wales and taught their national touch teams, and we played in the European championship. We were with such a great bunch of people, and I learned to love the game again. That trip cost $8000 each. My bro gave us $16,000 and he didn't tell a soul. He just wanted me to get my love for the game back.

When my brother saw me down, he helped me up. That speaks volumes to me over and above what he has done on the field. – Niall Williams

I wasn't sure getting into the national rugby sevens team would even be possible. I really had to sit down and think about what I was going to do next.

To me, he was Sonny my husband and closest friend first and foremost. I didn't take any notice of him being famous. He put enough pressure on himself in trying to stay injury-free, doing constant rehab exercises and treatments. You could never question his determination and willpower. So when Sonny set his sights on the Olympics, I knew he would do it. – Alana Williams

Being an Olympian really means being the best of the best, and for someone like me, who loved pushing myself, mastering a new game and learning something new, it was the ultimate challenge. The very best sportspeople ever have also been Olympians – people I admire like Usain Bolt, Muhammad Ali, Naim Süleymanoğlu, Hakeem Olajuwon, Hicham El Guerrouj, Saïd Aouita, Michael Jordan, 'Sugar' Ray Leonard and Mohamed Farah. The chance to win an Olympic medal wasn't something I thought would ever happen for me, but with the rugby sevens making its debut in the 2016 Rio de Janeiro Olympics, that dream seemed . . . possible.

So that was it. I locked on to that goal and spent most of that year doing everything I could to make the squad. I reached out to a few people, including New Zealand head coach Gordon Tietjens, to find out more about fitness levels and expectations, and I talked to some mates I'd played with at the Chiefs, like Liam Messam. I didn't know how I'd go and so was nervous about it at first, but once I had committed I was sure as hell going to go my hardest. I wanted to make the team but I wanted to do it well. There was no way I wanted to let anyone down. Like with the All Blacks, you have to honour the players who have been before you and pave the way for those to come. I knew I had the skill set, but rugby sevens is fast moving and fast running and there is nowhere to hide, so it requires full-on conditioning.

I have always trained hard and gone above and beyond what was expected of me, but Gordon Tietjens's fitness regime was the toughest I've ever done since my introduction to professional sport in my Bulldogs days. The conditioning levels were insane – but, then, the Olympics are a whole other level. To get there I had to play in six World Rugby Sevens Series tournaments to show my worth to the team. It is not until you play rugby sevens that you understand the demands asked of you out there. It is pretty much a sprint for seven minutes a half. Day-to-day training is gruelling and you have to commit. I truly gave it my all because I wanted to hear my name called out in that Olympic team.

There was a three-day camp in January 2016, and I lost three kilos in the prep for it. The first day we did an hour of fitness games after a beep test (used to measure aerobic power) and I knew I still had work to do. I wasn't where I wanted to be at that point, but that just made me train harder.

I've always had a sort of fear of playing against small, nippy guys because they're more elusive and fast, and usually pretty strong too. This was what I saw around me: a whole bunch of small guys – compared to me, at least. And the fitness required was a different kind of fitness; people don't understand the huge difference between fifteen-man and seven-man rugby. Sevens is so aerobic. That's why a game is two halves of seven minutes each, with a two-minute half-time break. You're running, tackling and being tackled the whole time. Missing one key tackle can cost your team the match.

I was trying to find the balance between being my usual physical self and playing a whole new game in which I had only six teammates to rely on and all that space to play in and be played against. To my delight, my offload worked in rugby sevens, and so did my physical tackles.

Titch was an amazing coach, a fanatic on fitness and very encouraging of me. His sessions were gruelling, but I just got on with things, and though I was worried, I was more than ready to make my debut in Wellington at the end of January. We won that tournament (yes, an offload or two and a couple of tries featured). It wasn't easy going, that's for sure, and I played in some serious rugby sevens tournaments, but was also sidelined by a few injuries. I played in the Sydney tournament, and we won the final against Australia.

And then, in July 2016, I was named in the All Blacks Sevens Olympic team. Alhamdulillah! Another goal achieved. But I wasn't the only member of the Williams family heading to Rio that year. I was really proud to make the team, but I was even prouder of my little sister Niall. She is a mother of two and when she first set her eyes on Rio, she wasn't contracted to any club. She would get up really early to train, spend the day looking after her daughters, and then train late at night. I think resilience and dedication must be in our genes, because we both did whatever it took to make the New Zealand Olympic team. Mum and Dad were proudest of all.

I was loving everything about playing sevens. I just wanted to stay healthy and injury-free and work with my teammates to bring the gold medal home. But I wasn't under any illusions: this competition was going to be fierce.

* * *

Walking into the Olympic Village in Rio was amazing. It's a massive place; you wouldn't believe the size of it. All these big high-rise accommodation 'hotels' had been built to house over 10,000 athletes. Walking around the village was a surreal experience for me, seeing all these athletes from different countries of every complexion and size – and, of course, with that heightened air of being physically aware of the space they're occupying that's common to all athletes.

We had designated hotels for each country in sections of the village, and New Zealand was sharing theirs with Ireland. The logistics of looking after and moving people around was mind-blowing. Some things worked well, but other things were tested just by the huge number of people. I remember there was a limited number of bikes to ride to the food hall. We soon learned you either had to grab a bike early or walk to the food hall and then eat fast so you could score a bike afterwards. That's what teammate Akira Ioane and I used to do.

Man, athletes give off their own aura, and I loved just riding around checking it all out. We'd pass a guy doing karate on the grass, someone doing stretches, a guy shadow-boxing, and that was where I saw an Olympic walker for the first time ever. I must have missed the walkers when watching the Games over the years on TV, and seeing that run/walk for the first time made us laugh because it looked so awkward. I wasn't laughing in a disrespectful way; it just looked funny with that hip action. It's so technical and the speed is impressive, but I know I couldn't do it; I would break into a run.

We heard rumours that the American basketball team had their own big luxury boat offshore to live on, and it turned out to be true. While most of the American athletes were in the dorms like us, the men's and women's basketballers were on a massive cruise ship. They'd come into the village every once in a while, superstars at the peak of their fitness and fame. One day, Akira and I were riding around and he went around a corner before me. I followed and nearly crashed into him. He'd stopped dead. Staring.

There, walking towards us, with no massive crowds of fans or minders, was Team USA, the American men's basketball team. Unfortunately, we didn't have our phones so we couldn't take any pictures. We caught ourselves staring at these exceptional athletes as we were avid fans. Kevin Durant got close to us and he stopped and said, 'How are you, guys? Y'all cool?' He greeted us and acknowledged us and it was a nice moment because I really liked that guy.

I loved my time in that village. Spain's hotel was next to ours. We saw Rafael Nadal and got a photo with him. Nice guy. I didn't know much about tennis, but I did recognise his achievements. Another time, I saw retired sprinter John Steffensen, who'd won a silver medal for Australia, in the food hall. He was at the Olympics in a mentoring role. John had a name for being fired up and calling out racism. Being a black man, he'd been on the receiving end too many times, so to see him now on the board of Athletics Australia was a sign that things were changing for the better. We knew each other, so had a good catch-up. He was staying with Usain Bolt and he invited me to come hang out with them later that night. I wanted to include some of my rugby boys, but I didn't want to impose on the big man, who was competing soon.

Usain Bolt is huge on the world stage and that was respected by the Olympics. He had an entire hotel floor to himself. Our whole team shared a floor. I turned up and we had a mad yarn. We talked about sport and politics. What I really like about him is the way he acknowledges everyone who is part of putting an event together. On the track he always gives a nod to the young kids who clean up the starting blocks after he runs or the volunteers who make things run smoothly. On the big stage, where it would be so easy to make it all about him, he takes time to make a young kid's day with a fist bump and a smile. That is what I really admire about him. It was a pretty enlightening chat. He is an impressive dude. Smart, likeable and funny, he was very aware of his position in the world, but also respectful to everyone, no matter who they were. 'It's one thing my parents would be really upset and hate about me, if I changed and stopped having respect. My parents would be crazy,' Usain said in an interview once. I know about that!

It was awesome to spend time with Usain, and as well as the chat, I do remember his feet. They were like huge plates. I figured he must have walked barefoot his whole life and he got his speed pushing off those big feet. The man is a champion and would go on to win three gold medals at that Olympics – in the 100 metres, the 200 metres and the 4 × 100-metres relay. And he'd done that at the previous two Olympics. He is definitely one of the greatest athletes of all time, and he worked hard, trained hard and pushed himself to become that. That's inspiring.

As well as the thrill of seeing sporting superstars everywhere you look, a big part of the excitement of the Olympics is the Opening Ceremony. Every athlete competing at the Games wants to be part of it, and I did too. But you can never lose sight of why you are there – to compete and to win. So I decided to stay at the hotel and watch the ceremony on television because I wanted to rest my legs. Now that I'd achieved the goal of being an Olympian, I had moved on to the next goal: winning gold.

* * *

On the first day of competition, the nerves kicked in. This was what I had focused on for a year. We were playing Japan at Deodoro Stadium and in the second half, I went into a tackle and didn't get up. I'd ruptured my Achilles tendon and had to be helped from the field. I was devastated, and more than anything I felt bad that I had let the team down. We lost that game 14–12 and would end up finishing fifth in the Olympic competition overall. There was no medal of any colour coming home with me. I was pretty gutted about that for the team and because of all the sacrifices that had been made to get to those Games. But that is sport. And elite sport takes no prisoners.

My sister Niall was there to help me through it. And the drama didn't end with the Achilles injury. The next thing I knew, I was hit with a stomach bug and diarrhoea. There was a little storage room at the back of the hotel where I had to kind of quarantine myself from the boys so they didn't get infected.

But the good news is there was an Olympic medal in the family. Niall and the women's rugby sevens team won the silver medal. Me and my family were so proud of her! She posted a message on social media encouraging me after her final:

This journey has been full of ups and downs, ins and outs, the known and unknown . . . but I wouldn't have wanted to do it with anyone else but him by my side. We both started this journey as a brother and sister who wanted to prove themselves in the [sevens] rugby game and are now able to call ourselves Olympians after representing New Zealand rugby sevens on the biggest sporting stage ever! No-one can ever take this moment we shared away from us and it's something we will treasure forever. Although his ended the way it did, I know he's not feeling sorry for himself and will be back better and stronger; with family, faith and will on his side, he is on the right track back. Silver wasn't the colour we wanted but a podium finish is nothing short of *amazing*. This medal is as much his as it is mine for the fact I wouldn't be here if it wasn't for the love, faith and support he's shown me from day one. Love you, bro. – Niall Williams

Love you too, sis. People can forget that disappointments don't just affect the athlete. Your family take that ride with you and are just as invested in achieving your goal. I was so proud of Niall but I was hurting for myself. I have to admit that after all the effort, the training and the preparation this Olympic injury hit hard. I'd wanted a medal so badly for myself and the team and once my Achilles went, I still hoped the team could play on without me and achieve gold. It wasn't to be.

Sonny trained and trained to make that New Zealand rugby sevens team so he could compete in Rio. He always put the training in, no matter what, but he also studied notes on the game's finer points and he was constantly away: gone for two or three weeks, home for two weeks, off again.

At the time I was thinking, *Why did this happen to Sonny, a dream destroyed after so much hard work?* We turned to our faith, looking for a reason. When he had the tests he was told by the doctors he had an injury that would take nine months to heal. So, he was at home in New Zealand doing rehab and, typical Sonny, was back to fitness in seven months. — Alana Williams

It took months to recover physically, but mentally it took almost as long. I couldn't train so I had to work hard to keep from sliding into a depression like I had previously. So much of what I do is about my physicality and training that I still struggle when I can't. Islam helped me deal with that. My daily prayers, keeping focused on the moment and being grateful for all that I had done and all that I had. My body was taking longer to recover and injuries were taking a toll. I knew the day was coming when I had some big decisions to make, but I wasn't quite there yet.

CHAPTER 13

Not ready to stop . . . yet

As I got older, my work ethic continued to improve. I knew what I had to do to play or box at my best. My motivation and desire to stay at the top meant I pushed myself. I was always looking at ways to make that one per cent difference, both on and off the field. That is what I had to do, both as far as my physical body was concerned but also for my mental wellbeing. On the field, that second effort can make a difference in a game; off-field, it meant the dreaded ice baths, stretches and yoga, on top of the usual training.

I am a team man, so if I can't train or perform as well as I usually do because of injury, it bothers me.

Dealing with injury and pain has been a big part of my career and any pro sportsperson will tell you the same: it goes with the territory. I always wanted to give myself the best chance so it meant countless operations and rehab and always pushing myself to recover quickly. In 2010, just before I went to New Zealand and started playing with the Crusaders, I had a routine clean-up of my knee to make sure I was fit and ready to go. After the op, the doctor told me he thought I could get it to the point where I would be able to play the 2011 World Cup but he couldn't guarantee anything after that. I decided I would do all I could to prove him wrong.

Many operations later, fast-forward to the start of the 2019 World Cup year. I had the regular routine check-ups to make sure I was in the best shape I could be. After some scans came back, I was told that with the way my knee was looking, I should probably start thinking about life post footy. The realities of that conversation hit me hard and got my mind racing. In the previous four years, I had dealt with an Achilles tear, a ruptured AC joint, broken bones in my shoulder, a few concussions and the old not-so-faithful knee on top of other small niggles, and every time I had done what needed to be done to be able to step back up. The mention of a possible end to my playing career was confronting. I still had the dream to play a part in winning three consecutive Rugby World Cups with the All Blacks, alongside Kieran Read, Owen Franks and Sam Whitelock, and this conversation seemed to be putting a line through that. I sat with those thoughts and then I realised I didn't have to agree to this outcome. I was going to put my faith in my Creator and in focusing on the one per cent wins and do everything possible to achieve this World Cup goal at the end of the year. If I spent two hours on the field, I'd follow that up with at least three hours preparing for the next day just to be able to train. I'd stand in the ocean for twenty minutes, no matter what the weather conditions or the temperature – cold, raining, three degrees, windy, it didn't matter. I'd get on a trigger-point roller and work my muscles before doing thirty to sixty minutes of yoga at home. To top it all off, I'd use the ice compression machine for twenty minutes every ninety minutes. I'd always have to ask Alana to fill it up for me, and she hated that machine almost as much as I did.

In my final All Blacks years, from 2016 to 2019, I was always willing. That Achilles injury was a huge setback, and coming back from that was a real grind. But I did come back. In 2017, I played in just about every All Blacks game, but that's when the media were at their worst.

As I said, even though I mostly ignore the media, you can't help but hear whispers. *He doesn't deserve his place. He should be dropped. What's he done to deserve being selected?* I blocked most of it out and just stayed focused on playing the best I could.

I remember once being at an event and encountering Colin Meads, one of New Zealand's greatest rugby players ever. He's so revered that everyone was trying to get a piece of him. I was too shy to go over and say hello, but he came over to me and said, 'I'm a big fan of yours, Sonny. I love the way you play, your physicality, your skills. Don't ever lose that approach.'

With all the negative media around at that time, those words really helped remind me I was bringing something different to the game – if my style of play was good enough for the most respected All Black to have ever played, I knew I was on the right track. It was a great confidence booster.

***

In a Test against Australia, I got a head knock in the first two minutes. Actually, I found out later I was briefly unconscious. The doctors watching that game in Sydney didn't come and check on me; they left me on the field. I actually played well in that game, too. (Johnny would have told me afterwards if I hadn't. We have this thing between us where he always gives me a frank and honest opinion – even if I don't always love hearing it.)

I couldn't even remember being knocked out, but after the game I had all these messages on my phone from Alana, my mum, my dad, Khoder. They were all angry that I hadn't been taken off the field. The footage from the game isn't pretty, and I am clearly disorientated and struggling to stand and walk straight. I can't remember much, but I do remember after the tackle telling myself, *Stand up, bro. Stand up.* I was wondering why I felt so tired. I had another seventy-odd minutes to play so had to pull myself together.

When we moved to New Zealand, I found the media there much worse than in Australia. It was very strange to me, because Sonny's a New Zealander, so I wondered why they wouldn't support him, be proud of him. This was a man who had done his country proud in rugby league and rugby union, and he was also a decent, caring human who always tried to give back.

But everywhere Sonny went in the country, people only showed him love. From seven- to seventy-year-olds, boys, girls, women, men — they loved Sonny Bill. It's because he's such a genuine person, and he is always willing to be photographed, to stop to talk and listen to people. They appreciated that. They were delighted he was approachable and a very nice, respectful person. I am very proud of my husband and very angry at those harsh critics who refused to admit they were wrong and who never failed to have a dig, whether in newspapers or on TV. What annoyed me the most was that Sonny never had a right of reply. He just had to suck it up and get on with it.

I remember that Test match against the Wallabies. After Sonny set up a try and played really well, Phil Kearns, the former Wallabies captain who won two World Cups said:

'This is the same bloke that the New Zealand media said was past it. The same bloke who made a world-record twenty-six tackles against the Springboks two weeks ago.' Was that a headline in his own country? No, it wasn't.

In that same Test, when he got that heavy head knock that turned out afterwards to have caused a concussion, he continued to play despite his dizziness. So many times Sonny's talent and dedication to win was ignored. – Alana Williams

The mainstream media always seemed to downplay my abilities and say I was not worthy of the black jersey. But, conversely, in the Pasifika and Māori community and media, I was always held in high esteem, which I will always be proud of. More than 50 per cent of players in general are of Pasifika or Māori background, yet this is not translated in their representation in New Zealand's rugby media and commentators. Sometimes you find people in prominent positions and you wonder how they got there. This thought seems to pass my mind more and more, regardless of whatever field I am in.

In my experience, usually the harshest critics are the ones who have the least credentials, so who should I take seriously? The voice of someone who has never played at the highest level? Or the words of someone who has the respect of the rugby-playing world, like Colin Meads or Phil Kearns? I will go with Colin or Phil every time.

We went on tour and played France, Wales and Scotland. I had built a solid combination with Ryan Crotty, a very underrated player whom the media called a journeyman. Crotts was a whole lot better than that; he was a player you could depend on who made very few mistakes. I could close my eyes and pop a pass knowing he'd be right there.

In the France game, I was up against Mathieu Bastareaud, a hard-running massive ball of muscle. Playing against him was exactly the kind of challenge I relished, and I went at it. I had always wanted to play with the All Blacks against France, in France. Now I was on the field.

Doing the haka before that game, I was pumped and ready to go. The French revere the All Blacks, but of course they cheer on their own team like tens of thousands of people gone temporarily mad. Later, when you see those same screaming fans sitting in restaurants, calm and composed, it is like you're looking at different people.

I had a really strong, solid game that night. The French fans cheered rather than jeered me. Whenever I played in Europe the fans gave me big love, I think because they appreciate someone who plays with passion. Their media treated me in a very special way too, as if I was one of their own.

But I did have a moment of reverting to my league days by knocking the ball out with my hands in the dead ball area. It got me a yellow card and France were awarded a penalty try. I knew I had stuffed up. In league you can knock the ball out, but not in rugby. It was an honest mistake in the rush of play, but later I was hammered for it and TVNZ's *Breakfast* host Jack Tame was right when he predicted that this one moment was going to enable the haters. It sure did. Some in the media called it inexcusable. I made sure I reread the rulebook. After a ten-minute sin-binning, I came back on and we won the game 38–18.

The next week we played Scotland, and everyone was predicting we'd thrash them. As All Blacks, we always put pressure on ourselves not just to win, but to perform well. Scotland had beaten the Wallabies not long before, so we knew this wouldn't be an easy game. It turned out to be real close, but none of us had come at the game with the attitude they were easybeats. No-one is. You have to respect the opposition no matter who they are. And I probably had my stand-out game of the year. Everything flowed; my little grubber kicks, the offloads, the hard tackling, all the little unseen things. It just came together.

Next we were playing Wales on their famous Cardiff Arms Park home ground. That is always hard. We had a cracker and won by a good margin.

***

By the end of 2017, I was feeling confident in my form, having worked my way back from the Achilles injury and receiving a team award for Players' Player. I know this doesn't mean much to most people, but to me, being acknowledged by my teammates is the greatest recognition.

Back home in Christchurch in 2018 with the All Blacks, we were doing a tackling drill when who should come flying at me and chop me low but my good mate Ofa Tu'ungafasi. I stood up and my bad knee had locked. I could hardly stand. I knew straight away this was not good.

When you've had knee injuries like mine, excess bone grows to cope with the trauma. And if any player was to give you trauma it was Ofa, one of the strongest players I've played with (although I would never tell him that!). I love my brother Ofa, and we have a strong bond. There was no ill will in that tackle. As soon as I realised my knee was stuffed, I was back in that dark mental space called injury. After surgery, the surgeon advised my best rehab was to get on the gym bike. I spoke to the All Blacks physio, Pete Gallagher, a great guy who thinks outside the box. His advice for the same knee in 2015 had been unorthodox. He told me I'd lost flexion, which basically means the ability to bend an arm or a leg, so he suggested that every day he sit on my leg to straighten it.

Within a week it was straightened, and within two weeks I was running normally. Prior to that, my whole body mechanics had gone into adjusting to compensate for the wonky knee. Pete's method changed everything; I felt like an athlete again.

So, of course I listened to him again. I got on the bike, and then Pete suggested I do a little bit of running. Brodie Retallick was coming back from an injury, too, and Pete suggested we train together. I hadn't run for two or three weeks, and Brodie is known for being a fitness man. I was running hard and the big man was fifteen or twenty metres in front of me. But I was in it for the long haul, and I was going to focus on beating Brodie.

I'd do another session with Pete, and I'd feel about 40 per cent better. I got back into my old habit of doing the extras. I'd always had this mentality that if you do the extra work, you will always be a little bit ahead of the others.

The next session I was another 40 per cent better. I started to see light at the end of the tunnel then. Brodie was no longer outrunning me. I told Pete I thought I was ready to go back to full training. I felt good. Actually, I felt better than good, as I was so relieved to be back to normal.

I had another week of hard training and then the starting team was named early the next week. Number 12, Sonny Bill Williams. Good old Shag Hansen had shown faith in me, when only a few weeks back I'd had no faith in myself. I thought I'd never recover in time.

That's one thing about Steve Hansen: he's not afraid to pull the trigger from time to time. For instance, look at Rieko Ioane getting his first chance against the Lions, or Julian Savea, and look how easily they stepped up to the level expected. All they needed was their shot, and Steve gave it to them with no hesitation.

So, next up we were playing France, and I was playing really well. Their number 12, Wesley Fofana, runs a short ball, and I'm thinking, *It's time to light him up! I love* when the opposition tries to hit a hole that's suddenly no longer there. Instead, I was flying at him. But my timing was out.

It was one of those unlucky situations. I hit him at the top of the shoulder just as he bent forwards. I popped my AC joint out and fractured all the little bones in my left shoulder.

That was the end of the season for me. I was out for a long time after that. I headed home. Alana was pregnant with Zaid and he was born a couple of weeks later. At least I was there for the birth. Alhamdulillah!

***

Although I had been out with injury for much of the 2018 Super Rugby season, I had worked tirelessly and got my body right so I could be involved in the end-of-year tour. But then, in the second game of the tour versus England, injury struck again. Although I was out for the rest of the 2018 end-of-year tour, I still had a whole off-season to get myself ready for the goal of making the 2019 World Cup squad. And the big upside was, it wasn't my knee! It was my shoulder.

This time, instead of injury throwing me down the deep well of depression, I had this mad sense of gratitude. I knew I had the strength to get back up one more time and not only heal, but become a better person in the process, getting closer to my Creator. It was a mindset that enabled me to grind it out, stay patient, take the long view and work towards being an even better teammate, husband and father.

I had a really good 2019 off-season from a training perspective. We had Phil Healey, our old trainer from the Chiefs, and Rieko Ioane and I were training together. Once we finished, I had achieved some really good markers. I was the fastest, the strongest and the fittest I'd been in several years.

I was training with the Auckland Blues, then Rieko and I would go off and train together. When Rieko Ioane is beating you by ten metres in sprints every day and the gap slowly closes, that feels like a win, confirmation of my fitness and steady improvement. That dark hole was way behind me. I went into the 2019 Super Rugby season with the Blues on a high. I felt I was going to finish off my All Blacks career at the top and was looking forward to getting to play with my old mates one last time. I was named as vice-captain then captain of the Blues, and was feeling really good out there on the field.

We played the Stormers at Eden Park. I came off the bench, made a break straight away, feeling good. We won the scrum, I ran a short ball, hit a hole and set up a try with an offload to Otere Black, who scored under the posts.

But in the tackle my knee hit the ground hard; I got up and I knew something wasn't right. I felt sick: it was the same old feeling of trying to walk back to position but knowing my knee was shot. I'd done the cartilage and I'd only been on the field ten or fifteen minutes.

Back in the sheds, the boys were asking, 'You all right?' 'You okay?'

Right then, I went into that mindset of determination to work hard and get it right. I told myself, *Just this last season, Sonny.*

I had to wait for the usual medical investigations, and I was at home when the Blues doctor called me. I had started the season in really good nick – physically, I'd been hitting markers I hadn't hit for years. Then, bang.

There goes my knee again. I knew this was serious. After some scans, the Auckland Blues doctor had bad news. 'This could be it,' he told me. 'This injury could be the one you don't come back from.' I acted all tough and said, 'Okay, cool.' Then I just sat there and got really emotional, eyes all watery; I didn't know my wife could hear, but she was standing the other side of the door, listening to the call. It was hard for Alana to watch.

After the Achilles, Sonny got injury after injury. I was at the game in Auckland and he was playing amazingly well, just flying. I was feeling so happy for him. Then his knee goes.

When he got the not-so-good news about the MRI scan, I walked out to the backyard and found him crying. Going to the World Cup meant so much to him.

I didn't really have any words to console him, and of course I was crying. I said to him, 'This isn't the end. It isn't going to finish like this.' I see it as my duty to be a mirror Sonny can look into and see the best version of himself and hear only positive messages coming back. Usually it doesn't take him long to get over things.

He called Khoder and they talked things through. They decided to call a meeting with the doctors and the physio from the All Blacks as well as the Blues physio and a surgeon to see if there was a rehab path he could take, checking on progress every week, or if it was better to have surgery.

It seemed to me nearly everyone was against surgery, but Sonny called the shots and said, 'Nah, I'm doing it.' I felt as if everyone had given up on him except Sonny himself. He had surgery and then he went at the rehabilitation as only he can do. That's Sonny. Every time he comes under extreme pressure, he finds a way to rise to the occasion. – Alana Williams

I was blessed to have Alana's support, and I was backing myself to get my knee strong enough to play at a high-enough level to make it into the World Cup squad. That old determination came back to me and so did the Islamic teachings of always being grateful for what you have. Rehab is no fun, but I had that goal and I pushed hard, did what the surgeon said, did what the physios said, and did what I had always done and stepped it up whenever I could. That year I played only the first and last games of the season for the Blues; that's how long it took to rehab back to form.

I got my body back to fitness levels that allowed me to play in the last game against the Hurricanes. Although I came off the field thinking I'd played well, I was pretty sure the powers that be would want me to play some park football to test out my fitness and boost my confidence levels, like they had done with Kieran Read. To my great surprise, that wasn't the case. I was handed the number 12 All Blacks jersey to play our next game against our greatest rival, South Africa.

ALL BLACKS v SPRINGBOKS:
SONNY BILL WILLIAMS MAGIC SAVES A HORROR SHOW

I played for fifty-eight minutes of that game, which ended up a 16–16 draw. I thought I had done my teammates and the black jersey proud. I was pleased with how my body performed and my skills were match fit. The headline that New Zealand media outlet Stuff ran suggested they felt the same. But Steve Hansen was obviously not impressed because I was called into a coaches' meeting with him, Ian Foster and Grant Fox. It was the first time I had ever been called out like that. Steve asked me to sit down and then told me that if they announced the 2019 All Blacks World Cup squad later that day, I would not be on the list. They carried on talking, but I wasn't hearing anything. All I could think was, *Why was I picked for that last game?* I'd gone from being in the starting fifteen to being told I would not even be named in the squad of thirty-two, all from that last performance? If I was to be omitted from the World Cup on how I played in that last game, I knew I'd done my best and I could definitely hold my head up high. But I was disappointed at how it was handled and thought Shag could have talked to me alone. I had played over fifty Tests and thought I deserved a little more respect than that. I guess he thought he needed Fox and Foster's support, but it didn't sit right with me.

I started thinking, *Couldn't you have asked me to coffee and been a bit more respectful about telling me how you felt? All of a sudden, I'm only good enough to play club rugby?* It was done in such an abrupt manner and I told myself it was just business. Not a relationship, not a bond between a player and his coaches. Just business. You are only necessary as long as you are useful. I know it happens to most players. One minute on top of the world, the next hurled off into outer space. It is brutal.

I was heading back to club rugby. But first, I had a frank talk with the coaches and told them exactly what I thought, how I felt the situation could have been managed in a better way. I explained that I knew it wasn't about me the individual, it was about the team, but they'd handled it wrong.

* * *

Park footy means lots of travel and playing in small towns in front of passionate crowds, often in pouring rain, and there is something about it that gets lost in the higher echelons of the game. They play with a freedom and happiness that is hard to find in those upper levels. It was good for me and reminded me what footy should feel like. Although I never openly expressed it at the time, deep down I was 100 per cent sure my All Blacks career was over.

Fast-forward a couple of weeks and the All Blacks were beaten by the Wallabies in Perth. They were getting savaged by the media. It was all doom and gloom, and commentators were predicting that we may lose the beloved Bledisloe for the first time in nearly twenty years. I was hurting for my brothers and sent messages of support to a few of the boys.

Then out of nowhere, I got a call from Shag.

'You're back in the team, Sonny.'

Just like that I was back training with the boys, and they were happy to see me. We were all pumped and ready to go. There is nothing more dangerous than a wounded All Blacks team. They named the team on the Tuesday before the game, and I was in the starting line-up. It was the biggest game of the year for the All Blacks, and I'd gone from being one of them to a club player and then back to the starting All Blacks squad in the blink of an eye. You'd never read about it – because it ain't meant to happen that way. Once you're dropped, you're supposed to be out of sight and out of mind.

We went to Auckland to play the Wallabies, who were on a high and pretty confident they knew how to beat us – and easily. Their number 12, Samu Kerevi, had an unbelievable game in that Perth outing, very physical.

I watched the game live and also in a replay. The whole time I was thinking, *Just give me a chance, because this is the type of battle I will thrive in.*

This was my shot, and I knew it was up to me. And I prepared as if it was my last game for the All Blacks ever, which it well could have been. As I always did, I prepared physically and mentally, but this time with even more intent. The game couldn't come quick enough.

The Aussie media were savage, with one headline on the back page of a Sydney paper reading, 'THE OLD BLACKS'. The headline was accompanied by a team photo, which the newspaper had altered with an app to age us and captioned with the words 'senior citizens'. I was the oldest in that team and I am pretty sure I won't look like that when I am an old man (though I wouldn't mind being that fit-looking at sixty!). It was a laugh for the boys and not too smart to try and rile us up. Disrespectful media like that can sting but it just adds another level of motivation for me.

We drove up to the stadium in our team bus and I remember getting off and thinking, *This is it*. In the changing room, I walked over to my jersey, which was hanging up ready, and got my boots out (I never, ever forgot them again after that first time!). The boys were all walking around or doing their own last-minute prep. I watched Ardie Savea and Rieko Ioane do their little dance moves. Big Sammy Whitelock had his head down, concentrating. Dane Coles, one of the players I respected the most in the squad and who I believed had the complete skill set that could have seen him play rugby league at the highest level, was putting on his boots. Captain Kieran 'Reado' Read moved around having a quick last word with all the players. I took it all in. I'm thinking, *I'm coming. I'm coming.*

Then we ran outside. It was raining and I thought the rain would impact my offload because of the slippery ball and the different tactics required to play in the wet. But I was too pumped to let that thought linger. I was just looking over at the Wallabies, picking out Kerevi who I considered one of the best centres in the world, and thinking, *Yeah, I'm coming for you.* A player with his talent needed my undivided attention.

I remember the day before I'd told my wife and Khoder, my family, that I was going to go out there and play hard and have fun. A steely resolve settled on us all.

I flew out of the line intent on making my presence felt from the off. But Kurtley Beale, world-class player that he is, outsmarted me and skip-passed to his outside man. Okay, but the start whistle had only just blown. I was in hunting mode. Made my tackles, and tried to be as physical as I could be, with or without the ball. We had to win to keep the Bledisloe Cup. And we did!

I love those big moments. We kept Kerevi quiet, and I played really well. I scored my twelfth try in fifty-three Tests and was part of a fierce team who beat the Wallabies 36–0. We received a standing ovation after the game and that is a mad buzz.

* * *

After that game against Australia, it was a great feeling in the sheds. I was proud of our resilience and how as a team we'd come through the struggles to put on such a dominant display.

Four weeks later, when they named the Rugby World Cup squad on the radio, I was at home with Alana and the kids, and Johnny was there too. Was I nervous? If it was purely based on my recent performances on the park against South Africa and Australia (not to forget my history in the black jersey), I felt like my name would be on the list. Despite the one conversation I had with the coaches, I knew my journey in 2011, 2015 and into 2019 meant I would be an asset to the team. I was no longer the shy, unconfident, mixed Sāmoan-Australian boy who had a 'yes sir, no sir' attitude to authority, whether they be right or wrong. I was now a proud, confident Pasifika man who knew he had earned his position in the squad. When the list was read out, my name was there. Alana was crying, Johnny was crying. I had very mixed feelings as I was happy to be going to defend the title and play in my third World Cup but I was also very disappointed for my good mate Owen Franks, one of our greatest ever props, and fellow Pacific brother Ngani Laumape – another former league player with whom I had a special rapport – who didn't make the squad. That made me feel a bit empty instead of full of all the joys. Two guys I was close to would not be joining us. That could have been me.

I'd been elevated back up, from club to elite and was in my third All Blacks Rugby World Cup squad. All the work, self-belief and heart had paid off. I look back to that young fella who arrived in Sydney with some talent but so much self-doubt and I am really aware of the way I have been able to shape my life. Key to all that was my belief in Islam; Islam helped me learn how to leave my torments behind. I was so grateful to be doing what I loved, living my life as a professional sportsman, and now I was united with my All Blacks teammates in wanting to make history. I knew that 2019 was going to be my last year in the All Blacks and I wanted to finish on a high note.

2019 Rugby World Cup Squad

Forwards: Ardie Savea, Sam Cane, Matt Todd, Luke Jacobson, Scott Barrett, Sam Whitelock, Brodie Retallick, Patrick Tuipulotu,

Nepo Laulala, Angus Ta'avao, Ofa Tu'ungafasi, Joe Moody,
Atu Moli, Dane Coles, Codie Taylor, Liam Coltman,
Kieran Read (c.)
Backs: Jordie Barrett, Ben Smith, Sevu Reece, George Bridge,
Rieko Ioane, Jack Goodhue, Anton Lienert-Brown, Ryan Crotty,
Sonny Bill Williams, Beauden Barrett, Richie Mo'unga,
Aaron Smith, TJ Perenara, Brad Weber

* * *

Imaan was turning five and this was her dad's last time in the
All Blacks, his third World Cup, and I was so glad I was there in
Japan to watch him. This was a huge achievement for Sonny after
his injuries. The way he got himself back to match fitness made
me proud. At thirty-four, he was the oldest in the team and was
on track to make history going after his third World Cup.

Things didn't go exactly as we all hoped. Losing the semi-
final against England was brutal. To keep Sonny off in that
game seemed a mistake to me and not because I'm his wife.
They got beaten in the first half, yet they didn't go to the bench
at half-time. When they finally did, Sonny came on but it was
too late, there weren't enough minutes left. So, the All Blacks
came third.

Sonny had a magic that could change a game because he not
only had the skills and physicality, but he could also see it, the gaps,
where the play was headed: he could read the game. If I'm watching

a game on television with Sonny, he'll say, 'Why are they doing that move? It won't work.' He took that ability into every game he played.

At the end of that Bronze-medal match against Wales, Imaan got to go on the field with her dad, and she carried his medal around. When we got back home to New Zealand, she took the medal to school; she was so happy and proud.

I think when Sonny's an old man he can look at those photos of him and Imaan on the field in Tokyo and be reminded of the importance of family and our cherished memories. — Alana Williams

It wasn't to be. We travelled to Japan looking to claim another World Cup, and after finishing top of the table in our pool we were ready to face Ireland in the quarter-final. I was on the bench for the start of that game, and, without disrespecting Ireland, it was a good feeling to beat them 46–14 and set ourselves up to play England in the semi-final. We were going in as reigning champions and, after beating our rivals South Africa in the Pool B match to get there, we were probably going in favourites. But nothing is ever certain on a footy field and England had a steely resolve that was evident as we performed the haka. They had a point to prove and they hit hard from the opening whistle. They did everything you have to do to win. At the end of eighty minutes, we were beaten by the better team, and as much as it always hurts to lose, they deserved the 19–7 win because they never let up. As our All Blacks captain, Kieran Read, said after the game, 'We gave our all, gave it everything we had, but just came up short. We're all hurting.' Steve Hansen backed him up, saying, 'There's no shame in it, but a lot of hurt which could all feed into a lot of All Blacks teams in the future.'

Like I have said before, there is nothing more dangerous than a wounded All Blacks team and that fire to win and reclaim that Cup will smoulder until 2023, when I have no doubt that it will ignite. But after the game, we all needed bulletproof vests when we sat down together to analyse what went wrong. It was a grim conversation, as the coaches pulled no punches, and the team had their say. Then we just had to get on with it.

That hurt fuelled us in the third-place match against Wales. We won that game 40–17. We hadn't come to win bronze. We wanted the gold medal and I wanted to lift the trophy for the third time, so I had some struggles in my head with that disappointment. But I played well in that game and did what I always want to do when I wear the All Blacks jersey: honour my brothers who have come before and build on a tradition for those who will follow. After fifty-eight Test matches, I don't care what my critics say: I gave all I could to that team and was very proud to represent New Zealand.

In an interview after the game, I said that while obviously it was hard to lose, there are more important things in life, and I wasn't going to sit and sulk over something that's not going to bring me happiness. I copped some flak over those comments; I think they wanted me to be crying in a corner. But I have learned that sport is only ever one part of a sportsperson's life, and it is not the only purpose. Sure, I go out to win. But if I play well, and give it my all, that is all I can do. Having my daughter with me on the field after the game against Wales, to sit and soak up the moment, and reflect on what it took to be there, was a beautiful thing. I was so thankful to New Zealand rugby, who had given me the opportunity to play those fifty-eight Test matches and also allowed me to keep boxing and to play rugby sevens. To play for the last time in the All Blacks jersey was emotional but I am forever part of rugby history and when I am an old man I will have lots of stories about the games we played and the people we played against. Alhamdulillah, I am so grateful for it all.

Do I wish we had won? Yes. But sometimes the Most High has other plans.

CHAPTER 14

Being where my feet are

After the World Cup, I had to think about what I wanted to do and how my body was holding up. Before that, I had told Khoder he could have conversations exploring other opportunities, but my focus had to be on the All Blacks and honouring that jersey, so I didn't want to discuss the future or know what offers were coming in. In the last few years, I really have tried to live by the saying: 'I try to be where my feet are.' Once I was back in New Zealand and Alana and I talked about it, I knew I was not ready to retire. At that point I thought I would stay in New Zealand and play another year of club rugby. Meanwhile, Khoder was sorting through offers and possibilities and he presented some to me for us to discuss. I decided the offer to join the Toronto Wolfpack, who were playing in the British Super League and based in the UK, was too good to turn down. Sure, the money was great, but the opportunity to return to playing rugby league and be part of the Super League was also a big lure. To transition back to league would be a challenge, but I am a sportsman and I need to have something to aim for. Importantly, that goal has to be worthy of all the sacrifices I ask my family to make to enable me to continue to play elite sport.

Talking to Toronto coach Brian McDermott and hearing his vision for Toronto in the Super League gave me a new sense of purpose. The aim was to succeed. And the fact that Toronto is a multicultural city and that I might help open up the North American market was another factor. I know what sport did for me as a youngster. If I can help young fellas find opportunities they may not have had otherwise, then I would be very happy. And Toronto wanted me not just as a player but for a leadership role; they wanted me to mentor the younger players and help where I was needed. It was a new challenge, and the challenge is always important to me. I want to push myself, stretch my skills and be a better player and a better person, and joining the Wolfpack ticked all those boxes. We wanted to win the northern hemisphere's premier rugby league competition in 2020. I was on board for that.

The team was based in Manchester, so it meant a move for Alana and the kids. That was a hard wrench for Alana, as while the details were getting sorted, she was pregnant with our fourth child. Dealing with three kids, a pregnancy (and hers have not been easy) and the thought of moving countries was a lot of pressure on both of us.

> Sonny was in Britain for six weeks. He came home two days before our son Essa was born. We thought the upheaval was over when we were all in the UK together, but one week later, everything went into Covid lockdown. – Alana Williams

It was an awful time for so many, and though we didn't know how bad things would get around the world, we all felt worried about what was to come. But Alana and I gave thanks to Allah that she hadn't waited to travel because if she had, the borders would have been closed and the kids and Alana would have been stuck in New Zealand and I would have been in Manchester without them.

As Alana said, within the first week of her and the kids arriving, the whole country was placed in lockdown and we had no idea how long that would be for. At first, it was full-on hectic with jet lag and a new environment. Alana and I pretty soon realised that with four kids in the house and limited outside interaction we had to put some structure in place, for all of us. We were home-schooling the older kids and so having activities at certain times of the day really helped to keep them on track. We were allowed to leave the house to exercise as a family and we were lucky as within the ten-kilometre radius that limited travel we had farmland and forest to explore. We went walking every day and it was lovely to be with the kids, checking out the natural world. Though the day Zaid and I were chased by cows is not the interaction with nature I was wanting to teach him about. I didn't know cows could run so fast. It was pretty funny! As tough as the pandemic has been for so many around the world, and my heart goes out to them, the world slowing down saw me able to spend uninterrupted time with my family. This has seen us flourish and has strengthened our bond. I just enjoyed being with them. Alana loved it too, because it was just us.

But I never forgot what I was there for, so my training never stopped. That was always part of my day. Weights, boxing, bike, yoga, stretching, running – everything I could do to maintain my fitness I did, always hoping that things would get better.

That wasn't to be and after five months, I was stuck in limbo, not able to play and not sure what to do. And that's when discussions with the Roosters began. The NRL allowed me to return to Australia. Packing up again was not quite as hard because we had barely unpacked, and the thought of being back in Australia brought comfort to Alana and me, though I think Alana would have liked to go back to New Zealand. So, we packed up the kids and committed to the two weeks' quarantine required to make a return to the NRL possible. The challenge of that and connecting with the Roosters boys lit me up.

I was pretty fit despite not being able to train with teammates for five months and before I flew back I had another clean-out of my knee to be sure it would hold up. I can't even remember how many general anaesthetics I have had, but it is a lot! I was looking forward to getting back on a field with the team and I was ready for another stint in the NRL. Especially after two weeks in hotel quarantine with the kids!

My first game was against the Canberra Raiders, and I came in off the bench in the second half. I loved being back out there, playing the game I grew up playing. I expected to be pushed, and I was. The rule changes to the game made it a lot faster, but nothing I couldn't adapt to. Post-quarantine, I still had to work on my fitness, but coming away with the 18–6 win was awesome. I played in the next three games then missed the qualifying final because of an injury to my neck, but I made it back for the do-or-die semi-final. We lost the match 22–18 to the Canberra Raiders, but the boys had given it their all to claw back to a near-win when it was looking bad early on.

We almost got there. I felt bad for the boys, but experience has shown that sometimes the fairytale doesn't happen. That is a hard lesson to learn but sometimes your best effort doesn't bring home the trophy. I had a chat about how to deal with that with some of the younger boys and how they can use that disappointment to fuel their efforts next season and beyond.

[Sonny Bill Williams] was fantastic tonight [in the semi-final]. He was a real success story this year. He came back and slowly got back to a situation where he could play. I thought he was big tonight. But he will be a success at whatever he does because he has the mindset and willpower. — Peter Sterling

All those who bagged [Sonny Bill Williams] in the lead-up — he stood up like a champion. Not bad for 35 with little prep. If that's his last NRL game, it's been a great career. — Danny Weidler

After the game I was asked if that was it for me, and at that point I didn't know. I had to see what was happening with Toronto, but so much depended on the way Covid-19 was controlled and it wasn't looking good in the UK or the US. And I had to admit that my thirty-five-year-old joints were finding it a bit tougher to get out of the starting blocks each week. I was doing everything I could to keep my body competitive on a footy field, but the injuries had taken a toll. I worked hard to get back to an elite level and I was proud of that, but even after the extra effort I was putting in to be ready for game day, I still had to take too many painkillers and drugs just to play. At one point, I had been taking so many painkilling drugs I ended up with burning in my gut and had to have an endoscopy to check out what was happening.

In that last game against the Raiders, I had so many drugs in my system and yet I still had pain in my neck, back and knee. I came in after warm-up and asked the doc for more. He said he had a duty of care to uphold and that if I had any more, I could overdose. Although I still had the drive, I knew my time in footy had come to an end.

Not long after, I was doing a boxing interview and I just came out with the news that I was not going to play league or union anymore. Every player fears injury will be followed by a loss of form and being dropped. I had worked hard to keep bouncing back but Alana and I had talked about it and we feared me being forced out rather than going out on my own terms. I've had anxiety about injury, as you know, since I was first told by a doctor my career might be over by age twenty-three.

I'm proud to say that my last game of league in Australia was at the highest level, playing in an NRL semi-final. My last All Blacks game finished on a good note too. It was time to step away physically from the game. And I had other things I wanted to do, and new challenges waiting. Leaving the game physically was easier than I thought, but mentally the game still lingers. In the end, the conflict between what my body could give and what my mind expected was just too distant. Combine that with all the painkillers and anti-inflammatories and I knew I couldn't play footy at an elite level anymore. I was in constant pain and I never wanted to be there just to make up the numbers. I always wanted to add value my way.

I am forever grateful to my Creator for giving me such a long career. And I've been fortunate to have played alongside some exceptional sportspeople. There are so many players who have given me friendship over the years and countless others who made an impression. I've always shown respect to every man I ever took the field with in the different rugby codes, as well as the brothers I have met through boxing. I've already paid tribute to a few, but I want to thank all the teammates who I played with over the years for allowing me to achieve dreams I never thought possible. I hope you all know I will always be supporting you from afar.

CHAPTER 15

Finding my voice

I am a very different person from the man I once was. I used to worry about saying the wrong thing or giving an opinion because I didn't believe that what I had to say mattered or would make a difference. That's down to the insecurity and low self-esteem I talked about earlier. I am in a good place now because of my faith and my family. But I have also grown up a lot. I have matured and everything I have experienced up to this point on my life's journey has created the man I am today. A man at peace with it all because of Allah.

When I started to gather information and brush up on all things Sonny Bill, I found a video on YouTube titled 'Sonny Bill Williams: 4 moments of charity/respect/humility'.

The first clip shows a Tongan girl approaching Sonny Bill on the field requesting something. He follows her to the crowd, where a Tongan player hands Sonny his baby so he can take a photo. Sonny is entirely in that moment, acknowledging a fellow Polynesian, knowing how good it makes the father feel. He touches the man's arm and walks over to acknowledge his family and other Tongans. It is a simple but beautiful moment.

The second moment points out that Sonny Bill had offered free tickets to any Syrian refugees who wanted to go to the 2019 World Cup. He proactively reached out to do that.

The third is after the All Blacks beat the Springboks in the 2015 Rugby World Cup semi-final. An inconsolable Jesse Kriel, Sonny's admirable mid-field opponent, is down on his haunches in dismay. Sonny goes to him, bends down and embraces him. It's more than a quick hug; he embraces the South African as one rugby brother to another, saying in the nicest possible way, 'This was our day. Tomorrow will be yours.'

Then, as the rain pours down, he helps Kriel to his feet, talking to him, his face close to Kriel's. For my money, that moment could have been freeze-framed and shown around the world as a lesson in aroha, respect, shown by one special athlete to another special athlete. *We fought a good battle, now we are no longer enemies but, rather, the opposite. Friends of mutual respect.*

The fourth moment is the one I described in the introduction to this book: Sonny's astonishing gesture of, first, spontaneous concern when a fourteen-year-old fan was tackled by a security guard when he ran out onto the field after the All Blacks won the 2015 Rugby World Cup.

The rest is history. That boy's hero put an arm around him and walked him back to his parents in the stand. Then he removed his gold medal and put it around the boy's neck.

Those moments – and I know there are many more – show the real Sonny Bill Williams, the man. No opponent ever got the better of him on the field, and he is a legendary sportsman. But what elevates him in my eyes is his heart, his empathy and his willingness to speak out for those who can't speak out for themselves. That is the true greatness of SBW.
– Alan Duff

In May 2020, the world was confronted by the shocking death of George Floyd while in police custody. The spotlight was turned onto the racism that still lives too close to the surface of our lives. For people of colour, this was more than a moment of outrage; it was an acknowledgement and understanding of the different ways you are treated because of the colour of your skin. Alan Duff and I have talked about how America has treated its black sports stars historically. Win the world heavyweight championship like black American Joe Frazier did in 1970 and then see if you can withdraw $10,000 from your own bank account. The answer was no.

Muhammad Ali dared to challenge the white establishment. He refused to be drafted into the US Army for service in Vietnam, even when he was threatened with jail and warned his world heavyweight title would be stripped from him. He was hated for daring to speak up, but he wouldn't be silenced. Strong-willed, he snatched the narrative and never handed it back. For the world to change, for equality to be real, we need people to speak up.

I am learning to do that: to speak out when it matters, or when I see injustice. I am determined to honour my principles. (I mentioned earlier that, with the All Blacks' blessing, I covered up the logo of one of our sponsors, a bank, because Islam does not permit interest.) I don't care who it is; if you are being held back, held down, you have a right to push back and keep pushing until you are treated as an equal.

Sport – and sportspeople – can help shine that light into dark places. It can unite, inspire and free. Look at Jesse Owens, an African American who, in the 1936 Olympics held in Berlin, won four gold medals. His incredible achievement in front of Adolf Hitler powerfully dispelled the dangerous Nazi theory of Aryan superiority. He showed that a person of colour could win the day. There is a lesson in that. Or the spotlight placed on racism and segregation in America by Tommie Smith and John Carlos at the 1968 Mexico City Olympics, as they raised their arms straight up in the air, each with their hand in a black glove in a Black Power salute. Or the Australian man next to them on the podium, Peter Norman, who wore a badge in solidarity, calling for an end to racism.

Rugby gave me an international profile, allowing me to thrive on the world stage. The love and tributes I received on announcing my retirement – from fans, fellow players, opponents, governing bodies, referees and even the media – made me feel empowered to follow my path more boldly. But I am just a man – I hope a caring man, with a heart. I have my flaws, and I know what it is to struggle. I was blessed and I found the light and the right partner and so I am on the path to be the better person I have always yearned to be.

Nowadays, I feel I most represent Polynesian and Māori people, especially the youngsters who are unsure what the future holds. Not all kids come from a privileged background. Not all kids have it easy growing up and many have to worry if there's food on the table. It is too easy for these kids to be left behind.

It needs to be understood how colonisation has affected Pasifika and Māori people, just as it has affected Indigenous Australians. Losing your culture, your way of life, has a drastic effect on any race, and this intergenerational trauma can echo on for generations. It can be seen today in our higher crime rates, worse health statistics, higher suicide rates, poor education outcomes, low home ownership – the list goes on and on. I'm glad that New Zealanders in general have lately made a major shift towards understanding our Polynesian culture, our outlook. And good on the media for promoting that.

This is not a demand for an apology. It is a plea for awareness. Colonisation is not just a moment in history with no after-effects.

When I was with Alan Duff in Auckland early in June 2021, working on this book, we ran into a Māori friend, Rua Tipoki – a former top rugby player who didn't quite make it to the All Blacks – and another mate, Quade Cooper. We chatted about various things, and my Māori brother expressed pride in me having done so well in sport. That talk moved on to the importance of self-belief – or the impact a lack of it can have. He recalled how, growing up, he was told that Māori don't quite have it; didn't have the fire or the work ethic or the ability. If you hear that enough, you start to believe it. He spoke about brown people these days turning a corner and starting to believe in themselves.

There were four of us standing there that day: Quade Cooper, the former Wallaby; Alan Duff, who has gone from serving time in jail to having his books published around the world; our Māori bro, who led his Irish club side in a haka before playing the All Blacks and came close to a major upset; and me. We were four brown people who'd come from difficult backgrounds yet made it. This is what we all want for young Pasifika and Māori. Self-belief that grows into success.

Here's a little story that, on the face of it, seems to be about my dad. But it goes way beyond that – and way back before it, too.

After I retired, I had an offer to become a rugby league and rugby union commentator for the Nine and Stan networks. I was ready to take on that challenge, and though I knew I'd have a lot to learn, I was ready to step up and do it. When I told my old man, he said, 'But don't you have to be a rugby person to do that job?' I was shocked and a bit dirty. I was the winner of two Rugby World Cup medals, winner of a Super Rugby championship, I had won two NRL grand finals and had played over 300 professional games in both codes. Wasn't I a rugby person?

I reacted strongly, even angrily, but when I thought about it later, I realised my father was just expressing that colonised Sāmoan outlook of, *We are not good enough.* It was his instinctive reaction, and it said more about the world he had grown up in than what he thought about me.

That kind of attitude has long been indoctrinated in Pasifika and Māori people. Those years of being downtrodden have an effect on your psychology; you automatically think in the negative. My father was the product of several generations of oppression. So even when all the evidence says his son is more than qualified to commentate on a sport he's excelled at, he still struggles to believe it. That's what colonisation has done.

If you look at how many Polynesians and Māori play in league and union teams in Australia and New Zealand, and increasingly in the UK and France, and then look at the lack of representation at an administrative and management level, you can see the problem. It would be good to see more brown coaches, board members and CEOs come through. It is important for our young people that Māori and Pasifika people are represented in all levels of society, because you can't aspire to be what you can't see. It is like me back at school, thinking I couldn't do anything that required an education. My focus was sport, because I had seen brown footy players on TV. I could aspire to be one of them because they were like me.

There are so many things in the world that need to change, and I am realising more and more that it is up to people with a platform – people like me – to call out what is wrong. The only way we can open people's eyes to injustice is to talk about it.

When Australia and New Zealand established the trans-Tasman bubble at the end of May 2021, allowing people from both countries quarantine-free travel, I flew back to New Zealand and headed for Queenstown. I was travelling with former Socceroo and refugee advocate Craig Foster.

We wanted to shine a spotlight on Australia's shameful treatment of refugees and asylum seekers. For too long refugee policy has focused on the politics of securing votes rather than the humanitarian focus it should have. Too many asylum seekers are housed in dismal camps on Christmas Island and in Nauru and Papua New Guinea. In 2021 alone, there are about 240 human beings imprisoned in offshore detention centres and $800 million has been allocated to be spent keeping them there. And one family of four, with two Australian-born children – Nades, Priya, Kopika and Tharnicaa Murugappan – spent over three years detained on Christmas Island before they were brought back to the mainland because Tharnicaa required urgent medical attention. The Australian Government has spent an incredible $10 billion keeping asylum seekers like this family in camps like convicted criminals.

These are people who committed no crime. After fleeing oppression and war in their home countries, they had legally sought asylum. Instead of being welcomed, for eight years they've been stuck in limbo. And the government doesn't give a damn. People's views on refugees have always baffled me. It really hits my heart that they are treated with such contempt.

In 2015, I visited a Syrian refugee camp in Lebanon, and it really opened my eyes. The first question we should all ask ourselves is: *What is a refugee?* When people understand that a refugee is actually a person seeking refuge from persecution, fleeing from a war or a cruel regime run by a dictator's brutal police or military, or a person fleeing from a society that would imprison and kill them for political or religious views, it will hopefully make them think differently.

A refugee doesn't really want to leave their homeland – few people do. Home is home. These people have been forced to leave their homes.

Why wouldn't the Australian Government let them in? Australia has been made better by the contribution of displaced people and refugees and until 2001, we were a country that mostly addressed asylum seekers with compassion. If we allowed these people to settle, we would see the benefits more than the disadvantages.

Visiting that camp in Lebanon made me question humanity as a whole. It was a devastating place. I watched kids play, like kids do the world over, only the mud puddles they were splashing in was raw sewage. You look into the eyes of the parents in a place like that and all you see is hopelessness. Bitterness. The profound disappointment of people who are forgotten, ignored. I saw some older kids, aged thirteen to eighteen, who had set up real basic makeshift schools in tents. These were kids grateful to be alive after losing most of their family to war.

With the help of an interpreter, I spoke to kids who told me they wanted to go back to Syria and not just survive but thrive. 'We want to go back to Syria and be productive in society, rebuild our lives.' Hearing that really hit me. Again, as I said, few people *want* to leave their homeland. It is an act of sheer desperation. Now they were in limbo. They couldn't go back to Syria, but they weren't Lebanese citizens. The adults had no opportunity to work, and though there were those makeshift schools in the camp, the kids had no access to a proper education. Where is the light at the end of the tunnel for these people? The sad truth is, there isn't one. They have to move on and keep moving on, maybe even to Australia, in the hope of finding a peaceful place to settle where they might rebuild their shattered lives. This experience has given me a deeper sense of gratitude for all that my family and I have.

So, Craig and I were in New Zealand while the Australian Prime Minister was there, wanting to look the politicians in the eye and ask them: 'Why?' And also ask them: 'Where has all the money gone? Ten billion dollars!' The workers in the camps are on about $10 an hour.

So why does it cost $800 million to house 240 refugees? That's $3.33 million per person. And the camps are not the Hilton. It makes me angry, and I can't see how that amount of money can be accounted for. I think we all have a duty to get our priorities right along with giving ourselves a big dose of humanity, and then to call on the government to change its policies. Imagine it was you, having to get up, leave everything you've known, grab your kids and your family, everything you've worked for in your life and flee. All we want is for the government to treat people in a humane way and give them a fair go.

I'm grateful to be blessed with such an amazing brother who is also such a decent human being. He's not perfect – who is? – and he has never claimed to be. But he's never made the same mistake twice and always learned from those slip-ups.

I'm so proud he uses his public profile as a platform to help others, like going to Christchurch to comfort and show compassion for his fellow Muslims who survived that awful massacre in March 2019. This same man donated his $100,000 boxing purse to the Christchurch Earthquake Recovery Fund. He is speaking out on behalf of refugees kept in dismal camps in offshore Australia and Nauru. He's not running around the A-list celebrity circuit partying on big yachts, wining and dining in fancy places. He's out there fighting for people who fled intolerable conditions in their own country just wanting a better

life in Australia. I am very proud of him. I love him heaps, even
when he introduces me as 'Nail', not Niall. I wouldn't have him
any other way. – Niall Williams

I was a late starter at watching my brother Sonny play footy.
I didn't go to his games till I was a bit older and was sent to live
in Sydney because I was wagging school in my rebellious phase.
Dad said come over to live with me and my partner, promising he
wouldn't be on my case.

Having two brothers there as well as my father meant I at
least had family support and so I went. I saw my brothers as
more my father figures; they let me know they had my back. While
I was at a bit of a loose end, Sonny paid for my early childhood
education diploma and offered to set me up with my own private
centre. I declined because, like a lot of Polynesians, the thought
of sitting exams and possibly failing was too daunting. I've been
in early childhood education eight years now.

I started to become aware of how popular my brother was
with the rugby league fans when I went to watch him play.
Everyone cheered madly for him, and it made me feel so proud.
When the media criticised him – which wasn't very often over in
Australia – I'd get mad.

It was Sonny who kind of coached me how to handle him
being criticised. He'd say, 'They don't know us. Who cares about
people we've never even met?' As I said, I was a late starter to
the SBW fan club but naturally I became a pretty avid one.

When he was leaving the Bulldogs, he took us family members aside to tell us. We were shocked, couldn't believe it. Dad was very upset; he just didn't understand it. I cried and we hugged, and he was off to France.

But he never ever forgot his family; he paid for me to go to Toulon, to Japan. Back to France. Paid mega dollars to get me from Sydney to Auckland because it was Christmas and last-minute fares were through the roof. He just wanted me home with Mum for Christmas; cost didn't come into it. Words can't express how I feel about him.

We live just twenty minutes away from Sonny in Sydney now. Dad and his partner live close by too. He loves my kids and my daughter, named after my sister, Niall, just adores him. She converted to Islam because of him. And there was no pressure from either me or Sonny. It was what she wanted.

I actually had no idea how big rugby league was in Australia. Or how big the All Blacks are in New Zealand – even their international opponents have huge respect for them. My brother a top league player, a Kiwi and then in the All Blacks?

I always watch his and Niall's games. And I kept the Bulldogs as my favourite league team even though he left them. If he's not playing for the ABs, I don't watch.

When he offered to put up the money for me to get my own childcare centre, I didn't have the confidence to do the extra study required. Johnny and I called ourselves the 'black sheep' of the family. But we turned out all right.

When I had a miscarriage, he flew Mum straight over to Sydney. He's helped us all out. In private, he's a goof. We've got videos of him dancing and doing silly, crazy things. He gets everyone involved. His body might have gotten a bit old, but his humour hasn't aged one day.

No matter how much pain he was in, how tired he was after a hard game, he always had time for us. I'm proud to talk about him. Proud to be the sister of such an exceptional, special man.

– Denise Williams

***

I've come so far from that teenager who couldn't speak up. Now I am using my voice to speak about injustice and also using my voice in a new career. My next challenge is as a sports commentator for the Nine Network in Australia and for Stan Sport. I am a big believer that without challenges, there is no growth, so pushing myself into this new space made sense. Sure, I could have just retired and led a quiet, comfortable life, but I am not one to sit back and let life go by. Is it daunting? Yes. Is it a little overwhelming? Yes. But that is what makes it interesting.

And, as I said earlier, over here in Australia there's no Islander representation in the media, at board level, as CEOs or sporting coaches. Islanders make up about 50 per cent of league and rugby teams, but zero per cent of the management jobs. I'd like to think I got the commentating role because I have runs on the board as a professional league and rugby player. I know both sports, but there are lots of Kiwi and Islander players like me; why haven't they found a place? It feels wrong that someone with my résumé should feel uncomfortable being in his own environment. It feels wrong that I should be invited to some official after-match function and look around to see I'm the only brown person in the room. So, I am really pleased and proud that Channel Nine has contracted me to their commentary team. I'm still waiting for the other channels to employ Pacific Islanders with proven sports records. There are heaps of them out there. Pasifika people need to see themselves represented in all aspects of society. They need their stories, their culture and their language to be treated equally in Australia and New Zealand. I am glad that is starting to happen.

As we worked on this book, Alan Duff and I talked about the incredible heritage of the Polynesian people. At least 5000 years ago – perhaps even 10,000 – our seafaring ancestors made their way from Taiwan, navigating by the stars to eventually settle every island in the Pacific Ocean. That strength, ingenuity and resilience is something all young Pasifika people should know runs in their blood. It shows that they are capable of anything they set their minds to and work hard for.

A French journalist, Karim Ben Ismail, once said about me, 'You can't stop the sun from shining.' While he might have meant it as an offhand remark, it stuck with me: not because it was about me, but because it is true. No matter what happens on the field, in the ring or in my life, it is a reminder that Allah does not burden a soul beyond what they can bear. It's a reminder to push through and keep going, keep trying, because the sun will keep shining and a new day will come.

If my story shows anything, it is that hard work and focus can make a difference. I hope I can encourage others to back themselves and be brave enough to walk through those doors. What matters most to me now is faith, family, friends and helping to point out injustice in the world. I have been given a gift and a profile, and I have to use them to make a difference. And I still love my sport!

I feel blessed. All those years ago, my one dream was to buy my mum her own house with that fancy wallpaper. I am proud that I did that and she has lived in that home for many years. My mum says she thanks her lucky stars for how life turned out. And so do I. Without the loving, supportive, inspiring figures like my mum and my nan, without the lessons I have learned from my father, without my brother and my sisters, without my wife and four beautiful children, I would not be the man I am today. I thank Allah for it all.

SBW: the Stats

RUGBY LEAGUE

Club Career	Years	Played	T	G	FG	Pts
Canterbury-Bankstown Bulldogs	2004–08	73	31	0	0	124
Sydney Roosters	2013–14, 2020	50	11	0	0	44
Toronto Wolfpack	2020	5	0	0	0	0
Total		128	42	0	0	168

Other Club Games	Years	Played	T	G	FG	Pts
World Club Challenge	2005, 2014	2	0	0	0	0
Total Club Games		130	42	0	0	168

Test Matches	Years	Played	T	G	FG	Pts
New Zealand	2004, 2006–08, 2013	12	5	0	0	20

| **TOTAL CAREER GAMES** | 2004–08, 2013–14, 2020 | 142 | 47 | 0 | 0 | 188 |

RUGBY UNION

Club Career	Years	Played	T	G	Conv	FG	Pts
Toulon	2008–10	33	6	0	0	0	30
Canterbury	2010–11	7	4	0	0	0	20
Crusaders	2011	15	5	0	0	0	25
Chiefs	2012–15	29	6	0	0	0	30
Panasonic Wild Knights	2012	7	2	0	0	0	10
Counties Manukau	2014, 2019	3	0	0	0	0	0
Auckland Blues	2017–19	17	0	0	0	0	0
Total		111	23	0	0	0	115

Test Matches	Years	Played	T	G	Conv	FG	Pts
New Zealand	2010–19	58	13	0	0	0	65

	Years	Played	T	G	Conv	FG	Pts
TOTAL CAREER GAMES	2008–15, 2017–19	169	36	0	0	0	180

RUGBY SEVENS

New Zealand	2016

BOXING CAREER

Date	Opponent	Result	W	D	L
27/05/2009	Gary Gurr	Won – TKO	1	0	0
30/06/2010	Ryan Hogan	Won – TKO	2	0	0
29/01/2011	Scott Lewis	Won – UD	3	0	0
5/06/2011	Alipate Liava'a	Won – UD	4	0	0
8/02/2012	Clarence Tillman	Won – TKO	5	0	0
8/02/2013	Francois Botha	Won – UD	6	0	0
31/01/2015	Chauncy Welliver	Won – UD	7	0	0
26/06/2021	Waikato Falefehi	Won – UD	8	0	0

Acknowledgements

Acknowledgements from Alan Duff

Thanks to Khoder Nasser for being so supportive and insightful. Thanks to Vanessa Radnidge for her tireless work and undying enthusiasm. Thanks to Jenny Rogers and the team at Transcription Services. Biggest thanks to Sonny Bill for sharing his story with us.

Acknowledgements from Sonny Bill

I would like to thank Alan Duff for helping me to tell my story. It was an honour to work with this Māori man to tell it the right way. And thank you to Mona Seiuli for the wonderful front cover photo.

Thank you to Vanessa Radnidge and the Hachette Australia, Hachette Aotearoa New Zealand and Hodder UK teams who have worked so hard to create this book with me. And thank you to all the hardworking booksellers who are helping to share my story.

For me to achieve my goals and aspirations while overcoming the doubts that once seemed all encompassing, the Most High has put many good people in my path and I would like to thank some of those special people here.

My love of sport was derived from my father's toughness and unrelenting desire to see his children succeed and reach heights he never did. I now know that he pushed us because he saw the God-given talent we possessed, even before we did.

Thanks to . . .

The special teachers who recognised my talent from a young age and pushed me in the right direction: Mr Waller and Mr Phillips from Owairaka District School, Mr Ball from Wesley Intermediate and Ms Mita from Mount Albert Grammar School.

The footy coaches throughout my childhood, whose support and encouragement will never be forgotten: Adolf Guttenbeil, Sheral and Julian Cameron, Tillam Kapsin. And, though they never coached me, if it wasn't for the commitment of the Lipscombe family to our small rugby league and athletics clubs, led by Ross and Anne, I and many other kids from poor households may not have been able to consistently play sport.

To the two Bulldog scouts who offered me that first scholarship, which was signed on Mum's little Honda Civic all those years ago: Mark Hughes and John Ackland.

Over the course of my professional career, these people I'd humbly say are the unsung ones who hold some of these successful franchises together:

Peter and Mary Durose: although they could never replace Mum and Dad, this couple looked after me and many other young aspiring players living away from home at such a young age and did their best to be there and make it better.

Fred Ciraldo was at the Bulldogs for years and he took a shy young Islander boy under his wing and it meant the world to me.

Garry Carden was my first-ever professional trainer and his relentless training methods really laid the foundations for my steely attitude towards the physical and mental training demands required over my career and that I'm still using in the boxing ring to this day.

Cathy King from the Roosters. This lady, who most of us lads call 'Aunty', is a big part of the club's success. Thank you for always going above and beyond for me and my loved ones.

Keegan Smith and Patty Lane are two of the most knowledgeable trainers I've ever come across. Their personal help over the years has helped keep me at my physical best.

Victoria Hood, from the Auckland Blues. Thank you for helping a fourteen-year-old high school dropout achieve something he never thought possible – getting a Bachelor degree. You have given me the confidence to give it a go and I can now show my children what they can achieve in this world through education not just sports. Thanks, Vic!

All Blacks manager Darren Shand, thanks for your support over the years, brother.

The Chairman of the New Zealand Rugby Union, Brent Impey, and the rest of the board for their support on and off the field, especially for me and the Muslim community after the Christchurch attacks. Your support will always be remembered.

Chris Lendrum, your honest and forward-thinking approach made my contract dealings simple and straightforward. Thanks, bro.

To the Nasser brothers: Ammar, Khoder, Amin and Ahmed. Thank you for your loyalty, wisdom and brotherhood.

To my mum, dad, brother, sisters, nieces and nephews. Alhamdulillah, I've been blessed with you all in my life.

My wife, Alana, and children, Imaan, Aisha, Zaid and Essa.

Alana, I appreciate all you do for me and the kids and your love and support doesn't go unnoticed. I love you. Insha Allah, Allah continues to help us with the wisdom required to support our children to succeed in this world and the next.

Imaan, Aisha, Zaid and Essa (and God willing a few more to come), thank you for all the joy and challenges you bring to our lives. Without you all, our household wouldn't be the loud, loving place that it is. And without the blessings of your little souls, Alana and I wouldn't have the natural growth one has in raising four Mashallah children.

My life has been a journey of many mistakes, many selfish acts and misdemeanours towards myself and others. For all those I have offended or mistreated, I ask for your forgiveness. I thank the Most High for allowing me to learn from my mistakes and change my selfish ways. I pray that the Most Merciful continues to shine that mercy on me.

Index

ALSO BY LAURENCE FLEMING

Fiction

A Diet of Crumbs
On Torquemada's Sofa
The Heir to Longbourn
The Summer at Lyme

Non-fiction

The English Garden (with Alan Gore)
The One Hour Garden
Old English Villages (with Ann Gore and Clay Perry)
Roberto Burle Marx, A Portrait

The Will of Lady Catherine

Laurence Fleming

dexter
haven
PUBLISHING

Published in 2010 by Dexter Haven Ltd
Curtain House
134–146 Curtain Road
London EC2A 3AR

ISBN 978-1-903660-07-2

Front cover image courtesy of the National Portrait Gallery, *Jane,
Lady Munro* by Sir Martin Archer Shee; all other images © Ken
Leeder, with thanks to the Geffrye Museum.

Typeset by Dexter Haven Associates Ltd, London
Printed in Great Britain by CPI Cox & Wyman, Reading RG1 8EX

To Barbara and Colin

The reader is asked to imagine that all the novels of Jane Austen began at the same time, the summer of 1814.

I

1822

Elizabeth could see Mr Darcy from where she stood at the window of her sitting-room, on his usual morning walk. He would go over the lawn at the front of the house, down to the stream, over the wooden bridge at the end of the pool, through the young beech trees and back up the drive again, over the stone bridge, a stroll which might take him half an hour.

Today, however, he had started by going down the drive and was just crossing the wooden bridge on his way back. He was carrying a letter; and Elizabeth's curiosity was aroused.

It was a particularly beautiful day, a light breeze moving thin clouds very slowly across the sky. There were little ripples in the pool—it was not quite large enough to be called a lake— and the grass on the hill above the cliff was long enough to have ripples of its own. There was still some blossom on the may trees.

Mr Darcy came straight upstairs.

"There is a letter today, my love," he said. "From Mrs Jenkinson."

"From Mrs Jenkinson! What can she have to say?"

"Something very much to the purpose, as you might suppose. Her name, you will find, is Amelia. I recall that we once decided, after a very long discussion, that it should be Matilda."

"Whatever her name, she has always had my deepest sympathy, squeezed in between your aunt and your cousin. For, although your cousin rarely speaks, whenever she does so it is always either a request or a complaint. And your aunt Catherine is a lady of stout, sterling qualities which are not readily ignored."

Mr Darcy smiled and said, simply: "Perhaps you would like to read it?"

It was dated, very precisely, from Rosings Park in the County of Kent, on Thursday the Sixth of June 1822.

You will forgive me, I hope, in thus writing to you unsolicited. Lady Catherine insists that there is nothing much amiss with her and that she will write to you herself when she has recovered. Her ladyship had a serious fall yesterday was a fortnight. She tripped over her train one evening and fell headlong down the lower part of the principal staircase. She arrived at the foot considerably bruised and unable to raise herself. She was rescued by two footmen and was immediately confined to her bed, where she has remained ever since. The doctor has been in constant attendance and is satisfied that nothing is broken. Lady Catherine herself has frequently remarked that people do not die from trifling little falls. My present anxiety is principally caused by her ladyship's extraordinary colour and the fact that she is unable to retain her food. I fear some serious internal injury, although the doctor assures me that such a thing is an impossibility and that rest and repose are all that is required. Under the circumstances I feel myself obliged to request a visit from you, and your lady, at your earliest convenience. Colonel Fitzwilliam is, I understand, still stationed in the Bermudas. I fear that the presence of one or other of you may shortly become imperative.

Elizabeth handed back the letter and said, without a smile: "There can be no question. We must go at once. We cannot respond with greater urgency than that."

"No, we cannot, though my aunt has never, to my knowledge, been indisposed before. It was always my mother who was ailing."

"What will become of your cousin Anne should the worst befall?"

"My cousin Anne, as sole heiress of her father and her mother, will be a lady of very large substance indeed. No doubt some impecunious younger son will feel able to fall in love with her."

They travelled fast and without mishap. The weather was fine and the days long. As they drove into the park at Rosings from the west, the setting sun shone on the windows to give the impression that the building was on fire; so that it was not until they drew up at the principal entrance that they noticed that all the blinds were down and all the shutters closed.

Elizabeth's heart sank. A slight pressure from Mr Darcy's hand indicated that he too had understood the message of the blinds and the shutters. He raised her hand to his lips.

"I am glad to have you with me, my love. We are, I fear, about to endure a difficult few days."

Elizabeth said nothing, merely returning the pressure of his hand. The steps were let down and, arm in arm, they walked up the broad, shallow flight to the front door. It was opened, before they reached it, by Heaton, Lady Catherine's butler.

"Mr Darcy, sir, and madam. May I say with all my heart that you have been quite sent by Providence? Allow me to take your hat."

"Mrs Jenkinson wrote to me last week," said Mr Darcy. "When did this sad event take place?"

"Less than two hours ago, I have to say. We have not had time to assume our mourning, nor yet to put up the hatchment over the door."

"It must have been quite sudden," said Elizabeth. "I hope she did not suffer very much?"

"As to that, madam, I cannot say. Her ladyship was unable to eat for some days, not even the many delicacies contrived for her in the kitchens. Her household, sir, as you can well imagine, is cast into the greatest confusion. Your arrival is quite in the nature of a relieving force."

Elizabeth removed her bonnet, as she was now a guest in the house, and it was placed beside Mr Darcy's hat, on a table in the hall.

"You will find Miss de Bourgh in the *Blue* Drawing Room," said the butler. "Mrs Jenkinson is with her and also, I must make haste to say, Mr Collins."

Elizabeth's heart sank a little further. Mr Collins, Vicar of Hunsford, distant cousin to her father and previous suitor to herself, was not a person to be welcomed at such a time or, indeed, at any other. The butler opened the door and announced them. She went in on Mr Darcy's arm.

There was a complete silence in the Blue Drawing Room. Mr Collins stood behind a high-backed chair almost as though it were a pulpit. Mrs Jenkinson, hands folded in front of her, occupied a hard-backed chair on one side of the fireplace, while Miss de Bourgh sat, as though stuffed, on a sofa on the other. Mrs Jenkinson rose quickly and came towards them, curtseyed briefly and said: "I cannot exactly welcome you to this house of sadness, but I must say to you that I am most grateful for your arrival."

"I received your excellent letter," said Mr Darcy. "We came as soon as possible and can only regret that we did not arrive in time."

"I doubt that Lady Catherine would have wished to see you," said Mrs Jenkinson, "neither can I recommend you to go and see her. Her demise was very rapid at the end and it is better that you remember her as she was."

Elizabeth and Mr Darcy bowed slightly to Mr Collins, who returned what would have been a deep obeisance had not the back of the chair been in the way, and they went over to Miss de Bourgh. She offered them each a hand, which they both kissed, but did not speak. Elizabeth sat down beside her. As Miss de Bourgh did not withdraw her hand she retained it, clasped between her own. The others remained standing.

After a moment Mr Darcy said: "Indeed, at such a moment, there is scarcely any comfort to be offered to you, my dearest cousin. But if you will allow me, I hope to remove all responsibility for the arrangements from your shoulders. I would wish there to be as little as possible to distress you."

The shadow of a smile passed over Miss de Bourgh's face and she inclined her head almost invisibly to Mr Darcy. Mr Collins said: "We must derive what comfort we can from the knowledge that her ladyship must even now be in heaven.

After such a blameless life, such devotion to the poor and to her family, it would be impertinent to question such a thing."

Once more Miss de Bourgh inclined her head, this time to Mr Collins; but, this time, there was no shadow of a smile.

Mrs Jenkinson spoke again.

"We hope to engage your good offices, Mr Darcy, in persuading my dear Miss de Bourgh to take a little nourishment," she said. "She would eat nothing this evening and had only a morsel of toast and an egg at breakfast."

Elizabeth turned to her neighbour on the sofa and said, with a smile: "Mrs Jenkinson is right, my dear Anne. We must all do what we can to keep up our strength and spirits. I hope we may persuade you to do that."

The hand within hers was removed. A bell beside her was rung and was answered, with what could be described as suspicious speed, by the butler himself.

"We will have our glass of wine in here today, Heaton," said Miss de Bourgh, in a voice of the most perfect calm. "And so will everyone else."

"Madam," was all the reply.

A silence of surprise ensued. Miss de Bourgh, the permanent invalid, had never been known to drink wine before.

"I know not what to say," said Mr Collins. "After only two hours. In conflict with the wishes of your late, your honoured, parent. I can only say I am astonished."

"You are right to be surprised, Mr Collins, and you will be even more surprised when you learn that this has been a happy ritual in my life for some years, known only to my dear Mrs Jenkinson and to our excellent Heaton. He has brought this vital refreshment to us himself, up the back stairs every evening, and one of the first things that I mean to do is to put carpet on those stairs."

"I can only entreat you," demurred Mr Collins, "not to take this dreadful step. The doctor, there is no need to tell you, has always feared the effect of any alcohol upon your delicate constitution."

There was a short silence before Miss de Bourgh replied.

"I have frequently had occasion to question," she said, "in my own mind of course, the nature of our doctor's medical knowledge. Now here he is again, once again, mistaken. My mother's death has clearly been caused by an internal injury; and that, he had declared, was impossible."

Elizabeth had never heard her utter so many words at once and neither, from the expression on his face, had Mr Collins.

"I have therefore decided," continued Miss de Bourgh serenely, "to do precisely the opposite to what he has been used to recommend. To drink wine when I wish to, to eat plenty of eggs and fresh meat, to drink milk, coffee and tea like everyone else, to eat butter, cream and cheese, to go out for a long walk every day and never to coddle myself. And while I shall continue at all times to respect the memory of my mother, I mean to begin my new diet immediately."

No one moved. Mr Collins did not speak; but, before the silence had lasted for too long, the butler returned with a laden tray.

"Thank you, Heaton," said Miss de Bourgh. "You need not wait. I can rely on Mr Darcy."

When the butler had left the room, Mr Darcy addressed himself to Mr Collins. He said, quite pleasantly: "I hope Mrs Collins is well?"

"Thank you. Yes, indeed."

"And the children? You have three daughters, I believe."

"Yes. Yes, indeed. Three daughters."

"Perhaps, if you were to go at once, you would be at home before it is quite dark?"

"Yes. Yes, indeed," said Mr Collins. "Although there is a good moon tonight."

Mrs Jenkinson, taking the hint from Mr Darcy, now rose from her chair.

"It was so kind of you to call, Mr Collins. We shall hope to see you tomorrow. Now that Mr and Mrs Darcy are come, we shall have their help to solve our problems."

Mr Collins started to offer his humble duty to her ladyship and then remembered. In some confusion he made for the door, where he turned and bowed. The three ladies graciously inclined their heads and said, in a unison which might almost have been rehearsed: "Goodnight, Mr Collins."

The door closed behind him, but no one spoke. Mr Darcy poured the wine and offered it first to Miss de Bourgh. Mrs Jenkinson, without hesitation, accepted a glass and Elizabeth thankfully accepted hers. Mr Darcy raised his glass and said: "To your health, cousin Anne, and happiness in the future."

They took their first sips in silence.

It was by now quite dark. The housekeeper brought in some lighted candles. She was followed by two footmen bearing trays with the paraphernalia required to make both tea and coffee and, to Elizabeth's great satisfaction, a large number of little cakes. The housekeeper then informed Elizabeth that she would conduct her to her bedroom whenever she should be ready.

"In about half-an-hour, perhaps," said Miss de Bourgh calmly. "And, when you have done so, I have some instructions to give about my breakfast."

The housekeeper acknowledged this and, rather more than half-an-hour later, Elizabeth and Mr Darcy bade good night to Miss de Bourgh and Mrs Jenkinson and followed the housekeeper out of the room.

As they mounted the stairs, Mr Darcy said: "And Lady Catherine? Where is she?"

After a moment, the housekeeper replied: "The doctor was most insistent that she be placed at once into her coffin, he being uncertain as to the cause of her death. This has been done, with the greatest speed, and she is no longer in the house."

Elizabeth was only too thankful to hear this. She smiled her gratitude to Mr Darcy for having asked the question.

The housekeeper opened the door of one of the principal bedrooms, where candles were already burning, expressed the hope that they would be quite comfortable and bade them "good night".

II

When they were alone, Elizabeth said: "What an evening of astonishments, indeed! I had never realised before that there was an embargo on wine in this house."

"It dates from the time of Sir Lewis de Bourgh," said Mr Darcy, "a person who is hardly ever mentioned but who, nevertheless, existed for some years. I remember him quite well."

"I suppose there is some interesting reason for this—shall we say, reticence?"

"There is," said Mr Darcy, with a smile. "A very good one. While watering his horse in the river Medway, on his way back from the Assizes at Maidstone, Sir Lewis de Bourgh fell off that horse and was drowned. At the inquest which followed, inevitably a source of acute embarrassment to my aunt, it emerged from the hosts of eleven public houses on the way, that Sir Lewis had generously refreshed himself at every one and indeed his own groom—on oath, you know—was obliged to confirm this. Since when there has been a noticeably short supply of wine at Rosings Park."

"I did notice, of course, the first time I ever came here, that only tea or coffee was offered in the evening. And I recall, too, that Sir Lewis was then mentioned, though only to say that no entail was thought necessary in *his* case. But at dinner I am sure that wine was served, though I do remember it was never given to Anne."

"You may perhaps also remember that, on those occasions, I or Colonel Fitzwilliam, or possibly both, were present. Lady Catherine would have regarded us as company, to use the butler's word. The Collinses, I think, and their guests, would not be so regarded and therefore the question would not arise. My cousin Fitzwilliam would always bring with him enough claret of the most excellent kind, for instance, to make certain that there was something fit to drink while he was here."

"I thought the new—Anne, I have to call her that though I can still only think of her as Miss de Bourgh—promised to be quite interesting. Do you think she will come to resemble her mother?"

"I must hope not, but she is in every way an unknown quantity. As I am sure she has been left with cousin Fitzwilliam and myself as trustees, at least until her marriage, we shall be glad to have someone of spirit to deal with, rather than the silent, withdrawn girl we all know."

"And yet—I would not call her a girl. How old is she?"

"My own age."

"Thirty-five! Indeed my heart quite bleeds for her. To have been prisoner upstairs for such a time is punishment indeed."

After a moment, Elizabeth continued: "I had not realised you were so close in age. I suppose that would be why your mothers arranged your marriage?"

Mr Darcy did not speak.

"I owe my information to Lady Catherine herself, you know—on her famous visit to Longbourn to prevent *our* marriage. She told me they had planned it in your cradles."

"I must be glad they did not succeed."

"But now—here we are with her daughter on our hands. I remember, when I saw her first, I thought how well you would suit. 'Sickly' and 'cross' I think were my words. Now, after this evening, I am delighted to think she has been playing games with us. I look forward to watching the petals unfold."

Elizabeth awoke unusually refreshed, after an excellent night's sleep. Her previous visits to Rosings had afforded little pleasure, but this one, despite its serious nature, offered to be quite different.

She watched her cousin Anne—no longer to be thought of only as Miss de Bourgh—work her way quietly through some slices of ham with scrambled eggs, some very good fresh rolls with honey and quince conserve and two cups of coffee. Mrs Jenkinson hovered but said nothing. Elizabeth found herself regarding her with more approval than before.

A hatchment had been set up and there was now a book of condolence in the hall, presided over by the two footmen who had picked up Lady Catherine from the foot of the stairs and carried her to bed. The whole household had assumed its mourning garb and two seamstresses had arrived from Sevenoaks to make up several black dresses for Miss de Bourgh.

Mr Darcy, closeted with Lady Catherine's steward, made all the arrangements for the funeral; and the butler was despatched, in one of Lady Catherine's carriages, to see what could be purchased from the vintner in Tunbridge Wells.

Elizabeth, whose maid had had the forethought to include her mourning, sat with her cousin and Mrs Jenkinson in the Blue Drawing Room, ready to receive any callers who might choose to come in. But, although there was a steady stream, on foot, on horseback and in the occasional carriage, no one ventured to disturb them. Her cousin Anne remarked on this.

"Although they must all know of my existence, I am acquainted with very few of them. None at all, indeed. They must be *seething* with curiosity. So their delicacy does them credit."

At six o'clock the main gates were closed and a mourning wreath was hung upon them. Freed now from all chances of intrusion, Anne asked Elizabeth to accompany her for a short walk in the park.

"I do not mean to over-stretch myself," she said. "Having been warned throughout my life of the dangers of over-exertion, it would be more than foolish to tax myself too heavily to begin with. I have had this plan of action in my mind for several years, you know, but never expected the chance to put it into operation quite so soon."

They walked across the lawn behind the house, to where a seat had been placed at the entrance to a little wood.

"I love this place," said Anne, as she sat down. "All my life I have done so. I have no intention of leaving it."

She turned to Elizabeth with a smile and said: "I should have been obliged to refuse your husband, you know, had he ever offered. I could not bear the thought of living in the north.

So I was always more than grateful to *you* for having removed all possibility of such a thing."

"Did you ever expect him to make you an offer?"

"My mother was quite certain that he would. Her own marriage, you know, was arranged in such a way. I believe, in fact, that it was a certain thing before they ever met. I should much have enjoyed being present at that meeting. My mother was the taller almost by a head."

Elizabeth could think of nothing to say. Her companion continued in the calmest way: "My mother cannot ever have been more than passably good-looking. 'A fine girl' is probably all they could have said. It was cousin Fitzwilliam's mother— your mother-in-law, you know—who was the beauty. Five years younger than my mother and married actually before her, though she waited some time for her first child. It was amazing that they remained on anything but the most formal terms. My mother quite doted on cousin Fitzwilliam, especially when he grew so tall and strong. And handsome. I hope you find him handsome?"

"I do so now, but when first I saw him I thought him insufferably proud and haughty. Now I am much inclined to think that he was only intimidated by the crowd of raucous girls that I am sure we were—all trying to capture his attention though without any appearance of doing so. It was at a public Assembly Ball. But perhaps you have never been to one?"

"No, indeed, I never have. The ones in Tunbridge Wells are, I believe, quite well attended and even by quite desirable people. But my mother always said I should find them too fatiguing."

"And what do you think now?"

"I think now," said Anne, with the widest smile that Elizabeth had so far seen, "that I should have found them too fatiguing."

They were silent for a little while. The sun was still high, casting a gentle golden glow over the north front of the house. In the softening light it seemed to Elizabeth less imposing, more inhabitable, than she had been used to think it.

"Of course," said Anne, "my own old nurse always said that a diet of beefsteak and porter would cure all my ailments. But, as you can imagine, no one paid any attention to *her*. They sent her off to live by the sea, at a place call Shoreham. I once had some thoughts of sending Mrs Jenkinson to join her—but she has become the greatest friend."

Elizabeth laughed.

"Of course you must keep her with you now. Once she sees that ordinary food no longer constitutes a danger, she may prove less solicitous. I like her more than I expected."

"She should stay, for propriety's sake. Single women do not live alone, no matter how advanced in years. I never had a sister, Elizabeth. Now I can see how useful one might be. I suppose you would not think of adding me to the large number of yours?"

"I will be your sister with the greatest pleasure. I hope that, when your period of mourning is over, you may think of coming north to see us, or at least give us the chance of inviting you to London."

"That I shall do—perhaps! But let us go in. It must be time to dine. For the first time in my life, I look forward to my dinner."

III

L ady Catherine's funeral took place on the following morning. Counting the tolling of the bell, Elizabeth was amazed to find that she had been sixty-four years old. The ladies remained quietly seated at home. Mr Darcy acted as Chief Mourner. Lady Catherine was placed beside her husband in the family vault and what Mr Darcy described as "a very respectable gathering" attended. The procession of well-wishers to sign the book of condolence continued throughout the afternoon and, at six o'clock, the gates of the principal entrance were closed once more.

Again, Elizabeth walked across the lawn with Anne, this time venturing a little way into the wood.

"Another soft, delightful evening," said Anne. "It is a treat for me to have someone like myself to talk to. Mrs Jenkinson, for all her excellent qualities, was always on her best behaviour and there was no conversing with my mother. She chose to regard me as a permanent invalid and to argue with her would have been a fruitless exercise. In the end I quite accepted my status as a delicate plant, liable to be damaged by the merest puff of wind."

"But were you not a very delicate child?"

"I was a delicate *infant*," said Anne, with some emphasis. "I know from my old Nurse that there was some difficulty rearing me at first. And when my birth was not followed by other children, and I stayed alone in the nursery, I became an object of almost sacred significance. I cannot blame them, in my heart, but now—all that is at an end. I am half-way already to my three score years and ten and do not intend remaining hidden any longer—though this, I must suppose, will depend upon the terms of my mother's will."

The lawyer came the following morning to read the will. Anne sat between Elizabeth and Mr Darcy while he did so. Its terms were perfectly simple. She was the sole heiress of her mother, but her property was to be managed by trustees until she "entered upon the married state". The trustees were named as Mr Darcy and their cousin, Colonel Fitzwilliam, and the existence of this condition brought about a certain silence in the room.

At last Mr Darcy said: "This stipulation is immovable, I suppose? There is no way round the condition?"

The lawyer assured him that there was not.

"It is not, my dearest cousin," said Mr Darcy, turning towards her, "that I object in any way to the responsibility that my aunt has placed upon me. It is rather a feeling of regret that she did not regard you as able to manage your own affairs. But you may be quite confident that I shall not dispute your doing anything you may wish, and I am sure our cousin will agree."

"Do not distress yourself," said Anne. "To begin with at least I must be grateful for any protection offered me from the wicked world outside. I hope your interest in my affairs, even if it is not quite voluntary, may give an excuse for frequent visits to Rosings by yourself and my *sister* Elizabeth."

"I am delighted to hear," said Mr Darcy, with a smiling glance at Elizabeth, "of this closer relationship. We shall do everything in our power to make you comfortable."

The rest of the day passed quietly. Mrs Jenkinson effaced herself and they were spared a visit from Mr Collins; but, on the fourth morning after their arrival at Rosings, the butler entered the Blue Drawing Room, where Mr Darcy was reading the newspaper and Elizabeth had taken up her embroidery. He asked if he might speak to Mrs Darcy.

"But certainly," said Anne, who was sitting alone and unemployed upon her sofa. "I hope there is no unpleasant news?"

The butler looked as though this might be a matter of some debate, but he said at once, to Elizabeth: "Mr Collins has called, madam, and begs the favour of a word with you."

"With me?" said Elizabeth. "What can have happened now?"

"Did Mr Collins include me in his summons?" asked Mr Darcy. "The effrontery of this man appears to know no bounds."

"His request was quite particular, sir. To *Mrs* Darcy."

"Do you have the strength to go alone, Elizabeth? Shall I come with you?"

"I think, perhaps," said Elizabeth, after a second's hesitation, "that I should go myself. But if I do not return within the quarter of an hour, you may certainly come to my relief."

She rose as she spoke and the butler said: "I have put Mr Collins in the Small Summer Breakfast Parlour, madam."

And then, in a lower voice to Elizabeth only: "You will be quite undisturbed there and I shall remain within call."

The Small Summer Breakfast Parlour was as far as possible from the Blue Drawing Room and it was hardly ever used. The butler announced her to Mr Collins, whom she found walking round the room. She seated herself on a chair by the window and the butler closed the door.

Elizabeth quietly decided that she would say nothing until Mr Collins spoke himself and so, for some moments, silence reigned. At last, and with the appearance of a great effort, Mr Collins said: "You can be at no loss, I think, Miss Elizabeth, as to the reason for my request to speak to you alone."

"You are mistaken, Mr Collins," said Elizabeth, in what she hoped was an indifferent voice. "I have not the smallest notion why you should wish to see me—and alone."

Mr Collins took a few further steps through the room and Elizabeth now noticed that his hat was lying on the table in front of her. Then, after an appreciable pause, Mr Collins said: "It is about your father's dreadful marriage."

Elizabeth judged it better not to speak.

"Apart from the absurdity of a man of his age entering into matrimony at all," continued Mr Collins, "to have chosen a woman of extremely doubtful reputation moves his action from mere folly into recognisable sin. And, as his heir at Longbourn, I believe that I should have been consulted."

"And would you have given your permission for the marriage, in that event?" asked Elizabeth.

"Most certainly I would not, Miss Elizabeth—Mrs Darcy, I should say. With your father's immortal soul in such jeopardy I should have opposed it with all my strength."

Elizabeth considered for a moment how best to refer to her stepmother, young, beautiful and only recently acquired.

"The present Mrs Bennet's previous marriage took place some years ago," she said. "As my father was in no way concerned in her divorce—they were indeed entirely unacquainted at the time—I can see no occasion for your objection."

"This is my complaint precisely," said Mr Collins, rather loudly. "You *do* see no objection. You and your sisters have, to all appearances, actually *welcomed* a convicted adulteress into your midst."

Elizabeth paused for a moment.

"If, Mr Collins," she said, "you could see for yourself the happiness that this marriage has brought to my father, not to mention the advantages that have accrued to his house and his household, you could not speak of my kind, delightful stepmother in such terms."

"As to that, my dear Miss Elizabeth, I would not risk contaminating myself by going within a mile of Longbourn—and you do not need to tell me that the present Mrs Bennet is daughter to a very wealthy man."

"Who has forgiven his daughter for her earlier transgressions, whatever they may have been. That must have been a matter of far more concern to him than it could ever have been to you."

"We are *all* concerned in her transgressions, as you call them. She was detected in adultery, in mortal sin, and now her sin includes your father. While her former husband lives they are sunk in adultery themselves. No one connected with them can escape the smell—I may even say the stench—of that open sin. But I will not allow it to spread further. I have not informed my dear Charlotte of your presence in this house and have only called to forbid you, so far as it lies within my power, to force your unwelcome presence upon her. And I must most strenuously urge you, in deference to the cloth I wear, never to see your father, or his present wife, again."

After the silence of a full minute, Elizabeth said, in a steady voice which rather surprised her: "Tell me, Mr Collins. Do you call yourself a Christian?"

"As an ordained priest in the Church of England, Madam, I must most certainly do so."

"You are acquainted, therefore, with the teachings of Our Lord? The parable of the woman taken in adultery? 'Let him who is without sin amongst you cast the first stone' were, I believe, His words. And you may remember the joy given by the one sinner who repented—I do not recall the rest of that quotation. Are you asking me to believe that you are yourself blameless in every respect?"

"Indeed, yes. I am certainly sufficiently without sin to cast the first stone. I can only pray for her instant destruction before she has destroyed your father's soul, and indeed his credit, for ever."

"You should rather pray that his marriage—which, let me assure you, is perfectly legal, even in the sight of God—should continue to prosper and that they should remain in love and charity with each other for the rest of their lives."

"The Book of Common Prayer makes no provision for such an eventuality. I should be reluctant to remain in orders if it did. I have written to your father, requiring that no further contact take place between our families, and this requirement I now impose upon you. Under no circumstances will you enter my house, on this or on any other occasion."

Elizabeth rose and rang the bell.

"Mr Collins, I have known your wife for many years longer than you have. If she invites me to *her* house, I shall have no hesitation in going."

"As I shall not inform her of your presence here, you may be certain that no such invitation will be offered."

To Elizabeth's intense relief, the butler now appeared. She handed Mr Collins his hat and said: "Good morning, Mr Collins."

The butler said, very firmly: "This way, sir, if you please."

But Mr Collins had not finished.

"A standard of conduct appropriate to Our Lord Himself is by no means relevant in these more enlightened days. I can think of no circumstances in which He could have approved your father's present behaviour. I repeat my prohibition to you. All contact between our families must cease."

"You may rest assured that it will do so, save upon invitation."

She sketched a curtsey and said again: "Good *morning*, Mr Collins."

The butler said, more loudly: "*This* way, sir, if you please."

And Mr Collins left.

Elizabeth stood still for a moment, fighting for composure, wondering if Mr Collins had finally taken leave of the very few senses she had previously supposed him to possess. She remained standing, staring out of the window, until aware of another presence in the room.

It was Mr Darcy.

"I am come to rescue you, my love," he said very quietly. "But you seem to have repulsed Mr Collins successfully—alone."

She took his arm, without speaking, and they returned to the Blue Drawing Room.

"My dear Elizabeth," said Anne, as soon as they entered, "you are quite pale, as if—but there are no ghosts at Rosings— though I sometimes think my father—but certainly *not* in the Small Summer Breakfast Parlour. Pray, what did Mr Collins have to say?"

Elizabeth sat on the sofa next to Anne and then said, very deliberately: "Mr Collins was complaining to me about the adulterous stench now emanating from Longbourn."

"Was he, indeed?" said Mr Darcy, in an ominous voice; but Anne went off into a peal of delighted laughter.

"He *could* not have done so," she said. "Even *he* could not have been so pompous—so *gothic*—so mediaeval."

"Oh, but I assure you," said Elizabeth, beginning to smile a little herself. "He has forbidden all contact between his family and ours."

"That, at least, presents *us* with no difficulties," said Mr Darcy.

"But poor Mrs Collins," said Anne. "How often has Mrs Jenkinson told me that your visits are the one thing she has to look forward to."

She smiled at Mr Darcy.

"Cousin Fitzwilliam," she said, "be kind enough to ring the bell."

Mr Darcy, who was standing by the fireplace, did so and the butler answered it.

"Tell me, Heaton," said Anne, "if you can remember so far back—what did my father commonly drink when he was feeling more than usually low?"

The question was so unexpected that the butler did not immediately reply. After a moment's consideration he said: "Sir Lewis, my lady—madam, I should say—at this time of the year was partial to what he called a Loving Cup. In the winter it was always a hot punch."

"And of what did this Loving Cup consist?"

"It was a blend of Madeira, madam, with brandy and champagne."

"And are we able to find such ingredients in our cellar?"

"I believe so, madam," said the butler without a smile. "Indeed, since my visit to Tunbridge Wells, I am quite certain."

"Pray, where is Mrs Jenkinson today?"

"She has walked across the park, I understand, on a visit to Mrs Collins."

"Then let us have this Loving Cup as soon as it may be contrived. And if, Heaton, this should occasion any remark below stairs, you may say that I am still recovering from the shock of my mother's death and that Mrs Darcy is recuperating from a visit from Mr Collins."

IV

I f Elizabeth thought she detected a slight spring in the
butler's step as he left the room, she was also aware of a
small rise in her own spirits.

"I know nothing of life outside this house," said Anne
pleasantly. "All my knowledge of real life is derived entirely
from the books in my father's library, so you may imagine how
strange they are. No additions have been made since my father's
death as my mother was rarely, if ever, seen in the vicinity of a
book. *Rasselas* remained for ever on a table in the drawing-
room, but it was *The Romance of the Forest* that she had beside
her bed. Indeed I am able to say, if only in a whisper and only
to you—I am most grateful to her for having taken no interest
whatever in my education."

"She placed no restriction on the books you read?"

"She did not. In my way I am quite a Blue-stocking. I am well
acquainted with the work of Sterne and Smollett, for instance,
but I have never read a word written by Sir Walter Scott or,
indeed, by Lord Byron. And I am sure I am the only person
now living in Kent who has read *right through Clarissa* and *also
The Man of Feeling* and *The Man of the World*. What do you
think about that, cousin Fitzwilliam?"

"I have read only the beginning and the end of *Clarissa*—I
am sure one can imagine what went on in between. The other
two I know quite well. But I hope you will not believe that they
bear any resemblance at all to men of the world, or of feeling,
today. In fifty years, one must hope that there have been a few
changes for the better."

"Well, I am relieved to hear you say that. One can become
quite confused, you know, between the adventures of Tristram
Shandy and Roderick Random and Tom Jones, for instance,
particularly if one reads them one after another. And there were

always some things which even Mrs Jenkinson could not explain to me. Although her husband was a clergyman, her father was a Captain of Artillery so not entirely unacquainted with the world. And as for what befell Pamela and Evelina and Cecilia and Camilla, not to mention poor Clarissa herself, it always made me quite nervous to think what might happen to me if I ever strayed beyond the edges of the parish of Hunsford."

Elizabeth laughed.

"Should you ever venture into the works of Sir Walter, I hardly think you will prefer the fate of *his* heroines. They nearly all lived in the greatest discomfort in the mountains of Scotland and one of them was actually obliged to walk all the way from Edinburgh to London."

"I am sure my mother would have disliked that extremely. I am sure she believed that there could be no harm in any of the books upstairs, as they had been selected by my father, or by his father."

"By which we are to understand that there *was* some harm in some of them?" asked Mr Darcy.

"She could not have known about such works as *Oroonoko* or *Moll Flanders*." replied Anne. "That is to say, I am sure she had never heard of either of them, but I found them and read them and did not know what to believe. I hoped they were inventions—like the Sleeping Beauty or Puss-in-Boots, you know, or even Robinson Crusoe and Gulliver, if it comes to that. But I fear that the truth is quite otherwise."

"The one about slavery and the other about transportation," said Mr Darcy, musingly. "I can only say that both continue to this day."

"I am sure I am better off in my own nursery," said Anne. "Which, however, I mean to refurbish in the latest mode as soon as ever I can discover what that is."

The butler now entered, with two footmen, one carrying a tray with the jug and glasses, the other with a small folding table, which he placed over by the window.

"Correctly, madam," said the butler, "the mixture in the jug should stand for at least half-an-hour before the champagne is added. And I must regret that there is no ice even in the ice-house. Her late ladyship, you may recall, saw no need for it."

"Well," said Anne, "I do not think we can wait for half-an-hour. But as I have no notion what it *ought* to taste like I hardly think I shall be disappointed. Pray add the champagne at once."

The butler did so. The footmen handed the glasses and they then withdrew.

"A toast," said Anne, as soon as they had gone. "To the next thirty-five years and to our closer acquaintance."

"And on our side," said Mr Darcy, "to the pleasure of meeting you, cousin Anne, for the first time in my life."

After a small, appreciative silence, Anne said: "Do we think this could be improved? I am quite willing that Heaton should try. He must have suffered sometimes from my mother's penurious habits when it came to wine. At least, however, he had the remains of my father's cellar to empty by himself, which I am sure he did—and now, my dear Elizabeth, tell us *exactly* what Mr Collins said. It is some years since I realised that he was not at all like the Vicar of Wakefield."

Elizabeth did so, with increasing enjoyment as her audience responded.

"And his last words were," she concluded, "that behaviour appropriate to Our Lord Himself had no relevance whatever to the present time, or indeed to Mr Collins's own situation. As he could not envisage approval being given by Christ Himself to my father's marriage, he felt it quite within his own rights, as a Christian, to condemn it entirely."

"I think," said Mr Darcy, "that there is a small confusion here. Had he nothing to say about loving his neighbour?"

"But nothing at all, of course. I said what I could about casting the first stone and the one sinner that repented. Then Mr Collins said that, as he was entirely without sin, there was *nothing* to prevent him from casting that first stone. The opportunities for sinning, as you can imagine, being quite rare in Hunsford."

Mr Darcy and Anne erupted together in a burst of laughter and Elizabeth, very shortly, joined them.

"I do remember," she said, when they had at last stopped laughing, "that when he heard of my sister Lydia's elopement, he wrote to my father advising him to forgive her as a Christian but never to admit her into his presence again."

"And only he," said Anne, on a suddenly more serious note, "could be unaware of the contradiction."

They sipped the Loving Cup in silence. Mr Collins's behaviour gradually seemed to Elizabeth more and more absurd and she decided to forget the whole episode.

"Although I have been dumb for twenty years," said Anne, "I have not been by any means deaf; and I can recall evening after evening listening to my mother and Mr Collins congratulating themselves on the excellence of their conduct and the infallibility of their principles. My mother has left me a fine pattern of behaviour, in fact. Whatever she did I shall not do and shortly, I have no doubt, I shall become the most popular person in the county. Though I suppose I must remain in black for at least another six months."

Mr Darcy offered to fill her glass again, but she refused.

"I must not be too greedy too soon," she said, "but, while I remember, I have to remark that Elizabeth's mourning is much handsomer than mine. Where, my dear sister, did you obtain it?"

"I think," said Elizabeth, after a moment, "that this dress was made in Bath. As part of the mourning for my mother."

"Bath is too far," said Anne. "But Audrey, my nurserymaid, tells me that there is a French dressmaker in Tunbridge Wells. And how do you suppose she came to know that? How little one knows of one's daily acquaintance, after all."

Elizabeth smiled. "I will not pretend to misunderstand you," she said. "Let us, by all means, have an adventure in Tunbridge Wells."

"An adventure!" exclaimed Anne. "If only one could. Though I doubt that a visit to Madame de Domballe, as I am informed she is called, would offer us *much* excitement."

"But perhaps," said Mr Darcy, "a visit to the High Rocks might constitute an adventure? We could try the waters, as I always like to do, and we might even pay a visit to an inn."

"Oh, I should like it of all things. Pray arrange it for me *at once*, cousin Fitzwilliam."

"This time I will do so, cousin Anne," said Mr Darcy very seriously, "but in future you will have to give your own instructions to your coachman—through your butler, you know."

"How very daring that does seem, to be sure, though I have had quite a success with Mrs Jenkinson *and* the housekeeper, neither of whom has said a word about my new diet. But vanquishing a *coachman, persuading* him to do what I wish, is *quite* another matter."

"You must try to convince yourself," said Elizabeth, "that your coachman wishes to be vanquished. He might even regard a visit to Tunbridge Wells as a pleasure as well as an adventure. Though surely he must have been there before?"

"The other day for the first time. My mother never went there. She regarded it as a hotbed of vice and immorality. All those people from London, you know, taking the cure and for such dreadful diseases."

She looked at Elizabeth and smiled.

"My mother, you know, had never a good word to say about *you*," she said, "which quite makes me feel how right I am to reverse *all* her opinions and to review *all* her conduct. I mean to repair all the cottages on the estate and even to build some new ones. When a tenant caught a cold, you know, my mother would send him some soup, but I would think it better to mend his roof and make sure there was some fuel to burn in his fireplace. What do you think, cousin Fitzwilliam?"

"I think, cousin Anne, that you are doomed to become a landlord of unparalleled excellence and I mean to enjoy myself watching it happen. But you need have no fear. I shall not allow you to reduce yourself to penury by spending all your money on other people. And I am sure our cousin Fitzwilliam will not permit it either."

"I keep hoping he will come back from the Bermudas with some vulgar Creole lady on his arm, one with a passion for purple satin, and diamonds, you know. But I fear he has not *quite* that sort of courage, though I am sure he is dreadfully brave in battle. And I fear, too, that vulgar Creole ladies may not have *quite* enough money to capture *him*."

V

Their visit to Tunbridge Wells took place on the next day, a particularly beautiful high summer day on which everything seemed to be smiling. The coachman and the grooms had put on black armbands but otherwise the signs of mourning had been kept to a minimum. Elizabeth, despite her own black dress, had to keep reminding herself that they *were* in mourning for Lady Catherine.

Mrs Jenkinson had regretfully excused herself from their expedition, on the grounds that she was promised to Mrs Collins and did not like to disappoint her. In her place came Audrey, now raised to the dignity of lady's maid and clearly very happy to be so.

They went first to the High Rocks, "a place I have long wished to visit," said Anne. "I am sure my mother never heard of Edmund Waller but he, you know, thought the Rocks the resort of fools, buffoons, cuckolds and whores as well as the wives and daughters of respectable citizens. You may imagine my difficulty in applying to Dr Johnson for elucidation. The dictionary was placed high on the shelf and was *extremely* heavy. I could only consult it when everyone was out. And the first time I did so, you may imagine my surprise when the book behind it fell out. It was *Tom Jones*. Whom do you think could have put it there and why? I suppose one may notice a buffoon or a whore when one sees one, but how, I ask myself, does one recognise a cuckold?"

"They are supposed to have little red horns protruding from their foreheads," said Mr Darcy perfectly seriously. "I think it most unlikely that we shall meet one."

In view of their mourning status they avoided the Maze, the Bowling Green and the Cold Bath and went straight towards the Rocks themselves.

"Quite high," said Anne, "and quite gloomy. Does this remind me of Sterne's *Journey through France and Italy*? I think them too sombre to have figured there."

"They must face the north entirely," said Mr Darcy. "I fancy the sun can never reach them."

Their attention was shortly attracted by the strange behaviour of a solitary man who stood on a high rock some thirty feet above them. He was particularly carelessly dressed and was pounding his chest with his right fist at regular intervals, something akin to a groan emerging at the same time. After a moment or two, however, he became aware of their scrutiny, stepped backwards and disappeared.

"They do say," remarked Audrey, "as how the High Rocks is the abode of the Devil."

"You may be quite sure, my dear Audrey," said Anne, "that the Devil does not wear a top hat."

They continued their walk in silence, the solid rocks on their right forming high cliffs, some of which were topped with trees and bushes. The dark mood of the place affected them all and it was Anne who said: "I am not sure that I wish to come here again."

As they approached the last of the rocks, before ascending the steps that led to the Aerial Walk, a figure fell from above them, landing on the sand only a few yards ahead of them.

He sat for a moment as though dazed. Then he shook his head several times, retrieved his hat, stood up only a little unsteadily, raised the said hat to Anne and Elizabeth, and walked past them without a word. Elizabeth was struck only by his extreme handsomeness. He was beyond competition the best-looking man she had ever seen. And there could be no doubt that he was the man they had seen on top of the rock.

But the incident disturbed them all. In unspoken agreement, they abandoned their visit to the Aerial Walk and went straight to the inn, where they did less than justice to the excellent meal that had been prepared for them there. Their spirits, however, rose perceptibly when they drove into the town, going first to the Dipper's Hall to taste the waters.

"Hardly palatable," said Anne, "but I cannot feel that they are unpleasant enough to cure anything of a really serious nature."

They were gathering themselves together prior to visiting Madame de Domballe, whose apartments were at the other end of The Pantiles, when Elizabeth noticed their acquaintance of the morning approaching the Dipper's Hall. He was by now respectably dressed and there were no outward signs of his earlier adventure; but Elizabeth's attention was entirely caught by the woman who accompanied him. She was, unmistakably, the Miss Crawford whom they had met in Bath on their last visit, and what had seemed like a great friendship had followed.

As soon as they entered the room, however, the man, instantly observing them, said something to his companion and they immediately left, so quickly that Elizabeth was unable to decide whether Miss Crawford had seen them or not.

"So," said Mr Darcy, "we have to suppose that that is the dangerous Mr Crawford."

"Indeed," said Elizabeth. "And if he is so then I think that much is explained. One might almost say—Lord Byron himself."

She turned to Anne.

"You have heard of my father's recent marriage," she said, "and to a divorced woman. Mr Crawford, if that is he, was the cause of all the trouble. My present step-mother was then very lately married, indeed a bride of only a few weeks, to a Mr Rushworth, when she ran off with this Mr Crawford; and they lived together until they could endure each other no longer. We have never seen Mr Crawford before, but we would regard Miss Crawford as a friend. His romantic and slightly careless appearance, I think, accounts for a great deal."

"I am sure it does," said Anne. "I could never decide, you know, what Peregrine Pickle and Roderick Random precisely looked like. It was difficult to imagine even some of the younger footmen and stable lads in such situations, as of course I never saw any other kind of male person. But I think that Tristram Shandy might quite resemble Mr Crawford—or the Lord Byron, of course."

She smiled at Mr Darcy.

"How indebted I am to you, cousin Fitzwilliam, for furthering my education in this way, though I am sure you could not have arranged for Mr Crawford to jump off that cliff. How chagrined he must have been to find himself so kindly cushioned by the sand. But now, I think, the moment has come to visit Madame de Domballe, as my impatience has quite overtaken me."

Madame de Domballe proved to be a lady of august and stately presence, very well-dressed herself and with hair elaborately curled.

"Indeed," said Anne later, "I wondered if I should not curtsey first."

Madame spoke indifferent English, but sharply and to the point.

"For how long will Madame mourn, I ask? It is not for a husband, I observe."

"It is for my mother," said Anne calmly. "I suppose full mourning for six months, perhaps half-mourning for a further three."

"Madame should not wear black. It drains the colour. As also grey. When the time is over, perhaps Madame will permit some suggestions?"

Elizabeth sat quietly while an animated conversation took place, principally between Madame and Audrey, with all of whose comments she silently agreed. Anne said very little, simply remarking, in the evening, that she quite looked forward to becoming a leader of the mode.

Mr Darcy joined them as previously arranged, having taken himself off for an invigorating walk across the Common. When they were again settled in the carriage, he said: "Once more I saw the mysterious Mr Crawford, but alone this time. I am certain that he saw me because, as soon as he did so, he turned round and walked off."

"But pray consider, cousin Fitzwilliam," said Anne. "Would you wish to be on terms with someone who had seen you jump off a rock and lose your hat? I really cannot blame him. I have heard of Lord Byron, of course, and if that is what he looks like then all becomes clear. We have none of his works at Rosings, I grieve to say. But I think we should forget the whole incident."

VI

As they awaited the summons to dinner that evening, Mrs Jenkinson handed Elizabeth a note from Mrs Collins.

"Dearest Elizabeth," it said. "I *must* see you. Pray come whenever you can."

She turned to Mrs Jenkinson.

"Is Mrs Collins quite well?" she asked. "This note is not like her."

Mrs Jenkinson did not immediately reply. Then, rather quickly, she said: "Mrs Collins is once more in the family way and very near her time. She has mentioned to me more than once that she feels there is something different this time."

"Perhaps it is a boy."

"I have suggested this but she is not convinced."

"Then I must see her, though how this is to be contrived when Mr Collins has forbidden me his house I do not know. I do not wish to encounter him again."

"I think I could assist you there," said Anne, who had been listening with great interest, "and how very delightful it is to be able to say so. I have only to send Mr Collins on some errand— as a great favour to me, you understand—which will absent him from his house for some time. There is a distant farm called Quarry End, at least three miles from here, quite at the end of his parish, in fact, and Mr Collins always walks within his parish. What can have happened there, I wonder, at this time of the year?"

She surveyed her hearers with a smile.

"It would be easier if it were the middle of winter. What do you think of a low fever? And would he be kind enough to observe the condition of the roof at the same time? A thing about which I know nothing. That at least is the truth. Perhaps

I need only to say that the report is that they are in trouble and would he discover what it is."

"And if they are not?" asked Mr Darcy, also smiling.

"Then, my dear cousin Fitzwilliam, I shall be only too happy to learn that the report was false. But why," turning to Elizabeth, "should she particularly want to see you?"

"She was my dearest friend before her marriage. I fear it may be something of importance."

"I will send the note over in the morning and instruct the messenger to remain within sight until Mr Collins has actually walked off. And I will drive you over myself, you know. I have never been inside that house for fear of infection—my mother would never permit it. But I will go at some time in the future. I believe she has made it very pretty."

This plan was closely followed. Soon after breakfast one of the stable boys returned with the information that Mr Collins had left the house and was on his way to Quarry End. The phaeton was at the door and, twenty minutes later, Elizabeth found herself alone with Mrs Collins.

She was quite shocked by her appearance. She was pale and her face was thin. She was lying on a sofa by the window and made no effort to get up, merely raising her arm and saying: "Oh my dearest Eliza, how *good* of you to come. You find me much diminished, I fear, but *pleased* that you could come."

Elizabeth went over to her at once, took her hand and kissed her cheek, murmuring only: "Dear Charlotte, I am more than happy to see you."

She drew up a chair to sit close to her, but she was no sooner seated than Charlotte began to cry, silently but with deep, painful sobs, covering her eyes with both hands.

Elizabeth, quite at a loss, for she had never seen Charlotte cry before, could only say, as kindly as she could: "Charlotte, dearest Charlotte, surely, surely there can be no occasion for this? Do, pray, tell me what troubles you?"

It was some time before this question could be answered. Slowly the sobs subsided and slowly a calm was achieved. Then in a low, desolate voice, she said: "I am *afraid*, Eliza. For the first time in my life, I am afraid."

"Then share your fears with me, my dear friend, and let us try to overcome them together."

"I am afraid of what I leave behind if I am taken this time."

"But—is there something different this time? Surely you are imagining this. I know, at this point, one often falls into a fit of the glooms, but I hope there is no very good reason."

"No," she said, "no, I am quite well, I think. I have the feeling that this child is not the same as the others—it is perhaps a boy. I have not been as well as before, however, and perhaps this has affected my spirits."

"I am sure that is all it is. I hope the doctor has not been bleeding you and prescribing only invalid food?"

"I have not seen the doctor," said Charlotte. "I have complete faith in our local midwife, who attended me before. I asked Mr Collins to ask her to come today, as he was to pass her house in his way this morning."

There was a silence between them, not uncomfortable. Charlotte put away her pocket-handkerchief and was once again her usual composed self. Elizabeth said: "How charming you have made this room, Charlotte. I think I have never seen these curtains before? But then, it is some time since I have been here."

"I am all too conscious of that, Eliza. I know Mr Collins does not wish it, since your father's marriage. It was Mrs Jenkinson who told me you were here—he has never said a word."

"I am sorry he has taken us all in such aversion, but I cannot otherwise regret the marriage."

"I know," said Charlotte, in a firmer voice, "that you blamed me for accepting Mr Collins; but, if I had not done so, I should still be at Lucas Lodge looking after my brothers and sisters."

"I always understood that," said Elizabeth. "I was sad only that it had to be Mr Collins."

"With all his faults, I have to say—I dote upon his children."

"Your children, too, my dear Charlotte. I think their charm owes very little to him."

Charlotte turned her head to look out of the window and said, absently: "I have always been very fond of this view. Our orchard has flourished and the house is as comfortable and pleasant as I can make it."

She turned back to look at Elizabeth and said, very quietly: "When I married Mr Collins, I looked no further than the fact. If I thought of children I thought of being always with them, caring for them, teaching them. I cannot endure the thought of leaving them."

"But Charlotte, dear Charlotte, this is only an irritation of the nerves. We all, I am sure, at such a time, have moments of despair."

"It is not that, this time. This time I have—what does the poet call it?—intimations of immortality, premonitions at the least. And that was why I wanted to see you."

Elizabeth could think of no comfort that she could offer and so remained silent. Charlotte continued: "I have never opposed him, you know. When our opinions differed, as they often did, I took refuge in silence and continued on my own way without referring to the matter. Lady Catherine supported him in all important things, with the result," and here she took out her handkerchief again and put it to her lips, "with the result that he has become so over-bearing and didactic that there is no enduring it. Last month there was a tragic case. A girl from the far end of the village, engaged to be married, gave birth to a child whose father, a thatcher, fell from a ladder and died before they could be so. And Mr Collins would not baptise the child."

Elizabeth, holding Charlotte's hand again, gave it a little squeeze.

"For the first time I remonstrated with him, saying it was no fault of the child's and to refuse baptism was to be needlessly cruel. Then, for the first time too, he turned on me, telling me, in fact, to mind my place and reiterating for the hundredth time his view of my duties as a wife. And it was then, too, at the height of his displeasure on that occasion, that he made plain his feelings about your father's marriage."

"He has made them plain to me, too, Charlotte. I think there is no changing them."

"In the end, of course, the girl took the child, a most beautiful little boy, to the vicar in the next parish, who baptised him without a murmur. So Mr Collins was left looking very foolish."

She sat up to be more upright and gave a sigh.

"Would you fetch the cushion off that chair and put it at my back? I find it difficult to arrive at a comfortable position just at present."

Elizabeth did as she was asked and Charlotte gave her a faint smile; but, when she was settled, she took both of Elizabeth's hands in both of hers and said, in a more agitated voice: "So this is why I ask for your solemn promise that, if I should go, you will not forget my daughters. The silly, pompous man I married is become a danger to us all," and, once again, the tears began to flow.

"Charlotte, dear Charlotte," said Elizabeth, now considerably concerned herself, "you have my solemn promise and you must believe me when I say there was no need to ask for it. Several times I have said to Mr Darcy how interesting I found your children and that I hoped we might be of use to them in future. And now that Lady Catherine has gone, and Mr Darcy is trustee to Miss de Bourgh, we shall be coming all the more frequently to Rosings."

Charlotte nodded and thanked her only with her eyes. Elizabeth, intent on changing the subject, said: "And do you have any knowledge of, or acquaintance with, Miss Anne de Bourgh? There she is, alone in that great house with Mrs Jenkinson, and quite unknown to anyone."

"We have exchanged looks several times, I suppose, and have occasionally agreed on the state of the weather. But beyond that I think I have never heard her express an opinion or offer any comment. She has never been inside this house."

"She emerges, to our great surprise, as quite a butterfly from the caterpillar she was before—if you take my meaning. I believe there is some intermediate stage. She has been kept in total subservience by her mother on the pretext of her own indifferent health. I think she had never had a square meal before last week and now increases in kindness for us, and us for her, each day. I shall be much surprised if you do not find her a very attentive neighbour."

They talked calmly for some time, about old days at Longbourn and about Elizabeth's life at Pemberley. The nursery-maid brought in a cordial for Charlotte, which she sipped slowly.

"But I must go, my dear Charlotte. I cannot run the risk of being found here by Mr Collins. Indeed I can hardly connect the man who came to us at first at Longbourn and the man who spoke to me the other day at Rosings. But do not upset yourself. Your fears, I must hope, are perfectly groundless but, in *any* event, you have my word that I shall keep my fondness for your children. And now, my dearest friend, good-bye."

They exchanged kisses and Charlotte, misty-eyed, said only: "I feel a little better now."

Pausing to blow a kiss to Charlotte from the doorway, and to say good-bye to the children, who were playing in the garden, Elizabeth left as quickly as she could, to walk, alone, across the park. In the middle of her journey she realised, with some surprise, that there were tears on both her cheeks.

VII

They were just finishing breakfast on the next day when the butler came in and asked, quietly, if he might speak to Mr Darcy. He was not away for long and returned with a very serious face, to tell them that Mrs Collins had given birth to a fourth daughter soon after midnight but had died herself just before sunrise. The child had been presented in breech. The midwife had delivered it successfully but had been unable to save the mother.

Elizabeth was sincerely distressed; Charlotte had been her friend for many years. She took some consolation from the hope that their conversation on the previous day had given her some comfort at the end.

It was not long, however, before it was known in the kitchen at Rosings, and shortly after that above stairs, and very soon after that in the Blue Drawing Room, that it had been the behaviour of Mr Collins himself which had brought on this tragic event.

Observing, from a distance, Elizabeth's departure from his house, he had fallen into a passion of rage, shouting at everyone and, in particular, railing so uncontrollably at his wife, that her pains had begun. She had fallen on leaving her sofa and again on ascending the stairs. A dreadful labour had followed, the child being produced only with the greatest difficulty and at final cost to the mother.

It was Mrs Jenkinson who brought this news.

"Those poor little girls," said Anne. "Has anyone courage enough to go and see how they do? Has the nursery there everything it can possibly need? Is there any alleviation we can make?"

"I had thought of going myself," said Mrs Jenkinson, "if you would not dislike it."

"And have you such courage, indeed? I fear that no one here can come with you—but do, by all means, go, and see what help we can offer."

"I understand that Mr Collins is locked into his study."

After a moment Anne said: "I think that we should offer them a haven here. Their nurserymaid is sister to someone in this house. They could undertake the care of them together and here is our nursery floor quite empty. It cannot be good for them to be alone in that house with their father in his present mood. What do you think, Mrs Jenkinson?"

"I think it an excellent scheme, Miss de Bourgh, and will do my possible to bring it about."

Mrs Jenkinson was shortly to be seen driving off in the phaeton. In the course of the morning she brought over the little girls, their nurserymaid, the wet-nurse and the new baby, together with a supply of clothes and their favourite toys. They were safely installed on the nursery floor with the connivance of the cook at the Parsonage and with the goodwill of all the servants at Rosings.

As she joined them at nuncheon with this information, Mrs Jenkinson added: "It has all been done without consultation with Mr Collins. I only hope he will not bring an action against me for kidnap."

"I will write him a soothing letter," said Anne. "If he is not completely out of his mind, he will realise that we have done him a great service."

The middle of the afternoon furnished evidence of how Mr Collins had been passing the time, locked into his study. Two notes from his hand were delivered at three o'clock. The first, addressed to Miss de Bourgh, said simply: "I could find no sign of occupation at Quarry End. The roof appeared to be in excellent condition."

The second, to Elizabeth, was in a different vein.

I humbly beg leave to inform you, Madam, that I hold you wholly responsible for the death of my dear Charlotte. With my own eyes I saw you leaving my house on the day she died, despite my previously expressed prohibition. It was this ill-advised and unnecessary visit that initiated last night's unhappy train of events which, had you had the grace to honour my declared wishes, might never have taken place. I shall pray to Almighty God that you will find the strength to live with this immovable stain upon your conscience.

Elizabeth's gasp as she read this was so audible that she was requested by Anne to let her see it. They exchanged their notes, Anne saying, as they did so: "If there was no sign of life at Quarry End, then there is something strange. I must send another messenger."

Then, having read Mr Collins's note to Elizabeth, she said: "Pay *no* heed, my dear Elizabeth. Clearly he is a little unhinged. It is a mercy that we have his children here."

Elizabeth, however, was sufficiently angry to wish to reply. Realising this, Anne indicated a desk by the window and said: "You will find everything there. I fear it is a very grievous loss to us all, as Mrs Collins was the only person in the world who could sometimes persuade him to act like an intelligent person."

After a moment's consideration, Elizabeth wrote:

My visit to your wife took place at her urgent request, conveyed to me by Mrs Jenkinson. My information is that it was your unreasoning, intemperate, unmannerly behaviour which began that tragic train of events. Whatever my father may have done, it was certainly no concern of your wife's.

I have destroyed your note. I shall forget that I received it. I shall continue to interest myself in the upbringing of *your wife's* children, in honour of the solemn promise that I gave to her yesterday.

She signed it only with her name.

The rest of the day passed quietly, too quietly, entirely without incident. As they came in from their evening stroll, Anne said: "I have instructed Heaton to make up some more of my father's cup. I cannot feel that Loving Cup is quite the best name for it and so have re-named it The Remedy—the Rosings Remedy, you know. I shall feel more comfortable with it under that name."

Mr Darcy joined them in the Blue Drawing Room just as the wine was brought in. He had offered his help to Mr Collins in making arrangements for the funeral, but had received no reply from behind the locked door of the study. He had therefore taken it upon himself to make those arrangements and had spent the afternoon conferring with the vergers and the sexton.

The burial was fixed for the following morning and a note had been sent to the vicar of the neighbouring parish, requesting him to attend in case Mr Collins himself should be unable to take the service.

Mrs Jenkinson came in later, reporting that all was well on the nursery floor and that the little girls had settled in. While they had asked several times for their mother, no mention had been made of their father.

"In short, Miss de Bourgh, I think we may congratulate ourselves upon the outcome of this morning's activities. But the wet-nurse is anxious that the new baby be baptised as soon as possible. She says she would feel it less of a responsibility in that case."

Mr Darcy attended the funeral alone.

He returned to tell them that Mr Collins had been there, had stood next to him, wrapped in his own grief and anger, and had spoken to no one. The service had been conducted by the visiting vicar; Mr Collins had recollected himself sufficiently to scatter earth upon the coffin; and that what seemed to be the entire village had attended.

"I have agreed with that other vicar to baptise the child—at eleven in the morning on the morrow. I told Mr Collins I would stand godfather, and that the two of you would be godmothers. If he heard me it was by good luck. I fear, my dear cousin, that you have an awkward time ahead, with him."

In the morning Anne, Elizabeth and Mr Darcy, with the baby and its nurse, travelled to the church in one of Lady Catherine's carriages. Mrs Jenkinson drove the little girls and their nursemaid and Mr Collins, accompanied by his own house servants, walked. He acknowledged his daughters without a smile, but recollected himself sufficiently to name the child Charlotte Lucasta.

As soon as the ceremony was over, Mr Collins bowed to the visiting clergyman and then walked off alone, without speaking to anyone. A few words were exchanged between the assembled servants; Miss de Bourgh thanked the vicar and the party then broke up, returning as it had come.

They were silent when they got back into the carriage, until Mr Darcy said, rather dryly: "Lucasta for the Lucases, of course. I wonder it had escaped me before."

"Yes," said Anne, smiling. "My other Collins godchild is called Anne Lucasta, you know. Catherine and Maria have Wilhelmina as their second name, for Sir William—and their own father, of course."

"Do you think," asked Elizabeth, "that Mr Collins will re-member to inform them at Lucas Lodge? I never saw a person so changed—and deranged. Should we perhaps undertake to do so?"

"No doubt Mr Collins will recall his family duties in time," remarked Mr Darcy. "If you were to inform your father the news would very soon be relayed to the Lucases. But I am so entirely out of charity with Mr Collins that I hope we may have no further contact, at least before we leave for Pemberley."

Their departure became the topic of the day. As they wound their way through the wood, on their evening walk, Elizabeth said to Anne that she must think of returning home; but, if there were any help or comfort that they could still give her, they would not think of doing so yet. Rather to her surprise, Anne replied at once. "No, my dear Elizabeth," she said, "you must go to your children. It has been one of the greatest pleasures of my life to have you and cousin Fitzwilliam here, and all to myself. I could not have supported the strains of the last few days without your presence. But now, I think, every-thing is resolved. I have only to discover who I am, and then invent a new, and more agreeable, way of life."

After a little silence she went on: "I have been considering my present situation for many years, you know. What I could not predict was how the household would respond to my mother's death, any more than I could predict how I would respond myself. I have been very moved to find them all so smiling and anxious to help and in Mrs Jenkinson a person of firm principles and excellent intentions, who has been, for many years, a friend. The changes of the last ten days are quite equivalent to a serious earthquake, but I think we shall survive them."

"Do you think you *will* make any changes?"

"Few, I think, if any. I have already settled into the *Blue* Drawing Room, a room my mother never liked, or used. I may change round some of the furniture—only to give it a different look, you know. And then I must accustom myself to being one of the sights of the neighbourhood. I suppose the callers out of curiosity will begin to arrive in a few weeks, after the first month of mourning is over. There are no younger sons at Hever or Knole, I think. Perhaps there may be some at Penshurst. It will be most interesting to see who calls the first."

"It will be something new for you to be a centre of attention to someone other than Mrs Jenkinson. No doubt you will receive some offers—but do you think any of them will be acceptable?"

"I would never contemplate leaving this house, but I am sure I would never have to. It is the property they would wish to marry."

She turned to Elizabeth and said, with a smile: "It is a great luxury to be able to talk in this way to you. How I shall miss it when you have gone! But I have some difficulties ahead of me. My mother was in many ways an admirable woman—that is to say, what she did was there to be admired; but she did it in such a way as to leave a scent of resentment behind her and this scent may prove a lasting legacy. It is sad for me that she had cut us off from our local society so completely. It must be at least six months before I can hold a rout party."

"And in the meanwhile—would you think of visiting us? If not at Pemberley, at least in London. We expect to spend two months there after Christmas, by which time, I think, your full mourning will be over."

"With all the pleasure in the world," said Anne, with another smile. "My mother would never allow it, for fear of infection, but I am growing stronger every day. I believe I would greatly enjoy—what do they call it?—coming to see the lions. And the thought of it will be like a great beacon at the end of these months of inevitable gloom."

They walked slowly across the lawn towards the house. Elizabeth had never admired it as a building but, softened by the setting sun, she could almost imagine that it was beginning to smile. Certainly, it looked much less formidable than before.

VIII

They left Rosings the next morning, after an earlier breakfast than usual. Sleeping one night on the road, they arrived at Pemberley in the late afternoon. The sun was still high, but the honey-coloured stone of the house was beginning to acquire its evening glow.

Elizabeth's heart always lifted a little at the first sight of that house, with gladness that it was still there, containing as it did so many of the chief objects of her affections, and with simple delight in its elegant proportions.

Although much had occurred in their lives to make it seem longer, they had been absent from home only a little over two weeks. Jane and Anne both had new dresses to display, and Alexander a new tooth. They all accompanied Mr Darcy on his evening stroll, and Elizabeth found herself wondering why they ever went away from Pemberley; although, as she quickly reflected, if they never went away they could never enjoy the overwhelming happiness of coming back.

She had agreed with Anne that they should maintain a regular and unreserved correspondence, but had not expected that Anne's first letter would arrive within the week.

Rosings, July 1st

My dearest Elizabeth will be, I know, quite astonished to hear that the reason why Mr Collins could find no sign of occupation at Quarry End was because the occupants were dead! They were a couple in late middle-age with no children, who seldom made contact in the village. For what reason we do not know, the man appears to have chopped his wife into little pieces and then hanged himself from a beam in the kitchen. I have never known such excitement in Hunsford, with magistrates and constables everywhere, but as they kept themselves so completely to themselves, no one is able to offer any suggestion as to why this gruesome event should have taken place. Mr Collins was lucky not to enter the house on that occasion as I understand the corpses were a dreadful sight. He has asserted himself as usual by declining to bury the man in consecrated ground, as indeed is quite his right, but under the circumstances he might have been better advised not to insist upon it. However, the affair has brought him a little back to life and restored him to his accustomed gloomy solemnity. He called yesterday to thank me for my kindness and hospitality to his daughters but did not seem to suggest that I ought to return them. I feel your absence every day. Pray let us meet again before too long if it can possibly be contrived. My warmest love to you and cousin Fitzwilliam.

Elizabeth showed this letter to Mr Darcy and replied to it before long, but she had little news. The month of July passed quietly, the weather particularly benign. She drove with her children every day, to picnic in the park, to join Mr Darcy wherever he was fishing, to make excursions into the woods. Her uncle and aunt Gardiner, who very often visited them at this time of year, were spending the summer by the sea, with their children, at Lyme.

They were to go, with their children, to Longbourn towards the end of August, for the christening of Elizabeth's twin half-brothers; and she was beginning to think about this, when a letter arrived from her father.

Longbourn, August 3rd

No doubt you will both be unsurprised to hear, after your skirmish with Collins, that Mr Edmund Bertram has declined to baptise my sons. He gives no specific reason. He just refuses. So my excellent son Morland has agreed to fulfil this office. I hope you may be able to convey him and his wife and son when you come yourselves. Maria says little but is certainly deeply hurt. I should have acknowledged your letter about the happenings at Rosings before, but I do not increase in enthusiasm for writing letters. We are also in some trouble with the church here, but will reserve this news until we meet.

Elizabeth always rather chided herself for having to be reminded of the existence of her sister Mary, whose husband, James

Morland, was Vicar of Kympton, some thirty miles from Pemberley. The living was in Mr Darcy's gift and he had presented it on their marriage. They lived in apparent comfort and contentment, had one son, and with a reputation in the village for kindness and compassion. Elizabeth was in no way surprised to hear that Mr Morland would perform the baptism. She chose to disregard her father's remark about being in trouble with the church, concentrating her disapproval on Mr Edmund Bertram, an ordained priest and brother to her step-mother—and whom she knew very slightly herself. How he could find it in his heart to refuse such an obvious, and pleasurable, duty she could simply not imagine.

Her father's letter completely changed the scale of their expedition and the next ten days were entirely devoted to arranging it. Their cavalcade set off precisely as planned, taking up the Morlands on their way, and spending one night on the road.

Elizabeth and Mr Darcy were alone in the first carriage as far as Kympton. As they went down the drive from Pemberley, he gave her a letter.

"Today's post, my love. From Anne."

"Then you must allow me to read it to you," said Elizabeth, as she opened it. "It dates from Rosings, August the 14th."

This whole countryside is in an uproar over the suicide of Lord Londonderry at Cray, I suppose not fifteen miles from here. I do not mix in political circles, as of course neither do you, but wonder what kind of society the politicians must keep to make such a thing possible at such a level. It has, however, had one immediate effect. I received a visit from someone I have never heard of, a mother and son from somewhere beyond Tonbridge, who were unaware of my mother's death and who called to discuss the matter with her. I do not entirely accept this as an explanation and rather think it was the first of the Investigating Visits that I have steeled myself to expect. The son could not have been two days over twenty-one and looked at me rather as he might have examined a very old gig suddenly discovered, dilapidated in a barn. His mother did all the talking, concluding by saying how sad she was to find that there was to be no Public Day this year, so I must suppose her to be on *that* list if only I can find it.

I am more and more pleased with Mrs Jenkinson, who bore much more than her share of that conversation. We laughed very much about it afterwards. The Collins girls are still here. Mr Collins is gone on a visit to his bishop but will be away only for a day or two. Mrs Jenkinson, I think, begins to love the little girls and to talk of engaging a governess for them. She has an inexhaustible supply of nieces so no doubt one of them could be persuaded. I quite dread the day when they must be told their mother is not coming back. At present they believe she is on a visit and we have not even put them into black ribbons, let alone full mourning, which I think cruel and dreadful for young children. The two elder ones now come with me every evening on what I think of as Our Walk. I am sure that I have never been so well. The dresses that were made for me six weeks ago are having to be Let Out and there are no more *caveats* from Mrs Jenkinson that such and such a dish may be too *rich*. Everything agrees with me. The excellent Heaton conjures up delicious marvels from my father's old receipt books—indeed I fancy we are working quite through them *all*—and altogether I have to say that I never believed I could be so happy.

"But who is Londonderry?" said Mr Darcy, when she had finished. "Oh, Castlereagh, I suppose. I believe there was some idiotic quarrel between his wife and Lady Conyngham, His Majesty's present peculiar. We may think ourselves lucky to be at a distance from all such intrigues, my love. How pleased I am that I have never felt the smallest desire to meddle in politics."

"I am glad to think of the little girls still being at Rosings. I wonder why Mr Collins wishes to consult his bishop? It cannot be about a *spiritual* problem, as Mr Collins does not have them. Could his bishop have heard of his disgraceful behaviour towards his wife and *summoned* him? My heart quite bleeds for his daughters and I think that Anne is right to keep them. I hope she may contrive to do so always."

"My cousin Anne astonishes me more and more. Who could have expected the mouse to turn into a lion? But she is, when all is said and done, the daughter of her mother. While they seem to be unlike in almost every respect, if she decides to adopt the Misses Collins, that is what will happen."

"As to *that*, my love, I also am a daughter of my mother. I trust you do not see too much of a resemblance there?"

"As to that, *my* love, your mother, with all her faults, had a very kind heart. And she was, I think, someone who thoroughly understood the finer points of housekeeping, which my own mother did not. If your mother's second daughter has transformed Pemberley into a model of domestic tranquillity, perhaps we should give credit where credit is due."

Elizabeth smiled and said only: "My mother's second daughter had some excellent material to work on. But I am glad you think it much improved."

"My mother was never perfectly happy here, I believe. Pemberley is a house and was built as one. My mother grew up in a castle, full of ghosts and draughts and dungeons. She was never quite comfortable being comfortable."

They did not linger long at Kympton. Everything, everyone, was waiting to take place in the appropriate carriage. Very shortly after they were on the move again, Mary said: "How pleased we are to be alone with you both, a luxury I had not quite expected. I wish to be extremely rude about Mr Edmund Bertram and hope that you will join me."

"We shall," said Elizabeth, "and completely. In every way. The only possible thing to be said in his favour is that it has been the reason for your being with us now. The relationship here is unusual. Mr Edmund is the babies' uncle. Mr Morland is their half-brother. I proclaim, if justice is to be done, that his claim is the prior one."

"And I am delighted," said Mr Morland, "that you think so. I believe his refusal may be put at the door of his bishop. We are most fortunate in ours. My dear Mary has even persuaded him to permit the singing of our psalms."

"I am become," said Mary, "if I may immodestly say so, a great performer on our organ. And our congregations are quite doubled, as the bishop wished. But I *also* think it owing to the excellence of my husband's sermons."

"I keep them down, you know," said Mr Morland, "to seven minutes. My father, a greatly admired preacher, limited his to ten—but that was in a much larger village, and in Wiltshire."

"You think those southern congregations may be more patient?" asked Mr Darcy.

"My father's parishioners were all farmers," said Mr Morland, "wedded to the land. He could tell them every week of any new discovery, or indeed that it was time to sow their turnips. My parishioners are quarrymen and coalminers and canal boatmen and I have yet to find that I know more about their lives than they do. But I make the effort. They are not articulate—but I flatter myself that am I making some progress."

"And if your congregations are quite doubled, you are succeeding," said Elizabeth. "But what could Mr Edmund's bishop have said to him to prevent such a quiet, appropriate family ceremony?"

"He could have said many things," said Mr Morland, "but all to no purpose if Mr Edmund *wished* to come. It is that which troubles me."

"Who knows what may not happen if nursery squabbles are allowed to continue into later life," said Mary. "We are lucky in that respect, I think, Elizabeth? I suppose you have no word from Lydia?"

"I have not," said Elizabeth. "I was about to ask you the same question."

"I do sometimes wonder how she goes on," said Mary. "Not only did she always want to run away, but she also wanted to be run away *with*. There is a distinction there, I think. Perhaps she is now within reach of a Moorish pirate—or indeed a Spanish bandit—who will come for her, you know, upon a golden steed."

Elizabeth laughed, but Mr Darcy said, sufficiently dryly: "Then she is in the wrong place. I believe the principal mode of transport in Gibraltar to be the donkey."

"Alas, poor Lydia," said Mary, smiling. "How my heart bleeds for her. But I have yet to be extremely rude about Mr Edmund Bertram."

"There is no need, my dear," said Mr Morland. "We are all agreed with you. I tell my flock that Christ came into the world to *mitigate* the fierce moods of the Great Jehovah, that repentance is the cure for all remorse. I do not believe, for instance, that the present Mrs Bennet—if I may so call her—ever means to run away again."

"And, after all," said Mary, "Our Lord would not have turned that water into wine—at that marriage, you know—if he had not intended us to enjoy ourselves sometimes. I believe his motives there to be frequently misunderstood."

IX

Mr Bennet, his butler and his housekeeper, all assisted at their welcome to Longbourn. An air almost of carnival invested their arrival. Quite happy to be Miss Elizabeth again, and to be told how well she looked and how beautiful were her children, Elizabeth received a particularly warm embrace from her father, who just said: "Welcome, welcome, my dear Lizzy. We lack indeed your husband's calm judgment—but now that you are both come everything will be resolved."

"Indeed it will," returned Elizabeth. "But where is Maria?"

"She still rests at this time of the day," said her father, "but I think might be grateful for a visit."

Leaving Mary and the nursemaids in charge of the children, and Mr Darcy and Mr Morland in charge of everything else, Elizabeth went immediately upstairs. She found Maria alone on a sofa in her bedroom, by the window overlooking the new flower garden.

As soon as their first warm greetings were over, Maria said: "Tell me truly, dear Elizabeth, how long did it take you to become yourself after Alexander's birth?"

"I would think quite three months," said Elizabeth. "He was born in December. I am sure it was at least the spring before my fullest energy returned. And you, my dear Maria, had *two* sons. I had only one."

"The air at Longbourn is very soft," said Maria. "It makes me feel quite sleepy. I am still feeding my sons, I suppose, which takes all one's best energies."

"And how are your sons? I think the whole party is gone upstairs to admire them."

"They are, of course, the most beautiful babies in the world. They bask in the smiles of their father—a species I have not met before. My own father was a distant figure at the best of times, designed to inspire respect rather than affection. But your father comes every day to the nursery and, I think, can accurately distinguish Henry from Thomas. And great pleasure does it give me to say so."

"As we are alone for one moment—and I am sure this may be the sole occasion—I would like to say that I hope he has made you as happy as you have certainly made him. How does everyone go on at Longbourn?"

"I think we are extremely well," replied Maria. "I am a little vexed to find that our people here no longer speak to those at Lucas Lodge. About the cause of the quarrel I can, of course, do nothing. Except, perhaps, to wish that it had never happened."

"Do not distress yourself, my dear Maria. You would find, did you choose to enquire, that they are all enjoying their uncivil war extremely. And lack of communication with the Lucases is scarcely to be regarded as a loss. My father must be enchanted."

Elizabeth now recalled that she was in the bedroom she had shared with her sister Jane until the day on which they both had married. It was a room of secrets shared, of comforts and encouragements given in moments of sadness and disappointment, a room which contained her childhood. She found it so entirely changed that her memories dissolved. She could only say to Maria: "How *truly* charming you have made this room. How glad I am to find you so at home in it."

She looked round again.

"I think you have done just what we would have done ourselves, though we talked for years about having new curtains. But we could never agree the colour."

Maria smiled and said: "I was more than a little fearful, you know, quite nervous to be invading the room which must hold so many memories for you and Jane. I hope the result is not *too* displeasing? I have to say it is the most restful room in which I have ever slept."

"Not displeasing, not displeasing at all," said Elizabeth. "I am delighted by its new life."

"You may see the beginning of my flower garden from this window," went on Maria. "It will one day be my pride and joy.

Even the gardener has said, in rather a guarded way, you know, that he thinks it may be quite pretty in the end. I fancy he was almost pleased to learn that I was imprisoned here upstairs when planting time came round. But I fancy he was *not* quite pleased when he found me talking to him from the window. However, there was no dispute this year about the plants. We could use only the ones we had. Next year I hope to be more adventurous—I quite drown in horticultural journals."

Elizabeth moved over to the window and found that an area of indifferent grass, on which they had been used to play battledore and shuttlecock, had been carved into an agreeable pattern of flower-beds, with a circular hedge about them.

"Mr Repton," went on Maria, "is unfortunately dead. Once, in a former life, I tried to persuade Mr Rushworth to employ him. But my adviser at Longbourn, you may be astonished to hear, is the owner of this house."

"Indeed, my father?" said Elizabeth in surprise. "How little one knows one's own family, after all. But tell me—what I really want to know, and what you could hardly put into a letter—has there been unpleasantness here—now that your previous marriage is known?"

Maria was silent for a moment. Then she said, very calmly: "Yes, I think I must say that there has. It was the Lucases, of course. I understand their eldest daughter is married to the man who would otherwise have inherited Longbourn?"

"Indeed she—was," said Elizabeth. "She was my dearest friend, but I have never quite reconciled the Miss Lucas that I knew with the Mrs Collins that she became. Her death is something that I cannot discuss. But what perhaps you do not know is that, the day before he proposed to her, he proposed to me."

"A man of the moment, I observe," said Maria.

Their eyes met and they both laughed.

"I am glad to laugh about it now," said Elizabeth, "but it was not at all amusing at the time."

"No, indeed, I can imagine not. But that of course explains a great deal. Fortunately our bride visits had all been paid before

Lady Lucas gave a series of evening parties from which we were excluded. The principal result of that was simply that the Lucases and the Bennets are no longer invited together—an improvement which, your father is kind enough to say—makes him regard his second marriage with even greater satisfaction."

"That sounds like my father, indeed," said Elizabeth.

"At the time I was afraid to think that I might be losing him many friends. But no—he seems quite pleased about it all. Those who no longer visit seem to be those he never cared for in the first place."

"No wonder he looks so well. He was never one to disguise his feelings and, if he found a person quite uninteresting, it would very often appear, at least to those who knew him."

"The Vicar felt obliged to call—to refuse us Communion, you know, and so of course we are no longer obliged to dine with him, or he with us."

"Which I am sure my father must regard as another great advantage. I know not how many times I have heard him inveigh against his own stupidity in bestowing the living of Longbourn on such a young, sanctimonious man."

There was a comfortable silence between them. Then Maria said, reflectively: "Even if we were to be ignored by all the world for the rest of our lives, there is enough here to occupy us. To return this house to former glories, to fill the garden with flowers and now, of course, to give life and happiness to my sons, must be enough for any but the most exacting woman. But that is not the case. We are visited by everyone we wish to know and I can only praise a generous God who has seen fit to anchor me in such an agreeable harbour."

"Oh, *how* pleased I am to hear you say so," said Elizabeth. "My father himself would not be discomposed if no one came to visit him at all. His own father, as you may not know, was a most notable recluse, but I am thankful to feel that, with you at his side, he will not become one himself."

"And can you approve of the changes I have made in this room? It spoke to me so loudly of you and Jane that I quite trembled to do anything."

"It is now a charming room," said Elizabeth, "and full of secrets. I daresay it may even whisper some of them to you. You have made it quite the prettiest bedroom in the country, and I am glad to see the old furniture looking so well in its new situation."

"As to that, the furniture in this house left nothing to be desired. Some of my own I brought from Matlock and a few favourite treasures. Your mother, I think, must have been a remarkable housewife. I have not altered any of her domestic arrangements and the old pieces, though plain by the standards of today, are all so perfectly preserved that they look as well in one room as in another. In short, my dear Elizabeth, you may count me as one of the happiest creatures in the world and one who will do her best to ensure that no shadow ever crosses the path of your father, or indeed the paths of his sons."

Elizabeth rose to take her leave.

"I must not linger too long up here," she said. "When I think of what is going on downstairs, I can only rejoice that we have been allowed this time together."

"I notice that you do not mention my brother Edmund."

"I do not mention him because I cannot understand him," said Elizabeth. "I think that much will be said about him in other quarters."

"I find it hard to come to terms with the fact that the only deep wound—in a situation full of such possibilities—should have been inflicted—and I use that word deliberately—by my own brother. A man of the cloth."

"Do not make yourself too unhappy, Maria, not in any way at all. Just remember, every moment, that everyone who has arrived today loves and welcomes you. We bring with us our own man of the cloth and, I do not hesitate to say, he is in every way what one hopes a man of the cloth will be. I think you have not met *him* before? I can only commend him to you."

They exchanged a kiss.

"I am glad you are here," said Maria.

X

It was Elizabeth's first visit to Longbourn since her father's second marriage and, everywhere she looked, she found small improving touches of which she could only approve. It was as though the house had previously existed in shadow. Now the curtains had been drawn back and the sunlight had come pouring in.

The new wallpapers upstairs were her principal envy and she resolved to put something like them on her own nursery floor. Downstairs the changes were few. In the drawing-room the curtains were those chosen by Jane and herself before their mother died and the result was as cheering as she could wish. A chair here was re-covered, a sofa there. Some pictures had been re-hung and some ornaments re-discovered from the attics. It was the same house, the house that she had always known and would always love; but it had been given a new lease of life and she could only admire the care and consideration which Maria had shown in all of it.

There could be only one topic of conversation in the evening. When Maria came into the drawing-room before dinner, Mr Bennet said: "Welcome, my dear Maria, and let me present to you your favourite sons-in-law. Darcy you know and cherish. But let me commend my son Morland to you, who seems to be, in every way, an ornament to his profession. His kindness and comprehension upon the present occasion are even beyond admiration."

Maria, Elizabeth thought, was looking particularly handsome and a covert glance informed her that her present sons-in-law thought so too. She shook hands with them, kissed Mary, and Elizabeth again, and then sat down saying, to Mary, as she did so: "I have received your sister Elizabeth's commendation for what I have done in her bedroom. I hope I may have your approval for what I have done in yours?"

"You may," said Mary, sitting down beside her. "I think I may speak for all my sisters when I say—you seem to have brought our dearest Longbourn back to life."

"I hope," said Mr Morland to Mr Bennet, "that all our arrangements for tomorrow are in place?"

"They are," said Mr Bennet, "and I will now recite them to you all—in case, you know, I should forget them."

Elizabeth found herself wishing for a glass of the Rosings Remedy at this moment, but was more than astonished when the butler came in with equipment to produce something suspiciously similar.

"No, no," said Mr Darcy, in an undertone. "It is ordinary champagne. My correspondence with your father is short, but to the point."

When the glasses had been handed, Mr Bennet said to the butler, who had arrived at Longbourn long before Elizabeth herself: "I believe you have adequate arrangements in the Servants' Hall?"

"We have, sir," said the butler, "and will drink a health to the young gentlemen with the greatest of pleasure."

"I have to propose their health myself," went on Mr Bennet, when the butler had gone. "I find myself," he said, after a moment, "very moved by all the occurrences here. I seem to have become a centre of goodwill which does nothing but amaze me. My son Henry is to have as his godfathers Mr Fitzwilliam Darcy and Mr Thomas Bertram and as godmother his sister Elizabeth. My son Thomas has his sister Jane as godmother and Captain William Price as his godfather. But as his other godfather I have been complimented to receive the acceptance of Mr Edward Gardiner, my late wife's brother."

There was a murmur of applause from Mary and Elizabeth here, and a glance was exchanged between Elizabeth and Maria, as it had been an accident to Mrs Gardiner that had eventually brought Maria to Longbourn.

"He is a man of whom I cannot speak too highly. His assistance in a certain matter, in collaboration with my present son-in-law," with a bow to Mr Darcy, "is something we must never forget. I wish, in this way, to keep him in the family, observing, at the same time, that an East India merchant, as he promises to become, can do no harm to a younger son. So I will ask you, please, to drink a health to Henry and Thomas Bennet and to wish them a long life and a happy one."

When the health had been drunk, Elizabeth noticed that Maria was mopping her eyes and went over to her.

"It is almost too much to bear," said Maria. "Surely something must go wrong soon?"

She was swiftly assured by everyone in the room that nothing would ever go wrong again and this comfortable, amiable mood lasted through the dinner.

Elizabeth, seated between her father and Mr Morland, marvelled as one favourite dish accompanied another and smiled across the table to Maria.

"Yes," said Maria, "my ally here is Mrs Hill, whose taste exactly echoes mine."

But a further surprise was in store.

As they waited for the tea and coffee to be brought in, Mr Bennet said, to Mary: "I have had our instrument completely tuned. I understand it to be in excellent order. May I ask you to prove that for us? I believe all your music is still there."

Elizabeth was standing next to Mary as he spoke, and heard her actually gasp; but, after less than two seconds, she said: "Yes, with all the pleasure in the world. I am glad you have had it tuned."

Elizabeth went with her, to turn the pages.

It was a performance which no one could have anticipated. In full practice, both on the church organ and on her own forte-piano, Mary did perfect justice to all the pieces which had rendered hideous many afternoons in the past, but which were now given with an accuracy, and even a passion, astonishing to them all.

When she had finished, Mr Bennet went over to her and said: "I think, my dear Mary, that I have never quite appreciated you before. I must ask you to forgive me."

He kissed her on the cheek; and Mary burst into tears.

XI

It was hot the next afternoon. The sun shone out of a cloudless sky and, as the church was only just at the bottom of the back drive, the whole company decided to walk.

Elizabeth was very moved to find that the entire household accompanied them. Her daughters came with her and Mr Darcy. Alexander Darcy and James Morland were carried by their nursemaids. The heir to Longbourn was in the arms of Elizabeth's own old nurse, and his brother in those of Mrs Hill, who had been their housekeeper as long as Elizabeth could remember.

They were received in silence by the Vicar of Longbourn at the entrance to the church. He exchanged formalities with Mr Morland, who then took over the service, the Vicar remaining in the background, looking rather shame-faced.

The font was at the back, but the church was full, not, Elizabeth was interested to note, with their friends and neighbours, but with their tenants and the village people. She turned and smiled at them all, receiving a kind of unexpressed acknowledgement which raised her spirits even further.

She and Mr Darcy made their vows together. Mary stood proxy for Jane and Mr Bennet for William Price and Mr Gardiner. The little boys expressed their outrage and fury at being deluged with cold water in a most acceptable way and the service came amiably to an end. Mr Bennet invited the whole congregation to refresh themselves at his house, remarking at the same time that he was very pleased to see them all.

Elizabeth had not expected this. Their own christenings she could not remember, although she would have been almost five years old when Lydia was christened; but they, of course, were all girls. She said to Mr Darcy: "This is an attendance which one good. I am sure the whole village, and all the tenants, are here. Do you think it is in compliment to my father, or are they merely rejoicing that the threat of Mr Collins has been removed?"

"The former, my love. You do not do your father justice. They come because he is an exemplary landlord."

"I am very glad to hear you say that," said Elizabeth. "I begin to realise how little I know my own father."

Cakes and ale were being served from long trestle tables and benches had been placed in various parts of the front garden. Elizabeth, moving among very old friends, was glad to receive compliments on behalf of her mother, principally in gratitude for the fact that there had been no interruption to the help available at the back door at Longbourn. This was a thing on which her mother had particularly prided herself. There had always been jugs of soup, or parcels of bread and cheese, for anyone who asked for them.

In the middle of the afternoon she noticed her own old nurse seated alone on a bench beneath a favourite beech tree, and went immediately to join her.

"A wonderful chance to talk to you," said Elizabeth. "We could not have been alone in the nursery today."

"But how pleasant to have it once again so full. It makes me feel quite young again."

"So—how do you all go on? I have been so happy to see my father grow so young again that I hardly considered what were the implications for this house."

"We go on very well, no trouble, never a word in anger. Our new lady settled in and put up no one's back. All the changes she has made have been those Mrs Hill had prayed for since my late mistress first fell ill."

"I know that is the truth," said Elizabeth. "Only you could have told me. And now, I understand, my father even visits the nursery?"

"Indeed, yes, which must be the most surprising thing of all. At first, you know, or at least I will tell you, he came up every day to admire Miss Jane and, after her, Miss Lizzy. You were, as I recall, most beautiful babies. But after Miss Mary I do not remember that he ever came. With Miss Catherine, a very sickly child, he had the door built at the bottom of the stairs so he could not hear her crying. And as for Miss Lydia—shall I ever forget the day he met us by chance in the garden, when I suppose she would be about four years old, and had to ask her what her name was?!"

Elizabeth suppressed a smile at this and only said: "But now he comes up every day?"

"He does indeed, and has never looked so well since he was a young man. I came, you know, into this house two weeks before Miss Jane was born, when he can have been scarcely twenty-two years of age. He will certainly live to see my little boys grown up."

"And can you tell one from the other?"

"I have embroidered a ribbon with H for Henry and T for Thomas and these I keep all the time upon their wrists. But their mother knows them both quite well, and even I very seldom make a mistake."

"I suppose it very important that they do not become confused, since only one can inherit my father's estate. I wonder what will become of the other?"

"My new mistress will take good care of him. Though perhaps I should not say so, I believe Sir Thomas Bertram has settled an enormous sum upon her."

"I am only too thankful to find her spending it upon the house. Nothing could be happier than what she has done in our old bedroom. I believe Sir Thomas has visited more than once?"

"He has. I overheard him to say to Mr Bennet that he blamed himself entirely for permitting Mrs Bennet's first marriage and that he would do all in his power to support and comfort her in her second."

"That was well done of him," said Elizabeth. "But—and I am almost afraid to ask—what said the household when the truth about that marriage became known? Through, as I understand it, the good offices of Lady Lucas?"

"Well, as to that, the servants here have always felt themselves to be above all those at Lucas Lodge. As they are indeed.

After the first surprise—my new mistress, you know, was presented by the Lucases as quite a scarlet woman—they dismissed the whole as a scandalous falsehood invented by the Lucases out of spite. And now that she has supplied two heirs to Longbourn, their devotion is complete."

This conversation was entirely satisfactory to Elizabeth. Any little doubts, or foolish reservations, were removed by it, and she abandoned herself to the simple enjoyment of being at Longbourn again.

She was especially pleased to find her father and Mr Morland entering into what looked like a close friendship. She had this confidence from Mr Bennet one afternoon, as they walked together in the garden.

"My son Morland has treated with our Vicar to such effect that he, the Vicar, called on me this morning, offering us Communion in private if we wished it. I can only say how much I regret being unable to feel it to be of the smallest importance—but I have, of course, accepted."

"So now I may leave you without a qualm," said Elizabeth. "Everything in place, everyone in harmony. What *can* you have done to deserve it?"

"I leave that, my dear Lizzy, to yourself to determine."

But he looked rather pleased.

The rest of their visit passed only too quickly. Not until the day before they were going to leave did Elizabeth find Maria alone in her room upstairs.

"Oh, I am so pleased," said Maria, "and especially so as I have a letter from my brother Tom today."

"I hope it is full of excellent news," said Elizabeth. "He is a very favourite brother-in-law."

"He says very little about himself. He is writing to the Darcys by the same post to invite them to Mansfield in October. Do you think that you will go?"

"Beyond any question—yes," said Elizabeth very quickly. "While we have been involved with your family at a distance for some time, we have yet—if I may borrow some words from the Duke of Wellington—to visit headquarters."

Maria laughed. "Headquarters it is indeed. I wonder what you will make of them all. My brother Edmund seems to have gone mad and, I suppose, his devoted wife with him. My father has changed beyond recognition in the last few years. Had he had any idea of the ferments brewing in our nursery upstairs, he might have visited us more often. And I can imagine no change to my mother except that, after thirty-five years, she might require a new sofa."

"It is a charming picture," said Elizabeth. "I quite long to meet her."

"My sister you will not meet. She has been banished, but with her husband this time, to a cottage near Dawlish. Just as I was, to Matlock."

Then, after a moment, she went on: "I was not the only one to make a foolish marriage. The Honourable John is a deep-died gamester who would have them both in a debtor's prison if he had his way. My poor father is beside himself to know how he can protect Julia from the results of her husband's idiocies. And this is now especially important as the money from the sale of my father's property in Antigua has, at last, come through."

"I am all ears," said Elizabeth.

"Well," said Maria, smiling, "there is not much more to say. My dear Tom, in fact, says nothing, except that an estate which marches with Mansfield on the north has become derelict and he would rather like to buy it. But it is slave money, of course, and my brother Edmund has almost too much to say about that."

"Do you think your father will ever allow you back to Mansfield? How old does a scandal have to be before it dies?"

"As to that," said Maria very solemnly, "it lives only until another, greater scandal puts it into eclipse. In this case it will always live until Mr Rushworth marries again."

"I believe, from my sister Jane, that he is still the scourge of London, with his two-and-forty speeches."

"I am surprised, in fact, that no one else has gobbled him up. Foolish he may be, but he remains one of the largest landowners in Northamptonshire. Do you think you will go to London in the winter?"

"I think perhaps in February, for six weeks. I cannot bear to leave my children any longer. But Mr Darcy has a cousin who wishes, in her own words, to see the lions and I think we shall much enjoy showing them to her—though I am by no means so happy about showing her to them."

Maria merely looked her question.

"A considerable heiress," said Elizabeth, with a smile, "or rather, now mistress of a very handsome property, aged thirty-five and coming into the world for the first time. She has been brought up entirely as an invalid, though now we find that she is no such thing. You can imagine the responsibility!"

"And is she as handsome as her property?"

"Difficult to tell how she will turn out. While she was living only on invalid food and was confined largely to the house, she seemed always very frail. Now one can only say—her features are perfectly good."

Maria laughed.

"How I envy you, dear Elizabeth," she said. "What possibilities it opens up! I must have a first-hand account of *all* your adventures. You will write to me yourself?"

"I shall, indeed, and with great pleasure. I just wish you could be there to support me."

XII

The invitation to Mansfield, to shoot partridge in October, awaited them on their return to Pemberley; and it was while she was discussing, in the nursery, what clothes it would be proper to take for the children—for they and their nursemaids were also invited—that a letter from Anne was brought to Elizabeth.

Rosings, Sept. 24th

It has taken all this time, dearest Elizabeth, for the intelligence to waft its way up the back stairs—I do not question either its source or its route—that Mr Collins was in fact *sent for* by his Bishop, that they prayed together for *three days* at the Bishop's residence—which I fancy is in Maidstone—and that he was in receipt of a sort of reprimand, though of course only of the holiest kind. I do not know how the Church behaves at such times, neither can I imagine how such information came to arrive in Hunsford. Perhaps it was the visiting Vicar, who conducted the service for poor Mrs Collins, who sent in a Report. Can you imagine such a thing? However, or for whatever reason, Mr Collins is quite changed. He comes regularly to see his daughters—who have *not* returned home—and I feel almost in charity with this new, *silent*, nearly modest person. Our principal other news must be that a niece of Mrs Jenkinson is now installed upstairs as governess and that she seems most happy to be so. She has been imprisoned for nearly seven years in the house of a Mrs Smallridge, near Bristol, a lady of quite unbridled vulgarity who treated her as though she were a servant—not eating at the family table and so on. She was required to give six months' notice but quite dreaded having to do so as they would have been even more unpleasant—if possible—during that time. In the end it was agreed that she could leave at once if she would forego the six months' salary already owing to her. I was very glad to be able to send her the money to travel post and to restore to her the lost salary when she arrived. She is a charming girl. She says she *thinks* she may have managed to teach something to her late charges but that the one principally in need of instruction was their mother! I suppose nothing good ever came out of Bristol. Already I begin to look forward to my visit to London with you. My period of full mourning will end just before Christmas so I am starting to assemble some clothes. I am become quite plump. Mrs Jenkinson thinks I have arrived at my proper size and I do indeed feel quite comfortable with it. Mrs Smallridge has been of use in an indirect way. She was a very *dressy* lady and wore her jewels and exposed her bosom every night, but not on Sundays. Her dressmaker, from Bristol of course, worked from books of French designs and so Miss Linton, the niece, has been able to bring with her copies of *La Belle Assemblée* which are *only one year old*. She does not admire the work of my Sevenoaks seamstresses but is full of praise for Madame de Domballe. I am happy to leave myself in her hands, particularly as she is a cool, elegant girl most becomingly dressed in gowns that I understand she made herself. I trust your journey to Mansfield may be taken without mishap. Pray send me your direction there in case I should have something of a sensational nature to disclose to you before your return to Pemberley.

When Elizabeth showed this letter to Mr Darcy, he said only that he was delighted to find her so interested in her life, but that he hoped her visit to London would not disappoint her.

"I must read *Tom Jones* once more, so that I know what she is expecting to find there. I am sure I could not endure *Evelina* a second time."

"And I am sure Tom Jones did not visit the Tower of London or the British Museum. Do you think that Anne will wish to go there? I wonder if you have ever been yourself?"

"Indeed yes, but not for twenty years. My tutor made it a point to take me everywhere of historical significance. I must be the only boy of fifteen in the country who was obliged to make a sketch of the Banqueting House, in order to reconstruct the scene of the execution of the King. But he was an excellent man in many ways. I recall that he also took me to Greenwich."

"I hope that Anne will not wish to be quite so adventurous, most especially not in the month of March. We must keep her at home in the warm, with charming parties and restorative doses of champagne cup."

"Perhaps you should ask her, in your next letter, for that receipt. Mrs Reynolds has not found anything comparable among our archives here."

"I will do that," said Elizabeth. "But what concerns me most is that her health should not suffer. Lady Catherine was not *always* mistaken. Perhaps as Anne is now more robust than formerly she will not be so prone to take infection."

"My tutor, my love," said Mr Darcy, "obliged me to gargle with salt and water night and morning, and I might recommend this practice to ourselves when we are in London. He, alas, must have neglected to follow his own advice for, when he left me, he became a master at Westminster School and died there—of a putrid sore throat."

"That is the kind of information that I prefer to be without, though no doubt you are right when you say he neglected himself. I mean to take the greatest care of us all."

"And I shall be most happy to assist you—in that, as in everything else."

XIII

It was a little over eighty miles from Pemberley to Mansfield. They started early, on a crisp, sunlit morning, and were able to arrive just as the evening was closing in. The children came with Rebecca—she and Jemima had had to draw lots as to whom should travel—and, after they had all been comfortably settled, the dinner was served only an hour later than usual.

The conversation was, to begin with, about Pemberley only. Georgiana had to be told everything in the smallest detail, so that the fact that Tom Bertram said very little was not noticeable until Elizabeth and Mr Darcy both remarked upon it when they were alone in their bedroom.

"I thought, too," said Elizabeth, "that he was by no means his usual confident self. He seemed, in fact, quite happy to take no part in our conversation."

"I hope we may not find ourselves taken up in a Bertram family wrangle," said Mr Darcy. "I agree with you completely— I did not even think him looking particularly well."

"I shall have Georgiana all to myself tomorrow," said Elizabeth with some satisfaction. "You may depend on me to discover *exactly* what is going on."

The gentlemen left early the next morning, as the day's shooting had been arranged at a considerable distance. Elizabeth and Georgiana breakfasted alone, and in the greatest comfort, a note being delivered just as they sat down.

"My sister Fanny," said Georgiana, in explanation. "She is in some alarm about Mary, her elder daughter. They are not very strong—their parents being cousins, you know—and both Edmund and Fanny are in a constant state of anxiety about them. I sometimes think they talk, and think, of nothing else."

"I thought you told me once that the elder daughter was called Maria—for Lady Bertram."

"Well, yes," said Georgiana, rather guardedly, "she was. But after all this kick-up—with the *other* Maria, you know—they have shortened it to Mary."

"I hope I do not wholly understand you, dearest Georgiana."

"I fear, I fear," said Georgiana, turning a little pink, "that you understand me only too completely. Both seem to have taken leave of their senses almost entirely on this subject. My poor Tom lectures Edmund endlessly—quite in reverse of the usual— but he makes no impression. One can only imagine that he *wished* Maria to remain in disgrace and seclusion for ever."

"Well," said Elizabeth, rather sourly, "he is a clergyman after all. But my brother Morland has no such antique reservations."

"Then let us rejoice about that. Fanny writes to say that she cannot sit with Lady Bertram today and will we go instead. In fact it is Fanny's week—we take it in turns as my poor mother-in-law cannot sit alone for longer than one hour at a time. But I grieve deeply that I must involve you in the life of the family so immediately. I hoped to have a whole week to ourselves to begin with; but do not, I beg, allow this to ruin your breakfast."

They set off an hour later, to walk through the park.

"Half-an-hour by the long route, twenty minutes by the short one. I use the long one mostly in the summer—but it is a fine day. I hope you may be feeling quite strong."

It was a delightful walk, the ground gently undulating, the woods and copses planted in such a way that the Great House was not in view until they were only five minutes from it.

"It was Sir Thomas's father who planted these trees," said Georgiana, "principally to screen his house from prying eyes. That Sir Thomas being inclined to dislike—*everyone* I rather fancy. This Sir Thomas has continued along the same road and *my* Sir Thomas has large designs upon some fields on the edge of the estate which seem to have lost their fertility."

Lady Bertram was discovered in the drawing-room, seated on a sofa and occupied with a long piece of embroidery. She put it aside and rose to greet them. She offered her hand at once to Elizabeth and said: "I have so looked forward to meeting you. I have to thank you for many kindnesses to my poor Maria."

She kissed Georgiana and then returned to her sofa, motioning them to sit on the one opposite.

"It was at all times a great pleasure to bestow those kindnesses," said Elizabeth as she sat down. "But I must hope, Lady Bertram, that you will no longer talk of 'poor Maria', since she is now as happy and contented as anyone in my acquaintance."

Lady Bertram looked at her and smiled rather distantly. As she did not speak, Elizabeth went on: "It is rather for us, I think, to thank you for the way she has rejuvenated—I think I may even say *renovated* my father, who is become quite another person since his marriage. There has been some reluctance, in certain quarters, to receive her, now that the fact of her first marriage has become known. But they are so contented, and complete, within themselves, that this becomes a matter of almost no consequence."

"Strange to think of my grandsons as your brothers. How do they go on?"

"They are as healthy, and as handsome, as any babies in the world. Maria dotes upon them, and my father too."

Lady Bertram smiled, rather more happily this time, and took up her embroidery.

"You will wonder at the odd shape of my work," she said, putting her needle in for the first time. "I am told it is an orphrey, much worn by the clergy in ancient times. My son Edmund means to wear it round his neck and I mean him to do so. It will remind him, I trust, that he is a Christian priest, a thing he seems to have forgotten."

She continued quietly sewing, while Georgiana related such details of her family life as had occurred in the four days since they had last met; and Elizabeth had leisure to look about her.

Lady Bertram was clearly Maria's mother. She was not so tall and she was plumper, but their facial resemblance was astonishing. Her face seemed quite unmarked by the passage of time and there was no sign of grey in the hair at her temples. She wore a very small, and very becoming, lace cap and her eyes were of an especially brilliant blue.

When her attention returned to the conversation, Elizabeth found they were talking about travelling.

"I believe you accomplished your journey in only one day, Mrs Darcy," said Lady Bertram in a tone of calm surprise. "I hope you are not too tired today?"

"Indeed, not at all, I am glad to say. We came in our own carriage and with our own horses for the first part of the way."

"But are not the roads still very treacherous and full of holes?"

"None that we encountered," said Elizabeth, with a smile.

"I can never forget the one occasion that my sister Norris compelled me to make a morning call at Sotherton. I was quite dreadfully jolted and the bruises lasted for a week. I have not ventured since beyond the park."

"With such a beautiful park all round you, the temptation to leave it must be very small," said Elizabeth. "But I am sure my father would be more than honoured, and Maria more than delighted, if your ladyship could ever feel able to visit them."

"Well, we shall have to see," said Lady Bertram, looking up without a smile. "My son Edmund informs me that it is a journey of quite fifty miles, not to be undertaken lightly. What I hope in my heart—and this is quite between ourselves—is that Sir Thomas will allow Maria and your father to visit *us*. But there seems to be, at present, little chance of that."

At half past one a cold collation was brought in and placed on a table by the window. At half past two, after doing it more than justice, Lady Bertram retired to rest.

"It has been such a pleasure to see you at last, Mrs Darcy," she said, once more offering her hand. "But we shall meet again. I shall tell Sir Thomas to invite you to dinner."

They returned to the Cottage by the short route, although it was a sunny afternoon.

"I have to say," said Elizabeth, as soon as they were well on their way, "how much I admire the appearance of Lady Bertram."

"Oh yes, indeed," replied Georgiana. "She is a constant pattern for us all. Not that it is entirely her own doing, you know. She has this devoted maid, called Chapman, who has been at Mansfield for ever and who looks after her as though she were the most precious thing on earth. Which for her, I suppose, she is. Always one step ahead of the mode—in Mansfield, that is to say. Nobody knows how she achieves that."

Then, as an afterthought: "I believe that Chapman grieved over Maria's adventure with Mr Crawford, and its outcome, longer than anyone else in the house. Of course she knew them both and had been making up Maria's dresses for several years before. Do you find Lady Bertram quite like her?"

"Very like, in face at least. Maria is taller and has more energy, though I was very interested to see how swiftly Lady Bertram moved to the nuncheon table."

"And you were *very* honoured, dear Elizabeth. She *rose* to greet you!"

Mansfield Cottage, viewed from the park, was a building of considerable charm, with identical new wings on either side of an old house. A verandah ran along the whole of the south front and, in the garden before it, all the children were to be found. Georgiana's son, now seen by daylight, proved to be a stout and happy child, eight months old and the apple of his mother's eye.

After playing for some time with the children, Georgiana took Elizabeth over the house, to find that all the principal rooms faced on to the park.

"I am singularly fortunate to be living here," said Georgiana. "Indeed, although I feel quite a traitor to say it, I am happier here than I ever was at Pemberley. As a little girl I found it very *large* and the climb up that staircase quite a labour."

"I must agree about the staircase," said Elizabeth, smiling. "That is our great secret, however."

"Then our secret it shall be!"

They talked of Rosings, and Hunsford, and their cousin Anne, of everything, in fact, except the true state of things at Mansfield. Elizabeth had forgotten that Georgiana had met Lady Catherine only the once, on her celebrated visit to Pemberley after Elizabeth's marriage.

"But she did approve my marriage, if only from a distance, and sent a handsome present of china, which we use most of the time. But Anne is someone whom I cannot imagine. Does *she* at all resemble *her* mother?"

"In no way at all," said Elizabeth, smiling again. "She is quite slight and will, I think, have a pretty face when she is in better health. We hope to give a dress party for her, in London, perhaps in February or March. Do you think we might have the pleasure of your company?"

"Not this year, Elizabeth. I could not leave my little Tom and certainly would not take him with me. The air in London, I understand, has all been breathed by someone else."

"I mean to go up after Christmas to make some changes in the house. It is a sad place, after all, hardly altered since your father's time. Your brother seems to live mostly at his club when he goes there, much to the disappointment of his cook. But I think he now means to go each year, so I must try to make it more cheerful. Your grandfather's furniture I can only admire, but the hangings in the drawing-room, and the silk on the walls of the ballroom, are certainly in no condition to be shown to strangers. No doubt I shall enjoy it greatly—I have *that* infection from Maria!"

XIV

It was perhaps three days later that Mr Darcy said, when they were alone upstairs: "I am quite certain that we are here on the edge of some family maelstrom and we must not let it suck us under too completely. Edmund does not shoot, but I observe a cloud to come over Tom's face whenever his name is mentioned. Sir Thomas, of course, treats me with the utmost politeness and as if I were a total stranger, but his shooting companions are not so circumspect. The position appears to be this. Sir Thomas has sold his West Indian property to great advantage. One of my informants puts it at a hundred thousand pounds, another at a hundred and twenty. The money has been a long time coming but has now arrived and a monumental family squabble has ensued."

"You scarcely had to tell me that," said Elizabeth. "One family is much like another in *that* respect."

"But wait until I tell you *all* the details," said Mr Darcy. "I am not perfectly certain how reliable my informant is. His land marches with Sir Thomas's somewhere to the west and I find him much too deferential, both to myself and to Sir Thomas, to be quite acceptable. But the situation is that Mr Tom Bertram means to acquire an entire estate just on the north, which has recently gone derelict, and put it down to timber. Mr Edmund Bertram wishes the whole sum to be expended on several schools and orphanages, as he says that only in this way can the stain and legacy of slave money be removed. And Sir Thomas himself wishes to settle most of it on his *other* daughter Julia, but in such a way that her gambler husband cannot get hold of it."

"In either case it is an enormous sum. I cannot believe that there is not enough for all three enterprises."

"So indeed one would imagine. But Mr Edmund is quite adamant, quite impossible to move. The money must be disposed

74

of in such a way that no benefit can come to the family. As slave money it must be tainted. No undertaking based on its use will prosper if profit is in view, and he will agree to nothing else."

"He refuses to see Maria. He refuses to baptise her sons. He refuses to listen to any other wishes, or opinions, than his own. What a very *intractable* person Mr Edmund Bertram must be. I am quite glad now that he would not dance with me at Georgiana's wedding."

"Between his behaviour and that of Collins one must begin to have misgivings about their notion of Christian charity. Only our brother Morland seems to have heard of it."

"And for that," said Elizabeth, "let us be most truly thankful."

Lady Bertram's instruction to Sir Thomas, to ask the party from the Cottage to dine, bore no fruit for nearly ten days. The invitation was then given for an evening before a day on which there was to be no shooting.

Elizabeth passed the time easily with Georgiana, playing in the garden, walking in the park, sometimes driving round it. They were advised not to call at the Parsonage, as Mary Bertram continued to give cause for alarm. They called each day on Lady Bertram, becoming more and more pleased with each other, admiring the speed with which her embroidery progressed and joining her in a series of delicious nuncheons.

On the night of the dinner they went to the Great House by carriage, it being too dusk and too dirty to consider anything else. Elizabeth much regretted that the light had almost gone by the time they set off as it was a journey of almost three miles, round the park and up the main approach. She would have liked to see this other aspect of the house.

They had not long been seated before Georgiana said, in a slightly uncertain voice: "It is so much easier to say this in the dark. I just hope that we may not find ourselves embroiled in some Bertram family turmoil, because I have not—I am truly unhappy to say—been quite open with you before. The reason we have not called upon the Edmund Bertrams is that Edmund himself declines to meet the daughter of the man who has married his errant sister. If they are there at all this evening some conciliation must have been achieved—someone must have given way. I just hope Edmund may not be too much on his high horse."

"Indeed," said Mr Darcy, in a tone of great annoyance. "So the contamination spreads to the edge of every family, does it? Even as cousin Collins said it would. I had expected behaviour of a more civilised kind from our Bertram connections."

Elizabeth was therefore in a state of some slight apprehension as she alighted at the Great House. Their cloaks were taken by the butler himself, who then said, directly to Georgiana: "My lady is in her drawing-room, madam." And then, in an undertone which they could all hear: "The rest of the family is with her."

The drawing-room was brilliantly lit and there was a fine, clear fire.

Lady Bertram sat alone on a sofa on one side of it, with a young woman whom Elizabeth assumed to be Fanny, alone on the one on the other side. Mr Edmund Bertram stood behind her, Sir Thomas and Tom—who was not yet in his evening clothes—behind Lady Bertram. It was as though battle stations had been taken up. The silence appeared absolute, but their entrance deepened it even further. They did not advance. The Bertram men did not move. The total silence continued.

After a very few moments Lady Bertram, no longer employed in putting away her embroidery, got up and came over to them. She kissed them both, gave her hand to Mr Darcy, called him by name and then said: "Come, my dears, and join me on my sofa. Sir Thomas and his sons are having a quarrel."

Mr Darcy had almost no choice but to stand beside Edmund, and he did so, folding his arms across his chest. Elizabeth thought she had never seen him look so stern. She offered a tentative bow to Edmund, whom she had not seen since Georgiana's wedding, but he did not return it. She settled herself perhaps a little too elaborately beside Lady Bertram.

After what seemed a very long time, Sir Thomas recollected himself. He said, to Edmund rather than to Tom: "I think we need not concern Mr and Mrs Darcy with what is purely a family matter."

"Mrs Darcy is a member of the family," said Edmund rather sharply, "with or without our consent. She is concerned."

"Then," said Mr Darcy instantly, "I must apply for membership as well. We go everywhere together."

His voice seemed to Elizabeth deeper than usual. In the silence which followed his words she had leisure to examine the Fanny whom she knew very well by report, but who had become, she now had to accept, a most formidable adversary.

She was, as Maria had said, very pretty but in a way which seemed to invite protection. She was not looking very comfortable. Their eyes did not meet. It would have been quite impossible, under all the circumstances, for a formal introduction to have been made.

In the end it was Georgiana who spoke. Elizabeth could feel her growing stronger as she did so.

"I have of course informed my dear brother and his dearest wife of all the causes of your dissensions. Since, as my brother Edmund so correctly says, they are a part of our family, I thought there could be no objection."

She paused, as though she waited for one. Then, as no one spoke, she went on: "I can only say that they would be happy to assist in any way possible to bring peace once more among you."

"In particular," said Mr Darcy, "I should be especially happy to assist in the matter of the orphanage, should assistance be required. I am informed, perhaps not too reliably, that the funds there are not quite sufficient."

"There are sufficient funds," said Edmund, a little too quickly. "If they are *all* given to the orphanage. It is my immoveable opinion that any money produced by the unpaid labour, by the forced efforts, of any human being, must be devoted to the work of God. Only in such a way can the stigma be removed. The acquisition of a new estate—or the support of an unfortunate daughter and her profligate husband—cannot be so regarded. But that is *not* the cause of our present dispute."

Elizabeth felt she had to speak.

"If, as I begin to understand, *my* presence here is a cause of that dispute," she said, as expressionlessly as she could, "as the step-daughter of a daughter of this house, then, of course, I shall be happy to relieve you of it."

She rose to go.

"By no means, Madam, I beg of you," said Tom, "by no means whatever. Let my brother Edmund explain to all of us the head and front of *your* offending."

Elizabeth remained standing but, to her great surprise, Fanny now put up her hand to Edmund. He took, and held, it while he was speaking.

"There is not even an argument here," he said. "In the eyes of God my sister Maria is wife to Rushworth, no matter how many foreign ceremonies she may go through."

"In the eyes of the law, however," pursued Tom, "her marriage to Rushworth being dissolved—admittedly by an earthly rather than by a heavenly authority—then she must be free to seek a husband elsewhere."

"And if that husband be already widowed then no objection can possibly stand," said Mr Darcy.

"The objection is quite simple," said Edmund, in a voice which Elizabeth could only describe as smug. "My sister is now living in sin and her children and their father with her. And this objection must extend to anyone connected with her or him."

"Which must include yourself," retorted Mr Darcy. "You can no more avoid being Maria's brother than Elizabeth can avoid being the daughter of her father. But, if this is your feeling, I am surprised that you declined to baptise those children. Would not that have diluted their sin? What could have been your intention there?"

Then in a deep, strong voice, he said: "I hope I could never treat *my* sister in such a way."

"You are not in orders," said Edmund; but his voice lacked strength.

"I am not," said Mr Darcy. "And I begin to thank God for it."

Elizabeth returned to her seat and was touched to find her hand taken by Lady Bertram, who smiled at her as well. Then, turning to Georgiana, she took her hand. Holding them both, and sitting up a little bit straighter, Lady Bertram said: "I am quite tired of all this fruitless bickering. I have survived a deep grief on behalf of a daughter, only to find myself deeply ashamed by the actions of a son. I miss my darling Maria and I want to see her again. And I want my dinner."

She spoke in her accustomed tranquil tone, but perhaps rather faster than usual.

"There is more than enough money—for everything. You have spoken of a gesture of reconciliation towards Mr Rushworth. Then let him supply the ground for Edmund's orphanage. It will merely mean that the poor little things will come from Kettering and not from Northampton. If Tom's trees and Julia's life turn out to be tainted by the slave money, then that is a risk that we, and they, must take. But in all this there is a condition, a condition that I most firmly impose upon my son Edmund, whose late behaviour one can only blush to remember. And it is this. That, in return for his share of this money—should he be fortunate enough to receive it—he ends for ever his childish, un-Christian attitude to Maria. That he remembers that she is his sister. That he remembers that he too is human and fallible. That Christ came into the world to save *sinners* and that He certainly did not intend *anyone* to preach only to the virtuous. Never—*never*—in a long life, has my faith in him been shaken so completely."

"But I cannot," said Edmund, the words apparently squeezed out of him. "I cannot. I have given my promise."

Quite possibly, Elizabeth thought, Lady Bertram had never in her life made such a long speech. She pressed her hand gently and the pressure was returned. Edmund now stood as though turned to stone. There was no movement from behind them. Mr Darcy leaned a little forward, as though in acquiescence, and put both his hands on the back of the sofa before him. The slight shifting of the logs in the fire, the faint roaring of the flames, were the only sounds in the room.

Then: "Yes," said Fanny. "On the part of a most beloved husband, I absolutely accept those conditions. We punish ourselves most unreasonably and all to no purpose. We should remember only that it is those motherless, fatherless children whom we attempt to benefit. Nothing else is of importance. Nothing else is of relevance. Nothing at all should be allowed to stand in our way."

Once more, nobody moved. It seemed to Elizabeth that nobody breathed.

At this moment, however, the butler, who must, Elizabeth thought later, have been listening at the keyhole, announced dinner.

The women rose, as one.

Without speaking they walked across the hall, each wife on the arm of her husband.

XV

Elizabeth was grateful, as she imagined everyone else to be, for the requirements of civility now placed upon them. The dining-room was also brilliantly lit. In the centre was a large round table with parlour chairs, so large in fact that it would be impossible to talk across it; and this, she could only feel, was an advantage not to be expected.

She found herself on Sir Thomas's right hand, with Fanny on her other side. The first few minutes were entirely taken up in deciding what to eat and drink and it was not until the whole company had made their decisions that Sir Thomas turned to her and said: "To attempt any adequate apology, my dear Mrs Darcy, would be impossible and, if you will forgive me, I do not propose to attempt it. You and Mr Darcy have been received into our family without formal introduction and you find us in a state of undress—if I may so put it—which would cause offence to many others. But I hope you may learn to think of it as a compliment, a compliment delivered perhaps with the left hand, but a compliment nevertheless. If I may add my admiration of your exemplary behaviour, and that of your excellent husband, you will gain *some* idea of my exasperated feelings. I hope that no comparable division may ever occur in your family."

"My sister Georgiana had of course explained to us both the nature of those divisions. What she did not do, because, I am sure, she did not know herself, was to tell us how deeply they had divided you."

"It is a matter perfectly beyond my comprehension," said Sir Thomas. "I cannot understand how my son Edmund, hitherto so kind, so conciliating, such a pattern of rectitude, in fact, could have been so entirely transformed since the marriage of my daughter to your father. In her disgrace, her banishment, her solitude, he visited her regularly, as indeed did my son Tom. Then, suddenly, her life is changed beyond all expectation—and through no instrumentality of his—and he takes exception to the whole process. All filial, all fraternal, feeling is jettisoned overnight, and we are left bewildered, trying to recognise a person whom we had previously supposed that we knew well."

"I can only hope that healing is now at least begun," said Elizabeth. "I have to say how greatly I admired the words of Lady Bertram."

"I watched my son Edmund's face as she was speaking, but not for too long. His misery was plain to see. Never before has he caused me the smallest anxiety. A living was held for him, another accidentally fell to him. His life was perfectly secure. He was strong enough to counsel others in distress or uncertainty, as indeed a man of his cloth should—or as indeed would be expected in any son of mine. I supposed that his visits to Derbyshire were for that purpose, to comfort Maria but also to help her see the error of her ways. Does he now consider her to be beyond his help? Unworthy of his notice? It is indeed a mystery past my solving."

Elizabeth could not immediately think of anything to say and so was grateful to him for continuing, in a slightly different tone of voice: "So let me welcome you at least to Mansfield. We find ourselves particularly happy in our acquisition of a daughter from your husband's family; but, even more so and, in spite of this evening's doings, the acquisition of a son-in-law from yours. How does your excellent father?"

"My excellent father," returned Elizabeth, smiling, "is in better health and spirits than I have ever known him. And this I, and my sister Jane, attribute entirely to his marriage to your excellent daughter."

"My excellent daughter," replied Sir Thomas, rather wryly, "had been a source of some shame, and some anxiety, to the rest of her family. But perhaps it is better to forget these things, to bury them in the past. I blame myself, in part, for having permitted her first marriage when I was aware that her heart was by no means in it. That she should have found happiness in her second is indeed more than she deserves."

"Oh pray do not say so, Sir Thomas. Her marriage has been of so much benefit to my family. My father has always been a man of independent thought—and indeed of action, when it was required. The opinion of his neighbours has never been one to concern him and we can only rejoice over the new life he has found with Maria."

"And we too must rejoice that a man of such unexceptionable standing, and understanding, has felt able to offer her the protection of his name and a haven in his house."

"Perhaps you refine a little too much upon it there. Of course old scandals do not die, but this one is, by now, surely a matter of history. It was indeed quite unknown in Hertfordshire at the time of their marriage and only an unlucky chance informed the neighbourhood. But, by that time, Maria had established herself at Longbourn and it was known only that she was your daughter."

"For which I give full credit to your father. Maria always was a headstrong girl, much indulged on account of her beauty, and anxious only to leave her home from a very early age. All this I realise now, to my own everlasting chagrin. When I consider what difficulties such a character *might* have caused, I can only shudder with relief that more damage was not done."

After a moment, as Sir Thomas ended there, Elizabeth said: "How little, how very little indeed, one sometimes knows about members of one's own family. My father, as I have said, is become someone we had never met before, and a cousin of Mr Darcy's, of Georgiana's I should say, is also quite transformed since the death of her mother."

"I think it especially handsome of you, and, I hope, your sisters, to accept Maria so kindly in the position of your mother."

"As to that, Sir Thomas," said Elizabeth, after a second's hesitation, "perhaps the less said the better. That my father long regretted his marriage to my mother I have known for some time, in my heart; and I think that is why he did not wish what he called a youthful indiscretion to poison the rest of Maria's life. He was released from his own hasty marriage only by my mother's death, twenty-nine years later."

"Then all I can do, Mrs Darcy, is to admire, and applaud, such generosity of spirit and to regret that it is not more widely to be found in human nature."

XVI

Not until the first course had been removed, and the bustle caused by the placing of the second one had died down, was Elizabeth able to turn to Fanny and say, very directly: "I hope we may begin our new acquaintance only by remembering that your brother is married to my sister."

To which she received the grateful, slightly smiling, response: "Indeed we may. I must hope your sister to be a better correspondent than my brother."

"Do men ever write letters, I wonder? There are, of course, so few of them in our family that I really have no notion. When last I heard from *my* sister it was to the effect that *your* sister—Susan, I rather think—still awaited the return of a certain handsome Lieutenant from the East Indies."

"Indeed yes," said Fanny, "and I am sad to say that she awaits him still. A fever acquired in the East Indies put him ashore at Simonstown, at the Cape, and for some weeks, I understand, his life was despaired of; but careful nursing, I must suppose, brought him through, though he was for many months too weak to go to sea. His ship was concerned in the evacuation of the French from St Helena—after their Emperor's death, you know—and he was able to rejoin it only when they returned to the Cape. And then they were ordered at once to go back to the East Indies. I do not know what their Lordships at the Admiralty can find for them to do there."

"I fancy you are not alone in wondering that," said Elizabeth, with a smile. "But I hope his fever is quite gone? I do not pretend that my sister *excels* as a correspondent, though her letters are always full of news and, I should say, gossip, when they come. But of one thing I am quite certain and that is that she and your sister live most comfortably together with, if I understand her letters correctly, never a cross word between them."

"I think they are both grateful for the company of the other. It seems to be the common lot of naval wives to be left quite alone for months at a time. Certainly Susan appreciates the delicacy of your sister in bearing with her impatience, as the period of waiting grows."

"I believe she was at one time sad enough to say that she feared she would never be other than an aunt?"

And Fanny laughed.

"Yes, but I think that period of low spirits passed when she received, at last, a letter from the Cape. And, whether she likes it or not, she is an aunt and will be many times more for, besides William, we have five brothers and a sister. It is most truly a fate that she cannot avoid."

"I am pleased to think that we are aunts ourselves, with a niece in common. Do you think she will always be Frances, or will she too be known as Fanny?"

"It is too early to say. It is my mother's name and I have always liked the sound of it."

"It is a charming name," said Elizabeth, "and if I may continue our conversation in this same tone of voice—do you think Mr Edmund can accept the conditions you have accepted for him?"

"I have no doubt at all," said Fanny, also keeping her voice very low, "that he will do so. It was an injunction laid upon him by his Bishop, one he should never have allowed him to impose."

"Which was?"

"That he should never again meet Maria or have anything to do with the family of her husband."

"Is he a Bishop of the Church of England?"

Fanny barely repressed a smile.

"He is indeed, wonderful to relate. But what, at that time, we did not know..."

She broke off. They were suddenly aware that no one else was speaking. Lady Bertram had maintained a steady flow of talk with her neighbours, Tom and Mr Darcy. Sir Thomas and Georgiana had been deep in conversation, while Edmund sat alone, unsmiling and unspeaking. Then Lady Bertram asked Mr

Darcy about Maria's house on Matlock Moor, allowed him to help her to some pears in brandy, and the moment passed.

"...was that the Bishop's own wife had run away from him not three weeks before."

A glance of the most perfect understanding passed between them. Successfully suppressing a laugh, Elizabeth said: "I hope you mean to tell me? With whom?"

"Oh," said Fanny, lowering her voice even a little more, "with a German baritone from Mainz. He had come over to examine some sheets of old English plainsong which had lain untouched in the Bishop's library for centuries; and he was resident with them for more than three months."

They laughed together, stifling it at once.

"Well, well," said Sir Thomas, "I will not ask. Your laughter has a very pleasant sound. I sometimes think our problems are too much of our own making."

The drawing-room had been, Elizabeth thought, very slightly re-arranged. The two sofas no longer confronted each other. The fire burnt brightly but there were not quite so many candles as before. She settled herself with Fanny on one sofa. Georgiana and Lady Bertram sat on the other and the men stood, or walked around the room. The tea and coffee were brought in immediately.

When the butler and the footmen had gone, Sir Thomas cleared his throat and said: "There is something I must consult you all about. I had the news yesterday that old Mrs Rushworth at Sotherton had died, and is to be buried there tomorrow. The question is quite simple. Do we go—or do we not?"

"We go," said Edmund, at once. "Whatever our quarrels have been in the past, the Rushworths are our neighbours."

"If," said Mr Darcy, "you think the presence of a stranger might render the occasion less awkward, I would be happy to be that stranger. I speak largely from self-interest, of course. I have read of Sotherton Court in the guide books and believe the plasterwork to be very fine."

"I doubt that we shall be asked inside," said Tom, "but you will find there are some very magnificent chimneys."

"We should indeed be glad of your company," said Edmund, still very stiffly. "And I am obliged to you for your previous offer of help. But I think my mother's suggestion may be the better. We will ask Rushworth for a piece of land."

"Then," said Sir Thomas, "I agree. I am most happy to agree. It would be right, I think, and proper."

It was decided that the carriage from the Great House would call for the gentlemen at the Cottage at ten o'clock exactly. The funeral was fixed for half past twelve. Fanny undertook to sit with Lady Bertram. She and Edmund left shortly afterwards, their parental anxieties being not wholly at an end; and, before very long, the party from the Cottage followed them.

There was a long silence in the carriage before Tom said, apparently through clenched teeth: "I have to say, I can only say, how my brother's—*intemperate*, yes, intemperate behaviour has wounded us all. How deeply I regret that you should have been exposed to it—and how grateful I am that you, my dear Sir, come with us tomorrow. I could not trust myself alone in a closed carriage with only my father between us."

"Something of the sort occurred to me," said Mr Darcy. "But I thought him slightly less intemperate by the end of the evening."

When they were once more alone, Elizabeth said: "How very acute you are, my love. Something did change Mr Edmund during the evening. Perhaps his mother's words. But he is not wholly to be blamed. An injunction was imposed upon him by his Bishop which, I think, his wife has decided to overturn—if that is what you do with injunctions."

"I thought she spoke up very well."

"She did. I like her. By no means the monster previously presented to us. But what *we* have to rejoice about is—that, until now our lives, miraculously, have not been very full of Bishops. Mr Collins is already in trouble with his and now Mr Edmund must be in trouble with his. I just hope we may manage to do without them entirely."

XVII

Elizabeth and Georgiana were comfortably alone at breakfast the next day when a letter was brought in for Elizabeth. It was from Anne and had been sent on from Pemberley. Elizabeth read it aloud.

Rosings, October 21st

I have quite mislaid your direction at Mansfield, dearest Elizabeth, and while I would like to think that a letter addressed to Mrs Fitzwilliam Darcy at Mansfield Park, England, would arrive, I have not yet learned to be so optimistic, or so trusting. So I must rely on the good nature of your people at Pemberley to send this on to you. Not that I have anything of cataclysmic proportions to impart to you, beyond saying that I continue very well. Miss Linton, that angel of light, comes with me on my visits to Madame de Domballe. They arrange a wardrobe of such sumptuousness and variety that I cannot begin to describe it. But you may rest assured that everything will be as perfect as possible since she is herself a person of impeccable taste, as is Miss Linton as well. With the two of them advising me I cannot look otherwise than *suitable* in any ensemble of their devising. We divide only on the subject of caps. Mme. de D produced many pictures of the latest sorts—I cannot at all like any of them. They are of three kinds, the Fetching, the Frivolous and the Imposing. Everything points to my adoption of the latter which I do *not* approve but no doubt we shall arrive at some compromise in time. My father's lawyer came last week to show me the family jewels that he has in his keeping. Why did my mother never wear them, I wonder? They are so magnificent that I think I have scarcely the courage to do so myself. They are to be cleaned at the jeweller's and some I shall certainly bring with me to London, no matter what the risk. The lawyer was kind enough to say how pleased he was to see me here and offered his services at any time, in such a way that I was able to believe he *meant* it! What a change is here. The Collins girls continue upstairs, much to my delight. I must try not to become too fond of them in case their father should recollect himself and recall that they are *his*.

The dreadful news is still from Quarry End. Much of the house is to be pulled down and built again and what should the workmen find but four infant skeletons in boxes in a cupboard. Mr Collins, on this occasion I have to admit, behaved admirably and buried them beside their mother without a murmur. But I could not but feel that their infant spirits must haunt any house on that site, so have directed that the whole building be destroyed and we will build again at a distance. I hope you divert yourselves exceedingly at Mansfield and that you will not die of a surfeit of partridge. My cook here, with whom I am now on the friendliest terms though this must remain a secret, tells me that you can roast them, or grill them, make them into escalopes, or quenelles "at a pinch" as she says, and that is all. I daresay my own fields are full of them. Next year perhaps my dear cousin Fitzwilliam will come and shoot them for me. Pray invite him on my behalf. I need not tell you both how much I *long* for February.

"Oh," said Georgiana, when Elizabeth had finished, "how charming she sounds. And how happy. I hope we shall contrive to meet one day—do you think she would contemplate a visit here?"

"No one can tell at present, I imagine. She unfurls her petals with such speed, and each one is more unexpected than the other. But from what she has told me I think she would regard Mansfield as being quite as far northward as Pemberley. I am not sure she even means to cross the Thames."

The gentlemen returned from the funeral in great good humour. Mr Rushworth, in the opinion at least of Mr Darcy, who shared it with Elizabeth when they were alone, scarcely seemed to recollect his former relationship with the Bertram family, and greeted them with calm amiability. Peace and kindness were once more established between the families and every available civility was advanced on both sides.

"We are not to dismiss Mr Rushworth," remarked Mr Darcy. "Foolish he may be, but not so foolish that he cannot employ a first-class steward. One knew immediately where the Sotherton property began, firstly because the road was suddenly excellent, and secondly because the fields on either side were in perfect condition."

"Did you catch a sight of the house as you went along?"

"No, there was only a distant view from the church. It stands very low, a stone building I believe from Elizabeth's time. One could see only gables and chimneys, not so many as I had expected. One must assume the mullions and the oriel windows. In no way comfortable to live in, I would think, but certainly a thing to be preserved. Rushworth did ask us up to the house but Sir Thomas judged it too soon, I imagine, as he declined. No doubt Rushworth will be calling here before long, even if there are no longer any prospective brides in residence."

Their visit, after this, drew very quickly to a close. They dined once with the Edmund Bertrams and, once, Lady Bertram and Sir Thomas dined at the Cottage.

"I think," said Georgiana rather dryly, "that we may thank my handsome brother for *this* piece of civility. Lady Bertram, in general, *never* dines from home; but I observed, when we dined there ourselves, how she blossomed in his company. I don't think she has been in this house once this year."

The dinner party took place happily, Sir Thomas being at his most amiable and Lady Bertram at her most conversable. The cook excelled herself and Georgiana was able to say to Elizabeth— immediately after the Bertrams had left, at ten o'clock precisely— that she did not remember such a pleasant evening in that house.

They returned to Pemberley two days later, leaving as the sun rose and arriving as it set. Elizabeth was aware that it grew colder as they neared home, but they were welcomed back as warmly as possible. The newly-papered walls on the nursery floor were approved by everyone, and Elizabeth found herself hoping that she would be as successful with the changes she proposed to make in the London house.

Christmas was to be spent with the Bingleys. In order to avoid Sunday travel, they drove over easily on the fourth day before Christmas, it being a distance of less than thirty miles.

Elizabeth found Jane as enthusiastic and as handsome as ever. Their husbands had been friends for many years; their children were always pleased to see each other. The sole impediment to perfect comfort had previously been the presence of Mr Bingley's sisters, the one a widow and the other a spinster; but this year, as Jane was quick to inform Elizabeth, there was to be a great improvement.

"I could not bear to put this in a letter," said Jane, when they were alone upstairs, "and it has taxed me exceedingly not to tell anyone else, but Caroline and Louisa are not coming here this year. And you will never dream where they are gone! Imagine this. To Italy!"

"To Italy! Are they perhaps in pursuit of the great Lord Byron? I recall that Louisa at least had formed a great passion for his poetry."

"Well, I know nothing of that, but the truth is, in its way, *quite* as diverting, and there *is* a Lord in the case, though I suppose he had better be nameless. But Caroline formed a great passion for *him*—you know they live entirely in London since Mr Hurst's death—and she sincerely believed he returned her passion. When what should he do but marry the daughter of a neighbour in the country who had suddenly been left thirty thousand pounds by her grandfather. I could find it in my heart to feel sorry for Caroline just that once—she was quite flattened indeed, though of course no one was supposed to know anything about it so of course we could not sympathise. They left in November and are settled at Leghorn, where people speak English, you know. And if they *are* in pursuit of the handsome Lord George, which I do *not* think, I believe he is quite handy, at Genoa."

"So then, my dear Jane, the house in Grosvenor Street is quite empty?"

"It is, my dear Lizzy, until Bingley and I go down to occupy it—as we shall do, I think, in January. Could anything be more delightful? It is a charming house and *they* will not be in it!"

"I mean to go myself immediately after Christmas, to make *some* changes. Then I shall come back, I think, as we do not mean to stay there until the middle of February. We are due to give a dress party for Anne de Bourgh, Lady Catherine's daughter, do you remember? As she is already thirty-five years old we are not exactly presenting her as a postulant, but I want her to enjoy her first visit to London. She does not mean to risk herself in the infectious airs of the metropolis until March, and I think she is quite right. I do not mean to take the children."

"Oh no indeed, and neither do I. How do you go on with Miss de Bourgh? I know you did not care for her before."

"I think I really love her, in a cousinly way. She never said a word before, you know, so one could not judge. Now everything she does, and says, seems to me exactly right, but in order to gain control of her fortune she is obliged to find a husband. So I think we must assist her there, at least."

"Well, we shall certainly come to your party. How very diverting it will be. How *very* diverting it will *all* be—no Caroline, no Louisa. Truly, I can hardly wait. But now, my dearest Lizzy, let us make this a Christmas to remember as well—our first without them—and, let us hope, the first of many."

Mr Bingley had bought his estate a year after his marriage, but in a very neglected condition. The land had slowly been brought back into excellent heart on the advice of the agent he had been wise enough to consult from the outset. The house had taken longer to restore, and extend, but was now the scene both of a domestic comfort as complete as possible, and of a generous hospitality much appreciated throughout a wide neighbourhood.

A children's party on Christmas Eve was followed by a ball on Boxing Day for tenants and neighbours, and the Darcys then returned to Pemberley, to give their own ball, on the third day after Christmas.

XVIII

It was not until the first of January that Elizabeth found herself in her carriage, with her maid, on her way to London. She had written ahead to give notice of her coming, a week earlier than she had intended, but when they drew up at the house they saw that the blinds were down and the knocker off the door. By travelling post, and sleeping only one night on the road, they had overtaken her letter.

Mr Darcy's house was in Brook Street. It was regularly inhabited by a butler and a housekeeper, a cook and two maids, other staff being taken on whenever the family came to London. They were therefore admitted by a startled, and very apologetic, butler, by no means in his best clothes. Elizabeth graciously agreed that her letter should have been sent off sooner, a conversation about the unreliability of the mails followed, and a flurry of activity began.

It was dark and dismal with the shutters closed. The furniture was shrouded in holland covers and the lustres tied up in linen bags. A chill pervaded the whole house, as marked in the drawing-rooms upstairs as in the hall. She asked that the smaller of the two rooms on the first floor should be got ready at once, and while this was in doing she retired, still wearing her travelling clothes, into the principal drawing-room. She sat down on one of the sofas, not removing its protective cover, and considered how best to bring the house to life.

Her aunt Gardiner had already furnished her with the names of two very reliable silk warehouses, which she hoped they would visit together. She was also a principal source of information as to where the best carpenters, plasterers, curtain-makers and upholsterers were to be found. Elizabeth was certain that, once the work was put in hand, it would be accomplished fairly swiftly but, as she looked round the silent, withdrawn room, she wondered if the six weeks she had given herself could possibly be enough.

She was interrupted in her gloomy thoughts by the entrance of the butler.

"There is a Mrs Wickham below, madam, asking to come up."

"Mrs Wickham?" echoed Elizabeth, in the greatest surprise.

"The lady informs me, madam, that she is your sister."

"I had no notion that she was in this country," said Elizabeth after a moment. "You had better show her in here."

Astonished, annoyed, completely discomposed, Elizabeth waited. Some two minutes later a female figure, heavily veiled and draped in the deepest of black mourning garments, slowly entered the room. Very deliberately she put back her veil, to reveal a face that seemed quite unchanged to Elizabeth, but which she had not seen for nearly four years.

"My dear Lydia," was all she could think of to say. "Welcome. Welcome back to England."

She had risen as Lydia came further into the room, and for perhaps ten seconds they stared at each other, face to face and without speaking. Then Lydia turned and settled into a chair opposite Elizabeth's sofa, also still in holland covers. When she was quite comfortable, Lydia said: "Well, Lizzy, you look quite stout. And I fancy that bonnet did not come very cheap."

"How does it come about, how can it possibly have happened, that you can arrive here, totally unheralded and, quite obviously, a widow?"

"As to that, my dear sister, it would have required a very *long* letter to give you all my news. And writing letters, you know, I have always found a more than tedious occupation."

"But—did you not write at all? Or has your letter gone astray?"

"In the end I did not write. But you are not entirely blameless yourself, my dear Lizzy. The last letter that I had from you was to say that my father's new wife had given birth to twin sons and that everyone was rejoicing. I did not even know he had married again."

"Then my letter to you, with *that* information, must have been lost. She is a young woman, scarcely older than Jane, and a daughter of Sir Thomas Bertram. I like her extremely and she has made quite a new man of our father."

"I fancy Mr Collins takes no part in the rejoicings," remarked Lydia. "How well I remember him coming to Longbourn to decide which one of us he would choose to marry."

"Let us not spoil the day by talking of Mr Collins. But tell me—how long have you been in London? And where do you stay?"

"One week," said Lydia, "and with Mrs Younge in Edward Street. A boy has been stationed in this street ever since—to give us the earliest intelligence of your arrival."

"He might have had a very long wait," said Elizabeth, smiling. "We do not mean to come until the middle of next month, you know. I am come this time to arrange such mundane things as new curtains and new wall-coverings. But enough of this. Tell me first—how long is it since Wickham died?"

"It will be six months at the end of January, but I mean to remain in full mourning for a year, you know. Everyone at Gibraltar told me how well I looked in black and at the moment I cannot think of acquiring a new wardrobe. The cost of everything here is quite outrageous."

"But I hope you were not very badly off at Gibraltar?"

"Indeed we were not. I have to say I was never so comfortable in my life. Mr Darcy's money enabled us to live on Rosia Parade, you know, quite the best address. Of course the house was haunted, so we got it a little cheap, but I paid no attention to the ghosts. It was the house where they brought Lord Nelson after the battle at Trafalgar and sometimes a door would shut all by itself. They said that that was Nelson himself come back to take a look at things. The cemetery there, you know, is full of the Trafalgar dead."

"I did not know," said Elizabeth. "But I am glad to think that they were quietly and reverently buried."

"But Gibraltar is a strange place, after all. It is not a bit like Brighton, or Newcastle. It was a little awkward to begin with when I found that the Colonel's wife was Sophia Goulding from Haye Park. You remember that girl with the huge nose and tawny hair who was always left by the wall at the Meryton Assemblies? And of course she knew all about my marriage to poor Wickham. But after quite a short time we became great friends, and she told me that she had had six thousand pounds."

"Then that might explain it," said Elizabeth, smiling again and deeply reluctant to stem the artless flow of Lydia's conversation. "I don't think I ever exchanged two words with her."

"We were a very *small* society," went on Lydia. "The Governor was the Commander-in-Chief as well and I suppose there were not more than twenty-five persons altogether, in society I mean. And some of the wives were not exactly of the sort one would have met with in *this* country, which is why Sophia and I became such friends. Then there was an Admiral, who was always at sea, and there was a Commissioner, but I was never perfectly certain what he did, but his wife was quite fond of amateur dramatics. And the Governor, you know, lived in a huge and handsome house called, of all things, The Convent. Probably the Spanish built it years ago. Wickham said he often saw the nuns flitting in and out—but only through the side door, of course."

"But, my dear Lydia, what could you find to do? How could you pass the time?"

"Well, as to that, there were some handsome buildings from the time of the Duke of Kent. Some twenty-five years ago he was Commissioner, you know. Strange to think his daughter may be Queen at last. So we could have balls and our theatricals there. None of the buildings is very large, because Gibraltar is steep, you know, all steps and stairs—*salitas*, they call them. But on the top of the Rock there was a beautiful flat place for walking and wild flowers, when it wasn't covered with cloud, you know. There was a sort of yellow cloud which would sit there for weeks at a time and made us all very ill and bad-tempered. But we had picnics up there when it was clear, and dined with each other, and tried to find new receipts for dishes and new patterns for dresses—indeed we spent much of our time just changing our clothes. And the officers played cards all the time, of course, sometimes for quite high stakes, and I was perfectly content until I discovered that not only was Wickham cheating at cards but that he had also invented a quite excellent system."

They were interrupted at this point by the entrance of the butler. He came to advise them that the little sitting-room had been prepared for them, that there was a good fire in it and that the housekeeper would shortly have some tea carried up to them. Elizabeth told him that Mrs Wickham would remain to dinner and that the carriage would be needed to take her home. He promised to give both matters his personal attention and preceded them out of the room.

In the better light, and with her bonnet off, Elizabeth could see that Lydia was looking remarkably well. She was handsomer than she had been at sixteen and her face now had some expression on it. This could be caused by a new intelligence, or merely by the action of experience, but in neither case did she seem to be the empty-headed, milk-faced girl who had eloped with George Wickham. She found herself regarding her youngest sister, if not exactly with affection, at least with something far removed from dislike.

The room was warm and the tea was hot.

"Brook Street," said Lydia, in a conversational tone, "is an excellent address, so Mrs Younge informs me. She remembers this house quite well. I believe she was governess to Miss Darcy, or some such thing. I have quite a large room in her house, at the back."

"But I think," said Elizabeth almost before she had finished, "that—as we shall probably never be so private again—you had better tell me *all* you have to tell me. And at once."

"Oh," said Lydia, "about poor Wickham, do you mean? Well, it was *very* awkward. I happened to notice him taking a card out of his sleeve, you know, and when I taxed him with it—but only when we were alone, of course—he admitted it. So I begged him to stop, or at least be more careful. But I also said that he must pay any substantial winnings to me or I should be obliged to inform his Colonel. And so in this way, I am glad to say, I was able to salt away a considerable sum which came in most useful when I had to purchase my mourning. Because it couldn't last, you know, and it did not. He was found out by one of his fellow officers and challenged to a duel."

Elizabeth had begun to pour herself a second cup of tea, but found that she was shaking too much to do so.

"Well, as I am sure you do not know, some ten years ago, a Lieutenant Blundell was killed in a duel, perfectly conducted according to all the rules. But afterwards his opponent, and both the seconds, were tried and condemned to death because no one had told them that duelling was now outlawed. The Royal Pardon was obtained in that case, but they all had to resign their commissions and so on, so of course our Colonel could not permit a duel."

Lydia got up and poured herself another cup of tea, helping herself to one of the little cakes on the tray.

"And indeed I cannot imagine *what* would have happened," she said, with her mouth full, "if we had not all gone for a picnic on top of the Rock a day or two later. After our luncheon, Wickham and one or two of the officers went for a walk, but they soon came running back with the distressing news that poor Wickham had slipped and fallen over a cliff. And the saddest thing was," she concluded, in a voice of the most perfect serenity, "that he had been trying to obtain a particularly pretty wild flower to bring back to me."

Elizabeth gasped and clasped her hands together.

"Well, I have to say," continued Lydia, calmly, "that Sophia Goulding behaved especially well. I think it was really she who prevented the matter going any further. She did mention to the Commander-in-Chief, when he began to get interested, that she had been surprised by the number of nuns she had seen going in and out of his Convent and she was quite a friend of his wife's, you know. Because it ended there. I got some money from the Colonel, for Wickham's commission, and I had all his ill-gotten gains, and the dressmakers were wonderfully cheap, so my mourning is quite handsome."

Elizabeth could only gaze at her sister, half in admiration, half in disbelief. Trying again, she managed to pour herself a second cup of tea.

"But if," she said quietly, "all this happened nearly six months ago, what have you been doing in the meantime?"

"Oh," said Lydia, "it was *very* awkward. When an officer is killed, on active service, you know, the Navy will very often convey his widow home. But this was not quite the case with us. I moved into another lodging and had to wait for the regular packet. There is one, you know, run by a Mr John Bibby—isn't that a charming name?—but it is on its way back from China or some such place and is not at *all* regular. In fact one does not at all know when, or whether, they will turn up, and indeed one was quite thought to be lost. But, however, two arrived on the same day so I took passage in one of them. To Liverpool."

Elizabeth could not save herself from asking: "And what do you mean to do now?"

"Well, my dear Lizzy, this is really why I have come. I cannot go back to Longbourn with the new wife. I suppose I could go to my sisters, three months here and three months there, and poor Wickham had no relations. But I think it will really be best if I find another husband and I rely on you to give me your help there. Though we shall have to be quite quick, you know. My mourning ends on the 26th of July and I really have no other clothes."

In spite of herself, Elizabeth laughed.

"What a *warning* you are to us all, my dear sister, as indeed our nurse has said a hundred times. And, as always, you are in luck. Jane and Mr Bingley are coming to London, to Mr Hurst's house—Caroline and Louisa are in Italy. A cousin of Mr Darcy's will be here to be introduced to London—so we shall all be giving some parties."

"Then I shall spend the next few weeks bringing my dresses up into the height of the mode. Mrs Younge is very good at that—indeed she quite enters into the spirit of my adventure. What excellent fun it will all be."

Over dinner Lydia talked entertainingly about Gibraltar, the apes on the Rock, the donkeys in the town, the strange custom of distributing Christmas presents at Epiphany, when the Three Kings would ride in on camels, throwing their gifts to the children. She was taken home almost immediately afterwards.

In the solitude of her own room, Elizabeth was able to agree that the best thing would be to find Lydia another husband. She did not at all relish the idea of having her stay at Pemberley for three months every year.

XIX

Mrs Gardiner arrived the next morning at eleven o'clock, and a procession of tradesmen and skilled workpeople followed her. Before too long, they had agreed exactly what was to be done and the work was put in hand immediately, Mrs Gardiner agreeing to oversee it all when Elizabeth returned to Pemberley.

After a small nuncheon in Brook Street, they set off, in Mrs Gardiner's carriage, to a warehouse in Spitalfields where some especially beautiful brocaded silks were to be found. Though the choice was considerable, it did not take long for Elizabeth to make her decisions, in every one of which Mrs Gardiner was able to support her. Having spent two hours in the warehouse, and a sum of money which quite frightened her, but which Mrs Gardiner assured her was not at all out of the way, they returned to the carriage, and Mrs Gardiner said: "I have directed him to return to Gracechurch Street, my dear Lizzy. I cannot endure the notion of your dining alone in that enormous house and as it is only ourselves, there will be no need to change."

Elizabeth gratefully acceded to this and a boy was sent off with a message to Brook Street.

When they were alone in Mrs Gardiner's own sitting-room at the back of the house, and drinking some of Mr Gardiner's excellent tea, newly arrived from India, Elizabeth told her aunt about Lydia's dramatic arrival in London and the circumstances leading up to it. Mrs Gardiner listened mostly in silence, limiting her remarks to exclamations of sympathy, or surprise, and then she said: "I truly thought we had seen the last of her and poor Wickham. Mr Gardiner, you know, at the suggestion of your father, was exploring the possibility of purchasing a commission for him in the army of the East India Company, as he is now become very well acquainted with many of its officials here. But now, I suppose, we must start all over again. What does the foolish girl propose to do? I recall only too well the time she spent with us here before her marriage. She would listen to no one's suggestions or consider the implications of her behaviour. Once her mind was made up, there was no altering, or reversing, it."

"Well, my dear aunt, there is no difference now. Her mind is entirely made up. She is come to London to find another husband and relies on us for our assistance."

Mrs Gardiner put down her cup and, after some five seconds, burst into laughter.

"One must admire her honesty," she said. "Truly there is no concealment with Miss Lydia. But what are her prospects, when all is said and done? She can have no fortune and she is only moderately handsome."

"I think we must not under-estimate my sister, or indeed put too low a value on her charms. She is handsomer than before, and looks her best, as indeed she informed me herself, in her widow's weeds. As to fortune, one can only guess—it would depend on Wickham's prowess at the card table."

"I cannot quite like to be a party to a plot against *all* the men in London. You and I, my dear Lizzy, have taken our pick from the top of the bunch, but I suppose there are men who deserve to be married to Lydia?"

"At least we shall not be put to any extra expense, or trouble. We are to launch Miss de Bourgh at several parties and have only to include Lydia in them. And Jane will be entertaining also, to celebrate the absence of her sisters-in-law."

"Well, I will enter your plot, though as you may imagine the only young men that we meet here are lawyers or are engaged in some respectable trade. But that, I fancy, would in no way deter Lydia—though she, perhaps, might be rather too feather-headed for them."

"At the moment she lodges with a friend of Wickham's—the Mrs Younge you told me of all those years ago. But when we are all settled here she can shuttle between us and the Bingleys— and yourselves, if you are willing. For the threat that hangs over us is that she will move, if nothing better should be on offer, from one sister to another, spending three months with each."

"And your father? What does he think of all this?"

"I imagine he knows nothing of it. Lydia was never a favourite of his and I cannot suppose that he would want to see her now."

A few days later she entered her carriage in the highest spirits, feeling that her week in London had been very well spent.

They travelled up the Great North Road as far as Stamford, where they slept. They then went across country to Melton Mowbray but, as they entered Derbyshire on the other side of Nottingham, the snow began to fall and they were advised to divert their journey to Ashbourne. Here they were obliged to spend three nights in what was fortunately a very comfortable inn, while the roads that led towards Pemberley were cleared.

She was therefore welcomed, five days after she had set out from London, by an anxious, not to say an agitated, husband.

"My love," said he to her as soon as they were alone, "never again shall I allow you to go anywhere without me. The visions of disaster that have assaulted me in the last few days have only served to remind me what my life was like before we married and to point out what it would be like again without you."

"Then I will certainly never do so, as you so dislike it. But this time I felt only that it was woman's work and that there would be nothing for you to do while I visited silk warehouses and talked to upholsterers. But, in one way, my love, I am glad you did not come. I had a conversation of the frankest kind which I think would not have taken place had you been there—to own the truth, with Lydia."

Mr Darcy did not move. He said only: "She has appeared."

"She has appeared," said Elizabeth, smiling a little at his reserve, "and in an entirely new guise. She is now Mrs George Wickham, romantically mourning a husband who died in a tragic accident while on active service. Nevertheless, she contrives to give the impression that she is a *consolable* widow and has asked for our assistance to discover another husband for her."

"Not one farthing," said Mr Darcy, after a moment, "did I ever grudge towards their maintenance, so long as they continued out of England. But to have her back upon our hands, upon our doorstep, is entirely another matter. I will certainly do what I can to help her. But perhaps you had better tell me all the *un*romantic details?"

Elizabeth did so as briefly as possible, her recital punctuated only by grunts or groans from Mr Darcy. When she had finished he said merely, and in the voice of a true philosopher: "Well, my love, at least the duel did not happen. I think we must congratulate ourselves there. Neither did he end his life upon the gallows, nor in a debtor's prison. I congratulate his Colonel on dealing so smoothly with such an unpleasant matter, and can only rejoice that Lydia seems to be so serenely unaware of what a tightrope she was walking. No doubt, even without our assistance, she will soon put another interpretation on this unsavoury catalogue of events."

"Should she fail to find a husband, her intention is to live with her sisters, three months with one, then three months with another."

Mr Darcy pretended to shudder. Then he laughed.

"I think we can safely say that she can count upon our fullest, and *most* enthusiastic, assistance," he said.

The next few weeks passed quickly, all taken up with preparations for the visit to London. Elizabeth had brought back with her patterns and materials and much of the time was spent in the sewing-room. Three women from the village were brought in to help—obliged, to begin with, to stay in the house, as the snow continued to fall—and within three weeks a series of morning and walking dresses of unparalleled elegance had been constructed, to the admiration and satisfaction of all. Elizabeth had already decided that she would purchase all her evening gowns in London, in order to make sure that no one was further ahead of the mode than herself.

Towards the end of the month a letter was received from Anne, with the intelligence that she was very similarly occupied.

Rosings, January 21st

I am come out of mourning, my dearest Elizabeth, and with what I believe is called a vengeance. The process of turning a stitchwort into a peony, or perhaps I should say a dandelion into a sunflower, is begun and affords us all the *greatest* pleasure. Miss Linton has long been determined that I should be in full health before any decisions are made and now I have to say that I am. My hair, in particular, is quite changed. We spoke, at one time, of washing it in turpentine, like poor Queen Caroline, but I do not believe she ever did so as it was always an enormous black wig, so the idea was put away and I seem to have been living on *apples* for as long as I can remember. No matter. My hair is now bright and obedient and Mme de Domballe informs me that my colouring is similar to that of the late Queen—of France, I mean, not England. She must be fifty years old, so perhaps she does know, but I am not sure that it is a connection that I *welcome*. However, she—Mme de D— has chosen all the materials for me and they are all cream and buff and very pale yellow and I have to say that she is right about them all. The great ball dress is to be made of a heavy silk—"peau de nymphe", apparently a favourite colour of Marie Antoinette. I had expected a nice healthy pink, as of a nymph who had spent the summer disporting herself in the fields. But not at all. *This* nymph has clearly been hiding under a tree trunk in the *darkest* dell and if we were to see anyone with skin of that precise shade we should all be seriously alarmed. It is quite *sallow*. The dress, however, is a triumph, with large tucks in the bodice, a knot of ribbons at the breast and ruching and piping above the hem which is *padded*. This makes the skirt stand away from one's ankles, which I think an excellent innovation, especially in view of what happened to my mother. I am to wear white satin slippers. Perhaps I should not dwell on all my projected finery, but am quite surprised to find how much it all interests me. There was talk, of course, about engaging a lady's maid, a thing I have never had. I suppose as I rarely went into company my mother thought it unnecessary. There has always just been Audrey from the village. However, Mrs Jenkinson says that she and Audrey will be able to do all I need and I hope they are right. Mme de Domballe quite surprisingly offered to make a dress for Mrs J and I have accepted this. It is a very dark blue and makes her look "très grande dame" says Mme de D. Of course the greatest fun was with the jewellery. There is a most beautiful gold necklace with diamonds and pearls and five enormous sapphires. When I put it on Mme just shook her head and said they made my eyes—which, as you may not remember, are a kind of grey—*disappear*. So the sapphires are now replaced by enormous golden topaz. The jeweller who did it clearly thought we had lost our minds, but was gentleman enough to say, when he brought back the finished article, that it suited me to perfection. We go quite often to Tunbridge Wells, to see Mme and the jeweller, of course. It is a charming place and I cannot think why my mother never went there.

Mr Collins now breakfasts every morning with his daughters and reads to them from the Bible afterwards. He is so assiduous that I begin to wonder if he may not have an eye to Miss Linton, a most beautiful, elegant girl. I think I must arrange for her to be seen by one of my suitors, who now arrive in droves—in spite of the weather, though we have not suffered anything comparable to your snowdrifts and blizzards—and are always accompanied by a mother or a sister or, in one case, two sisters-*in-law*. It is very difficult to know what to do with them. Heaton has tried out many receipts from my father's book and he now makes them all in quarter quantities, adding economy to exhilaration. He is himself always extraordinarily cheerful as indeed is everyone in the house. How I long for my visit to London. May we arrive the 5th of March? Myself, Mrs Jenkinson and Audrey. I will send the carriage home again as I am sure there will be no need for it and as sure that you can have no room for it.

Elizabeth wrote at once to confirm this arrangement, but observed rather crossly to Mr Darcy, when she saw him later, that she thought Anne had not yet perfectly understood that it was *she* who was inspecting her *suitors*.

XX

They arrived in Brook Street, in excellent order, on the fifteenth of February, to find that all Elizabeth's innovations had been carried out and that the house was consequently a lighter and more cheerful place.

"I know not how it is, my love," said Mr Darcy, as they went upstairs together, "but you have the art of showing me things I have known all my life in quite another light. I have never cared for this house before. I found it large and gloomy and lived in it mostly alone with my tutor. My mother did not like it, my father came to it only when his affairs dictated. Before I married you I much preferred my club. Now, you put up new curtains and change the covers on the chairs and—suddenly—all the old ghosts have gone."

"That," said Elizabeth, with her warmest smile, "is just what I hoped you would say. We owe something, though, to my aunt Gardiner, who has helped to bring so much of this about. I hope she will come to see us soon."

Mrs Gardiner, in fact, called the following morning and found both Elizabeth and Mr Darcy at home.

"I have been quite in my element here," she said, as she sat down. "I have been able to admire all the materials that were chosen and in this I was joined by all the workpeople concerned. I have to congratulate you myself and to convey their approval as well."

"Certainly," said Mr Darcy, "a transformation has occurred, and we have to thank you for all the time it must have taken you to oversee the changes."

"Well, as to *that*," said Mrs Gardiner, half-laughing, "it was the greatest pleasure. Spending other people's money has a certain satisfaction of its own—and then, you know, the changes began to appear so swiftly, and the improvements were so immediately obvious. By which I would be understood to mean that I enjoyed every moment of the last six weeks and I look forward to the time when everyone can see the house in all its splendour. When does Miss de Bourgh arrive?"

They had not been seated very long before another arrival was heard and in two minutes the butler announced Mrs Bingley.

"Oh my dear Jane, how pleased I am to see you," said Elizabeth, as they exchanged a kiss. "I hope you are quite happy in Grosvenor Street?"

"Yes, indeed, quite happy," replied Jane, "but a most extraordinary circumstance occurred last week and I am come at once to tell you about it before our dear Lydia does so. Those curtains are quite the prettiest I have seen this season and you, my dear aunt," as she kissed her, too, "are looking better than ever. I hope it is not merely that desirable bonnet that makes you look so well?"

"I think," said Mrs Gardiner, "that the desirable bonnet may be a little responsible, but it is more probably my delight at seeing my two favourite nieces together in London."

Jane and Mr Darcy exchanged a greeting and then she sat on the sofa, next to Elizabeth.

"It was like this," said Jane. "Lydia and I were sitting upstairs, as we are, you know, and she was telling me more about her life in Gibraltar. She is much improved, do not you think, my dear Lizzy? At least her talk is no longer only about men and Gibraltar is certainly a place that one knows nothing about. When all of a sudden the butler announced a caller for Mrs Hurst and Miss Bingley."

She looked round as though about to disclose some information of the most secret kind, but no one spoke.

"We had not previously had any of those, though we had been there a fortnight, so my curiosity was a little aroused—and who should it be but Mr Rushworth, just arrived in London. As he was waiting below I thought it no harm to ask him up, as we were already slightly acquainted, and so up he came."

"Do, pray, continue," said Elizabeth, with an encouraging smile.

"Well," said Jane, returning her smile, "I have to say that Lydia was looking quite her best in her black clothes—as she quite well knows herself—and Mr Rushworth sat down opposite her and did not take his eyes off her for one moment. Indeed, when he left at last, he carried her hand to his lips and expressed the hope that they would meet very often as he was to be in London for six weeks. He was still in half-mourning, so I presume—his mother?"

"Yes," said Mr Darcy. "His mother."

"So," said Jane, "the embargo on women with fair hair no longer stands, I suppose? You remember she would only let him make friends with women with dark hair when we were here before?"

But it was at this moment that Lydia herself was announced and she came rather quickly into the room.

"Oh, my dear Lizzy, how much better this room looks than it did in holland covers. Quite charming indeed. And how are you, my dear aunt?"

She exchanged a kiss with Mrs Gardiner and then offered her hand to Mr Darcy, who bowed over it in great seriousness.

"It is quite an age since I saw you, Mr Darcy."

"An age indeed, Mrs Wickham. How well your mourning becomes you."

There was a short silence in the room while Lydia settled herself in a chair next to Mrs Gardiner, facing her sisters. Mr Darcy continued standing at the back.

"Well," said Lydia, "Jane will have told you of my great good fortune last week and now I must ask for your help in this important matter. But first I must know if anyone can tell me the name of the play which had Mr Rushworth's two-and-forty speeches in it?"

"Yes," said Elizabeth, "for I had the whole history of the theatricals at Mansfield Park from Georgiana, while we were there last autumn. And the play, if I recall correctly, was called *Lovers' Vows*."

Lydia almost clapped her hands.

"Then it is even better than I had hoped. For you must know that we performed it at the Commissioner's in Gibraltar."

"I understood it to be a rather immoral play, unsuitable for ladies to appear in," said Elizabeth.

"I think I have never heard of it," remarked Mr Darcy. "Pray, what is it about?"

"Oh," said Lydia, "it is not at all immoral. It is just the sort of foolish subject you would find in any novel from the circulating library. There is this wicked German Baron, you see, who fathers a son and then deserts the mother and goes off to France to marry someone else. Then he comes back twenty years later with a daughter, who is being courted, for her money of course, by a wicked Count. But the daughter is in love with a clergyman, her tutor, I suppose. And the son draws his sword on his father, without knowing who he is, when he refuses him money for his starving mother. But it all comes right in the end. The Count goes off. The son is acknowledged and his mother is given something to eat and so she forgives the Baron his disgraceful behaviour."

"Scarcely, one would think, material for a three-act play," observed Mr Darcy.

"Has it ever been upon the London stage?" asked Mrs Gardiner. "Not that I think I should have attended it if it had."

"The advantage at Gibraltar was that there are only three women's parts, and I have played all three of them."

Mr Darcy sat down.

"Pray, tell us all about it," he said. "Here is a talent that we know nothing of."

"Well," said Lydia, "there are two main women's parts. Agatha is the deserted mother and Frederick is her son. And when they meet, you know, there is a great deal of hugging and kissing, so the Commissioner, or perhaps it was the Colonel, decreed that these two parts must be played by a married couple. But Wickham would never learn his words, although I learnt all mine, so in the end we were not allowed to do it. But they had been so impressed by my acting that I was given the part of Amelia, the wicked Baron's daughter. Because she has only to kiss the Baron's hand, you know, so this was quite acceptable. But there is a scene between Amelia and Anhalt, the clergyman, which is almost a declaration of love, and the man who was playing Anhalt, one of the Captains, said he preferred to play the scene with his wife, no matter *how* ridiculous, as she was more than thirty and Amelia was only eighteen. So then I became Cottager's Wife," finished Lydia rather sadly, "and did the prompting, you know. But it was a great success. We gave eight performances."

"So, if Mr Rushworth had two-and-forty speeches, what part could have been his?" asked Jane.

"I fancy he must have been the Wicked Count," said Lydia, "with hardly a single speech more than two lines long."

"I seem to recall, from the one occasion when I heard him reciting, that one of them was 'Is it Hebe herself, or Venus?'" said Mr Darcy. "You can imagine that that being said, in the most romantic tones, after several glasses of port, might well bring a pause in the conversation."

"Then it is indeed Count Cassel," said Lydia. "Because then Amelia says to him 'I cannot help laughing at your nonsense'. And then he says something about having travelled the world but still being able to admire Amelia. And then she says she is sorry she has not seen the world and he asks her why and then she says, quite sharply you know—'because *I* might then, perhaps, be able to admire *you*'."

They all burst out laughing at this, so well did Lydia speak her last words.

"She does not like the Count?" suggested Mr Darcy.

"No, no, she is in love with the clergyman. She and the Count have some other exchanges. It is a very small part, after all. But I am sure I could give him all his cues."

"Then you expect to see him again?" said Elizabeth.

"That is one thing we mean to consult you about," said Jane. "If you would not all dislike it, I propose to ask him to dinner."

"But," said Elizabeth, "can you mean to further this romance? Surely you cannot have forgotten?"

"Forgotten?" said Lydia. "What?"

"That Mr Rushworth's former wife is married to our father."

"Yes," said Jane, remorsefully. "I think I had forgotten."

"And as I never knew," said Lydia, "I cannot be said to have forgotten."

"You never knew?" said Elizabeth, astonished. Then, after a moment: "Of course, it would be in that letter that never arrived, I suppose. But I think it makes a difference."

"Only a very small one," said Lydia, after a short pause, and neither put out nor to be put off. "It will merely mean I could not go visiting at Longbourn with Mr Rushworth, and Longbourn, as you know, was never a favourite haunt of mine. I have this enormous advantage over every woman in London and I mean to press it. If Mr Rushworth is there to be caught, then I mean to catch him."

"Well, that is to speak plainly indeed," said Mrs Gardiner. "Do you mean to conduct your courtship in your widow's weeds?"

"Indeed I do, because, as I have already told Lizzy, I have no other clothes to wear."

After a short silence, Mr Darcy got up and, once more placing his hands on the back of a sofa, said: "In fact, I think it an excellent scheme. He is looking for a wife; you are looking for a husband. Should you manage to catch him, to use your own word, you will do so, I venture to think, with the good wishes of a great many people in London. So—" he said, looking down into Elizabeth's astonished face, "how shall we set about it? Will you, my dear Jane, ask him to dine first, or shall we? And we all rely on you, my dear aunt, to support us in this, with your valued husband, as your presence will certainly add an air of sobriety to what might otherwise appear a rather reckless undertaking."

Mrs Gardiner merely bowed.

"I have almost engaged him already," said Jane. "If he should be free, would Thursday of next week suit us all? And I think, my dear Lydia, that you should take up your residence with us a day or two before that."

"Oh, do you mean it, dearest Jane? You will all help me?" exclaimed Lydia. "I scarcely expected such a speech from you, Mr Darcy, but I do recall all your great kindnesses on a previous occasion. This time, however, I mean to behave a little better."

Mrs Gardiner, who had come in her carriage, now offered to convey Jane and Lydia, who had both walked, to their different doors, and very shortly Elizabeth and Mr Darcy were once more by themselves.

"Before you say one word, my love," said he, "consider all the advantages of the situation. Mr Rushworth is by no means to be sneezed at. Half the town of Kettering, a very up-and-coming place, is built upon his land. With a wife at home he may not spend so much time in London—indeed we may never have to see him again. And it will be much to *our* advantage if Lydia will commit all her future indiscretions in the country. She is by no means as empty-headed as she appears. In fact, I am inclined to think her quite as shrewd as your late mother, though in a rather different way."

"True, my love, quite true, though I cannot really like it. Do you think that Mr Rushworth has any notion that Jane and Lydia are his late wife's step-daughters?"

"I am sure he has not, neither do I think it would make the smallest difference to him if he had. Were his mother alive the matter would be quite different, but his mother is not alive. And perhaps, if we are clever, we need not involve your father. Lydia is of age and your father's lawyers can do all that is required. Should it *be* required, that is to say."

"Shall you be able to endure the performance of *Lovers' Vows* that will be given every time we go to Sotherton? Perhaps you may even be offered a leading role?"

"As I am sure will you! But, as I understand it, I should be obliged to play the part either of your son, or your father, and as I seriously doubt my proficiency in either role, I shall choose to remain in the audience."

"But the clergyman? Should you not enjoy making a declaration of love to Amelia?"

"No doubt I should, were you my Amelia. But I do not mean to wait quite so long before I do so, or upon *that* as my opportunity."

He came a little closer, and kissed the top of her head.

XXI

Thursday of the following week seemed to Elizabeth to approach rather more quickly than Thursdays commonly did. By six o'clock they were being conveyed to Grosvenor Street, where they found Mr and Mrs Gardiner before them. Jane and Mr Bingley welcomed them with their customary kindness and the ladies sat down to await the arrival of Mr Rushworth.

Elizabeth was happy to observe how well her family was looking. Mr Gardiner, her mother's younger brother and, even now, hardly more than forty, increased in elegance and distinction as he grew older. His wife echoed him in elegance and distinction and Jane, never less than beautiful, had on a new dress and a diamond ornament in her hair; but it was Lydia who continued to give her the greatest surprise.

The youngest, and tallest, of her sisters, she had had, as a girl, a disappointing tendency to bounce, to say the first thing that came into her head. Her life in Gibraltar, among both military and naval wives, seemed to have taught her some discretion and, from somewhere, she had acquired a considerable taste in dress. She wore a simple necklace of jet and a jet ornament in her hair, but her evening gown, in defiance of the current mode, still swept the floor.

"I have not yet had time," she said to Elizabeth, observing her observing this, "to turn up all my hems and pad them, but I shall certainly do so before your party."

Elizabeth had only once been in company with Mr Rushworth and had no recollection of him. He arrived at exactly a quarter of seven and proved to be slightly taller even than Mr Darcy. His fair hair was modishly cut and his half-mourning in the height of fashion. His eyes were of the palest blue and he smiled frequently, an agreeable impression of vacant amiability being unintentionally given.

"We thought you would not disdain a family party, Mr Rushworth," said Jane, after Mr Bingley had performed the introductions. "With your bereavement, and my sister's, so recent, we thought you might prefer it."

"Yes, I am most thankful," said Mr Rushworth. "One cannot be better employed than sitting comfortably among friends and talking. A small dinner party is exactly what I like."

With Mr Rushworth the principal guest, he was able to be placed next to Lydia with no appearance of contrivance. To begin with Jane, on whose right he sat, claimed his whole attention. Not until she turned to Mr Gardiner, on her other side, was Mr Rushworth able to face towards Lydia and offer her his accustomed opening speech.

"'Is it Hebe herself, or Venus?'" he asked, lowering his voice a little.

Lydia laughed gently and said: "'But who can help laughing at your nonsense?'"

Mr Rushworth was so astonished that, for a moment, he did not speak.

"Then the Baron has to say, you know," said Lydia, converting her laugh into a smile, "'neither Venus, nor Hebe, but Amelia Wildenhaim, if you please'."

"'You are beautiful, Miss Wildenhaim,'" said Mr Rushworth, laying down his fork. "'Upon my honour, I think so. I have travelled, and seen much of the world, and yet I can positively admire you.'"

"'I am sorry not to have seen the world,'" said Lydia, in a tone of regret entirely at variance with the character she was assuming.

"'Wherefore?'" asked Mr Rushworth.

"'Because,'" said Lydia, with another smile, "'I might then, perhaps, admire you.'"

"'True,'" said Mr Rushworth, "'for I am an epitome of the world. In my travels I learnt delicacy in France—enterprise in Italy—prudence in Spain—hauteur in Russia—in England sincerity and in Scotland frugality. And in the wilds of America, I learnt love.'"

"'Is there any country where love is taught?'"

"'In all barbarous countries. But the whole system is exploded in places that are civilised.'"

"'And what is substituted in its stead?'"

"'Intrigue.'"

"'What a poor, uncomfortable substitute,'" said Lydia, in a tone of further regret. "But I fear, my dear Count, that you have the results of your travels a little confused."

"Well, as to that," said Mr Rushworth, suddenly himself, "I never could get them right or in proper order. But do, pray, Mrs Wickham, be kind enough to instruct me."

"With all the pleasure in the world, my dear Sir. I rehearsed both Agatha and Amelia, you know, but in the end appeared as neither and became the prompter. You learnt delicacy in *Italy*, *hauteur* in Spain, enterprise in France—which always seemed to me a little strange—and *prudence*, of all things, in *Russia*! Then, quite admirably, sincerity in England and frugality in Scotland. I never did agree with the author on all these points—he was German, of course. And as for learning about love in the wilds of America—what *could* be more improbable?"

"But at least this time the words were right, even if the order was wrong?"

"Indeed they were. You have an excellent memory, Mr Rushworth. It is some years since you performed?"

At this point Mr Darcy, who was seated opposite Lydia and who had listened to this exchange with the greatest surprise, said to her: "What are you talking about, over there?"

"'Of war, Colonel,'" said Mr Rushworth, obedient to his cue and quite oblivious of the fact that Mr Darcy had not intended to join in. Lydia laughed and said to Mr Darcy: "You have quite taken the part of the Wicked Baron, Mr Darcy. You have only to ruffle your hair a little, but your timing was quite perfect. I believe the correct words are 'What are you talking of there?'"

"'Of war, Colonel,'" said Mr Rushworth again.

"Well," said Lydia, "I will be the Baron also. 'We all like to talk on what we don't understand,'" she said, in a voice as deep as she could manage.

"'Therefore,'" said Mr Rushworth, "'to a lady, I always speak on politics, and to her Father, on love.'"

"'I believe, Count,'" returned Lydia, once more in her bass voice, "'notwithstanding your sneer, I am still as much of a proficient in that art as yourself.'"

"'I do not doubt it, my dear Colonel,'" said Mr Rushworth, "'for you are a soldier: and since the days of Alexander, whoever conquers men is certain to overcome women.'"

"Indeed?" said Mr Gardiner, unaware that Mr Rushworth's words were borrowed. "I cannot quite agree with you there, neither do I understand why you should speak to a lady's *father* upon love."

"Oh, the Count is very correct, you know," said Lydia, "speaking to Amelia's father before courting her. And that is just what she is afraid of, because she doesn't like the Count, you know."

Then, as Mr Gardiner still looked extremely puzzled, she said with a smile: "It is all from a play, my dear uncle. Mr Rushworth and I were just rehearsing our words."

"Were you so?" said Mr Gardiner, returning her smile. "Then I have to say, my dear Lydia, that your talent has been hidden, for I had no idea that you were acting."

"But pray continue," said Mr Darcy. "Your audience is held quite spellbound. What next has the Wicked Count to say?"

Mr Rushworth looked a little uncomfortable for a moment, but Lydia said, in her gentlest voice: "'Bravo, Colonel! A charming thought!'"

"'Bravo, Colonel! A charming thought!'" said Mr Rushworth immediately. "'This will give me an opportunity to use my elegant gun; the butt is inlaid with mother-of-pearl. You cannot find better work, or better taste. Even my coat-of-arms is engraved.'"

"'But can you shoot?'" said Lydia, in her Baron's voice.

"'That I have never tried,'" said Mr Rushworth, now well into his part, "'except with my eyes, at a fine woman.'"

"'I am not particular what game I pursue,'" continued Lydia, as the Baron. "'I have an old gun; it does not look fine; but I can always bring down my bird.'"

"Bravo! Bravo!" said Mr Bingley, amid the general laughter and applause, for the attention of everyone at table had been caught. "My dear Lydia, you have quite missed your vocation. When may we expect to see you at Drury Lane?"

"You must give me a little longer, Mr Bingley," replied Lydia. "I have rehearsed only Agatha and Amelia. It will take me some time to get up the role of the Baron."

"Which I am sure you could," said Mr Bingley. "But pray continue. What more has the wicked Count to say?"

"Well indeed," said Lydia to Mr Rushworth, "shall we go on?"

Receiving Mr Rushworth's nod, Lydia said, as the Baron: "'I shall be ready in a moment.'"

"'Who is Mr Anhalt?'" said Mr Rushworth.

"'Oh, a very good man,'" said Lydia, now Amelia.

"'A very good man,'" said Mr Rushworth. "'In Italy that means—'" and he paused.

"'That means a religious man,'" supplied Lydia. Then, in almost a whisper: "'In France...'"

"'In France,'" said Mr Rushworth, in a louder voice, "'it means a cheerful man; in Spain, it means a wise man; and in England it means a rich man. Which good man of all these is Mr Anhalt?'"

"'A good man in every country, except England,'" responded Amelia.

"'Then give me the English good man,'" said Mr Rushworth triumphantly, "'before that of any other nation.'"

"Correct, correct, Mr Rushworth," said Lydia, applauding. "You have the words exactly."

"A very admirable sentiment," said Mr Gardiner, "whether in your own character or the Count's. I do not seem to have seen this play—at least, I think not?"—to his wife.

"No," said Mrs Gardiner, "and to my deep regret. We have denied ourselves a great treat."

"It is some time since it was performed," said Lydia. "The date was on my copy but I think I left it at Gibraltar. But it was in the last century, you know, and at the Theatre Royal."

The conversation became general for the remainder of the dinner. Mr Rushworth, they learned, had grown tired of hiring houses for the season in London; he had never found one that really suited his mother. He had now bought one in St James's Square, which he liked very much, and to which he hoped to invite them all soon.

"But not until the six months is up. I do not wish any disrespect to appear, even by mistake," he said.

"I hope," said Elizabeth, "that your mourning will not prevent your presence at a dress party we mean to give for a cousin of Mr Darcy's early in March? I am sure there could be no objection, so long as you did not dance."

"As I am in the same case," said Lydia, "perhaps we could sit out together? If you think," to Elizabeth, "our dark clothes would not cast too great a gloom?"

"Certainly we cannot do without you, my dear Lydia," said Elizabeth. "Perhaps if you sat in the card-room conversing together, no one would think you guilty of any discourtesy."

"One cannot be better employed," said Mr Rushworth, "than sitting comfortably among friends, and talking. Pray, when is your party to be?"

"We have not yet quite decided, but we think about the tenth of March."

Mr and Mrs Gardiner did not stay long after tea and coffee had been served in the drawing-room. It was a dirty night and they offered to convey Mr Rushworth, who had walked. He declined this, but civilly hoped that he would meet them again. He left very shortly afterwards, Jane having expressed the hope that they might meet him after morning service at St George's, Hanover Square, on Sunday; and he promised to be there.

Alone in their carriage, on the way home, Mr Darcy said: "You must not feel *too* sorry for Mr Rushworth, my love. Lydia is a kind-hearted girl and for her he will be a great change after Wickham. He is quite honest, almost, one might say, dangerously so. He will do her no harm and, I think, she will do him no harm either."

"I am glad to hear you say so, indeed, and I hope you may be right. It is just that I cannot be quite happy taking *both* the Rushworths into the family. Imagine—if they should ever meet!"

"I truly think we are clever enough to prevent that. If your father wishes to see Lydia, he can always visit her alone."

With this assurance Elizabeth forced herself to be content. She saw very clearly all the advantages that would accrue, should Mr Rushworth make an offer to Lydia; but she would have been a great deal more comfortable had she been able to think that he was not going to do so in her house.

XXII

They all walked to St George's on Sunday, the day being dull but not wet, and they were by no means the only members of the congregation to do so. From the remarkably small number of carriages, and the very large number of persons, it was possible to conclude that there were many people there who did not think it right to expect their servants to drive them to church on a Sunday.

Lydia sat between her sisters, with Mr Darcy at one end of their pew and Mr Bingley at the other. Mr Rushworth, seated at a distance, bowed to them as he arrived and joined them afterwards outside the church. They walked very sedately, two by two, to the door of the house in Brook Street, where Elizabeth smilingly handed Mr Rushworth his invitation to her dress party on Tuesday of the week following. She had in fact sent out her invitations the day after their last meeting, but had decided to give him his personally.

He accepted gracefully and continued onwards with Lydia and the Bingleys to Grosvenor Street, where a nuncheon awaited them and to which he had been tacitly invited.

Four days later Anne de Bourgh arrived, on a very fine afternoon, her luggage separately conveyed behind her. Elizabeth went down to the hall when she heard all the racket of their arrival and found her in a high state of pleasurable excitement.

"Oh, my dear Elizabeth, here at last I am and how noisy everything seems to be. And what shall I call it? The *scent* of the Thames as we came over Westminster Bridge would have knocked us all over had we not already been seated. But I am charmed to be here and even more charmed to see you looking so delightfully well."

"I need not say welcome, my dear Anne, as you must know how anxious I have been to introduce you to London. I only hope it will not disappoint you."

"Impossible, I hope. But here is Mrs Jenkinson and Audrey, who, I think, is even more astonished than I am by the size, and the smells, and the noise. But I am very glad to observe the excellent pavements."

The few days before the party passed quickly. Elizabeth took Anne shopping in Bond Street and on one particularly fine afternoon they were driven into Hyde Park.

All the arrangements for the ball had been made. The consultation with the confectioners was complete, the precise constitution of the orchestra agreed and the nature of the decorations decided. Elizabeth was especially interested in the music. The waltz was now generally danced at private parties, but dancers had been hired to demonstrate a reel Mr Darcy had seen in Edinburgh, when he had gone there for the marriage of her father; and she hoped that perhaps some of the younger guests might be tempted to try it.

On the night of the ball, they dined very early in a morning-room at the back of the house. As she went into her dressing-room, Mr Darcy called to her and put into her hand a flat morocco case, which he took out of his pocket.

"My love," he said, "for *our* first ball in London, you must allow me to give you this trifle of an ornament for your hair."

It was a spray of single roses, entirely worked out in diamonds, but with a large pearl at the centre of each flower. She could only smile, as the tears pricked her eyes; but at last she put up her face to be kissed and said: "How you spoil me, dearest love. And how much I enjoy being spoiled. Nothing in the world could be more beautiful."

She then hurried away, but not, she hoped, too obviously, as her hair would now have to be altogether re-arranged in order to include the diamond spray. Her ball gown had arrived that morning from the dressmaker, a most elegant garment in pink satin, trimmed with another pink satin of a slightly paler shade. It was perfect in every particular. When her dressing was complete, even her own maid was moved to say: "I do not think, madam, that I have ever seen you look so well."

The invitation was for nine o'clock, but no guests were expected for at least one hour. Nevertheless, she was waiting in the drawing-room at exactly that time. Two minutes later Anne came in, accompanied by Mrs Jenkinson, giving Elizabeth leisure to think how very different was the Anne de Bourgh now in front of her from the whey-faced, diffident girl she had been used to meet at Rosings. Clearly, Madame de Domballe was a lady of exquisite skill and taste; the jewellery, as altered, suited her exactly; and she carried a very pretty fan.

"I found it, you know, in one of my mother's boxes upstairs," she said. "It will take several generations to go through them all, but this we found in one of the first that we opened and I thought it more than suitable. They are nymphs, as you can see, but dressed in rather more than their skins, I am happy to note. I could not resist it."

After a moment she added: "I do not mean to dance, you know. Though I am in every way much stronger than I have ever been, I should be quite knocked up by more than one country dance. I hope you will not be put out by this?"

"Not at all," replied Elizabeth. "Ten years ago, and in the country, you would have been obliged to open your own ball, at least. Now I think we shall find the dancers will arrange themselves. I only hope that receiving the guests, and standing for hours at the top of the stairs, will not be too exhausting for you."

"I think not. I hope not! We do not have to stay there, I trust, until *all* the guests are come?"

"No, indeed, but we may be stranded there for quite an hour."

"I suppose," asked Anne, a little nervously, "as the newest heiress, I do not expect to receive an offer quite at once?"

Elizabeth and Mrs Jenkinson laughed together.

"No, my dear Anne, not quite at once. Indeed, we have said nothing of your inheritance, but these things get about."

"What shall I do—if I do?"

"Well," said Elizabeth, half-laughing, after a moment, "you must say: 'Pray, Sir, do not inflict such violence upon your knees. I have no thoughts of matrimony at present.'"

"Oh," said Anne, delighted, "how I should enjoy saying that. Let us hope I have the chance to do so."

"But you must say it with your sweetest smile."

Mr Darcy came in shortly, and after a very few minutes the first guests could be heard arriving, long before they had been expected. As they moved together towards the top of the stairs, Elizabeth was able to say: "I hope you will allow me to say, my dear Mr Darcy, how much I enjoy being married to the handsomest man in London."

"You may, my love," he replied, smiling, "because I can return the compliment exactly. No one could look more beautiful than you do. And as for my cousin Anne, I can hardly believe my eyes."

The three of them stood together, Elizabeth receiving the guests, Mr Darcy introducing them to "my cousin, Miss de Bourgh". The ballroom was in the charge of a Master of Ceremonies and, before long, the orchestra could be heard striking up for the first dance.

The evening went without a setback. If Elizabeth was puzzled by the immense number of acceptances, she could not be otherwise than flattered.

The Bingleys and Lydia arrived at about ten o'clock, just as they were considering moving from their post at the top of the stairs. Jane and Mr Bingley were as exquisite, and as elegant, as ever, but on this occasion it was Lydia who took the eye. She wore on her head a black lace mantilla, secured by a black tortoiseshell comb, and she carried a large black fan.

As Mr Darcy said later, she looked as though she had come straight from Madrid; but all this Spanish finery in no way detracted from, indeed rather emphasised, her beautiful English skin. She still wore her jet jewellery, but in her ears, tonight, there were diamond drops.

Commenting on these later to Jane, Elizabeth received the dry reply: "Well, my dear Lizzy, from everything I hear about him, it seems that our poor Wickham was a much cleverer villain than we had any idea of."

Mr Rushworth arrived alone very soon after the Bingleys, and very soon after that Elizabeth and Mr Darcy were able to dance for the first time, she with Mr Bingley and he with Jane. That their party was the greatest success was already apparent. They began to receive congratulations on it long before it was over.

The Gardiners, and many of their older acquaintance, arrived only in time for supper. Elizabeth quickly introduced the Gardiners to Anne and Mrs Jenkinson, who were already the centre of a group seated in the drawing-room. It was not long before they were joined by Lydia and Mr Rushworth and, when the time came, they all went down to supper together. The supper was, Elizabeth was glad to find, one of unexampled excellence. Contrived between a professional caterer and her own kitchen, with their butler and Mr Darcy himself in charge of the cellar, there was clearly no need whatever to concern herself with the welfare of her guests. Delighted cries and satisfied smiles appeared all round her and she was able to snatch two minutes to talk to Jane.

"All I want to know, my dearest sister, is how Lydia got those diamonds."

"Well, it seems that for some time Wickham was doing very well at cards and giving his winnings to her—not an event which one would exactly expect. And he also knew of several dubious merchants in Gibraltar—in fact, I do not like to question her *at all*, you know, about the strange people Wickham knew. At all events, she turned her money into jewellery and this is some of it—sewn into her stays, you know, for the journey and she never took them off from Gibraltar until she arrived in London. Three weeks, she says. But I fancy the washing arrangements on board ship are not very convenient and she spent most of the voyage prostrate on her bed."

"And what has Bingley to say about her new romance? I seem to recall that he did not much relish the prospect of Mr Rushworth as a brother-in-law at one time, when the bride would have been his sister Caroline."

"On that head, dearest Lizzy, it is wisest to be silent. I have no doubt that it will all come to pass, just as Lydia has planned it, so the time to complain will only be, I think, if and when it does not."

The two subjects of this conversation were to be seen seated on adjacent chairs, consuming large quantities of the several desserts and conversing animatedly when they were not eating. Elizabeth said nothing, merely exchanging a sisterly smile with Jane.

The new reel was demonstrated immediately after supper and three sets were formed as soon as they had finished. So popular did this prove to be that it was asked for again. Six sets were made up the second time, in one of which Elizabeth joined. Dancing once or twice more herself, conversing here and there with her guests, many of whom she was meeting only for the first time, the evening passed both quickly and happily.

Towards two o'clock she came into the drawing-room, to find Anne comfortably ensconced upon a sofa. Elizabeth sat down beside her and said she hoped she had never lacked a companion.

"Not for one moment, dear Elizabeth. I have been hugely entertained. Solicited as a dancing partner more often than you can imagine—and the supper downstairs! Never have I participated in such a sumptuous feast. One day I must do something like it at Rosings. No one, I grieve to say, has injured his knees in my pursuit, but"—and here she spoke behind her fan—"I have observed the gentleman so interested in your sister doing violence to his. I could not truly quite believe my eyes—so different from Tom Jones."

Hardly had she finished speaking than Mr Rushworth himself approached.

"Pray, Mrs Darcy," said he, slightly out of breath, "m-may I have the honour of two words with you?"

"Do, please, sit down, Mr Rushworth, and tell us what is troubling you," said Elizabeth, smiling up at him.

"As to troubling, nothing at all. I have asked your sister to marry me and she has said she will. I am concerned only—to whom should I apply?"

"There is no necessity to *apply* to anyone, dear Mr Rushworth. Lydia is of full age and all her family must be only too glad to welcome you into it. Let me, indeed, be the first and I am sure Miss de Bourgh will join me."

She motioned to one of the very attentive footmen and asked him to bring three glasses of champagne.

"But—but—but," said Mr Rushworth, "the formalities?"

"As to that," said Elizabeth, in her serenest manner, "I believe it best that you consult with Mr Darcy and Mr Gardiner. They will know where the lawyers are to be found. Perhaps you could call here tomorrow morning, about noon?"

"Yes, yes, indeed, I will, indeed. I am much obliged to you indeed, Mrs Darcy."

They drank the champagne as though they were united in a conspiracy together. Anne engaged Mr Rushworth in conversation, and Elizabeth was free to go and find both Mr Gardiner and Mr Darcy, to tell them of the treat that was in store for them.

The last guest did not leave until four o'clock. The food in the supper-room was all eaten up, in perfect tribute to those who had prepared it, but coffee, champagne and wine were still to be found. Elizabeth and Anne stationed themselves in the drawing-room, in full view of anyone going downstairs, should they wish to take their leave.

When the last one had gone, Anne said: "I need some more words—so glad, so pleased, so charmed, so delighted—and there it ends. There were times when I quite wished to say 'You should *never* wear sapphires with *that* shade of green' or rubies with that shade of blue, you know—but I hope I did not actually do so. A wonderful party, dearest Elizabeth, dear cousin Fitzwilliam. I thank you very much. I am alive, at last, and shall remember your ball always, as a model for some I mean to give myself."

XXIII

Mr Rushworth was punctual to his appointment, as, to their everlasting credit, were Mr Gardiner and Mr Darcy. After a short consultation in the drawing-room, the three men went off to the Temple, where Mr Gardiner's lawyer, who also handled the affairs of the Longbourn family, had his rooms.

Having seen them safely off, Elizabeth and Anne left, in the carriage, to call formally on Jane and Lydia, and decide what was next to be done.

"It is indeed like a romance," said Anne, "though not like any that I have read. Do you mean to consult your father in all this? I cannot but feel that *he* might have something to say."

"It is above all things what I wish to avoid," replied Elizabeth. "My father never paid much attention to Lydia, except of course when she ran away, and then I quite thought he would go off in an apoplexy, so furious did he become. There must be some problem about Mr Rushworth's marriage, as a divorced person, but I think it may be done before a registrar; and it will be wisest to wait until the arrangements are all made before informing my father."

They found Lydia in a glow of satisfaction, calmly discussing with Jane the acquisition of a new wardrobe: "because I hardly think it acceptable to be married in black when the mourning is for a previous husband."

"Did he—did Mr Rushworth—tell you anything of his house in Northamptonshire?" asked Elizabeth.

"Yes, indeed. *Indeed* he did. I collect that it is a huge and draughty mansion in some seven hundred acres, but I am sure, with his money, that I can make it perfectly comfortable. I am quite conscious, you know, of my great good fortune and mean to put on a performance—as a great lady, you know—which will astonish you all."

"I am sure," said Jane, "that you are well able to do that and any support that you may need will always be yours. I am only distressed as to when we should inform my father, and precisely what we should tell him."

"I mean to write to him from Sotherton," said Lydia, "and tell him all that has occurred. I doubt that he could *assist* the present situation and I cannot bear the thought that he could impede it."

"As far as that is concerned," said Elizabeth, "you may rest quite easy. It is a match which even my mother could not have contemplated for you, and I do hope, my dear Lydia, if I may be your elder sister for a moment, that you will do justice to Mr Rushworth and not involve him in any ill-considered escapades."

"As far as *that* goes," returned Lydia, "you too may rest quite easy. I mean to take the greatest care of him and I can only pray that, this time, I may have children."

The conversation soon turned towards the previous night's ball and a very lively discussion took place, by the end of which they had agreed that it had been quite perfect in every respect and should be repeated every year.

"In fact," said Jane, "I can see no reason why we should wait until next year. Louisa and Caroline may not go to Italy every year and I should dearly love to give a ball without them. I will speak to Bingley as soon as he comes in. How long does Miss de Bourgh remain with us?"

"To the end of this month," said Anne. "I cannot altogether deprive myself of the spring at Rosings, but have to say that London, in many ways, exceeds my *wildest* expectations."

"And," said Elizabeth, smiling, "as Anne and I are agreed to be sisters, you must be her sisters, too. Do you think," turning to her, "you will ever have courage to visit your sisters in the *north*? Because this," she added, in explanation to Jane and Lydia, "is the first time she has ever crossed the Thames."

"It is," said Anne, smiling also. "I feel myself here to be quite in foreign parts. But the journey was in every way so much

easier than I had contemplated, and so very much more interesting, that I think I may soon discover the courage even to
cross the Trent—particularly when I may expect to find *three*
welcoming sisters at the end of my journeys."

Their visit did not last much longer after this and they
returned to Brook Street, to find the house miraculously restored
to its accustomed order and tranquillity.

As they sat alone in the small drawing-room, Anne turned
to Elizabeth and said: "There is something, my dear Elizabeth,
that I do not quite understand, and as we are in private I must
ask you to explain it to me."

"But of course," said Elizabeth, wondering what could be
coming next. "Pray tell me what it is."

"I had always thought, you know, that it was only necessary
to be married to have children. This is to say, you were married
and the children would appear. But I have often wondered why
Mrs Jenkinson, who was married for some years, had only
nieces and here is your sister praying that, *this time*, she may
have children. So what could she possibly mean?"

Elizabeth's heart sank a little at this artless question. She
said, very lightly: "There must be an element of chance in the
matter of children. Sometimes the two parties do not mix."

"That is just what I do not understand."

"But, my dear Anne," said Elizabeth, after a moment, "did
your mother never tell you?"

"My mother never told me anything. You may safely assume
that I know nothing."

Elizabeth's heart sank a little further. Then, gathering her
courage, she said, as matter-of-factly as she could: "In the first
place, then, men are not made quite like us."

"No," said Anne. "I have seen the statues. They have a leaf
between their legs and their chests are quite flat."

Elizabeth smiled a little at this, but went bravely on to
explain what lay behind the leaf. She managed her recital with
some dignity, though her little speech was punctuated by
squeaks of surprise from her listener, some gasps and some
moments of complete silence. When she had finished, there

was a long pause before Anne said: "I cannot at *all* believe it, Elizabeth. Pray tell me that you have invented the whole?"

Elizabeth quietly assured her that she had not.

"But that would mean—do you mean to tell me—cousin Fitzwilliam?"

Elizabeth merely nodded.

"And he so kind and well-behaved. I cannot quite believe it. Is it not—surely it must be—quite an assault?"

"Not, my dear Anne, where there is affection. Of course it can be an assault, but where there is true love between two people, I can only say it is something to be treasured."

After a small silence, Anne said: "So *that* is what happened to poor Clarissa. How my heart bleeds for her. How *much* it must have hurt."

Elizabeth said nothing.

"So everyone's parents—I *cannot* believe it—my own father, indeed," she went on, clearly in the deepest turmoil. "Oh, how extraordinary!"

Then, suddenly changing her manner, and removing the handkerchief from in front of her mouth, she laughed out loud and said: "But how, I wonder, did he manage? He would have needed a ladder."

They laughed together and the air of distress that had invaded the room disappeared. After another pause, Anne said: "But there is even something else I need to know. This monthly affliction that you speak of—does it only affect married women?"

"By no means," said Elizabeth, in the greatest astonishment. "It affects every healthy woman in the world. It is a universal curse."

"Well, I, for one, have never experienced it."

"Never?"

"Never."

A complete silence followed this admission. Then Elizabeth took Anne's hand between hers and said, as kindly as she could: "I think, my love, in *that* case, that we had better consult a physician."

A long discussion followed, during which Elizabeth divulged more information about the nature of childbirth, again incredulously received. At the end, Anne said simply: "I honour you more than I can say. I am sure I could not endure the half of what you have been through—and when I think of poor Mrs Collins, I wonder how I can bear it."

Realising that Anne was indeed very much shocked by what she had heard that afternoon, Elizabeth was about to ring the bell, to ask the butler to assemble the Brook Street version of the Rosings Remedy, which they had sampled once or twice, when she heard the gentlemen return. Some minutes afterwards, the three of them came into the drawing-room, when Mr Darcy informed her that he had already done what she had proposed to do.

It was, however, Mr Gardiner who said: "Mr Rushworth is the soul of generosity, my dear Elizabeth. I do not scruple to say that your sister Lydia is a very fortunate girl and we are all invited to share in her good fortune by a visit to Sotherton in the autumn."

"I am charmed to hear you say so, my dear uncle. I have already welcomed Mr Rushworth into the family and am now delighted to be able to do so again."

"Mr Rushworth is anxious to be married as soon as possible," said Mr Darcy. "Perhaps Lydia should put off her mourning before that."

"I believe," said Elizabeth, "that she has every intention of doing so."

"My poor Mrs Lydia has suffered enough," said Mr Rushworth rather emphatically. "I wish to convey her quickly to Sotherton, where she may be quite safe."

"I am sorry to hear of her sufferings," said Mr Gardiner. "Pray, where did they take place?"

"In foreign parts, I need not say," said Mr Rushworth. "It was hot, so hot she could not sleep. And there was this rock, you know, so big it kept the cool breezes away and with wild monkeys upon it, and sometimes a thick yellow cloud which made them all ill. But she will be quite safe at Sotherton. There are only cows and sheep and horses there."

"I have once been at Sotherton," said Mr Darcy, directly to Mr Rushworth. "Perhaps you may recall—last October? I thought the building very fine."

"It is fine," said Mr Rushworth, "and very enclosed. There is nothing to be afraid of there."

"I am sure there is not," said Elizabeth, who could think of nothing else to say. "I long to see it, very much."

The butler now entered, with a footman. The glasses were handed and they wished every happiness to Mr Rushworth, who then very shortly departed, to prepare himself to dine in Grosvenor Street, where he was already engaged.

When he had left, Mr Gardiner turned to Mr Darcy and said: "We seem fated to attend the weddings of Lydia Bennet together. Let us hope that this one will have a happier outcome. At least one can say that the omens are infinitely more propitious."

"With special licenses and civil marriages, the whole affair is much simpler than formerly," said Mr Darcy, with some satisfaction. "With Rushworth in such a hurry, we may well be bidding them farewell within a fortnight."

As Anne continued very silent, Elizabeth asked her, as they went upstairs to change for dinner, if she would prefer to have something sent up to her room.

"No," she said. "I am shocked, perhaps, but not horrified. I think that a quiet evening at home, and one of your excellent dinners, is all that is required."

Elizabeth did not forget to send a note to Sir William Knighton, the King's physician, requesting him to call at his earliest convenience; and she was surprised to receive one in return from him before the evening was quite over. He would be happy to call at eleven o'clock on the following morning.

After giving the matter some urgent consideration as they sat together, reading or sewing, after dinner, Elizabeth decided that she must ignore Lydia's wishes and write to their father herself. Just before she went to bed, when she was alone in her dressing-room, she sat down and wrote:

Brook Street, March 11th

You will be so astonished, my dear Father, by the contents of this letter, that I must beg you to sit down if you are not already seated. What I have to tell you relates principally to Lydia. When I came to London alone in January, who should appear but she, draped in the darkest of widow's weeds. It seems that her dear Wickham accidentally fell off a cliff at Gibraltar, in circumstances which are better not examined too closely. On a visit to Jane earlier this month—the Bingleys are in Mrs Hurst's house in Grosvenor Street—she encountered Mr James Rushworth, of Sotherton Court in Northamptonshire. I fancy I do not need to tell you who *he* is. And the long and the short of it is that they are now engaged to be married. Mr Darcy and my uncle Gardiner are taking care of the formal arrangements and seem perfectly satisfied with them all. I write therefore only to say that, should you wish to see her before she leaves for her new home, she will continue with Jane until she does so. She is much improved, especially well-dressed and with rather less to say of herself than formerly. She will be quite angry with me for informing you of all this, for her intention was only to write to you when she got to Sotherton, as she remains quite unaware of any awkwardness in the situation.

Should you wish to come, pray invite yourself to stay with us as we shall be, as always, delighted to see you. I truly hope that all is well at Longbourn.

XXIV

Elizabeth received Sir William Knighton in the drawing-room, where she explained, as briefly as possible, the nature of Anne's condition. She then escorted him upstairs to Anne's bedroom, where she sat with Mrs Jenkinson, wearing only her wrapper. When Elizabeth offered to leave the room, Anne particularly requested her to stay, so she sat with Mrs Jenkinson while the examination took place.

Sir William had brought with him the latest instrument, which he called a stethoscope, for listening to the heart and lungs. Having done this, with every appearance of satisfaction, he asked Anne to be kind enough to open her wrapper.

He looked at her intently, but briefly, and then motioned to her to close it again.

"Thank you," he said. "I think we do not need to look any further."

He then, without speaking, seemed to ask Anne if he should say what he had to say in front of Elizabeth and Mrs Jenkinson; and she, also without speaking, consented.

"Then I have to tell you, Madam, that you are in general in the finest of health, your heart, your lungs, in unimpeachable order. But I have also to say, and I hope this will not be a source of too much distress to you, that there is a small malformation of the lower regions and no conjugal union would be possible—certainly, one must never be attempted. In all other respects, I have the happiness to say that you have every prospect of a long and healthy life—and indeed I must tell you that your prospects are very much better than most, as it is what we must call the female organs that are the principal seat of any troubles that may occur in later life."

"I hope I misunderstand you, Sir William," said Elizabeth, as Anne remained silent.

"I regret to say that I think not, Mrs Darcy. I believe they have been omitted altogether."

Then, seeing Elizabeth's look of disbelief, he went on: "It is by no means unknown, you know. I am in this case only surprised that my patient should have had to wait until now to be informed. It must have been apparent from the moment of her birth."

"And there is nothing to be done?" asked Elizabeth.

"Nothing at all, I grieve to say. It is not possible to create what Nature, in her wisdom, has seen fit to leave out."

"Then," said Anne, after a moment, "we have only to thank you, Sir William, for your time and your courtesy."

Sir William bowed.

"With your permission, Mrs Darcy, ladies," he said, "I will see myself out."

He left a complete silence behind him. After what seemed like minutes to Elizabeth, Anne said, to Mrs Jenkinson: "And did my mother never say anything to you?"

"My instructions from Lady Catherine were very clear," said Mrs Jenkinson. "I was never to discuss with you the functioning of your body. I think, on reflection, that had you ever asked a direct question, I would have answered it. But in general, you know, your health was so poor that it was impossible to tell whether you suffered from a monthly indisposition or not."

"But my old nurse? Did she never speak to you?"

"I fancy she was similarly sworn to secrecy. Certainly, she never discussed the matter with me. Though it pains me to say so, the one whose duty it was to inform you was Lady Catherine herself."

"She could never have brought herself to do so," remarked Anne, with no hint of criticism in her voice. "It would have been to admit that she had given birth to an imperfect child."

After a moment, she went on: "But I prefer that it remain a secret between us. I do not even intend to inform Audrey. Cousin Fitzwilliam, if you like, Elizabeth, but he too must agree to remain silent."

Then, gathering herself up, she said: "And now I think I should like to be dressed and, if it should be at all convenient, to go for a drive in the Park."

An hour later, Elizabeth and Anne left in the carriage, to be driven sedately round Hyde Park. They sat in silence, hand in hand, for the greater part of their journey; but, at last, as they were leaving the Park to return home, Anne said: "I am trying to decide, you know, whether I am upset or not—if I should be more distressed than I am. After what you told me yesterday, dear Elizabeth, I can only think myself fortunate to be spared everything that you, and other mothers, have to go through. If my role in life is simply to be that of a Lady Bountiful—whom I recall from one of those plays at the time of the Restoration, and which I must read again since I *now* know what they are about—then so be it. I have much to be thankful for, though I fear that, for my cousins Fitzwilliam, their trusteeship will have to last my entire lifetime."

"They will not mind, my dearest Anne. That I can vouch for personally. You have a beautiful house. I believe that Mrs Jenkinson is most truly a friend. Your servants are devoted to you—and you have the Misses Collins."

"Yes," said Anne, after a moment, and as if it had not occurred to her before. "I have the Misses Collins."

They spent the day very quietly after that, but at night, when they were alone, Elizabeth told Mr Darcy everything.

"I believe there must be a problem of that kind among the women of that family," he said, when she had finished. "My mother waited five years for me. Lady Catherine had only the one child. There are ten years between me and Georgiana. My mother, too, was never quite well after Georgiana's birth—though happily Georgiana herself seems not to have inherited that."

"I think I have never admired Anne so much as I did this morning, when she received all that Sir William had to say without flinching, or blenching. If he had been speaking to me, I am sure I should have been in hysterics. We must take great care of her, my love."

"We must," said Mr Darcy. "But I begin to suspect that my cousin Anne is more than able to take care of herself."

Elizabeth's letter to her father was answered, two days later, by his appearance in Brook Street. He arrived while they were still at breakfast, having left Longbourn before sunrise. Elizabeth was very pleased to see him, asking for fresh coffee at once, and indeed requesting a repeat of the whole repast for him. She and Mr Darcy made small talk while Mr Bennet made an excellent meal, after which he said, when the servants had gone: "So, my dear Lizzy, let me have the pleasure of understanding the farrago of nonsense that constituted the substance of your letter. It seems that she lost Wickham less than a year ago and is now already contracted to Rushworth. I do you the justice to believe that you could not have *invented* this extraordinary set of circumstances, but am come, as you see, to discover the truth of them—without informing my dearest Maria."

Elizabeth and Mr Darcy both laughed at this.

"You may well be surprised, my dear Sir," said Mr Darcy, "but I do assure you that what you have just said is quite true. And I must further add that the engagement has the unqualified approval of ourselves, the Bingleys and Mr and Mrs Gardiner."

"Well, upon my soul," replied Mr Bennet, "I never thought that Lydia could *still* have the power to surprise me. Can it be that she is not aware who Mr Rushworth is?"

"Oh, she is aware of it," said Elizabeth, laughing, "for I told her myself. But she said it would only mean that she could not bring Mr Rushworth to see you at Longbourn. What I am not so certain of is whether Mr Rushworth is aware who she is—the name of Bennet has probably never been mentioned."

"It has been mentioned," said Mr Darcy. "Clearly, in all the contracts she is referred to as Lydia Wickham, formerly Bennet. But Mr Rushworth did not remark upon it—indeed I wonder if he noticed it."

"And are we to countenance this marriage? Is not this James Rushworth a very foolish fellow?"

"Not foolish, I think," said Mr Darcy, "but simple, in the better meaning of that word. Generous and unsuspicious, and if

I had had any idea that Lydia could be making a game of him, I could not have done what I did to further the match. I believe I can say, however, and no one can be more surprised than I that I should do so, that they will contrive very happily together. His estate, as I have seen for myself, is in the most excellent order."

"Well, this is a day of wonders, indeed," said Mr Bennet. "No one could cavil at Lydia's wanting to marry him, but on his side—can he truly *wish* to marry her? And not one word of regret for poor Wickham?"

"As to poor Wickham," said Elizabeth dryly, "I think the less said about him the better. We do not know *all* the circumstances surrounding his death, and I rather think we should seek to enquire no further. Suffice it to say that we have all been spared a disagreeable scandal and that Mr Rushworth's appearance on the scene is a dispensation of Providence almost too desirable to be accepted."

"And Lydia herself? How is she?" asked her far-from-doting father.

"She is much improved, quite changed indeed," said Elizabeth. "She will not be pleased that I have told you of her intended marriage, as she did not mean to inform you of it until it had been accomplished. But, if I may presume to offer you advice, my dear Father, I believe you should ask her to come and see you here, where you may tell her everything a loving father should. There will be no danger of meeting Mr Rushworth here, and I think perhaps you owe it to her. My aunt Gardiner told me of your plot to send them out to India."

"As far as that goes," said Mr Bennet, with an unrepentant smile, "it would have been the ideal solution. They would have been a permanent charge on all our purses and a possible source of trouble and embarrassment as long as they lived. But now, my dear Lizzy, I will take your advice if you will lead me to some paper. I hope I may stay the night?"

Elizabeth assured him that he could.

"And in conclusion," said Mr Bennet, with another, almost conspiratorial smile, "I can only say—how *delighted* your mother would have been."

They laughed quietly together.

The carriage conveyed Mr Bennet's note to Lydia and remained to bring her back to Brook Street. Elizabeth intercepted
her in the hall to offer an apology for informing their father of
her forthcoming marriage, and was surprised when Lydia said:
"No, no, my dear Lizzy, it is just what I would have wished,
though I had no notion that he would want to see me. I am
glad to have this chance to talk to him alone and must thank
you for bringing it about."

Elizabeth went out in the carriage once again with Anne who,
having breakfasted upstairs, was not aware of the morning's
occurrences. They stopped briefly in Grosvenor Street, to invite
the Bingleys to dine, and then continued into the Park.

"I am glad to think I am going to meet your father," said
Anne. "More and more I begin to realise what a sheltered life
I have had and more and more I begin to wish to spread
my wings. You and your sisters are quite a revelation to me.
While I do not find you at all alike, there is a confidence
between you that I can only envy; but to be included in your
family, as you have already offered to do, can only give me the
greatest pleasure."

"And I am sure the pleasure will be returned on our side,"
said Elizabeth. "You are as much at the beginning of a new life
as is Lydia herself, and we shall all do our best to make sure that
you make up for lost time."

On returning to Brook Street, they found Mr Bennet and Lydia
on better terms than they had ever been, each quite enjoying
the company of the other.

"I could never have imagined," said Mr Bennet in an aside
to Elizabeth, "that Lydia, that hoyden of hoydens, could have
turned out so well. Not only is she now both handsome and
elegant, but she seems to have acquired from somewhere some
common-sense and information; and I scarcely think we can
give our poor Wickham credit for that."

"I could hardly have supposed," said Lydia in an aside to
Elizabeth, "that my father could ever be quite so conversable.
He seemed to have an interest in what I had to say about Gibraltar

and spoke to me at all times as though I were no longer a little girl. Can it be that Maria has brought about this change?"

The dinner party went off easily, with no awkward silences and no cessation of comfortable chat. A very affectionate farewell passed between Mr Bennet and Lydia, and he returned to Longbourn on the following morning.

Lydia's marriage to Mr Rushworth took place before a notary in the City rather less than ten days later. She was accompanied by both her sisters and Mr Darcy and Mr Bingley were witnesses to the wedding. A breakfast was held by Mr and Mrs Gardiner in Gracechurch Street and the bridal pair left immediately for Sotherton, in a carriage specially purchased for the occasion.

Lydia had put off her mourning and both she and Mr Rushworth appeared to be so delighted with themselves, and with each other, that they made indeed a very handsome couple.

In the evening the wedding party, with the addition of Anne and Mrs Jenkinson, attended one of the theatres, returning to Brook Street for a late-night supper.

XXV

Anne's last engagement, before returning to Rosings, was the Bingleys' Ball, which took place three weeks after Elizabeth's, on the last day of March. New ball dresses were commissioned, new dancing shoes acquired and the occasion enjoyed perhaps even more than their own ball, as they had no responsibility for it.

Jane had found a different orchestra, and another caterer had been discovered, so that the two events should not appear too similar; but, in terms of gaiety and happiness, there was little to choose between them. Elizabeth was especially pleased to see a small group of admirers, many of whom had attended her own ball, clustered round Anne, who blossomed and glowed in their company. Mrs Jenkinson sat comfortably among the dowagers and their whole party went early down to a supper that was even more delicious than Jane had led them to expect.

As they said goodbye, Jane invited Anne to come and stay with them in the summer and Anne almost promised to do so.

"But I am lost for words to describe my enjoyment of your party and in return must hope that you and Mr Bingley will one day visit me at Rosings. In the few weeks before coming here, I particularly began to feel how very large my house is, and how empty—so I hope you will be able to give me this pleasure."

Jane replied suitably and they left, among the first, as Anne had decided to travel the next day. Her carriages had already arrived from Kent, and their party departed, as intended, precisely at eleven o'clock on the following morning.

"Once more, I have no words," said Anne. "You have shown me a new world, not only of elegance and excitement, but of kindness and consideration as well, which I have never met before. Promise that you will not wait too long before coming to me again; and I, on my side, will concentrate on raising my courage to a point where I may come and visit you."

Kisses, embraces, were exchanged and they drove away in great good humour, but with some regret.

Alone together, Elizabeth and Mr Darcy settled in the small drawing-room and, for some moments, simply stared into the flames of the excellent fire.

"I cannot be quite happy about poor Anne," said Elizabeth, at last. "Should she decide to face life alone in that society, will the married women come and visit her?"

"Certainly, my love, unless my understanding of her situation has progressed beyond the real into the cynical. She has much to offer. Should she choose to set herself up as a great hostess she will never lack for respectable company. And despite the best efforts of Madame de Domballe, and of everyone else, she does *not* look to be the kind of female who is going to run off with their husbands."

"Oh no, certainly not that. Though you must allow that her appearance at all times was precisely right. Perhaps she will become a pattern for dress and behaviour in the county of Kent. I can quite imagine it, you know. And her courage, as I have already said, in accepting the verdict of Sir William Knighton, is hardly to be admired enough."

"I fancy she does not lack for courage. She was always liable to be married for her money and estate, but her situation being what it is, I think her too honest to accept an offer in the ordinary way. Though, one must admit, there are loveless and childless marriages enough."

"I want only to see her content with her own life and surrounded by those she can trust."

"She is already half-way there. While I, and my cousin Fitzwilliam, do not exactly surround her, at least no one can make off with her fortune while we live."

"I fear only that she will be too solitary."

"My love, pray recollect two things. The first is that she has always lived upstairs, seeing no one and making no friends. The second is that you and your sisters grew up in a freedom which Rousseau himself might have envied. The air of conviviality which invests you all is one of your greatest charms. So what looks like loneliness to you may merely seem tranquillity to her."

"I hope, indeed, that you may be right," said Elizabeth, with a smile, "and I look forward to hearing who this Rousseau is. But do you not think the time has come—to talk about our return to Pemberley?"

After a calm and quiet discussion, the following Monday was fixed on.

As Elizabeth sat over her breakfast coffee on the Saturday, the butler brought in a letter. It was in a perfectly plain envelope with the one word "Elizabeth" written on it. Opening it quickly, she discovered it was from Anne.

"Pray, how did this arrive?" she asked the butler in astonishment.

"I understand, madam, that it was brought up by one of the grooms from Rosings. He waits for your reply."

"I hope he is being looked after?"

"He is, madam. I have attended to the matter myself."

"He must have left very early to be here so soon."

"I understand, madam, that he left at dawn. He has ridden all the way."

Elizabeth's heart misgave her a little. Surely only bad news could be so urgent? The letter, however, was quite short.

Rosings, April 3rd

My dearest Elizabeth and my dear cousin Fitzwilliam will, I hope, forgive if I entreat, request, even demand their presence as soon as is humanly possible. A sudden inspiration has overtaken me which I have not courage enough to put into practice alone—or even indeed to put upon paper. If you are not yet gone to Pemberley, pray come and see me at once.

Your agitated Anne.

"Is Mr Darcy gone out?" said Elizabeth, when she had read this, the butler fortunately still being in the room.

"He is on his way, madam. I believe he is even at this moment in the hall."

"Then pray intercept him or—if you are too late—send after him to call him back. He goes to his club."

Within five minutes, Mr Darcy entered the room and Elizabeth showed him her letter.

"Well," said he, "as we are already packed up, and tomorrow is Sunday, we had better be off immediately."

An hour later they drove off, the groom from Rosings accompanying them.

Elizabeth's mind was so busy, conjecturing this, puzzling about that, that they were drawing up at Rosings almost before she was aware of it. They were welcomed, as always, by the butler but, no sooner had he finished speaking, than Anne herself came into the hall.

"Oh," she said, "how could you be here so soon? My dearest, most amiable friends. But come in, I beg you. Here is an excellent fire in the Blue Drawing Room and Mrs Jenkinson is upstairs. A perfect opportunity to unfold my stratagem to you."

Her stratagem turned out to be, to the stupefaction of both her hearers, a proposal of marriage to Mr Collins. Neither could utter a word.

"Before you say anything at all," Anne went on, "just consider the conveniences of the situation. I can have no children. He has four, of whom I am very fond. In order to have full control of my fortune—and pray do not misunderstand this, my dearest Fitzwilliam—I must 'enter upon the married state'. No other condition is demanded, neither consummation nor any other kind of conjugal behaviour. I was closeted yesterday with my attorney and, while I cannot say he recommends this course of action, he does not absolutely prohibit it. So—what do you say?"

Elizabeth spoke first.

"Can you arrange for him to continue living in his own house? I know you feel that this one is both large and empty, but to have Mr Collins permanently fixed in it is a penance not to be contemplated for a moment."

"An excellent notion," said Anne. "I had not thought of it."

"And you know, my dear Anne," said Mr Darcy, "that my trusteeship is no kind of burden to me. I cannot help but feel that the steps you propose are unnecessarily drastic simply in order to be rid of it."

"Ah," said Anne, "I was afraid you would feel it so. It is not that I think you would not enter into my philanthropic schemes, but consider it in this light. Here is this immense sum of money, so immense that it produces an *income* of more than five thousand pounds a year. In order to avail myself of that money—my principal, my attorney calls it—I must have the consent not only of you but of my other cousin Fitzwilliam, at present in the Bermudas and liable to be sent I know not where else in the world. The time required to obtain *that* consent must be anything up to a year, even supposing the necessary letters not to be lost at sea."

"That I understand," said Mr Darcy. "Perhaps I might also wish to join in your philanthropic schemes."

"I saw such dreadful things in London, things I could not imagine, only living here—dirty, ragged children, hungry and alone. I could not find it in my conscience not to try to benefit them in some way."

Her words brought about a complete silence. At last Mr Darcy said: "Yes, indeed. You are perfectly right to wish to do something of the kind."

"I knew you would agree," returned Anne, smiling. "You have a generous heart."

"But if you marry," said Elizabeth, "would you take the name of Collins?"

"I should retain my father's name and try to restore to it a little of its lost lustre and glory."

"Then certainly," said Mr Darcy, "there can be no quarrelling with such an intention."

"I will send a note to Mr Collins, asking him to join us after dinner. I did not feel I could make the proposal by myself. I need to feel your support in the background. And I must do it while my courage is still high. He must have completed his sermon for tomorrow by now."

Alone upstairs, and changed for dinner, Elizabeth said: "Perhaps she found this idea in Peregrine Pickle, or Roderick Random, do you think? Or even in this Rousseau that you mentioned?"

"This Rousseau, my dearest love, was a Frenchman who did not write that kind of novel. Indeed while it would not be true to say that he *caused* the revolution of the French, he did not appear to object to it."

"Then," said Elizabeth, "I do not wish to hear another word about him."

They were joined at dinner by Mrs Jenkinson and by her niece, Miss Linton. The conversation centred largely on the talents and behaviour of the Misses Collins and Elizabeth was particularly glad to feel, for Charlotte's sake, that they had fallen into such excellent hands.

As they lingered a little over the dessert, Anne said, with a satisfied smile: "I did not tell you, my dear Elizabeth, about the proposal I received at your sister's ball. He was perfectly drunk, of course, but still quite upright, you know, until he chose to do full violence to his knees, just as you said he would. But he kept on calling me Miss de Vere—was there such a person at the ball, perhaps? Whatever the situation, I did not accept his proposal. The words you gave me acted like a charm. He rose—not without difficulty, you know—and murmured his compliments should we ever meet again. And then he really *tottered* away. I cannot help feeling a little disappointed that he did not tell me who he was. I might have become a Duchess."

As the laughter spread among them, Anne said, directly to Mr Darcy: "Perhaps it was that that gave me my idea."

XXVI

Mrs Jenkinson and Miss Linton took their tea upstairs and Mr Collins punctually arrived.

After exchanging bows with him, Elizabeth and Mr Darcy kept themselves a little apart, settling with their coffee in a corner of the room distant from the candlelight, while Anne dispensed the tea to Mr Collins. As she handed him his cup, she said: "Do, pray, be seated, Mr Collins."

Mr Collins sat down, without a word.

For some moments, perhaps even for some minutes, there was silence in the room. Then Anne said: "Mr Collins, I have a proposition to put to you, which I hope you will think not unworthy of your acceptance."

"I am all ears, Madam," was his answer, "and entirely at your disposal."

"The proposal that I have in mind is of a somewhat delicate nature. May I offer you a second cup of tea?"

"Indeed you may," said Mr Collins, rising and going over to the tea-board. The tea was poured and Mr Collins's seat resumed. Elizabeth was suddenly conscious of the beating of her heart.

"You are aware, I think," continued Anne, "that I am the sole heiress of both my father and my mother. It is a large and prosperous inheritance, which I would wish to share—to scatter my good fortune among others."

"I can only honour the generosity of your intention, Madam," said Mr Collins.

"While in London lately, I had the sadness to discover that I am unable to bear children."

"I am distressed to hear it. The will of God is sometimes hard to understand."

"My own distress was very fleeting. My aim is now to benefit those who are already in being, as many as are within my orbit.

And foremost among these, as I am sure you are aware, are your own daughters."

There was a silence. A cup was replaced on a saucer and put down on a table.

"Do I understand, Madam, that your wish is to adopt my daughters?" asked Mr Collins, in a voice which suggested that he would offer no opposition.

"No, Mr Collins, I do not. My proposition is more complicated than that and its consequences more far-reaching."

Again there was a pause and Elizabeth held her breath.

"My intention," stated Anne, in a firmer voice than before, "is to become their step-mother."

The ensuing silence lasted longer than the others. Elizabeth's hand sought that of Mr Darcy. He squeezed it, comfortably.

"You honour me beyond my desserts, Madam," said Mr Collins, at last. "I must only regret *deeply* that I cannot accede to your proposal."

"I have spoken too soon. Your excellent wife is too lately dead for you to consider such a thing?"

"It is so, certainly. But for other reasons I can only state it to be quite impossible."

"From your own point of view, Mr Collins, the advantages are far from trifling. The advantages to your daughters, however, I would consider overwhelming. I would educate and dower them, preparing them for marriage at the highest level. In the end, no doubt, my estate would be left entirely to one or other of them."

"I can only regret, Madam," said Mr Collins, in a voice of agony. "I can only deeply regret."

"Let me be rightly understood, Mr Collins. I do not offer a marriage in anything but name. I would expect you to remain in your parsonage, though we should meet here every evening at dinner. There would, indeed, be no interruption in your normal mode of life. Your daughters, I believe, will be happy to continue here, seeing you each day as they do at present. Later, of course, they would spend some time with you at the Parsonage. I consider it important that they should experience some other way of life."

"I grieve, I regret, I can neither assist nor accept," said Mr Collins, in an increasingly tortured voice. He got up and began to pace about the room.

If Elizabeth had formed no opinion as to how this interview would proceed, she had to acknowledge a feeling of astonishment at its development. The objections she had imagined to be all upon the other side. A marriage even of this kind to a clergyman would run the risk of ostracism in the highest circles; but Anne herself had lived her life so entirely alone, and so completely outside society, that this was hardly a consideration with her.

At last Anne said: "I hope you do not mean to tell me, Mr Collins, that you have some other lady in view?"

"No, no," said Mr Collins, in a voice of increasing desperation. "It is quite otherwise, indeed."

"I am aware that Miss Linton—and indeed that you are thrown very frequently together—and your daughters are no doubt very fond of her—"

"No, Madam, no, indeed," interrupted Mr Collins. "I have to confess—I have no option but to confess, that I have promised the Bishop—"

"You have promised the *Bishop*?" said Anne, disbelief and disapproval strong in her voice.

"I have promised the Bishop," said Mr Collins, breathing rather heavily, "that I will not marry again. He requires that I remain celibate."

"But," said Anne, instantly, "the marriage that I propose would in no way interfere with that. A part of our contract would be the complete renunciation of conjugal rights, on both our sides; and we are all aware of your views upon adultery."

Mr Collins did not speak. He began his pacing again, backwards and forwards behind a sofa.

"I could not find it in my conscience," said he, at last, "to benefit in any way from such a marriage."

"But there would be no benefit to you," said Anne, in a voice which increasingly reminded Elizabeth of Lady Catherine. "Not one farthing of my fortune do I propose to make over to you. In order to have control over it I am required to enter into the married state, though to acquire that control I must certainly have the consent of any potential husband."

"There would be no benefit to me?" asked Mr Collins, in a voice combining relief with disappointment.

"None whatever. I intend that the marriage remain secret. I propose to retain my own name. I propose that we continue to live in our separate houses. As step-mother to your daughters, whether acknowledged or not, I am the better enabled to make provision for them. My influence with the Bishop, should you perhaps wish to become one yourself, will be the more powerful if our marriage is unknown. I have five livings in my gift. All I am asking you to do, Mr Collins, is to sign a piece of paper before an attorney. Your way of life will scarcely alter, except that, with the education of your daughters accepted by me, you will have more money to expend upon yourself."

Then, as an afterthought, she added: "And I can certainly promise you a most excellent dinner every evening."

Mr Collins now stood perfectly still. Clearly there were feelings at war within him. He began to pace up and down again, to stand still, to pace up and down again, to stand still. At last, and after a silence quite as uncomfortable to Elizabeth as it must have been to Anne, he said: "Then, Madam, in all humility, I must accept your offer."

It was a small, vanquished voice, from which all expression had been drained. With a great effort, he added: "I believe it is what my dear Charlotte would have wished."

"I am obliged to you, Mr Collins," said Anne, with a calm that Elizabeth could not but envy. "It remains only to put your name at the top of our contract and to place your signature at the bottom and this, I grieve to have to inform you, must be done at Maidstone. Would the day after tomorrow, in the morning, be convenient?"

"The day after tomorrow it shall be," said Mr Collins, in a strangled voice. Then he bowed to her and said: "I will wish you a very good evening."

And he vanished into the night.

It took some time for peace to return to the room. Elizabeth poured some more coffee for herself, but it was by now almost completely cold. They could see only Anne's back from where they sat, and she was quite silent and still. Then Mr Darcy took Elizabeth's hand and they went over together, Mr Darcy raising Anne's hand to his lips.

"Well, my dear cousin," he said quietly, "as I believe them to say in the Navy, you have certainly burnt your boats."

"I have," she replied. "But without regret. I have acquired a family and a fortune. But I shall hope for your help, cousin Fitzwilliam, and your advice, about the schools I shall found and the orphanages I shall build. And as for my little girls upstairs," she said, with a radiant smile, "I shall be able to indulge them to my heart's content."

"And that, I know," said Elizabeth, "will be the greatest pleasure of all."

They did not remain downstairs much longer. When they were again alone in their bedroom, Elizabeth said: "I hope you are fairly happy, my love, with the arrangement that Anne has made?"

"I am. The only danger lies in the secrecy—it is always awkward when a secret leaks out, as I suppose this one is bound to do. I do not anticipate any trouble from Collins. His constant presence at her dinner table may at least discourage her suitors. His promise to the Bishop is a safeguard we could not have expected. She is now in full control of her own life and I can only rejoice that she feels able to be so."

"There are times, my dear Fitzwilliam, when you remind me very much of my father. I could almost hear him saying what you have just said."

"I take that as a high compliment, my dear Elizabeth. Your father is a practical man, without pretence or flummery, and, as I have told you many times before, I am more than proud to be married to his daughter."

They travelled to Maidstone in the Darcy carriage, taking up Mr Collins on the way. It was Anne's idea that they did this, since the Darcy servants would be less open to gossip than her own, though she candidly said that, as was the case with most secrets, no doubt the news would be all over the county within a fortnight.

The contracts were signed and witnessed; the marriage was concluded. Anne was remarkably composed; Mr Collins looked pale and a little nervous, though his signature was perfectly firm. They left him at the gate of his parsonage after arranging that he would come in the evening to dinner.

They were welcomed, as always, by the butler, but there was such a knowing look on his face that Elizabeth could not help wondering if he had overheard Saturday night's scene with Mr Collins.

However, he said only: "I have prepared the Rosings Remedy today, madam. It awaits you in the Blue Drawing Room and requires only the final touch."

"My dear Heaton," said Anne, with a distinct sparkle in her eye. She took off her hat and handed it to a footman. "Pray add the champagne immediately."

XXVII

In the course of the afternoon Elizabeth sent off an express to Longbourn, to say that she hoped they would be with them again on Thursday. She had not intended to visit them this time, on their return journey to Pemberley; but the events of the past month—even if one of them were to remain for ever a secret—provided topics of sufficient interest to give hours of fruitful discussion.

She was reasonably certain that her father, despite all appearances to the contrary, regarded Lydia's marriage as a very good joke; and she was also quite sure that, with that being the case, he would have shared the joke with his wife. Elizabeth found that her curiosity to know what Maria thought about it had become quite overwhelming. A visit of three nights was proposed.

Mr Collins dined at Rosings that evening, still in his unaccustomed, strangely subdued state. A smaller table had been placed in the great dining-room, with comfortable room only for six people, and Mr Collins took his seat at the foot of it. Elizabeth had particularly asked Anne not to put her next to him, so this privilege was accorded to Mrs Jenkinson and Miss Linton.

But she need not have worried. Mr Collins no longer advanced his opinion on every subject, or endorsed every comment of Anne's as he would have done those of Lady Catherine. He listened attentively to the conversation of Mrs Jenkinson and Miss Linton, particularly when they discussed anything relative to the well-being of his own daughters. He gave his opinion only when applied to, was civil to Elizabeth but not too apologetic, and was in every way such a changed person that Elizabeth could hardly prevent her astonishment from being visible.

Her satisfaction was complete when he returned to his parsonage before the tea and coffee were brought in; and Mrs Jenkinson and Miss Linton withdrew very shortly after they had finished theirs. Alone with Mr Darcy and Anne, Elizabeth was able to say: "I feel we shall leave you in very calm waters, my dear Anne. I cannot imagine what has brought about this immense difference in Mr Collins, but I am more than happy to observe it."

"I believe we must thank his Bishop for this," replied Anne. "Of course, I can have no notion what was actually *said* to him, but certainly the alteration seems to stem from his visit last summer."

"A visit to Maidstone his road to Damascus?" remarked Mr Darcy, smiling. "Let us hope his conversion is as complete, and as permanent, as was Saul's into Paul. And I must agree with Elizabeth. I believe the new life developing round you will be one that will satisfy you in every respect. The joy and happiness that you propose to spread around you will be the source of great joy and happiness to you."

"I must hope you are right, cousin Fitzwilliam," said Anne, very seriously. "Today has suddenly brought home to me an all-pervading sense of the responsibilities that are now mine; but I believe I shall be able to discharge them, and in such a way that no one will be the loser."

"If you can do that," said Elizabeth, "you will be in the way to sainthood. One can only wish your projects every success— but I hope you will not exclude us from them?"

"Indeed I shall not," replied Anne. "One of the greatest pleasures of the past few months has been to find myself so close to both of you. And you may certainly live to regret it," she finished, laughing, "as I shall consult you at every turn."

The next two days passed peacefully. Mr Darcy and Anne went into Maidstone each day, to wind up the trust and discuss anything outstanding with the attorney. Elizabeth walked with the Collins girls and Miss Linton in the woods, where the windflowers and primroses were now in bloom.

She was more and more pleased with Miss Linton, with her excellent sense and exemplary patience, her sense of fashion and her sense of humour. On Charlotte's behalf, she felt that Miss Linton's presence could scarcely be improved on and, as they walked back across the lawn, with the girls a little ahead, she said so.

"That is indeed kind, Mrs Darcy," said Miss Linton, "and I thank you. Though, on my side, I am obliged to say that no one in my situation could ever have been made more welcome, or more comfortable. I hope you can have no notion of what I endured at the hands of the Smallridge family, and were the Misses Collins ten times more troublesome than they are, I would still rejoice in my good fortune. But perhaps I could ask you," she said, rather diffidently, "something about their mother? I believe you knew her very well."

"Yes, in a manner of speaking, we grew up together. Her parents lived within walking distance of mine and she became a friend many years ago, though she was six or seven years older. She was the eldest of a large family and, I think, was frequently only too happy to leave them behind and come on a visit to us."

"Did she play, or sing, or draw? In short, what talents am I to look for in her daughters?"

"As to that," said Elizabeth, after a moment's thought, "I think you look for good humour and an amiable disposition rather than for any stirrings of genius. I do not recall that any of the Lucases could play or sing or draw. Charlotte herself was a notable needlewoman and her presence in the kitchen was by no means unknown. Lady Lucas I think I may describe, I hope without condescension, as a good, plain woman, but Sir William must have had more than common ability, since he made a genteel fortune for himself in Meryton. We were never, however, precisely informed in what way."

"So there are aunts and uncles there, who might later take an interest?"

"There are indeed, and grandparents as well, though I am not certain of what value they could be. Miss de Bourgh has wise ambitions for them here. As for the talents, or abilities, that they may inherit from their father, I can only say—that your guess must be quite as good as mine! The girls may have every advantage that money can bestow; but—perhaps— neither brains nor beauty?"

"Well, I will not pretend to misunderstand you, Mrs Darcy. I had no knowledge of Mrs Collins but I have been told that she was one of the kindest women in the world. And Mr Collins—if one may regard him dispassionately—is by no means unhandsome."

"I fear," said Elizabeth, "that I am *quite* unable to regard him dispassionately."

"By which I would be understood to mean," continued Miss Linton relentlessly, "that his eyes are of excellent colour, only without expression; his nose is by no means too large and his hair of a tone and a texture that many an aspiring beauty might envy. He needs only to have it cut. Of his teeth I must certainly say nothing, but Miss de Bourgh assures me that the water at Rosings is particularly beneficent and that rheumatism on the estate is almost unknown."

Elizabeth, astounded completely, could think of nothing to say.

"You stare, aghast," said Miss Linton, broadly smiling. "I may explain by saying that Mrs Smallridge employed a dancing master and a drawing master for her daughters and, while those daughters quite certainly learnt less than nothing, they both taught me a great deal. Which must explain," she went on, and with a direct glance at Elizabeth, "why I am able to regard Mr Collins with dispassion. As the possible subject for a portrait, I have to say that the construction of his head is particularly fine."

"If only there had been something in it!" exclaimed Elizabeth, recovering and suddenly laughing. "But he is a distant cousin of my father who is still, I do not hesitate to say, one of the handsomest men I have ever seen."

"Then let us hope that my little girls will inherit only the best qualities from both sides."

"I have perfect confidence in leaving them in your kind, capable and competent hands. I am sure that any small spark of talent will be observed and fanned into a flame. But we shall be frequent visitors, my dear Miss Linton, so I look forward to a longer, deeper and closer acquaintance with *you*."

They shook hands with great cordiality.

XXVIII

They were able to leave Rosings on the Thursday morning, without misgiving. The stitchwort, in Anne's own words, had become a peony, the dandelion a sunflower. It seemed to Elizabeth that they left behind a happiness possibly unknown in that house before; and she could only rejoice in the fact. To their great surprise, Mr Collins appeared at the gate of his parsonage, to doff his hat and wave them on their way, but they returned his farewell as obviously as possible.

The day was fine and the roads were dry. They arrived at Longbourn long before sunset.

"I love this house of yours," said Mr Darcy. "It looks better now than it has ever done and I must always be grateful to *it* for having nurtured *you*."

"I am glad to hear you say so. Perhaps a part of me will always live here. Perhaps I realise now, too, how happy we all were for most of the time."

Mr Bennet and Maria greeted them as soon as they got down from the carriage and they were taken upstairs to the drawing-room. Tea was brought for the ladies and wine for the gentlemen, and before long Mr Bennet took Mr Darcy off to his book-room. Elizabeth put in a request to be taken up to the nursery to see her brothers, but Maria said, in a rather firmer voice than usual: "Later, if you would not object. Just now, we need not move—we shall be quite private here."

Although Elizabeth knew quite well what was to come, she simply smiled and looked a question.

"You can have no doubt, I think, why I should wish to be so private," said Maria. "Indeed, there is no one else in the world to whom I *can* speak on this subject—but you must tell me all you know about Mr Rushworth's recent marriage."

Elizabeth suddenly realised that she had been thinking of that event as Lydia's marriage, rather than Mr Rushworth's. She gathered her strength and said, easily: "There is little to tell, in fact. He saw my sister quite by accident and seems to have fallen in love upon the instant. I believe her situation as a young, romantic widow did her no harm. He had only himself to please and on her side there could be no possible objection."

Then, as Maria did not speak, she added: "If his marriage seems to you a little hasty, I have to say that I think there is every reason to hope for their happiness."

"Your father scarcely seemed to recommend Lydia as a wife," remarked Maria.

"She was by no means a favourite of his, certainly, but her first marriage cannot have been easy and she has been—what can I call it?—*matured* by it. Like wine, she has been much improved."

After a short silence, Maria said: "I am astonished to find that I am in any way concerned for his happiness. It is guilt, I have no doubt, guilt for the great wrong that I undoubtedly did him. To marry one man while in love with another, though doubtless it does happen very often, is not behaviour of which one can be quite proud."

"I had not understood that," said Elizabeth.

"Oh yes," said Maria, unbending a little, "it was not Mr Rushworth who made a woman of me. I could not bear to touch, or be touched, by him. From that point of view, your sister has a virgin bridegroom, though of course that cannot be the case. The contrast, then, between the two men, was that of a wineglass filled with a strong red wine, and a beaker full of very pale ale."

Elizabeth could not help laughing.

"In that case Mr Rushworth has not changed too much," she said. "We had little conversation with him, indeed none at all, alone; but his one purpose at present is to make my sister safe and happy, and no woman could object to that."

"I understand his mother is now dead?"

"Yes, last autumn—while we were there at Mansfield."

"Well, that can only be an improvement," said Maria. "There was no one to compare with her precious James. I believe she took my defection even harder than he did. She was a clumsy, jealous woman bent only on vengeance, quite ready to tear to pieces anyone who slighted her son."

"Come, my dear Maria," said Elizabeth, at once, "you must forgive yourself, and her. So much has happened since that time. While it is quite extraordinary to me that I should say it, I have no more doubt of my sister's happiness with him than I have of your happiness with my father. And if their conversation should ever run a little thin, you know, they can always rehearse *Lovers' Vows* together."

"What can you mean?"

"Only that Lydia appeared in it at Gibraltar. I understand that there were three women's parts and that she learnt them all, only to become, at last, the prompter. So not only could she give him all his cues, when he recited his two-and-forty speeches, but she could also tell him which one to say next."

Maria, after two seconds, burst out laughing.

"The picture!" she said. "The picture is altogether too exquisite—and entertaining! Did you ever see her doing this?"

"Most certainly I did. *We* did. At the dinner-table one night, at the Bingleys'. And so beautifully did she do it that I knew then that the die was cast."

"Then I think I am now quite happy. No one who could do that could wish him any ill."

"That I am sure she does not. And her first husband being what he was, it must be now like coming to port after a storm. He was very handsome, indeed—at one time I must confess to a partiality there myself. But he was unreliable in every way, selfish, thoughtless and, ultimately, a common cheat. She is lucky to have lost him."

"With all his faults, I cannot say that James Rushworth was any of those things. I never doubted the goodness of his heart."

"Of that I, too, am certain. And indeed his amiability is such that he may well come to forget how you were connected and invite you, with my father, to visit him at Sotherton."

"Well there," said Maria, very positively, "I would have to draw the line. It is a house I never wish to see again, but I hope your sister will be happy in it."

They rose together, left the drawing-room arm-in-arm, and went upstairs to the nursery.

XXIX

On the following morning, just as Elizabeth was trying to steal secretly out of the house, to visit her favourite haunts by herself, she was approached, in the hall, by the butler.

"Excuse me, Miss Elizabeth," he deferentially said, "there is a visitor in the morning-room who particularly requests your presence."

"*My* presence!" said Elizabeth, in astonishment. "Who can it be?"

"I am sworn to secrecy, Miss Elizabeth. But I can at least tell you that the visitor arrived on foot and presented herself at the garden door."

"Someone from Lucas Lodge, I suppose," said Elizabeth. "Do you think I should go?"

Elizabeth and the butler were old friends. A look of complete understanding passed between them and the butler said: "While I cannot exactly recommend it, madam, I believe it will be best if you do."

They went together to the morning-room.

"I shall remain on hand, Miss Elizabeth, to show your visitor out the way she came in."

He opened the door. A dark figure rose from a chair by the window, put back her veil, and Elizabeth found herself alone with Lady Lucas.

She had not expected this. She had supposed that one of Charlotte's younger sisters might have ventured to call, but had never anticipated the possibility that Lady Lucas might come herself. She was at first too angry to speak and a total silence ensued.

At last Lady Lucas said: "I should not have come."

"No, Lady Lucas, you should not."

"I heard you were here. There is something I must ask you."

"It would have been wiser to write—to me, at Pemberley."

"I could not allow the occasion to pass without trying to see you."

"You appear to have consulted no one's wishes but your own."

"I came in through the garden door. I do not believe I was observed."

"You were admitted by the butler. All the servants must know you are here."

"He was never one to go about spreading tales."

"I have certainly never known *him* to do so."

"I must sit down again. I do not feel well."

"Then pray do so."

Elizabeth remained standing. Lady Lucas sat down and searched in her reticule, at last producing a vinaigrette. She took two deep breaths and applied a handkerchief to both her eyes. Elizabeth was suddenly aware that she was being extremely impolite to a woman whom she had known most of her life and with whom she had never quarrelled before. She sat down herself and said, in a softer voice: "If it is about Charlotte, Lady Lucas, you may ask me whatever you like."

Her remark was greeted with a watery smile, which turned, almost instantly, into a sob.

"I know so little," said Lady Lucas.

"If Mr Collins is your only informant, then that is hardly surprising."

"That was why I had to come."

Elizabeth forced herself to recollect that she was talking to Charlotte's mother and not to the woman who had done so much to destroy Maria's credit.

"Reluctantly," she said, "I must admire your courage, Lady Lucas. What is it that you wish to know?"

"I wish to understand," said Lady Lucas, suddenly alert, "why Charlotte, who is built exactly as I am myself, should die of a fourth child. I am the mother of ten, as I think you know, and not one of them gave me any trouble."

"The child was presented backwards, Lady Lucas—in breech, I believe they call it. And no doctor was present."

"But the midwife—surely she—?"

"I believe that Charlotte herself was in some distress at the time. I saw her on the day of her confinement and she told me that she had not felt as well as usual."

"You mean that that dreadful man had been more unpleasant than usual."

"I did not say that, Lady Lucas."

"There was no need to, Mrs Darcy."

Lady Lucas fumbled once more in her reticule, producing another handkerchief. She mopped her eyes again.

"I keep all Charlotte's letters, you know," she said presently. "As mention of Mr Collins became more and more infrequent, what else could I suppose?"

"I was always, in my heart, opposed to Charlotte's marriage."

"It seemed so prudent at the time; and Mr Collins's prospects were so good."

"I understand you, I believe."

There was another silence. Lady Lucas sniffed again into her handkerchief and wiped her eyes. At last she said: "Is there nothing else that you can tell me?"

Elizabeth was by now in something of a turmoil. On the one hand, Lady Lucas had a mother's right to know all the circumstances surrounding a daughter's death. On the other, she was aware that she could only be so informed by reducing Mr Collins's credit even further. She got up and moved over to the window, saying, with her back to Lady Lucas: "I saw Charlotte, at her most urgent request, on the morning of the day she died. She already had, as she told me then, 'intimations of immortality' and admitted that she had not been as well as in the other cases. I should say that Mr Collins had already forbidden me his house but I went, nevertheless, to see Charlotte, as she clearly wished it very much. Most unfortunately he saw me leaving. A terrible scene ensued between them, her pains began, with the result that we both know."

"But I do not understand why Charlotte was so anxious for your visit."

Elizabeth turned round.

"She wished to receive my promise, Lady Lucas, if I may be perfectly candid with you, that, in the event of her death, I would not desert her children."

Lady Lucas no longer attempted to restrain her tears. She sobbed unashamedly for the inside of a minute, her weeping ending on the words: "I knew it. That is to say—I was afraid. I thought it might be something of the sort."

When she had collected herself a little further, she said: "And I am sure that you gave her that promise?"

"I did."

"You were always a very kind girl."

Elizabeth did not speak. Lady Lucas, after a moment, said: "And the children? I am almost afraid to ask."

"The children are now resident at Rosings, Lady Lucas. They have been ever since their mother died. I do not say that Miss de Bourgh will adopt them as her wards, precisely, but certainly she means to bring them up as daughters of her own. They have an excellent governess, charming quarters and Mr Collins sees them every day. If you do not wish to lose sight of them altogether, I suggest that you write to Miss de Bourgh proposing yourself and Sir William for a visit."

"Could I be so bold, I wonder?"

"You are their grandmother, Lady Lucas. Nothing can alter that."

"And Miss de Bourgh? Is she as proud and impatient as her mother?"

"She is not. Indeed she is quite the opposite, in almost every way. The little girls could hardly be more fortunate. And if I may presume to offer you further advice, Lady Lucas, it is that you call upon Maria here and apologise for making her previous history generally known."

"But it was only the truth."

"Which is why it was so damaging. Old scandals are best left alone, I think, particularly as my father was not involved in this one."

Lady Lucas rose from her chair and put down her veil.

"I shall tell Maria to expect you," said Elizabeth.

Lady Lucas moved over to the door. With her hand on the handle, she said only: "How you have grown, Elizabeth."

Elizabeth heard the butler say something, and Lady Lucas reply, though she could not distinguish the words. From the morning-room window, Lady Lucas could shortly be seen walking down the path which led to the little gate into the lane, the lane which led, at last, to Lucas Lodge. She moved slowly, with never a backward glance.

Elizabeth stood very still for some moments, taking deep breaths to calm herself, torn between admiration of Lady Lucas's conduct as a mother and condemnation of her behaviour as a neighbour. After perhaps five minutes she went to the door, to find the butler hovering outside it.

"I think this must be our secret," she said to him. "I shall inform my father of this visit, but no one else. Then he can decide himself whom he wishes to tell."

"I think that very wise, Miss Elizabeth. Though I fear her departure will have been observed from upstairs."

"I seem to remember, from the old days, that our Nurse was sometimes most conveniently blind."

"As you say, Miss Elizabeth. I will remind her when I see her."

Elizabeth now put on her bonnet and pelisse and went out for her walk, trying to convince herself that she had not been so rudely interrupted, that the incident had not occurred. She made her way towards the Hermitage, only to find, and to her great surprise, her father walking towards her.

"My dearest Lizzy," he said, as soon as they were within speaking distance, "*what* can have happened to discompose you so? I never saw you look so upset."

"I had intended to break it to you rather more gently, Father, but I have just sustained a morning visit—from Lady Lucas."

"Indeed?" said Mr Bennet.

"She came to the garden door. I saw her in the morning-room."

"On the track of what new scandal did she come, I wonder? Your mother always said she had the longest nose in Hertfordshire."

"Only information about Charlotte's death. One cannot be surprised, after all."

"She could have written, I believe. Your address at Pemberley is not a secret."

"Precisely what I said to her."

"And how did she know you were here? Your mother also thought she had the sharpest eyes in England."

"We drove past yesterday. It is a new carriage and there is always a little Lucas in one of the front windows."

"So what did you tell her?"

"I told her the truth and advised her to write to Miss de Bourgh."

"And was that *all* your advice, my dear Lizzy? I think I perceive a certain look in your eye."

"No, it was not. I advised her also to call on Maria and make an apology."

"Oh, my dear child," said Mr Bennet, "how cruel, how clumsy, how *in*considerate! Life without the Lucases is so *very* pleasant. I cannot believe this of you!"

Against her will, Elizabeth laughed.

"I am sorry, my dearest Father, I *had* not thought! But no doubt her courage will fail her."

"My lovely Maria is redoubtable indeed should one happen to offend her. In this case one can certainly do without the Lucases, entirely. Should she follow your advice, however, I shall think the better of her; and the glory of it is that, even in that case, we shall only ever have to ask them on the most formal of occasions. So I forgive you. Your intentions were, I am sure, as always indeed, quite excellent. But what are you doing up here?"

"Exploring, perhaps. Renewing my acquaintance with my old haunts. A part of me is always here. I should have turned in a moment. I might enquire the same of you?"

"Your remarkable husband has been with me to discuss some changes that are to be made in the Lower Meadows. His ideas are so much better than mine that I have left him to expound them to everyone concerned."

He took her arm and they went down the hill together.

"I never cease to be amazed," said Mr Bennet, "by the skill of my daughters in catching desirable husbands. What do we have to say about Lydia's latest exploit? Has anyone heard from her?"

"Not yet, indeed, though perhaps a letter is waiting at Pemberley. I have no doubt that Lydia will one day astonish us all."

"I am much inclined to think that she has done so already."

"By which I mean—she has promised a performance as a great lady which, I am sure, she is able to give—and I think it will be best if we just sit back and watch her. I believe her to be genuinely fond of Mr Rushworth and, in his eyes, there is no one to compare with her."

Mr Bennet smiled.

"I shall certainly not quarrel with him there," he said. "I trust indeed that Lydia is unique. But perhaps she too will have five daughters?"

They laughed together as they returned to the house, all thoughts of Lady Lucas effectively banished from Elizabeth's mind.

The winter had only just departed from Pemberley. A few tips of green could be seen in the hedges, but the beech trees remained stern and leafless. Elizabeth, delighted as always to be home again, congratulated herself that, even with all the unexpected events of recent weeks, she had not deprived herself of one moment of the spring. Everything was yet to come.

XXX

Elizabeth was quite right. A letter from Lydia was waiting for her.

Sotherton, April 8

My dear Lizzy, I take up my pen in some surprise as I do not recall that I ever wished to write a letter before, to you or to anyone else. But my amazement at all the circumstances of my new life is so great that it demands to be shared and, because of the good understanding lately set up between us, I write to you rather than to Jane. Also I believe your feelings on arriving at Pemberley must have been like mine on my first sight of Sotherton. Had you any notion it would be so big? I certainly had not. However, I must say first of all that I am extremely happy. If I am dazed by the size of the house—and the number of rooms!—I can hardly be complimentary enough about the kindness and civility of the whole household. The late Mrs Rushworth, listening between the words, if I may so put it, seems to have been a lady of no charm and very little beauty, not much regarded in the neighbourhood. But her house-keeper, a Mrs Whitaker, is a person of some excellence and—beyond telling her that I cannot eat mutton, you know—I have had no reason to alter any of her arrangements. Everything is done here, in the kitchen, or the dairy—a delicious cream cheese—or the still room. There is no going into Meryton should we run short of a thing; indeed I am sure there are provisions in these cupboards for a siege of several months. But I do not complain about this as I am sure no one could be looked after any better. My performance as a great lady is demanded of me every day and it is one that I shall be able to perfect in time. Everywhere I go there are curtseying girls or boys touching their forelocks and my cheeks begin to ache with all the smiling.

The gowns that I ordered in London are here already and are required every day, as bride visits are paid by everyone of note within a circle of thirty miles. That I should be a great curiosity is no surprise and I can only trust that I do not disappoint. With the help of a maid, also engaged in London, and those gowns, and the others that we copy from them, I am able to pass myself off as a beauty. Sir Thomas and Lady Bertram have called, both their sons with their wives, the Duchess of Rutland and the Countess of Coventry and more neighbours of a less exalted kind than I can keep any track of. Tomorrow we go in fact for me to lay the foundation stone of some orphanage that interests the Bertrams which is to be built on Rushworth land. We shall have to give a grand reception in the early summer as I would hope to hold it at least in part outdoors. The garden round the house is a series of walled compartments, which I like very much, ideal for this purpose. I do not think they have been touched since first made in the reign, so Mrs Whitaker tells me, of James the Second. Perhaps *you* know when that was? There is also a chapel from that time but I am thankful to have been spared a Great Hall. The house is quite as draughty as I had expected and I dread the thought of a real winter here; but perhaps we could migrate to London. I find that my dear James is renowned in the district as an excellent shot and, what has surprised me very much, a "bruising rider to hounds", if I have the phrase correctly. But I know him, at the moment, only as a superb whip and we drive out every afternoon. He is determined to shield me from every adverse breath of wind and I cannot quarrel with this. Our conversation is not quite of the first quality but he will listen over and over again to my tales of life in Gibraltar and I sometimes read to him aloud. As the days begin to get longer I will embark on a series of dinner parties for those within the distance of a drive. In short, my dear Lizzy, I cannot thank you sufficiently for your support in London, and I am your happiest and *most* obliged sister,

Lydia Rushworth.

Lydia's handwriting was large and this missive exactly covered a double sheet; but a further piece of letter-paper was enclosed, on which was written:

The rest of this letter was written to be shown to Mr Darcy or my father or anyone else, to save me the trouble of writing, you know, but what I have now to say is for your eyes only and may be put straight into the fire. I was perfectly dumbfounded to discover that my dear James had never lived with his first wife. They had separate bedrooms from the beginning. What he has been doing in the meantime I can only conjecture but I was, in any event, obliged to show him *what to do*. Fortunately my poor Wickham had been an admirable instructor all those years ago and I have to say my pupil was a very quick learner. I now find myself sustaining visits from him three or four times a day, or night. By good luck, all the mattresses in this house were renewed at the time of his previous marriage (though I find that they never lived here at all) as I cannot at all imagine doing this in a *feather* bed. But how am I to discourage all these visits? I have really no energy for anything else. I remember that husbands were used to lock their wives into chastity belts when going to the Crusades, but have never heard of a wife doing this to herself. And even if I could bring myself to do such a thing, *where*, do you suppose, are such contraptions to be procured? I cannot quite see myself soliciting such a thing from the local blacksmith—or would it be a saddler? I am sure I am already in the family way but shall not be certain for another two weeks.

With love, my dearest Lizzy, Lydia.

Stifling her laughter, and slightly ashamed of it, Elizabeth read this over twice and then, as there was still an excellent fire in the morning-room, did as Lydia had asked. Her problem was certainly one which Elizabeth had never envisaged and it was one which seemed to admit of no solution. She knew of no one who could be consulted any more than Lydia did herself; but she amused herself by considering whether the blacksmith or the saddler should be approached, concluding that it would require a collaboration.

It was a particularly sweet home-coming. The children were well; everyone was pleased to see them. When Mr Darcy had completed his several consultations with his steward, he accompanied them on their excursions and expeditions into the park. The spring arrived quite suddenly, almost overnight. Bluebells followed the primroses, and there were cowslips on the slopes below the woods. By the end of the month, they were able to go out without their coats.

She wrote to Lydia, a letter which could be shown to anyone, as she could think of nothing to say on the private subject. She wrote to Maria and to Anne, simple letters thanking them for their hospitality; but nothing that had occurred, not even in recent weeks, had prepared her for the news contained in Anne's first letter to her.

Rosings, April 28th

I am sitting here quite stunned, my dearest Elizabeth, helpless and breathless, wondering if indeed what has just transpired has really happened; or if I have not just imagined the whole. Perhaps if I write it down I shall be able to believe it, so I will do so now. Mr Collins, at the suggestion of his Bishop, is to lead an Anglican Mission to the Coromandel Coast, that is to say, in *India*. He leaves the country at the end of next month, embarking at the North Fleet in Kent, less than thirty miles from here, so that at least is quite convenient. His voyage is to last for quite four months, with calls at Madeira, St Helena, the Cape and Mauritius, ending at Madras, where their Mission is to be established. He is to be accompanied by two younger clergymen with their wives, and *he* is to accompany the two young daughters of a Mr Bird, Collector of Masulipatam. All this I have understood, but it is not yet *digested*! Of Madras I know nothing, beyond its calicos and muslins, save that it is hot, sultry and unhealthy. Mr Collins would appear to be signing his own death warrant and, as a Christian (I do not say as his *wife*!) I asked him if I had contributed towards his arrival at this extraordinary decision. He replied that I *had*, but only insofar as I had relieved him of the responsibility of his daughters. He was now able to devote the remainder of his life to the Lord. Had the Bishop *pressed* him to agreement, I asked him further. Had he been obliged to confess his marriage? He hesitated a little there, finally replying that he had not. The Bishop considered his single condition ideal for the situation and he himself felt it would be easier to remain celibate in India than it would be in Hunsford. In the end he confessed to me, as I think he could see how much discomposed I was by his news, that he believed himself entirely responsible for the death of his wife and he hoped the Lord would accept the rest of his life as a sacrifice.

29th. Reading what I wrote yesterday makes it all clear. The decision is made. I cannot alter it nor do I think I would do so if I could. I do not think his daughters will miss him. I am sure I shall not but I cannot entirely accept a situation very advantageous to me without feeling it will have to be paid for at some time.

Enough of this. We are all well. I told Mrs J. and Miss L. today at breakfast and said frivolously that I must look about me for a new parson. Whereupon Miss Linton instantly said that she knew of an excellent young man now a curate somewhere in Bristol. In whom, she did not add, she had an interest. But I think we should wave farewell to Mr Collins first. It would be entertaining all to go and see him set sail. I shall suggest that he inform the Bishop of his marriage just before he does, as being the best safeguard for his daughters. If Miss Linton should indeed marry and settle in the Parsonage here the view from the nursery will be almost *too* beguiling!

I have decided not to rebuild the farm at Quarry End, but to build instead a small orphanage for twenty girls, who should be trained in all the domestic arts with a view to going out as housekeepers. Quite where they are to be found I do not know at present but no doubt they will have been discovered by the time the roof is on.

It is not yet one year since my mother died. I do not believe anyone ever had twelve months so full of unusual events, not the least of which is my improved knowledge of you and cousin Fitzwilliam. Pray let us meet again before the summer is quite over. Meanwhile this letter brings to you the love of your devoted sister,

Anne.

Five minutes after she had read this for the second time, Elizabeth heard Mr Darcy come back from his morning walk. She found him in one of the smaller drawing-rooms and handed him her letter. He read it through quickly and then returned to the first part, without speaking. When he gave it back to her he said, with the smile that could still cause her heart to flutter: "Well, my love, I think we can no longer have *any* cause to doubt—that there is a God in Heaven, even if He appears to have selected His chosen instrument somewhat at random."

"I cannot quite feel that he is the one person to be sent—to advertise the Christian religion."

"Perhaps, if he listens carefully enough to his own sermons, he will learn to behave better."

"And the greatest glory of it all is that, no matter what disasters may befall him, we shall not be there. It appears to be a situation entirely without drawback and I only hope that my poor Charlotte is able to see it."

"Of course she is, my love. She and Lady Catherine are sitting together, looking down—on a very substantial cloud."

"Oh, please do not jest about that—*my* love. I just trust that you may be wrong. More than enough to make one change one's mind—about trying to go to Heaven. It is enough indeed to make one think—about going elsewhere."

Mr Darcy laughed.

"But Lady Lucas might be there," he said. "George Wickham, certainly. Mr Crawford. Maria's aunt in Buxton. The possibilities do not end. Better, I think, just to go on as before."

"Well, I suppose," said Elizabeth. "You must be right, of course. As always. But—what about those Bishops? How are we to avoid them?

"I leave that to yourself to decide," said Mr Darcy.

Words for Today
2009
Notes for daily Bible reading

Words for today 2009

IBRA

International Bible Reading Association

Words for Today aims to build understanding and respect for a range of religious perspectives and approaches to living practised in the world today, and to help readers meet new challenges in their faith. Views expressed by contributors should not, however, be taken to reflect the views or policies of the Editor or the International Bible Reading Association.

The International Bible Reading Association's scheme of readings is listed monthly on the Christian Education website at www.christianeducation.org.uk/ibra_scheme.php and the full scheme for 2009 may be downloaded in English, Spanish and French.

Cover photograph – Sarah Bruce
Editor – Nicola Slee

Published by:
The International Bible Reading Association
1020 Bristol Road
Selly Oak
Birmingham B29 6LB
United Kingdom

Charity number 211542

ISBN 978-1-905893-02-7
ISSN 0140-8275

Designed and typeset by Christian Education Publications
Printed and bound in Slovenia by 1010 Printing

Contents

Editorial

I am writing this editorial on Palm Sunday, not long back from church where we have had the traditional, long dramatic reading of the Passion story – this year performed by a group of young people. What better occasion to remind me of the power of scripture, particularly when read aloud, and read well, to move, to challenge, to disturb, to unsettle, to get under the skin? Though I know this story well, I can never feel comfortable or complacent as I join in the part of the crowd, shouting 'Crucify him!' and listen to the unfolding tale of betrayal, violence and self-offering.

Yet, powerful as scripture is to speak to us, it needs commentary, explanation and thoughtful study to interpret its message. There's a wonderful saying of the rabbis that Solomon had three thousand parables to illustrate every verse in scripture. And even God is pictured, by the rabbis, as studying the Bible, as if the very author of the word expects to find new things there! In my own church and in thousands throughout the world, Christians will spend the next week reliving and exploring just some of the layers of meaning of the Passion story. We'll do so in many ways: in sermon, meditation, silence, symbolic gesture and action (such as the foot-washing and the Good Friday walk of witness), in song and hymnody, in credal response and intercessory prayer. And many people will help in that task of opening up and reflecting on the scriptures – not only the trained clergy and lay ministers but others, too, like the young people who performed the Passion story today in my church, and a whole host of those who will take part in bringing the liturgy of Holy Week to life.

In a similar way, I hope that the many different writers assembled for you in this year's *Words for Today* will help you to open up the scriptures and unlock some of their power – a power that is both ancient and ever new, a power that speaks in many different voices to the many different contexts and needs of our contemporary world.

Nicola Slee – Editor

Prayers

O God, give me a spirit of expectancy as I read the scriptures, a wise, enquiring mind and a heart attuned to your presence. Speak to me today a new word of life: whether that be a word of comfort, challenge, disturbance or surprise. And give me the courage to put your word of life into action.

Nicola Slee

O Lord, be gracious unto us! In all that we hear or see, in all that we say or do, be gracious unto us.

Beduin prayer

From the unreal lead me to the real. From darkness lead me to light. From death lead me to immortality.

The Upanishads

Lead me, O God, and I will follow, willingly if I am wise, but if not willingly I still must follow.

Early Stoic prayer

Even if I have gone astray, I am thy child, O God; thou art my father and mother.

Arjan, seventeenth-century Sikh

Thou, O God, canst never forsake me so long as I am capable of thee.

Nicolas of Cusa

How to use a 'quiet time'

Pay attention to your body Take time to slow down, consciously relax each part of your body, and listen to your breathing for a while.

Use silence to relax and empty your mind of all that's going on around you. Know that God's loving presence encircles you, your family, your community and the world. Learn to enjoy God's presence.

Have a visual focus – a cross, a plant, interesting stones, pictures or postcards.... Create a prayer table on which to display them with other symbols.

Read the **Bible passage** for the day several times, perhaps using different translations, and then the notes. Allow the words to fill your mind. Try to discover their message for you and the world around you.

Listen Remember that the most important part of prayer is to hear what God is saying to us. God speaks to us through the words of scripture, the daily news, and often through people around us.

Include the world Hold the news of the day in your mind. Enter the situation of those you hear or read about and try to pray alongside them and with them.

Pray without ceasing Prayer is not only 'the quiet time' we set aside. It becomes part of the whole of life, a continuous dialogue between God and ourselves, through all that we do and think and say: a growing awareness of the loving presence of God who travels with us and never leaves us.

Acknowledgements and abbreviations

GNB   *Good News Bible* (The Bible Societies/Collins Publishers)
– Old Testament © American Bible Society 1976; New
Testament © American Bible Society 1966, 1971, 1976.

NIV   Scripture quotations taken from *The Holy Bible, New
International Version* © 1973, 1978, 1984 by International
Bible Society. Used by permission of Hodder & Stoughton
Limited. All rights reserved. 'NIV' is a registered trademark of
International Bible Society. UK trademark number 1448790.

NJB   Taken from the *New Jerusalem Bible*, published and copyright
1985 by Darton, Longman and Todd Ltd and Doubleday &
Co. Inc., and used by permission of the publishers.

NSRV *New Revised Standard Version* © 1989, Division of Christian
Education of the National Council of Churches of Christ in
the United States of America.

REB   *Revised English Bible*© Oxford University and Cambridge
University Presses 1989.

RSV   *The Holy Bible, Revised Standard Version* © 1973, Division of
Christian Education of the National Council of Churches of
Christ in the United States of America.

BCE   Before the Common Era. BCE and CE are used by some
writers instead of BC and AD.

*   indicates that a reading appears in the Revised Common
Lectionary for that week.

Photo on p.88 ©Helen Lambie

Who is Jesus?

1 Epiphanies of Jesus

Notes based on the New Revised Standard Version
by Peter Privett

Peter Privett is an Anglican priest and European co-ordinator for Godly Play. Godly Play seeks to honour the spiritual lives of children and offers a safe space for them to explore and question their religious experience. It offers the languages of play and story so that children can be supported to make meaning for themselves. Adults and children are seen as co-teachers and -travellers on the journey. (See Jerome Berryman, The Complete Guide to Godly Play, *Living the Good News, 2002.)*

Definitions of the word 'epiphany' from the *Oxford English Dictionary* include: 'to reveal, to bring to light, to make known, to declare, to expose, to make manifest'. There is a sense in which the very act of being is itself an epiphany. It is. I am.

Linked to the declaration of the revelation is a response, some perception, awareness, or understanding of that which is revealed. But this may take time, as the initial revelation often is so intense that a variety of emotions is experienced. It is. I see.

The language of epiphany is also varied. It is rarely to do with logic and argument. Words often slip and slide in their meanings and sometime evaporate into thin air. Other language systems come into play. The languages of image, symbol, drama, myth, poetry, song, and the non-verbal give form to the Epiphany of Christ.

Who is Jesus?

Divine drama

It seems like a divine drama, and the mode of the Epiphany takes on theatrical qualities. It begins in darkness, a group of outcasts waiting and watching. Suddenly there is a creature of light that evokes a deep sense of fear. Feelings of fear are met with a message of deliverance from fear, focused in the word 'Saviour'. The sign is a baby.

It is quite ordinary on one level. Here is Jesus. But then the drama is intensified as the ordinary is understood on another level. The dark veil, the night-painted curtain at the front of the stage is drawn back to reveal the glory of God, and not just one creature of light but a multitude, a whole host.

God's presence enters the world. Glory shines around. An ocean of sound sings glory to God. But this is not a static song. It's a hymn of up and down. The angels are the movement of God. Glory goes up to God. The peace from God comes down to the earth. Heaven and earth are wedded together. Here is Jesus. Glory and peace will again be sung at the beginning of the Passion story (Luke 19:38).

This deep epiphanic experience of union prompts the shepherds into action. They go and see the reality and again on one level it is an ordinary scene of a birth of a newborn. But this double vision produces wonder and more glory. The heavenly chorus is now accompanied by the choir of humanity singing the same song.

Glory to God in the highest and peace to people on earth.

Divine song

If yesterday's epiphany was drama then this is song. It's glory again, in song. The passage is littered with stanzas from the psalms.

What might the glory God be like? Words can't capture it entirely because, when confronted with glory, words dissolve. So singing glory might do it. Song is the language, poetry the language, of vision. Truth is encapsulated in the songs we sing in worship.

Christ reflects the glory of God. With glory comes light. The originating light is beyond vision, is too much. A beamed image, reflected likeness, is bearable – just.

The composer John Tavener, in his composition *Ikon of Light*, uses voices to create the incredible intensity of searing, penetrating light. Sometimes the first movement, called 'Phos', is so harsh and intense it becomes unbearable at times to listen.

Christ bears the same stamp of God's nature. He is the imprinted seal, the carbon copy, a duplicate. He is the reproduction, the replica, the divine facsimile, a mimetic emulation of the holy.

'Angel' doesn't do it justice. It's not enough. The songs call for closer, more filial and intimate, understandings for the musician of creation. The songs give glimpses of ethical implications too, the hymn of righteousness against lawlessness. The songs remind us of the things both temporary and eternal.

This is epiphanic song, songs of ecstasy, rapture, bliss, of imaginative vision, of joy, of losing consciousness even…

Sing: Gloria, gloria, gloria.

Who is Jesus?

Divine painting

The image of the invisible God (verse 15) connects to the previous passages. It's almost the same subject matter, but the message and truth can be expressed in a variety of media.

What might epiphanic painting lead us into?

The passage speaks about Christ not only being the agent, the means, the process of creation, but also the holder, the focus, the gatherer, the vessel, the receptacle, the frame. Painter, picture and frame are gathered together into one.

Before you paint a picture you need a creative idea, something as yet unformed, a wisp of the finished picture. The idea moves though the painter and into the raw, unformed material of pigment, clay, paint, canvas, paper or wood. The paint and materials are transformed and become something other than themselves. The process itself shapes and changes the painting and the painter. The process has a life of its own. Canvas and frame contain and gather together the intricate and multitudinous process.

The artist has to be *in* the process to reconcile the disparate natures, to reconcile the incongruence. Before all things the artist is there, before the painting. Before all things raw materials are there, before the artist. Before all things there is the silence of what might be.

This process then is the model for those who follow. It's archetypical, the ruling principle. It is the principle at the heart of the divine nature. The process that goes into the painting becomes the model for those who view.

In Christ and by Christ, through Christ and for Christ.

Silent drama

The declaration of the nature and work of Christ is seen in the two words 'Saviour' and 'Emman'u-el' (God with us). The meaning of these words is revealed in the emotional life of a betrothed couple, a couple in crisis, in distress.

Saviour and Emman'u-el can be made known in the emotional life of any couple.

It's in the relational, situational reality of the day to day. Saviour and Emman'u-el are found in the emotions of doubt and betrayal, in faithfulness and decency. Salvation and reconciliation are spoken to each other in this silent drama.

Scene 1: Severance. Mary and Joseph stand side by side, front of the stage. Both look at one another, then Joseph looks away. Mary looks down. Mary moves to the back of the stage and covers herself totally with a dark veil.

Scene 2: Dream. Joseph falls prostrate on the ground. He then kneels. Mary comes from backstage, removes the veil and kneels with Joseph. There is some distance between them. Neither looks at the other.

Scene 3: Saviour. Both characters continue to look ahead, still kneeling. A newborn child appears between them. The child has outstretched arms. Both characters turn to look at the child, ignoring each other.

Scene 4: Emmanuel. The two adults move towards the child. Both gently pick the child from the floor and together hold him. At last they face and look at each other.

Save us, God with us.

Who is Jesus?

Collage

Truths can be recognised, perceived and understood when disparate images are gathered together, compared and contrasted. Epiphanies happen when similarities and differences, comparisons and divergence are placed side by side so that insight can emerge.

Matthew seems to be creating an epiphanic collage in this narrative as he seeks to meditate upon the nature of Christ. There is the struggle between Herod and Jesus, which by association adds images of the struggle between Pharaoh and Moses. There is the worship of the Magi, foreigners who recognise the king, the ruler of the universe, set alongside and in contrast to the jealousy of Herod, who shares the same nationality as Jesus, yet wishes to annihilate the child.

These contrasts represent the struggle of different ways of seeing. There is perception that is based upon the preservation of the present order, the guarding of power, leading to panic, self-interest and jealousy. Contrast this with those who see something new and act upon it, without thought of guarding their own power. Their purpose is worship, and the consequence is a change of direction.

The collage is covered with joy, not just ordinary joy, but *great* joy: an excess of joy, vast, huge, over the top joy; ecstatic, blissful, delight-filled joy. And it leads to the central image – the child.

Perhaps excess, abandonment, the leaving of the inhibitions, lead us to see the child, whose dwelling becomes a sacred space filled with gold and incense, a mysterious house of our nobility, our holiness and our death.

Give us an excess of joy.

Mythological song

The reality of an epiphany is often so mysterious that the language of logic fails and evaporates. The language of logic can lead into paths of debate and argument, of uncharitable decisions as to who is orthodox and who a heretic.

In contrast, this passage explores the nature of Christ in poetic and deep mythological language (see J L Houlden's Pelican Commentary, *Paul's Letters From Prison*, SCM, 1977). This mystical poem tells the mysterious story of Christ. It enters the realm of the symbolic, the territory of the transcendent. As it is sung, the hope is that it will directly affect those who sing it.

Modern research has suggested that people are not persuaded by sermons, logic or argument. Story, song and mythic language have a far more profound effect.

This is a song of opposites: descent and ascent, service and exaltation. It is a song of two epiphanies. Where does reality lie? The song doesn't ask us to choose one or the other. The truth of Christ lies in the mysterious 'therefore' (verse 9): the place where these two songs intertwine. The hope is that the singer and the song should become one.

The Epiphany of Christ is revealed when the song is enacted in the community. The song is no soloist's preserve. It is about community singing.

Take me down, down, down… Raise me up, up, up….

The divine dance

This passage brings to mind those wonderful black and white films featuring Gene Kelly or Fred Astaire. One person begins to tap out a rhythm in the dance, and the other copies, then waits for more of the design. Gradually the dancers build up into a symbiotic dance of connection where teacher and pupil become a dynamic force of creativity. A similar story could be told of the prima ballerina who, in later life, passes on the steps to a generation of new dancers. The dance that once was alive in her now lives in them, and her delight is seeing their creative energy flow out to others.

Dance is embodied, articulated flesh. The heart beats fast, the blood flows powerfully around the body, muscles are taut and energised. Dance brings the body alive. To really dance is to let go, to give oneself totally to the rhythms of the divine. There's no holding on.

In the dance anything is possible: the lame leap for joy and even the dead live.

The divine dance is a direct challenge to all that would paralyse, those deathly powers that encourage fear and prevent us from functioning.

The power of the dance is an invitation to join in. Can you prevent your feet from tapping, your body from leaping – no matter how strongly you grit your teeth and clasp your arms tightly across your chest? Go on, admit it, those toes are beginning to wiggle ever so slightly!

Dance then where ever you may be.

From 'Lord of the Dance', by Sydney Carter

Sacred calligraphy

Thomas Merton is famous for his spiritual writings, but perhaps less known are his meditational drawings. The later drawings are more calligraphic and abstract and are linked to his growing interest in the spirituality of the east.

A key eastern meditation involves the freehand drawing of a circle, the letter O, with brush and ink. This is the last image used in Merton's *Dialogues and Silences*, edited by Jonathan Montaldo (SPCK, 2002). The never-ending circle, the zero, the O, could be the epiphanic calligraphy to set alongside this passage by Paul.

The calligrapher explores each part of the circle. The brush stroke of each minute arc is linked to the next. The brush strokes trace the journey of Christ, the journey of humanity. The circle starts with Christ being raised; this small arc also stretches back to the beginning of humanity. Death and life flow through the ink.

This is a cosmic drawing where power and authority cease to have relevance and meaning. The circle of resurrection has structural, systemic implications. The final struggle for existential meaning is over, for death itself is finished. The last part of the circle is a cosmic consummation, celestial completion. Even the Christ is consumed into the great O.

O silence, golden zero
Unsetting sun

                           Thomas Merton, Dialogues and Silence.

Saturday–Sunday 10–11 January   *Luke 9:18-22*

Side by side

The declaration at Caesarea Philippi challenges us to answer the question, 'Who do you say that I am?' The readings of the past week have offered a rich menu of understandings. What happens when we place all these readings side by side? How might they speak to each other?

What happens when babies and children are set alongside the one who is the means of creation, the holder and frame of the created order? How does the first fruit greet the obedient servant? In what way does the glory of God enlighten the one who enters into life-giving conversation? What does 'Saviour' really mean? How is God with us?

The possibilities of this exercise are endless.

Spend some time going back over the readings and ask the question: What might be the epiphany here? Which image speaks most strongly to you? Which is the most important? Which image of Christ could you never do without?

Who do you say that I am?

It is.

I am.

I see.

Who is Jesus?

2 A window to God

Notes based on the New Revised Standard Version
by Peter Privett

Windows let light in, sight out and vice versa. The
dictionary says that they are openings in a wall, they are framed
for the wind's eye.

Sometimes our diary says that we have a window in time,
an opportunity for action. The computer window frames
information. Opaque windows prevent sight and with darkened
windows you see out but not in.

Windows divide and separate. They create protective threshold
spaces. They sometimes enable an exchange, a two-way process.

The eyes are said to be the windows into the soul.

In this week's readings we consider different kinds of window,
and different aspects of the imagery of windows, as we reflect on
Christ as a window into God.

Who is Jesus?

Window onto love

The window opens in today's passage to reveal love.

Love is something that can be seen. It's not a feeling or an abstract idea. It has to be made concrete, enfleshed, incarnated. In the musical *My Fair Lady*, Eliza Doolittle shouts at the end of the musical: 'Don't speak of love. *Show me!*' She's had enough of talk, she wants some action.

The view from this window is the action and being of Christ. But then something more happens, because this is not a static view: it is dynamic. In the viewing, the viewer is taken over, incorporated and empowered to act in the same way as Christ.

This indwelling, dynamic vision is a vision of God. This vision of God is not one of an isolated being but a God made known in movement and empowerment. The divine is a profound power source that generates the action of love in others.

This is a powerful window, and perhaps it is not a window after all but a high-speed revolving glass door – a door that enables the viewer and the viewed to become one.

Look through a window in your home. Pray for the things that you see.
How might they become part of you and you with them?

Windows onto fragments of perception

I'm confused by this reading. It feels like walking along a dark corridor filled with small windows that only give glimpses of what might be outside. The windows are like small mysterious openings on to something that feels much bigger and larger, but as yet I don't see the whole picture.

First, there is a glimpse of a child and then, in the next opening, the parent. The space between the windows separates them but the next gives the view that they are intimately entwined and appear to be one. The subsequent window reveals that they are not alone but surrounded by a great company, connected through the dialogue of life-giving love.

A further opening reveals that love, as in yesterday's readings, is not an abstract idea but includes our ethical behaviour, the ways in which we organise and live our life together. The commandment of love is not about a negative way of life but a response to the other, a desire for connection and relationship.

Other openings reveal water and blood. They are the stuff of the real world. Love is when water and blood come together, in birth and death, in baptism and Eucharist. Love is sacramental, in that it is physically shown and declared in actions and matter, yet reveals something deeper, eternal, life-giving and more mysterious.

These fragmentary windows of perception are glimpses of part of the picture but not the whole. The view outside might be one window into the inseparable nature of things.

Create a small frame from a piece of paper. Place it on a newspaper and use the fragments as the inspiration for your intercessions.

Wednesday 14 January

John 6:35-51

A window on to highs and lows

The reading is filled with John's theology of up and down. These are not necessarily physical spaces but two dominating orders or principles. *Down* represents the egocentric activity of humanity where manipulation and control are key. I want to keep you down. *Up* has at its heart the spirit of compassionate, relational love. Which gives sustenance? In what ways does Jesus reconcile them and give hope?

The window for today's reading is one of those glass lifts on the side of a vast modern many-windowed tower block. The work of the lift is to travel up, to carry us from the depths of self-centredness to the upper reaches of love, from the ego – I – to the one who is – I AM.

I AM is not about egocentric activity but the gathering of all things to be raised up. Nothing is worthless.

This is a pretty expansive lift and the invitation is generous. There will be those who don't see any reason for travelling upwards. The view at ground level seems to be fine. But the work of the I AM, the one who comes from above, is to raise up that which is below. The process is sustaining. It is the bread of life.

The power of this many-windowed lift is sourced by the purpose of God. The irresistible draw of love attracts like a magnet. The lift that encompasses the creation of God is raised from death to life. The escalator takes us up to the top window to glimpse that which is above – who will be drawn down so that we may be drawn up.

Go to the lowest room in your home and pray for the things below. Climb up to the highest part and pray for the things above.

A window onto heaven

The window today is heavily curtained with material that has the closest weave possible and is heavily lined. The view from the window is so intense that the curtains can be parted for only a fraction of a second at a time. The response is fear and falling.

This scene is crucial in the tradition of Orthodox icons. The icon is a window into heaven. The material objects of pigment, water, egg, animal hair, wood – the substances of the earth – enable the vision of heaven. The proportions try to come close to perfection. The Transfiguration is the primal icon, and one that many writers of icons paint first. Christ is surrounded by a halo of two lights. In many old icons the pigments have aged into dark indistinguishable colours. Originally they would have been green and blue, the colours of the earth and the heavens, the divine. The window reveals in searing light the wedding of earth and heaven.

The story has these same two elements. There is the crassness of earthly ordinariness in the desire to build shelters, contrasted with the divine theophany of the shining cloud. This intense, extreme light – severe light, force-full light – cannot be endured for too long. The curtains have to be drawn across for relief. But perhaps a small peek is permitted to reveal ordinary, safe light, to reveal a view of care and compassion.

The work of Jesus is to raise up. It's the phrase used in the gospel when the sick are healed and the dead are raised. The curtains are pulled back to reveal an opening into the future, the climax of the Jesus story, a story no longer confined to time and place.

Close the curtains and pray.

Open them for a short time and pray. Open the curtains of time and pray.

Who is Jesus?

A window on to the soul of the universe

Here's another time window. It takes us back to the beginning of creation and much more. This window is like a crystal – it's multidimensional. It is the window of windows, the window from which all definitions of window might come. This opens up a space to provide a window on to the very intention of creation. This is a *big* window! This is the mystical window into the soul of the universe.

The view is not just about then but about every time and every place. This window is so huge that we can see the unity of being. 'In', 'with', 'and' merge together. 'Was', 'is', and 'will be' become one in the creative dialogue of mutuality. Difference is not seen as competitive; separation is not conflictual. Difference and separation are about completion and celebration. This is the intention, the meaning and purpose for the universe.

In fact, when this window is opened, it virtually disappears because there is no threshold, no barrier any more. Yet look again and the opposite happens. The truth of the first opening is narrowed down into the particular and the specific, as seen in the lives of John the Baptist and Jesus. Their light continues in those who live as they did. Those who live the way of letting go and receiving back receive the power of eternal life.

Open the door wide to pray. Stand at the threshold.
Imagine the window into the soul of the universe and pray.

A window onto two world orders

Here we are being offered alternatives: two windows of opportunity. One is labelled 'world' and for John this opening is unattractive, murky and uninviting. The word has negative connotations. It is based on the clash of egocentric desires. It is represented by power games and politics that consume much of our personal and social interactions. The world belongs to the realm of below, its territory is the land of 'down'. It is symbolised in the antagonism of the Pharisees' encounter with John the Baptist, and will be explored time and time again in the gospel. It dominates our relationships and is often seen as being the only real order.

John's ministry begins with a denial of the 'I'. I am not the Messiah, Elijah or the prophet (verses 25-26). This is the other opening that is offered. He points to one who will be the Lamb of God who takes away the sin of the world.

Many religious paintings have an image of a lamb carrying a flag. This is often depicted as a strong lamb, not one who is ready for the sacrificial altar, but a lamb that is powerful, one who leads. An alternative translation of verse 29 is 'the lamb who takes *up* the sin of the world'. Here is one who carries the frailty of human nature into the great glass elevator that we travelled on Wednesday. Here is one who understands and offers us another order in which to operate, an order that operates with up and down, that is humane and divine, that knows water and spirit.

Through this window heavenly doves will come and rest with us also.

Pray for the order of water and spirit, of humanity and divinity.
Pray for the realm of accompanying doves.

Widows, orphans and aliens

1 The sacred duty to care for the alien, the orphan and the widow

Notes based on the Revised English Version
by Jan Sutch Pickard

Jan Sutch Pickard is a writer and storyteller living on the Isle of Mull, and a Methodist local preacher. Having worked in the last few years as Warden of the Abbey in Iona, as a writer in residence at Southlands College in London, and as an ecumenical accompanier in Israel/Palestine she says she has now settled down, to try to be a good neighbour in a small local community.

'Women and children first' is supposed to be the rule as people make for the lifeboats in a shipwreck. Such people deserve extra care. Yet the news in any week will show that these are the first to suffer in warfare or domestic violence.

It is moving, therefore, to see how Jewish tradition and law, from very early days, emphasised the duty of caring for the most vulnerable. This week's passages make rules to live by, appeal to experience, show how the early church grew in awareness of the need to be inclusive, and reflect on the nature of faith, and of God.

Throughout, we are never allowed to forget the symbolic figures of the widow and the orphan, who have also always been real people with real needs.

Widows, orphans and aliens

Take care

'Widows and orphans,' said the woman from the printer's, as we were proofreading a book of poems. 'What do you mean?' I asked. 'That's what we call odd lines like this one: it really belongs at the end of the verse on the previous page. These "widows and orphans" are untidy. We need to watch out for them. We have to look after them – make sure they don't get lost – or we'll lose the meaning, too.'

The teaching in Exodus is not about lines of poetry but people: real widows, grieving and lonely, children who have lost their parents, with all the distress and deprivation that means; strangers in the land, who may be refugees or economic migrants and/or members of an ethnic minority. They need and deserve care. Those who neglect them – or, worse, wrong and exploit them – will feel God's anger. This passage is emphatic about that.

In Exodus we see God through the eyes of a different and often violent society. This God's justice, we're told, can be relentless. And what is the outcome when human beings try to exact God's justice? More widows, more orphans. We need to make sure we don't lose the meaning.

God, you see the sparrow fall, and know where human tears are falling too; may we never lose sight of those most needing care, nor miss the meaning of your love.

Widows, orphans and aliens

Remember!

'Bear in mind that you were slaves in Egypt and the Lord your God redeemed you...'

The message from Exodus is repeated and underlined here – and in many other places in the Old Testament. *Remembering* is a strong reason for the Israelites to act with compassion. They should know what it feels like to experience injustice or exploitation, to be marginalised. Their liberation has been a sign of God's justice. God's mercy did not leave them excluded as aliens.

But, just as in families there can be cycles of abuse, so in society – and even between nations – those who have suffered injustice often inflict the same on others. The State of Israel, which came into being as a place of refuge for a suffering people, has occupied and exploited the neighbouring Palestinian Territories for forty years; settlers take the land and soldiers often use force against unarmed civilians.

A group of Israeli citizens, the Women in Black, demonstrate every Friday in the centre of Jerusalem, with signs saying in Hebrew 'Stop the occupation'. One woman, Anna Colombo, was still demonstrating in her nineties. She lost all her family in the Holocaust, and is quoted as saying, 'My entire family was killed in Auschwitz. I was revolted that we are causing suffering to others that I myself experienced ... that is why I stand with Women in Black.'

If you can, learn more about the current situation in Israel/Palestine. And hold on to the truth about which Anna reminds us: that in many situations remembering, though painful, is vital to our humanity.

Remember some way that God has set you free. How can you pass on this blessing?

Do not oppress

In the library of books that is the Old Testament, we move to a different section. Centuries away from the books of history and law, we're among the intense visions of prophets, speaking to a suffering people, in a troubled time. But the message is consistent: one of justice and compassion.

Widows and the fatherless are mentioned again. The need to care for those with no one to protect them is recognised by many cultures. Today people in Britain take for granted a state pension and social services for the elderly, child-protection legislation and – where needed – fostering and adoption services. Counselling and self-help groups are available.

In case we take too much for granted, we need to remember that, in many parts of the world, women, often widows, often with few resources, are the main support for grandchildren and neighbours' children orphaned by AIDS. Thank God for their compassion and resilience!

What about 'the poor'? Poverty can be divisive. Instead of caring we can become guilty or judgemental. And what about 'the alien in our midst', different in language, culture, faith – an asylum seeker, maybe?

How often do we turn our backs? What do we find difficult? How might our actions oppress them? What could we do instead?

Call to mind a person you know by name, or have seen in the street, who belongs to one of these groups. Remember that he or she is also a child of God. Hold this person in prayer.

Widows, orphans and aliens

Leave no one out

Dear Peggy,

Thank you for your Christmas letter. It's good to keep in touch, especially since you lost Henry, and my Tom died within the year. I wish we lived nearer to each other. It's a lifeline to have someone to talk to, folk who understand, who speak the same language. I feel so disappointed. Tom and I wanted to move here when we retired. On holiday, it seemed a home from home. But now I'm on my own I feel an outsider, left out. Even in church – they won't let me help. I don't feel welcome.

I need company and conversation to keep my mind alive! Peggy, what can I do?

Love, Jane.

Jane's present-day problem reflects a situation in the early church, which was keeping up time-honoured Jewish traditions of looking after the most vulnerable. 'There was never a needy person among them' (Acts 4:34) because, after Pentecost, resources were shared in a new, more radical, way.

But problems still developed. In a cosmopolitan city, this Jewish community included 'incomers' who spoke Greek. Some were widows, struggling to survive. While Jane's letter is about emotional support, also important, these women in Jerusalem needed daily bread. When food was shared, the 'outsiders' were missing out. So the disciples reorganised the church – appointing deacons – to make the sharing fairer.

Do you see people being left out in your community? If so, what can you do?

Thank God for those who speak a language that we can all understand: the language of love.

Widows, orphans and aliens

Act on it!

The passages we've read this week are strong on practicality – about the widow's cloak (how else would she keep warm?), the detail of gleaning in cornfields, and at olive harvest; readiness to reorganise the church to be more inclusive and effective. Faith is spelled out in the small print of social caring.

This very frank letter of James, circulating in the early church, goes further. It declares that religion that is uncaring is worth nothing. A form of words, or a superficial observance, isn't religion at all.

Religion is an interesting word. From the Latin, it contains ideas of tying things together – making connections. What does this letter mean by 'religion'? Not just a faith group; something deeper than an intellectual position or a formal statement of belief. It brings together a whole bundle of meanings: reading scripture (or listening to it) (verse 22); recognising the truth (verse 23); remembering (verse 25a); relating to God and to other people (verse 27); really acting on what you believe (verse 25b).

And who gains from this making of connections, this putting faith into practice? The most vulnerable people – widows and orphans among them. And also ourselves, as we discover our integrity and act with compassion.

I look in the mirror. What do I see?
Me – that's enough, isn't it? I know what I look like.
But who am I?
The answer is more than skin deep:
I am a child of God.
Father, show me just how I am like you;
help me to do what you would do.

Widows, orphans and aliens

Celebrate God's compassion

Yesterday's reading reminded us that caring for those most in need is at the heart of our life as believers. If we need a reason, then we can listen to the psalmist celebrating God's generous love.

This powerful God, maker of heaven and earth, is, says the psalmist, a much more reliable source of help than any earthly ruler, however benign, for they are all mortal and fallible. The corruptions of power seen in our own century have had their equivalents through the years. But 'God's faithfulness is for ever'. God's power, which is used in the cause of justice, satisfyingly 'thwarts the course of the wicked'.

God's priorities turn those of dictators upside down, with an option for the poor. So this psalm, which has much in common with the Magnificat, sings of a God who cares most for the least: for people who are oppressed, the hungry, prisoners, those who are blind, bowed down with illness, poverty or grief, for strangers/outsiders – and for widows and fatherless children.

All week we've remembered the duty of each society to care for the vulnerable. We call such actions humane actions. Such compassion is also integral to God's nature. The apostle Paul, whose feast day is today (Sunday), wrote to the Corinthians about love – human love and God's love, reflecting each other: 'At present we see only puzzling reflections in a mirror – but one day we shall see face to face' (1 Corinthians 13:12).

Reflect on Paul's words.

Widows, orphans and aliens

2 Sojourners and aliens

Notes based on the Hebrew Bible and the Revised
Standard Version by Rachel Montagu

*Rachel Montagu has worked as a congregational rabbi.
Now she is the Scholar in Residence at the Council of Christians and
Jews and teaches biblical Hebrew for Birkbeck College's Faculty of
Continuing Education.*

The relationship of those who are temporary residents – not, or
sometimes not yet, full citizens – and those among whom they
live, is an important biblical theme. When the matriarchs and
patriarchs travelled from their birthplace to Canaan, at first they
were strangers among those who were already there. Because
the patriarchs found wives from their family of origin, Sarah,
Rebecca, Rachel and Leah were all newcomers to Canaan. Isaac
and Jacob were born there but lived as new immigrants among
the Canaanite tribes. Ruth accompanied her mother-in-law
Naomi from her homeland in Moab back to Bethlehem; her story
has been described as a counterblast to Ezra and Nehemiah's
rulings against foreign marriages (Ezra 10:2-5, Nehemiah
13:23-27). The word 'ger' means sojourner or temporary
resident. In post-biblical Judaism, *ger tsedek*, righteous sojourner,
is the word for converts. The book of Ruth is read in synagogues
on Shavuot, which commemorates the covenant and giving of
the Ten Commandments; this tells Jews that those who enter the
Jewish community through conversion are as much part of the
congregation as the descendants of those who stood at Mount
Sinai. However important national boundaries are to us, Isaiah
reminds us that God says, 'my thoughts are not your thoughts'.
Jonah 4:10-11 and Amos 9:7 teach that all humanity are God's
creatures under God's care.

Widows, orphans and aliens

Abraham – patriarch or pimp?

This is the second of three 'my wife, my sister' episodes (see Genesis 12:10-20 and 26:1-16) in which Abraham and Isaac pretended their wives were their sisters to protect themselves from attack by foreign hosts who might covet these beautiful women. Both times Abraham received substantial gifts – immoral earnings? Isaac was unmasked when King Avimelech (a long-lived monarch or a dynasty using the same name?) saw him and Rebecca 'playing'. Abraham's deception was revealed by God sending the king either a plague or a dream.

Pharaoh and Avimelech seem nobler than the patriarchs here. Traditional Jewish interpretation teaches us that, though the first time Abraham consulted Sarah, this time he does it 'without her will or consent'. Sarah's feelings alone in Avimelech's or Pharaoh's palace can only be imagined; sexually vulnerable and doubly alienated, she is the alien Abraham's alienated wife, their relationship is unacknowledged and her beauty feared as a mortal risk to her husband rather than a source of delight.

God tells Avimelech that Abraham is a prophet and will pray for him; this is the first reference to prophecy or use of the verb *hitpalel*, pray, in the Bible. One of the themes of Abraham's story is recognising the holiness of the other; Abraham, Avimelech and Melchitsedek recognised each other's awareness of God across their cultural differences.

When considering how to help refugees and asylum seekers, do we consider sufficiently carefully men and women's different experiences and needs?

Blessed are you, Eternal our God, who lifts up those bent low.

Widows, orphans and aliens

Ups and downs between Israel and Egypt

Jacob and his sons moved from living among others in Canaan, the land God promised them, to living as temporary strangers in Egypt. The word Jacob used for his lifetime, *m'guri*, is from the root 'gur', meaning newcomers and temporary residents, although a more straightforward word for 'dwell' is used when discussing with Pharaoh where Joseph's family will live. Joseph exploited the Egyptians' dislike of shepherds (46:32-34) to negotiate an area where his family could live without mixing. Historians debate how integrated they later became into Egyptian society.

The Holocaust originated in Germany, which had one of the most integrated Jewish communities in the world, although it later destroyed Jewish communities elsewhere in Europe who lived lives very separate from their fellow-citizens.

Ancient Egypt did not grant sojourners' rights; the Pharaoh who appointed Joseph to rule over his land (41:40-43) was happy to welcome Joseph's family but when 'a new king arose who did not know Joseph' (Exodus 1:8) he was able to enslave them, exploiting xenophobia. The bitterness of their lives as slaves led to the command in Leviticus 19:34 to treat strangers and temporary residents as equals and love them 'because you were a stranger in the land of Egypt' and should understand how it feels.

For action

- Find a local organisation that helps or campaigns for refugees and asylum-seekers, and help its work.

- Read a book by someone who came to your country as a refugee.

Blessed are you, Eternal, who loves righteousness and justice.

Widows, orphans and aliens

A house of prayer for all

The role of the prophet is to pass on God's message; the call to act justly and with righteousness is a recurring theme in the prophets' books, as is the hope that all will recognise God. In this chapter, eunuchs (excluded from the community in Deuteronomy 23:1) and foreign converts, who might consider themselves without any future hope from God, are explicitly included in the imminent salvation. Chapter 58 prioritises feeding the hungry over fasting and sacrifices; both there and in this chapter the sabbath is not a ritual less important than helping those in need but a vital part of God's covenant and a way to delight in God's presence (58:13-14). The foreigners here are those who have converted to Judaism to serve and love the Eternal. However this is still a universalist passage; God's house will be open for all to pray there.

The Hebrew used here for memorial, *Yad VaShem* – literally 'hand and name' – is the name of the Jerusalem Holocaust Museum where those of all nations who helped rescue Jews during the Holocaust are commemorated on the Avenue of the Righteous. They were people who ignored the thinking behind Nazi persecution, that Jews and gypsies were aliens, not part of the countries in which they were citizens and could be separated out for persecution, and risked their lives to love their neighbour (Leviticus 19:18).

Blessed are you, Eternal, whose name is goodness and whom it is pleasant to praise.

Ruth – vulnerable foreign widow or ruthless pursuer?

'Foreignness' is a key theme in Ruth. Did Naomi try to send her daughters-in-law home because they would be happier in their own culture? Because the rules designed to protect childless widows (Deuteronomy 25:5-10) would complicate their lives? Because her reintegration would be harder accompanied by foreigners? Ruth is portrayed as loyal and loving to Naomi but hints appear of the fear of the sexual immorality of foreign women, common in many cultures. Were they so poor they needed the corn Ruth would glean (2:2), meant as subsistence for the most vulnerable, widows, orphans and strangers (Deuteronomy 24:21)? Or is her prime purpose finding another husband? Ruth reports that Boaz said she should stay close to his young men; Naomi tactfully suggests working with his young women (2:21-22).

In 2:10 Ruth describes herself as *nochriah*, a far stronger word for foreigner than *ger*, the word used for the patriarchs in Canaan and in Leviticus 19:34. Ruth's undertaking to Naomi (1:16-17) became a prototype for conversion but she is obviously still regarded as 'that Moabite'.

Boaz, whose name means 'with strength', (contrasted to Machlon, 'sickly'), clearly understands what Ruth has done: like Abraham, she has left her family and birthplace. His blessing reflects his religious character as clearly as 'not as one of your handmaids' (verse 13) is Ruth's signal that she deserves better.

How can we learn to challenge ourselves when we stereotype people because of their origins?

Blessed is the Eternal who shelters us under the wings of the Shechinah, the divine presence.

Friday 30 January

Widows, orphans and aliens

God's shepherd, God's anointed

Jewish high priests and kings were consecrated to their task by anointing with oil (see Leviticus 4). Was Cyrus the Persian king similarly consecrated or does *m'shicho*, 'his anointed', here simply mean God appointed him to the task of rebuilding the temple? Cyrus is also called 'my shepherd', a title resonant with symbolism: the patriarchs, Moses and David were all shepherds. 'Shepherd' and 'anointed' explain 'I have given you an honoured title' in verse 4. Just as Nebuchadnezzar, the king of Babylon who destroyed the temple, was God's agent, punishing the people for idol-worship (Jeremiah 25:7-9), so Cyrus was seen as God's agent in rebuilding the temple, doing so because he recognised God – see Ezra 1. 'You did not know me' does not contradict Ezra – 'you did not know me before' – (understood) but you have come to know me. Is this an early example of interfaith co-operation?

There is a word play in Hebrew in verse 1 that does not survive translation – the word for 'loose' or weakened loins is the same as 'open' doors. The words on God's nature in verse 7 are quoted in Jewish liturgy but with a significant alteration – instead of 'create evil,' the prayer says 'create all'. This verse can be read as an attack on dualistic Persian beliefs in a god of light and a god of darkness.

Blessed are you, Eternal our God, who spreads a shelter of peace over us and over the people of Israel and over all the world.

How to be good?

Jesus quotes Leviticus 19:18 and Deuteronomy 6:5 as the summary of the commandments. Concisely summarising all the biblical commandments was popular among the early rabbis. Rabbi Akiva also suggested that 'Love your neighbour as yourself' was the greatest principle of the Torah. 'Love your neighbour' was included in the Book of Jubilees' version of the seven commandments the righteous of all nations must keep to earn eternal life.

Rabbi Lionel Blue has said that our hands must be the hands of God, working in the world to give others the help they need. New immigrants, temporary residents and minorities should give and receive as well as those who are part of the establishment, 'the great and the good'. The Samaritans were defeated by John Hyrcanus c128 BCE and later supported the Romans against the Jews during the Bar Kochba revolt 135 CE. Hence they were not collectively the friendliest of neighbours to the Jews; yet this Samaritan overcame any prejudice to give help, fulfilling Leviticus 19:18 and 34.

In Avot de-Rabbi Natan, it says: 'Who is the greatest hero? One who turns an enemy into a friend.' By helping him, the Samaritan sees the robbed and wounded Jew as a friend. Those of us like the priest and Levite, whose lives are so busy we cannot easily make time to help others, may thus deprive ourselves.

How do we decide how much of our time and money we can spare for others?

Blessed are you who provides for my every need.

Widows, orphans and aliens

3   Widows and orphans

Notes based on the Revised English Version
by Godfrey Chigumira

*Godfrey Chigumira is an Anglican minister-trainee
at St Michael's College in Cardiff, researching on the empowerment
of women against HIV/AIDS. He grew up in Zimbabwe, southern
Africa, a region where HIV/AIDS has left many women widowed
and children orphaned, where he worked as a pastor supporting
women suffering from HIV/AIDS.*

This week's readings on widows and orphans remind us of the
widows and orphans affected and infected by HIV/AIDS in the
world today. HIV/AIDS has created a difficult moment not only
for the widows and orphans, but for the church as well, by
shaking the very foundations and meaning of life: individuality,
family, culture, community, religion itself. The plight of widows
and orphans brings the church face to face with its strengths,
failures, sinfulness and frailty. The church is cornered, with no
place to hide and no way of pretending to be what it is not. What
is best and worst in the church is being exposed.

For some, the church is falling from grace. Yet HIV/AIDS is
also a moment of grace and opportunity. The church can show
its salvific colours by ensuring that widows and orphans are
empowered to overcome their tragedies. It can more resolutely
seize the opportunity to care, to provide hope, and to nurture
the lives of devastated widows and orphans. To curb the
multiplicity of social, cultural, economic and political evils that
nurture the infection, the church also needs to work towards
changing the whole complex worldview of domineering powers
and institutions that shape society and make widows and orphans
vulnerable to HIV/AIDS.

Dismissed without favour

Anna's marriage must have been painfully short, and the rigours of 'worshipping night and day, fasting and praying' (verse 37) must have made her widowhood difficult. No doubt many in her position would have opted to remarry.

For many women widowed through AIDS, however, marriage can last no longer than a year, and their widowhood no longer than Anna's seven years of marriage. With most infected, remarrying is no option. Their own temples they never leave are the orphaned children left in their care. Their daily fast is the hard labour they endure in hunger, poverty and sickness to feed the children. Unlike the contented Simeon, too often their day of the Lord's coming happens prematurely and they are dismissed without experiencing much of the Lord's favour.

Jesus answers Anna's years of longing, waiting and hoping by his appearance to her in person. In his physical body, already over-shadowed by the cross, Anna saw the world as saved and God's glory shining on all. Yet in our day and age still, many widows experience unimaginable condemnation, torment, toil and pain in their bodies.

What tangible difference can I make to the lives of widows desperate for AIDS drugs and human dignity?

Lord, may my physical presence in this world prompt me to make a difference to the lives of widows living under the darkness of HIV/ AIDS. Dispel from me lack of courage to make your glory shine on all damaged, distorted and broken lives.

The reluctant Elijah

Women widowed through HIV/AIDS may relate to the widow of Zarephath's circumstances in many ways. Like her, many live in a drought situation, their lives bordering on starvation; they alone must provide for themselves and their children, without help. Many are hopeless and in despair, ready to surrender to death.

God, however, shows he did not want this widow and her child to starve. Neither does God want women widowed through HIV/AIDS to starve. There is more than enough food for all. Thirty to forty per cent of the food processed in the developed world is thrown away. While many poor widows die of malnutrition-related illnesses, obesity is becoming an 'epidemic' in some parts of the developed world. A third of children underweight in Africa will never achieve their full potential, while a third are overweight elsewhere. All God needs are 'Elijahs' who will get his providence and food to the starving. Unfortunately for many widows and children, 'Elijah' very often never comes and some starve to death.

How can I be a non-reluctant Elijah?

Help us, dear Lord, to cultivate self-value, self-confidence and self-esteem in women. May our churches, cultural, social and political institutions, business and charity organisations desist from nurturing images of women that show little care for their own wellbeing.

February

HIV/AIDS is largely an injustice!

Christianity easily identifies with peace, soft-heartedness, readiness to forgive or to turn the other cheek. Concepts of toughness, aggressiveness, fighting on and never giving up seem to depict violence and to contradict Jesus' meekness. Often this understanding makes Christians ineffective in bringing about change, incapable of facing challenges, and even vulnerable to oppression. Hence Christians have often worried and prayed long against injustice, but have actually done little to support their prayers. Perennial questions such as why many women are poor, become vulnerable widows, or lack education, medicine, food, housing, property ownership and employment are frequently at the heart of Christian thinking and worship, but not so much of Christian action.

Hence 2000 years after Jesus started transforming the world, we still find it acceptable that some people die of preventable diseases and lack of medicine. The parable of the persistent widow can illustrate how the injustice of women's infection, suffering and widowhood can continue unabated if not importunately confronted. Unlike the popular Christian attitude, this widow refuses to accept her vulnerability. She is an aggressive fighter of revolutionary integrity. She is not afraid of sweating and tiring her legs on her way repeatedly to make her plea. And so she attains justice!

How can justice be attained for women against violence, cultural male superiority, economic dependence on men, international trade agreements or debts and governmental under-representation?

Lord, help us to grasp our capability to ensure justice for women against HIV/AIDS!

Widows, orphans and aliens

The Christian challenge of gender imbalance

In societies most affected by HIV/AIDS, the majority of women are communal farmers providing most of the hard labour and producing most of the food. Land is one of the most fundamental resources for women's empowerment against HIV/AIDS. Yet land and property access is largely indirect, through men. Lack of entitlement to land and property restricts women's economic options, reduces their personal security and their collateral, increases violence against them, and causes their poverty and homelessness.

The request by the daughters of Zelophehad shows how laws can be challenged and changed to rectify gender imbalances, even in the most patriarchal culture. The daughters knew how to interpret the law. Our challenge is to overcome women's socio-economic difficulties such as illiteracy, lack of training, of management experience and advice. They had the courage to challenge injustice. Our challenge is to bring change to those societies often bent on making women ever more docile through intimidation, retaliation and allegations of turning against one's culture. The procedure the daughters used of going before Moses, the priest and the whole congregation – rather than sending a male representative – was simple. How can we help women in our day who often go through complicated procedures of resolving property-grabbing that presuppose plenty of time, literacy, patience, access to shelter, knowledge of rights and resources for travelling?

Dear Lord, Moses gave these women a listening, sympathetic ear and was supportive. May we be responsive to women who face unsympathetic judicial officials, irresponsive administrations, police unwillingness to prosecute property-grabbing, or lack of written wills.

Rescue them or they die

If Jehosheba had not rescued Joash, Athaliah would have killed him. If we do not rescue children orphaned by AIDS, AIDS and its impacts kill many. It is as simple as that.

As more young women die, older women, often widows, usually impoverished, and some psychologically overwhelmed by HIV/AIDS, now look after a lot more orphans than before. The orphans, not surprisingly, usually do not get enough of the care, medicine and food they need.

2 Kings 11 can remind us that children orphaned by AIDS are in need of every little effort we can contribute to their wellbeing. Joash's seven-year hiding in the temple symbolises the period of peace, innocence and protection children should enjoy. We should not be content with most of our excuses when the suffering of most innocent children is preventable.

Great reforms often begin with one person. Jehosheba can be credited with preserving from extinction the royal seed through which God had promised the Messiah, and her single life began the religious reforms directed by Joash.

Jehoiada provided the Lord's written instructions for a king and presided over the renewing of the national covenant. Does not our duty with orphans extend to bringing them up according to God's law?

Jehosheba's environment had become ruthless to children. Even when surrounded by social and cultural indifference to orphans, may we still make a difference to children's lives.

Lover of sinners, inspire us to love the innocent.

Widows, orphans and aliens

The sexually enslaved

In Esther's society, it seemed a great privilege for any woman to become the king's wife. It is, however, difficult to overlook some parallels between her life experience and the experiences of abused girl-children orphaned through AIDS.

In some societies men are allowed to have sexual relations with many women, and they use their power and money to lure orphaned girls for sexual favours. Many orphaned girls are valued not for what they are as persons, but for what they can offer sexually. Some orphaned girls are given up by their relatives and guardians for the sex trade or trafficking as a survival strategy.

A few contrasts between Esther's situation and that of many orphaned girls can be made as well. While Mordecai brought up Esther 'as his own daughter', some orphaned girls cared for by relatives are treated as a burden to be got rid of. While Esther gave herself up to the king as part of the king's edict, some relatives of girl orphans and guardians allow child trafficking for their own economic gains. Whereas Esther's relationship with the king led to her empowerment and that of the Jewish people, many orphaned girl-children end up becoming infected themselves, thus leading to even greater enslavement.

How can Christianity make a difference in such cases?

Lord, may your grace enable us to fight against child abuse, especially exploitation of girl-children, who often become vulnerable because of deprivation. Show us how we may become involved in the fight against the AIDS pandemic that has ruined the lives of many girl-children.

Nehemiah

I Rebuilding the walls of Jerusalem

Notes based on the Hebrew text by Pete Tobias

*Pete Tobias is rabbi of the Liberal Synagogue, Elstree, in Hertfordshire. In addition to his ministerial duties, Pete is also an author of books (*Liberal Judaism: A Judaism for the Twenty-First Century *was published in 2007) and many articles. Pete can be heard regularly offering a 'Pause for Thought' and other reflections on BBC Radio 2. Pete is a devoted fan of Watford Football Club!*

Two and a half thousand years ago, the people of Judah were exiled in Babylon. The Persians, who defeated the Babylonians some seventy years later, offered the exiles the opportunity to return to their ancestral home. Many took up this invitation; more remained in Babylon.

Nehemiah, who enjoyed a privileged position in the court of the Persian king, was in the latter category. When Nehemiah heard that the city of Jerusalem was in ruins, he determined to return to the home of his ancestors and his religion to rebuild the city and re-establish its cultural and religious life.

This was an enormous challenge. The nature of that challenge and Nehemiah's success will be more closely considered in next week's readings. This week's thoughts are focused on the challenges we set ourselves. Nehemiah was devastated by the news of Jerusalem's destruction but turned that devastation into an inspired project of reconstruction. As we follow his achievements, let us consider what are our visions – personal, communal and global – and how we enlist the support and deal with the opposition of others as we seek to implement them.

Nehemiah

February

Prayer must lead to action

How often has the arrival of distressing news forced us – often despite ourselves – to think of praying? No matter how cynical or dismissive people might be about the existence of God, the words that most often fall from the lips of those receiving bad tidings are 'Oh my God…' This was Nehemiah's response to the news about Jerusalem. Nehemiah had a strong belief in God, so his words were genuine and his response – weeping, fasting and praying to God – entirely consistent.

Another human reaction to such bad news is to seek an explanation for catastrophic events. Nehemiah does this also, reminding himself of the sins of the people of Judah that led to their exile. Having prayed, and reached this conclusion, he might then have been consoled and returned to his work as the Persian king's wine taster.

But prayer is not meant only to console us. It should also inspire us to act. The true test of the strength of Nehemiah's prayer lies in its effect on him: as a result of it he is inspired to return to Jerusalem to begin his awesome challenge of reconstruction.

Let us learn to see prayer as a call to action and let us test the sincerity of our prayer by what it encourages us to achieve.

'Words only lead us to the edge of action. But it is deeds that bring us close to God and humanity.'

Rabbi Albert H Friedlander z'l (RIP)

Dream on!

Convincing ourselves of the need to take action is difficult enough; convincing others can be even more challenging. Nehemiah finds sympathy for his concerns from the king and is encouraged to undertake his task of rebuilding the walls of Jerusalem. His first request is for royal letters to guarantee his safe conduct from Persia to Jerusalem. The opposition to his task is also highlighted for the first time in the persons of Sanballat the Horonite and Tobiah the Ammonite. These gentlemen, whose motives are unclear, display implacable and unwavering hostility to Nehemiah's vision of a rebuilt Jerusalem.

Each of us has, at some time, sought to build our own Jerusalem, to achieve a goal that we have set ourselves. Having found within ourselves the courage and determination to undertake the task, we invariably encounter opposition. We may not have access to a king to grant us letters guaranteeing our safety. But we can seek such encouragement and protection from a deeper source: from the God who dwells within and beyond us, giving us guidance, safety and determination to move forward with our task.

Nehemiah was not put off by the schemes and plans of Sanballat and Tobiah, nor was he dismayed by the immensity of the task that confronted him when he saw the desperate state of Jerusalem. Let us similarly rise to the challenges we face in our lives.

'You may laugh and mock my dreams! But my dreams shall yet come true'.

Saul Tchernikovsky

Nehemiah

Jerusalem wasn't built in a day

We would all like to change the world. We each have our own vision of Jerusalem – an idealised picture of how we would like the future to be. The first task in realising our vision is to enlist the help of those who share with us the aims we seek to implement. Human dreams cannot be fulfilled in isolation from other human beings; any task intended to benefit a community must be shared by members of that community. It is in working together towards a common goal that human beings demonstrate what is most noble, most worthy, about our species.

But we know that the world is such that not everyone will agree with us: we must invariably encounter opposition. Change can be achieved only gradually: to use the cliché, Rome was not built in a day. And so it is also necessary to establish limits to what we believe we can achieve, in order to protect our own hopes. So it was that Nehemiah's first action was to ensure that the gates of the city were rebuilt and secured.

Let us never be dismayed by the immensity of the challenge that we face. Just because we might not be able to do everything that we might wish, let us not use this as an excuse to do nothing at all.

'It is not for you to complete the work, but neither are you at liberty to refrain from it.'

Pirkei Avot 2:16

February

Self-defence

So we have convinced ourselves of the value of our vision, persuaded others to share it and set reasonable limits to it in order to ensure it can be achieved. Now we have to face the reality that not everyone shares our vision and, indeed, some oppose it – even to the point of violence. It is a sad reality of human existence that the free will with which we have been endowed must necessarily lead to disagreements. God has given us free will and it is up to us to exercise it – and also to deal with the consequences of the conflicts that might emerge from it.

Nehemiah is left in little doubt that those who have already voiced their opposition may seek to put their words into action. And so he instructs his workers to ensure that half the men work while the other half stand to protect them.

The visions we have may face opposition from many places – beyond and within us. Let us seek to overcome self-doubt as well as those who challenge us to find the determination to implement our vision.

O my God, guard my tongue from evil and my lips from telling lies. Even when others curse me, may my soul be silent and humble as the dust to all. Open my heart to your teaching and make me eager to do your will. Dissuade those who seek to harm me and let not their plans prevail.

> *Siddur Lev Chadash (Liberal Judaism's daily and Sabbath prayer-book)*, Liberal Judaism, *1995, p.146*

February

February

Unless the Eternal One watches over the city, its builders toil in vain

The work of building Jerusalem is almost complete – but Nehemiah is beset with complaints from many of his impoverished countryfolk. It soon becomes clear that there is poverty among the inhabitants of the new Judah and that much of this is caused by the practices of the wealthy nobles.

So begins the transition from the physical building of the city of Jerusalem to the spiritual and communal values that are needed to underpin it to ensure its survival. The bricks of the walls that will soon be finished need more than cement and mortar to hold them together. They require justice for those who dwell within them, else the walls will surely collapse. Nehemiah realises this and immediately calls upon those who are exploiting their brothers and sisters to desist. The building of the city cannot be complete until justice is established and questions of poverty and debt are confronted.

So it is for our own vision, our project that we have set ourselves. If the aim of this project requires the exploitation of others or fails to respect their rights, it is not worthy, it will lack God's support and cannot succeed.

Let your favour, Eternal One, our God, rest upon us and may our work have lasting value. O may the work of our hands endure.

Psalm 90:17

You're making it up!

The final resort of those who would seek to frustrate our schemes is to spread false rumours about our intentions and attempt to discredit or even ensnare us. Even as the wall surrounding Nehemiah's Jerusalem is being completed, his detractors are declaring that he intends to lead a rebellion against Persia and declare himself king. Others try to lure him into dangerous meetings that can only end in harm.

Just as the announcement of a vision can invite hostility, so its success will arouse jealousy. There is an alarming range of negative human emotion that needs to be overcome in order for a vision to be realised.

It is most important that we should not lose sight of our own goals – and even our own selves – when confronting such negativity. Nehemiah dismisses the words of those who make false claims about his intentions by declaring 'You are making it up out of your own head!' (verse 8) Nevertheless, such attitudes can discourage us. Let us seek to find enough confidence in ourselves – the same confidence that first inspired us to seek to attain our goal – in order to see off the jealous disapproval of others.

It is easy to feel dismayed by the criticism or opposition of others. Our prayers should help us to protect ourselves from self-doubt.

Doubt, even while it lasts, need not debilitate us. The sense of right and wrong persists, and there is always work to be done.

Siddur Lev Chadash, p.301

Nehemiah

2 The religious life of the city

Notes based on the Hebrew text
by Pete Tobias

Nehemiah's project is completed and it has been an extraordinary success. The walls around Jerusalem have been rebuilt in just 52 days and the city is secure. The people of Judah who were exiles in Babylon now have the opportunity to return.

Nehemiah's focus now switches to the quality of life that will be enjoyed by the residents of his newly secured city. A people that has been exiled from its home for three generations needs a range of measures to ensure that it can safely return.

Nehemiah's measures seek to encourage the residents of Jerusalem to recognise their past, to recall the stories and traditions of their ancestors and rediscover the identity that was threatened by years in exile. The manner in which he seeks to achieve this can be divided into various elements: recalling the past, taking responsibility for remembering it, participating in events to acknowledge it, celebrating it and implementing measures to ensure it will continue to be recalled by future generations.

These elements of community-building do not necessarily seem at first glance to guarantee that Nehemiah's objectives will be achieved. But, as we follow his words during the coming days, we will see how the tasks of remembering, taking responsibility, participating, celebrating and maintaining are essential for the identity of communities and of each of the individuals within them. As the efforts of Nehemiah reach fulfilment, look for ways in which his vision and actions can work on a personal level in the life of every individual.

The most important people

Having completed the building of the city wall and placed doors in the gates, Nehemiah now sets about the task of organising the structure of the religious community that will live within those walls and gates.

His priority in terms of selecting key people is revealing: the first appointments are the gatekeepers, the singers and the Levites. This can serve to remind us of how a religious community – or even a personal religious venture – should be structured. First of all, it is important to establish boundaries defining the nature and identity of our religious belief. Commitment involves discipline and we need gatekeepers to remind ourselves of our own limits. Then come the singers: the voices of joy that well up within or beyond us to help us celebrate and appreciate the beauty and worthiness of our chosen religious path. And finally the Levites: the organisers of the religious structures within which we will observe our religious beliefs. Without guidelines – and guides – our faith lacks focus and direction.

It is important that we have an understanding of how our faith should contain and guide us as well as offer us opportunities to celebrate. In our dealings with our world, ourselves and our God, let us always have in mind the gatekeepers, the singers and the Levites – the religious organisers – of the faith that sustains us.

May the One who blessed our ancestors bless all who occupy themselves with the needs of the community in faithfulness.

Siddur Lev Chadash, p.214

Nehemiah

Serve the Eternal One with joy!

This event is an extraordinary moment in the development of the Jewish people. It documents the first public reading of the Torah, the Five Books of Moses. Those hearing this reading 2500 years ago were unknowingly establishing a tradition that is still an element of Jewish practice. Orthodox Jewish tradition holds that this document being read to the people of Judah was several centuries old, having been given to Moses at Mount Sinai. A liberal, scholarly, perspective would say that it was a product of the Babylonian exile, compiled and produced to maintain the people's identity. Whatever its origin, the effect of hearing the Torah at this moment was a powerful emotional one. Safely returned to the home of their ancestors, the people of Judah gathered together as a community, and they wept.

But Nehemiah and those with him seek to divert the people from grieving and focus on celebration. The ancient harvest festival is a time of joy and the commandment to celebrate joyfully is contained in the words of the document. From this we should learn to focus on the positive aspects of our religious heritage, to recognise our good fortune and the gifts that have been given to us, even as we acknowledge the suffering that may have come before.

May we always take the opportunities for celebration that are granted to us and always seek to put our sad experiences into perspective.

Those who sow in tears shall reap in joy.

Psalm 126:5

A link in the chain

Having already understood the importance of celebrating, even in the face of sadness, the next stage of the project to re-establish the religious identity of those returning to the city of Jerusalem is undertaken. The Levites, the priestly group charged with the responsibility for overseeing the religious development of the people, remind the listeners of their historical roots. Here was a group of people whose recent ancestors had been uprooted from their home being encouraged to recall a more ancient past. The pain of their recent experiences and their own failings are put into a broader context, reminding these individuals of their connection with the past and their role in the continuing development of the Jewish people.

This reminds us of our duty to remember and respect the efforts of previous generations of our community and of our responsibility to pass on their wisdom, faith and love to those who will come after us. We are all bound together.

How can we honour the memories and the efforts of those individuals and communities who have, in the past, sought to implement God's will? How can we recognise and fulfil our role as a link in the chain of human development?

'Remember the days of old; consider the generations long past. Ask your parents and they will tell you, your elders, and they will explain to you' (Deuteronomy 32:7).

We give thanks that you, Eternal One, are our God as you were the God of our ancestors.

Siddur Lev Chadash, p.144

February

Rights and responsibilities

The task of establishing a religious identity continues. The returned exiles have fixed boundaries to contain and protect themselves, they have recognised the religious duty to celebrate and seek positive expression of their faith and have made the connection with their past. Now they must acknowledge their responsibility to uphold their religious traditions and practices.

In our increasingly troubled world, the accepting of responsibility is becoming less apparent. We often hear of people – quite legitimately – demanding their rights, be they social, political or economic. And one of the purposes of religion is to demand that human rights are respected. But a commitment to a religious faith carries with it responsibility: it places upon us duties.

Some of those duties seem mundane, perhaps even irrelevant, when set against the scale of suffering and need in the world. But our religious faith should encourage within us a sense of discipline and structure in our personal observance and practice in our everyday lives. Once we have taken this responsibility, we are then more able to focus on our religious duty to bring meaning and hope to those around us and the world beyond us.

In what way does my own religious practice make me more able to recognise my responsibility to my community and to those less well off than I?

If I am not for myself, then who will be for me? But if I am only for myself, what am I? And if not now, when?

Pirkei Avot 1:14

Do not separate yourself from the community

Nehemiah's task is almost completed: the Jewish community of Jerusalem is now re-established, its safety and identity are guaranteed and its responsibility to itself and others has been set out.

We often take for granted the religious structures within which we express our religious belief. Somewhere behind the communal institutions and events that perhaps we take for granted is our own version of Nehemiah: committed individuals whose work provides us with the opportunity to express our faith securely and with dignity.

Perhaps we are those organisers, leaders of our local community. Or perhaps we take such leadership for granted, enjoying and benefiting from the efforts of those who take that responsibility. If that is the case, then we should, like the people of Jerusalem, join in with the activities of the community and be sure to participate in every aspect of its life.

What do I give to my own community? Do I make my full contribution to its life and its activities? How might I become more involved and play a greater part in the lives of those with whom I share my faith?

Eternal God, we come before you surrounded by members of our community. With them we share our happiness and it becomes greater; our troubles and they become smaller. Let us not separate ourselves from the true strength of our community: the experience and wisdom of old people, the hopes of the young and the examples of courage and care that sustain us.

Siddur Lev Chadash, p.122

Nehemiah

Love your neighbour as you love yourself

It would be good to be able to conclude this study of Nehemiah's work on a positive note. Nehemiah's achievements are, without doubt, worthy of admiration and gratitude – for, without them, the faith of Judaism and its offspring would have disappeared in the sixth century BCE. Nehemiah has supervised the rebirth of his people's historic tradition and has ensured that its adherents have safety, a connection with their past and a responsibility to uphold it.

But Nehemiah discovers, as do all committed religious leaders, that not everyone shares his enthusiasm or commitment. Having devoted his efforts to protecting the people of Jerusalem from outside influences, Nehemiah now finds opposition from within. His response is angry, even violent.

We may sympathise with Nehemiah's anger and frustration at the failure of his co-religionists to treat their heritage with the same respect that he does. But his actions to enforce his beliefs cannot be condoned. The true test of any religious faith must be its ability to tolerate those who do not adhere so totally to its practices. In the end we shall be judged not by our own religious practices and beliefs but on how tolerant we are of those whose practices and beliefs differ from ours.

How easily can you accept the customs of someone whose religious tradition and practice is different from yours?

Remember me with favour, O my God.

Nehemiah 13:31

Johannine images

I Source of light, life and love

Notes based on the New Revised Standard Version
by Nicholas Alan Worssam SSF

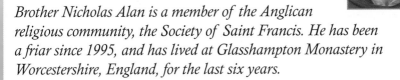

*Brother Nicholas Alan is a member of the Anglican
religious community, the Society of Saint Francis. He has been
a friar since 1995, and has lived at Glasshampton Monastery in
Worcestershire, England, for the last six years.*

In our community, when we recite the psalms, we finish the
recitation by saying together the doxology: 'Glory to the Father,
and to the Son, and to the Holy Spirit; as it was in the beginning,
is now, and shall be forever. Amen.' This refrain calls us back time
and again to the Holy Trinity that breathes life into our worship.
There is, however, an alternative doxology that begins: 'Glory to
God, Source of all being, Eternal Word and Holy Spirit.' The first
is traditional and has the echoes of the centuries in its words,
uniting me with all those who have summed up their worship of
God in this way for nearly two millennia. The second reminds
me that God is the ultimate source of all that is, here and now
in this very moment, holding all things in being with his attentive
presence of love. God is the first cause, as the theologians used
to say, the ground of our being and fountainhead of life. The
readings this week explore this aspect of God, seeing how the
universal religious images of light, life and love inform us about
the God who is closer to us than the blood in our veins or the
breath in our lungs.

Quotations, except for Thursday, are taken from *Drinking From
the Hidden Fountain: A Patristic Breviary* by Thomas Spidlik (New
City, 1992).

Johannine images

In the beginning, God

> *This Good is the beginning and the end of all things. It is involved in all existence. It creates from nothingness ... It is Providence and perfect Goodness. It transcends being and not-being. And it has the ability to turn evil into good.*
>
> *Dionysius the Areopagite, sixth century*

Saint Francis of Assisi, the inspiration of the community to which I belong, loved to call God by the name 'Good'. In one of his prayers he says to God: 'You are Good, all Good, supreme Good, Lord God, living and true.' The goodness of God was the theme of his life.

In Genesis we read that the beginning of all things was the creation of light, and that 'the light was good'. It could be said that our essence is in fact the energy of light, a light visible in and to the saints, shining out as in the face of Moses or Jesus in their transfiguration, energising us to the practice of the good. This light is poised over the expanse of darkness, of nothingness: the non-being out of which we came to be.

But God is beyond both being and non-being, beyond all names. We say God is providence and goodness, and this is true, we really can trust God in all things; but still God transcends even these categories of our understanding.

Let us then put aside all thoughts, all rationalisation, and return to the primal light of our creation, to the God who says, 'Let there be...'

O God, of your goodness, show me yourself.

February

Fountain of life

We ought to celebrate Life eternal, from which comes all other kinds of life ... This divine Life is the Beginning of all life, the only Cause and Fountain of life. Every living thing ought to contemplate and praise God.

Dionysius the Areopagite

Life is very precious because in all life is found the Life that is God. Because of this, all things should be treated with respect, even with an attitude of veneration for the one whose living waters birth them into existence. Nurture and non-violence are the ways to echo God's steadfast love, to shelter others as God the mother bird shelters her young under her wings.

God gives life itself, enlivens all that she touches. This life is not static: it is exuberant and overflowing, like a fountain throwing its spray into the wind. It is a fountain of living water, flowing water that forms a river from which all may drink and be refreshed. How much of our lives are really like this? So often we try vainly to hold on to the blessings God gives, as if to create a lake for our own recreation. But God will have none of this. God's blessings are meant to be shared, to be given away like water flowing over the palm of a hand. We could not hold God back even if we tried.

Is there some act of kindness you can perform today that will bring to light God's love?

With you is the fountain of life; in your light we see light!

Johannine images

You desire truth in the inward being

Those who are engaged in spiritual warfare must always keep their hearts tranquil. Only then can the mind sift the impulses it receives and store in the treasure house of the memory those that are good and come from God.

Diodochus of Photica, fifth century

Today is the beginning of Lent, the day when Christians have traditionally received on their forehead a mark of the cross, made from the ashes of palm crosses from the previous year. It is a reminder of our earthly nature, accompanied by the words: 'Remember that you are dust and to dust you shall return. Turn away from sin and be faithful to Christ.' Repentance begins with an acknowledgment of our frailty and sin, of having fallen short of the glory of God; but it doesn't end there. God washes us clean and puts a new and right spirit within us, restoring to us the joy of salvation.

The work of penitence can indeed be joyful as the grime of our sin is washed away and our true nature of light shines out from within. Christ is our light, the truth of our inward being, teaching wisdom secretly to all who have ears to hear. And of course this process is not finished on a single day. Day by day, moment by moment we need to return to Christ, recollecting our awareness amid the distractions of the world, cultivating the tranquillity within which we can hear the treasures of wisdom whispered secretly in the heart.

Teach me wisdom in my secret heart!

February

Living water

It was for this that intelligent beings came into existence; namely, that the riches of the Divine blessings should not lie idle. The All-creating Wisdom fashioned these souls ... that there should be some capacities able to receive his blessings and become continually larger with the inpouring of the stream ... The fountain of blessings wells up unceasingly.

Macrina of Cappadocia, fourth century, in
Nicene and Post-Nicene Fathers, *Oxford, 1893*

Here in John's gospel Jesus talks with a Samaritan woman and, in the quotation above, Macrina and her brother Gregory of Nyssa discuss the mysteries of human creation and destiny. Both dialogues direct us to the wisdom that gushes out from within in rivers of blessing for all people. This wisdom enlarges us, opens us up to our neighbours such that their lives and ours are seen to be not separate but two eddies of a single stream. It is for this that we are created, that we might channel the blessings of God, carrying all to the ocean of God's eternity.

But if we are to reach that sea, then we must be prepared for the shallows and rapids on the way. It was not easy for Jesus to approach the Samaritan woman, and the disciples are scandalised by his action, even as she herself is surprised. Sharing our blessings can feel like a diminishment at first, but only for a moment, as in the instant of true sharing we discover that God is in fact an inexhaustible spring.

Is there one thing that you can give away today?

Lord, give me this water always!

February

Johannine images

I am the light of the world

> *The Father is light, the Son is light, the Holy Spirit is light;*
> *one light, timeless, indivisible, inconfusible, eternal, uncreated,*
> *illimitable, invisible, lacking nothing, above and beyond*
> *all things, a light no one can ever behold without first being*
> *purified. And by contemplating it, we can receive it.*
>
> *Simeon the New Theologian, tenth century*

One early image used to describe the Trinity is to compare the three divine persons to the flame, light and heat of a fire. Here Simeon reminds us of the absolute unity of the Trinity: one light enlightening all creation. But, to be able to see this light, first we must be purified, by which he means practising penitence and keeping the commandments of God. In this way we grow in humility and self-knowledge, and can receive the grace of the gifts of the Holy Spirit.

The man born blind in today's reading encounters Jesus, and God's work of healing is revealed. So we too, meeting Jesus in the sacraments of the church and in each other, have our eyes opened to the light from which we came. God's grace irradiates our world: and we think that our skies are perpetually grey! But first we must stoop to the ground, to the spittle and the earth of everyday life in community, to discover the healing touch of Christ.

What is there in your life that you would like to be healed?

Lord, open my eyes!

He opened my eyes

Unceasing prayer means to have the mind always turned to God with great love, holding alive our hope in him, having confidence in him whatever we are doing and whatever happens to us.

Maximus the Confessor, seventh century

Sometimes we think that we understand Jesus, but he always surprises us. He changes our life, then disappears into the crowd. We do not know where he comes from or where he goes. But still we can return to him, invite him further into the house of our life, and offer to him all that we have to give.

The discipline of prayer, working towards the unceasing prayer recommended by Paul (1 Thessalonians 5:17), is a way of inviting Jesus into our lives. In this way we hope in God and have confidence that whatever happens works for our ultimate good (Romans 8:28). This way of praying may focus on a repeated phrase, such as a verse from the Psalms, or a single word like the name of Jesus; but whatever practice we follow, moment by moment, breath by breath, we are called to give ourselves wholly back to God. Then the witness of our lives will speak louder than any words can tell, and the light within us will shine throughout the whole world to the glory of God (see Matthew 5:16). For without God we can do nothing.

Spend some time in prayer this weekend, silently asking God's love to shine out in your life.

Lord, I have seen, and believe.

Johannine images

2 The Good Shepherd

Notes based on the Russian Orthodox Bible by
Lucretia Vasilescu

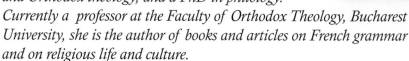

*Lucretia Vasilescu has degrees in French language
and Orthodox theology, and a PhD in philology.
Currently a professor at the Faculty of Orthodox Theology, Bucharest
University, she is the author of books and articles on French grammar
and on religious life and culture.*

In the Old Testament, Yahweh is rarely attributed the title of
shepherd directly, but he is evoked in this capacity through his
relationship with the chosen people. Thus Jacob, on blessing
Joseph's children, invokes the Lord, shepherd of Israel (Genesis
48:15-16). God is head of Israel's shepherds, while Moses, Aaron,
David, are the Great Shepherd's shepherds. The intervention
of God, the shepherd of Israel's flock, is often direct: he tends
the flock, judges the sheep, criticises and condemns the bad
shepherds (Ezekiel 34), and stands against the violent shepherds
who act as tyrants, abusing their power.

In Jesus' time, shepherds were judged differently. Unable to
observe the commandments of the Law because of their duties,
they were regarded as negatively as robbers and thieves. Yet, the
chosen people's memory retained the image of the Shepherd
yet to come, and in the earliest Christian centuries the image of
the shepherd became a dominant one for Jesus. Jesus is the one
who fulfils the expectation of the good shepherd, sent to the lost
sheep of the house of Israel (Matthew 15: 24). He is the great
shepherd of the sheep (Hebrews 13:20), the chief shepherd
(1 Peter 5:4), who gathers, by his death, the flock in Galilee
(Matthew 26:32; Isaiah 40:11; Zechariah 13:7). Led by him, we
reach our home, the kingdom of the Father.

March

God, the great shepherd

Psalm 23 is the chant of a worshipper at the temple, a person who finds peace in constant intimacy with God. It is a hymn dedicated to rest as a symbol of spiritual regeneration and stability in faith. Rest is not relaxation but renewal and regeneration of the exhausted ones. The place of rest is a place free from servitude and constraint, where one enjoys the liberty of God's chosen ones (Revelation 14:11-12).

The water of rest is the living water imparting eternal life, which people receive from God through Christ (John 7:37); it is a spring of water welling up to eternal life (John 4:15-16). Bodily thirst is easy to appease, while restlessness, the thirst of the soul, sends one seeking for God's everlasting rest.

The shepherd's care drives away fear from the heart of the faithful one, whose unwavering trust is thus rewarded. Observing the covenant brings about peace of soul. Anointing one's head with the oil of God's magnanimity is a sign of joy.

Augustine imaged the church as the flock led by the Good Shepherd, Jesus Christ, to the holy pastures of the Eucharist. Baptism in Christ – the waters of rest – imparts strength and health, opening up the path of salvation. Doing the will of our Christ is to find the path to spiritual bliss and eternal life.

For as much as thou art thyself the fulfilling of the law and of the prophets, O Christ, our God, who didst accomplish all things appointed of the Father: fill our hearts with joy and gladness, always and for ever and unto the ages of ages.

　　　　　　　　　　　The Holy Liturgy of Saint John Chrysostom

Johannine images

The shepherd and his sheep

The metaphor of the shepherd, deeply rooted in the Judaic tradition of a nomadic people (Deuteronomy 26:5), presents the theme of authority, the leader's authority as well as the authority of the life companion, based on loyalty and love. The shepherd is the able, strong one, well aware of the flock's necessities and always ready to defend it against any danger.

Those merely seeking the honours of a position are the false shepherds, those dubbed robbers and thieves. The robber regards the sheep as his property, belonging to him, for him to exploit. He is only interested in himself, rather than in the care of the sheep. By contrast, those worthy of receiving the authority of rulers are those elected by Christ. By faith and by knowledge of the divine word, those united with Christ become true leaders. Christ is the door, the only way that others may become shepherds, with him, of his flock. Whoever wishes to be a good shepherd must pass through the door that is Jesus. Jesus is both the door and the doorkeeper, says Cyril of Alexandria, 'to show that there cannot be steadfast leadership for those who do not accept this office through him, as a God-granted gift'.

Jesus remains the shepherd, and the flock belongs to him alone, even though others may share in his work of care. The only intercessor, Jesus, fulfils the Law by 'a revelation filled with more grace than Moses', according to Cyril.

O Lord Jesus Christ, Son of the living God, both Shepherd and Lamb, who takest away the sins of the world; who didst remit the loan unto the two debtors, and didst vouchsafe to the woman who was a sinner the remission of her sins: do thou, the same Lord, loose, remit, forgive the sins, transgressions and iniquities, whether voluntary or involuntary, whether of wilfulness or of ignorance, which have been committed unto guilt and disobedience by this thy servant.

From the Confession, Orthodox liturgy

March

Jesus Christ, the servant of God

The beginning of this passage refers to the disciple, also called the servant. It is the disciple who learns from the master and carries on his teachings. The title of servant, particularly Yahweh's servant, presupposes a different status. In the Old Testament, the name 'servant of God' is attributed to righteous ones, to good, blameless and upright people such as Job, to the prophets and those loyal to God.

Although some have thought so, the servant is not a collective character; he is also more than a mere pious man or some kind of mythological figure. He has a clearly defined role in the divine economy, God's servant being the Messiah (cf. Zechariah 3:8).

For Christians, Christ is the servant. Humble, obedient and fulfilling the heavenly Father's will, he suffers in order to vanquish death through his life. As the prophecies foretell, the great priest's servant will slap him in the face, others will spit at him, Pontius Pilate will have him whipped and allow him to be crucified. All the prophecies will be fulfilled.

The wise person will hearken to the voice and follow the teachings of Jesus Christ, the one who calls himself 'the servant' of God (Philippians 2:7).

O All-Ruler, Word of the Father, Jesus Christ, thou who art perfect, never in thy great mercy leave me, but ever abide in me, thy servant. O Jesus, Good Shepherd of thy sheep ... enlighten my mind with the light of understanding of thy holy gospel. Enlighten my soul with the love of thy cross. Enlighten my heart with the purity of thy word. Enlighten my body with thy passionless passion. Keep my thoughts in thy humility. And rouse me in good time to glorify thee, for thou art supremely glorified, with thy eternal Father, and thy most Holy Spirit for ever.

From the Evening Prayer of St Antioch

Johannine images

Jesus Christ, the bread from heaven

'Things given by divine grace must be heavenly and worthy of God's great magnanimity', proclaimed Cyril of Alexandria. The bread coming down from God is such a gift, being the very body and person of Christ himself, given in the Eucharist. Being immortal and endowing the receiver with immortality, it will feed believers for ever. The manna given in the wilderness was not from heaven in this sense, which is why it decayed, and those who ate it were seized by death.

Christ, the source of all spiritual values, avows his divinity publicly, clearly and fearlessly, in the synagogue and in Capernaum. His teachings require the assent of those being taught. Only spiritual people are able to understand the meaning, the depth and the beauty of the sacrament: that through the holy Eucharist, Christ invisibly imparts life. Christ's body, received by believers, is life-giving, filled with the Spirit's life-giving workings. Those who obey the word of the only-begotten Son, the one Lord, Jesus Christ, live in spirit, in communion with God and their neighbours. Those who are in communion with Christ's body are also in communion with Christ's Spirit. It is through faith that Christ dwells in us while we, those united with the Son, those called to adoption through grace, are also God's children by virtue of our likeness to him.

Let our mouths be filled with thy praise, O Lord, that we may sing of thy glory; for thou hast made us worthy to partake of thy holy, divine, immortal and life-giving mysteries. Preserve us in thy holiness that we may meditate on thy righteousness all the day long.

The Holy Liturgy of Saint John Chrysostom

David, the shepherd of God's flock

David is a luminous image in the biblical tradition. In the beginning, he is merely the suitable man to lead his father's sheep in Bethlehem, but God's plan was different, for David was the one chosen to become a king, 'shepherd of my people Israel' and 'prince over Israel' (2 Samuel 5:2).

Today's story is marked by simplicity: David's plain clothes that suit him for his fight with Goliath, his plain weapons in combat. Freed from heavy armour, he is able to handle his simple weapon, a sling and a few stones, allowing him to employ the tactics that bring about his victory. Spontaneity and ease, granted by God in order to overcome life's adversities and hardships, are characteristic of David's faith (Psalm 17: 32). Spiritual harmony stems from this simplicity and from David's trust in God.

David's deeds are a lesson to the faithful of both present and past times. Shedding the heavy shield and the royal weaponry that weigh one down – in other words, shedding the sins and encumbrances that get in our way – this story illustrates the ease with which a Christian can bear Christ's yoke. David's lightness of bearing and swiftness of movement become symbols of the alert, receptive spiritual openness to the divine will that should mark every Christian's life.

Jesus, my hope, forsake me not;
Jesus, my helper, reject me not;
Jesus, my creator, forget me not;
Jesus, my shepherd, lose me not;
Jesus, Son of God, have mercy on me!

Akathist hymn to our Lord Jesus Christ

March

Christ, the Good Shepherd

The core of the Saviour's discourse here is the laying down of his life in redeeming self-sacrifice (verse 11). The cross is not presented as a violent act, imposed from the outside, but as Christ's own self-offering. Jesus transforms the violent, exterior act of crucifixion into an act of free self-giving to others. Jesus does not offer some material thing, but gives his very self. By so doing, he imparts life.

The sheep, God's creatures, do not belong to the shepherd as if they are mere objects. No, rather the shepherd knows them, loves them and wants them to live in truth and righteousness. The shepherd and his sheep are united in knowledge and truth, a knowledge situated within Jesus' own relationship with the Father, so that Jesus' disciples become taken up with him into the life of the Trinity. Thus, the church and the Holy Trinity make a whole. Despite all its diversities and conflicts, the church is one through its one shepherd, Christ, the Son of God, who was made human in order for people to have life and have it abundantly (John 10:10). Here we have a vision of the church triumphant, under the staff of its Good Shepherd.

We thank thee, O Lord our God, thou good lover of mankind and physician of our souls and bodies, who painlessly bore our infirmities, by whose stripes we have all been healed; thou Good Shepherd, who earnestly seeks the wandering sheep; who givest consolation unto the fainthearted, and life unto them that are crushed … Do thou forgive, as the good God that remembereth not evil, not leaving us to fall into a dissolute life, neither to walk in the paths of destruction.

From the prayer of anointing in the sacrament of Holy Unction

Johannine images

3 The way

Notes based on the New Revised Standard Version
by David and Kathleen Wood

*Kathleen and David Wood are both Methodist
ministers serving in Lancashire. Before entering the
ministry, Kathleen was a special needs teacher. Much
of David's ministry has been in theological education.
Part of their 'way' has been care for Peter, their son
with profound and multiple learning difficulties.*

This week's image from John is Jesus the Way. Last
week we reflected on Jesus the Good Shepherd. Part of that
picture was of the shepherd going ahead of the sheep to lead
them. Walking with the shepherd therefore means following
his path. John uses the picture of Jesus the Way in a number of
different contexts, which we shall explore this week, with the
help of two well-loved psalms. Ultimately, John understands
Jesus to be the one who leads us through death on a way into
the unknown. This road is so closely identified with Jesus that he
personifies it. So, for John, *he* is the way, the truth and the life.

March

Jesus – the only way?

The tourist asked a local farmer for directions. When the farmer was unable to give them, the tourist became very exasperated. 'Ah!' said the farmer, 'but I'm not lost'! Knowing the way to God is vital and, for John, that way is Jesus.

Today's passage contains one of the great 'I am' sayings. In the previous verses, Jesus has spoken of himself as the one who leads us through death to the Father. This is the journey Jesus himself is about to make, but he seeks to reassure his friends that he goes to prepare a place for them. Where he leads, they can follow.

Little wonder that this passage is the one most often chosen at funerals. But then, Dr Who-like, the future becomes strangely present. For those, like Philip, who want to see and know God now, Jesus is also 'the way'. Experience of God comes through following the way of Christ, which is the way of faith, costly obedience and sacrificial love.

The real question concerns whether Jesus is the *only* way. In a multi-faith society, Jesus' word that he alone leads to the Father sounds most narrow and exclusive. The prologue to the gospel has sounded a more inclusive note. Jesus is the incarnation of the universal Word, present in all creation, that enlightens everyone. Also, we do well to remember that John is writing to Jewish Christians with the reassurance that Jesus really is the expected Messiah. Yet John reminds us that in our own experience Jesus is the human face of God.

Lord, we thank you for showing yourself to us in Jesus. Help us to discover more about you by following him more closely.

Johannine images

Pilgrim's progress

Many years ago, quite by chance, I walked the Pilgrim's Way across the sands to the Holy Island of Lindisfarne. Becoming aware of the countless saints and worshippers who had made the same journey before me, I became deeply moved and had a real sense of God's presence.

Today's psalm is an exuberant celebration of the joy of pilgrimage. Like some other psalms, it was sung by worshippers on their way to the Jerusalem temple, perhaps for the Feast of Tabernacles. Using emotional and powerful poetry, it sings of a deep yearning for God and the sheer delight of communion with him. You sense that this pilgrim party has nearly arrived at journey's end. The pilgrims anticipate their arrival in the temple, house of blessing for all God's people. But they also reflect on the pilgrimage itself, which has been a source of strength and renewal.

This psalm reminds us that seeking God, our exceeding delight, is the goal of our life. Yet the way to seek him involves a physical, active going – going to church, going on retreat, going secretly into your room to pray, going to those special places where heaven and earth seem to meet. And, whatever your Lenten discipline, it should be about seeking God, not making you feel virtuous!

Take time this week to go on a prayer walk, seeking God through the familiar sights and sounds of your neighbourhood.

The agony and the ecstasy

Life with our profoundly disabled son has been a hard road. Love for him has meant an acceptance (sometimes very grudging!) of the lifestyle he brings. Yet the struggle has been life-changing. We have learned and experienced so much of God, faith and joy. In and through the agony there has been ecstasy.

A God-man has to do what a God-man has to do! That is the reality Jesus now faces. He has known all along that opening the way to God will involve his suffering and death. But now the hour has arrived – Gethsemane – and the full horror of it strikes him. In a sense, his only choice is that he has no choice. Yet, with echoes of both his baptism and transfiguration, there comes a deep and divine reassurance. The way of the cross is the way of glory. In and through the struggle, the life-giving love of God will be revealed. His lifting up will be the magnet drawing all to God. And so Jesus accepts the way of humble obedience, knowing that, through his agony, others will find ecstasy.

There is a mysterious yet wonderful truth here. I sometimes wonder why life for God's people is so hard. Any advance, change or success in mission seems to come at such a cost! And it can get you down. The cross reminds us that, in the economy of God, that's how it is. This is the light in which we need to walk.

Lord, help us to find you in our struggles, seeing them as the way to your kingdom.

Johannine images

From where will my help come?

'My money's all in property,' said a woman, 'These days the financial markets are so unpredictable!' 'Well, we've set our daughter up in business so she can care for us in our old age', replied a couple across the table, perhaps rather tongue in cheek! This was one recent conversation I overheard about the source of future help.

Another such conversation can be read in Psalm 121. This confident, joyful 'psalm of Ascents' would probably have been sung by pilgrims either on their way to festival worship in the Jerusalem temple, or on arrival at the temple gates. The anxious question (verse 1) and reply (verses 3-8) address this fundamental issue: in a life with so much difficulty, danger and uncertainty, where does my help really come from? The answer is clear and certain: not from the hills themselves (referring perhaps to other gods worshipped at hill shrines, or dangers to be encountered in the hills on the return journey, to other securities or to the hills surrounding Jerusalem), but from the one true God, the creator of the hills, the maker of heaven and earth. On the journeys we make in life and on the journey of life itself, the only safe way is with God.

Lord Jesus, help me to see clearly those things in which I trust, rather than in you. May you and I together remove them from my life, so that my journey may continue in confidence and joy with you and into you alone.

Johannine images

The way of risk

Alfie had been in a steady relationship for several years but the love they had once felt for each other had gone – and yet for many months they continued together. Eventually Alfie made the painful decision to leave their shared home and for a while it seemed as though he had died inside. However, within 18 months he had met and married Jessica; now his disposition is transformed and he is more fully alive than he had dared imagine or hope.

In deciding to return to Judea, Jesus was taking a huge risk – and his disciples were horrified. Their 'misunderstanding' in verse 13 (a typical Johannine device allowing for further explanation) demonstrates their failure to realise that the journey was, in fact, for their sake. That way they might believe more fully who Jesus truly was and experience a fresh revelation of his glory. This journey was going to be a critical one, a journey to death, through death and beyond death, for the life of the world. They would need to walk in the light of Jesus.

Perhaps in reading Thomas' words we might see the challenge to ourselves and our churches – following Jesus means a willingness to die, to risk what we already have for the greater glory that awaits us.

Thank you God, for the faith and courage of Thomas and those today who are like him [name some known to you]. Help me to follow you – whatever the risks.

The way of humble service

Yesterday we read of Thomas' brave choice to follow Jesus to Jerusalem whatever the risks. Today it is Peter's turn to volunteer to journey with Jesus, even if it involves laying down his own life to do so.

Grand gestures can sometimes be easier to make – more obvious, more noteworthy – than quiet, faithful obedience. Almost twenty years ago, when I was looking after two young children at home, and adjusting to the fact that one of them has severe and profound learning difficulties, it felt as if life was utterly crowding in on me and I was sinking fast. A church member called to see how she could help. Did I want to talk with her, sharing things I trusted to no one else? I thanked her and said that she *could* help by collecting my charity envelopes; that would be one pressure less. Unfortunately, she declined to do that. Somehow I sensed she wanted to be known as the heroine who saved the sanity of the minister's wife; an anonymous collecting of envelopes didn't quite fit the bill!

In today's passage, Jesus is sharing with his disciples how they are to behave when he has gone from them and until they can follow him into that uncertain future. Loving, sacrificial, humble service towards one another (demonstrated by foot-washing) is the way of Jesus.

Today, try to carry out a simple act of unnoticed kindness for someone else.

March

Johannine images

4 Life that is stronger than death

Notes based on the New Revised Standard Version
by Tom Arthur

*Tom Arthur is a Presbyterian minister from the USA
serving the United Reformed Church in the UK through the PCUSA's
Worldwide Mission Division. City URC, Cardiff, where he currently
works, is an 'open and affirming' church doing significant work
with destitute asylum-seekers in the community, providing, through
a team of volunteer barristers, free legal advice for those who have
exhausted normal channels of support. Tom teaches New Testament
Greek through City's adult education programme and has recently
written a course for new Christians called 'The Way: An Introduction
to Christianity as a Way of Life'. Retiring in January 2009, Tom is
married to Marieke. They have three children and five grandchildren.*

The 'way' of Jesus leads through life and death to a life beyond
our imagination. He gives us access to the life, love, grace and
truth of God, a power beyond our comprehension. We trust in
this power for our ultimate safety. Lazarus is raised as a sign that
we can all be raised. Nevertheless, there is no 'short cut' to this
life. Jesus goes before us on a narrowing way. Just as the seed
'dies' in the earth and a woman risks death in the pain and danger
of childbirth, so the disciple must face death in various forms –
in self-denial, adversity, persecution, even martyrdom – before
reaching the place of light and peace prepared for us.

Life beyond our understanding

Scientists are saying that not only are human beings still evolving but, in the last five thousand years, are evolving more rapidly than ever before. Changes include lighter skin and blue eyes in northern Europe and partial resistance to diseases such as malaria among some African populations. We are like other parts of this dynamic, various universe that are subject to natural selection. Life forms emerge, interact, modify. They flourish for a while and, sometimes, like the dodo, disappear.

Humanity is neither unique nor at the centre of all this. God, who made the crocodile, is at the centre. When Job questions God's justice, God's answer out of the whirlwind is simply to point to the crocodile. The crocodile has been around a lot longer than Job has, and might just be around a long time after the last human being has shared the fate of the dodo. Kind of puts us in our place, doesn't it?

What is amazing about being human is the capacity to see such a stupendous and dynamic universe and wonder about it, think about it and talk about it, write about it and sing about it. How miraculous life is! How wonderful is the majestic otherness of God and the intimate here-ness of God. Have eyes ever seen, ears heard or mind ever imagined a God who made all things, with whom we could sit down and engage in deep conversation and debate?

Which creatures in the universe cause you greatest amazement? Take your amazement into your prayer.

Johannine images

Power beyond comprehension

'It was a dark and stormy night' is one of the most unimaginative ways to begin a story there is; an annual celebration of bad writing invites otherwise serious authors to have fun imitating pulp fiction by beginning their stories with this very tired phrase.

When John uses such an opening to introduce Jesus walking across the water, however, he creates surprise and amazement. The question is what kind of power Jesus represents. The conventional thinking in this story is represented by the crowd's desire to make Jesus king. That's the way people ordinarily understand power and authority, and even today our hymns often betray that this is the kind of Jesus we still want to worship.

But John portrays Jesus as embodying a power infinitely more wonderful than the power of a king. John is saying Jesus is like 'the spirit of God … moving over the face of the waters' at the moment of creation (Genesis 1:2). There is something elemental, creative, world-making about Jesus. His is not the political power of worldly monarchs. The power he embodies is power beyond the reach of our ordinary understanding and yet, paradoxically, a power that is at work in each one of us, re-creating us, and, through the bold creativity of our discipleship, re-creating the world. We will not settle for what is merely conventional.

Pray for those who wield power in your local community, country and in the wider world, that they may embody the kind of power Jesus demonstrated.

Resurrection life

John Updike describes the often-repeated Apostles' Creed as 'a path worn smooth over the rough terrain of our hearts'. Martha meets Jesus' assurance of resurrection with a recitation of the formula she has accepted and memorised as a creed: 'Oh, I know that he will rise again in the resurrection on the last day.' The conventional answer does not seem to be giving her much consolation. She misses her brother *now*.

But Jesus says, 'I am the resurrection.' Resurrection is not something to believe in so much as it is the shape of a person's life, and it is therefore a present reality, not a distant possibility. Those who believe in him, Jesus says in another place, do what he does (John 13:14-15), embracing the honest stench of our humanity as the object of God's love. Resurrection is a way of coming fully into life, like being born again.

Martha gets the point, and recognises that Jesus is the Messiah 'who is coming into the world'. Resurrection is a way of coming into the world, a 'coming out', as it were, no longer bound by or buried under the formulae or labels of conventional living but released to live in a way that is authentic, honest and therefore fully alive. It's not something to wait for. Resurrection is to be lived now.

Give me courage and grace to live your resurrection life now – and to share it with others.

The 'death' of the seed

Almost thirty years ago I travelled to England as a tourist – my first trip across the Atlantic. I decided not to take my camera. Taking photographs was a big part of my work managing publications at McCormick Theological Seminary, and I was only too aware of how stopping all the time to take pictures seemed to take the life out of things. The habit seemed to strip things of their temporal dimension and the possibility of interaction, framing them in a lifeless objectivity. I didn't want to be a camera-snapping tourist. I wanted to immerse myself in the world my Sunderland grandparents had lived in before they had emigrated to the States seventy years before.

The Greek tourists in this story want to see Jesus the way tourists always want to see things, preserving the memory in their little box of mental souvenirs. But Jesus says the way to 'see' him is not to preserve a moment in timelessness but to do what he does, to become so immersed in the process of living that the whole idea of stopping and holding on to any particular moment disappears from our thinking.

This is what it means to live as Jesus lived. We are invited to leap into life as the grain of wheat falls into the ground, with a sense of abandon, propelled into the world by love with more regard for others than for preserving our own safety. This is the way of life that bears fruit, a way of life in which death has no sting, as Paul would say, and the grave no victory.

Show me how to become so immersed in the process of living that I can risk letting go of everything that holds me back from your costly, risky, glorious life.

Johannine images

The 'death' of childbirth

I'm really unsure about the propriety of including limericks in daily meditations on scripture, but one of my favourites goes like this:

> *There was a young lady named Wild*
> *Who managed to stay undefiled*
> *By thinking of Jesus*
> *And noxious diseases*
> *And the bother of raising a child.*

Clearly, the pain of childbirth is an experience Ms Wild would wish to avoid at all costs. And her attitude towards Jesus is a set of values enabling her not just to retreat from life but to deny it.

But Jesus is able to use the pain of childbirth as an image of something that lives at the heart of being Christian. 'When a woman is in labour she has pain … But when her child is born, she no longer remembers the anguish because of the joy of having brought a human being into the world' (verse 21).

From slavery in Egypt to exile in Babylon, and even into our own day, the consciousness of pain is part of the creative act. In the Beatitudes, Jesus calls those who are poor in spirit 'blessed', meaning perhaps that those whose spirits are crushed because of oppression or abuse can imagine the way to liberation when others cannot. In Isaiah the 'suffering servant' is the one who can give the lead in a new life lived faithfully with God.

The Christian way of life is no escape from pain into some leafy spiritual suburb but an immersion into life in all its richness, where the deepest sorrows and the deepest joys of the world meet, to create something new. It's the way of the cross, and the way to resurrection.

Pray to have the courage to enter into the deepest sorrows and the deepest joys; and for those you meet there.

Jesus will welcome us home

For a predecessor of mine at City Church, who was instrumental in setting it up, the theme song of Cardiff's Huggard Centre, a shelter for homeless men, is 'There's a place for us,' from *West Side Story*. The song continues to inspire us. Today our church's 'open and affirming' policy gives a wide-open welcome to all sorts of marginalised people who may be shunned elsewhere, as many of them can testify. We believe that, if there is a place in God's heart for each of us in the breadth of our diversity and uniqueness, then there ought to be a place for each of us in the church. We shouldn't have to wait for our funerals before they sing 'There's a place for us'.

Our church had tee-shirts printed with a picture of Jesus on them with wide-open arms and the words 'WELCOME HOME … SUPPER'S ON THE TABLE'. When Jesus tells Thomas he is the way to get there, we think of those wide-open arms. We believe living like Jesus means welcoming people in their diversity and uniqueness as God's children. Living like Jesus means living together in such a way as to open up a welcome, accepting, affirming home where broken and shunned people can rediscover their full God-given humanity.

The world needs to know Christianity is not just for funerals. It's for living. And it's for everyone.

What can you do to help someone realise today that 'There's a place for us'?

Johannine images

5 The beloved

Notes based on the New Revised Standard Version
by Chris Budden

*The Reverend Dr Chris Budden is a minister of the
Uniting Church in Australia. He serves in a parish in the Newcastle–
Lake Macquarie (NSW) area. He is an Associate Researcher within
the Public and Contextual Theology research group of Charles Sturt
University. He is currently working on a contextual theology that
takes seriously the claims of indigenous people.*

The theme for this week's reading is the way in which John's
gospel and the other readings reveal God's extraordinary love
and generosity, the passionate desire to call human beings into a
life in the heart of God's life. Jesus shows a care for his disciples
that is far beyond what one would expect of a teacher or master.
His is a love for a friend, a yearning love that aches for the love
to be returned. It is not love from a distance, an act of goodwill
from Jesus to another. It is a close up and personal love. It is love
that flows from the knowledge that, without this love offered and
returned, life is incomplete both for God and humanity. It is risky,
vulnerable and hopeful love. It is a love that makes hard choices
to care for the poorest and most vulnerable, God's ordinary
people, and calls leaders to account for their failure to care for
such people. It is love that seeks to evoke a response of love and
commitment to God.

March

Johannine images

To love an unfaithful people

The prophet Isaiah is deeply concerned for the people of Israel and Judah. God has lavished attention on this people who have been called to be God's particular people. God has rescued them from slavery, and taught them how a liberated people should live. But they have repaid this care with constant disobedience and unfaithfulness. Most serious among their misbehaviour is the constant violation of the rights of the ordinary people, and the amassing of wealth by a very few (verse 8). This was not the inclusive, equal, caring community God had called them to be. In this situation the people, the ordinary people, cannot be cared for and protected. What more could God do for this people?

In our passage Isaiah says that the two political communities will be destroyed because God will withdraw God's presence and care from the people. The political community that is the nation and its leadership must end. Yet we would get only half of Isaiah's picture if that is all we heard. He has spoken too passionately of God's love for the people to imagine that God could just walk away. Later Isaiah will speak of a more hopeful future that will come after this perverse social situation has collapsed.

In what area of your life are you most likely or tempted to fail to return God's love for you?

Loving God, you nurture us like a tender vine. Allow us to bear the right fruit, to return your love.

Johannine images

More than intellectual assent

Faith can never be just intellectual assent, a cool weighing of the evidence about who Jesus is. Faith is about knowing, relating, having one's whole life rooted in Jesus Christ. In this passage, that relationship is imagined in terms of a vine and its branches. The point of the vine is to bear fruit, and the source of this fruit is not the branches but the main stem of the vine and the roots it sends deep into the soil.

Where I live it is easy to see the cycle of the vine: the buds springing forth, the grapes appearing and growing, and the harvest. Then, after a break, there is a critical decision: which branches must be pruned back so that the food and energy provided by the roots will nurture more fruit and not just ever-growing branches? Which branches must destroyed? On their own, the branches are useless, of no use as timber or for decoration. Their only purpose is in being part of the vine.

Our life is found in relationship, in what happens between us and Jesus, in the shape of the discipleship he calls us to live. It is this that honours God and the love God has for us.

What one thing could you do each day or week that would help you abide more fruitfully in Christ?

At times we think we would be better off on our own, gracious God. Keep teaching us that it is not so.

Johannine images

No false boundaries to God's love

It is not clear whether the Song of Songs is an allegory, drama, series of love songs, a Syrian wedding ritual, or a Hebrew poem influenced by Canaanite fertility rituals. It is clearly a statement in praise of love, expressed in romantic and radiant language. It is simple, sensuous and passionate; and appears to speak of the way of a man with a maiden. Actually, it only got in the canon of scripture because the rabbis said that it spoke of the mystical love of God for Israel.

Regardless of its origins, the Song of Songs does give us helpful images of God. It speaks of passion and sensuality, of relationships that are deeply intertwined – the sort of relationship we should have with God through the Holy Spirit. The free and erotic language employed opens up a space in which people can cross social boundaries and challenge occupational status. There are no false boundaries to the love of God. The poem speaks of gender equality, of the passion and claims of the woman. It also challenges racial stereotypes. The woman is black (like the tents of Kedar) and deeply beautiful (like Solomon's lavish tents). There is love offered and love returned (see verses 7-8).

How do you react to the idea that you are to love God passionately? How could you do that?

Passionate love is scary, God. It wants to catch us up totally, to draw us into its whole life, to enfold us with breath-taking feeling. Give us courage to love you like that.

Jesus cares for ordinary things

This is an extraordinary picture of care. Jesus has been cruci-fied, stripped naked, humiliated, and left in shocking agony. The disciples had nearly all run away; only John remained. Near the cross there was a lonely vigil. Jesus' mother had come to see her son die, to watch her hopes disappear. With her were a couple of faithful friends. Jesus sees his mother and John. In spite of his own agony he says to them, 'you are now mother and son; care for each other'. And John takes Mary into his home.

Of course there is some church politics underlying this story. John wanted to show that his community was a valid and faith-ful one even if it did not accept the authority of the apostles like Peter. He is establishing his own, and his community's, authority; he stayed with Jesus, and he cared for Jesus' mother, and so his testimony can be trusted.

Yet there is also another message. It is easy to turn the Christian faith into something that is simply concerned with eternal life. Jesus is concerned with daily life and ordinary things. He cared for what would happen to his mother and how, as a widow, she would survive in that society.

Small acts of care are as crucial as grand schemes. What small act could you and your church do to offer care in your neighbour-hood?

Lord, it is easy to be so concerned for the big things that we miss the needs at our feet. Help us to care for ordinary things.

Love without bounds

John's gospel is quite clear: women can be included among Jesus' closest disciples. Mary and Martha are loved by Jesus (11:5). In our reading the beloved Mary makes a response of extraordinary generosity. It is a sign of love without measure or restriction. It is not just about words or emotions, but involves the things she owned and which were valuable.

We are reminded in Matthew's well-known parable of the sheep and the goats (Matthew 25:31-45) that Jesus is cared for as those in need are cared for. This passage, in contrast, reminds us that love of God cannot be reduced to love of people. We do love God as we love others, and we do discover the mystery of Christ's presence as we care for others, but that is not the whole story. We are to love God by the relationship we enter into with God through the Spirit, by the prayers we offer and the worship we give. It is to be a love without bounds and excuses. This is a love that can build cathedrals even in a world in need, for it is a love that knows hope and reality beyond our living. Indeed, it is a love that builds cathedrals and has money for those who are poor; neither being too busy with good works to love God, nor too heavenly minded to love the world in which we live.

What one thing can you do to make sure you keep loving God?

Teach us, O God, to love you with endless enthusiasm.

The discernment of the Spirit

At the beginning of the chapter, Paul tells the Corinthians that he wants their faith to rest on the power of God, and not on his clever words. He does know God's wisdom, for it has been revealed through the Spirit who knows all things, even the depths of God (2:10). But these things cannot be spoken to those who rely on human wisdom and who wish to live naturally and apart from God's Spirit. Such people cannot understand the gifts that come from the Spirit and, indeed, see such gifts as foolish things (verse 14).

Truly to understand the gifts of God's Spirit, to know the wonders of the Christian life, we must enter into it through the Spirit. You cannot gaze on the Christian faith from outside and expect to know what it is about. To understand Christ and the Christian life it is necessary to take a risk, to enter into a relationship through the Spirit, to live the life so that its truth is revealed in the living and the Spirit. We need to be so connected and tied to Christ that it can be said that we have his mind. That is real wisdom.

Where in your life do you hold back, waiting for more understanding, rather than taking the risk and sharing Christ's life?

Gracious God, break down our false barriers and pride, and enable us to see with the mind of Christ.

Holy fools

Notes based on the Revised English Bible
by Neil Paynter

*Neil Paynter has been a teacher, a nurse's aide, a
night shelter worker, a mental health worker, a farm
labourer, a fruit picker, a security guard, a bookseller, a
hospital cleaner, a stand-up comedian and a musician. Presently he
is an editor at Wild Goose Publications, the publishing wing of the
Iona Community (www.ionabooks.com), and editor of* **Coracle***, the
magazine of the Iona Community.*

In my work, I have met many 'holy fools': folk in rest homes and
in night shelters who were to me the most prophetic and Christ-
like. They taught me so much. I want to introduce you to some
these friends in the coming week.

*Jesus, as we accompany you into Holy Week, help us to meditate on
the fruits of God's foolishness. And when we meet the holy fools of
our day – in the city streets or out on the exiled edges in places like
psychiatric hospitals – give us the openness and strength not to mock
and crucify them.*

Holy fools

Mark

It took a long time for Mark to find a church he could dance in – rocking and turning and spinning in his wheelchair. 'People are afraid, I guess,' he told me. 'Afraid of joy.' It's not for himself that he dances, Mark says. It's for God, to express his gratitude and thankfulness, and how he's chosen joy finally.

Mark spent six months in hospital with double pneumonia and pressure sores from lying that cut to the bone. Just to move was painful. He cried for entire days. Asked God, 'Why?' 'When can I get up again?' And God said: 'When you learn. Finally, really learn.' He wanted to die. But God said: 'No, you can't die, I'm not finished with you. You have work to do.'

Mark told how, lying propped and positioned between locked bed rails, he was forced really to work through his feelings from his past: his separation from a woman born with a disability, his hurt. His drinking. Above all, his broken relationship with God.

Then – after six months of lying broken in sorrow, with ulcers and sores eating him – Mark resurrected healed and whole, and God said, 'Dance. Stop abusing yourself, stop punishing yourself and others. Stop sitting with words. Dance for all God's disabled people and for their liberation.' Mark doesn't care what people think, he has to dance. It's his purpose, his mission.

Lately he's been dancing figure eights, he says – big, free figures. Flowing, spinning, gliding. 'For a while I was trying to figure out why exactly. And didn't know, so then stopped thinking about it and just danced. Feeling the flowing freedom of it. But then it came to me: If you put a figure eight on its side, you know what it's the sign of? … Infinity. It's infinity. It's dancing infinity.'

Teach me how to dance, dear God.

Holy fools

What kind of a relationship is that?

I can't imagine that Hosea was exactly an exciting man to be with. And then, when he takes his wife, Gomer, back, he informs her they won't have sexual 'relations'. Well, what kind of relationship is that? No wonder Gomer had gone searching for a fuller life elsewhere.

And what kind of relationship is God proposing in this book? One minute he says: 'I am not going to let loose my fury … I shall not come with threats' (Hosea 11:9). The next minute: 'Now I shall be like a panther to them, I shall prowl like a leopard by the wayside; I shall come on them like a she-bear robbed of her cubs and tear their ribs apart, like a lioness I shall devour them on the spot, like a wild beast I shall rip them up' (13:7-8). Well, which is it?

It's hard to have a relationship with a (psychotic) God like that – a God in need of therapy. And it's difficult to *really* believe in God's calls for, and commitment to, social justice when he speaks and acts like that.

So many people today are searching. But they get turned off Christianity because the God we embody is 'loving' and 'accepting' one minute, sin-obsessed and judgemental the next: a narrow, life-denying God unable to embrace modern life in all its fullness. The King of Guilt and Shame. A false idol.

Do you ever feel stifled or abused in your relationship with God and Jesus? Is there anything that you need to speak to God and Jesus about? Or to the church? Do you ever contemplate leaving Jesus Christ or the institutional church for a fuller life elsewhere? Where else might you find (have you found) God and community?

Read Luke 15:11-32 and the Song of Songs.

A time when justice and peace will flourish

Jeremiah's book is censored and burned and he has to go into hiding. He is arrested, beaten and interrogated, imprisoned in a pit beneath a house and starved. Finally, he is dumped down a deep, muddy well.

This could easily be a description of the treatment of a prisoner of conscience today, in 2008 (as I write) – in Burma, Guatemala, Palestine, Guantanamo Bay. Poets, novelists, journalists, union organisers, politicians, teachers, doctors, religious leaders like Jeremiah – people imprisoned for their beliefs. People who, out of deep inner prompting, must speak out, who can do no other. Modern-day prophets who struggle to hang on to hope – to a vision of a time when peace and justice will flourish in their beautiful, tortured lands.

Write an Amnesty International letter in support of a prisoner of conscience somewhere in the world. See current appeals at: www.amnesty.org.uk. Or write to Amnesty International for more information and a letter-writing guide at Amnesty International UK, The Human Rights Action Centre, 17-25 New Inn Yard, London EC2A 3EA.

Living God, you have taught us that faith without works is dead, so temper our faith with love and hope that we follow Christ and give ourselves freely to people in their need: then the lives we live may honour you for ever.

From the Iona Community Worship Book, *1988*

April

Holy fools

The rainbow man

I met the rainbow man working in a night shelter for homeless men. The rainbow man dressed in bright colours – tie-dyed tee-shirts, purple hair, pink nail polish. Spoke in colours. It was a depressing, colourless place – dingy, dirty yellow walls; clouds of grey smoke hanging. He was labelled mentally ill, schizophrenic. At one time he had studied fine arts at college, somebody said, had worked masterfully in oils and acrylics. Now, he worked in Crayola crayon. Drew like a child: dogs and cats and upside down pink-orange flowers planted in clouds. He got beaten up by the men a lot.

One day he brought a leaf in from a walk he took (he was always taking long walks) and held it up to me and said 'To look, see the light in the leaf pulsing, dancing still.'

I was busy and tired and had forgotten how to see, and said: 'Yeah, it's a maple leaf, so what.' I was oppressed and harried: there was someone buzzing at the door again, paperwork, so many important things to do. 'The light in the leaf,' he said again and danced away in a whirl of wind.

And when I sat down and stopped, I realised that what he meant was: look and see that energy, that essence, alive in the leaf. He could see it. He was supposed to be disabled but he was able to see the light of God in a leaf and to wonder at it. After weeks of running blind through my life, I learned from the rainbow man to open my eyes and heart again. To trust.

Pray for those who are rejected by the bulk of society.

Maggie

'Maggie, you've got your teeth!' Maggie stands and smiles, modelling them for us. 'Madonna, eat your heart out,' she says, and laughs in her husky, earthy way. It's quite a contrast: the false perfection of the new, white-white teeth against the brown, wrinkled background of her crooked, beaten face.

It only took a year. 'Wait for your cheque.' 'Wait for your teeth.' Maggie has learned patience. Like everybody here in the night shelter, she's had to. She knows it takes a long, long time for anything to trickle down to a shelter in a basement. Having no teeth is a trial, but after so many trials and losses – abusive men, dead-end jobs, poor housing, psychiatrists and social workers, breast cancer, a best friend who lost all hope, a good friend who was murdered – you learn to endure, and to live with little things like having no teeth.

'You really look great, Mags,' I say, setting up for bingo.

'Well, thank you dear, but they're just a plug in a leak, you know. The body dies, the soul is eternal, as they say. But at least I can chew now, no more soup and mush,' she says, and smiles brightly again.

'Alleluia,' I answer, and stop and gaze at her. But it's not her new teeth I'm struck by – although I'm very happy she finally has them – it's her old laughing eyes and the light that has never left her. The beautiful, strong light that no one has been able to blacken, or rob, or put out, or take away. The miraculous, amazing light she has, somehow, never lost faith in.

Pray for those with many crosses to bear.

Holy fools

Elizabeth

I met Elizabeth while working in a psychiatric hospital. It was a place where few people kept track of the days. Either they were unable to – lost in a fog of heavy drugs – or, because the days were all the same, they didn't bother.

Elizabeth had an amazing and inexhaustible wardrobe and made a point of dressing up extravagantly. She sometimes changed as often as four times a day! Standing smiling, in a long, flowing, golden gown, a floppy hat (both too big for the short old woman who looked like a little girl trying on her mother's outfits), in long white gloves, bright-red lipstick, costume pearls, dangling earrings in the shapes of moons and fishes – she explained proudly: 'I dress this way darling because the days are all the same. And if the dirty old days won't change then, by Jesus, I will!'

Through the long afternoons she danced. In the dirty, fold-up dining room. To a music only she could hear. All around her gathered the ghosts of the place – the suicides, the walking dead.

I danced with her sometimes when I was on duty, and she taught me new steps. Taught me how to open up and hear the music. Taught me how to dance no matter what.

Jesus, teach us how to dance – no matter what.

Readings in Mark

1 To the cross and beyond

Notes based on the New Revised Standard Version
by Maxwell Craig

*Maxwell Craig, a minister of the Church of Scotland,
has served parishes in Falkirk, Glasgow and Aberdeen.
From its launch in September 1990 to December 1998, he was
General Secretary of Action of Churches Together in Scotland; and,
in 1999 and 2000, served as minister at St Andrew's Church in
Jerusalem. He is a member of the Iona Community, and a chaplain
to the Queen in Scotland.*

Mark's is my favourite gospel. It was probably the first to be
written. The other gospel writers may well have had it on their
desks as they wrote. I asked all those who came to be members
of our church to read it through, preferably at one sitting. In
these last three chapters, Mark describes the tumultuous time
that led to the cross and beyond it.

Christians throughout the world see the cross as the distinctive
symbol of our faith. People wear it; hymns proclaim it; churches
are never without it. Yet the cross was a brutal form of
execution, widely used by a tyrannical regime. What the cross
and the resurrection are saying is that Jesus was more than a
great teacher; more than a caring, loving person; he was, as Paul
puts it in Colossians, 'the image of the invisible God'; 'in him all
the fullness of God was pleased to dwell' (1:15, 19). The cross
and the resurrection proclaim this truth, so that we in our day
can be convinced of the ground on which our faith stands.

Betrayal

Jesus' final week in Jerusalem was packed with paradox. He and his disciples were there for the Passover festival, recalling that death had passed over the Hebrew people in their Egypt enslavement. They were also there for the culmination of Jesus' ministry on this earth.

What was to be the climax of those three tumultuous years? It begins with betrayal. Our lives are linked with those we love and those by whom we are loved. When that cup of love is dashed from our lips, we're deeply hurt. The disciples had been formed into a team of varied talents: the practical ones and the thoughtful; the bolder ones and the quieter. They were drawn from different strands of Jewish conviction, but they were at one in their devotion to their Lord. As they shared the sacred Passover meal, Jesus told them: 'One of you will betray me.' It was impossible, inconceivable that one of his closest friends could do this. How could one of them be the instrument of his downfall? Jesus knew it meant his death: there could be no 'passing over' for him. God's kingdom was calling (verse 25); and the coming days would see the breaking of his covenant of love with one of his own. So the pain of Passion week begins.

Lord, can it be me who betrays you? Grant us the grace, we pray, that we may remain faithful to you in our day.

The agony of Gethsemane

It's a beautiful garden, Gethsemane. It stands on the Mount of Olives over against Jerusalem's old city, with its Wailing Wall, its Church of the Holy Sepulchre, and its Muslim Dome of the Rock. In Jesus' time it was much the same, but with the Jewish temple alone bestriding the Temple Mount. During my 16-month stay in Jerusalem I went often to Gethsemane, simply to sit and pray there. Some of the olive trees look so gnarled and gnawed by time that they may well have been there in Jesus' day.

In Gethsemane that night, Jesus knew that his betrayal was taking place; he would have to face the outcome alone. He asked Peter, James and John to come with him. 'Stay awake, while I go and pray,' he said. He was disappointed later to find them asleep, tired out by the tumult of their past days. When someone we know is in trouble, at home or in hospital, they long for a visitor; not a doctor or a nurse, simply a friend who need say almost nothing. Their presence itself speaks volumes. Jesus knew he had to face his passion alone. He prayed that his cup of suffering might pass from him. Yet still he was able to pray: 'Not my will, but yours be done.' That is the glory of Gethsemane.

Help us, O God, to keep awake, to be alert for what you ask of us. Grant us the will to pray, with Jesus, that your will, not ours, may be done.

Courage and denial

It is clear, as soon as they had him arrested, that the high priest and his colleagues were determined to have Jesus executed. They had no power of their own to do that, but they could recommend it to the Roman governor. The dice were loaded against Jesus before the trial began. His courage stands unrivalled throughout that trial. There was another with courage that night. Mark tells us 'all of them deserted him and fled' (verse 50). Not Peter. He had the temerity to follow all the way to the high priest's courtyard. Maybe we criticise Peter too readily. But when he is accused of being one of Jesus' disciples, his courage fails him. Three times he denies he's ever known him.

How do we know that? Tradition has it that Mark's gospel was based on Peter's retelling the story of those three, for him, life-changing years. Peter is saying: I failed him; I denied him that night. Yet still he loves me; he has forgiven me, in spite of my faithlessness. What an amazing grace that is for us to know, when we fail to honour our Lord or witness to him as our Christ! We too can honour Peter's courage and learn from his denial.

Lord, we confess that we've failed to honour you in our living; we've failed to witness to you as our Saviour. Forgive us, we pray; and give us the grace to serve you with Peter's courage.

The poison of envy

At daybreak the chief priests brought Jesus to the Roman governor for trial and for what they hoped would be his speedy execution. As governor, Pilate would have heard about Jesus. He spotted their envy at once. One of their own was more popular than they. When he questioned Jesus he could find no fault in him. He wondered what to do. He thought there could yet be a fitting outcome. It was his custom, at Passover, to release a prisoner. He could outwit the chief priests and give the people their choice – Jesus or Barabbas – confident that they would make the popular choice. He had reckoned without the chief priests and their poisonous envy. They had made sure that, when the crowd was asked to choose, they would shout for Barabbas. And so it was. Pilate was astounded. 'Why, what evil has he done?' (verse 14). But when the clamour rose even further, he delivered Jesus to be crucified.

Envy is a corrosive poison. What about us? We're tempted to look sideways, to compare ourselves with others. They may have better talents, more money, better luck. The truth is that there is no need for envy. God loves all his children without favour, because he is our Father. He calls us to shun envy for his Son's sake on this Holy Thursday.

You've taught us to love our neighbours and we envy them. Help us, Lord, to turn that envy into love.

April

April

The killing

The killing was cruel. The cross was cruelty personified – and the person an innocent man. Crucifixion was a long, slow, barbaric form of execution. So why call it Good Friday, this day of Christ's killing? Because it's the proof that Jesus emptied himself of his divine power and became obedient unto death, even death on a cross (Philippians 2:7-8).

Death is the taboo word for us. We shun it, forgetting that life itself is a terminal condition ending, through our nature, in death. We shun it as if life led to a dead end. Yet we believe that, through Christ's dying for us, death is the door to a new tomorrow. We know nothing of that tomorrow, except that the Lord who has promised to be with us to the end of time will be with us then.

What more can we say about this savage killing? Just this. Jesus was the one free man. He freely accepted his dying. Through it he has made us free to walk his way, to speak his truth and to live his life. Dare we claim that freedom? Would we rather shun his dying gift?

O Christ, the master-carpenter, who at the last, through wood and nails, purchased our whole salvation, wield well your tools in the workshop of your world, so that we who come rough-hewn to your bench may here be fashioned to a truer beauty of your hand. We ask it for your own name's sake.

Celtic prayer

Resurrection

The women had waited all day at the cross. They watched his agony, despaired over his dying; then, Sabbath-bound, wept over their loss of him. Now, on the first day of the week, they go to the tomb to perform death's dues. They can't do it. He's not there. They're told he's risen. They're to tell his disciples. But Mark states: 'They said nothing to anyone, for they were afraid' (verse 8). The other gospels record that they did tell the disciples. It was their privilege to be the first witnesses of the good news of God's victory over death. Later manuscripts couldn't leave verse 8 as Mark's last word. So other verses have been added.

Yet 'terror and amazement' were appropriate responses to their experience of the Friday, the Sabbath and Easter morning. That the women were able to rise from their fear and give us the good news is testimony to the truth of Easter Day. The resurrection is the central pillar of our faith. Because Jesus died and rose again, we can have confidence as we face our own death. More, we can have the same confidence every day of our living. The witness of the women is the shining star that will guide us.

Lord Jesus Christ, the chains of death could not hold you. Give us your confidence, that the chains of our self-centred living may be broken and our lives set free to serve you and the neighbours you have given us.

April

Readings in Mark

2 The good news of Jesus Christ

Notes based on the New Revised Standard Version by Maxwell Craig

The three opening chapters of Mark's gospel present a breathless beginning to the story of Jesus' life on this earth. Breathless, because Mark omits so much of what the other evangelists wrote. There's nothing about Jesus' birth or his genealogy; nothing about his boyhood; nothing about his upbringing or his parents; nor anything as philosophical as John's great prologue. He is proclaimed as entering the world's stage fully mature, with Mark's all-embracing opening words: 'The beginning of the good news of Jesus Christ, the Son of God' (verse 1). Indeed, the climax of Mark's account issues from the lips of an alien, the Roman centurion in charge of his execution, who says: 'Truly this man was God's Son!' (15:39).

Recent translations suggest this verse should read 'a son of God'. For me, that won't do. The Greek text is, and grammatical rules confirm it: 'Truly this man was God's Son.' Mark states this at the beginning; and each following chapter is geared to proving, like a Euclidean theorem, that what was to be proved has been proved. That, I believe, is why the pace of this gospel is so breathless. There can be no waiting, no distractions: all is thrusting towards his final conclusion: Jesus the Christ, crucified and risen, is the Son of God for us and for all time.

The church a team?

The opening verse is electric: 'The beginning of the gospel of Jesus Christ, the Son of God'.

At once Mark sketches the forerunner. John the Baptist is preaching out in the desert; people flock to hear him and to be baptised in the Jordan. When I was working for a spell in Jerusalem, my wife and I went one day to the Jordan. We saw a relatively small river, because so much of its water has been drained off for irrigation purposes. John's purpose is to prepare the way of the Lord. 'I have baptised you with water, but he will baptise you with the Holy Spirit' (verse 8). But Jesus himself comes for baptism; then goes into the Judean desert to prepare for his ministry. When he returns, John has been arrested. This is the signal that Jesus' ministry must now begin. He goes to Galilee and begins to form a team.

For any worthwhile enterprise, a team is vital. Jesus knew that his time on earth would be limited. It was crucial for him to find the right team. Is your church a team? The priesthood of all believers has become a shibboleth. But when a church becomes a team, the difference is immense. Every member a witness; every new day an opportunity for witnessing.

Will you offer yourself, your time and your talents, to be one of your local team in your church? If you do, you will make that difference count.

April

The authority of Jesus

The breathlessness of Mark's writing captures our imagination. In thirteen verses the phrase, 'and immediately' (in Greek, *kai euthus*), is used seven times to demonstrate the effect of Jesus' presence and his preaching. This is a new authority, way beyond that of their traditional leaders. He teaches the crowds; he heals the sick; his fame spreads around the whole region. The expenditure of energy is personally demanding, yet still the crowds gather on into the evening. It's not surprising that he's exhausted. So, early the next morning, he goes out alone and finds a place of quiet. There he prays. His disciples seem unaware of this need. He's gone, so they go at once to find him. Even for Jesus, a time of rest and of prayer is needed, reminding us to set aside time for quiet and for prayer.

The authority of Jesus shines throughout this passage. Even the unclean spirits recognise that authority. The irony is that the church accords to priests and ministers an authority that is not their due. I know, from my own experience, what a thrill it was to be called 'Abuna' by the Arab members of our Jerusalem congregation. I should have quenched that thrill with a douche of Presbyterian cold water! We have one authority, Jesus Christ the Lord.

Take from us, Lord, the misuse of authority within the church, so that we may fully recognise your authority over all your people.

Jesus as healer

Here are two of Jesus' healings. The first is that of a leper. Leprosy was common in Palestine. There was the disease itself, but on top of that was its social exclusion. There's a community a short distance south of Edinburgh named Liberton. It was the 'leper-town' where lepers were obliged to live, at a safe distance from the healthier majority. Jesus' first reaction, when the leper approached him, was to touch him: by doing so he declared that no human being is beyond the reach of God's grace.

Mark then records a second healing. This time it's the resourcefulness of the victim's friends that captures our attention. They can't get him near Jesus, because of the crowds gathered around the house. So they clamber up to the flat roof, made largely of brushwood packed with clay between the roof beams. It was probably quite simple to dig out the filling between the beams and lower the paralytic safely to Jesus' feet. But it is *their* faith, not that of their friend, which moves Jesus to have compassion on the paralytic and heal him. For me, this is a compelling sign that praying for someone is both natural and necessary. What we're doing in such a prayer is precisely what his four friends did for the paralytic that day.

Pray for someone known to you who is seriously ill. Jesus calls us to do just that – and with that prayer follows the action that best fits it.

Three challenges

The crowds are still gathering. It concerns the Jewish leaders; and they look for faults to criticise. First they condemn his choice of a taxman, Levi (aka Matthew), as a disciple. And they're not alone. There's a powerful painting by Caravaggio in Rome showing Jesus' call of Matthew. The picture shows three pointing fingers: Jesus points to Matthew – You, he says; Matthew points to himself – 'You can't mean me', with his other hand firmly on his money; Peter points at Matthew – 'Surely not him?' It's the sinners I'm here for, says Jesus.

Then his disciples are seen eating and drinking freely, with little sign of asceticism. The bridegroom is with them; they have to celebrate. Third, the disciples pluck grain on the Sabbath, breaking the sacred law. Jesus quotes David's action when he was hungry; and his critics are silenced. Silenced, but no less hostile. Already Mark recounts the growing hostility that, so soon, will bring Jesus to the cross.

Our day sees the church facing many challenges. How we deal with these challenges is crucial. Do we dodge them? Or do we recognise that these were the very challenges Jesus faced throughout his ministry? We can draw confidence from knowing that, when we face up to these challenges, we are following the way of our Lord.

Lord Christ, give us the courage to face up to the challenges that threaten your church in our day and refuse to be scared of them.

Team Jesus

The hostility towards Jesus escalates. Now the Jewish leaders are sending their agents to watch him. He defies the law by healing a man on the Sabbath. Infuriating to the scribes and the Pharisees, but highly popular with the people. So the crowds swell even more; so much so that he needs a boat to be moored handily to get away from the constant crowding. Then, in the silence of the hills, he chooses his moment. Knowing that the hostility he is facing is likely to cause his death (verse 6), Jesus takes his first major step towards ensuring that his gospel will continue to be heard after his death. He appoints his disciples, his team. They are to be his constant companions; and to dare to show it – not an easy thing to do when he is already at odds with the authorities.

He gives them two things. First, a message: someone with a message demands a hearing. Second, he gives them power. This is true delegation, recognising that, without newspapers, books or the internet, the only way to spread the message will be through his chosen disciples.

How many of our leaders, how many of us, can trust our colleagues sufficiently to give them both the responsibility and the power to carry that responsibility through?

Lord, give us the grace to delegate such authority as we may possess, so that in humility we may reckon others to be worthy.

April

Opposition nearer home

Jesus' friends, even his family, now turn against him. They see him drawing crowds and consorting with undesirable people. For the good name of the family, perhaps, they want to restrain him, keep him out of the public eye. The scribes see this as their chance. They accuse him of casting out demons through demonic power. Jesus' response sounds deeply shocking.

The unforgivable sin. What really is that? If we look to Jesus and the Holy Spirit and see them as evil or demonic, we've become morally blind. We've put ourselves beyond penitence, because penitence grows out of the awareness of wrongdoing. If we fail to see the difference between right and wrong, we cannot repent. Without that repentance, we cannot be forgiven. But Jesus goes further. His own family are questioning his rightness, even if their motive might be considered caring. He declares the gospel of his incarnation by stating that God's purpose goes way beyond the ties of family or kinship.

Jesus says: those who do God's will, they are my mother, my brothers, my sisters. We try to dodge these verses, because they offend what is natural. And yet we recognise their truth: we are called to step out of what is natural and into what is Christian.

Lord, give us awareness of our wrongdoing, so that we may offer our repentance and be forgiven. We ask this in Jesus' name, through the power of the Holy Spirit.

Politics of God

1 Justice, power, and the state

Notes based on the New International Version
by Jonash Joyohoy

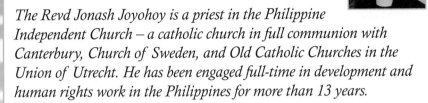

The Revd Jonash Joyohoy is a priest in the Philippine Independent Church – a catholic church in full communion with Canterbury, Church of Sweden, and Old Catholic Churches in the Union of Utrecht. He has been engaged full-time in development and human rights work in the Philippines for more than 13 years.

Situated throughout the globe, more and more Christians find the politics of God a very interesting topic to deal with and get involved with. Why not? The politics of the world are getting more frustrating every day; we need to look for guidance about the structuring of human affairs to God. Yet there are people, politicians and Christians alike, who seek to reduce God's role in politics by dichotomising the social and the spiritual, as if they were utterly unconnected. This should not be the case. Society and Christianity do not exist in two different compartments but in the same environment, the one world that God created. Everyone can live the Christian faith while engaging in politics.

Christians therefore should not distance themselves from politics. 'Politics are too serious a matter to be left to politicians,' General Charles de Gaulle once said. Indifference to politics amongst Christians should be seriously challenged, and Christians should be encouraged and helped to engage seriously in political debate, action and witness. This week's notes may be one small contribution to this debate and to action.

Politics of God

God acts in history

The passage speaks of God's anointing of Jacob and his descendants as leaders of Israel. Consequently, and according to biblical history, Israel's leadership went on under the bloodline of Jacob. Here we can see God revealing himself through the establishment of authority and leadership. Naturally, those so appointed by God are expected to reflect God's love and concern to the whole of humanity and the world.

On the other hand, the passage also portrays the historical reality of God and the subsequent relativisation of human authorities under such a set-up. God makes it clear, 'I am the first and last and besides me there is no other God' (verse 6). Thus, while God anoints leaders, his authority over them is absolute. The powers of those appointed by God are temporary and conditional before the ruler of history.

It follows that faith in God who is ever active is a challenge to all to become active participants of history as well. The people should not allow themselves to be relegated to passivity or disenfranchised of their right to involvement, but should engage in and for good governance. After all, nations and histories are being constructed by the toils and creativeness of those who labour. Participation in the work of building of God's kingdom is then for all, not only for the appointed leaders.

O God who created and nurtured the world, may we appreciate your presence in our lives and the significance of our part in shaping history. Make us builders of your kingdom, and keep us happy in your sight.

The call for us to act with justice

If the previous reflection was about active participation in building the kingdom, in this passage we learn about correct participation and the divine measure or standards in ensuring it. In contemporary times, people are often cynical about social participation. They are alert to the dangers of being misled or misused into serving the ends of certain individuals or corporations. Yet their conscience tells them that they must take the risk of getting involved anyhow.

The passage tells us that justice is God's measure of correct participation. It is the mark that distinguishes those who are God's from those of the devil. Moreover, justice must be pursued in humility if it is to maintain its objectivity (verse 8). Without a genuine humility, the pursuit of justice carries the risk of miscarriage, or worst, being aborted altogether, colonised by the desire for one's own good or name. Humility here means transcendence of one's limited self-interests, and the willingness to be used as a channel for God's truth.

Some workers in rich countries may be annoyed at migrants who compete with them for job opportunities. Unless they are able to rise above their own narrow self-interests, they fail to see the bigger picture. If, however, they try to see things from the vantage point of the migrants, the affected locals will realise that one of the key reasons for the migrants' leaving their families and homelands is that those same lands have been made barren by years of North-based corporate exploitation.

To get at the truth and be on the side of justice, one has to free oneself from narrow personal, sectarian, or racial perspectives and try to grasp the wider picture.

Transcendent God, teach us to rise above our selfish interests and perspectives in order to see the truth according to your standards. Be with us always as we pursue justice in your world.

Politics of God

Abuse of power in the Old Testament

The Bible contains various narratives about the abuse of power. The story of King David masterminding the death of Uriah to take advantage of Uriah's wife Bathsheba is a most glaring example. This is a centuries-old illustration of the adage, 'power corrupts, absolute power corrupts absolutely'. Interestingly, this abusive deed was performed by a God-anointed, and the most influential, king of Israel!

Even in recent history, we see that no one is safe or free from the tendency to abuse power. Those in power, including those with religious and ideological power, are vulnerable to committing abuse. Experience tells us that dependence on the mystical Spirit alone is not enough to stop abuse. God's sovereignty over history means that the divine wisdom may also be found in human knowledge – including the social sciences. Social science can provide reliable systems to avoid or minimise abuse in ways consistent with faith and prayer – neither replacing nor being an alternative to these, but working in harmony with them. Right political and social systems can provide necessary checks and balances so that those in authority are constrained in their human tendency to abuse.

Uriah and Bathsheba would have been spared if the constant prayers in the temple had been complemented with the institution of appropriate checks and balances in governance!

Loving Parent of all, abuses of power are happening because of our indifference. Free us from the guilt of not doing what should be done, and strengthen us as we change our ways.

Abuse of power in the New Testament

The phenomenal increase in numbers of Jesus of Nazareth's followers prompted the Sanhedrin – the temple-based council that represented the Jews to the Roman Empire – to meet in session. And, according to John's account, it was no less than the high priest who, in his official function, prodded the council into making the decision to kill Jesus. This time, however, it was not God's anointed who abused power as we saw in the story about David and Bathsheba. On the contrary, it was God's anointed, Jesus Christ, who turned out to be the target and subsequent victim of power abuse by the establishment. According to John, the death of Jesus was sought by Jewish national leaders in fear of their imperial masters. In short, the Jews had the impression that the Roman Empire was the ultimate target of the ministry of Jesus.

This point can be illumined further by the earlier narrative about the birth of Jesus. Putting aside its dramatic elements, the birth of Jesus happened at the time when 'Caesar Augustus issued a decree that a census should be taken of the entire Roman world' (Luke 2:1). The birth of the saviour occurred at the very time of Rome's systematisation of imperial subjugation via the census. At a time when the great power seeks to exert even more influence on the peoples of the world, God sends a world saviour to counter the world oppressor.

In relation to justice, power, and the state, this story may also come as a reminder that not all human and political authorities are representative of God.

Lord of justice and mercy, people are being killed and abused in many places because of greed. May your saving presence embolden us to function as your stewards; make us courageous channels of your peace.

The Christian duty to support the state

This famous passage appears to be in tension with yesterday's reflection. Relating to the same 'governing authority', the Roman Empire, this passage apparently demands submission instead of opposition. Ironically, these words were penned by a direct victim of state power – Paul, the apostle to the gentiles, who suffered all forms of persecution because of his faith. Why would a victim support his oppressor? Was he coerced into writing the epistle?

If we probe more deeply into the narrative by looking at the context from the standpoint of Paul as victim, we may see a more revealing angle. While, on the surface, Paul calls for submission to authorities, he aptly describes 'God's servant' as bearing a sword against the 'wrongdoer' and not 'for nothing' (verse 4). Those who do wrong and who do not do good should be the ones who are to suffer the sword of God's servant – a responsibility grossly violated by the Roman Empire. In so writing, Paul actually exposes the evils of the establishment. And more than that, he articulates and raises the requirements for the establishment to become true representatives of God, in deed as well as in word.

Supporting the government by means of service, lawful obedience and payment of taxes is axiomatic among Christians. That is not to say that this passage commands unthinking or uncritical loyalty.

God of truth and equality, teach us to see deeply into things. Allow us to support and follow authorities as they deserve, and to be critical of practices that compromise the welfare of your people.

The Christian duty to challenge the state

The final passage for this week visualises those who were martyred 'because of their testimony for Jesus' and the gospel, and for refusing to worship the beast or its image. Writing in the same century when Jesus and his followers were martyred and when persecution of Christians was ongoing, the Revelation writer is presumably referring to Paul, Peter, Stephen and the rest of the early Christian martyrs as those 'seated and given authority to judge' (verse 4). Those who took up their cross and followed Jesus Christ in advancing the gospel are portrayed here as models and recipients of divine reward.

Revelation's affirmation of the martyr's exemplary works holds before us the validity and necessity of the Christian being both 'dove and serpent', both gentle and cunning. In the biblical context and likewise in today's context under neo-liberal globalisation, to be as gentle as a dove and cunning as a serpent is a pastoral necessity. Christians in many places have to assume the role of prophets and defenders in order to be consistent with the gospel call to follow the Good Shepherd against robbers and thieves who kill and plunder.

In the contemporary world when the gap between the rich and poor gets wider and wider, the Christian duty to challenge those responsible is growing clearer than ever.

God of love, through Jesus Christ you gave us grace and show us a concrete example of how to be of service to your kingdom. Free us from worldly standards of happiness, give us freedom to sacrifice our own goods for others, and direct our human energies for the benefit of your kingdom.

Politics of God

2 Marks of God's kingdom

Notes on the New Revised Standard Version
by Lesley George Anderson

*Lesley George Anderson is the President of the United
Theological College of the West Indies (UTCWI),
Jamaica, and Chair of the Praesidium of the Caribbean Conference
of Churches (CCC). He is a member of the World Council of
Churches (WCC) Pentecostal Joint Consultative Group and a former
District President of the Panama / Costa Rica and Belize / Honduras
District Conferences of the Methodist Church in the Caribbean and
the Americas (MCCA).*

God takes the initiative to reach out to us in truth and love.
Sometimes we evade him as we evade each other. We set up
barriers based on race, colour, religion and nationality. We close
our borders to foreigners or those who look different from
ourselves.

The desire for peace is overshadowed by vicious wars. The
world is in political turmoil. There is no genuine unity. Humanity
is fragmented. Distrust is rampant and fear is dominant. The
politics of God throughout history and in every culture is
based on an understanding of God's sovereignty. In the world
of politics, God is the supreme ruler. This belief is what gives
believers absolute confidence in him. In this week's readings we
will see some manifestations of the remarkable imprints or marks
of God's kingdom and the revelatory evidence of God's truth.

As you read and ponder, ask yourself: What implications does this
have for my own politics? Do I consider myself politically active
or not? If not, what does this say about my commitment to God's
world and the community of which I am a part? If yes, do I need
to reconsider my political commitments and priorities?

Be of one heart and soul

Through the power of the Holy Spirit, Jesus prayed for the unity of believers (John 17:32) and 'those who believed were of one heart and soul' (verse 32). The early church, the community of faith, was Christ-centred. With Jesus at the centre of their lives, the believers exhibited a unity in all their relationships.

By an act of God, on the day of Pentecost, the believers were of one heart and soul. Not even their various languages could separate them. Their unity was their strength.

The oneness of the believers was grounded in their common faith in Jesus. As they were united in faith, so they were united in heart. They had the willingness to have the mind of Jesus: to live, talk and walk like him. Their ultimate desire was to love him and proclaim him as their resurrected Lord. They were ready to follow him in humility (see Philippians 2:7-8) and serve him without reserve. There were no barriers to separate them. They even shared their possessions (verse 32). They were one in heart and soul!

In what practical ways can you work with God for the unity of your society?

Lord, help us to achieve the genuine unity of the early church.

April

The truth crucified and glorified

Jesus sends his disciples into the world to proclaim the message of truth. This is what he said: 'They do not belong to the world, just as I do not belong to the world. Sanctify them in the truth; your word is truth' (verses 16-17).

The disciples do not belong to the world but are being sent into the world with the truth. The 'world' in Greek is the *kosmos*, the whole creation of God (see John 3:16). The truth is Christ himself. He said, 'I am the way, and the truth, and the life' (John 14:6). John the Baptist bears witness to Christ and, paradoxically, to the truth (5:33).

Jesus bore the truth in his person. He wrestled with the bitter cup in the Garden of Gethsemane. He suffered and died on Calvary's cross. Through the power of the living God, he was resurrected. The marks of the wounds in his hands and side are evidence of his love for us.

I met a Methodist preacher in Costa Rica who was very ill. He could not walk. When he was healed, he stood on his feet and bore witness to the saving power of Jesus. Today he testifies to an unchangeable truth: Jesus is able!

How effective can a Christian society be politically if it belongs in the world but is not of the world?

O God, we believe that your Son, Jesus Christ, is the truth crucified and glorified.

There is a way out

From time to time I have encountered people who told untruths and used trickery to trap me into giving them money. A few used 'crocodile tears' to break my heart. Jesus was confronted by spies with trickery as well. Their motive was to 'trap him' and get him into trouble with Pontius Pilate, the governor. They asked, 'Is it lawful for us to pay taxes to the emperor, or not?' (verse 22).

The term 'taxes' has a religious origin and the Greek *phoros* means 'payment to a state'. Roman taxation was burdensome, extreme and cruel. If Jesus agreed with Roman taxation, the public might turn against him. If he disagreed, the Roman authorities might consider him a freedom fighter against Roman domination. It appears there was no way out for Jesus.

Jesus considered their question crafty and requested a denarius, a Roman silver coin. '"Whose head and whose title does it bear?" They said "The emperor's." He said to them, "Then give to the emperor the things that are the emperor's and to God the things that are God's"' (verses 24-25).

Jesus' answer is tremendous. The word 'give' in this context means to pay and fulfil your contractual obligations (read Romans 13:1-7). Christians are obligated to pay their taxes to the state. At the same time, being made in the image of God (Genesis 1:27) requires us to love him with our entire being and to worship him in spirit and in truth (read John 4:24).

Make a commitment to pay honestly your taxes due the government.

O Lord, when we find ourselves in difficult and hopeless situations, help us to rely on you for a way out.

Politics of God

The choice is yours

Caiaphas and the leaders found Jesus guilty of blasphemy (read Matthew 26:57). They led him to Pilate who had the authority to put a person to death. Pilate raised a provocative question with Jesus: 'Are you the King of the Jews?' And Jesus answered, 'You say so' (Mark 15:2). Jesus' response was marvellous and, lest there be any mistake about his person, he said: 'My kingdom is not from this world … my kingdom is not from here' (John 18:36). His kingdom is not earthly – it is heavenly. Truth is a king and Christ himself is that king. 'Everyone who belongs to the truth listens to my voice' (verse 37). Those who love the truth will hear the truth. But, 'what is truth?'(verse 38).

There comes a point in our lives when we must make choices. Sometimes we make right choices. Sometimes we make wrong choices. It was the annual Roman custom to release a Jewish prisoner during the Passover Feast as an act of goodwill. The people had the choice to choose the 'true' son or the 'false' son. They chose to crucify Jesus, the true son, and set the convicted murderer, Barabbas, the false son, free. The name Barabbas is Aramaic for bar 'abba' – 'son of the father'.

When we blind ourselves from seeing the truth and close our ears from hearing the truth, the cries of 'Crucify him, crucify him, crucify him' still reverberate around the world.

Why do some people make wrong political choices? And how do we discern what is such a choice?

We thank you, O God, for your gift of truth in Jesus Christ, your only begotten son.

Christ Jesus is our only mediator

Paul tells us: 'For there is one God; there is also one mediator between God and humankind, Christ Jesus, himself human' (verse 5). Jesus is the only mediator between us and God. He is the way, the truth and the life. No one comes to the Father except through him (John 14:6).

One of the most beautiful places to visit is the Caribbean, with its lovely islands, majestic mountains and exquisite sunny beaches. It is a melting pot of many races, cultures, languages, indigenous and major religions. We pray for each other. We pray for our elected officials. We pray in the power of the Holy Spirit and in the name of Jesus, God's gift of salvation (eternal life). He is mighty to save. He is the only mediator. This is a fundamental truth.

When my brother, Guillermo, drowned, followed by the death of a nephew, Luis, and a cousin, Alfonso – one after another – the experience of death was overwhelming. In those crises of life, Jesus Christ became our family's refuge. In our sorrows, he gave us comfort. In our despair, he gave us hope. In the storms of additional sorrows, he gave us strength to cope. He was there for us. He will be there for you too. He is our only mediator. Hold on to that truth.

Do you pray regularly for elected officials in your community and country?

Lord, you gave yourself a ransom for all, desiring that all may be saved. Save me, I pray! Save me! And bless those who lead us and seek to serve us.

May

Jesus' standards of happiness

We live in a world in which power and wealth, social standing and political leadership are regarded as some of the manifestations of happiness. The view that success equates with happiness is false. Jesus presents a different worldview of happiness. To people who desire true happiness, he gives the Beatitudes.

Many people are hurting from the sorrows of war, painful marriages, broken friendships and conflicts of interest. Some children suffer from abusive teachers and drug-addicted parents. How are you reacting to these situations? Are you angry? Are you ready to retaliate? Are you able to forgive?

When we are hurt and wounded in spirit, some of us will seek revenge. Others will wait patiently for the right time and place to retaliate. Pride will soar to protect our shattered personhood. Put such attitudes to death. They are a barrier to spiritual growth. Jesus says: 'Blessed are the poor in spirit, for theirs is the kingdom of heaven' (verse 3). Christ will give strength and grace to the humble. Cry out to him (see Psalm 34:17-18). In him your victory is already won!

Think of examples of ways in which Christians can turn the world upside down by living out the Beatitudes.

Lord, cleanse me of the sin of pride and give me a forgiving spirit.

Oneness of humanity

1   One human family

Notes based on the New Revised Standard Version
by Brian Haymes

*Brian Haymes is a Baptist minister who has served
in several pastorates, the last in London, and has also taught in
two theological colleges. He is married with two daughters and two
grandchildren. He lives in Manchester, England.*

A seriously sad fact about our world is the deep divisions
between peoples. In some contexts this can be a matter of life or
death. News broadcasts tell of people being wounded or killed,
made homeless and refugees, because they were from the wrong
tribe, nation or group and in the wrong place at the wrong time.
It is part of the tragedy of our humanity.

In contrast, the Bible offers another visionary picture, of one
human family. That does not imply a situation where everyone
is the same, for the Bible asserts and values diversity. But it does
show ways, before God, that we might learn to live together. We
shall see how God is creatively at work, holding together what he
has made and restoring what is broken. Given what is reported
to us in our papers and on our screens, this is good news.

Questions for reflection for the coming week

- Why do we make so much of our divisions in the human
  family?

- In what ways can Christian people demonstrate the faith that
  we all have the same parent?

- What differences would this make as we practised this faith?

Oneness of humanity

Made in God's image

On the sixth day God creates humankind, in God's image! What can this mean? Some have argued that it refers to character, that unique spiritual capacity that they and God have in common. Others have stressed the ability to reason, related to the role assigned to us in the purpose of creation.

It is one humanity that is created in the diversity of male and female. Only as one humanity is the image of God present. There may be important sexual differences but male and female are united in the humanity created by God. It is this that urges Christians to say that all people, everyone, is sacred and of unspeakable worth.

Being made in God's image also probably carries the meaning of humankind being in a representative role in God's creation. We are given responsibility, to help creation come to fulfil its life. We have a calling of stewardship and care. Nowhere is humankind called to dominate within God's creation. All forms of domination – sexual, economic, racial – indicate that something has gone wrong and the one humanity is scarred. This is a serious matter because being made in the image of God also means that humankind is called to mediate God's presence in the world.

Creator God, divine parent of us all, thank you for sharing your life with us. Help us to reflect your love and care for all your children made in your image.

Be fruitful and multiply

That story of the great flood, shall we think of it as divine judgement on a disobedient humanity, already fallen into division, murder and oppression? Or might the story be mainly about anguish in the heart of God?

What with Cain and Abel and the advent of murder, followed by the beginnings of tribalism and the enmity that can bring, God's purposes for all humankind seem to have been distorted. Now again the sanctity of all human life is reaffirmed by God. Human blood is not to be shed, an affirmation underlined by the prospect of capital punishment. Christians disagree about that policy but, in the text, it underlines the importance of human life to God. Nothing must cheapen what God has made in his image. Said John Calvin, 'God deems himself violated in the violation of these persons.' All humans are sacred in the eyes of God.

Verse 18 refers to Ham. A horrid tradition once tried to apply the curse pronounced on Canaan to all people of African descent in an attempt to justify slavery and apartheid. It is a wicked distortion of the Bible's message. Thank God, God remembered Noah, one who did right by the purposes of God, so that after the grief of the flood the covenant of the faithful God is renewed for all.

Covenant God, thank you for your faithfulness to all your children.

Oneness of humanity

The inclusive Spirit

In Genesis 11 there is a story of humankind trying to build a tower up to heaven to make a name for themselves. It was an attempt to take control, something that has happened several times in our history as dictators have tried to force their will on the rest of us. God recognised the danger in all this and came and scattered humankind over the earth and confused their languages. This was an act of judgement but also, at the same time, of grace. God affirmed human diversity and taught that unity was not something any of us could impose.

But in today's passage we read of God creating a new unity in the light of the death and resurrection of Jesus. The Holy Spirit, promised not just to the few but to all, comes on the disciples and the result is that Babel is overcome. All hear the good news of God's grace in Jesus, without their differences being destroyed. Peter the preacher did not create this amazing happening. God did it.

The Holy Spirit is always the Spirit of unity, bringing and holding together what might otherwise fly apart. This unity is not something we create but receive in the light of Jesus. Pentecost reveals how God sees the divisions of humankind.

Gracious God, thank you for every expression and vision of one world you give us.

God has no favourites

This is such a crucial story that Luke tells it twice in two chapters to make sure we get the point. It is a common feature of all humankind, often expressed in our various religions, that we divide people and things into good and bad, acceptable and unacceptable, clean and unclean. Sadly, this sometimes has more to do with ancient prejudices and fears than with religion. Peter thought his response to the food in the sheet was proper. Certainly his distancing himself from gentiles, the peoples of all the other nations, was taken to be a godly way of living.

Now God opens his eyes. God is obviously at work in the life of others. The whole story emphasises the activity of God in bringing Peter to the realisation that God has no favourites and what he has done in Jesus he has done for all. The proof of that is in his gift of the Spirit to the peoples of the nations and not just to Israel. This is a momentous development in the life of the early church. Now the story of God must be shared in all the world. There is no place for a God of exclusive love. And the people of the God known in Jesus are called to live out this truth.

Surprising God, keep us alert to what you are doing when and where we least expect your presence.

May

Oneness of humanity

With peoples of other faiths

Paul does not mock the religious variety in Athens. It was not unusual for an altar to be left undesignated, to avoid offence to a god not yet known. Paul simply recognises the seriousness with which the people of the city may be taking their religion. He has no desire to give offence by his own attitude.

Paul proclaims the truth that all humankind is God's creation. We all have one ancestor and are prompted in our religious search by the same God. Paul quotes a pagan philosopher, to drive home his point. The truth of God is not confined to his own religious history.

But Paul does have a particular point to make to these religious people. The restricting of God to a particular place, form of words or images is wrong. Idolatry is always wrong because it reduces the wonder of God to what we think is manageable and desirable. Anyway, explains Paul, the living God, the only God worth honouring and serving, is alive among us. This he has shown in raising Christ from the dead. Paul is not ashamed of this exclusive claim. It is witness to the God who would save us all. The urgency of this message is for all people everywhere.

Give us wisdom, courtesy and courage in our witness to others who know something of you by other names.

God is one

Here is another aspect of our human solidarity. All have sinned. It is the painful truth about us. But Paul makes this point only to drive home another even more significant one. We are all justified by God's grace as a gift. It is God who does what is needful and right. It is God who establishes the right relationship with himself that we have marred and scarred. We are not, however, left to ourselves in despair and failure. In Jesus Christ, God does what is right and restores the fundamental relationship again. God's promises are kept in covenant love.

Our life in God is not a personal or corporate achievement. We have nothing to boast of before God when it comes to salvation. Amazingly, as the one-time slave trader John Newton knew, it is grace that reaches out and saves us. God offers his grace to Jews and gentiles alike. And we are right with God by faith, which is trust, receiving the gift offered in Jesus. Our careful religious observances are not without their value but there is nothing for any one, any religion, to boast about. Our hope and peace in God come as a gift: grace – amazing grace.

Saving God, thank you for the gift of faith and quiet trust you have given us. Help us to celebrate and grow in your love as we serve and worship you this weekend.

May

Oneness of humanity

2 All one in God – barriers are taken away

Notes based on the New Revised Standard Version by Brian Haymes

Last week we realised that the humanity we share is united in several respects. We are all the creation of the one God. We are, each one, made in the image of God and so are of infinite value. Sadly, we also realised that we are united in the fact that we are all sinners, those who have not trusted God enough to share his vision and ways.

This week our readings help us see what God does about this disunity that affects both our relationship with him and with one another. To restore our broken humanity seems to be beyond us. Just think of the deep divisions that are part of our continuing story. Bringing us together, reconciling us, is a task for God alone. How does God overcome our divisions and heal our brokenness?

Questions for reflection this coming week

- Where do you see reconciling work going on in the world today?

- What divisions do think are the most threatening to the peace of the world and how do you think the church should help to overcome them?

- Do you have any further reflections on the unity of the church, not least in your locality?

Oneness of humanity

Abounding grace

In some parts of the world the dominant way we understand ourselves is as separate individuals. We accentuate personal freedom and liberty. Our goal is to become as independent of others as we can.

By contrast, the emphasis in the Bible is on our solidarity, our interdependence. We are not so much individuals, or part of a group or nation, as fundamentally one humanity. In this passage Paul is using this way of thinking to proclaim a great gospel conviction.

He draws the contrast between life in Adam and in Christ. We all are part of humanity as in Adam. This humanity is marked by sin, disobedience, condemnation, legalism and death. It is a form of humanity where there are divisions of hate, indifference and murder.

In contrast, Paul points to Christ. Christ is not a direct counterpart to Adam, for something much more wonderful happens in and through him. Being in Christ is marked by justification, grace and life, the result of Christ's obedience. Though he does not mention it, Paul has the cross of Jesus in mind. Being in Adam contributes to crucifixion. But in Christ, the result is not death but the free gift of God's renewing grace. Through Christ we are reunited with God and one another.

Thank you, loving God, that you long to save us from our life in Adam by meeting us with your abounding grace in Christ.

May

Oneness of humanity

Unity in diversity

Notice the Trinitarian way in which Paul speaks. God gives gifts by the Spirit and activates them all in the service of the one Lord. Christians speak in this way of God. God is a unity with diversity. With these varied forms of self-expression Paul drives home his points about the unity and diversity in the church.

The church in Corinth was a divided church. Too many boasted of their spiritual superiority. Others had no regard for the serious economic differences within the congregations. There were power struggles and too much human pride. Paul argues that whoever has a gift of the Spirit at work in and through him or her reflects the work of the one God. The source of gifts is one. And we are talking of gifts, not our own human achievements. A serious mistake is made when people think that the work of God in them gives them a special status. All in the church are debtors to the one Spirit who is at work in all who are in Christ. So Paul uses the metaphor of the body. It has identifiably different members but it is one body and the members have no life apart from the body. So it is with Christ. Here is the deep unity of the church in the unity of God, maker, saviour and sustainer.

Forgive our indifference to other Christians. Help us grow deeper as the body of Christ.

When water is thicker than blood

We are all of us shaped by our upbringing. For Paul that meant being in a community whose members believed they were more significant than the gentiles, being male was more important than being female and being a free person vastly superior to the life of a slave. Paul would have taken in these assumptions with his mother's milk. They would have been part of normal life.

Now read verse 28 again. Something new has happened in Paul's view of the world. True, there were still Jews and gentiles, men and women, free people and slaves, and a great deal of this mattered in the everyday life of the world. But not in the church, this new humanity gathered in Christ.

Here is a new society or family where the old distinctions that mattered so much are transformed and their significance substantially changed. If you are baptised into Christ then you share a new humanity where the old economic, religious and gender distinctions do not apply. You are not more of a Christian if you are a Jew, or male or free. The church, this new way of being the human family, is different. Outside Christ you might say that blood is thicker than water, my family comes first. But in Christ we find the baptismal waters are thicker than blood. A new humanity is being shared in Christ.

Help us, Lord, to live out our baptism.

Oneness of humanity

The vision of peace

This passage (which can also be found in Micah 4:1-3) is the subject of a sculpture at the United Nations Building in New York (you can see it online at www.un.org/av/photos/subjects/art.htm). It is the kind of vision that captures the hopes of many, perhaps all of us. It inspires peace-keeping initiatives all round the world.

At its heart is the worship of God, and people make pilgrimage to the mountain of God. In coming to worship they recognise their dependence and indebtedness to God the maker of all. They come to worship, to offer themselves. They come to learn of God's ways, to discover how to be obedient. They do this not as an abstract theoretical reflection but that they may walk in God's paths. They are not submitting to a world leader or some theory of world government. They come to worship God, acknowledging God's claim upon them all.

And in consequence they await God's judgement on the nations. God's word is what matters. So they will change the weapons they have used to settle disputes and gain power and turn them into productive farming tools. They will not teach their children to fight in war ever again.

On another mountain, Jesus once said, 'blessed are the peacemakers, for they will be called children of God' (Matthew 5:9).

Lord, grant us your peace. Help us so to trust in you that we become peacemakers.

An uncountable multitude

John's vision is stunning. Here is a huge congregation at worship, with people from every tribe and language, an unlimited international gathering. It isn't just the size that is so amazing, it is the nature of the congregation. All the old divisions have gone. Here in the triumphant worship of God are all those whom God has redeemed and called. It is the triumph of the Lamb.

The whole of Revelation makes this astonishing claim. The meaning of history hidden in the great scroll is not understood by any of the great empires and their leaders. They come and go, inevitably leaving the havoc of hatred and bitterness in their wake. They do not give us the key to history's meaning. The only one who can unlock the scroll is the Lamb, Jesus, with the scars of crucifixion for ever on him. But it is this Jesus who now unites what is divided, healing what is broken. The purposes of God are revealed in the Lamb through whom together we approach the throne of God.

Those early Christians for whom John was writing must at times have felt very vulnerable in their small congregations. But then, and now, comes the realisation that we belong to something immeasurably big, that multitude that no one can count.

Gracious God, give us a greater sense of the universal nature of your church, spread across all time and space, centuries and cultures.

May

Oneness of humanity

Down go the dividing walls

Walls are built to keep some people out and others in. They set boundaries. Think of the Berlin wall that once divided Germany and became the symbol of much fear, hostility and death. Or the wall built between Israel and Palestinian territories. These are hostile walls, dividing off the enemy, walls of bitterness and strife.

There have always been such walls, real or metaphorical. One of the most basic in the years of the early church was the wall between Jew and gentile. But what happened in the life, death and resurrection of Jesus, in the gift of the Holy Spirit, was the pulling down of this wall of hostility. People could never have imagined it happening, but here, in the early church, Jews and gentiles were brought together, in the peace that Christ gave. They were no longer strangers, as if they came from different alien worlds, but were together becoming the place where God's presence is known on earth. One new humanity was truly coming into being in Christ.

A church without walls was coming into being, a church with a strong centre, Christ with the apostles and prophets, an open church where the Christlike God made his dwelling.

O God, whose desire it is that all your children should be saved, enable your church to live out its calling in Christ, calling others into the new humanity made one in him.

Eucharistic themes

1 Thanksgiving and thankful living

Notes based on the Revised English Bible by Barbara Glasson

May

Barbara Glasson is a Methodist minister working with an emerging church that makes bread. She works with people often considered 'on the edge' of city life. She is also Director of the face2face project at The Centre for Theology and Health, Holy Rood House, Thirsk, working ecumenically with survivors of sexual abuse. These reflections are born out of a recent visit Barbara made to bread projects that are being developed in Soweto, South Africa, as a result of the bread-making initiative in Liverpool.

'Nobody is a nobody to God'. We can say this with our mouths but what does it actually mean? Working with people on the edge is a real blessing; it makes sense of the gospel imperative to live lives of generosity and grace. This is not just so that the powerful can redistribute wealth and live justly, although that is important, but so that the radical edge of the gospel can transform all of us. In a recent trip to South Africa I came back once again to this sense of blessing. Seeing the bread rise under the African sun (and moon) brought me to wonder at this great connection with the poorest across the earth. When we say 'Make poverty history', it is not simply a plea to eradicate differences – as Jesus said, the poor will always be with us – but rather to understand that God is entwined within the history of the poor. It is mysteriously within this ambiguity that I believe the Jesus of the gospel is most alive.

Putting our ears on

A small hut at the end of a dusty road in a place called Everton. A gathering singing in the harmonies of South African rhythm. A translator sits behind a table. A woman comes forward and sits on the bare wooden bench. She is going to tell her story. It is time. She tells of the security forces kicking her pregnant sister in the stomach, of her fear of going to hospital, of how she raises her dead sister's family. This is a meeting of Khulumani – 'the speaking out' – part of the truth and reconciliation process in South Africa. Afterwards the counsellor talks of 'being midwife to the stories'. 'It is a labour', he says. He embodies a daily commitment to bring these things to birth.

Later, back in Liverpool, I hear a story of a closer Everton, a place with forty per cent unemployment and an endemic drug culture. Shootings are no longer surprising, some get into the national press. We hear of young people crying out for attention. 'What they need,' says the weary local councillor, 'is a good listening to!'

Today's psalm speaks of God giving the psalmist a hearing (verse 2). Eucharist is the embodiment of Christ's story within our stories, a chance to bring our daily struggles into God's hearing. In the Eucharist we are challenged by the echoes of God's brokenness in the ordinary stories around us.

Today, God, please give me the opportunity to be midwife to somebody's story. When you are silent, God, help me to be thankful that you are listening.

May

Bearing the load

We wait on the steps of the theological college. It is not a hardship to sit in the sun and chat. A woman is walking past with the whole week's laundry on her head. Amongst a lot of hilarity we amuse ourselves by trying to balance the basket as she does. Later, our companion scolds us for admiring someone by the road carrying a bundle of logs larger than she is. 'If we were meant to carry so much weight on our heads, God would have strengthened our spines.'

It is true that, in a country where over one thousand people a day die of AIDS, it does seem that some people have far too much to bear. We meet with a teacher whose class comprises eighty per cent orphans, and hear of a grandmother of 82 who is unable to give up her gardening job because she is the sole wage earner in her family of twelve orphaned grandchildren. We can be far too glib about 'bearing one another's burdens'.

Back in Liverpool, the city councillor reminds us of the need to avoid the language of 'us' and 'them'. 'We are all together in this,' she says. The newspaper headlines all too often call the young people of Everton 'animals'. The weight of prejudice and struggle undermines whole communities. Bearing each other's burdens means raising our heads and looking in each other's eyes.

How can we bear the world together?

For your kingdom's sake help me banish the 'them' word.

Eucharistic themes

Everyday Eucharist

The bread is rising outside in the sun. We have joined the women of Soweto who are making loaves to feed their community. Later, as a seemingly endless queue forms, we are invited to share in the distribution. We place vegetables and maize meal into upturned sandwich boxes until the sun sets. The thanks with which this modest food is received is hard to bear.

There are no simple answers here. In this African context we appear rich but in our own cultures we are just ordinary people with modest incomes. We want at the same time to give what we can and not appear to be white Westerners who have everything. Giving and receiving is everybody's responsibility and only comes with honest dialogue and a longing for things to be different. It is about relationships that share power.

Back in Liverpool, as we make bread alongside the street homeless, a new lad with long blond hair stands beside me at the table. I apologise that I have forgotten his name. 'It's Jason,' he reminds me, 'but my friends sometimes call me Jesus!' At prayer time, as Jason and I light our African candle, I am reminded that giving and receiving are not simply the material exchange of goods but consist rather of transformed, sacrificial, everyday relationships that come into being through the possibility of all strangers being Jesus.

When we give and receive, how are we given and received?

Enable us to live everyday Eucharist, around ordinary tables, with anyone who might be Jesus.

Blessings

There is a curious mixture of death and blessing in the church. In the UK, numbers dwindle through cultural transformation, apathy, suspicion and honest scepticism. In South Africa, the church dies through 'the sickness', the unspoken devastation of AIDS. In September, fifty candles were lit for the members of the younger women's meeting lost since last year. In England we don't light candles for the lost ones, because in truth we can't really remember who is missing.

In Soweto we baptised and confirmed fifty new members. Last Sunday in Liverpool, I baptised one. We will have to wait and see if she will grow up to have a faith. In the meantime, we have promised to nurture her and love her as best we can. She is a great blessing to our bread-making community.

In church we spend a lot of time worrying about whom we should bless. We forget that we are surrounded by blessings, blessings that come from the free and generous outpouring of God's love. It is God who blesses, not us.

At the end of Luke's gospel the disciples are blessed when they feel most desolate. How this blessing transforms them! Fired up with praise and enthusiasm, they are told to wait. Ascension Day is about holding fast in the face of death, and giving praise for our blessings in the waiting times.

How are we blessed?

Jesus, help your church not to ask, 'Whom should we bless?' but rather exclaim, 'How we are blessed!'

May

Outpouring

After a precarious border crossing, approximately 1500 Zimbabweans have taken refuge in the Methodist Mission in Johannesburg. In the daytime they go looking for work; at night they sleep in the church. On the stairs, in the corridors, in every corner, exhausted people try to sleep. At the communion service we were invited to assist the bishop with the anointing of those coming forward for healing. As we marked with oil those many upturned hands, a mother passed me her tiny baby. With the child wrapped in rags nestling in my arms, I made the sign of the cross. I will never know her name, but I will always remember her.

Into the bread mix the Liverpool bakers pour Palestinian oil. As they write their initials into the bread they remember other places where oil is poured: squatter camps, overcrowded sanctuaries or sectarian cities. Wars fought over oil. They write the names of the nameless ones into the bread – an act of simple solidarity with the poorest of the world.

Jesus not only knew that the poor would always be with us but also that we would need to be prompted to remember to live lives of reckless generosity. As the Methodist bishop of Johannesburg preached, looking out over that sea of destitute people that had poured into his church, 'Nobody is a nobody to God.'

How do we embody the belief that 'nobody is a nobody to God'?

Name-knowing God, anoint our impulses with open handed generosity.

Wisdom from scraps

As darkness fell, one African woman said gently, 'We must listen to what the bread is saying to us!' The others nodded, the bread rose gently after its pummelling in large plastic bowls. Looking up at the moon, and being so far away from home, I remembered my son's comment when, as a little lad, I had taken him out into the garden to look at the moon. We had just moved to Liverpool and we were all homesick. I pointed up to the thin sliver of light in the sky. 'Look', I said, trying to comfort him, 'a new moon!' After the kind of pause only six-year-olds know how to make, he replied, 'No, mummy, it's the same moon we had at the old house!'

Yes, it is the same moon, over Africa and over Liverpool. It feels like a different world, but it is the same world. It feels like different bread, but it is the same bread.

The Liverpool bakers celebrated communion at the Methodist Conference. We had enough bread for everyone to take home but still there was some left over. At the end of the service someone asked, 'Would it be OK for us to take the remnants to a party we are giving for refugees?' It was the end of the miracle – or more likely just the beginning.

How can I live more generously?

God of the heavens, help us to recognise we all live under the same moon.

Eucharistic themes

2   The shape of our life together

Notes based on the Jerusalem Bible by Bernadette
Arscott

*Bernadette Arscott is a Sister of the La Retraite
Community, which was founded in 1674 to provide
retreats for women, and today continues to respond to the human
and spiritual needs of our time. Bernadette is a spiritual director and
retreat giver, and lives in Birmingham.*

The readings for the coming week invite us to reflect on Jesus at
table; Jesus sharing food; his relationships with his guests and his
hosts; his values of hospitality and how we are intrinsically part
of his being. He challenges us to become the 'body of Christ' by
being in relationship not just with him, but with all our brothers
and sisters – and indeed with all of creation.

Mealtimes with Jesus are challenging and transforming – the
ultimate nourishment and resource of love. That resource is
what we take with us when we leave the table, and is the gift of
the Holy Spirit empowering us to share this nourishment with
others with generosity and thanksgiving.

The Holy Spirit of God hovers over the whole of creation and we
who are sons and daughters of the Creator live and breathe, eat
and drink in a relationship of love with that same Spirit. It is this
relationship that compels us to take our part as members of the
whole body that is the world, the cosmos, the universe.

Eat, drink and be – in relationship!

Jesus took some bread… As he took bread and as we take bread, we are invited into a relationship with all creation.

Look into the bread – see the wheat growing in the soil of the fields, feel the sun as it ripens the wheat, smell the yeast, the leaven of the flour, pour in the oil and the water and add some sweetness, honey perhaps, and hear the hum of the bumble bee… The whole of creation is here. And Jesus says, 'Take and eat. This is my body.' So be in relationship with the whole of creation.

When we share in the food that Jesus offers, we become part of the body of Christ that recognises every other person as a unique revelation of God. Every person is invited to this sharing of the gift of creation. This is a blessed and sacred sharing. This is the meal of thanksgiving.

When I think of sharing the Eucharist, is there anyone I would not want to invite to the table? Jesus invited the one who would betray him, the one who would deny him and those who would abandon him. Jesus didn't just invite *everyone*. Jesus invited *anyone* to his table.

How about me?

May we walk in Christ's truth and love one another as Christ has loved us.

Christ Jesus, in sharing the bread that is blessed and broken for sharing, may we become responsible to and for each other.

May

Jesus made as if to go on – what if he had?

Is there such a thing as a chance encounter? If we look back at the unexpected meetings we have had over the years, and see them in the light of Jesus with the two disciples on their journey to Emmaus, what might we draw from *our* experiences?

As a young adult, I was on a railway station, deserted except for a woman with two small boys. When I saw that she was weeping I felt embarrassed and started walking as far along the platform as possible. Eventually the faces of the two bewildered children got to me and, feeling in my pocket for some change, I went and asked the still weeping woman if I could offer her a cup of tea. She accepted gratefully and we all went into the station buffet and sat down together. She began to tell me her story and continued when we got on the train, while I entertained the children, now considerably more cheerful.

She accepted me – a stranger. She trusted me with her story and she stayed in touch until the boys were grown up, though I never saw her again.

What if I had stayed at the end of the platform? I would have missed her story, a special encounter, a revelation of God.

Jesus, living Lord, send us your Spirit that we may see how our lives are shaped by meeting others. Help us to embrace every opportunity to break bread with friends and strangers.

Be my guest

Those who invest in relationships also begin to shape their lives around communion of life together. They begin to take on the identity of a 'body'. They have characteristics and values that mark them out and distinguish them.

I know that I am at ease in someone else's house when I am 'at home' there. The hospitality of the host is such that I no longer feel 'the guest'. I feel comfortable enough to make myself a cup of tea and to offer to make one for my 'host'. The guest and the host become interchangeable. This is only one of the marks of a true relationship.

As we come to share and give generously, so we are enabled to receive humbly and thankfully. As we are content with what we have, so we can make space for prayer and praise. As we are faithful to the truths and values we have received, so we can be open to the Spirit, who can do infinitely more in us as the body of Christ in relationship with others, than we can ever ask or imagine.

Where, and with whom, in the shape of my life, do I feel most 'at home' and where do my Christian values become strengthened and shared?

Spirit of God, give us those gifts that empower us to make true and lasting relationships. May those who seek your love and generosity find in each of us a warmth of welcome and an open and compassionate heart.

Eucharistic themes

Not the 'sell-by date', but food that will last

When I visit a friend, nothing gives me greater pleasure than to take a gift in the form of bread that I have made myself. As I gather the ingredients, I start to think about the forthcoming visit and the person I am going to see. As I begin to mix the dough, I think about our friendship and what it means to me. The dough begins to come together and I start to knead. I am focusing on the love I want for the people who will eat this bread as I knead and I knead. Soon it is ready to be left to rise.

Later I return to find the dough has doubled in size and I give it a further knead before shaping it ready to bake. More love, more prayer of thankfulness for this relationship. God is present. This is the bread of life.

When we are seeking Jesus, are we not looking for love? For the only nourishment, the only food that gives life, is love itself. Why are we, who are physically well nourished, still hungry?

Do we, who know we are loved and have so much love to share, give enduring love to others in whatever way we can? Or are we still living by the 'sell-by date' in our lives?

Jesus, bread of life, be our sustenance always, that we may nourish others by the love we show in our everyday lives.

'Because you're worth it'

So says the advert…

The centurion, who earlier in Luke 7 so impressed Jesus with his faith and humility, said the words, 'Sir, I am not worthy to have you under my roof, but give the word and let my servant be cured' (Luke 7:6-7). The centurion believed in the worth of his servant. Jesus saw this and commended not only his faith, but also his humility.

Here, in this parable about the wedding feast, Jesus shows us how easy it is for us to think that we find our 'worthiness' by being like or near the person we judge to be important. The guest who seeks the highest place has lost faith in her/himself and tries to find value by identifying with another whom they perceive to have high status.

If I, as guest at the table, keep my eyes fixed on the hospitality of the host, with gratefulness and a sense of loving relationship with the other guests, I will not be concerned with where I am sitting. I need only rejoice in being invited to the table of the Lord.

In each of my neighbours I can find the presence of God – and then I can hear the voice of God saying, 'My friend, move up higher, you are worthy.'

How concerned am I about the kind of people I know? In a culture obsessed with the famous and those who are called celebrities, how do I find the worth of true relationship?

Lord Jesus,
make me humble of heart,
not seeking after greatness,
only rejoicing in friendship with you and with those you love.

Eucharistic themes

What is your Pentecost experience?

There is a worldwide movement called 'Conversation Café' that invites people to come together – in a café, or wherever – to share, with their host and those who are gathered, their dreams and longings for a better world. The first time I took part in one of these gatherings we were about eleven people who came in 'off the street' into a little café in Bournville, Birmingham. There were eight different nationalities and cultures present, and we each expressed and listened to ideas and suggestions for a better world: a sharing that made our 'hearts burn within us'.

It was for me a Pentecost moment. The signs of the Spirit were there for me in the companionship and welcome of strangers; in hearing the gifts of hope, optimism, compassion, concern for peace, desire for justice and, above all, a willingness to listen.

God's Spirit blows where it wills and the power of that Spirit can manifest itself in the most unexpected places.

Do I expect to be visited by the Spirit only at Pentecost? – or can I discover my own Pentecost experiences? What are the gifts of the Spirit that are manifest in others around me? – and do I know and acknowledge my own?

Come Holy Spirit,
your Spirit of love can change our hearts.
Teach us to reverence in one another the gift of life that we share,
and let us walk in union with your Spirit all the days of our lives.

Eucharistic themes

3   Living eucharistically

Notes based on the New Revised Standard Version
by Donald Eadie

Donald Eadie is a retired Methodist minister living in a multicultural neighbourhood in Birmingham. He lives with a serious spinal condition and has a room within which he offers a ministry of stability and availability. He listens to people who want to ponder life and its meaning, search for a sense of direction and wonder what God is up to in the world and in our lives.

For some people, the faith journey includes moving away from the centre of the busyness of the church into the borders or the margins of church life and, paradoxically, coming nearer to the heart of things. The borders become the new centre, the place of discovery and of exploration.

 The mystery of the Eucharist is not, as is often thought to be the case in our churches, hidden under a fair linen cloth on a communion table approached only by the ordained. The bread and wine are signs of a reality that is always and everywhere present – present in all things, present in and for all people. In the Eucharist we say: God is for us. God gives God's very self within the ordinary things. This is the nature of God.

The invitation is for us to discover resonances, echoes of Eucharist among the people whom we encounter. What is shared in the next few days emerges from listening with those who enter the mystery of bread on the edge.

Transformation through an openness to receive

The story of the foot-washing and the interpretation that follows have become a model for what some choose to call 'servant ministry' and a charter for the church serving within a variety of ways within the wider community.

There is also an interweaving paradox of humility and harshness here. The issue is not just humble service to each other. It is as if Jesus is saying to us, 'Unless you are prepared to expose yourself to encounters where you are open to receive what you have not expected from God – to *receive*, not just give – then you cannot be a follower of mine'. There is within us a deep reluctance to receive, a reluctance to face those encounters that could transform us.

Eucharistic living includes being open to receive the gifts of God through dark and light, through the creative and destructive, through the essential otherness of those who are different. This could mean laying ourselves open to receive through people of the different world faith communities, different sexual orientation or different cultural backgrounds. The challenge is to receive and to lay ourselves wide open to the possibility of transformation.

In the Eucharist we say: God gives God's self within the membranes of life and draws us into the mystery of providing within unexpected ways and unexpected places.

We are told 'It is more blessed to give than receive.' What is your response?

Jesus, you kneel at our feet. Help us also to be open to receive.

Eucharistic living

It has been suggested that the original meaning of the 'this' in 'This is my body, this is my blood' refers back to the whole sequence of gestures connected with the bread and wine. In making the gestures of receiving, thanking and sharing, Jesus explains, 'This is me, this is my life'. And this is still the way God gives new life.

Michael Wilson was both a doctor and a priest. He was also nephew of Edward Wilson, who went with Scott to the Antarctic. In the concluding period of Michael's life he asked that I be his 'eucharistic person'. He suffered with a huge cancerous tumour on his neck. I assumed there would be discussion of choice of liturgy and practical procedures to do with receiving communion. I quickly learned that I was being drawn into much more than a prearranged devotional slot on a Thursday afternoon.

Michael was more interested in eucharistic living than eucharistic liturgies. And on those weekly visits we naturally settled into that pattern of receiving, thanking and sharing. We asked, 'what has been received in the last few days that has been a source of relish, wonder, and thanksgiving?' We realised that the mystery into which we enter is not only one of remembering but also one of incarnation, the incarnation of mystery.

Eucharistic living is about receiving, expressing gratitude and also about sharing. 'The unshared remains unredeemed.'

Where have been your moments of relish, wonder and thanksgiving in the last few days?

Jesus, receive our gratitude and deepen our generosity.

June

The God who prays

After the tsunami, the Sri Lanka Christian Council urged that the people of the churches meditate on Psalm 46: 'though the earth should change, though the mountains shake in the heart of the sea; though its waters roar and foam, though the mountains tremble with its tumult … The Lord of hosts is with us; the God of Jacob is our refuge' (verses 2-3, 7). Our shared testimony remains: the Spirit is brooding within the world's chaos, creating, forming, wooing and calling into being.

God's Spirit groans within the whole created universe as in the pangs of birth. It is a continuing groaning within the bewildering travails of our time. We are right to shudder and also to wonder when we proclaim the eucharistic affirmation: 'Heaven and earth are full of your glory.' There is an old Jewish prayer: 'Blessed art thou, Holy one of blessings, whose presence fills all creation.' And an old hymn that includes this line: 'In all life thou livest, the true life of all.'

Some of us need reminding from time to time that prayer is more than something we do when we curl up in some religious corner. Prayer belongs to the nature of God. God's Spirit prays within us, prays within all our faculties and not just those with religious labels attached.

Spirit of God, hover over the chaos as you did the first chaos, and bring out of it life and hope.

Gerard Hughes after 9/11

June

Being and doing

We were living in the family's much-loved simple wooden cottage by a lake in the forests of central Sweden. My wife's family has lived in that forest area since the sixteenth century. And we were asked one day, 'But what do you do here?' And the mischievous part of me replied, 'We be.'

Of course there are lots of things to be done: water to be fetched from the well, wood to be chopped for the fire, mats to be scrubbed clean in the lake, clothes to be washed and food to be cooked. And it is also a place for being, a place for gazing, for pondering, a place for wondering about the being-ness of things, the birch-ness of the birch, the blue-berryness of the blueberry, the orchid-ness of the orchid, the squirrel-ness of the squirrel, and the elk-ness of the elk. And for wondering about the encounter with the being of God within the being of creation. And the being-ness of God within the being-ness of human beings.

In a world with so much waiting to be transformed, we may wonder about the significance and the power of being. There is a description of God that some of us never quite understood but have never forgotten. It appeared in the writing of the theologian Paul Tillich and was made popular by Bishop John Robinson – God as 'the ground of being'.

Perhaps the being and the doing are more interwoven than some might imagine.

'I have given up thinking and taken up gazing.' How do you respond?

Help us, Lord, with both the being and the doing.

The God who prays

A friend who is a South African nun speaks of the significance of waiting and watching during end times, of the end of some familiar institutions and organisations – religious, educational and social – and the need to help them to die well. And also of our need to wait and watch for birthings, emerging new patterns and forms belonging to resurrection.

We were taken early one morning to a women's empowerment project in Kandy in central Sri Lanka. For years the dark, rundown building had lain empty. A handful of courageous and mainly elderly women from the local Methodist church, some former midwives, nurses and teachers, had transformed the derelict house into a home for destitute younger women who had suffered abuse and rape. They were taught hygiene, nutrition, childcare and self-esteem. They learned to care for their babies, for themselves and for each other. The aim of the project was to build up resilience, to affirm confidence and skills for work and to rebuild bridges towards the families that had rejected them.

The invitation of Jesus is to be communities of resurrection. We should encourage each other to share our stories from around the world, from the neighbourhoods where we live, and from within our own lives: stories of birthing, of uprising, of surprise. Resurrection stories are often elusive, confusing, messy, wobbly – mysteries.

I believe in the resurrection of the dead. Do we?

Jesus, open our blind eyes to see buds of resurrection.

You are set free

The promise is not, 'one day you will be free', but, 'you are free.' It was a wet winter night and there was an invitation to leave the warm and set out towards a party. Local Muslims were throwing a party to celebrate a marriage. The groom was a community worker who had helped refugees and migrant workers to find a place to gather, a place to pray. The bride was a teacher who had travelled the world, working in Argentina, India and Sweden. Now she worked in one of those schools in the back streets of Birmingham, a primary school for Asian children.

The local Muslim community wanted to say, 'thank you', as they looked back on hard days. The school hall was a feast of cultures: dancing and singing by Indian women in beautiful costumes, Irish folk music, including bagpipes and whistles, and dance. People of very different cultures and languages, from Pakistan, India, Ireland, Uruguay, Sweden, the Caribbean islands and Britain, no longer spectators appreciating the contribution of others but participants prepared to leave their corners and to share in dance and music – women and men, young and old. The food was prepared and served by the men.

A foretaste? A Eucharist on a winter night in a school hall?

Jesus, help us to live as those set free to live our thanksgiving

June

Readings in Mark

3 Parables and healings

Notes based on the New Revised Standard Version
by Doff Ward

*Dorothy Ward is a retired teacher who has recently
celebrated 25 years as an Anglican lay reader. She
spends time learning and working in the field of spirituality in an
ecumenical setting.*

The readings for the coming week, taken from Mark's gospel,
cover a wide variety of incidents and involve a great many
people. They offer us an opportunity to meet and ponder some
of the doubt, certainty, agony, fear, joy, surprises and tests of
strength that people long ago lived through when coming face to
face with Jesus.

Living in today's world we are separated from them by the
passage of time and many of us by our culture, upbringing,
lifestyle and status, but in common with them, meeting with
Jesus can arouse in us many of the same, or similar, inner joys and
conflicts that have been felt by men and women throughout two
thousand years since those original gospel events. We owe them
– both the ones in the gospel stories and the ones who came
after – a debt of gratitude, for they offer us a great panorama of
what it can mean to be living and learning, avowed and active
followers of Christ. If we are willing to learn from them, they
have a great deal to teach us.

Just imagine!

Today's reading brings us to one of the best-known stories that Jesus told and the opportunity to consider how best to respond to the parables when we meet them. Some, like the parable of the sower, can be heard, appreciated and applied to people in every age, whereas others are set very firmly in the time when they were told. What they hold in common is an invitation to do two things: first, what Jesus often asked, to listen; and second, to use our God-given gift of imagination.

Many of the parables provide a snapshot of the kingdom of heaven. Because snapshots are very commonplace to many people today and frequently come to be viewed in sets rather than singly, we tend to go through the pile quickly, allowing each one only a cursory glance. In this way we miss much of the background and detail they offer.

We can view the parables in much the same way since they too tend to be grouped together in the gospels. They can be a richer source of wisdom if we discipline ourselves to reflect on them singly, taking time and allowing our imagination to lead us into the story and provide 'spectacles' through which we see what they have to say to us where we are.

Lord Jesus,
help me to give my whole attention to your word,
that your Holy Spirit may enlighten my inner eye.

June

Looking for the unexpected

There is an emphasis in today's reading on the need to listen. Because there is so much for many of us to take in and respond to in the modern world we can become superficial listeners. One practice that can help to counterbalance this tendency is to read scripture aloud. This habit can sometimes help us to notice and hear the unexpected word or detail that, on a surface reading, can seem insignificant or throwaway.

Why today, for example, might Mark have included the fact that the disciples took Jesus with them in the boat 'just as he was?' (4:36). Using that phrase today we might refer to someone not at their best or someone in comfortable leisure clothing, not dressed 'for the occasion'.

To take Jesus 'just as he was' was to have a very different meaning for the disciples. They took with them someone tired, apparently clapped out for the moment, likely to be without drive or energy. When the storm arose and they were in danger, they discovered what it meant for Jesus to be 'just as he was'.

Who for you today is Jesus 'just as he is'?

Lord Jesus,
I come as I am,
bringing my needs, my gifts,
my strengths, my weaknesses,
to you, just as you are.

Go or stay?

In today's reading Jesus is faced with a request that to us may seem strange. The people who saw the demoniac transformed into a perfectly rational man responded by asking Jesus to leave their neighbourhood.

Many of us gifted with average intelligence and competence can find it difficult to know how to relate to people with severe learning difficulties. We greatly admire those who are trained in their care, or know instinctively the right balance between kindness, respect and guidance. The temptation is for us to stand back and leave it to them.

Perhaps recognising this gives us the key to understanding the people who, seeing the demoniac sitting clothed and in his right mind, asked Jesus to leave their neighbourhood. His action had exposed their apparent deficiency. They had been sure that nothing could be done for the man and had resorted to shackles and chains. Jesus, with the faith that they lacked, had brought about the transformation using, as it seemed, only the right words. Did that leave them feeling uncomfortable and inadequate? Do we wish to turn our backs on people and experiences and situations that make us feel uncomfortable and inadequate?

How might those people have fared if they had asked Jesus to stay in their neighbourhood and he had done so?

Lord,
ever present in my neighbourhood,
help me to recognise you,
welcome you,
and learn from you.

Go for it!

Why hope when there is none?
When all investment in hope
had yielded nothing?
Yet hope's flow could be stemmed no more
than the flow of blood from my body.
Meagre leavings, hope and shame,
to penetrate the crowd surrounding him
and make my silent plea
(for uncleanness has no voice).
Yet at his turning, speech came;   *a frenetic flow of words.*
And shame met mercy,
hope met love,
grief met peace,
the insidious flow of blood
secretly staunched.

If we go back in time and hear the facts of the case, how would we rate the chances of a healing for the woman with the haemorrhage? Jesus was on his way to save the life of a dying child and so surrounded by crowds that he was virtually hemmed in. Women at that time and in that culture were not favoured by their status in society, and this woman would not have had the physical strength to push her way through a demanding and excited crowd. Even had the crowd been sympathetic towards her, the disciples were not encouraging all and sundry to get close to Jesus. And yet the woman managed to get close enough to touch the hem of his garment! Even allowing for that achievement, was Jesus likely to have delayed his vital journey for someone whose need was not urgent? Yet he did!

Gracious Lord, give me the strength to keep faith when problems crowd in on me.

A part to play

At the point when news of the child's death is announced, Jesus finds himself in company with people with a whole range of beliefs, opinions and feelings. Some would have been totally dismissive of a healing being possible, some desperately trying to hold fast to their faith, some flooded with doubt, some reluctant to abandon diminished hope and some already grieving.

This is an illustration of God being in the midst of a whole sea of human emotions, an inner as well as an outer tumult. Christ's reaction was to bring order into it: first to reassure; next to select those whom he wished to accompany him who, between them, had strong feelings of love, desire, faith and hope; third, to exclude the mockery and noise and go in to the child with those focused on healing.

After the child had been restored came the practical instruction to give her something to eat. Here was a gracious handing over to the mother with the reassurance that she had a part to play in the healing. Never would food have been prepared with a heart so filled with relief and joy and thanksgiving!

Many people have a part to play in healing and, however modest that part may be, their work can be appreciated and strengthened by our quiet, thoughtful prayer.

Healing Lord, help us, as and when we can, to be alongside you in the healing of body, mind and spirit.

June

Travel light

Because the twelve disciples setting out on their mission were told to take the minimum to ensure their physical comfort, protection and provision, they were forced to depend not upon what they had, but upon who they were. Distant in time as they are from us, it is possible to build up a fair picture of who they were: twelve individuals who came from different backgrounds, had different strengths and weaknesses of disposition, intellect and upbringing, had been called by Jesus and had responded positively, had become members of the community of his followers.

As members of that community they had the opportunity to *observe* Jesus closely, noticing how he acted and reacted towards people; *be influenced* by him, learn from him and question him; *absorb* and remember what they learned; *appreciate* where and when and how he prayed; *grow closer* and more caring towards him and each other.

Through the attentive and prayerful reading of the gospels the opportunity *they* had has been extended to *us*. Unless we are too weighed down with things we choose to carry on our journey, we can find time and space to hear God's call, receive and accept his love, authority and direction for *our* journey.

Heavenly Father, be my protector,
Lord Jesus be my model,
Holy Spirit be my guide,
that I may travel light and in good heart.

4 Stirrings of conflict

Notes based on the New Revised Standard Version
by Doff Ward

> *Listen! I am standing at the door, knocking;*
> *if you hear my voice and open the door, I will*
> *come in to you and eat with you, and you with me.*

Revelation 3:20

Through sermons and reading and hearing what other Christians have to say, we are introduced to many different portrayals of God. They can range from an indulgent and kindly Father Christmas figure to a fierce and seemingly vicious policeman, and we can harbour a very confused picture in our minds.

Set against this we have a strongly drawn portrait of Jesus, the Son of God, in the gospels. To look at this portrait closely and hear and absorb what he taught we have the opportunity to do more than clear our minds: we are offered the means of building, rebuilding and strengthening the most important relationship that life has to hold out to us.

In the readings for the coming week, continuing in Mark's gospel, we shall reflect on Jesus as the central figure of the narrative. In doing that, we can be reassured that we shall be working in harmony with him for, in the words of St Paul, 'In Christ God was reconciling the world to himself' (2 Corinthians 5:19).

June

165

Let me introduce you!

Although our reading today centres on John the Baptist, we could be offered no better guide for getting to know Jesus better. Speaking to his disciples, John said of Jesus, 'He must increase, but I must decrease' (John 3:30). We shall be well advised to follow his lead by setting aside our own concerns and busyness for a time and allowing ourselves space to move into the situations in which we shall meet Jesus in the days ahead.

Today gives us an insight into how different people would react to Jesus by considering how Herod reacted to John the Baptist. Although John was his prisoner, he aroused in Herod fear, attraction, perplexity, the acknowledgement that John was righteous and holy and the desire to protect him. What, in John, evoked this reaction?

John's message was not selling himself, but Jesus. As we know that he taught his disciples who Jesus was (John1:29), it seems likely that he spoke on the same subject to others and we know that Herod liked to listen to him. Had he not allowed pride to rule his action one wonders whether Herod would not have had John killed, but retained him as his prisoner in order to hear more of his message.

In what ways can pride be a barrier, preventing people from getting to know Jesus today?

Lord, help me to recognise anything preventing me from getting to know you better, and empower me to step over such barriers.

Whose problem?

The prospect of a period of rest and renewal for Jesus and the disciples seems to have been denied them by the will of the crowd. The natural reaction would have been frustration and anger, and perhaps that was so for the disciples, but in Jesus the persistence of the crowd aroused compassion. He discerned a greater need.

When it grew late, the disciples recognised that the crowd needed food, the sensible answer being for Jesus to send them away and for their need to be served by the action of the people themselves. In their sight this was not a spiritual issue but a situation needing a practical solution. Were they in effect saying, 'It's not our problem'?

Jesus had a different viewpoint. He too saw the need of the crowd. Did he also see complacency in his disciples? He reacted not only by teaching the crowd, but teaching his disciples that they had a part to play in providing God's children with their daily bread. Where the disciples saw their own inadequacy, Jesus saw their potential.

Lord, help me to offer willingly what I have to offer, little as it may be, in answering need in today's world.

June

Time to move on?

Can a miracle harden hearts? It seems for the disciples that this had happened. Perhaps their recent successful ministry of healing and casting out demons (Mark 6:13) had convinced them that they were fully trained and needed to learn no more. The feeding of the five thousand had shattered that illusion. It had been incomprehensible to them, leaving them out of control, a state that most human beings find difficult to accept. Letting God be God can be a challenge, arousing a desire in us to reclaim control by hardening our hearts and putting trust in our own rational explanation of things.

The disciples had yet to grow in faith if they were to proclaim the full meaning of the good news. Seeing them in difficulty, Jesus sets aside his original plan of passing them by on the water, intending, it would seem, for them to draw their own conclusions from what they saw. Instead, in response to their fear, he offers them reassurance and they are moved on from witnessing a miracle that answered the needs of others to a miracle in answer to their own need.

If, like the disciples, we need to grow in faith, what might be the first step to take?

Lord Jesus, help me to seek you in the unexpected and to accept you as a God of surprises.

Must it be this way?

Earlier in his gospel Mark paints a picture of the growing popularity of Jesus and his teaching, but he later introduces the attitude that Jesus aroused in the establishment. The behaviour of his disciples offered an opportunity for the growing tension to be given a voice and from Jesus there comes a strident voice, speaking out against hypocrisy.

The legal experts, or scribes, were genuine and passionate in working to define the written Law in such a way as to offer guidance for its interpretation. In many ways their work was valuable but, as Jesus pointed out, it could lead to foolish misinterpretation so that the focus became small issues rather than greater human need. There could be no greater contrast to that misinterpretation than in the behaviour and teaching of Jesus, whose focus was always on the needs and care of the people he met.

Ritual and disciplined behaviour has a place in the lives of most people and in the life of the church, and it is of value provided it fills the role of servant. Keeping our focus on the life and teaching of Jesus guards us against it taking on the role of master.

Gracious Lord, may the restriction of habit never hold me back from following your way of truth and life.

June

Here and now

Today's reading offers us the rare privilege of being in company with the disciples and having Jesus explain his teaching to them. Often we meet passages in the Bible that we can find difficult to understand and we would welcome the opportunity to have Jesus explain them to us in the way that he talked to the disciples on the way to Emmaus (Luke 24:27). One way that many people have found this opportunity opening up to them is through an ancient way of praying called *lectio divina* (holy reading). The method is simple; the fruits can be very rich. A time of say 10 to 20 minutes each day spent praying in this way with the passage for the day can help to relate what we read to our own time and our own lives. Try the following simple method.

First, read the passage through several times. Then ask yourself: is there a word or phrase that seems to be significant for me? Stay with what comes for a few minutes, repeating it in your mind. Does the word or phrase relate to where I am in my life now? Does it offer any kind of invitation or sense of direction for me? Listen out for the word of Jesus speaking to you here and now.

Lord, I ask that your word may find me receptive, and bring forth in me the fruit of righteous living.

Don't be put off!

Drained and drawn,
child of mine,
while I have a voice
to curse or cry
those devils
shall never claim you.
Gentile scorned
shall not submit.
Woman challenged,
with womanly wit
shall sponsor her child,
daughter of God,
to be rightfully claimed
by the healing word
of this wondrous,
whispered, Son of God.

We read of many instances in the gospels where Jesus was approached by people of determination whose wish and will for themselves or others to be healed gave them the strength and ingenuity to overcome obstacles. We hear nothing of those who were not prepared to stir themselves or take the risk of being deterred or disappointed, yet they must have been many. Some who heard of others being healed or their lives being changed may well have lived to regret their own lack of motivation when the opportunity had been there for them. Others were perhaps prepared to follow the crowd, but not to fight their way through it like the woman with the haemorrhage (Mark 5:25). Although they do not appear directly in the gospels, Jesus captures such people in the parable of the sower (Mark 4:2), and in our own time we can meet them everywhere.

Loving Lord, give me the determination, as well as the will, to serve you.

Burden bearers

1 Friends and supporters

Notes based on the New Revised Standard Version
by Jim Cotter

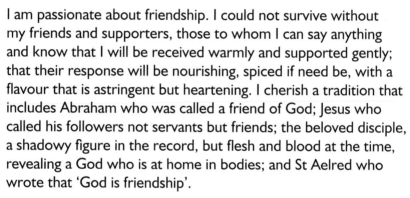

*Jim Cotter is an ordained Anglican who ministers
in the parish of Aberdaron in north-west Wales to
householders and to visitors, and who writes and
publishes as Cairns Publications. See www.cottercairns.co.uk.*

I am passionate about friendship. I could not survive without
my friends and supporters, those to whom I can say anything
and know that I will be received warmly and supported gently;
that their response will be nourishing, spiced if need be, with a
flavour that is astringent but heartening. I cherish a tradition that
includes Abraham who was called a friend of God; Jesus who
called his followers not servants but friends; the beloved disciple,
a shadowy figure in the record, but flesh and blood at the time,
revealing a God who is at home in bodies; and St Aelred who
wrote that 'God is friendship'.

I also relish the challenge that we be 'godfriends' to one another
(like 'godfathers' and 'godmothers'), those whose deepest
concern will be the ultimate wellbeing of the other. And each
of our friendships is unique, a mixture of 'chemistry' (a word
we use for something mysterious!), affection and goodwill.
That 'chemistry' may well be diffused sexual desire, the desire
that sometimes flares into greater intensity, and more often
remains gently and subconsciously in the background, nurturing
the friendship, even perhaps making it the most indissoluble of
human relationships.

June

King or friend?

A shepherd boy, one of the lowest of the low, and the prince, one of the highest of the high. Is a friendship of equals possible between the bottom of the kitchen table and the top of the banqueting table? Yes is the answer here. David is the king's servant but the prince's friend, and the prince saves his life and risks the wrath of his father. Jonathan even invests David with his clothes and his armour. What gossip did that provoke at court? And you can't have a closer relationship than is implied by the binding of souls and the loving of another as much as one's own soul, as much as one's own life.

Here is an extraordinary love, a 'sacred covenant', touching the very core and marrow of the being of two friends. And the prince tricks the king, an act of treason against the polity of the state, and saves the life of his friend. To the king, his son has brought shame to his family; to the prince, his friend has brought out in him a sense of honour that speaks of a higher loyalty. Which of them is closer to God?

Would you betray your country to protect your friend?

God of friendship, deepen my loving that I may one day lament with David that my friend was greatly beloved to me, surpassing the love of spouse and family. I pray this in the Spirit of the One who laid down his life for his friends.

June

Burden bearers

Conditional or unconditional?

When will we see a church notice that invites the stranger to join 'the company of the disreputable'? Those seeking to do the will of God find support amongst those unthinkable to the ones who have a reputation to build, who depend on the approval of society, who want to walk the corridors of power. God is not a God of the pure, with clean hands. He mixes with spies and prostitutes. And there is no indication in the story that either the spies or Rahab changed their working practices after their exchange. Much to the dismay of the respectable, Rahab even finds a place in the genealogy of Jesus, according to Matthew, along with three other questionable women: Tamar, Ruth and Bathsheba (Matthew 1:1-17).

Friendship may grow from the support that we calculate will be to our advantage, even the mutual support that is to both parties' advantage. And few are the friendships that can be completely equal. But no matter. We can at least be honest about our mixed motives and be glad that we are not pure-bred, but mongrels.

What support have you received from a friend that feels like a debt you can never hope to repay?

God of truth, give me the honesty to admit that I am not mature enough to give unconditional love to my friends, all day and every day. I pray this in the Spirit of the One who incarnated that amazing love.

Homestead or unknown land?

Oh the pull of convention! Ask yourself what are the accepted norms of your society, the ones you grew up with. Then reflect on Naomi and Ruth and Orpah: how powerful for them were the particular forms of marriage and family, tribe and territory, that were taken for granted.

Without husbands, women had no secure place in the community. Doubly so if you had come from another tribe and another territory: you were estranged from your original family and you could not worship your god – gods in those days being thought of as having only one bit of the earth as their domain.

Imagine the three women in border country, being pulled this way and that, Orpah back to her own homeland, Naomi back to her original homeland, and Ruth uncertain which way to go. It is her love for her mother-in-law that triumphs over all the powerful messages she had no doubt imbibed.

Who can fail to be moved, even at this distance of time, by anyone who says this to another? 'Where you lodge I will lodge; your people shall be my people, and your God my God' (verse 16).

Who is more important to you than your family?

God of challenge, give me courage to question what I have never questioned, and to act as I have never acted, despite what the neighbours will say. I pray this in the Spirit of the One who left his family for his friends.

Burden bearers

Advice or presence?

I sit down to write to a friend who is troubled. I am at a loss for words. Hmm. That may be good for both of us. I make do with clichés and feel uneasy. Perhaps I can write that words alone can never satisfy. Perhaps something like, 'Words fail me and I can but sit here in silence holding you to my heart.' Perhaps there is more consolation in silence, even more if the silence is given along with my presence. Yet how hard that is! To sit in silence, to give no advice, to feel helpless, and maybe to hold a hand. (A friend of mine ruefully muses that in hospitals visitors are often more dangerous than viruses!)

Even if Job's friends turned out to be false comforters when they could stand the silence no longer, at least they didn't speak for a week, but simply sat with him. (Have I taken that in? For a week!)

How often have you sat with a friend and said nothing? If never, why not?

God of the calm at the heart of the storm, give me the patience with myself to lay on one side the anxieties that rise within me when I am faced with distress, and give me the courage to sit in silence, and not to run away. I pray this in the Spirit of the One who taught us to take no anxious thought for tomorrow.

Wealthy and skilful or poor and useless?

Somebody has got to look after him. It's all very well, this 'nowhere to lay his head', this wandering around the countryside not knowing where his next meal is coming from, telling people to look to the birds of the air and trust that God will provide. Somebody has to do the cooking. And have you seen the state of his shirt? He never notices.

Oh, I know. There's never been anyone quite like him. You've known his healing touch, Mary, and you're calm at last. Joanna, you're always listening to him, trying to work out what his stories mean for us. (By the way, is Chuza's job safe? You've raised quite a few eyebrows at court by your enthusiasm for Jesus.) I just wish he'd recognise how much it costs to keep nomads moving.

Men, Susanna, they always find it hard to receive. But it's tough for us too, who have resources to spare. We don't realise how much we need the contributions of those who've been taught they've nothing to give.

What is the difference between one-sided and equal friendships?

God of justice, even in small things, open our eyes and ears that we may recognise how much we owe to others, not least in the skills that we ourselves do not have, however hidden they may be. We pray this in the Spirit of the One who was supremely aware.

June

Burden bearers

Favourite or focus?

Was I his favourite? He seemed to need something from me that nobody else could give. He said things to me that nobody else heard. He trusted me with what troubled him.

I was younger than most of his closest followers: I always felt inferior when I was with them. They were tougher, more knowing, plenty of experience to draw on. Yet he often singled me out, I still don't quite know why.

But I know why he was special to me. I didn't really trust anyone when I was a child. I was locked into myself. It was as if I merely existed, sealed off in some dark, tomb-like room. But I wasn't quite dead. There was something alive, deep inside me, that I wasn't aware of. But he was. He spoke to me, waking me up, calling me into the light of day and the warmth of love. It made all the difference.

Now I am old, and I'm amazed that the stream of life still flows through me, that his love and mine are so intermingled that I can't separate them. I hope it touches everybody else in my life.

Does your closest friend increase the amount of love you give to others?

God of friendship, keep me from being sealed off from others, widen and deepen my friendships, and so increase the amount of love in the world. I pray this in the Spirit of the One who never stopped loving.

Introduce a friend to

Light ^{for our path} 2009 or *Words* ^{for today} 2009

For this year's books, send us just £3.00 per book (including postage), together with your friend's name and address, and we will do the rest.

(This offer is only available in the UK, after 1 June 2009. Subject to availability.)

 **IBRA**
International Bible Reading Association

Order through your IBRA representative, or from the UK address below.

Do you know someone who has difficulty reading *Light for our Path*?

Light for our Path and *Words for Today* are both available to UK readers on cassette.

For the same price as the print edition, you can subscribe and receive the notes on cassette each month, through Galloways Trust for the Blind.

Please contact the IBRA office for more details:

International Bible Reading Association
1020 Bristol Road, Selly Oak, Birmingham B29 6LB

0121 472 4242

sales@christianeducation.org.uk

IBRA International Appeal

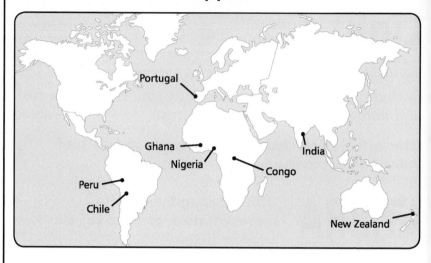

In five continents you will find Christians using IBRA material.

Some will be using books and Bible reading cards translated into their local language, whilst others use books printed in English. As well as our current overseas partners there are many more organisations who would like to print the books and cards themselves.

The IBRA International Fund works through churches, Christian groups and Christian publishing houses overseas to make these Bible reading resources available. Each year we receive more requests for help from the IBRA International Fund for assistance in producing these materials, but the only money we have to send is the money you give, so please help us again by giving generously.

Place your gift in the envelope provided and give it to your IBRA representative or send it direct to

The IBRA International Appeal
1020 Bristol Road
Selly Oak
Birmingham
B29 6LB
United Kingdom

Thank you for your help.

Burden bearers

2   Mentors and teachers

Notes based on the New Revised Standard Version
by Mike Holroyd

*Mike Holroyd is currently pursuing doctoral studies in
Disability Theology. However, Mike has previously 'done time' in the
classroom, teaching both religious education and music in secondary
schools in the south-west of England. Mike is both an Anglican and
a committed member of the Metropolitan Community Church. He is
currently exploring ways of integrating the call to ordination with his
own sexuality and disability.*

The role of the rabbi in both Old and New Testaments is much
revered – though this week's readings go beyond teacher as
conventionally understood, and include political as well as
religious leaders, parents and spiritual guides. The readings this
week not only tell important stories, but also encourage us to
take a closer look at ourselves as teachers and learners, mentors
and apprentices.

June

Moses and Jethro

It's amazing how someone slightly removed from a situation can shed some extremely helpful new light. Moses, tired and overworked, begins to tell the story of the Exodus – he has become so wrapped up in it all that he fails to recognise the blessings that Israel has received. But Jethro sees straightaway and praises God. He offers some extremely practical advice. Moses has continued to try to get involved in every detail of every little problem that faced his community. We do not know the reason for this, but it is clear that Jethro was concerned about Moses becoming burned out. So, the solution was simple: learn to delegate – not just to anyone, but to suitably qualified people who can be trusted. Importantly, Moses was not to give up his responsibilities – rather he was to use his wisdom and expertise to sort out the most complicated issues.

Sometimes the greatest wisdom comes from those one step away from the everyday activity of our lives. It takes someone to point out the potential harm we may do to ourselves if we carry on the way we are. Many of us find it difficult to delegate, perhaps because we are afraid that no one can do it as well as we can, or that we may become dispensable if we step back from a particular role.

Have a good look at all the responsibilities you carry. Do you need a Jethro to give you some pointers so that you can avoid burning out and have enough space to recognise the goodness of God in your life?

June

Moses and Joshua

Change is here to stay – these are discomforting words for many a congregation and the source of much discussion and dispute. But change is inevitable. Moses was unique, a charismatic founder whose wisdom and leadership inspired a community for scores of years. However, the community had to come to terms with an indisputable truth – that Moses would one day die, and the people would have to get used to life without him. So, a suitable successor was found, and Moses started the process of the handover.

I am about to take a sabbatical from my work. One of my tasks will be to hand over my role to my successor. I am no Moses, I can assure you, but these verses have reminded me that we all have a responsibility to enable others to develop their leadership in a way that reflects their own gifts and abilities, not ours. I will need to take care to hand over appropriate facts and tools, without expecting the person who follows me to run the project in the same way as I have done. There will always be core values and objectives that need to be carried forward, but those of us responsible for handovers need to take a step back once this has been done – though perhaps not in such a final way as Moses did! Objections to change can often be about an overdependence on charismatic figures. Moses knew that it was time to start looking for someone else to take over the reins – we too need that wisdom.

Think about some of the roles you have – are you still a beacon, guiding others, or have you become a pillar, getting in the way? Are there things you need to hand over to others?

Deborah and Barak

This story must surely inspire the surprise of many a woman – a man actually listens to and acts upon sound advice! Female judges are not unknown in the book of Judges, but in Christian history as a whole I think we can safely say that the contribution of women to salvation story has been understated.

The NRSV appears to convey at least a neutral interpretation of the collaboration between Deborah and Barak – sadly the NIV interpretation views the partnership as shameful. This reminds me of a conversation I had with a street evangelist who was convinced that God used Deborah only because 'he' had exhausted 'his' supply of good men. However, the truth is that, despite cultural norms, Deborah's God-given insight contributes to a temporary lull in the oppression of the Israelites. Time and time again, God uses people often thought to be cultural outsiders to convey a crucial spiritual wisdom.

We need to reclaim the truth of this story – that God can use anyone in the pursuit of justice and peace. Those who are marginalised often bring the most profound insights into situations and communities. Collaborative ministry built on sound relationships of trust and respect will always achieve more than arrogant autocracy.

As a church, will we continue to silence the voice of the marginalised, or will we embrace them with open arms, in order that we may cherish their words, and realise our common salvation?

Eli and Samuel

This is a much-quoted story, but rarely do we register its full significance. Although things had not gone well on Eli's watch (to put it mildly)(1 Samuel 2:22-36), he was still able to play a crucial role at the start of Samuel's prophetic ministry. His loss of sight was no barrier to his ability to offer wisdom and guidance. It was Eli who had the task of teaching Samuel to hear the voice of God, even though this was soon to take the shape of hard words for Eli and his descendants (verses 12-14). The final part of the story reads as a confirmation of Samuel's moving from apprentice to fully fledged prophet.

It takes all kinds to build the kingdom of God – young and old, disabled and non disabled. There is a definite transition in this story, from Eli to Samuel, from one generation to the next, one style of leader to a new one. But there is also a mutuality of giving and receiving – the roles are complementary and dynamic, each needing the other in different ways. So it is with us.

Do those of us who have had faith for a long time always welcome the words of those who are at the start of their journey? Does God sometimes have things to say through them that our dependence on experience has blotted out?

July

Burden bearers

Mary, Joseph and Jesus

I have seen parents panicking when their child has disappeared into a crowd for just five minutes. It would not have been unusual at the time of Jesus for the whole community to take responsibility for children – so it's not surprising that it took some time to realise that he was not with them on the way home after all. It must be hard for parents to empathise with Jesus. 'I thought you'd know where I would be' is hardly a fitting response to distraught parents who have been searching high and low, scarcely able to hope for the best whilst fearing the worst. But, whilst this is one of those all-too-human stories that evokes all kinds of emotional responses in readers, its purpose is of course to remind us about the parent that is in every son and daughter, and the teacher that is in every child.

How many times have you heard a child say something that is profound in its simplicity? Sometimes children have an amazing talent for being able to identify quickly the important things in life. Jesus knew the importance of the relationship between himself and his heavenly Father, even though he may not have anticipated the amount of anxiety he caused his earthly parents.

Although they may not always follow all the appropriate protocols, children so often have things to say that we would do well to hear. Perhaps by paying a bit more attention to the voices of children, we might also get more in touch with the child within each of us.

Paul and Timothy

Timothy was clearly a popular man amongst the faithful, but he had to pay a high price to become an accredited leader, for some would accept him only if his Jewish inheritance was as undisputed as his good character. Paul had high hopes for Timothy, wanting to make sure that he did not end up like those others who had, according to Paul, gone astray.

Mentoring can be a tough role. We need to be careful to allow other people to develop in a way that enables them to grow, but we also want to steer them away from making the same mistakes as others have made, or that we ourselves have made. Parents have a huge responsibility to guide their children, whilst allowing them the freedom to explore and find their own way through the maze of life.

We all have those we look to for inspiration, challenge, wisdom and comfort – and we all have the potential to offer those gifts to others.

O God our Mother and Father, you nurture us as your children and mentor us as your disciples. We give thanks for those who have inspired us by their words and by their actions. We praise you for those who have gone before us in faith, leading the way and encouraging us to follow. We offer our gratitude for those who see the potential in us and use their experience to draw out your gifts in us. We pray that, by your grace, we will inspire others through our love, our commitment and our stories.

Burden bearers

3   Colleagues and peers

Notes based on the New Revised Standard Version
by Laurie Richardson SSC.

*Sister Laurie is an Anglican contemplative nun of the
Society of the Sacred Cross, Tymawr Convent, in rural Wales. Before
joining the community in 2002, she worked in theatre and the arts in
Canada.*

Sometimes we need our eyes opened to see that we are not
sufficient unto ourselves. We try to do it all, or cover up, or do
without, rather than see that maybe we are not meant to be
self-sufficient in all that God asks of us. If we allow ourselves
this thought we may begin to see that there is a gift for us in the
other. Living in community, day in day out, with fellow Christians
is a continual opportunity to see this gift of the other in daily
life. As Christians, we can only really come to know who we
are through the process of relating to one another in Christ. We
cannot be whole without the other. We are not autonomous
individuals. Rather, we are essentially bound up with and in
each other. We are one body; branches from the one vine who
is Christ. We need to know how to be dependent, how to
ask, how to receive. These readings all show us a way to learn
and grow in the truth of who we are through another person,
through recognition of our mutuality and equality.

Bound in brotherhood

Here is a model of the kind of mutuality into which God calls us. Moses is insecure despite God's reassurances. So much depends on him and he has no confidence. Aaron is given to him in his need. Where there is a need there is always a gift, if we can but find it. Aaron becomes one with Moses in the intimacy of speech. Together they make a new relationship with God. God creates a new relationship and accepts them as one. And through this the people come to believe and worship the Lord.

Maybe two can do what one cannot. There is something about Moses and Aaron here that is very touching. The older brother steps in, stands in for his sibling, providing a stability and confidence that sometimes only family can.

Am I able to admit my need? Can I risk showing my vulnerability?

I acknowledge my need; may I open my eyes to your gift.

July

The gifts of friends

Here is such a crowd of heroes, each named with his deeds of bravery. This is a community of equals, united in fidelity to their common cause and in their mutual respect. Each sees the other as honourable and worthy. They are David's protectors and each would give his life for the king. Indeed, this is what three of them risked as they drew water from the well at Bethlehem. Because of this, David would not drink the water; instead he poured it out for the Lord.

Their sacrifice became his sacrifice, their oblation his oblation.

Giving life for life is the ultimate gift. By their act, the water was made holy. But their other gift to him was to reveal his humility. David has eyes to see that, though he is their king, he is not their superior.

Do I want to hold myself back and stay within the accepted hierarchy or am I ready to recognise – and celebrate – true mutuality and equality?

Help me to know that we are all loved absolutely by you; may I embrace this radical freedom.

Together in patience and persistence

Moving to a new level of maturity in a relationship is always a challenge. Discerning the right time is key.

Three times Elijah says that he is called to go on while Elisha is to stay behind, but Elisha will not leave him, will not let him go. Elisha knows that the time has come for Elijah's departure, yet he is not ready for the moment of transition. Elijah asks him what he wants; Elisha must make his desire known, he must speak and confess to the other.

Elisha feels he is the one to whom the mantle of prophetic spirit and authority is to pass. But there is the risk that he might be wrong. The outcome is uncertain.

We sense that both accept the outcome in stages, knowing it is not theirs to decide. Together, Elijah and Elisha wait on God and God's time and God's will. Elisha attains maturity through this mutual focus and trust.

Help me to wait with another, to share my spirit and to hear your word.

Bound in faith and trust

This is another story of a step forward in relationship. Jesus shares his ministry with his followers by sending them ahead to all the places he intended to go.

What is he asking of them? What are they to learn? They go out to warn, to prepare, to bring in more labourers for the harvest. Jesus wants to show them the bigger picture – the kingdom at hand, the world in need, and the world's blindness to its need.

The disciples will undoubtedly be strengthened by the experience. They go with nothing: 'I am sending you out like lambs into the midst of wolves' (verse 3). All they have for the task is peace, and the good news. They are to share what they have and accept what they are given. They go with faith and with one another, and so discover what it is to be one body. There is certainly no self-sufficiency here, and no reward except survival and the joy of the good news. If there is to be a community it must be strong and courageous, and Jesus invites his followers to see that they are equals in his work.

Open my eyes to see the amazing power of faith. Open my heart to the fellowship that surrounds me.

The strength of goodness

Quite simply, Paul could not have done without Barnabas. Paul was certainly confident and capable, but he could be prickly too, and his reputation as a persecutor of the church could not be ignored. Someone had to vouch for him in Jerusalem where the disciples, quite reasonably, were afraid of him. Barnabas told his story, defended him, and said he was sincere. He stood up for him and became a bridge, an intermediary, a mediator. He provided a support for Paul, and was a counterpoint to his character and personality.

Together, they were more than two strong individuals. They needed each other. When Barnabas saw the growing church in Antioch he went to Tarsus to find Paul to help him in the work. Barnabas was known as 'a good man full of the Holy Spirit and of faith' (Acts 11:24), a 'son of encouragement' (Acts 4:36) – trustworthy and full of courage, heart. This is a profound and important gift, truly life giving. In the company of such a person we feel safe and heartened ourselves, and we can go on to do so much more than we thought.

You are the great heart of all. May I live in this strength and so be an encouragement to others.

July

United beyond conflict

Being the body of Christ always calls us to go deeper; it is never all finished and decided, with all the troubles sorted. This story is an illustration of the kind of challenge and discernment we are still presented with today. James, Peter and John, and Paul, Barnabas and Titus have acknowledged their mutual respect. Their ministries differ but all is the work of Christ. But when Peter visits Paul in Antioch he eats with gentiles until people from James come, then he loses nerve. Others begin to be swayed – even Barnabas.

Paul is always concerned that no one be a stumbling block to another. The other's weakness is of more concern than one's own need; we must adapt our actions to be of support to the other. Peter's dilemma is that he would like to support both the gentiles and his fellow Jews. Yet for Paul this is inconsistent with the truth of the gospel – that we are one in Christ.

Unity does not mean lack of conflict. Because he values and trusts absolutely their unity in Christ, it allows Paul to challenge Peter to stick to what he believes and to accept the consequence of conflict. Paul does not question Peter's apostleship: he is not coming from a place of judgement, but of deep mutuality. Underlying his challenge is a deep and abiding love.

When the possibility of conflict next arises, push yourself further than you are comfortable with to move into it and trust the Spirit to lead you into a deeper awareness of unity.

I want to live into unity. Open my eyes that I may follow you.

Burden bearers

4   Challengers and critics

Notes based on the *Bibel in gerechter Sprache* (Bible in Just Language, Gütersloher Verlagshaus, 2006) by Antje Röckemann

Antje Röckemann is a minister of the Evangelical Church of Westphalia, Germany, and works as co-ordinator for women's affairs in Gelsenkirchen. She is co-editor of the feminist theological journal Schlangenbrut. *She is engaged in feminist inter-religious dialogue and in the development of a spirituality focused on body, movement and dance.*

The biblical texts for this week focus on conflictual relations: arguments, quarrels, even hostilities and enmities. To live an upright, honest life causes conflict. One who sees and speaks clearly will quickly become unpopular; one who has a firm belief should not be surprised to meet barriers and opposition.

The selected stories are mostly concerned with male actors, for example, a prophet who gives his opinion to the king. In most stories there are just two parties: the 'good' and the 'bad'. In two of the stories, however, one of the main actors is a woman. Is it merely a coincidence that these stories don't use the scheme of a good and bad player? In fact, these stories tell of a dialogue of equals and include a kind of 'happy ending'. It's interesting to ask, what are the Queen of Sheba and the Canaanite woman doing differently from the men? What can we learn from them to enable us to enjoy more successful encounters with others?

Criticising the king at the expense of Bathsheba

Who can stand up to such a power-hungry person as King David? Who can stop him? Bathsheba, a woman and a foreigner, could not. David saw her, desired her, raped her and afterwards made her a widow, so that his adultery did not become public.

The prophet Nathan tells a parable to confront David with his failure. David understands immediately and admits his deed. So far so good: the prophet proves to be a good friend helping to straighten David's relationship with God. But at whose cost? David's child is the innocent victim in the story, as are his wives (notice the plural!).

This story is a popular sermon text in my church, but with the notable omission of verses 11-12. And indeed, how can the preacher explain that David's guilt is atoned through the public rape of his wives? And why must the child die? What kind of God is this who acts in such a way, and how is God distinguishable from David?

I find I must dissociate myself from this God and this solely male story of violence and vengeance – yet hope nevertheless that power-hungry persons, particularly power-hungry men, are stopped by courageous people.

Where do I have power – with the danger of misusing it? Where can I take the role of a prophet?

We ask you, God, for those who have power,
that they use it with respect for every human being.
We pray for those who experience injustice,
who suffer from violence and misuse of power.
Help them, also, through us.

Praise and criticism alike

This mythical story that has inspired many writers and artists shows the fame of Solomon's kingdom, which represents the epitome of cultural blossoming. Under his reign Israel became a player on the stage of international politics and culture. In biblical terms, Solomon had *chokmah*, wisdom.

Yet throughout the story the Queen of Sheba takes the initiative. Her wealth and her intelligence are quite equal to Solomon's, and their meeting is a kind of intercultural dialogue, an international meeting at the highest rank. It is an encounter of equal partners, her equality being perhaps the best gift that a foreign visitor could give. The intensity of the experience and the erotic nature of the encounter is suggested in verse 13.

The queen's long speech is full of praise. Perhaps later editors added verse 9, with its hint of criticism, subtly implied. Although the source of Solomon's wealth is no subject of the dialogue, it can be assumed that this wealth arose by exploitation of the population. The queen alludes to this indirectly by speaking of the criteria for the good use of Solomon's power: justice and righteousness.

The desire for wealth is rather a taboo. But aren't culture, beauty, art, music and happiness part of the 'abundance of life' that most of us desire?

God, we ask you for the women and men
who are able to live in abundance and with happiness.
Be near those without any such expectation.
Let them encounter friends
who encourage them to believe in their own possibilities.
Let us discover this strength also in ourselves.

Burden bearers

Omnipotence versus justice

Here is a criminal story, uncovered by Elijah in the name of
Yahweh. A greedy king and his greedy queen instigate a judicial
murder so that they can cultivate vegetables in a nearby vineyard!
This doesn't make sense – a king hardly cultivates his own
cabbages! The story is in fact a novella. Its political as well as
religious background is the contradiction between a kingdom
run on absolutist lines and the traditional, Israelite way of life
regulated by laws that protect the people. The contradiction is
enshrined in the meeting between the prophet Elijah and the
king Ahab, who is rightfully addressed as the guilty, responsible
person.

The prophet tries, though with little success, to make the king
act faithfully and thereby protect the rights of the Israelites.
The king's failure is punished – with loss of power and public
humiliation. Ahab's repentance at the end of the story only delays
the punishment to the next generation.

However, this story is not so much about individuals' actions
and motivations as raising questions of communal righteousness
and justice concerning the limited rights of kings and the greater
significance of faith in Yahweh.

Which religious or secular prophets or prophetic groups are
you aware of who act to challenge political power as Elijah did?
Which ones do you support?

God of justice,

the ear for our concerns,

hear us into speech,

that we may talk even without words,

that we may act to realise your dream for our world,

of a life lived in freedom and justice.

To face the truth

In 597 BC Jerusalem was conquered, and many Jews were exiled. In 586 Nebuchadnezzar destroyed Jerusalem again, and displaced its inhabitants. This is the time of the prophet Jeremiah.

The prophet relentlessly uncovers the religious, social and political deficits of his time; he predicts a catastrophe. Jeremiah is a great performer, acting as well as speaking his words, to make doubly sure he is understood. His opponents were kings, priests, other prophets, the people – in fact, everybody. They call him 'crazy' (Jeremiah 29:26).

The priest Pashhur imprisons Jeremiah. His job is to prevent the announcement of total disaster. Facing military conflict with the Babylonians, he cannot let the prophet undermine the morale and the strength of the people. Coming from a priestly family, Jeremiah should know and understand the consequence of his actions.

Jeremiah's estimation of the political situation was correct. Resistance was useless, the conquest was total. But how could his contemporaries know his predictions would be proved right? We shouldn't condemn Pashhur. One of the most difficult decisions is to know when the ordinary doing of one's duty is right and when it is wrong. Who is right is only shown by history – in hindsight…

Franz Werfel's *Hearken Unto the Voice* (German original 1937) is a fantasy historical novel about the prophet Jeremiah, which I commend to readers. Associations with present-day political systems are deliberate.

God, you expect us to face the truth
but it is often hard to bear.
Teach us soberly to observe reality
and to discern the difference between
the soothsayers and those who speak the truth.

A new perspective

In this text Jesus is presented in a shocking manner: he is ignorant, nationalistic, misogynist even. Why does Jesus reject the woman's request so openly and in such an insulting way? How is this request for help any different from other requests? Because it is from a woman? Because she is a Canaanite and thus not Jewish? The offence culminates in the comparison of the woman with a dog. It is intolerable!

Nevertheless this story remains one of my favourites, for it shows Jesus learning. He does not stick to his original view, but he dialogues, he listens to the reasoning of the foreign woman of a different faith. And as a result he changes his attitude. The nameless woman argues skilfully, at first agreeing with and confirming Jesus' view, accepting the image of children, bread and dogs he uses to humiliate her. 'Yes,' she says in verse 27. But then continues with 'however...' and adds a new facet to the image – the crumbs. She proves herself as theologically adept as the rabbi – and she makes Jesus extend his horizon to a world and human beings outside his own people.

This is the only story in the gospels in which Jesus changes his view in a dialogue – remarkably with a woman and foreigner. All other 'disputes' with (male) theologians are 'won' by Jesus.

Try – just for one day – to listen to someone with a different background, faith or ethnicity. What do you learn – about them, about yourself?

God, we live between wisdom and cleverness,
between justice and self-interest.
Sharpen our ability to recognise
what is really helpful to others and ourselves
to bring us together across our differences.

One faith, many opinions

This chapter is a report from the Council of Jerusalem in which the apostles discuss the relations between Jewish Christians and gentile Christians (you may compare Paul's report in Galatians 2:11-21). From this we learn that there are already different groups and opinions in the early church. The Jews among them naturally follow the rules of the Torah. Besides them there are the non-Jewish Christians – should they also follow the Jewish law?

Paul and Barnabas represent one extreme position: faith alone is sufficient, the commandments of the Torah are not necessary. The Jerusalem party on the contrary thinks the observation of the Jewish law is compulsory. James, the brother of Jesus, represents a compromise view and this is the decision they all agree on. The gentile Christians need accept only some basic rules.

In this debate reasons are not given, there is no reference to Jesus – and indeed, no argument of Jesus is quoted as relevant to this question. Despite the council's decision, all in all the position of Paul became the generally accepted view. But Christianity thereby lost its solidarity with the Jewish sisters and brothers and a whole part of the inheritance of Jesus was lost. Things could have been very different today if James' decision had won out.

What would you like to learn from the Jewish faith, from the Torah? How does it help to be a Christian if you know about Judaism?

God, source of all the living, we all look to your son Jesus, the Messiah, the Christ, although we belong to many peoples from all around the world. Let us value our diversity, and praise you in all our different ways and words.

July

Ezekiel

1 The call of Ezekiel

Notes on the New Revised Standard Version
by Ann Conway-Jones

Ann Conway-Jones is an Anglican, living in Birmingham, involved in Jewish–Christian relations. She is studying the early Jewish and Christian mystics who used Ezekiel's imagery in their descriptions of heaven.

In 597 BCE some of the most capable people in Jerusalem were rounded up by the armies of the Babylonian King Nebuchadnezzar, and made to walk the thousand miles to Babylon. Among them were King Jehoiachin and Ezekiel, the son of a high-ranking priestly family. From exile Ezekiel followed the deteriorating situation in Jerusalem. The new monarch, Zedekiah, reneged on his loyalty oath to Babylon, and planned rebellion, entering into an alliance with Egypt. This provoked a furious Nebuchadnezzar to return to Jerusalem, and after a long siege, in 586 BCE, the city and its temple were captured and burnt. A second wave of its inhabitants was taken into exile. There are allusions to these political manoeuvres in the book, but Ezekiel tries to make sense of current events from the perspective of God's holiness. His understanding of God, at times bizarre, even grotesque, is far removed from our historical and scientific knowledge. Do his fantastical visions, strange actions, and emotional intensity still speak to us? You will have to decide for yourself.

Some of the same imagery, and the same range of emotions, are to be found in the psalms. After each day's notes I have quoted a verse or two from the psalms. You may like to look up the whole psalm, and use it in your prayers.

God's throne chariot

The book opens with a surreal vision, drawing on ancient oriental imagery for God. God is depicted as riding in the sky in a chariot made up of living creatures. Wind, clouds, fire and lightning accompany God's appearance, as they did at Mount Sinai (see Exodus 19:16-18). Later in Ezekiel we learn that the 'living creatures' are cherubim (see 10:20). The Bible describes God as 'enthroned on the cherubim' in several places (see 2 Samuel 6:2 or Psalm 80:1). The ark of the covenant in the holy of holies of the tabernacle was surmounted by two cherubim, and God would speak from between them (see Exodus 25:18-22). Ezekiel's cherubim are different from those on the ark, which is maybe why he does not recognise them immediately. But that is part of the point: nothing about God can be pinned down.

Notice how many times the phrase 'something like' appears in the chapter. What is being described is beyond description. But whereas we might use abstract terms like 'transcendence', here theology is conveyed through concrete imagery. The God whose majesty fills heaven and earth can also appear in one place. God is holy and unapproachable, but also free, mobile, and eternally watchful – notice all the eyes on the rims of the wheels.

With what kind of imagery would you describe God?

> *God bowed the heavens, and came down;*
> *thick darkness was under his feet.*
> *He rode on a cherub, and flew;*
> *he came swiftly upon the wings of the wind.*

Psalm 18:9-10

July

Eating the scroll

The references to traditional biblical imagery continue: the dome, as in the dome of the sky (see Genesis 1:7), sapphire, as in the pavement under God's feet (see Exodus 24:10), the bow in a cloud, as in after the flood (see Genesis 9:13). But the nearest Ezekiel gets to God is at three removes: he sees 'the appearance of the likeness of the glory of God' (verse 28). And then he hears a voice, and is given his calling: he is to be sent as a prophet to the people of Israel. He is not only to hear the words of God, he is to ingest them, to take them into his very self. A scroll appears, and he has to be told three times to eat what looks like indigestible papyrus. The scroll contains words of lamentation and warning and woe. Ezekiel has been warned, and so have we! Well over half the book (chapters 1–32) is virtually all doom and destruction. Only after the calamity has happened, and Jerusalem has been destroyed, will we get words of hope and restoration. Unsurprisingly, Ezekiel is not to expect a warm reception. His task will be like walking among thorns, or sitting among scorpions. And yet when he eats the scroll, it tastes as sweet as honey.

As you read Ezekiel, can you taste honey amidst the lamentation, mourning and woe?

> *How sweet are your words to my taste,*
> *sweeter than honey to my mouth!*

> *Psalm 119:103*

Ezekiel is overwhelmed

Ezekiel is in the grip of a mighty whirlwind of a God. Notice the expressions for his experience: 'the spirit lifted me up and bore me away', 'the hand of the Lord was upon me', 'the spirit entered into me'. No wonder he is stunned. God has plenty to say to him, but Ezekiel never utters a word. The message even seems contradictory: one minute he is told to speak God's words to the house of Israel, the next that his tongue will cling to the roof of his mouth. Maybe his stunned seven-day silence is an overwhelming empathic experience of God's fury and anger. But he is not a puppet: he has to choose to accept his responsibility. And it has limits. He is to be a sentinel, warning the wicked. How they then act is their choice. Talk of sentinels evokes the guards standing on the city walls of Jerusalem. But whereas Jerusalem is soon to be besieged by the Babylonians, here it is as though God on his war chariot were riding against the people.

This picture of God may not be one we are comfortable with – it may well stun us. We may have to keep silence, as we give ourselves time to work through our reactions to Ezekiel's descriptions of divine rage.

How do we know when to speak and when to keep silent?

> *I am silent; I do not open my mouth;*
> *for it is you who have done it.*

Psalm 39:9

Jerusalem under siege

Ezekiel, though living in Babylon, is back in spirit in his beloved Jerusalem. He lives out the content of his prophetic message. Drawing a map of Jerusalem on a mud brick, he becomes the besieging army. He is told to place an iron wall between himself and the city, recalling the hardening of his face in 2:8-9. Then he was being protected from people's reactions. Is he now playing the part of God, refusing to be softened by pleas? Next he symbolically bears the punishment both of Israel in the north (overrun by the Assyrians back in 721 BCE), and Judah in the south. He enters into the coming plight of Jerusalem by eating the people's meagre rations. A city under siege soon runs out of firewood, leaving only human dung to cook on.

Suddenly Ezekiel emerges as a character and speaks for himself, shocking us into realising, yet again, the gap between his thought world and ours. He is a priest, concerned above all with honouring God's holiness, and his horror is not at the plight of the people, but at the violation of the purity laws. God relents, allowing him cow dung. There is no relenting for Jerusalem: the people are to waste away under their punishment.

Stick to a subsistence diet for a day.

> *For I eat ashes like bread,*
> *and mingle tears with my drink,*
> *because of your indignation and anger;*
> *for you have taken me up and thrown me aside.*

Psalm 102:9-10

The sword of judgement

This is possibly the most difficult of this week's passages. God shows nothing but anger and fury, promising no pity. By a vivid gesture involving shaving his hair, itself a symbol of wartime captivity, Ezekiel prophesies the fate of Jerusalemites: some will die of famine or plague within the besieged city, some will be slaughtered once it falls, and some will be exiled. All in order that people may know that the Lord has spoken.

The Christian response to such passages has tended either to make a false distinction between the God of the Old Testament and the God of the New, or to join in the condemnation of Israel. It is one thing when a religious tradition preserves self-criticism, another when one religious group perpetuates vilification of another.

We might see things differently by remembering that experience often precedes theology. Caught up in regional power politics, Israelites, whether in Babylon or Jerusalem, were experiencing traumas, with more on the way. They were losing their land, monarchy, and temple – all central to their religious belief. Explaining events as a punishment from God safeguarded faith. Better to think of God as in charge than the rulers (and gods) of Egypt and Babylon. It is still not uncommon for traumatised people to feel punished.

How would you respond if told, 'This tragedy [a death, flooding, an epidemic…] is a punishment from God'?

> *We are consumed by your anger;*
> *by your wrath we are overwhelmed.*

Psalm 90:7

Ezekiel

Abominations in the temple

Ezekiel has another vision of the fiery figure seen in 1:26-8, and he is transported by the spirit, or wind (the Hebrew word is ambiguous), to Jerusalem. The glory of the God of Israel is there – whether this is still the fiery figure is not clear. God speaks, and directs Ezekiel through the temple, showing him four abominations, each more offensive than the last.

The vision may have been provoked by reports reaching Babylon of priests belonging to the Egyptian Pharaoh being stationed in Israel, which happened in 592 BCE. But it reads more like a montage of what to Ezekiel were the worst pagan rites ever conducted in the temple. The 'image of jealousy' (verse 3 – a statue of a goddess?) seems to have been there a long time. These abominations have driven God from the sanctuary and sealed Jerusalem's fate.

Ezekiel's vision is leading up to the departure of the glory of the Lord (see 10:18-19, 11:22-23). According to his understanding, the Babylonians will be able to capture the temple only because God has already abandoned it. He sees the foreign invasion as a heavenly cleansing of an impure city. Only then will a new start be possible. The book will end with the glory returning to a future restored temple (43:1-5).

What would you consider to be an abomination, offensive to God?

> *O God, the nations have come into your inheritance;*
> *they have defiled your holy temple;*
> *they have laid Jerusalem in ruins.*

> *Psalm 79:1*

✹IBRA
International Bible Reading Association

1020 Bristol Road, Selly Oak, Birmingham B29 6LB, UK

Order form for 2010 books

Name: _____

Address: _____

_____

_____

_____ Postcode: _____

Telephone number: _____

Your order will be dispatched when all books are available. Mail order only (post included).

Code	Title of Book	Quantity	Unit Price	Total
	UK customers			
AA0922	Words For Today 2010		£8.50	
AA0921	Light For Our Path 2010		£8.50	
AA0923	Light For Our Path 2010 large print		£12.00	
	Overseas customers in Europe			
AA0922	Words For Today 2010		£11.00	
AA0921	Light For Our Path 2010		£11.00	
AA0923	Light For Our Path 2010 large print		£16.00	
	Overseas customers outside Europe			
AA0922	Words For Today 2010		£13.50	
AA0921	Light For Our Path 2010		£13.50	
AA0923	Light For Our Path 2010 large print		£17.50	

Payments in pounds sterling, please.
Please allow 28 days for delivery

Total cost of books	
Donation to IBRA Fund	
TOTAL DUE	

☐ **I enclose a cheque (made payable to IBRA)**

☐ **Please charge my MASTERCARD/VISA/SWITCH**

Card Number: ☐☐☐☐☐☐☐☐☐☐☐☐☐☐☐☐ **Issue Number:** ☐☐

Expiry Date: ☐☐ ☐☐

Security number (last three digits on back): ☐☐☐

Signature: _____

Website: www.ibra.org.uk Email: sales@christianeducation.org.uk
Tel: (+44) 0121 472 4242

The INTERNATIONAL BIBLE READING ASSOCIATION is a Registered Charity

Please, tell us about yourself...

Age: ☐ Below 30 ☐ 30-49
☐ 50-64 ☐ 65-80 ☐ Over 80

Gender: ☐ M ☐ F

Denomination_____

Do you attend Church? ☐ Every Sunday ☐ Frequently
☐ Occasionally ☐ Rarely

How long have you read IBRA? _____ years

Do you read the IBRA notes:

☐ Every day ☐ Frequently
☐ When feel the need / time allows ☐ Very occasionally

Would you like to see:	More	Same	Less
Whole OT Books / Gospel / Epistle	☐	☐	☐
Weeks using poetry	☐	☐	☐
Wide variety of writers	☐	☐	☐
Commentary rooted in personal experience	☐	☐	☐
Critique based on academic study	☐	☐	☐

Other comments

What national Christian periodicals do you look at?

☐ Reform magazine ☐ Woman Alive
☐ Methodist Recorder ☐ Families First (Home and Family)
☐ Magnet ☐ Christianity magazine
☐ Baptist Times ☐ Universe
☐ Church Times ☐ Third Way

Other _____

THANK YOU

Ezekiel

2 Words of warning

Notes based on the New Revised Standard Version
by Renato Lings

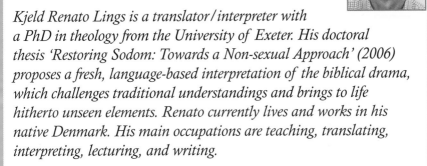

*Kjeld Renato Lings is a translator/interpreter with
a PhD in theology from the University of Exeter. His doctoral
thesis 'Restoring Sodom: Towards a Non-sexual Approach' (2006)
proposes a fresh, language-based interpretation of the biblical drama,
which challenges traditional understandings and brings to life
hitherto unseen elements. Renato currently lives and works in his
native Denmark. His main occupations are teaching, translating,
interpreting, lecturing, and writing.*

The theme of this week is words of warning. Ezekiel speaks with
great intensity about the wrongs of Israel and what it takes to
right them. He is particularly concerned about idolatry, violence,
and falsehood. The prophet's stark warnings may well echo
our own doubts and fears about the role of humankind in the
future of this planet. This week's notes mirror some of these
doubts and fears. In the light of Ezekiel's concerns, it is time to
issue a warning about our present-day idolatry, which takes the
form of materialism. World trade is organised in such a violent
manner that the poorer countries literally subsidise the rich.
In addition, the long-standing conflict in many churches over
same-sex relationships is detrimental to the gospel message.
Current church policies are incapable of solving this issue in all its
complexity.

July

Idolatry and change

In the face of global climate change, I and many believers wonder what it takes to restore the ecological balance that the planet has clearly lost. The excessive accumulation of carbon dioxide in the atmosphere is directly traceable to human activity. Dramatic change is on our doorsteps and the voices of warning are multiplying. What are we to do?

Perhaps Ezekiel offers a clue. As the prophet wrestles with the trauma of deportation and exile, he is aware that the Eternal is willing to restore the people of Israel to its former homeland. But, at the same time, a clear warning is issued. The Israelites must give up their proclivity for idol worship. This is the *sine qua non* for being granted a new heart and a new spirit. If they stubbornly hold on to their idolatrous ways, says Ezekiel, the Eternal 'will bring their deeds upon their own heads' (verse 21).

Modern civilisation as we know it seems to have arrived at a fateful crossroads. If we continue to do business as usual, the consequences for ourselves will be dire. For our children and grandchildren it will be far worse. The time is coming to take a long, hard look at the way we conduct ourselves on Planet Earth. Are we willing to heed the voices of warning and let the Eternal transform our lives?

Can you make a difference in the face of climate change?

Eternal God, enable us to discover the elements of idolatry that confuse us. Open our hearts to your purifying healing.

Our violence

Ezekiel is a master of arresting imagery. His preparations for exile are highly graphic. To me this passage brings home the plight of millions of people around the world threatened by the effects of climate change. We know that, before too long, sea levels are going to rise and considerable portions of dry land will be inundated by salt water. The land will be 'stripped of all it contains' (verse 19). This, in turn, will threaten the existence of the people living there. Hundreds of thousands will go into exile. Unprecedented international turmoil is likely to be the result.

The situation Ezekiel describes has a simple, yet complex cause: violence. I often think that my generation is treating our planet with precisely that violence. So many aspects of modern living are based on exploitation, including depletion of natural resources and the slavery-like conditions of underpaid labour in industries around the world. In the global economy violence is a major ingredient.

At the same time, 'solutions' to many international conflicts of a political nature are being sought by violent means. Such misguided policies produce tragedy and destruction. As I write, the primary example is Iraq. Following the Western invasion, untold numbers of Iraqis have lost their lives, and millions have been uprooted from their homes. While Ezekiel was deported eastward to Babylonia, Iraq's ancient predecessor, many of today's Iraqis have fled westward to Jordan and Syria.

Have you thought of becoming a peace builder?

Creator of the universe, enable us to see the violence we foster. Teach us to build true peace.

July

Ezekiel

Innovation versus orthodoxy

Christianity seems to be for ever caught in the tension between innovation and orthodoxy. Whenever new ways of interpreting scripture and Christian tradition appear on the horizon, reactions tend to be divided.

Ezekiel's reflections remind me of a hotly debated current issue, namely, the controversy about same-sex relationships. For years opinions have clashed, and a number of Christian churches have reached theological deadlock. One group finds same-sex relationships acceptable in the light of the gospels. Another group is convinced that the inclusion of same-sex partners runs counter to other parts of the Bible. As both sides appeal to scripture, they seem to think their message is 'prophetic'. Which is true and which is false?

What is missing from the picture is an honest, completely unbiased evaluation of the effects of current policies. Believers of all persuasions need an approach to sexuality that leads to joyful, loving, productive lives in God's service. The Bible reminds us, 'You will know them by their fruits' (John 13:35, 15:4). I am yet to meet a lesbian, gay or bisexual Christian who has felt empowered by those who try to recreate them in their own heterosexual image. Instead I have known gay people who committed suicide and others who have attempted it. Their pain and grief, caused by ignorance, prejudice, exclusion and bullying, are with us daily.

Are you ready to listen to the concerns of lesbian, gay and bisexual Christians?

O Eternal, grant us the gift of discernment. Enable us to yield fruits that are acceptable in your sight.

Any injustice in my life?

When modern Christians read this passage of warning, many of us are likely to think: 'No problem. I do not worship idols, I am no adulterer, I do not steal, I support different charities, and I believe in justice for all. Ezekiel does not have people like me in mind.'

Perhaps it is an inherent part of the human condition to think that for law-abiding citizens everything is fine. Yet, the more I ponder the passion underlying the prophetic words and apply it to my own context, the more I begin to suspect that not all is well with me and my privileged Western community. We may not practise idolatry in a religious sense, but how free of iniquity are our lives? For example, our pervasive consumerism is materialistic and generating a tremendous amount of waste. Yet it is allowed to continue. Isn't this a form of idolatry?

Similarly, we may not regard ourselves as hard-hearted or thieves. However, I was dumbfounded when I discovered that, in terms of overseas aid, for every penny we in the West give to the poorest countries, we receive that amount tenfold. Such blatant abuse is generated by the current rules governing world trade. In actual fact, the poor countries are subsidising the rich. It is time for us to start wondering why this crucial matter is largely ignored. What exactly does it mean to believe in justice for all?

In what way(s) is your life being affected by unequal trade?

Loving God, grant me insight into the injustices around me. Let me be hungry for your justice.

Parents and children: letting go

According to Ezekiel, children are not responsible for the actions of their parents. Likewise, the parent should not be held accountable for what a child does. In terms of logic, the principle works. But how many modern readers are comfortable with this? I for one have been raised in a culture in which parents are responsible for the education and behaviour of their children. At the same time, children are liable for any debt left behind by deceased parents. Ezekiel and modern legislation seem to be at loggerheads.

Thankfully, I have never had to answer for anything my parents might have done. They were respected members of our community. However, I must admit there are certain things I wish they had done for me, and never did, while I was young. Should I hold them responsible now, after all these years? I know some people who remember their deceased parents with bitterness.

I like to think this is not my case. Rather, what sometimes haunts me is a feeling of sadness and nostalgia of what might have been. Yet I am aware that there is no going back. Many ancient fairy tales and biblical stories show us that backtracking is, literally and figuratively, not the way forward. Perhaps Ezekiel can help me put it in better perspective: 'Turn, then, and live' (verse 32). As I let go of the 'sins of omission' of my parents, I can free myself of the burden of the past and face life today.

Are you at peace with your parents and/or your children?

Gracious heavenly Parent, enable me to forgive and be forgiven.

The challenge of growth

At a recent film festival I watched a shocking documentary describing the coming-out processes of CJ and Tim, two young high school students in the United States. What they had in common was a scenario of vicious, anti-gay bullying coupled with collusion on the part of school authorities. The gay victims were punished for being honest about themselves and blamed for the abuse they had to endure. Thanks to the support of their parents, both young men survived the ordeal and were able to challenge the injustice.

Another moving documentary showed the coming out process of Shulamit, a Jewish high school student in Massachusetts. I was particularly touched by the loving attitude on the part of Shulamit's parents. They fully accepted the long, difficult journey upon which their lesbian daughter was embarking. I will never forget the powerful message Shulamit received from her mother: 'My child, you were created *betzelem Elohim*, in the image of God.'

Personally I feel it was God who prompted Shulamit to bring up the sexuality issue with staff and students at her school. The fruits of her labour speak for themselves. At this high school, Jewish believers with very different backgrounds, opinions and attitudes could slowly begin to grapple with the thorny issue of same-sex attraction and scripture. The overriding concepts that brought the different sides together were love and respect and the willingness to grow in knowledge and understanding.

Is your religious community able to engage in respectful dialogue about sexuality and scripture?

God of all nations, grant us willingness to accept your call and the grace to grow with the challenge.

August

3 Words against foreign nations

Notes based on the New Revised Standard Version by Rachel Mann

Rachel Mann is an Anglican priest and poet based in South Manchester. Her writing has appeared in magazines, journals, books and newsprint. After a period of major ill health, she is looking forward to enjoying more of the good things of life again.

Political and economic power and its impact on human existence is a reality as old as human civilisation. These reflections, liturgies and meditations move between time and space – backwards and forwards through history, both real and imagined. They are written from a variety of perspectives – both powerful and marginalised. In doing so they seek to get closer to the hope and promise that lies in the living God: a hope and promise that it so easily marred when one speaks too literally or becomes absorbed with what are usually called 'the facts'. The people of God have known this for a long time – their rich use of poetry and song continually reveals it.

To reflect on in the coming week

Spend some time reflecting upon who, for you, are the modern-day powers who oppress the weak and poor. Pray for change.

- Who are God's prophets in our world? What are they proclaiming?
- How might you, in a world where the strong seem to succeed and exploit power, account for God's apparent failure to 'act' for the poor and vulnerable?

Spend time in prayer inviting God to help you break free of your own perspective to encounter the world from someone else's viewpoint.

The costliness of waiting

Everyone is waiting: beyond the gates and city walls the soldiers wait for the final assault; inside we wait for our fall – for the arrival of the tanks and flame throwers, for the rapists and looters. Smoke rises from their camp. Our children hide or cower; some have been forced into service guarding the walls, surely an empty sacrifice of unlived lives. Now is the doom of the world and, for those of us who survive, captivity awaits. I cannot see how any of us will be able to sing God's song in a strange land. God, it would seem, would even deny us the comfort of tears and mourning: our holy man says that grief – the bread of suffering – is not to be ours.

What kind of God is this who promises destruction, but would not let us lament over our downfall? Perhaps it shall be so complete there will be none left to mourn; I know many of us have been faithless and lacked love and prayer, but I cannot make sense of this God.

Dawn is breaking; I try to pray. May the end come quickly. The bombardment begins – they are coming. Will God ever grant us the gift of celebration, of tears, again?

Faithful God,
in the costliness of waiting,
in our failures to love as we should,
grant your suffering people
the assurance of your faithfulness,
now and always.

The unsinkable ship of power

How can anyone say that God is against us when we've been blessed with so much wealth and power? Don't you see, if God didn't want us to have it, he would have ensured we had less. So, you will forgive us if we don't take the proclamations and lamentations of the odd, marginalised prophet too seriously. Frankly, we're too busy for that – trying to ensure that the world has what it needs. OK, so some of what we produce and trade in is weaponry, but the world will always need arms and armies. Only foolish dreamers like prophets imagine otherwise. The most important thing for us is to ensure that we are secure and that our position in the world is maintained – we must maintain our borders because, although we are wealthy, we don't have room for everyone. I like to think of our land as a kind of ship: it's large and powerful and it's going places. But not everyone can get on board, otherwise it would sink.

What's that you say? Do I think we're unsinkable? I should think so. Whoever heard of a ship of our size going down?

Gracious God,
help us accept the gift of humility
and grant us the foolish wisdom
of holy dreamers. Lead us away
from the prison of selfishness
towards the promised land of love.

Woe to you, woe to us...

*Woe to you who lord it over others, who behave as if you
are gods.*

*Woe to you, you peddlers of landmines and tanks, whose hope
is conquest.*

*Woe to you profiteers and loan sharks, woe when you build
fortunes on the tears of the poor.*

*Woe to you who neglect the demands of love, who sup
champagne whilst children starve.*

*Woe to you nations who support unjust regimes for your
own ends.*

*Woe to you politicians who deceive your nations into
unjust wars.*

*Woe to you who withhold medicine from the needy, who close
your eyes to those broken by treatable diseases, who turn your
back on those with HIV/AIDs.*

*Woe to you who would deny shelter to the homeless, the asylum
seeker, the refugee.*

*Woe to you people when your hunger for position, money and
power destroy your compassion and solidarity for the poor.*

*Blessed are you when the holy food of grace breaks open your
life and you become a feast of hope for the world.*

Compassionate God,

bless us with the grace

to become bread for the world;

keep us from the poverty of self-centredness

and make us hungry for the food of justice.

The economics of necessity?

You see, what so many people fail to understand is that what *we* – my people and I, our business community, our banks and manufacturers – actually seek is simply stability and peace, the ideal conditions for trade and commerce. We have no interest in exploiting others. We want poorer nations to do well so that they can buy our goods. We try very hard to develop the smaller nations but they are so backward, and frankly rather corrupt. Should my people be made to pay because they have got ahead through their own industry and commitment to hard work?

I know there are people among the nations we work with (I believe that their people sometimes call them prophets) who think we exploit and take advantage. But I would not get very far if I suggested to my people that they give up their hard-earned standard of living. I believe it is fashionable these days to talk of fair trade and such like. But how fair is this so-called 'fair trade' to my people and to the growth of the economy? Surely a fairer world is one in which people are encouraged to maximise profits (no pun intended!) and allow the excess of their earnings to trickle down to the poorest?

God of justice,
keep us from treating the exploited
with contempt. Make us fierce friends
of the poor. Make us agents of your love.

The axe shall fall

I rather admire them – the protesters, I mean. They are, after all, *essentially* harmless and they are a rather colourful and amusing bunch. They have this chant they use at their demonstrations – 'God will take an axe to the trunk of the powerful and plant a holy people for himself' – which goes to a *very* amusing tune. Now I know that these words could be understood in a quite threatening way, but when you see the rag-bag bunch of vagabonds and fools who are singing them, how few they are, it's hardly a cause for alarm. And frankly their voice is so small, so marginalised, one can't take them seriously. Have they no idea what they (and their god) are up against? We are the greatest nation on earth – the roots of our power and our wealth reach so deep into the past that I cannot see how we should ever be felled. The most beautiful cedar, the most ancient oak is as a sapling compared to us. So, in the end, all shall weep in the face of our empire which shall last for evermore. And should these amusing little troublemakers ever become really threatening we shall deal with them, and their annoying little god, as we shall see fit.

God of courage and hope,
when we are tempted to lose heart
in the face of worldly power,
help us to be faithful to the beautiful, tattered ways
of your love, compassion and peace.

The failure of love?

There are people here who have chosen to forget their names. They say it is easier that way: for if you no longer have a name, then you can no longer be called a human being. And given what we have come to, it is perhaps more liveable if we no longer consider ourselves human. I have seen women and men hurl themselves against the electrified barbed wire rather than live like this. Our guards laugh. We have become victims of the powerful; forced into poverty and slave labour. Our hope is death. We are nobodies living off what we can steal to bring into the camp. The beauty of our lives is daily snuffed out by the anger of rifle butts in our faces. Murder has become ordinary, unexceptional. Our captors ask from us a song of hope, and spit in our faces. God is dead here. We are abandoned. Who will stand with us? Who will come to heal the sick? Who will seek out us, the lost, and show us the way home? Come God, if you are still listening, show us the face of your saviour.

Living God,
who seeks out the broken,
who stands with the poor,
who weeps with the abandoned,
who gives hope in the face of death,
reveal to your desperate people your face once again.

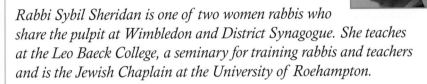

Ezekiel

4 Words of hope

Notes based on the Hebrew text (Jewish Publication
Society, Philadelphia 1999) by Sybil Sheridan

*Rabbi Sybil Sheridan is one of two women rabbis who
share the pulpit at Wimbledon and District Synagogue. She teaches
at the Leo Baeck College, a seminary for training rabbis and teachers
and is the Jewish Chaplain at the University of Roehampton.*

Ezekiel's visions extend through times of great destruction.
He saw the departure of the glory of God from Jerusalem's
holy temple in a vision and then witnessed the prophecy
come true. We see in this week's readings – found towards
the end of the book that bears his name – that the prophecies
change and Ezekiel offers words of hope. He sees a time when
the destruction will be reversed and even history itself runs
backwards as humanity is recreated; God's presence returns
and 'all will be Eden again' (words of Judy Chicago in a poem
reflecting on the hope of a recreated earth). In all this Ezekiel
goes beyond the historical into spiritual time and offers a vision of
reconciliation that has more to do with a heavenly Jerusalem than
an earthly one. While it is hard to see his vision being realised
in the context of any real world, in terms of our own spiritual
development, Ezekiel does indeed offer us words for today.

The prayers throughout the week are taken from the Jewish daily
prayer, the *Amidah* as translated in *Seder Hatefillah* (Movement
for Reform Judaism, London, 2008).

August

The good sheep

When Moses was tending Jethro, his father-in-law's flocks, he noticed one day that a small lamb had gone missing. He searched high and low for it until he found it, lost and far away from its mother. He picked it up, held it close to his breast, and carried it back to the others. 'This man, Moses,' declares God, 'shall lead my people. Because he took so much trouble to care for the smallest and weakest of his flock, he will take care of the smallest and weakest of my people.'

From the midrash, the collection of rabbinical commentary on the Hebrew scriptures

The lesson of Moses, lost on the people of Ezekiel's time, should not be lost on us. Where the strong bully the weak, where leaders not only look after their own interests first, but actively ruin what resources are left so that the poor have nothing; there, all suffer punishment – the guilty and innocent alike. In the future, we are told, God's punishment will be on the guilty alone, while the innocent, the weak and the oppressed of the people will thrive with the leader they deserve.

Restore your judgement of righteousness in the world. Turn away from us sorrow and pain; rule over us with love and mercy; and judge us with righteousness. Blessed are you God, the ruler who loves righteousness and truth.

The holy land

> *The earth is the Lord's and all that it holds, the world and all its inhabitants.*
>
> *Psalm 24:1*

Just as God created all humanity yet chose the nation Israel to be a holy people, so too God chose the land Israel as a place of special holiness. The land is both a metaphor for the people, and a separate entity whose fortunes are intertwined with theirs. It has been invaded and destroyed just as the people have been exiled and persecuted. Yet at the same time, the land is independent; it is the land that turned against its people in its sin and punished it for its disregard of God's commandments.

Ezekiel promises a new world order where land and people are reconciled. There will be a permanent connection of people and land bound together in peace and prosperity. It is a vision that, in our war-torn world, seems remote but one we know to be possible if only we could bring ourselves to act in the ways we know to be right.

Sound the great horn for our freedom, and raise a banner to restore all of us who experience exile. May the voice of liberty and freedom be heard throughout the four corners of the earth for all its inhabitants, for you are a God who redeems and rescues. Blessed are you God, who sustains your people Israel.

Re-creation

The Lord God formed man from the dust of the earth. He blew into his nostrils the breath of life, and man became a living being.

Genesis 2:7

Just as in the original creation, so in this vision God puts life into lifeless objects. However, in the first creation, the source of humanity was the earth. Here old bones are recycled. This is less a new creation than a re-creation. We are all re-creations of the past. Our culture and heritage, the stories of our forebears and the habits of our parents live on in us and we become the personification of our ancestors.

Ezekiel's vision also promises restoration to the land. In modern-day Israel, biblical towns live again and the language of the Bible is once more spoken in its streets. The new nation of Israel is faced with the same dilemmas as its ancient namesakes. Its people have the same choices, the same possibilities and the same opportunities to share in God's reconciliation. The people and its leaders need our prayers to ensure they fulfil the promise of Ezekiel and not resume the sins of their ancestors.

Bring forth soon a new flowering from your servant David, a 'flowering of righteousness' (Jeremiah 33:15) and a 'doorway of hope' (Hosea 2:15), for we wait and work for your salvation. Blessed are you God, who makes the power of salvation flourish.

God's great jubilee

In the seventh month on the tenth day of the month – the Day of Atonement – you shall have the horn sounded throughout your land and you shall hallow the fiftieth year. You shall proclaim liberty throughout the land for all its inhabitants.

Leviticus 25:9-10

Ezekiel's vision of the new temple takes place on the Day of Atonement, the day of the year when Jews, ancient and modern, repent of their sins and ask forgiveness. But Ezekiel's vision takes place in the year of the jubilee: the fiftieth year in which all debts were cancelled, all slaves went free and all peoples returned to their ancient tribal lands.

The jubilee was a foretaste of the Messianic age. So the scene is set for God's return. The temple, symbol of God's indwelling with Israel, is restored at that moment where freedom is declared and all peoples, individuals and nations, return to the perfection that was once theirs.

Turn in mercy to Jerusalem and may your presence dwell within us. Rebuild it as you have prophesied; then it shall indeed be called 'city of righteousness, faithful city' (Isaiah 1:26). Help us to establish it as a place worthy of prayer for all peoples. Blessed are you God, who builds Jerusalem.

Ezekiel

Glory glory

Exalt the Lord our God and bow towards his holy hill.

Psalm 99:9

God's sacred presence had been with the people from the time they left Egypt. At that time, it had been indicated in the pillar of cloud and fire that accompanied their journey through the wilderness and settled on the tabernacle. When Solomon dedicated the first temple in Jerusalem, God's presence as cloud descended to take up residence there. When the temple is restored, God's glory will return to its place at the spiritual centre of the nation.

But in Ezekiel's world the presence does not come in the form of a simple cloud. The complicated details of the chariot described in his first vision bring the glory of God back to the people. The first temple was described as God's footstool, the new temple is God's throne. Thus God is both more near and more glorious than before.

Nothing ever returns to what it was. Experience changes everything, so the restoration is coloured by the experiences brought about in exile and the circumstances that created exile. Our sins, once forgiven, can bring us closer to God, yet our sins also make God more fearful to us.

Our living God, be pleased with your people and listen to their prayers. In your great mercy delight in us, so that your presence may rest upon Zion. Our eyes look forward to your return to Zion in mercy. Blessed are you God, ever restoring your presence in Zion.

Eden again

A river issues from Eden to water the garden and it then divides and become four branches.

Genesis 2:10

The rebuilding of the temple and the return of God's presence is not the end of the story. The supernatural river that here issues from under the temple and which flows with healing in its waters the length and breadth of the country makes the land a more fertile and abundant place than it ever was.

For those of us living in rainy climes, water, the source of blessing, is not sufficiently appreciated; but for most of the world it is the difference between life and death. The garden of Eden is defined by the river that runs through it, that divides into four rivers and gives life to the world. Now, Israel becomes Eden, with an abundance of fruit trees reminiscent of those in the first garden.

But water as life extends beyond these qualities. In the Judaeo-Christian tradition *mayim chayim* (living waters) are the waters of baptism, of *mikqwe*. Each individual who enters them emerges as from the placenta, reborn – a new being – with all the possibilities and opportunities of the first human, Adam.

Bless this year, our living God, and may all that it brings be good for us. Send dew and rain as a blessing over the face of the earth, bring life-giving water to all the earth, satisfy all the world with your goodness and bless our years as good years. Blessed are you, God, who blesses the years.

August

Readings in Mark

5   Training the disciples

Notes based on New Revised Standard Version
by Paul Nicholson SJ

*Paul Nicholson is a Roman Catholic priest belonging
to the Society of Jesus (the Jesuits). He is currently Director of
Novices in Britain, and has worked since ordination in the fields of
spirituality and social justice.*

The readings this week bring us to the heart of Mark's gospel. In
many ways, the disciples Mark pictures are a sorry lot. Slow to
understand, quick to argue, fickle, vain and fearful. Not at all the
strong foundations upon which you might have expected Jesus to
build his church. Yet perhaps their very mediocrity can make it
easier for us to identify with them, to imagine ourselves standing
in their shoes. I'm no saint; nor do I (usually) pretend to be one.
But if I'm honest, I can recognise in myself something of Peter's
impetuosity, the belligerence of James and John, or the hesitant
faith of Thomas.

Even so, each of us, like each of them, has heard and responded
to a call to discipleship. That call is not without consequences.
We, too, are expected to continue to grow in faith, to allow
ourselves to be taught by the Lord. This week's readings contain
an invitation. It is an invitation to a contemplative kind of prayer, a
prayer that looks intently at Jesus as he goes about his daily tasks.
As you watch Jesus training his disciples in the gospel over these
days, ask yourself what it is that he might he be wanting to teach
you – here and now.

August

Your hands are God's hands

In this variant of the familiar story of the feeding of the five thousand, Jesus more than satisfies the hunger of four thousand people with seven loaves and a few small fish. It's a vivid picture. A lakeside setting, with crowds of people captivated for three days by Jesus' teaching. His disciples, by turns practical and impatient. On the sidelines, a group of Pharisees, carping and resentful. And at the centre, Jesus himself, prayerful, confident, very much in control. Notice the different ways in which he involves the disciples in what he is doing here. They are the ones who actually distribute the food, the ones who collect up the left-overs. So they are the ones who experience at first-hand the people's reactions to what is taking place. What are these reactions? We're not told, but can perhaps imagine astonishment, questioning, awe and delight. What would it be like, to be handing out the food that Jesus has blessed in this way? How would you feel, to be caught up in this story?

The sixteenth-century mystic, Teresa of Avila, said 'Christ has no hands today but yours'. What is it like for you to be doing God's work in the world today?

Lord, I ask you to show me during the course of this day the ways in which I am acting as your disciple. Help me to see more clearly the various ways in which I am bringing your gifts to the people around me.

Growth by trial and error

When I was a scout, we sang a chorus that began: 'My eyes are dim, I cannot see, I have not brought my specs with me...' This is the starting-point for both halves of today's reading. In the first, the disciples cannot see what Jesus is getting at. His image of yeast, the corrupting influence of the Pharisees and Herod, is beyond them. In the second, a blind man, unusually in the miracle stories, comes to full sight only slowly and in stages.

It would be nice, wouldn't it, to become the perfect disciple overnight? Knowing what Jesus wants of me and carrying it out promptly at all times. By contrast it is frustrating to find myself repeatedly in the condition Paul describes in Romans 7: 'I do not do the good I want, but the evil I do not want is what I do.' Jesus may be able to accept that my growth in discipleship proceeds in fits and starts, often feeling as if I take one step forward, two steps back. The key question, though, is whether I can accept this in myself, over and over again, without becoming disheartened.

To be able (in the words of another song) to 'pick yourself up, dust yourself off, and start all over again', not just once, but daily, monthly, and even decade by decade, is a real gift. I invite you to pray today for that gift for yourself and for those around you.

'Who do *you* say...?'

Poor old Peter! It's easy to sympathise with him here, isn't it? At first he does so well. The other disciples report conventional responses to Jesus' question. He's another of that long line of prophets, like Elijah, or the more recent Baptist. Peter's answer represents a real breakthrough. Jesus isn't just a prophet among prophets. He's the Messiah, the Christ, singled out and sent by God. Peter isn't simply relaying village gossip. Looking deep into his own experience of being with Jesus, he comes to a clear vision of who he is.

Unfortunately for Peter, although it's a vision that's clear, it's also only partial. Jesus goes on to spell out the surprising implications of what Peter has glimpsed, implications for Jesus himself and for those who would follow him.

If Jesus puts that same question to you, 'Who do you say that I am?', how do you reply? Do you offer the stock responses from catechism or creed? Or can you draw on your own experience of being with him, of trying to be his disciple, to offer a fresh answer of your own? And if you can, what are the implications, for your own life or the lives of others, of the description that you give?

Lord, you ask me, as you asked Peter, 'Who do you say that I am?' Help me to draw on my own experience to give an answer that spells out something of what you mean to me.

On top of the world

Some years ago the actor Alec McCowan toured with a one-man show, reciting the whole of Mark's gospel. He used the King James Version, which links different scenes with the one word 'straightway'. The overall impression was one of great activity – Jesus always on the move. This reading gives the same impression: up the mountain, Jesus transfigured, Moses, Elijah, the Father's voice, down the mountain. But at the centre of all this movement is a single still point, a point that can offer a focus for prayer.

The voice of the Father is heard. It says of Jesus: 'This is my Son, the Beloved.' And in that moment, the disciples see only Jesus. Maybe you can get a sense of what it must have been like for Jesus to feel himself acknowledged as the beloved child of God. To have a moment when that awareness came to crystal clarity. For in a sense those same words apply to us, to all disciples. You yourself are God's beloved daughter or son.

What is it like for you when that awareness comes to a clear focus? Peter's response is 'It is good for us to be here.' Would those words capture your own response to this? Or are there others that speak more accurately of your own experience?

In a moment of quiet today, ask God to help you realise more deeply that you are his beloved child. Keep a note for yourself of how you respond.

Faith/healing

Our theme this week is Jesus training the disciples, so it is worth asking of a passage 'What have the disciples learnt here?' To answer this question, it again helps greatly to put yourself in their place. What might you have learnt of Christian discipleship, if you had been caught up in these events?

Today those disciples who were not with Jesus at the Transfiguration have been trying to cure a sick child, without success. In response, Jesus refers repeatedly to the need for faith, although whether it was the disciples themselves or the crowds who lacked faith is perhaps not clear. What does Jesus mean by faith? In context, it seems to have to do with trust in God, confidence that God will act for the good of his people. Then that confidence is linked to prayer: only through prayer can this level of trust in God be built up and maintained.

Different Christians see the miracles of Jesus differently. Were they signs particular to Jesus, of the reign of God breaking into our world? Or extraordinary demonstrations of God's power, to continue among Christ's followers, but rarely? Or a normal part of everyday discipleship, requiring only that the disciple believes? This passage doesn't address such questions directly. It does give those first disciples a lesson of the need to pray, and pray often, if their own faith in God is to remain a powerful force in their own lives.

Lord, I believe: help my unbelief!

The look on Jesus' face

What little teaching I have done suggests to me that, when you have a lively, responsive group, engaged and full of curiosity, it can be a real joy. Conversely, a poorly motivated, obtuse group, uninterested in what you want to convey and counting the minutes until the end of the session, is little short of hell on earth. The disciples in today's passage are closer to the second category than they are to the first.

Jesus tries to explain to those who have been closest to him his understanding of the path they're taking. They don't understand it, don't like what they do understand, and are afraid to ask too many questions. If that's not bad enough, no sooner do they get home than this dull, resistant band start arguing among themselves about who is number one! In the circumstances, Jesus' response seems remarkably restrained.

If this scene were a film, imagine a single frame near the end of the story: Jesus centre-stage, with a little child in his arms; the disciples standing round, maybe shame-faced and sullen. What expression do you see on Jesus' face here? What does that expression suggest is going on in his mind and heart? And what does that tell you about your own discipleship, your call to be a 'servant of all'?

Speak to Christ for a few moments now, as openly and freely as one friend speaks to another, about your reactions to what you have seen here.

Readings in Mark

6 Going up to Jerusalem

Notes based on New Revised Standard Version
by Paul Nicholson SJ

There's a sharpness, an impatience even, in the
Jesus we encounter this week. He's not in a mood to pull any
punches. Straight questions get straight answers, while those
deserving of criticism are not spared it. To be a disciple of Jesus
at this stage of his ministry would have been challenging indeed.
And the stage of his ministry gives the key to what is going on.
'They were on the road, going up to Jerusalem, and Jesus was
walking ahead of them' (Mark 10:32). Jesus is on the path leading
to his final confrontation with all that opposes the reign of God;
and he travels that path eagerly, not letting the disciples' faltering
footsteps hold him back.

Ignatius Loyola, Renaissance nobleman and founder of the Jesuit
order to which I belong, knew that ultimately only desire could
motivate people. Without desire, will is toothless. He recognised,
too, the power of imagination to elicit desire. By letting my
desires reveal themselves in prayer I can inspect them, sift
through them, and decide which to follow and which to temper.
So in one of his favoured methods of prayer, he invites you to let
the scriptural scene become real for you, noticing what desires
are stirred up in you: to become more Christ-like, to serve as he
did, to confront in your own life whatever opposes the kingdom
of God. As you read and pray this week, notice those desires that
God has planted in your heart.

August

Jesus the extremist

Civilised communities tend to be wary of extremists, and rightly so. People prepared to kill and maim in support of a belief system need to know that what they do is unacceptable, and cannot win God's approval. Yet the Christ we meet in the reading today, with his talk of millstones around necks, severed limbs and torn-out eyes, is a long way from the 'gentle Jesus, meek and mild' beloved of nursery piety.

What seems to be at stake here is a question of priorities. The time of being 'salted with fire' is upon us. There's no longer the luxury of being able to dither, to sit on the fence or refuse to take sides. The disciple is called to devote himself or herself to the reign of God, and anything that gets in the way of that devotion must be set aside.

There is a particular challenge in this to those parts of the world that are comfortable. The opposite of extremism can easily become a world-weary *laissez-faire*, anything for a quiet life attitude. Maybe it takes the experience of being brought up short by the violence of Jesus' imagery to re-awaken my own desires for change, to unlock the energy that will enable me to move forward as resolutely as Jesus is doing here.

Lord, let your words, as the old adage says, 'comfort the afflicted and afflict the comfortable', both in my own life, and in the world into which you send me today.

Jesus the radical

How can you simultaneously uphold high moral standards, yet make compassionate allowance for human weakness? Any finding themselves called upon to preach, or to exercise any form of Christian leadership, cannot escape this question for long. Jesus faces the two sides of the question here when confronted with a debate about marriage. He holds that God's plan is for marriage as a life-long, indissoluble union of two people; yet he acknowledges that there was reason behind Moses' allowance of divorce. So what is his own view? Here in this passage of Mark he comes down heavily in favour of indissolubility. (Other gospels represent a more nuanced stance by Jesus.)

But look at the context. The Pharisees' questioning is hostile, seeking only to trap Jesus. Jesus himself is on the road to Jerusalem. This is no time for shades of grey. God makes radical demands of those who would follow him, and it is important that those demands are heard with clarity. This is neither the time nor the place to discuss follow-up strategies for those who set out to meet God's demands but fail. Elsewhere, Jesus will model great compassion for such people, and call upon those who come after him to show equal compassion. But today the demand must be made clearly, and as clearly acknowledged.

What are the radical demands the gospel makes of you (whether or not you manage to keep them)? Which of these might Jesus be inviting you to reflect upon today?

Jesus the lover

Going up to Jerusalem, Jesus is a busy man. Everybody wants just a few minutes of his time: to answer a problem, to heal an injury, to give a word of advice. Unsurprisingly the disciples find themselves operating a filtering system, trying to send away the less deserving, keeping time-slots for the more important. Jesus doesn't seem to object to the idea in principle. It's the disciples' judgement of who is important that he thinks has gone awry.

First he insists on meeting the little children. Perhaps encouraged by this, a young man makes his approach. Challenged by Jesus with the commands of the Jewish law, he guilelessly blurts out his conviction that he has kept them all. Does Jesus contradict him, challenge him, or at least check up on his claim? Not at all! Jesus sees something in him that touches his heart. He sees the best in this man, loves him for it, and seeks to draw out of him something still better.

Isn't that typical of Jesus, the way that he treats you and treats me? Put yourself into that place where Jesus, looking at you, loves what he sees. Knowing all that you've done, and all that you hope for and dream of, he looks at you with great encouragement and love. For that moment, you are the centre of his world.

Try to return to that place two or three times today. Notice what goes on in you when you are there.

Jesus the poor man

A few years ago I lived for some time in a hard-to-let apartment on a council housing estate in north London. When I had been there for maybe a year, the estate became the target of 'prosperity preachers', a group who promised wealth and worldly success for all who truly believed in Christ. For a while they attracted a popular hearing, just as those who promised cheap loans did. But they made few long-term converts. Why? Because it didn't work. Faith in Christ alone was not enough to raise the living standards of those who had the cards of society stacked against them from birth.

It is difficult to see how anyone can read this section of Mark 10 and believe that faith leads to material prosperity. To be sure, Jesus doesn't say that the rich cannot enter the kingdom of God; but he says that their path will be difficult. Moreover, he goes on to encourage those who have voluntarily left behind some of their own supports and resources, in order to help others come to faith.

Are we perhaps given a glimpse of Jesus' own experience here? At this juncture, as he approached Jerusalem and the end of his earthly ministry, could he recognise himself as having been given the hundredfold as he had journeyed on his way?

What securities has your discipleship called upon you to leave behind? Can you recognise any ways in which you have been more than compensated by God?

August

Jesus the challenger

On another occasion, you feel, Jesus might have treated the sons of Zebedee more gently. But now he is going up to Jerusalem; there's no time to tread lightly. So they get their wish. They will share the cup that he has to drink. Even though they don't realise what they have asked for. Even though they, and the others, seem unable to take in Jesus' talk of his forthcoming passion.

But they don't have to drink that cup yet. It will be after Jesus has returned from the dead, after the Spirit has come, after they have become fearless preachers of God's word. Only then will they have to honour the commitment entered into almost unthinkingly today. And, tradition suggests, nine of the ten who here express their indignation at being pipped for the top posts will also know what it means to drink the cup of suffering that their master drinks.

For many Christians, setting out on the road of discipleship resembles signing a blank cheque. You say 'Yes' to what God invites you to with little idea of where it will lead, or what it will ask of you. Years or decades may pass before you realise the full implications of your Christian calling. Yet Jesus never takes advantage of this situation. He will never ask anything of you until he knows that you are ready for it.

What might it mean for you, to drink your share of the cup Jesus drinks from?

Jesus the healer

For six years I worked in a retreat house, helping people to deepen their lives of prayer. Often this involved broadening their repertoire, introducing new methods and techniques of prayer that might, on a given occasion, make them more aware of God, who, active in scripture, was also active in their lives. The story of Bartimaeus was a favourite here. It's easy to imagine that Mark wrote it with this aim in mind.

With whom do you identify as you read this passage? Most, I suspect, would think themselves presumptuous to take on Jesus' role. And the crowd is too distant, too much a cast of extras, to invite a strong sense of identification. But Bartimaeus, the blind beggar, he is surely just right. A man aware of Christ as his last, best hope. A man called out to stand before Jesus. A man hearing the words addressed to him: 'What do you want me to do for you?'

And maybe that's where the story shifts. No longer are you acting the role of another, compelled to follow the gospel's script. Suddenly you speak your own lines. Your prayer becomes a frank confession of all that you need from God, all that you hope for, all that you dream of. You rest in Christ's loving gaze as he gives you everything you need. And in response, you, too, follow him along the road.

Hear Jesus address you now: 'What do you want me to do for you?'

Idols

1 The many guises of idolatry

Notes based on the New Jerusalem Bible
by Joseph G Donders

Joseph Donders, a Dutch Roman Catholic priest of the Society of Missionaries of Africa, is Emeritus Professor of Mission and Cross-cultural Studies at the Washington Theological Union. He was formerly Head of the Department of Philosophy and Religious Studies and Chaplain to the Catholic Students at the State University of Nairobi, Kenya.

The term 'idol' occurs more than 150 times in the Bible. The best-known occurrence is most probably the time that the people melted the gold they had and poured it into a mould, making it into the statue of a golden calf. They danced around it singing: 'Here is your God, Israel, who brought you out of Egypt' (Exodus 32:8). They danced around a thing they had made, forgetting about God, and at the same time forgetting their real selves as ones created in God's image. Neither God nor they themselves were the centre of their lives any more, but a thing, an idol, a piece of gold, something made for profit and gain. They lost themselves dancing around that idol.

It is a story that repeats itself again and again in all kinds of ways and disguises throughout biblical and human history. It is bad news, but the good news is that there are and always have been people who centre their lives on God and God's reign – both in their own hearts and in the wider world. May we be among their company.

Making a name for ourselves

The temptation is great. In a certain way, everyone is correct in considering her or himself as the centre of the universe. Everything that happens seems to refer only to him or herself. You hear of a traffic accident and you refer it to yourself, thinking 'Thank goodness I am safe.' You read about the outbreak of a dangerous contagious disease and you are relieved to hear that it is on another continent.

Not only individuals, but even nations often reason and react like that. Only what happens to them, or what affects them, is of importance. It is a kind of matter-of-fact politics.

In Babel it was that same thought, that same temptation, that willingness to relate the whole of reality only to themselves that made the people decide: 'Let us make a name for ourselves' (verse 4). It is what they did; it is what so many are still doing today.

Constructing their Babel, their stress was not on the tower but on the fact that it was *their* tower and nobody else's. It was then that Yahweh interfered. Their course of action that seemed so fine and so 'natural' was, in fact, an error, a mistake. Just like any sin, their sin was, in the final instance, a lack of judgement, albeit an acute one.

God interfered, not to punish them, but to correct them, to help them understand the reality of their relationship with God and neighbour.

Let us pray to understand that spiritual maturity is to be aware of our dependency on, and relationship with, God and neighbour.

The cost of prosperity

Laban and Abraham's son Jacob were both experienced cattle breeders. Jacob was working for his father-in-law, Laban, to pay off his debt to him. There was something else they had in common. Laban was convinced that his own prosperity was due to Yahweh's favour upon Jacob, and was therefore dependent on Jacob's presence. That is why he did not want Jacob to leave once he had paid off his debt. So the two made an arrangement that compelled Jacob to stay for a longer period. But Laban deceived Jacob, and Jacob in his turn played a trick on Laban by using some of his rather strange breeding skills. It is interesting to note that both related their tricksy prosperity to Yahweh's blessing!

Some years ago a small book was published entitled *The Prayer of Jabez*, referring to a character in the book of Chronicles (1 Chronicles 4:9-10). Jabez is another biblical farmer who prayed for prosperity, for land and animals. The book became an overnight best seller. Its message was simple: 'Pray for prosperity and you will be heard.' It is only one example of a contemporary prosperity approach to the 'good news'.

Yet, does praying like this not seem to make God a means to get something that is in danger of becoming more important than God? Does one not risk that what one is asking for becomes the centre of one's life, around which all else turns?

Think about the place of money and prosperity in your life. Is it a blessing for you and others or…?

Idols

When idols take hold of the heart

It is not that the elders who came that day to Ezekiel did not believe in Yahweh. They did and that is why they had come to Yahweh's prophet. They hoped that he would do what a prophet is supposed to do, not so much to foretell the future, but to speak God's word, to speak 'for God', in God's name.

And, indeed, the word of God came to the prophet. It told them that God refused to be consulted. The reason for that refusal was given, too: 'These men have enshrined their foul idols in their hearts, why should I let myself be consulted by them?' (verse 3). What would be the use? Let them first stop their double-crossing and get rid of those idols!

Bible stories are like mirrors. We often see ourselves in them. Hearing and witnessing those stories, we ask ourselves: where do I see myself in this story? Do we not risk being in the same situation as those elders of old when we are looking for God's word in our own contemporary situation and praying for justice, peace and the integrity of creation? Are we willing to get rid of our addictions to the way we live, travel, spend, consume, eat, drink, clothe and try to protect ourselves?

Why is it that God seems often to be silent in our day and age, in our churches and communities, and in our everyday life?

September

Loving money

In Paul's first letter to Timothy we catch a glimpse of a difficulty in the early Christian communities: a difficulty that still threatens followers of 'the Way', even after two thousand years.

Paul warns Timothy against those leaders who use 'the Way of Jesus' to profit themselves. That is why they argue, are jealous, and have unending disputes. They think, Paul writes, 'that religion is a way of making a profit' (verse 5). He then broadens his argument by not only speaking about church leaders, but also by warning all those who have decided to follow 'the Way'. Indeed, he writes, following the Way of Jesus is profitable, but in a different way. It connects them to all those charged with Jesus' Spirit. It should not be seen as a way to get rich. People who think so are going to get in all kinds of situations that will lead them away from the faith. Loving money, they will try to get richer and richer instead of being content with what they have and need. He then pens that oft-quoted saying: 'The love of money is the root of all evils' (verse 10). In fact, this is a saying that is often *mis*quoted and shortened to: 'Money is the root of all evil.' No, it is the *love of money* that makes money a harmful idol!

Jesus said: 'There is more happiness in giving than in receiving.'

Acts 20:35

Lovers of self and more

Paul, to whom this letter to Timothy is attributed, uses the term 'the last days' (verse 1). This could mean the days at the end of time, days in the future, but it may mean 'in the days we are living in now'. When Peter addresses the crowd in the street after Pentecost he uses those words in the second way, when he says: 'In the last days I pour out my Spirit on all humanity' (Acts 2:17).

That gift of the Spirit, however, must be rightly understood. If misunderstood it might lead to the idea that every individual – without any further ado – can be equipped with his or her particular and exclusive knowledge. This is the kind of supposed knowledge that one can find on the shelves of present-day bookshops, usually in the 'self-help' or 'Body, Mind, Spirit' sections, touting esoteric and arcane wisdom in all manner of guises.

Paul does not hesitate to use harsh words in his warning to Timothy. He writes that this so-called 'wisdom' can make people self-centred, boastful, arrogant, disobedient, ungrateful, reckless, and demented by pride, following one craze after another, and never coming to the knowledge of the truth, preferring strange human information to God's revelation in Jesus Christ. They will keep the outward appearance of being religious, but reject or misunderstand the inner power of it: the power the Lord gives as we share together in his Spirit.

The Lord will rescue me ... and bring me safely to his heavenly kingdom.

2 Timothy 4:18

Idols

Wrapped up in self

Did you hear the African story about how sickness and death came into the world? In the beginning nobody ever died. God gave people life in this world and then, after a well-spent life, an angel was sent with the invitation to join God in the heavenly glory. Everyone had always been happy to see this angel and glad to switch over from this earthly life to the glory of the next.

Until, that is, the day the angel was sent to a rich man who had just had a bumper harvest. He had pulled down his old barn and built a huge new one. The very night that he had safely stored his harvest, the messenger came to him with God's invitation. But the rich man said that he was not going to come, he still had much to eat and to drink. And he did not go. When the angel returned to God, God asked, 'Where is the man I invited?' The angel answered, 'He refused to come. He told me that he had too much for himself to be willing to leave it all and come.'

God became very upset and decided then and there to send sickness and old age to people before sending the angel, so that we would be softened up and prepared for the life to come.

Fool! … So it is when somebody stores up treasure for themselves, instead of becoming rich in the sight of God.

Luke 12:21

Idols

2 Making the appropriate choice

Notes based on the New Revised Standard Version
by Neneng Paniadomogan

Neneng Paniadomogan is an ordained pastor of the United Church of Christ in the Philippines (UCCP), based at Magpayang-del Rosario, Tubod, Surigao del Norte, Mindanao island. Her concerns and interests focus on the wellbeing of women, children and the environment. She also conducts Myers-Briggs Type Indicator (MBTI) workshops.

Making any kind of choice is often not easy. Making the appropriate choice is especially difficult when we consider the demands of our Christian faith on what we believe and how we live. Like the people of the Bible, we are called to make choices all the time in many aspects of life. The basic call of our God is to choose life over death, adversity over prosperity, truth over lies, sharing over hoarding, integrity over falsehood and trust over anxiety.

May the glimpses we get from this week's biblical texts give us insights and pointers as we wrestle with the dilemmas we face and the choices we need to make. The wooden and golden idols of ancient times may not look like our own idols today, but anything that competes with our loyalty to God and draws us away from God's commandments is potentially an idol. To prevent us from becoming idolatrous, let us choose God! Let us choose LIFE!

September

Idols

Where is your heart? Where is your treasure?

Twenty-four hours a day, we are bombarded with words, pictures and music designed to attract and manipulate our thoughts and emotions and entice us to acquire some particular item, attitude or 'lifestyle accessory' that will make life easy and happy. We may be tempted to 'listen' to our eyes and accumulate things we think will provide satisfaction and security. It is instructive to take a look at our kitchen cabinets and shelves and see how they are filled with various things accumulated through the years. And we find it difficult to let go of them; they have become our security blankets.

I asked a woman who lives in a poor slum area in our city why she and her family worked so hard and incurred debts so that they could have various appliances, which they displayed in their living room. She replied, 'With these, at least we will feel we are also decent people.'

We are so anxious to have all these things that our eyes can see and desire. But they are temporary and soon moth and rust and thieves will take them away. The temptation is great but our Christian faith challenges us to choose that which will last: love, righteousness, justice and peace. These are meant to be shared not hoarded. If these are our true treasures, our heart will open our eyes to the realities that endure.

O God, help us to let go of things that have captured our eyes and hearts and given us false security. Remind us that these treasures are temporary. You alone are eternal and the values of your kingdom outlast all things.

What is life?

An advertisement on our TV screens says: 'Coke adds life.' I would say that this statement is a sacrilege. It runs contrary to our belief that God alone gives, sustains and extends life. It is indicative of the way consumerist society manipulates the mass media to sell their products and instil in people's minds the belief that without this particular product – these kinds of food, appliances, clothing or vehicles – we can't have life. We realise how destructive such advertising can be when we think that many women from developing countries are tempted to feed their babies manufactured milk from bottles, rather than their own breast milk, because they think it is healthier and 'classier' – as, of course, the manufacturers want them to think.

In my few visits to Western countries, I have felt envious of the way that people are able to fill their grocery carts with huge quantities of drink and food, of many different varieties – yet still many of them complain about how difficult life is. Then I think of my people back home, many of them hardly eating three meals a day, yet trusting and hoping that somehow God will provide the next day's meals. Which of these really has life? The saying, 'live simply so that others may simply live', is a hard challenge for those who worry so much about what they will eat and wear; yet it is the challenge of this passage, in which we are invited to 'strive for his kingdom, and these things will be given to you as well' (verse 31).

Dear God, remind us that we need little on which to live. Help us not to equate life with material things such as food and clothing. In you only can we find true meaning in our living.

Idols

Strange versus the familiar

Paul challenges those in Athens to wake up, to look around and to see which idols give meaning to their existence. They have become so familiar with the various images of the gods in their city, but he wants to introduce a new one, a stranger, the 'unknown god'.

How familiar are we with this unknown god? We have acquired so many idols today, things that seek to replace our ultimate loyalty to God. As my seminar professor, Dr Levi Oracion, says, 'Our idols do not have to be carved wood or graven images; they can be tiny things such as cell phones, computers or Nike shoes, or they can be huge things like power, riches, success and self.' The Philippines has been tagged the number one text capital of Asia and almost everyone has a cell phone, even those who have difficulty in feeding themselves and their family. It has become an idol for both the rich and the poor, young and old. I myself seem to be lost without this 'little thing'.

Take a moment now to pause and become aware of what 'little things' have become a familiar and seemingly essential part of your everyday life, without which you could not imagine functioning in your day-to-day life. Where and what are your idols? Let us discern and seek to know the 'unknown god' who is above every idol. Let us search out and know this unknown god who has, in fact, searched us out, and come to us in the form of a human being; who dwelt among people and showed us the way, the truth and the life.

Reign in our hearts, O God, so that no other idols can replace you. Let our highest loyalty be in you alone and to no one else.

September

'Wow body!'

How do we love our bodies? How do we take care of them? The image of the body presented by Paul is so beautiful. It reminds us that each part is important and has an essential role to make the body function well. This image is also appropriate for a family, a church, a nation and indeed the whole creation.

But the bleak reality that contradicts this beautiful image is that people's bodies – especially women's and children's bodies – are being abused, desecrated and violated across the world, because of poverty, and cultural and social pressures. On the other hand, some people seem to worship their bodies as if they are all that matters in life. With endless gadgets, ornaments and fashions available to decorate and pamper the body and every kind of food and drink available to satisfy our bodily cravings, nevertheless, the rich and developed countries promote a lifestyle that actually diminishes the health and wellbeing of our bodies, exposing it to new dangers and risking desecrating the 'temple of God'.

• List the ways in which you take care of your body.

• What new ways might you practise to improve your body's condition, such as learning to meditate, doing some form of exercise or eating a more healthy diet?

We confess our sins against our bodies; we have not taken care of them well enough. Encourage us to appreciate your gift and to nourish our bodies with love and care, without making them into idols. Enrich us with your Spirit.

Idols

Eat your fill and bless the Lord

'You shall eat your fill and bless the Lord'! What a beautiful assurance! It is also a challenge, perhaps especially for people in the West who have so much food freely available, stocked in freezers and refrigerators and yet may have lost the ability truly and wholeheartedly to praise and thank God for the abundance they enjoy.

Paradoxically, it is often the reverse in countries where people have much less. Many Filipinos, especially the poor ones, are very thankful for any food they eat, though they do not have the luxury of eating their fill. Most of them pray before eating, even when the food on the table is only porridge and some salted fish.

God desires that all people are able to eat and be filled. Unfortunately, many in the world go to bed hungry and go around in the daytime with empty stomachs – perhaps because other people have made food their god and deprived many of their basic needs.

A co-pastor, the Reverend Rudy Beley, led this prayer over a meal, which has stayed in my memory: 'Some people have appetite but no food; some have food but no appetite. Thank you, God, that we have both.'

O God, bless us with the food we need to be filled. Thank you for your creation that sustains us. Help us to be mindful of the many who are in want of food. Help us to share what we have with the hungry.

September

Choose life

God has given us the choice: to choose life or death. But God has set a requirement also: to obey the commandments of the Lord your God. Consider the following acronym on the word 'life':

Life is possible only if our Loyalty is to God and God alone. A person's highest loyalty must never be to any other person, organisation or cause. To be loyal to God is to follow God's teachings, which promote life and enrich our bodies.

Integrity propels us to be consistent with what we believe and how we live; to be able to withstand pressures, believing that God wills peace, justice and righteousness and shuns greed, hatred and lies. Integrity enables us to stand up for what enhances life and celebrates creation.

Faithfulness to God and God's commandments is crucial. Idols will try to draw us away from God. We must be strong to resist these temptations; we must strive to cling to God. Faithfulness is to believe that whatever it takes to live simply and justly is pleasing to God.

Endurance to stay focused on God rather than on the gods of this world is something we all need: endurance to press on with courage and strength, to learn and grow in the journey towards wellness and life, to walk with those who choose life and together create a life-friendly world – not only for now but for the generations to come.

For those times and situations when we have chosen death and adversity, forgive us, O God. Enable us to choose life and prosperity. Give us the wisdom to know the difference and guide us to those things that please you alone.

Idols

3   Countering idols and idolatry

Notes based on the Revised Standard Version
by Ben Knighton

*Ben Knighton works with research degree students
from the Two-Thirds World Church in Oxford. He has published
a monograph on* The Vitality of Karamojong Religion *and is
researching Gikuyu history*

Idolatry seems an alien, antiquated practice today, so that the
second and third commandments may appear the easiest of the
ten; but the New Testament and especially Jesus apply the trend
away from act to motivation begun in the tenth, about coveting,
to the rest, deepening the challenge of this commandment.
God-substitutes do not need to be graven; the human, not
excluding the Christian, heart can in practice have many things
before God, above all in this personalist age, which redefines
self-will as freedom. What no personality type can escape is the
temptation to put oneself before God. To succumb is the most
ancient sin, the primordial attempt in the garden to usurp God
by *Adam*, all humankind, not just Eve, in order to 'be like God'.
This subtle temptation is the prerogative of beings who are made
in the image and likeness of God, yet can be misled by their own
desires to grasp at equality with him.

It is in laying ourselves transparent to the searchlight of scripture
that we can expose the great idols and invisible vestiges of our
selfish and devious inner motivations. How can people of faith
– those who walk the Jesus way – counter the grip of idols and
idolatry? The readings offer insights into God's counter-script
through Jesus of releasing human beings from these shackles. If
we will let the Holy Spirit minister to us thus in private, it will
save us from our unredeemed motives being exposed later in
public.

September

The Jesus way

Luke follows Mark in placing this passage after Peter eventually tumbles to who Jesus really is, 'the Christ of God' (verse 20). Jesus at once responds to this divine revelation to the fisherman who had been open enough to receive it, by speaking about the stumbling block of the cross and the mysterious resurrection that would follow. Of course we know from the other gospels that Peter gags at this, for he wants to be a leading supporter in a strong, publicly successful Messianic movement, as did Judas Iscariot. Such a priority Jesus exposes as satanic, as diabolical as the realisation of his anointing was divine!

Jesus' teaching here is central and clear, however paradoxical. Each who would save his or her own life will lose it, while those who will give it away to follow Christ will save it. There is no room for Christ under the sovereignty of the ego. Until the 'I' has been crossed out of our priorities, there is neither cross nor Christian salvation. Until this cross is voluntarily picked up, 'daily' Luke emphasises, there is neither discipleship nor sanctification. This is the way to open the narrow gate. All are invited to do so, but not all are willing, and there are many who refuse at this fence. It requires no theological erudition, for the requirement is brief and simple, but so hard to desire, when we want our own way.

Have all digested this open, but scandalous, secret of the cross? Have I?

Lord, not my will, but yours be done!

Idols

Renewing minds

If yesterday we saw that 'self' was the roadblock to salvation, today the renewal of our minds that Paul enjoins opens our eyes to pride as the root of all sin. Every single use of 'pride' and 'proud' in the Authorised Version is deeply pejorative; pride is most irrevocably opposed to God and it is, therefore, what God in the end must remove. In Paul's opening chapter to the Romans, the proud are haters of God and inventors of evil (1:30). Pride does not consist of act or appearance, but of an attitude of mind that refuses to give its life to God. Yet Christian Britons can be so quick to talk of pride in a school, in their children, in some tradition or achievement, with little thought that to be proud of these implies disdain for others.

I was appalled when I heard that a Kenyan priest, who had followed me all the way to a Durham doctorate, then told his students that they needed *his* epistles, not Paul's! Had my learning taught him this? Paul's idea of transformation and renewal does not allow any Christian to think more highly of self than one ought. His authority for saying so lay not in any human qualification, 'but by the grace given to me' (verse 3). *Charismata* are of use to God only if they arise out of his uniting *charis* (grace).

Do I communicate pride to others, however unconsciously?

Lord, show me how to exercise my gift, so that others may be blessed by it!

Life in the Spirit

In this early epistle Paul is hot on the consequences of the emancipation of the gospel: freedom, servanthood, love, and eight other fruits of the Spirit. Yet even the Christian is not necessarily released from any one of fifteen and more works of the flesh. Because the Christian Galatians, who were brought to Christ by Paul's own mission in the middle of what is now Turkey, are being taught by others to base their salvation on the law, Paul is seriously worried for them. He is afraid that they are going to miss the gospel altogether – the good news that does not consist in adhering to any code of observable behaviour and which is rooted in no particular culture. This allows Christian faith to be wonderfully universal, being tied to no one culture, whatever the Judaisers in Galatia may insist upon.

Paul contrasts the desires of Spirit and flesh: those given by the sanctifying Spirit yield great qualities such as patience and kindness, whereas those of the flesh result in very different ones.

If Europe's churches have been gradually emptying for a century, might it be because the idols of rank, class, denominationalism, nationalism and racism filled the empty buildings and because Christian self-conceit, provocation and envy were the 'passions and desires' of the flesh that needed crucifying?

How can Christians in my church beware of pride of status and the idolatry of social esteem, which lead us to 'bite and devour one another'? What can I do?

O Lord, give me the fruit of your Spirit so that my work for the church turns not to dust!

Idols

Faith and faithfulness

The greatest idolatry of our day revolves around celebrity. In Kenya, radio presenters just out of school are paraded in glossy magazines and on election platforms. Celebrities acquire fame sometimes merely because they are famous, yet the pressures of stardom are enough to ruin anyone's life. None of this would be possible if the masses, including many a Christian, did not idolise them.

To idolise is more than to admire an exceptional talent, such as Whitney Houston's voice; it is to adore without knowledge, to worship the unworthy, and to trust in the unstable. Similar idolatry can be found in every time and place. A century ago there was a Dodoso herder in Karamoja who joined a cattle raid to Sudan. The raiders suffered a counter-attack that picked them all off bar one, who returned with all the livestock. He became so famous in the region that people would walk scores of miles just to see his herds of cattle, which were marked out by a certain distinctive colour. So also in the Jerusalem church it was tempting to celebrate the rich man in the hope of sharing in the glories of this world, with the inevitable resultant dishonouring of the poor.

At which points does my church, and my own giving, show the sin of partiality identified by James?

O Lord, give me faith in what is not seen, in the immortal and invisible, that I may show mercy to those who need it most!

Living with enough

The psalmist deals with a strange yet common idolatry. Not a few people come to make, if only subconsciously, fear to be their idol. This does not have obvious immediate rewards, so can appear as impartial as the Christian faith itself. Yet there are compensations, for fears and worries (and there are always grounds for some) can evoke attention and pity. Responsibilities can be alleviated. The Christian leader or preacher can be excused for his lack of courage, being commended for his prudence instead. Yet if the Christian does live a self-sacrificial life that deliberately does not reward people in the way the world expects or demands, tension or opposition is bound to arrive.

Psalm 23 is not a sentimental, pastoral idyll, one reason why it was a favourite in the First World War. The valley of the shadow of death is there to be walked. The banquet must be eaten in the presence of enemies; if fear reigns, it cannot be enjoyed. The key is to look to God himself and his care and provision, so that 'I fear no evil', even though it is tangible – not because we are excused it.

What is it precisely that we fear about the future? Where do we need to act and where do we need to trust in our Father for provision?

O Lord, teach us that where you are guiding us has all we need in this life, so that we will fear no lack!

Living the Go(o)d life

Another perennial idol enjoying a golden run today is success. It depends not on being celebrated, for we may want to succeed only for the satisfaction of our own pride or for another. A colleague once told me that there was nothing wrong with ambition, and indeed the desire for a bishopric is commended in 1 Timothy 3:1. Yet trying to further an ambition by causing trouble for others, weakening competitors' positions, breaking confidences, using deceptive and devious tactics, makes the motive selfish, however veiled, and not for the common good. Selfish ambition in one's heart goes hand in hand with jealousy (verses 14 and 16), fuelling both the desire to have what is not yet owned, and covetousness.

According to James, being driven by wanting power and goods for oneself will end in disorder, division, and war. Such motivation is not merely carnal and unspiritual but 'devilish' (verse 15), yet this is the common scenario of the workaday world in which Christians must earn a livelihood, and too often of the church. In verse 6 of chapter 4, James cites Proverbs 3:34 for the solution for the godly life: 'God opposes the proud, and gives grace to the humble.' Such an attitude will not remove an enemy at once, but it will give true wisdom that is open to reason.

How do I respond unselfishly to my brother or sister in Christ, when their desires for success seem motivated by pride?

Lord, teach me to discern pride and avarice whenever they appear among my motives and give me grace to choose meekness!

Readings in Mark

7 Jesus in the temple

Notes based on the New Revised Standard Version
by Sam Peedikayil Mathew

*Dr Sam Peedikayil Mathew has been a teacher of the
New Testament for twenty years. He serves as Professor and Head of
the Department of New Testament at Gurukul Lutheran Theological
College, Chennai, India. He has authored several books and articles.
He has a keen interest in contextual biblical interpretation.*

In the gospels Jesus is presented as a controversial figure from
the beginning of his ministry in the northern district of Galilee
until the end in Judea. Mark, chapters 11 and 12, gives us
information on the Judaean section of his ministry. Jesus' entry
into Jerusalem is marked by a royal welcome given to him by
the common people. In contrast to this we find the politico-
religious leaders and their supporters questioning Jesus and
trying to trap him in his answers to hotly debated issues of
the day. In these chapters, Jesus dares to confront the temple,
which was the centre of religion, politics and economics. He
does not hesitate to discuss controversial issues and make his
views on the topics clear. He doesn't shy away from pointing out
corruption and injustice – not only in the temple but also among
the politico-religious leaders themselves. In these episodes we
see the enemies of Jesus come all out against Jesus, seeking ways
to destroy him. For them Jesus proves to be a leader who is
different from the war heroes, a leader with non-violent views
and ways. He subordinates religious rituals and practices to the
love commandment, and privileges the poor, the marginalised
and all oppressed people.

September

A leader with a difference

Jesus' entry into Jerusalem riding on a colt made him a unique leader among the Jews. Common people considered Jesus to be the expected Messiah and they associated all the popular messianic expectations of a victorious king with him. They welcomed Jesus, just like any leader of the Maccabean revolt who came victorious in their war against foreign rulers a few centuries ago, by spreading their cloaks and leafy branches on the road. But Jesus showed that he is not a warrior like the Maccabean war heroes who came riding on horses after their victory. He refused to follow the path of violence and force. Instead, he chose a colt, a symbol of humility. Jesus presented an alternative model of leadership in the midst of popular expectations of a militant leader.

Mahatma Gandhi was a leader who proved to be different through his simple lifestyle and philosophy of non-violence in the struggle against British colonial power in India. Although his lifestyle and non-violent freedom struggle came under severe criticism and ridicule from his own contemporaries, his life and teaching had a great influence in the struggle for justice for the blacks in the United States and in the fight against apartheid in South Africa.

Make a list of leaders in your locality who have made a difference in the lives of ordinary people and see what they have in common, if anything, with Jesus.

Lord, grant us grace to resist the temptation to be carried away by popular expectations.

Protest against injustice and exploitation

The temple at Jerusalem was the centre of religion, politics and economics for first-century Palestinian Jews. Jesus' action and words in the temple conveyed his disapproval and protest against the economic activities within the temple premises. His driving out of those buying and selling in the temple was a direct attack on the priestly aristocracy who owned shops in the temple precincts to provide for the needs of the temple worshippers. These shops extracted maximum profit by fleecing the worshippers. The overturning of the tables of moneychangers and the seats of dove-sellers showed Jesus' protest against such exploitation of the poor and weak. Jesus was so angry that he did not allow people to carry anything into the temple for a while. His words, however, were more damaging than his actions. The temple, which was supposed to be a 'house of prayer', is turned into a 'den of robbers'. No wonder that the rulers of the temple, the chief priests and the scribes who were their supporters, sought a way to kill him.

Following in the footsteps of Jesus, we are challenged to confront unjust structures and to challenge their custodians to change their ways, even if suffering and death itself are the consequences.

Identify areas where exploitation and oppression take place in your church/society. What do you plan to do as a true follower of Jesus?

Lord, give us courage to protest against injustice and exploitation in your name.

September

Protest movement as the basis of Jesus' authority

Immediately after Jesus' severe criticism of the temple, his authority is questioned by the chief priests, scribes and elders, who were Jesus' opponents from the beginning of his ministry. Jesus asks them a controversial counter-question regarding the baptism of John – whether it is from heaven or of human origin. John the Baptist, who identified with the prophetic tradition, called people to repent and gave them 'baptism of repentance for the forgiveness of sins' in the river Jordan. John's movement led ordinary people to forgiveness of sins without need of the temple, sacrifices and the mediation of priests, and free of cost at that. Now Jesus bases his authority on the popular protest movement of John the Baptist. Jesus identifies with John's movement when his authority is questioned. Just as John's movement had divine sanction rooted in the prophetic tradition of Old Testament, Jesus indirectly implies that his temple action also had divine approval.

No wonder Jesus met the same fate as John, who was killed by the political authorities. When our actions for the cause of justice are rooted in the commandments of God, naturally there will be popular support, although opposition from the political powers cannot be avoided.

List some commonalities between a movement for justice in a context with which you are familiar and Jesus' struggle for justice.

Gracious God, enable us to face opposition with courage and base our struggle for justice on the movements that already exist in our contexts.

Leaders are accountable

Jesus intensifies his criticism of Jewish leaders using the parable of the wicked tenants. The prophet Isaiah had, centuries earlier, depicted Israel as a vineyard that produced sour grapes (Isaiah 5:1-7). The leaders of Israel mismanaged the temple-state, headed by the religious aristocracy of Judaea, by refusing to give the produce to the owner. They even dared to kill the servants and the heir of the vineyard and assumed ownership of the vineyard. Therefore God will punish them.

The religious leaders understood this parable as a direct attack on their power and position and sought to kill Jesus. His criticism of the religious leadership and their supporters is attested in many other places in the gospels. Earlier in the temple action, as we saw, they were criticised for robbing the people through the temple. In Mark 12:40 the scribes, who are the supporters of the temple leadership, are accused of 'devouring the houses of widows'. They are addressed as 'blind guides', 'whitewashed tombs', 'brood of vipers' and murderers (Matthew 23:24, 27, 33). Jesus did not mince words when the religious and political leaders of his time deviated from their divine calling and became selfish and corrupt. He taught that all are accountable before God, irrespective of their power and position.

How could you help to make people in your locality aware of corruption among their leaders?

Lord, enable our leaders to realise that all are accountable before God and grant them power and grace to live up to your standards.

Opponents are silenced

Jesus silences the Pharisees, the Herodians and the Sadducees who come to trap him through his answers to burning political, economic and theological issues of his day. The Pharisees and the Herodians try to trap him by asking Jesus the question about the legality of paying tax to Caesar. For the Jews, the imperial tax, which was a visible symbol of political oppression, was not only an economic burden, but also a religious offence. Jesus' answer, 'Give to the emperor the things that are the emperor's, and to God the things that are God's' (verse 17) does not give his opponents a chance to catch him out and brand him as enemy of the Romans. It is an enigmatic saying, but perhaps implies that the primary allegiance of the people – created in the image of God – must be to God.

The Sadducees' question about the resurrection is wisely answered by pointing to the scriptures. Thus the supporters of Herod and the temple are given a fitting reply by Jesus through his wit and wisdom. Jesus' sharp response to his critics teaches us that controversies are to be faced with courage and conviction in the faithful word of God.

What are the different ways in which opponents of the gospel in your locality can be confronted?

Gracious God, grant us wisdom and understanding to discern the intentions of all critics of the gospel and to face them with wisdom and courage.

Religion is subordinated to love

For Jesus, the greatest commandment of God is to love God and fellow human beings. A scribe who is an expert in the Law is told that the love commandment is more important than whole burnt offerings. The worship, offerings and sacrifices in the temple are clearly subordinated to the command to love. The scribe's summing up of the two love commandments into one command in verse 33 is accepted by Jesus. Thus Jesus seems to say that primary importance must be given to loving God through loving one's neighbour as oneself. In Luke 10:27 the love commandment is presented as one command – to love God and neighbour. Jesus stands well within the prophetic tradition that emphasised that observance of festivals, offerings and sacrifices in the temple are meaningless without practising justice (e.g. Amos 5:21-24). Active love and concern for fellow human beings is more important than worship in the temple. One must be able to see God's face in the neighbour, as seen in the parable of the good Samaritan.

Once a rabbi was asked, 'How does one know when the day ends and night begins?' He replied, 'When you see your sister or brother on the face of others, then the day begins. Till then it is night.'

What would be your response if you witnessed an accident victim on your way to Sunday worship?

Lord, enable us to rise above the boundaries of our religion and practise your command to love others.

Readings in Mark

8 The days are coming

Notes based on the New Revised Standard Version
by Sam Peedikayil Mathew

Any discussion of the end time arouses human
curiosity as well as anxiety. Biblical teaching
regarding the last things is often misunderstood as mere
information about fantastic future events. However, a careful
reading of the New Testament shows that the teaching on the
end time is not concerned with times and seasons so much as
directed to believers to strengthen their faith and to live in the
present time meaningfully and with hope in the final triumph of
God.

The people of God are exhorted to be watchful of the hypocrites
and deceivers who cheat believers in the name of religion.
They are called upon to keep their hopes alive in the midst of
seemingly hopeless situations. Since God is in full control of
the situation they can be courageous in the context of trials
and tribulations. The preparedness and the eager expectation
of the last days can make their lives more meaningful, both to
themselves and to others.

The end time beckons the people of God to be watchful for
the enemies of the gospel and on guard against them. The signs
of the end are to be discerned by transcending reason and
exercising faith in Jesus so that believers can co-operate with
God's mission in the power of Jesus.

Religious hypocrisy and true piety

The scribes are verbally attacked in this passage in several ways. First, the scribal interpretation of the Messiah as the Son of David is called into question. Then, after having rejected the scribal theology regarding the Messiah, Jesus criticises the practices of scribes. He warns against the social and religious power exerted by the scribes in the worship places and marketplaces. In verse 40 he accuses them of exploiting widows' houses and making hypocritical prayers. Thus the theology and unjust practices of scribes are roundly questioned and condemned by Jesus.

In contrast we find a poor widow who puts two copper coins into the temple treasury. Although she puts in a small sum of money, Jesus comments that she has put in more than the rich – 'everything she had, all she had to live on' (verse 44). Totally unaware of the exploitation and oppression going on in the temple, she expresses her devotion to God by contributing to God's house all she has. Therefore she is commended by Jesus for her sacrificial giving to God.

So Jesus finds both hypocritical religious leaders and truly pious and sincere worshippers in the temple. Even today religious hypocrisy is not hard to find at the top levels of church leadership, whilst true piety may often be discerned at the grass roots. Inequalities of faith, as well as wealth and privilege, are still glaring realities in Christian circles.

What do you think are the consequences of exposing hypocrisy among religious leaders?

Lord, help us to distinguish between true piety and hypocrisy in religious circles and to respond accordingly.

September

Readings in Mark

Be watchful and courageous

Curiosity and anxiety about the future are found among most people. In India, fortune tellers who use horoscopes, astrology, palmistry, face reading, numerology and other such methods are seen everywhere. They exploit the curiosity of people to know their future and in the process deceive and mislead many people. Today's text warns us against all kinds of deceiver. Although Jesus does not give specific dates and times for the end time, he offers some signs of the end. These include the appearance of messianic pretenders, increasing violence between nations, and natural calamities. Believers are exhorted to be watchful and courageous in the midst of persecution by the religious and political authorities. They are comforted that the Holy Spirit will assist them in their crisis. Conflicts are to be expected – even in one's home, between close relatives. Perseverance is called for in the midst of these trials and tribulations.

In Christian circles one can also find those who mislead people by specifying the exact dates and places of the end time. Biblical teaching regarding the end time is directed towards strengthening believers who are at present in the midst of trials and tribulations, rather than offering certainty about future events. It warns believers against deceivers and strengthens them to face adverse situations.

How would you identify those who deceive believers in your locality?

Lord, grant us grace to be watchful of deceivers and persevere courageously till the end.

September

Be hopeful amidst hopelessness

Suffering and persecution will be at its worst during the end time. The poor and the weak will suffer the most, Jesus warns. The suffering will be so intense that people will have to flee. But the believers are comforted that the days of intense suffering will be short because it is the Lord who determines the number of days of suffering. Nature will also join in intensifying the suffering of the people. The heavenly bodies will fail to perform their functions. Nevertheless, amidst political and religious opposition and natural calamities, hope is not lost for the people of God. The Son of Man will come in the clouds to gather the people of God from all corners of the world.

It is significant that the Son of Man is described as coming with great power and glory. The message for believers is the final triumph of God over all the forces of evil. God's people will suffer temporarily, but the final victory belongs to God. The forces of evil will do their worst, but God is in full control of the situation. The destiny of the people of God is determined neither by earthly political powers nor by heavenly bodies. Their destiny is safe in the hands of God.

List some of the ways in which you as an individual, and your church, can help to keep hope in God alive.

Lord of the universe, enable us always to keep alive faith in your final triumph.

Be always ready

The people of God are expected to read the signs of the times and understand that the end is near. No human being knows the exact time of the end. The secret of the end lies with God. Human beings cannot manipulate nor predict that. The people of God are exhorted to be vigilant at all times, like the doorkeeper who waits for the coming of the master at any time. Believers are expected to prepare themselves for the final coming of the Son of Man and the consummation of their salvation. This leaves no room for relaxing and taking things easy. They need to live their lives with alertness and eager expectation. Such vigilance will enliven their hopes and make their lives more meaningful.

The early Christian community depicted in the Acts of the Apostles (2:41-47) was one such vigilant community, expecting the end very soon. They pooled their resources and had everything in common. In that sharing no one lacked anything. The eager expectation of the end time changed their religious, economic and political life. Such an attitude made a radical change in their perspective to life.

What gets in the way of your leading a vigilant life? How might you combat these hindrances?

Lord, give us your divine perspective on our life so that we may live with vigilance and hope.

Friends and foes of the gospel

In Mark's depiction of the last stage of the earthly ministry of Jesus, the friends and foes of Jesus are brought into sharp focus. Whereas the chief priests and scribes, who are staunch opponents of Jesus, seek to arrest him and kill him, a marginalised person receives him as his as guest and an unidentified woman anoints him with very expensive ointment. It is noteworthy that, although the leaders and the powerful people, like the chief priests and scribes, seek somehow to kill Jesus, it is the marginalised and the weaker sections of society who welcome him and accept him. Church history also testifies that generally it is the poor and the downtrodden who have responded to the gospel positively. They are the people who gladly receive the good news, perhaps because they know well their need of it. Mark uses irony to show that, while the religious leaders and their supporters were trying to kill Jesus, a woman prepared him for his suffering and death.

In Christian ministry too, opposition to the gospel is a reality wherever one remains true to the gospel of Jesus Christ. The followers of Jesus will have to face such opponents courageously, as Jesus faced them. It is a comforting thought that in the midst of hostility and opposition there will be people who support and protect God's people – even though they may not be the powerful of the world.

What can you do individually and as a group to make enemies of the gospel into friends of God?

Pray for those who oppose the gospel through their words and deeds.

October

Signs of the end time

The disciples of Jesus were reluctant to believe the testimony of Mary Magdalene that Jesus had been raised. Even after Jesus' appearance to two other women, they refused to believe. Jesus had to appear to the disciples and reprimand them for their lack of faith, and their stubbornness. Whereas the three women disciples believed in the resurrection easily, the other disciples were not willing to believe. John's gospel describes how the apostle Thomas insisted that unless he saw and touched the marks of crucifixion he would not believe. Jesus made it clear to them that only those who believe will be saved. Those who believe in Jesus and his resurrection will perform signs that Jesus performed, such as casting out demons, healing the sick, speaking in tongues and having power over snakes and poison. The power of Jesus is given to those who believe in him.

Belief and unbelief are the signs of the end time that have already begun with the coming of Jesus. His disciples are expected to have faith that transcends reason. Those who have such faith will be able to see the risen Jesus and experience the power of God in a new way. The risen Lord will work with them and do wonders.

How does the risen Lord work today in our midst? Think of specific examples.

Lord, grant us your grace to go beyond our reasoning to see, hear and understand your signs in our present context.

Visions of abundant life

1   Creating abundant life

Notes based on the New Revised Standard Version
by Barbara Calvert

*Barbara Calvert is a Methodist minister. Previously, she
was an RE teacher. She then worked for Christian Aid, followed by a
period as chaplain to international students in the three universities in
Glasgow.*

The life of God is abundant in every way. It appeals to every part
of ourselves; it is rich with every possible form of promise and
potential. As John's gospel says 'I came that they may have life
and have it abundantly' (John 10:10).

The ancient Israelites believed they should make the vision of
abundant life real in practical ways, through creating a society
where prosperity given by God was to be shared as widely as
possible.

For reflection and action in the coming week

• Read *Unbowed: My Autobiography* by Nobel Peace Prize winner
  Wangari Maathai (Heinemann, 2007).

God's sensual gifts

As I write, in today's paper is the obituary for Dame Anita Roddick, the founder of The Body Shop. As I read of her life, fragrances of Raspberry Ripple bubble bath, White Musk shower gel, Brazil Nut face wash, African Salt body scrub and aromatherapy lavender oil waft around in my memory. Anita made it OK to indulge our bodies. None of her products was tested on animals and she sought supplies from poor and marginalised groups throughout the world, providing them with much needed income.

And then we read in today's psalm of 'oil to make the face shine' (verse 15)! How beautiful is that? A God who, long before the Body Shop, indulges us with sensual gifts, everything our hearts and bodies could desire, even 'wine to gladden the human heart' (verse 15)! A God who thinks of our every need, but, recognising the danger in such generous and abundant provision, also provides the rhythm of our days to regulate our indulgence: day and night, darkness and light, cold and warmth, work and leisure, sunrise, sunset.

Can we cope with such God-given generosity or, like greedy children in the tuck shop, do we try to grab it all for ourselves, overindulging and consequently being the harbingers of our own destruction?

O Lord, how generous are your works!
May our gratitude be reflected in our just sharing of all that you provide.

Trees of life

Virgin rainforest. Thick, hot, verdant green leaves dripping with moisture, unexploited, with the four mighty rivers of Pishon, Gihon, the Tigris and Euphrates flowing slowly towards the beckoning sea. This is the picture we are given of the Garden of Eden in Genesis 2. God, lovingly, trustingly, tenderly places man in this garden 'to till it and keep it'.

Before long the trees have been uprooted, the forest cleared for mining, for there is gold here, bdellium and onyx stone. Huge profits are to be made and the forest that had provided for humanity's every need – juicy fruits, protein-filled nuts, canopies for shade, wood for shelters, canoes and cooking, medicines, ointments, a rich habitat for an abundance of wildlife – is lost and the earth returns to dust.

But the tree, which according to this account of creation is the first plant created by God, has become again the symbol of life and hope. In Haiti, mango saplings are given freely to those who will 'till it and keep it'; in the Holy Land, new olive trees are nurtured, a symbol of both resistance against aggression and of hope for the future; and in Kenya, the women, led by Nobel Peace Prize winner, Wangari Maathi, have resisted fierce and often violent opposition from ruthless developers, to plant millions of trees and bring fresh life and hope to arid lands. May we be granted the wisdom to nurture and respect the fruits of the earth.

O Lord, how plentiful are your works!
May our gratitude be reflected in our purposeful respect for all creation.

October

Costly yet free

What is the picture given here of life in the promised land? Harmonious, peaceful, people living in right relationship with one another and with God, loving the Lord with all their heart, with all their soul and with all their might, and passing that love on to their children. This is an idealistic picture, far from real human experience. There is no pain or want here. God's side of the bargain is to provide a land flowing with milk and honey, pure and sweet – delicious foods provided freely without human toil. It is a picture reminiscent, is it not, of the Garden of Eden? And, like Adam and Eve in the Garden of Eden, the people of the promised land fail to keep their promises.

As the story of God's people continues, the picture becomes discordant, ruptured – until in the gospels we have the images of milk and honey flowing freely without cost replaced by the costly images of bread and wine. Bread requires wheat, yeast, kneading, waiting, baking – and wine requires vines, pruning, picking, trampling, and again waiting until all is ready. And then the bread is broken and the wine is poured. At great cost, these gifts are offered to us again freely. Costly but free! For all who partake of the feast of life, God's covenant promise is renewed and life in abundance restored.

O Lord, how costly are your works!
May our gratitude be reflected in costly response to all your promises.

Enjoying the sabbath

A friend of mine was reminiscing about her 1950s' childhood growing up on a farm in north Devon. Her parents worked long and hard on the farm during the week and there were chores for my friend and her brother to do when they got home from school. Then on Saturday it was baking day. Logs were fed into the firebox to keep the oven hot as all the baking was done for the week ahead – cakes, pies, bread and even the Sunday joint was roasted on Saturday. Sunday came and it was a different day. Time to spend together, going to church, visiting family and neighbours and Sunday dinner was the cold roast baked the day before with just a simple salad and bread.

Today's verses, part of Deuteronomy's version of the Ten Commandments, command the people to keep the sabbath. In the more widely known Exodus version, the people are commanded to remember the sabbath because God rested on the seventh day of creation. But here in Deuteronomy the people of Israel are reminded of the time when they laboured long and hard as slaves in Egypt.

Sabbaths – in our case, Sundays – are a gift from God. Not a day to be endured when you are not allowed to do anything, but a day of rest from the labours of the week, a day to enjoy God's bounty. How do we express this in our worship? And how do we share this positive vision of Sunday as a valuable gift to our society today?

O Lord, how restful are your works!
May our gratitude be reflected in quiet reflecting on your gift of rest.

Visions of liberty

On the wall of my study hangs a Palestinian embroidery. In the middle of the embroidery is an olive tree created out of neat green cross-stitches for the leaves and branches and black for the trunk of the tree. Above and below the tree, again picked out in neat green stitches, are the words 'The earth is the Lord's'. I was reminded of these words on a recent visit to the Holy Land.

I was standing on the Mount of Olives, overlooking the walls of the old city of Jerusalem. Today a new, three metre high, grey concrete wall is to be seen snaking its way across Palestinian land, separating farmers from their fields, families from their olive trees, workers from their means of employment, children and students from their schools and colleges, the sick from medical centres, and dividing peoples from the hope of justice, reconciliation and peace.

In today's passage, the Lord of the earth proclaims a year of jubilee when 'you shall return, every one of you to your property and every one of you to your family' (verse 10). We do not know if this vision of a jubilee year was ever realised but it is a vision of liberty that God wills for us, that we might sound the trumpet and be released from the burden of conflict over land that belongs to the Lord. Is it possible for this vision to apply to Palestinians too?

O Lord, how just are your works!
May our gratitude be reflected in living out your vision of freedom for all.

Naked and exposed

The worn-out boots and bloodstained clothes of the warriors (verse 5) – these are images of conflict. A naked, newborn, vulnerable infant (verse 6) – this is an image of peace.

Peace has no weapons, clothes to hide behind, clever strategies or grand plans. Peace is pictured in the near-naked, shaven heads of the Buddhist monks in Burma who dared to confront the military dictatorship, not with any grand plan or strategy, but simply by standing alongside the poor in naked solidarity. And in Burma too we have peace represented in the vulnerable figure of a woman, Aung San Suu Kyi, feared by the powerful, spending 11 of the past 18 years under some form of house detention. Aung San Suu Kyi has been described by the Nobel Peace Prize committee as 'an outstanding example of the power of the powerless'. Far from drawing attention to herself under difficult personal circumstances, she refused even to leave the country as her husband lay dying in a British hospital, for fear of not being allowed to return and continue the defence of democracy.

Those who seek to oppress the poor with guns, tear gas, brutality and torture long for those whom they oppress to take up weapons. They would know how to respond. It is the nakedness of those who seek the way of peace that they fear most.

And so God comes to us, naked and exposed: the newborn infant, the Prince of Peace, ushering in God's kingdom of endless, abundant peace.

O Lord, how exposed are your works!
May our gratitude be reflected in solidarity with all who are oppressed.

Visions of abundant life

2 The vision of abundance: for ourselves and for others

Notes based on the Good News Bible by Dafne Plou

Dafne Sabanes Plou is a freelance journalist from Argentina and a member of the Methodist church. She works with women's groups, particularly in Christian education and evangelisation. She is also a member of her church's Communications Committee.

What does abundance mean in our society today? Sometimes I feel that consumerism has invaded our lives utterly, causing us to think that abundance is being able to fill our supermarket trolleys with all kinds of goods, shopping freely in malls every weekend and queuing up for hours to purchase the latest model of the latest hi-tech appliance in the market. Whenever we go out, our children are likely to badger us with their requests: 'Please, buy this for me' – whatever 'this' happens to be. And if we say 'no', they are not deterred but simply ask again as soon as they see something else they fancy. There's so much to choose from, that we never seem satisfied.

In this market-driven era, do Jesus' words mean anything to us at all? Life in all its fullness (John 10:10) is more than what we can afford. Are we ready to take his promise and live according to his mandates? Or would we rather opt for the market's materialist promises and be satisfied by its shiny offers?

Go to a land that I am going to show you

Sandy and his family accepted the challenge. A new Methodist congregation had been formed spontaneously by migrant workers in Rio Gallegos, in the south of Patagonia, in Argentina, where winds typically blow at 100 km per hour. The new congregation needed a minister to work with them in their consolidation and growth. It wouldn't be easy for Sandy and his family to leave the big city, their comfortable home and many belongings to travel more than 2000 kilometres to face the unknown.

Their neighbours and workmates regarded Sandy as a 'rare specimen'. He was not an ordained minister himself, so why give up his comfortable life to go far south to that barren land with such unfriendly weather? But there was something in the call that enticed him, and also drew his wife and children: the promise that the Lord would be with them, blessing their work. A long way from shopping malls, surrounded by fishermen, shepherds and their families, they learned what life in all its fullness might mean. They discovered the friendship and solidarity that can grow between men, women and children who are far from their dear ones in a vast and lonely territory and who know their need of one another. Sunday services in the chapel were a celebration, where people shared in abundant hope.

Are we willing to leave aside our way of life so as to share our abundance with others?

October

Visions of abundant life

Don't be afraid

In the film *Babel*, Mexican film maker Alejandro González Iñárritu features the misfortune of a Mexican maid who loves the two children she's looking after but makes a mistake so that she is left with the children in the middle of the desert on the border of her country with the United States – a deadly place where illegal migrant workers have suffered the worst of fates. Under a strong sun, with no water and no clue about where to go, the maid leaves the children on their own, under a tree, and walks away to find help. Like Hagar so many centuries before, she doesn't want to see the children suffering.

The situation is distressing and the audience gets the feeling that the poor of this world have no chance, even when they are desperate to find 'abundant life' in a sort of 'promised land' advertised to outsiders as an ideal place where money flows like honey. The film raises many issues, such as lack of communication, spiritual emptiness and loneliness in our so-called developed societies. Under a bright, shiny surface, our world today seems often to have no heart.

Hagar and her child were also victims of rigid traditions, callous rules and unkind, envious feelings. But the Lord was with them. And in the middle of the desert, God offered them fullness of life.

Beloved God, help us to open our hearts and hands to those who need our love.

Not alone

It was an unsettling sight. Something was wrong in the neighbourhood. The locals observed groups of people, foreigners, going for a walk at midday, coming out from what seemed to be an abandoned warehouse. They would walk two or three blocks and then return to the building, not to be seen again till the following noon. What was going on? They were men and women, young and old. They never spoke to anyone, just looked ahead with fear in their eyes.

Neighbours murmured quietly about it at first, but then discussed the situation openly when they met at the butcher's, the grocer's, in the coffee shop. Some of them thought of calling the police, but others were afraid. What would happen to them if they denounced what was going on? But those grim faces! They couldn't stand the sight of them any more. They could see the people were suffering.

The police finally came and with them, the press, radio and TV reporters. It was a national scandal. Illegal workers, foreigners, kept like slaves in that old warehouse, working 18 hours a day, with just one short break at midday.

'I have heard them cry out to be rescued from their slave drivers,' said the Lord, and sent Moses (verse 7). The Lord also heard those modern slaves and sent the neighbours who, like Moses, obeyed.

Give us, Lord, open eyes and a brave conscience, ready to respond to injustice.

October

Visions of abundant life

Dignity

Women from the church in the shanty town were going to participate for the first time in the Women's Guild Day in their city. Most of them were cleaners, maids or casual workers. They promised to provide lunch for everyone, bringing meat pastries they would cook. The food was delicious and there was plenty for everyone. When the meeting ended, organisers offered to pay for the pastries. 'Why should you pay? You are not charging us for the tea and coffee, the cakes, scones and biscuits that you have all brought. We want to share with you. Accept what we have cooked as our contribution to this joyful day.' And there was dignity in these women's eyes.

The Lord had prepared this banquet for these women from the shanty town and, by their equal participation, had taken away the disgrace they had suffered for years. God had removed the cloud of sorrow created by social divisions, class prejudices and discrimination. He had offered fullness of life to all the women – both those who were better-off and those who were working hard for a living – so that they would encounter each other on equal terms, with respect and appreciation for what each of them could contribute to their Christian community: a community called to be loving, open and inclusive.

Are we ready to overcome the stereotypes and prejudices that keep us apart from each other and from God?

October

Turning mourning into joy

She has terrible memories of her youth. When she was a teenager, her neighbourhood, which used to be peaceful and friendly, was taken over by drug dealers. There were gang fights in the streets. People from all over the city and further afield would come to buy drugs. One could find youngsters lying on the pavements with the needles still in their arms. It was terrifying. Neighbours feared for their lives.

One day, a Christian group came to preach about changing lives. This group had a passion for working with youth and recovering former addicts for a new start. It was a courageous enterprise. Pastors and volunteers walked the streets talking to people, offering a new way to live, telling them that there was hope after all.

After several weeks of difficult and persistent witness, one of the drug dealers joined them. He changed completely. His home was transformed from a drug den to an open place welcoming all who were seeking help. The neighbours put aside their fears and joined forces to support him. More people joined. The mood in the area changed for good. Children could now play in the park again; people could walk in the streets and enjoy their surroundings once more.

Preaching the good news and accepting Christ as Lord had turned the mourning of this community into joy, their sorrow into gladness. God had satisfied the needs of his people and was guarding them as a shepherd guards his flock.

Even in our sorrow and despair, help us to know, God, that you are there so that we will not stumble.

October

The commitment to abundant life

In the Bible readings during this past week we have gained a good picture of what people commonly see as abundance: a banquet where no one is left out and every person can enjoy the fruits of the land: gifts of grain, wine and olive oil, plentiful sheep and cattle. The dancing, the joy, the wiping away of tears and the overcoming of sorrow are also part of this vision of abundance. At a time when water is becoming ever more scarce, the image of a well-watered garden is soothing to the spirit and to the imagination. Full inclusion of all reflects the results of God's blessing: young women and men, as well as the elderly, the blind, the lame, pregnant women and those about to give birth are all called to become part of God's great nation. They will all be guided to streams of water and to smooth, safe roads.

But before this happens, there has to be commitment to change things. In the synagogue at Nazareth, Jesus announces his commitment to change the world and the society we live in. He is ready to start his ministry by bringing good news to the poor, proclaiming liberty to captives, curing the blind, setting free those who are oppressed and announcing salvation to all people.

When he calls us to join him in these actions, he knows that our commitment, sustained by his power, will pave the way to the great banquet, where every woman, man and child will enjoy the abundance of life that he has promised us.

Challenge us, Lord, to true commitment to abundance of life for everyone.

Visions of abundant life

3   Abundant life for all

Notes based on the New Revised Standard Version
by Barbara Calvert

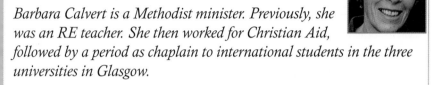

*Barbara Calvert is a Methodist minister. Previously, she
was an RE teacher. She then worked for Christian Aid,
followed by a period as chaplain to international students in the three
universities in Glasgow.*

God wants us to share the gift of abundant life with other people.
But which other people? In response to the question, 'Who then
is my neighbour?' (Luke 10:29), Jesus told the parable of 'the
good Samaritan'. So our question is, who is to be included in the
sharing of this gift of abundant life? The Old Testament answer
varies, but Jesus taught that the plenty of God is so vast that
there is enough for everyone. God's wealth is to be shared by all,
without exception. The challenge of Christian discipleship is to
live as if this is true.

For reflection and action in the coming week

• This week is One World Week. Reflect on one simple thing
  you can do this week to symbolise that God's world is one –
  perhaps just a simple word of greeting to a stranger.

October

The green covenant

God tells Noah no fewer than five times that God's covenant is 'between me and you and every living creature that is with you, for all generations'. In a significant way, this covenant is different from the later covenant with Abraham. The Abraham covenant is a personal relationship with Abraham. *This* covenant is universal, comprehensive, embracing all created life – a green covenant.

When I was living in Devon the churches together produced a Lent course called 'What on earth are we doing?' The course encouraged us to recognise ourselves as part of God's universal creation and our responsibility for that creation. Our lifestyles were challenged as we recognised how we had contributed to the threat of global warming facing God's world. This caused some discomfort, and the next year it was decided to do a more 'biblical' course!

We had a similar experience at our church in Paisley in Scotland when we opened a fairtrade shop and decided to call the shop 'Rainbow Turtle'. Turtles are a vulnerable, threatened species, as are many producers in the poorest countries of the world, and the rainbow is God's universal symbol of hope. Some members of the Town Council asked us to consider changing the name as they thought it wasn't very Christian!

So often we try to exclude our creator God from God's own living, dying, decaying, growing, renewing green creation – isolating God in a pietistic, sterilised, lifeless church.

God saw everything that he had made, and indeed, it was very good. Let all creation be glad and sing for joy.

October

Holiness equals humanness

Leviticus expresses its concern not only for ritual holiness but also for community holiness. The refrain 'for I am the Lord your God' shows that the direct implication of believing in the one God is caring for the whole community. The Holiness Code of Leviticus requires holiness not only in the temple but all the time, including living rightly with one another: justice for the poor and the alien, and love for your neighbour as you love yourself. The concept of holiness is expanded and applied to the whole of life; holiness and humanness are called to be soulmates. Perhaps it all sounds rather daunting, even impossible, as if failure is built in to the system.

For Christians, however, Jesus is our perfect embodiment of holiness and humanness. In him, holiness becomes so much more than a moral code and becomes a glorious way of life. In Jesus, we discover what it is to be fully human and also holy. The two can be lived together, sharing the same breath so that we experience life in all its fullness.

For Jesus, holiness was not life set apart but life lived to the full: feasting, laughing, befriending everyone – shepherds, fishermen, women, widows and tax collectors. 'Life in all its fullness' is living justly, humbly, lovingly, compassionately; feasting, laughing, having fun, showing God by being both truly human and truly holy. In Jesus, the Holiness Code of Leviticus comes alive.

God saw everything that he had made, and indeed, it was very good. Let all of our being, body, mind and soul, be glad and sing for joy.

October

The natural world in a hazelnut

One Christmas when I was a minister in Devon, I was given a large recycled sweet jar full of hazelnuts. The farmer had collected them when they were falling from the trees; there had been a prolific abundance of nuts. I started to eat my way through them. They were sweet and delicious but by the summer I was still only halfway down the jar! But then I found another use for them as I prepared our harvest services.

The nuts reminded me of Julian of Norwich's vision, in which God showed, in the palm of her hand, a little thing round as a hazelnut. Julian lived at a time when the Black Death was causing devastation throughout medieval England; she shared in the general anxiety about life. In the vision, Julian is told by God to look at the little thing in her hand. Julian asks 'What is it?' and the answer came: 'It is everything that is created.'

Isaiah's vision too is of everything that is created. It is a vision of the ideal king whose just reign extends to the natural world, even to creation as a whole. This ideal king, understood by Christians as a prophecy of the Messiah, restores the wholeness of the creation. And so, as we celebrated harvest, each of us holding one of last season's nuts in the palm of our hand, we reflected on the words that Julian heard in her vision: 'It endures and ever will endure, because God loves it.'

God saw everything that he had made, and indeed, it was very good. Let even the smallest parts of creation be glad and sing for joy.

Visions of abundant life

Jump – for joy!

Come and eat! This is not the message of health educators to overindulgent Britons! Rather, they are telling us that half the population of the UK could be obese in 25 years' time, leading to frightening health problems and the stark warning that today's children will die at a younger age than their parents. So we are urged to exercise more, with children being encouraged to play sport. It doesn't have to be hockey or netball, associated in my mind with the awful gym kit of my school days. Any sport will do – even frisbee!

Physical inactivity was not a problem in Isaiah's day. Food for the table was the result of human sweat and toil, and water had to be collected and carried. So this passage is full of both physical and spiritual energy and activity: 'come to the waters', 'come buy wine and milk', 'seek the Lord' (verses 1, 6).

The abundant life freely offered to us by God can be received only if we respond. We receive God's gift and the gift, in turn, draws out from us more activity. Our response is to 'go out in joy', to 'burst into song' and 'clap hands' (verse 12). As seeds that are sown bring forth fruit, so shall God's life given in abundance not return empty. There is certainly no lack of activity in Isaiah's invitation to abundant life! But it is activity freely undertaken as a response to God's love, not a regime recommended by your personal trainer at the local gym.

God saw everything that he had made, and indeed, it was very good. Let every human activity respond to God and be glad and sing for joy.

October

Visions of abundant life

The old party is over

Imagine the six stone water jars lined up, each holding twenty or thirty gallons. That's roughly 165 gallons – well over three thousand pints. Another image of life in abundance! The old jars of Judaism are transformed into jars overflowing with the new wine of the kingdom.

Two years ago at the Greenbelt Christian Arts festival (held each year at Cheltenham race course), Ann Morisy preached at the Sunday morning communion service on this story of the wedding at Cana. With something like fifteen thousand people gathered for this open air celebration in the late August sunshine, there was a celebratory party atmosphere. Images of life in abundance and jars overflowing with wine seemed appropriate for this eucharistic celebration.

In her address, Ann reminded us that many of us in that congregation had overindulged. She reflected on the story as a threefold drama: the wine has run out; the party is over; the call is simply to do as he says. We have raped and pillaged the earth, filled it with noxious gases, altered our very climate, drunk ourselves silly, with no regard for those who come after, our own children and grandchildren – and the game is up. The renewal of the celebration will come when we repent of our selfish excesses and begin to take up God's work.

God saw everything that he had made, and indeed, it was very good. Let every vineyard in God's creation be glad and sing for joy.

We can still dare to sing

'Let the nations be glad and sing', 'let all the peoples praise you' (verses 4, 3). These beautiful words bring One World Week to a close. Frequently we feel insecure and anxious about the many challenges facing us, either real or imagined. In truth, the oil is running out, there is increasingly a lack of water or cultivable land; sea levels are rising. Some parts of the world are experiencing overcrowding, increase in gun crime, proliferation of nuclear weapons and terrorism, whether state sponsored or from rebel factions. The reality of our world can seem at odds with these words of the psalmist.

In 2007, Alan Johnston was taken hostage in Gaza. He was held for several months in a bare room. The only people with whom he had any contact were unpredictable, desperate young men, their identity concealed in headscarves. Sometimes he feared the worst. But hope never died. He remembered his childhood in Africa and the story his mum had told him of Ruth reaping the grain left at the edges of the fields. Everything was so strange, he felt as if he were like Ruth, a 'gleaner in alien grain'. This picture kept coming back to him and gave him strength and comfort.

Throughout the generations, a story from the Bible can be like the face of God shining upon us. In a world of discord, strife and injustice, we need One World Week moments every day of every week to remind us of the psalmist's vision.

God saw everything that he had made, and indeed, it was very good. May God continue to bless us; let all the ends of the earth revere him.

October

Hebrews

1 Jesus our great high priest

Notes based on the New Revised Standard Version
by Lori Sbordone Rizzo

*A native New Yorker, Lori Sbordone Rizzo has been a
'journeyman-teacher' preparing at-risk youth to pass
their high school equivalency tests. Theologically, she describes herself
as a revolutionary evangelical lesbian mystic. In 2009, she hopes she
will be doing more preaching, writing and fishing.*

The Epistle to the Hebrews is a sermon for a community in
trouble. Its original audience comprised Jewish Christians who
were just beginning to experience persecution. The reality that
their confession could lead to social alienation, political and
economic disenfranchisement, arrest, even torture, has shaken
their faith. The writer is one of their pastors. He (or she – there
are several women who could have penned this tract) longs
to deliver this message in person, but has decided that it is too
pressing to wait.

Preaching is pastoral care, and the pastor knows that what
the community needs most is Jesus. But who was this Jesus,
anyway? This was the question of the day. The preacher gives
his congregation a theology of Jesus that upholds his divinity as
the eternal Son of God, while at the same time emphasising his
compassion as one who became fully human so as to identify
with our condition and lift it to heaven upon his return. Sounds
like some tightly knit rhetoric, and it is. Hebrews gives us the
finest Greek in the New Testament, but at its heart there is a
pastor who knows that people need a God who is powerful
enough to overcome darkness, as well as one who will have
compassion on them when fear has caused them to fall.

Who is Jesus? How does your answer to this question shape how
you pray and how you live out your faith?

October

Rescue

This summer, we rescued a hatchling turtle from a pedlar who had him in a dirty basin on a crowded city street. We gave him a spacious glass aquarium on a sunny windowsill with plenty of fresh water. We bought him nutritious pellets, and we waited for him to eat. He ignored them. We tried other foods, brought in a lamp and heater to create the most comforting environment, but nothing seemed to motivate him. Finally, he snapped at a dried shrimp. We were ecstatic!

I pushed my best chair next to him; this little turtle has huge power to delight me. I wonder if he knows this, if he can even see me smile through the glass. He will live his life out on our windowsill; better than a basin on the street to be sure, and in these comforts perhaps he will feel our love for him. I have come to this conclusion: that if our effort has done little more than embody love for him, it is enough. We are all eternal. Life is not fleeting; opportunities to love and know love are.

God is more completely other to us than we are to turtles. He is not limited as humans are; he can do all things except lie. He has taken a 'by any means necessary' approach to embodying his love for us. The creator and sustainer of the universe is on our side.

O God, help me to know your love, and to allow that knowledge to change me.

Kenosis

Jesus enters human history as a comet. His birth sets the midnight sky ablaze in light. His death darkens midday. In his Sermon on the Mount, Jesus exhorts us to 'let your light shine before others' (Matthew 5:16). He pours out his own unto the last dregs. Theologians call this *kenosis*, from the Greek verb 'to empty': the love that Jesus showed when he emptied himself of his divine status in order fully to embrace our dilemma. The author of Hebrews says this was necessary 'so that he might be a merciful and faithful high priest' (verse 17). It is because Jesus laid aside his divinity and lived as one of us that we can trust him to understand our propensity to screw up. His human life is the seat of his mercy because in it he can comprehend who we are and where we are coming from prior to passing judgement.

It is uncomfortable to shift our thinking from Jesus our brother to Jesus our judge, and this is precisely because we know that we sin all the time. If I have to stand before Jesus today, the best I have to say for myself is this, 'With all the sincerity my twisted heart can muster, and with all the devotion my conflicted will can claim, I have sought to do your will. Even so, dear Lord, have mercy on me.' Kenotic spirituality is not losing yourself but yielding to the will of God, and so becoming united with him.

So God, where shall we go today?

Lost and found

There was a Lent of losing in my life. It started with jewellery, then a student, finally my partner and the home I knew with him. I leapt from friends' couches to squats in abandoned buildings to naps under trees in the park as one amongst my fellow vagrants. Every homeless person I met had a story. Here's mine.

In between coping with squats I was applying to be a full-time student at an Episcopal seminary. For months, I had been dreaming of a house in the woods where I could study scripture. I put in the application, all the time thinking, 'Am I crazy? I don't even have an apartment.' Then, a miracle, I was accepted and my tuition was paid in full. So I moved to Pennsylvania; the seminary found me a place to crash temporarily, but when I went to registration, my address form was blank. Then someone called me on the phone. There was a house in the woods outside of town; I could have it rent-free for the year. When I saw it, I fell on the ground. There was the house I'd seen in my dream. I remember telling God, 'All the time I was freaking-out about being homeless, you were standing there just waiting to drop this on me!' It stood in my future, like a great rest, waiting to reveal God's love to me. If life in that house is but a foretaste of heaven, O joy!

Today, if I hear your voice, let me not harden my heart.

Jesus our priest

Through ages and cultures, priests have been people who stand in the gap between humankind and God. The priest's job is to represent the people and hopefully convince the Almighty to look kindly and not wipe us out. The priest enters into the holy space with utmost reverence and leaves offerings. If all goes well, the priest returns with blessings. Obviously such a person must be called by God, otherwise they are not getting in the door, but you would also want a priest to share your experience because this way they can fully represent your dilemma to the Almighty. The God of whatever religion you choose can't grasp sin, nor can God comprehend what it is like to live surrounded by human failure.

In Jesus, we have a priest who is powerful to save precisely because he has firsthand experience of life within our reality. He knows who we are behind our most clever self-deceptions, and even in this he loves us. His love makes us want to be true. The author of Hebrews exhorts his congregation to approach God with a bold frankness (verse 16). The word in secular Greek suggests conversation between free citizens. It is used here to invite us to speak openly to God, not protecting him from our emotions or shaping our prayers as one would in a letter to one's boss. By the ministry of our great high priest, we can approach even the Almighty God with confidence.

O God, you know me and love me anyway. Help me to trust you to be honest in our conversation.

Falling away

I had an encounter with the love of God in college, but the church, as with all human institutions, bit me and the venom went straight to my heart. There were moments when I could sense the danger, but I didn't care; I was done with religion. One night, I was with some homeless friends sharing a beer around a trash-can fire, when someone tossed a Bible into the flames. 'Brilliant!' proclaimed my comrades, but to my great surprise, the sight repulsed me. Before I knew it, my hand thrust into the fire and yanked it out. My friends were aghast. I fobbed it off as a knee-jerk reaction to book-burning, but as I turned the charred volume over in my hands, I knew there was more. Something about it felt decisive, as if watching that Bible burn, joining in with my friends' ridicule as I always had, would take me to a place I could not get back from.

Who knows if this is true? It could easily be born of the high drama of youth. But if we believe ourselves to be in relationship with the living God, then we are wise to heed the writer's warning lest we take that relationship for granted. Maturity in the spiritual life is not naïve about danger. Thanks be to God, we walk in the watch of our Good Shepherd.

Jesus, you are a sure and steadfast anchor through times when I have been neither. Bind my heart to your hope.

October

Foreigners

My grandfather Tony arrived in New York from Italy, although in a very real way he never left. As immigrants before and after him, he sought out his townfolk (*paisans*) and developed a circle where they could eat, speak and act as if they were still in the old country. He learned English reluctantly and hated the food. I remember passing him a peach once and he spat it out; then babbled on about 'the peaches in Italy'. He squirrelled away cash for a ticket home; then at the moment of escape, when he found the money had been stolen, he drove his car into a wall. Life in the foreign place was unbearable.

Abraham was an immigrant. Like Tony, life was often difficult; it's not easy being a foreigner. Unlike Tony, Abraham's home was always before him. No thief could keep him from it. Like all immigrants, Abraham carried in his heart a picture of his homeland, but it was a place he knew only through faith.

Life within the kingdoms of this world often feels strange to me. Much of what it offers I spit out like bad fruit. Through prayer, in fellowship with *paisans* from the 'new country,' I have tasted much better fruit than anything this world has to offer.

We are all strangers and foreigners in a land where we don't quite fit, watching for the inbreaking of the kingdom, which we will at once recognise as home.

Comfort the homesick among us today, good Lord, and hasten the coming of your kingdom.

Hebrews

2 Faith, hope and love

Notes based on the New Revised Standard Version
by Lori Sbordone Rizzo

In its secular context, 'faith' is reserved for things
that are proven. My faithful fishing lure is the one
that produces fish. Anglers refer to it as their 'go to plug'. Every
cast is an act of hope, but with my 'go to' on the line I hope with
substance because I have the memory of prior results. On the
other hand, when I walk to the shore with unproven tackle and
there are no birds working the water and no signs whatsoever of
fish around, hope is hard to sustain.

Fishing teaches me about prayer. Fisherfolk set out to encounter
fish. If I didn't catch a fish at least once in a while, I'd probably
quit. When I pray, I set out to encounter God. If there wasn't at
least one time in my life when I felt a hit, I doubt that I could have
continued. God does not ask us to 'hope against hope'.

The author of Hebrews says 'Faith is the substance of things
hoped for' (11:1). Faith is the superstructure, the foundation
upon which our confidence rests. God has proven himself in
history and in my life. The memory of his faithfulness sustains me
on days when there are no signs whatsoever that he is around.
It empowers me to believe big things, for myself, my community
and the whole world for that matter. When our lives testify to
God's faithfulness, we give people the substance to hope for
themselves. If you ever need a 'go to prayer', tie this one on: 'O
God, glorify yourself in my life today'. It never fails.

*In what ways has God proven himself – in your life, in the lives of
others, in stories and in scripture? What conclusions can you come to
about the character of God?*

Faith in action

The roll-call of faith folk continues: ordinary people who found the courage to act in accordance with their confession. Next up: Moses – the Prince of Egypt who renounced personal power to identify with slaves. If this self-emptying love reminds you of Jesus, the preacher is smiling. In verse 27, he tells us that the reason why Moses was able to do these things is because he 'saw him who is invisible'. Moses acts like Jesus because Moses is in mystical communion with him. Apparently the transfiguration wasn't the first time these two met. In this mystical fellowship, Moses took on the likeness of Christ. He found it impossible to enjoy his privilege while others were being oppressed. He was unafraid in the face of Pharaoh and his chariots. He stayed on task and trusted God.

The preacher does not bring such giants of faith to this stressed-out community to humiliate them by comparison and so shame them into action. Rather, he uncovers the source of their courage – Jesus. All these believers – from the big shots to the forgotten – drew their strength from divine union with Christ before he ever took the trip to Bethlehem and was born of a virgin.

As God did for Moses, so God will now lift them into this divine dance that transforms short-sighted and scared human beings into the next generation of disciples.

Restore your divine likeness within me, O Lord, that I may act as you would in my day today.

Freaked

Christopher Street is the main drag for the gay community in New York, and the home stretch for our pride parade. Churches along the route usually close their gates early on that third Sunday in June, but one congregation decided to open theirs and asked me to preach. I pressed my alb, put a cross and a rainbow around my neck and stepped out into the celebration. People looked at me as if I was the freakiest drag queen on the block! Then I invited folk from the parade in, and they were dumfounded. A few climbed the steps, but fear stopped them at the door. You would have thought they were entering a horror show. 'If I walked in there, miss, the walls would fall down.'

I thought, 'What have we done to the church of God to turn it into a house of horrors?' Queers – be we gay, lesbian, transgender or simply strange – have been so hated by so-called Christians that in the eyes of the church we cannot imagine ourselves to be anything but dirty. Who needs it? We stay home, read our devotionals, and talk to God on our own terms. But we miss much by denying ourselves community. We miss the glimpses of heaven that corporate worship can give us.

When these shadows fade, and we, by grace, join the heavenly chorus, some people might be shocked by the company they are keeping. Oh well.

Jesus, you are the true priest. Have mercy on me, and write your law on my heart.

Actions have consequences

What's this connection between shedding blood and forgiving sins? The idea is somewhat of a relic. That actions have consequences, however, is a timeless truth, and our actions are not always done with the best intentions. The consequences of bad actions always cost somebody something. Blood is costly. It is the vehicle of life. Behind the arcane practice of ritual sacrifice is the painful observation that every one of our misdeeds, be they ignorant or willful, has unleashed bad consequences into others' lives. We have set consequences in motion that, to some extent, have drained the life out of people. As the ancients gazed upon blood pouring to the ground, perhaps they grasped the gravity of their actions and so resolved never to do them again. They went away trusting that they were right with God, not because some unsuspecting animal went in and paid their debt, but because in the course of that liturgy they resolved, by the grace of God, to change.

For those of us who confess Christ, the cross is where we look to understand the consequences of our misguided actions. And from the cross, Jesus looks at us and says, 'I know what you've done, and I love you still.' This is one way the cross heals: it reveals a love so huge that it cannot fail to change us. God willing, we will extend the mercy we have been shown to all we meet.

Lord Jesus, Son of God, have mercy on me.

God is not like us

If God was as I am, he'd be late. He would always have you stressing about whether he was going to show up on time. He'd be impossible to speak with in the morning until he had his coffee. If God asked me to leave heaven to live and die as a human being so that people who leave trash on the beach can be redeemed, I'd have suggested that he take that idea somewhere else.

The side effect of 'humanising' God is that we read into him all our limitations. We fail to comprehend his faithfulness, because we are not faithful. We refuse his forgiveness because we can't understand how anyone could be that merciful. We miss his love because our hearts cannot fathom its depths. If we cannot conceive of God as being more reliable than we are, it's small wonder that we lack confidence.

Scripture reveals a God who, from our first conversations, has been unswerving in his devotion to us and unyielding in his insistence that we can be far more than we imagine. It is the power of this story that the preacher recalls for a fearful congregation, so that they might find within it the almighty God and creator of the universe who, as it turns out, has been with them all along. How cool is that?

Today, God, I ask you to help me believe that you are as big as you say you are.

Hebrews

Juiced

The preacher has just finished invoking the names of those who stood for God's kingdom while they walked the earth, and have gone on to the church triumphant. They now become a grand cheering crowd that surrounds this community in the contest they must wage. If you get confused along the way, says the preacher, simply look to Jesus. Ask yourself what he would do, and then do it. Many take exception to this counsel, arguing that Jesus' unique parentage gave him special fuel that made radical obedience easier than it would be for mere mortals. The preacher of Hebrews would remind us that Jesus emptied himself of divine advantages before his birth.

Through the Spirit, we have the power to do anything Jesus did while he lived as a man, from feeding the poor to always choosing the Father's will, despite the personal cost. To quote both Jesus and Spiderman's Uncle Ben, 'From everyone to whom much has been given, much is required' (Luke 12:48). We have been given the power and authority to bring the kingdom of God into people's lives, just as Jesus did. When we fall short, it is not because God gave his Son performance enhancers and outlawed them for us. We have all we need to complete our task and join the immortals; if we feel faint, we need only reach out to grab a cup of water from the many saints who surround us.

God, I am no superhero, and I can't even imagine how to live like you today, but I am willing to try.

Outside the camp

They were suspicious of him, this rabbi who claimed his only teacher was Yahweh. There were questions about his family, his friends, his 'lifestyle choices'. Did they really give the man a proper hearing? Were they ever open to accept him as a gift? They just moved him from 'different' to 'dangerous'. In no time at all, he was outside the camp.

In Jesus' time, 'they' were the religious and political establishment. Now we are the 'they', the ones who miss gifts brought by people who are turned away from our churches because they smell or talk or pray funny. As the preacher says earlier in this chapter, 'Do not neglect to show hospitality to strangers, for by doing that some have entertained angels without knowing it' (13:2).

It is good to remember that our faith began outside the camp. Fundamentalists from Texas to Teheran have bad-rapped radical devotion to God; postmodern society wants 'reasonable religion', if any at all. How do we hear this call to revolutionary discipleship? Che Guevara observed that revolutionaries are driven by love. When you stand outside the camp, you realise that the camp cannot stand, and because you love you know that you have no choice but to make a better place for people to run to and be safe.

It sounds crazy, but can we love enough to become fools? That's hard to ask anyone, especially a New Yorker, but I am reminded that there's a new world coming, so we'd best get prepared.

Fit us for heaven, O God, even if it means that you must unfit us in our lives here.

Christian love

1   The greatest commandment

Notes based on the Good News Bible by Magali do Nascimento Cunha

Magali do Nascimento Cunha is a Brazilian Methodist, a journalist and an educator. She is Professor of Ecumenism and Church and Society at the Methodist School of Theology in Sao Paulo, Brazil.

'Love', as the old song says, 'is the greatest thing' and, when asked about the most important commandments, Jesus affirmed love as the greatest one. Although love has become for many just an overworked word in today's society, the sentiment is still true. God's love for us – that one unchanging certainty – is at the heart of our world, endless and to be relied upon. God's love for us is so great that God sent Jesus to show us the way of love, that we too might love one another. From love is born every good impulse we have: kindness, generosity, putting the other person first, refusing to give up on someone. We try and sometimes – often – fail to love, and yet tomorrow we will go on trying: because God first loved us. Further, we are to try to love our enemy, the person who insults us, whom we want nothing to do with. Everything in us wants *not* to love that person, and yet this is what God asks of us: because God first loved us.

To reflect on in the coming week

- 'Love' is a very common word in Christian circles, but frequently it seems that these circles remain locked into the abstract idea of love as a sentiment. What you think about this?

- Love of the other is to give one's life for him or her. This was taught by Jesus. Whom do you know – in your local community or more widely – who seems to exemplify this practice most fully?

The commandment of unlimited love

In this passage, when Jesus refers to the commandments of love, the Greek word is *agapao*, the verb 'love' that is related to the noun *agape* (love). This is not love as the feeling that a man has for a woman or vice versa (romantic love); nor the deep friendship among friends (philial love); nor the feeling of a father or mother for their offspring (parental love) nor that of a brother or sister for their sibling. *Agapao*, the word used by Jesus, means to love or to express love to someone who is near, to the compatriot, to the companion, or most widely, simply to the other.

When Jesus recovers God's commandment of love, there is novelty in his teaching. He emphasises the relationship with the other – the wide meaning of love that those who serve God must have. A Jewish tradition had limited this love to the one who was near, the compatriot from the land and the foreigners who inhabited the land, but not those from outside. Jesus enlarges this understanding, widens it to go beyond the boundaries of kinship or nationality. He recovers the meaning of love that is directed to the other. All are a target for this love, because God loves all people. This love is well expressed in the gospel of John when it refers to God's love of the world – 'so much that he gave his only Son…' (John 3:16).

Agape love is love not merely for this or that group, but for the whole world; a deep, not a superficial love, that gives of the uttermost. This is God's love – and God expects us to love in the same fashion.

God of all love, thanks for being the loving God who sent your Son to show us how to love according to your will.

Christian love

Doing as Jesus did

Presented by Jesus as the greatest commandment, love for the other was something lived out by him in his daily life. How did Jesus love others? By being among the people, especially those considered the worst or nothing at all, by talking and eating with them, by healing the sick and those considered impure, by releasing those imprisoned by evil spirits. These are just some examples.

Jesus, then, knowing that he would not remain much longer with the disciples, asks them to remain in his love (verse 9). And he does more: he tells them to love one another just as he loved them (verse 12). What can we conclude from this teaching? That to follow Jesus means to do as he did, to love as he loved. It means to be ready to give one's life for the other, sympathising with his or her needs, identifying with his struggles, rejoicing with her success, being among people as Jesus was, healing, releasing and so on. What a challenge for Christians, who identify themselves as Jesus' followers!

For those who answer the challenge and are faithful to the commandment, there is a promise: Jesus calls them no more servants but friends, those who know the will of the Lord (verses 14-15).

Dear Lord, it is not easy to love as you do. We ask for your mercy and patience so that we may learn to be your faithful disciples and good friends.

Love versus revenge

'Love' is a very common word in our world, found often in songs, movies and advertising. The word is also very common in Christian circles, frequently preached and sung about. However, we can notice that both in Christian circles and in wider society, the predominant idea of love is an abstract one: love as sentiment. In contrast, when teaching about love as a commandment from God (the will of God), Jesus speaks in a very concrete way. Living his own ministry as a sign of love, he teaches that to love as God does and wishes people to do implies humility, forgiveness and openness to the other – even if the other is an enemy.

We live in times when people learn revenge as a response to hatred, especially to violent acts. In armed conflicts at the national or international level we see leaders calling for revenge, justifying their call by appealing to the notion of the 'just war' or calling on biblical texts such as Exodus 21:24, 'an eye for an eye and a tooth for a tooth'. In countries where urban violence has made many the victims of robberies, murders or kidnaps and has created hatred and mistrust among citizens, revenge has a strong appeal, and even the death penalty is presented as a solution to violent crimes.

What do Jesus' words say to us and to our world today? Will Jesus' teachings find committed Christians to make them concrete in a world of violence and revenge?

Lord, make me an instrument of thy peace;
where there is hatred, let me sow love;
where there is injury, pardon;
where there is doubt, faith;
where there is despair, hope;
where there is darkness, light;
and where there is sadness, joy.

The Prayer of Saint Francis

November

Christian love

Making a difference

How does a Christian make a difference in our world? When I was a teenager it was very common to hear questions like this in the Protestant Sunday School class I attended. In Brazil, where Protestantism was brought by missionaries, most of whom based their preaching on puritan and pietist approaches, the answer to be learned was something like the following. A Christian is different by keeping Sunday holy, by avoiding drinking, smoking and dancing – which effectively meant distinguishing oneself from the majority of the other people, especially the Roman Catholics! As I matured in age and in faith, learning more about Jesus' teachings, I began to develop new understandings about the meaning of making a difference as a Christian. The apostle Paul helped me a lot with his writings. He says that we Christians, the people of God, must clothe ourselves with compassion, kindness, humility, gentleness, patience and tolerance, adding love to all this list, as it 'binds all things together in perfect unity' (verse 14).

Far more than an external appearance, as the Pharisees would have stressed in Jesus' time, God values attitudes that are faithful to his will and that keep love actively alive. It is this that really makes a difference in our world, especially in times when individualism, selfishness, arrogance and competition are dominant values.

Loving God, I wish to make a difference in the world, your creation. Help us, your followers, to keep compassion, kindness, humility, gentleness, patience and tolerance as our main values in life, and to demonstrate love in all that we do.

Good Samaritan or a Samaritan who was good?

I am sure that most readers of these notes will be very familiar with this parable, and will have heard many sermons on it. I heard one myself recently from a colleague and was struck by his approach. He raised the question: is this a good Samaritan or a Samaritan who was good?

In Portuguese, as in other languages, when we put the adjective 'good' before a noun referring to a person, we are usually saying that the person does everything that is expected of him or her, fulfilling all social and filial expectations. We speak of a good student, a good teacher, a good cook, a good doctor, a good father, and so on. In Jesus' times and context, a good Samaritan would be a person who would not relate to Jews (they were considered enemies), would worship God only in their own space (Mount Gerizim), would pass Jewish borders in a hurry to get out of Jewish environments, and so on. My colleague made us realise that, in fact, in order to be truly good to the other – his neighbour, the man who had been attacked on the road – the Samaritan had to forget all such ideas, deeply ingrained in his upbringing, and act in a completely contrary way, actually act as a 'bad Samaritan' in terms of his social and religious code of conduct. He had to relate to a Jew in order to help him, spend more time in a Jewish environment, show solidarity to a Jew in need, and so on.

I learned a new lesson from this famous Bible passage. Telling this story, Jesus was trying to teach a teacher of the law that sometimes we have to break conventions and do the unexpected to put love for others into practice.

Lord God Almighty, how great and wonderful are your deeds! King of the nations, how right and true are your ways.

Revelation 15:3

Christian love

Fighting with love

A song composed during the dictatorship in Brazil, when the armed forces were in power, expressed the people's hopes for change and the return of democracy. The refrain of this song went: 'my battle is, as the youth says, to stop with poems the mouth of the machine gun and to cover with flowers the rifle's barrel'. Military groups had used weapons to take power in Brazil and continued using them to keep that power for two decades, decades in which the people suffered grievously. The poet invited Brazilians to fight against the regime by using different weapons: weapons of love and tolerance (poems and flowers).

Paul, too, had been a soldier and weapons had been his tools of warfare, producing suffering. As a Christian, a follower of Jesus, Paul transforms his past experience and now uses the metaphor of the weapon to invite his brothers and sisters to engage in the cause of the gospel with love. Paul teaches that the world through sin produces fighting and jealousy, orgies and drunkenness, immorality and indecency, yet he invites Jesus' followers to face all this with love. Love is the only obligation that Christians have to the other. 'If you love someone, you will never do them wrong; to love, then, is to obey the whole law' (verse 10). Therefore, 'take up the weapons of the Lord Jesus Christ' (verse 14). That means mercy, dialogue, humility, tolerance, patience, indignation, compassion. These are the only weapons Christians need.

We offer you, dear Lord, our lives as your tools to make love a concrete experience in every place in the world. Receive this living offering.

2 What love means

Notes based on the New International Version by
Eun Sim Joung

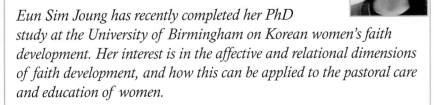

*Eun Sim Joung has recently completed her PhD
study at the University of Birmingham on Korean women's faith
development. Her interest is in the affective and relational dimensions
of faith development, and how this can be applied to the pastoral care
and education of women.*

We live in a world with many opportunities to learn. From cradle
to grave we are learning to live in many ways, whether we realise
it or not. We also live in a world of 'love deficiency'. Many relationships and families are broken and many individuals suffer
mentally because of this. Most of us are anxious to seek and
receive love of any kind. However, we rarely train ourselves in
how to love others.

Throughout the Bible, the message is focused on one word –
'love'. A number of words connote God's unconditional love for
us, for instance, intimacy, compassion, affection, mercy, forgiveness, redemption, and so on. This week's Bible passages help us
to learn to appreciate God's love for us and our need to love one
another.

For reflection during the coming week
• What kind of love have you been looking for in relationships
  throughout your life?
• Was or is there anything that stops you from loving others as
  God loves you?
• What was or is it?

For action and prayer
• Imagine you are a child of a loving God.
• Feel the warmth and intimacy.
• Imagine you are a carer like our loving God.
• Feel the compassion and rejoice.

November

Christian love

A high standard of action

This passage is also found in Matthew's famous sermon on the mountain, which was the first message that Jesus gave to the twelve disciples after he called them. Jesus asked his disciples to love their enemies, not the ones who were good to them. He expected a high standard of action from his followers. How high? Jesus commanded, 'Be merciful, as your Father is merciful.'

Today's Bible passage reminds me of a story about a Korean minister, Yang Won Shon. During the politically chaotic time before the Korean War, while taking care of lepers, Minister Shon resisted communism and sometimes got himself imprisoned. His two sons followed in his footsteps, and were mercilessly shot and killed by insurgent rioters. A few days later, one of the students who killed his sons was arrested. Minister Shon pleaded for the release of the boy from execution. After this was granted, he adopted the student, who later graduated from Bible school and became an evangelist. When the Korean War broke out in 1950, Minister Shon did not seek to escape but remained to look after the leper congregation. He was arrested and executed by the communists.

This man was a shepherd and a martyr who loved his enemies and was merciful as God is merciful, a true example of the kind of standard of love Jesus demands.

Take your time and think of people who have hurt you. Pray for them and for the grace to forgive. In what way can you can express forgiveness and love for them?

With actions and in truth

We sometimes experience our life as disordered, very dry or lacking any meaning at all. This is because we have lost touch with true love. We easily forget how much our family, friends and, most of all, God, love us.

In the last moments of his life in his farewell message, the writer of this epistle gently but firmly challenged first-century Christians, and also today's Christians, to love one another with actions and in truth. Love is the only command, both old and new (1 John 2:7) and without love no life is found in us. Only love can make us pass from death to life. John contrasts two love stories here: Cain's story in which his burning jealousy brought hatred and murder; and Jesus' story in which his life-giving love brought forth life. Jealousy is a form of misused love. In fact, love has the power to bring death when misused, but life when well used in truth.

John speaks of a love that is practical and concrete. That is, love is not expressed in words or by the tongue but in actions and truth. Love is not a passive emotion or attitude but a meaningful relationship and activity (3:17-18). It is not a state but an action. The actions, however, require a truthful heart. Without heart any actions are 'a resounding gong or clanging cymbal' (1 Corinthians 13:1). Love without actions is fake, yet good deeds and sacrificial actions without the whole heart are a waste. Both actions and heart should go together.

Lord, help us love you and the people around us with actions and in truth.

Christian love

The source and the norm

In today's Bible passage, John tells us about the love that comes from God and which is the essence of Christianity. This is an altruistic and self-sacrificing love that respects others and springs from the depths of the heart. John tells us two facts: that God is love and that love comes from God alone, who first showed his love for us by sending his one and only Son. He explains that this love is made complete in us if we love one another. In other words, we need to remember that we become complete only inasmuch as we love other people.

John mentions 'fear' as the opposite of love. It is not an exaggeration to say that all the problems in relationships and mental illnesses we experience in this world are caused by fear of receiving and/or giving love. Today's message declares that love that comes from God drives out our fear, as light does darkness. In marriages, friendships and communal relationships, God wants us to encourage each other and fulfil each other's needs. In fact, loving God and loving others cannot be separated because all unconditional love comes from God. Furthermore, loving oneself is not separated from loving others, because loving others makes us complete.

Take time to think about people who need love, and look for a special way to show your love for them this week.

Lord, let us always remember that you are the source and the norm of love.

Tired and wanting to blame?

This letter was written when Nero's persecution of the first-century Christians became severe. Peter encourages the Christians to be strong and to build each other up with love. Looking after each other while they were all suffering, they must surely have been tired and have blamed each other, even though they had seen Jesus' miracles and his resurrection and ascension. So Peter told them to serve one another with the strength God provides. He also asked them to offer hospitality and speak as if speaking words from God rather than grumbling. Like John and Paul, Peter urges love among the Christians, saying 'above all, love each other deeply, because love covers over a multitude of sins'.

True love endures others' faults. Love also guarantees others' freedom or privacy. Love surely sustains and enables others to stand, by offering help. Love does not dwell on faults or call to mind difficulties in relationships, so that close friends separate, but covers over an offence (Proverbs 17: 9). It builds and recovers one's relationship with others. It tolerates conflicts, differences and contradictions. It certainly enables us to endure and transcend our own fragility and sufferings, which will then enable us to take care of others' pain and needs. In this way, sufferings can be a gift to enable us to strengthen our own character, to come closer to God and to reach out to others.

Lord, have mercy on those who are suffering in body, mind, finances or relationships! Let them be strong and filled with love. Let them have hope that their sufferings will turn into blessing.

Christian love

Feeling awkard about receiving?

Jesus washed his disciples' feet just before the Passover feast and just before he was arrested by Roman soldiers, knowing that one of his disciples was going to betray him and he would be crucified. In this action, Jesus sets his disciples an example that they should serve one another.

The whole situation was awkward for the disciples. A conversation between Jesus and Simon Peter is described in particular detail (verses 6-11). In the conversation, Jesus challenges Peter, saying that the washing of feet is a symbol of love and of being in relationship with him. So having his feet washed by Jesus is receiving his sacrificial love and becoming a part of him. What an honour and privilege this is! The hands touching the disciples' feet were the same hands that caused many miracles. Jesus wanted his disciples to experience the privilege of this gracious act and he also wanted them to do the same for one another.

Today, we find many people, even Christians, who feel awkward about receiving love. People who have experienced rejection by parents from their early childhood particularly find it difficult to receive their wife or husband's love, or the love of a close friend. Overcoming their struggle to forgive their parents is a big issue in their growth in faith.

The ability to receive love is an indication of our maturity. One who can receive love can truly love others. One whose sins are forgiven is able to forgive others' sins. One who has a real relationship with God can make true relationships with others.

Imagine you are one of the disciples having your feet washed by Jesus. Feel the warmth and intimacy.

On the basis of love

This is Paul's private letter to Philemon asking him to welcome Onesimus, a slave, as a brother. From the passage, it can be deduced that Onesimus has run away from Philemon, so bringing financial loss to him and causing him offence. Onesimus, however, has changed and become useful after meeting Paul. On the basis of love, Paul now asks Philemon to do something that went far beyond custom, law and the cultural norms of those days – that is, to accept him, the runaway slave, as a brother. Paul says, 'welcome him as you would welcome me' (verse 17).

This letter is full of affection with heartwarming tones, describing Onesimus very dearly: 'my son', 'my very heart', 'very dear to me' are phrases indicative of Paul's great love for him. In the parable of the prodigal son, Jesus spoke of God's love for us in similar fashion. On the basis of love, the father demonstrated his forgiving, accepting intimacy and rejoicing to the son, giving no indication of the immense pain and grief he had suffered all the time that his son was away.

Today's passage teaches us there is no limitation to love. We ought to love people, whoever they are. On the basis of love, we can overcome differences of ideology, class, race, tradition, culture and also religion. Today discrimination and exploitation still exist in different forms, such as genocide, economic exploitation of the poor, child labour and sexual trafficking, and so on. We must remember that we are to treat others on the basis of love, whoever they are and whatever they have done.

Lord, forgive our ignorance, prejudice and insensibility towards the differences in others! Let us become instruments of your love.

November

Christian love

3 What love does

Notes based on the Revised Standard Version, Good
News Bible and Greek text
by Brenda Lealman

*Brenda Lealman has been a religious educator, adviser
and school inspector. Her special interest has been the place of
spirituality in education, and the place of the arts in spiritual growth.
She has published work on this, and she is also a published poet and
currently the chair of the UK organisation, the Creative Arts Retreat
Movement (CARM). She has travelled widely, including staying in
ashrams in India; as guest of the Diocese of Vellore, Tamil Nadu,
India; and as guest lecturer at a theological college in the Canadian
arctic. She is retired and lives on the North York Moors.*

Time and again the New Testament tells us that *agape* love is
communal; love becomes concrete in actions and expressions
of mutuality and interdependence. Love comes by grace and
by intent. It flows from our experience of God's love for us
or, put another way, when we sense that we live in an I–Thou
universe. The amazing discovery of so many people is that
through loving we know more and more deeply that we are
loved. Love is reckless, beautiful, challenging; it takes risks, and
brings often uncomfortable but wonderful growing. Irenaeus, an
early Christian writer, said that the glory of God is a human being
fully alive. Love is about coming fully alive. Most of us can only
dream about what that means. But to dream; to be excited by
possibilities and stretched towards action: isn't that part of loving?

Love is reckless gift and reckless giving

This is the story of people who have been stopped in their tracks and changed. They have fallen into love; into the wild energies of the Spirit; into fellowship, community. With reckless generosity they sell their possessions, provide for the needs of all – not just of those who belong within the fellowship. They are free and freed: freed from anxieties about loss of status, goods, lack of security; freed from self-assertion; from the need to justify or legitimise themselves; from power-seeking, competition, greed. They are freed into a radically new, creative way of living. The marks of this new community are fellowship, common life; teaching (sharing their intoxicating experiences of life in the Spirit); breaking bread together (which in the New Testament becomes a technical term for the early Communion service); sharing meals in their homes; worship and prayer. These people have been overwhelmed by the gift of abundant life that overflows in joy, praise and gratitude.

A golden age? A passing paradise? Is there anything in this for us? Too impracticable? Too unrealistic? We're opened to how we, too, could be taken by surprise and transformed. We are given a glimpse of alternative ways of being. We are given the possibility of joy; an expectation, a dream, to fire our hearts.

Give thanks to God.
Weave your thanks and/or dream into words, paint, music, embroidery…

Love is interdependence

Twenty years on from yesterday's reading and we're in Corinth, a prosperous city: two harbours, docks; shows at the theatre, music at the odeion; a colourful nightlife. Troubles in the church were enough to make any pastor resign: divisions; an avant-garde who saw no conflict between Christian commitment and a licentious lifestyle; marital troubles; visits to prostitutes; cliques following different brands of Christianity. Paul's response here is gentle and circumspect. Simply: get on with making the collection you started for the poor Christians in Jerusalem. Understand that what is needed is partnership, interdependence. Be a community of hospitality, accepting and sustaining one another; treat each other equally; meet needs without distinction. What is needed is sharing, caring, serving the common good. No need to make yourselves poor; to redistribute wealth.

Nothing exciting or radical here, you might think. But isn't this only the minimum they can do? Paul goes deeper: the gift and the pattern is the poverty of Christ who emptied himself to express love that seeks nothing. In Christ's poverty be emptied of self-absorption. Through mutual acceptance and reciprocity all will have riches; none will be the losers. Does such mutual recognition, esteem and sharing of burdens have the potential to become abundant generosity?

Name divisions/conflict in your local community or church, or nation. Pray for their healing.

How could you help someone to turn his/her loneliness/disability into a gift to share with others?

Love transforms

Family life and good household management were important in Roman society; they were signs of good citizenship. By law and convention, the household was patriarchal; in law a wife was her husband's property (and so were wives in England until the nineteenth century). Paul appears to accept this situation; to overthrow the social order isn't his priority. But the guidance he gives on family life is potentially subversive.

The bride prepares herself for her wedding day by having a ritual bath. Through washing and cleansing, Christ prepares the Christian community to come to its full stature and beauty. A husband should love his wife with the care and respect that he shows towards his own body, the marriage reflecting the mystery of communion between Christ and his church. Husbands must love their wives, and wives respect their husbands.

The Greek verb from *agape*, self-giving love, is the one used throughout this passage. Perhaps you're disappointed that the verb used of the wife's response to her husband's love is *phobatai*, 'to reverence' or 'revere'. Nevertheless, are there seeds here for the transformation of family life? For moving away from damaging possessive or codependent love to mutuality; to equality of family members within the fellowship of Christ; to recognition of uniqueness and mystery in all human beings.

Give thanks for those who have generously allowed you to grow; allowed your soul to break and bud, and grow shoots of glory, as one poet put it.

Do you try to affirm people? If so, how? How do you encourage people to value themselves and to go on growing?

Christian love

Love takes risks

From a worldwide perspective, the majority of Christians today are poor; many are discriminated against; many fear persecution or are persecuted. Here is a letter from an unknown writer to an unknown Christian community, possibly in Italy, and almost certainly one that has suffered ill-treatment, lack of popularity; at risk from persecution (perhaps near or in the time of Domitian, about 85 CE); in danger of giving up the struggle to be loyal to Christ. The letter inspires: 'Faith is to be certain of the things we cannot see.' But the unseen is reached only through taking risks in love (the Greek word used here is from *philia*, 'friendship').

For a moment let's stand alongside these poor, vulnerable, quite frightened people. Insecure, but we're urged to offer hospitality, to welcome strangers into our homes (how much easier to be censorious towards outsiders, backsliders). Suffering, we are reminded to be compassionate, to attend to others who suffer, who are in prison. Poor, we are told not to want more; but to be satisfied with what we have.

In Tamil Nadu, India, 95 per cent of Christians are dalits (outcastes); in various ways dalits are still discriminated against. I have stayed with these people; most are very poor indeed. But out of their poverty and insecurity come overwhelming hospitality, generosity, cheerfulness, joy. From such people we learn so much about what it is to be human without relying on the props of goods and status.

Find out more about present-day persecution on grounds of religion – for example, where there is persecution of the Christian church.

Help us, God, to live with less.
Could you live with less? What could you get rid of and why?

In love we grow to full stature

1 Corinthians 13 is like a mirror; across it move the shadowy figures of the Corinthian Christians: the elite, self-inflated, shaping church and faith to accommodate themselves; the poor, not 'our sort', especially when it comes to breaking bread together. Others who pride themselves on their advanced spirituality and gifts such as ecstatic speech, secret knowledge of inner truths; or on their celibacy. Perhaps we see ourselves somewhere in the divided church of Corinth (see verses 4-7).

Paul doesn't upbraid the Corinthian Christians for their failures. But, even genuine spiritual gifts, knowledge and prophecy are, without love, as hollow as the clanging of the bronze artefacts made in Corinth. Self-sacrifice in martyrdom is worthless without love, that is, *agape* or self-giving love that is of both grace and intent; that intentionally works for goodness; for those qualities that don't divide but unite, and serve the common good (verses 1-3).

The Corinthian Christians are living in a shadowland. They value qualities that are temporary, incomplete. But love gives undreamt of capacities, moves us into seeing from new perspectives that are more than personal. There's a mirror in fairy tales: you look into it but it isn't yourself you see; in this case, it's a glorious you, you grown to full stature in love (verses 4-7, 8-13.)

Make us hungry, God, hungry for goodness and beauty, and for…
Reflect on or discuss with a group: What is goodness? What is love?
What is damaged love; how does it manifest itself?

Christian love

I am the stranger who is knocking

Advent reminds us that we live precariously in the presence of the absent Christ. Precariously because the absent Christ comes, continually comes, and will come; and we have to decide: do we want the baby? Are we willing to allow him to grow up; to go where he leads us?

Matthew uses apocalyptic images: an imagined scene of judgement reveals what God expects of us. What matter are obedience, actions, deeds, justice. And justice means showing mercy to 'the least'. When did we feed the hungry, invite the outsider into our home, look after the destitute and sick, visit those in prison? There is a twist: we serve Christ through serving these 'least'. And, then, an even more remarkable twist: the Son of Man (Messianic title for Christ) is the 'least', the marginalised, the needy. How?

But Matthew would ask: what can we do? About the third of the world's population that has no toilet facilities? About the carer next door who gets little or no respite? About the helpless and rejected? About slavery, oppression of women, the armaments trade, and…?

Faith requires terrible decisions followed by actions. Let us pray that such actions are made in the context, not of calculation, not only of the possibility of suffering, but of reckless generosity, gratitude, joy – of love, in other words.

God, we are the needy. Have mercy. Help us to recognise what our needs are.

Make a list of the injustices you care most passionately about. What action could you take?

Is it that even a prayer, deeply felt, can change, in some way, a little bit of the world?

Readings in Revelation

I Letters to the churches

Notes based on the New Revised Standard Version
by Marilyn Parry

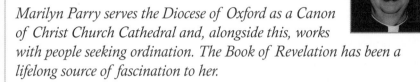

*Marilyn Parry serves the Diocese of Oxford as a Canon
of Christ Church Cathedral and, alongside this, works
with people seeking ordination. The Book of Revelation has been a
lifelong source of fascination to her.*

The Book of Revelation is a frustrating pleasure. It offers
encouragement for the Christian journey, but much of its
meaning is obscure and many of its passages are downright
offensive. We can never assume that we have understood the
text! Yet, the theme of the Apocalypse is relatively simple: John
wants to encourage folk to hang on to their faith in difficult
circumstances. However, John is not writing to churches
under persecution: the problem his hearers face is much more
subtle. They are Christians living in a well-ordered, stable and
prosperous society. How should they relate to their context?
Should they collaborate with it and live at peace, keeping the
faith in a quiet, personal, inoffensive and individual way? Or
should they resist, challenging the powers-that-be by insisting
that faith has public and corporate consequences?

John is critical of authority and suspicious of the forces that
sit behind it. He encourages discerning resistance rather than
blind obedience. This makes him the odd man out in the New
Testament. Unlike Paul or Luke, John does not think that the
ruling powers are divinely ordained and supported. He goes
further than criticism: he thinks that their downfall is essential to
God's purposes. The coming ordeal is the necessary conflict that
will usher in the kingdom of God.

November

Who's in charge here?

I need to keep on reminding myself that the Apocalypse was originally a 'heard' text (look carefully at Revelation 1:3). The strong images, repetitions and exalted language all make the spoken word stick in our heads. The text is most alive when the mind's eye images the words and remembers them.

The first vision is typical. John is earthbound on Patmos when suddenly the veil is ripped aside and the divine is disclosed. I wonder what you 'saw' as the event was described? Did you hear the images and remember Daniel's description of the Ancient of Days?

John is a man of his time and background. His vision of God must be interpreted through what he knows and expects. This way images are reborn and made fit for the present audience.

There are no half measures here: the Book of Revelation is an all-or-nothing text. Every element of this passage drives home the point that there is only one being running the show, the Lord who is the true author of the Apocalypse. The message comes from the God who is outside and throughout time. There is no one else worth a hearing. No wonder John is poleaxed!

What do you think you would see if you had a vision of God? How does your context shape this?

Lord Jesus Christ, you have loved us, freed us and made us into your priestly kingdom. To you be glory and dominion now and for ever.

School reports

When I was at school, I used to dread those times in the year when the progress reports went home for my parents to sign. There always seemed to be more complaints than compliments in the comments of my teachers. The letters to the seven churches (which we begin today) form a sort of report on their work. Because John wants to help his listeners, he uses a memorable pattern to structure the letters. As each angel is addressed, a bit of the description from yesterday's reading is borrowed, an assessment is made of the strengths and weaknesses of the particular church, and a reward is named. Each time, folk are urged to listen to what the Spirit says. This emphasises the solemn nature of the reports and their significance.

Even a quick reading makes it clear that the churches have work to do. Most have their good points, like endurance, but they also have their faults. The Ephesians are said to have lost their first love – they have slipped into complacency. Their faith is not passionate enough to hold true under test. They must try harder!

Through the next few days, make a short list of the strengths and weaknesses of each of the seven churches. Reflect on the significance of these characteristics.

Lord Jesus Christ, you are the Alpha and Omega, the one who is and who was and who is to come. Help us to love you passionately. To you be glory and dominion now and for ever.

Must pay attention!

Christ is in terrifying aspect here. Pergamum and Thyatira each have their strengths, but each church behaves in a way that comes under judgement. Food sacrificed to idols was a major issue for the earliest Christians, as was promiscuous sexual activity. Food caused problems because of its origin. If folk wanted to eat meat, they had little choice but to buy something killed in honour of an idol. Paul suggested not asking too many questions about the source of meat, unless someone's conscience was troubled (1 Corinthians 10:25). Then, a vegetarian diet was the only option.

The second issue, of sleeping around, is a double matter of faithfulness: to God and to one's lifelong partner. Both careless sexual behaviour and thoughtless consumption seem to be encouraged by some folk at each church (Nicholas and Jezebel), and this teaching is tolerated by others. But these behaviours blur folk's allegiance to Christ and entice them towards collaboration with that which is not God. The challenge is to see through these things to the truth. The churches need to be more single-minded in their devotion to Christ. Their report reads: must pay attention!

Christians worry a lot about sexual behaviour but, for the Apocalypse, carelessness about purchases is far more important. How does faith affect what you (or your church) buy?

Lord Jesus Christ, you pierce us with your sword. Help us to live as you would have us do. To you be glory and dominion now and for ever.

International Day of Disability

Fat or fit?

This passage doesn't concern the temptations of shopping. Rather, the focus is on health and fitness. For most of my life, I have been overweight, a problem that has grown over the years. While others think that I am happy, the truth is that I've been embarrassed by my shape and rather sad about it. Some time ago, I told someone the truth. She and others have helped me to make little changes to my life that are beginning to mount up. I hope that it doesn't take as long to get slim and fit as it did to get fat!

As it is with the body, so it is with the soul. The church at Sardis has a certain reputation: it looks alive and lively. But the truth is that it is decaying inside. If they don't act, they will soon be fit only for elimination. Changes will have to be made! On the other hand, little, weak Philadelphia is truly a hidden tower of strength. If it can keep on holding on, it will be a pillar raising the temple of God.

Collaboration and an easy life lead to flab. Resistance training leads to better things.

How are you on the inside? What *one little thing* can you change to improve your spiritual health?

Lord Jesus Christ, you are the true and holy one. Help us become fit for your kingdom. To you be glory and dominion now and for ever.

Risky behaviour

Today's reading makes it sound as if the church in Laodicea is a bit boring. They don't have enough faults to make them interesting, and there is nothing good enough about them to merit comment. They are tasteless, not worth eating. They are so dull that they don't even know that they have problems. As a friend of mine would say, 'they're so laid back, they're horizontal'. Only, horizontal isn't good enough for God.

The Almighty wants souls who will indulge in risky behaviour. After all, the calling is to imitate Christ, who lived about as dangerously as possible. Self-satisfied complacency isn't in it; remaking the self in Christ's image is what is demanded. But what does this mean? For the Laodiceans, the challenge is to be discerning about their own place. The things that they are offered by Christ are the very products and services that have made Laodicea wealthy. They specialise in eye ointments and fine cloth! The good Christians need to see their condition and their commodities clearly. They need to learn to strive for the real thing, the disciplines of faithful living that contributed to the establishment, not of the church, but of the kingdom of God.

You've now seen seven assessments of churches. Try writing an eighth letter, to your own church.

Lord Jesus Christ, you pierce us with your sword. Help us to live as you would have us do. To you be glory and dominion now and for ever.

On God's territory

Up to this point in the Apocalypse, we've been on firm territory, the physical earth. Now, we are about to enter an area that is much more explicitly God's territory. As we follow John into heaven, we step outside time into the always present reality of the Almighty. When we step through heaven's open door, we are home, even though we may not recognise it at first. God's territory is our territory; it is the place we are made to inhabit. Its worship is our worship.

Now we begin to understand the challenges facing the seven churches. Things earthly are much more real and attractive to humankind than things heavenly. Assimilation seems the best way of making a home in a strange land; it is the easier task. It is hard to keep on working towards kingdom location. Souls get weary – we've been refugees for a long time. There is the danger!

Nevertheless, now we know that heaven is our home and the vantage point of the visions, so earth becomes known as the place where evil gets the chance to suck folk away from the place where they belong. Discernment is essential; resistance is the only possible course!

Joining the worship of heaven is a way of reinforcing resistance. Perhaps it would help to use the heavenly anthem regularly to remind the soul of its true home.

Holy, holy, holy, is the Lord God the Almighty, who was and is and is to come.

Readings in Revelation

2   Seals, trumpets and woes

Notes based on New Revised Standard Version
by Ian Boxall

*Ian Boxall is tutor in New Testament at St Stephen's
House in the University of Oxford. A lay Roman
Catholic, who has taught in two Anglican theological colleges, he
teaches and writes widely on New Testament themes.*

Many people find this section of the Book of Revelation
disturbing, with its terrifying horsemen, plague-like trumpets
and dreadful woes. Perhaps it is good that we do so. But it is
important to hold on to the fact that Revelation is an apocalypse,
that is, an 'unveiling'. It unveils the truth about our world,
including its more disturbing aspects. In the kaleidoscope of
John's visions, the fragility of our worldly security is unveiled,
and the darker side of our political arrangements unmasked. As
vision after vision flashes before our mind's eye, we are invited to
reassess our own commitments and priorities.

But all this is located against a higher perspective. John sees the
heavenly throne room, which is the source of true power in
our world. God, and not any rival claimants, sits on the throne.
Moreover, the way in which God chooses to exercise this power
is revealed in the self-offering of Christ, and those who follow
Christ's way. The paradoxical way of the cross – the way of
power-in-weakness – is never very far from what John sees.

The power of weakness

What does true power look like? We tend to look for it in parliaments and royal palaces, in synods and university lecture halls. But earthly power often obscures its darker consequences: the plundered land, the silenced voice, the prison chains and the torture chamber. One struggles to hear the tears and cries of its victims, echoed in the bitter tears shed by John.

But John receives insight into another way of exercising power: God's way. The terrifying lion of the tribe of Judah is revealed as a slaughtered lamb. Yet, paradoxically, this sacrificial victim is powerful. His seven horns signify perfect power. He stands, despite having been slaughtered. His power lies precisely in giving his life.

And those who follow the Lamb's way respond by singing a song of worship. Singing, whether of protest songs or hymns expressing national or religious aspirations, is a powerfully subversive activity. Singing is what dictators move swiftly to quash. Similarly, true worship is not a flight from the real world, but entering more deeply into it. Moreover, this song of worship is infectious. The twenty-four elders are joined by thousands of angels, until the whole creation is caught up in this joyful and transforming song. John witnesses the apparently impossible; yet with God, all things are possible.

Lord, teach us your way of authentic power, that we may sing of this way in our hearts, and allow it to transform our actions.

Seeing our treasured worlds collapse

Four terrifying horsemen come galloping across the sky. At first they might seem unfamiliar to us, the stuff of fantasy novels or blockbuster movies. But watching them again, their faces begin to look only too familiar: military conquest; the removal of peace; human bloodshed; famine; death. These tragedies are so present in our world, and so bound up with human choices, that they have human faces.

Yet whose bidding are these horsemen doing? God's? But then, what kind of God rejoices in such human misery? Or are we seeing, in visionary form, the inevitable consequences of the worlds we ourselves create, constructed around our false gods? The result of such world-making is the opposite of God's creative action: a collapse from order into chaos.

Yet there is an antidote. God puts the slaughtered Lamb in control, accompanied by his army of martyrs, in order for God's new world to come to birth. But where would we rather locate ourselves in John's vision? Among the souls of the slain under God's altar, crying out 'How long?' Or among those under the rocks, preferring to be suffocated by their collapsing world? The fear of the Lamb's wrath is only too real: for there is nothing so terrifying as unconditional love. But the alternative is even more terrifying.

Are there aspects of your 'world' that you need to relinquish in order to make way for God's kingdom?

Lord, give us courage to surrender all that stands in the way of your kingdom, and to embrace that new world that you are bringing about through your Son.

A surprising multitude

Churches, like other human communities, have sometimes divided along social, cultural and ethnic grounds. We often prefer the purity of the 'in-group', the security of those who are the same as us. Certainly there is a purity demanded of God's people, a setting apart from others. Hence John hears that the servants of our God are to be sealed, marked out. God's people are marked out like the Exodus generation (Exodus 12), or the righteous of Ezekiel's Jerusalem (Ezekiel 9), marked with the cross-like *tau*. Moreover, in this call-up for battle, their ethnic origin seems very precise: twelve thousand males sealed from each of the tribes of Israel.

But again, John's vision challenges our horizons. What John actually sees is 'a great multitude that no one could count' (verse 9). The people set apart is not a small select group, but an innumerable company. It is composed of men, women and children, all willing to join the Lamb's battle. It is especially heartening that John is able to detect different languages and tribal characteristics within this colourful multi-ethnic band. Cultural and linguistic difference is not absorbed into some monochrome conformity. The church is so much greater than we would often make it, rarely less so.

Lord, our horizons are often so narrow, our attitudes parochial. Grant us a wider vision of your universal church, so that the world may believe.

The sound of silence

Many of us are afraid of silence. For too many, our frenetic, restless lifestyle hardly allows it. The relentless noise of our daily lives ensures that we generally avoid it. Hence the idea of a silence lasting about half an hour sounds intolerable. Yet silence, as our mystics and visionaries teach us, is golden. It brings us face to face with ourselves, in all our inadequacy and frailty. It prevents us running away from reality, and therefore brings us face to face with God. It takes us back to the beginning of all things, when out of silence God spoke his creative word.

Most importantly, silence in heaven enables the prayers of God's people to be heard. Like the prayers of the Exodus generation, which brought judgement plagues on Egypt, these prayers herald the trumpets of judgement. When God answers cries for justice and salvation, all that stands in the way of justice is judged. And that includes the ways in which we ourselves frustrate God's just and gentle rule.

So this passage sharply poses this question to us: do we really want God to answer all prayer, or only some prayer? When we pray 'Thy kingdom come', do we truly want our prayer to be heard?

How much space do you make in your life for silence?

Lord, lead us more deeply into silence, the silence that reigned when your Spirit hovered over the waters. In the silence, may we be recreated into the likeness of your Son.

Confronting the nightmare

John's Apocalypse can easily turn into a nightmare. Perhaps that is why it has particularly appealed to artists and poets, who are attuned to the deepest of human fears. Like the darkest of ghost stories, or the best of fairy tales, Revelation brings these fears and anxieties to the surface. In opening up the door to the bottomless pit, it enables us to confront and overcome them.

These fears may take very strange forms: grotesque demonic locusts with human features and scorpion stings; millions of frightening horsemen on fantastic hybrid horses. Whatever form they take, they can exercise a powerful grip on us, and even paralyse us. But God can release us from their control.

Nor are the demons only external to us. They can also be located deep within the human heart. There is a darker side to each of us that we rarely care to acknowledge. John's nightmare forces us to confront the demons within. It calls us to repentance. This, after all, is the basic call of the gospel. Confronted with the nightmare, we receive that gospel invitation to turn back, to change our minds and our hearts so that we can welcome God's kingdom with joy.

What do you find disturbing about these visions from Revelation? How might you reconcile them with your image of God?

Lord of freedom, set us free from all that enslaves us and terrifies us. Calm our fears, and hold us in your loving embrace.

Killing the prophets

No one really likes a prophet. Whether a Jeremiah, an Amos or a John the Baptist, prophets disturb us and enrage us. The prophet's fate is a salutary reminder of how even good, religious people can be driven to murderous hatred. Throughout history, God's people have persecuted, and even killed, God's prophets. We don't like what they say. We fear that they might see us as we really are. We hate their refusal to be tamed. We want their voices to be silenced.

In today's reading, John echoes the cry of William Blake: 'would to God that all the Lord's people were prophets'. The two witnesses, boldly prophesying, dressed in the sackcloth of repentance, symbolise the church's prophetic vocation. God's people are called to courage. God's people are called to speak God's word. God's people are called to witness to God's alternative kingdom.

And like prophets throughout history, the prophetic church is also the martyr church. Indeed, our word 'martyr' comes from the Greek word for 'witness'. There are many places in today's world where God's people know this only too well. Other parts of the church, however, are marked by timidity and bland respectability. Perhaps our own witness is like that. 'Woe to you when all speak well of you,' says Jesus, 'for that is what their ancestors did to the false prophets' (Luke 6:26).

Find out about Christians in today's world who suffer persecution for their witness to Christ. Name them before God in prayer. In what other ways can you show solidarity with them? What can you do to make others more aware of their plight?

Lord, give us courage to speak your word with boldness, to ourselves first of all, but also to the world.

Readings in Revelation

3 The triumph of the Lamb

Notes based on the New Revised Standard Version
by Christopher Rowland and Zoë Bennett

*Christopher Rowland is Dean Ireland Professor of the
Exegesis of Holy Scripture, University of Oxford.*

*Zoë Bennett is Director of Postgraduate Studies in
Pastoral Theology at the Cambridge Theological
Federation with Anglia Ruskin University.*

For biographical details see p.358.

The book of Revelation provokes a mixture of
incomprehension and perhaps distaste. The imagery is more
akin to the fantasy world of science fiction than religion. Reading
Revelation is much like reading a good political cartoon, which
pierces to the heart of the pretence of our political processes
in a way that the well-argued editorial often cannot. Instead of
supposing Revelation is a problem, perhaps we ought to ask
ourselves why we have so much difficulty with the book. Is it
asking awkward questions of our view of the world that we
would prefer not to face up to? How can this text illuminate our
deepest fears and hopes? Have there been times (perhaps in a
dream or nightmare) when we have experienced such intense
feelings of solace and relief?

John sees his vision in exile and writes to churches, some in
situations of persecution, but elsewhere, the issues seem to
be more concerned with churches who (like many down the
centuries) have lost the cutting edge of following the Lamb
wherever he goes.

Readings in Revelation

The way of the Lamb

Above the high altar in Westminster Abbey these words from Revelation meet the worshippers. Here in a church full of the tombs of the kings, queens, princes and the great and the good there is a reminder of the message of the book of Revelation: those who are the great and the good in their generation have to learn the ultimate truth of the way of life of the Lamb who himself was a victim of the cruel tyranny of the representatives of the kings of the earth of his day. This is the paradigm that Christians are called to follow. Down the centuries there have been many who have pointed to such a way and paid the price.

Prisoners of conscience, like Aung San Suu Kyi in Burma, have seemed a fragile response to military power and might. Revelation reminds us that it will not always be thus and that such testimony, even if quenched, will have its contribution to history under God.

The following prayer could be used throughout the week.

O God, give us courage to stand up and be counted, to stand up for those who cannot do so for themselves when it is needful for us to do so. Let us fear nothing more than we fear you and let us love nothing more than we love you – for thus we shall fear nothing also. Let us have no other god before you, whether nation or party or state or church. Let us seek no other peace but your peace, and make us its instruments, opening our eyes and ears and hearts, so that we should always know what work of peace we may do for you.

Jim Cotter, Prayers at Night's Approaching, *Cairns Publications, 2001, p.64*

Anything for a quiet life?

The message is a simple one: a pregnant woman is threatened by a dragon. She gives birth to a male child who is precious to God as the Messiah (cf. Psalm 2:9). The story of persecution is followed by the account of another struggle in which there is war in heaven between Michael and the dragon who had persecuted the woman. Michael and his forces prevail, which means that there is no longer a place in heaven for the dragon.

The vision suggests that a heavenly struggle is closely linked with the earthly struggle of those who seek to be disciples of Jesus and to maintain their testimony (verse 10). The maintenance of that testimony in the face of the temptation to a quiet life is another way of speaking of the overcoming of the forces of darkness in heaven by Michael and the angels of light.

As the letter to the Ephesians puts it, the struggle that those who seek God's will are involved in is with 'principalities and powers, (Ephesians 6:12). Revelation challenges us to see that our true struggles are not the resisting of petty temptations or peccadilloes but the resisting of those larger forces of evil that bring death to others and to society. We are part of a much larger struggle to offer life, hope and human flourishing.

What might it mean to maintain the testimony of Jesus? How would we explain our choice to someone and what justification would we offer on the basis of the Bible?

Standing out against the crowd

The consequence of the defeat of Satan in heaven is that he is thrown down to earth (cf. Luke 10:18 and John 12:31). John, inspired by Daniel 7, shows us the particular manifestation of that activity in the vision of the two beasts.

The beast attracts universal admiration for acts that appear to be beneficial (verse 3). Public opinion goes along with the propaganda of the beast and its supporters (verse 11). There is pressure on people to conform and be marked with the mark of the beast (verse 14). Those marked with the mark of the beast have freedom to go about their activities, whereas those who refuse to be so marked, and side with a different way of life that takes a stand for justice and community, are persecuted. Those who persevere (an important theme of Revelation) are shown that the might of state power is fragile, and its affluence, so attractive and alluring, is destined for destruction – destroyed by precisely that power which has maintained it (as we shall see later).

In the run-up to the Iraq War, hundreds of thousands of people around the world were stirred to go on to the streets and protest at the imminent war, protesting against the spurious reasons (as it turned out) given for the invasion, and the fear, death, destruction, terror and injury caused.

Where are the activities of the beast in 2009? Are we willing to stand up to be counted? If not, why not, and how does Revelation help us to judge?

Understanding the consequence of our choices

As in chapter 7, where John sees the vision of the multitude that none can number, so here too those who conform to the ways of the beast may achieve a respite and prosperity. But it is only temporary. John's vision here offers hope to those who stand firm (verses 1 & 12). Those who have compromised realise the error of their ways (verse 6).

In rather brutal fashion the vision brings home the ultimate character of our choices and our apparently harmless actions. We may think the odd bit of compromise with society's values is nothing, but Revelation asks us to take seriously the consequences of our choices. This may mean nothing less than being marked by the beast (verse 9). It is not good enough to say 'we were only doing our duty', or 'we were only being good citizens', or 'I had to look after my family and my interests; what else could I do?'

We may imagine that we can sit back and feel that we are there with the Lamb on Mount Zion. But the book of Revelation doesn't allow us the comfort of such complacency. The Laodiceans in chapter 3 were reminded that, though they were good church people, Christ stood outside the door and was knocking to gain entry – even as they remained unaware of his call to service and witness.

Save us, O God, from complacency and conformity to what is less than Christlike, so that all our choices may be good and true.

Reaping what we have sown

Support for injustice at the expense of integrity and a way of life that promotes justice for all will reap its own reward (verses 15ff), for the message of Revelation is that God's righteousness and truth will ultimately prevail. The terrible images and the violence here are off-putting. But as so often in Revelation they present us starkly with the ways in which our life choices have consequences for the world and for others. Our wellbeing may be at the expense of others. Judgement in Revelation is not about feeling all right with God but about appropriate actions – not going along with the crowd, being prepared to stick one's head above the parapet.

As you look at passages about judgement in the New Testament, consider the criteria. In Revelation 20:12 the judgement is according to what we have done. That is exactly what we find in the awesome judgement scene in Matthew 25:31-45.

What life choices do you make personally and politically that promote the wellbeing of the majority of the world's population?

Exulting at liberation

When the people of Israel reached the other side of the Red Sea they sang a song giving thanks for their political liberation (Exodus 15). That song is echoed in Revelation 15. Like the slaves who escaped from Egypt with nothing but trust in God and God's advocacy, so those who remain committed to the cause of justice can hope for vindication.

Those who have been in slavery, whether literally or metaphorically, have looked and longed for their vindication. Many have rejoiced, anticipating their liberation – whether their hope was realised or not – in ways similar to what we find in this chapter. And the vision of vindication we find here has sustained many, down the centuries, to endure horrendous conditions of enslavement and to trust in the one who ensures their final liberation and release. Perhaps there is a sense in which only those who have known something of enslavement can know the depths of joy of which this chapter speaks.

Do we have the right, or find it in our experience, to sing this song? Or are we enslaved to a culture that is enslaving others and condemning them to a life of poverty and death?

Readings in Revelation

4 God's wrath and God's salvation

Notes based on the New Revised Standard Version
by Christopher Rowland and Zoë Bennett

*For many years Christopher Rowland has been
studying the thought world out of which the Book of
Revelation emerged and believes that it pretty accurately
represents the thought world of Jesus and Paul. He
has written of the way Revelation has been interpreted
down the centuries in art as well as in theology, and has*

*just completed a book on one of the great interpreters of Revelation,
William Blake.*

*As well as her academic career, Zoë Bennett is a reader in her local
Anglican church and a member of Women in Black, an international
women's peace movement.*

The passages we read from the book of Revelation in this coming
week offer us shocking contrasts: on the one hand, images of
wrath, punishment, intense pain and horror; on the other hand,
images of rich beauty, of joy and of intimacy. God is the bringer of
all this 'weal and woe'. God is in charge.

What does it mean to live and act in this world against the
backdrop of this kind of vision? As we move towards Christmas,
and beyond Christmas, what does it mean to say 'Emmanuel:
God is with us'? In these readings we reflect on the pain of the
world, and on what it might mean to think of God's involvement
with us and with this world, both in judgement and in intimate
communion.

Who is writing the script?

This passage is full of shocking reversals of what we might expect. Angels bring pain. There is blood to drink. Plagues come by God's authority. The river Euphrates dries up. As the seven bowls are poured out on the earth, the reality of God's wrath is hammered home in escalating horror.

In Advent of 2002, in the run-up to the invasion of Iraq, my daughter who lives and works in the Middle East remarked, as she watched the television news, 'I don't know what they are discussing this for; the script is already written.' She meant: the script has been written by Bush, Blair and Saddam Hussein. I had to preach an Advent sermon the next day; I was expected to say that the script had been written by God. I was left with two questions: who is writing this world's script? And, given that it is a script of pain and blood, of darkness and agony, what does it mean to say God is writing it?

How would you preach the 'true and just judgement of God' in the midst of the intense pain of situations like that in Iraq? How would you have preached the next day after hearing my daughter's remark?

Write a letter or email to a person who is writing the script in your context, pointing out an issue of injustice, and the action you would like to see them take.

Lord, have mercy.

"'Tis pity she's a whore'

This is a passage about violence, about the abuse of power, and about the assault on God's ways and God's witnesses. Central is the image of the great whore of Babylon, the sexually promiscuous woman, drunk with the blood of the saints. The promiscuous and dangerous woman, who destroys the individual man and endangers the public social and moral order, is a commonplace of our social imagination. We see her extensively in literature, in mythology and in religious imagery – for example, in the prophecies of Hosea and Ezekiel. This damaging image often leads us to dwell on the supposed fickleness and destructiveness of women. But this 'whore' will later be killed by the very people who have used her (verse 16). Thus the image of the whore also leads us to reflect on the ways women are abused, privately and in the public realm. Prostitution, 'whoredom', in all its forms, is a symptom of the disease of patriarchal society. Women are used and abused.

What images of women as sexual persons are most commonly used in your context? Are these positive or negative? Are they in any way connected with images found in the Bible?

O God, who sees with the eyes of wisdom and compassion, look in mercy on all those who are abused – by the violence of the state, by the violence of persecution, by the violence of sexual domination.

A cargo of human lives

The image in verses 12 and 13 of a cargo ship in which human lives are carried like just so much iron, olive oil and cattle reminds me of the horrific scene in Michael Winterbottom's documentary film *In This World* where the refugees and asylum seekers are packed into an airless cargo hold and begin to die. This chapter paints a grim picture of what the wealthy part of the world does to everyone else, living in luxury founded on the poverty and slavery of others. Whether we look at arms dealing, climate change, extraordinary renditions or trading policies, we see the rich and powerful exploiting the needy and powerless. In this chapter we have a potent vision of the great city fallen, the reversal of fortunes, wealth laid waste, and the judgement of God. The contemporary singer and social activist Garth Hewitt sings of how the rich countries 'love to invest' in unjust systems that reinforce poverty and war for millions.

Watch a film that illuminates the injustices perpetrated and condoned by those who enslave others and trap them in pain and poverty: for example, *In This World*, or *Lord of War* with Nicolas Cage, which looks at arms dealing, or perhaps *Lilya 4Ever*, which deals with sex trafficking.

God of judgement, we pray you will act on behalf of those whose lives are traded for wealth, and goad us also to act.

'I a child and thou a Lamb'

The image of the Lamb as a symbol of Jesus Christ is central to the book of Revelation. The Lamb is the one who was slain – a difficult image for us as animal sacrifice is not part of our culture, although images of lorry-loads of penned animals and foul slaughterhouses may come to mind. The Lamb is also the innocent one, the one who is 'meek and mild', a subversion of the violence of God presented in the text.

In Blake's poem, 'The Lamb', which gives us today's title and prayer, the little child talks to the Lamb, saying how alike they are, and blessing the Lamb. It is a picture of human and divine gentleness and harmony. As we have read the book of Revelation, it may have seemed to us that God's answer to violence and evil is just more effective violence against the enemies of God. The image of the Lamb undermines that picture, reminding us of what we also know from the life of Jesus – that the one whom we worship is in the end one who is crucified, not one who goes around crucifying other people.

As we think this Christmas Eve of the marriage feast of the Lamb, of the 'salvation and glory and power' of our God, and of the angels who give testimony to Jesus, we remember the vulnerable little child born in Bethlehem.

Little Lamb, God bless thee.

Images of intimacy

Emmanuel: God with us. Today's passage is filled with images of intimacy that evoke in us a sense of what it might mean that 'the home of God is among mortals' (verse 3): sexual and social union, comforting someone who is mourning, wiping the tears from someone's eyes, a trustful relationship, giving water to drink, or a child who inherits. These familiar images of human life awake a sense of longing and belonging. Here we have comfort, nourishment and protection; these are basic human needs we all have. God's ultimate capacity to meet these, even in the face of death, is proclaimed. Verse 8 is more difficult: we all long to belong to the 'in crowd', but is it at the price of excluding the outsider?

As we celebrate the beginning of Jesus' life today we remember that Jesus had these needs too – needs for intimacy, belonging and protection. He also faced death and found resurrection; and he did not exclude the outsider.

This Christmas Day take one deliberate action that gives the gift of human intimacy to another person. It could be one of the actions that are used as images in this passage.

Intimate God, we thank you today that you have made your home among us. We remember Jesus born as a baby. Help us to live in intimacy with God and our fellow human beings by the Spirit of Jesus Christ dwelling in us.

St Stephen

I remember as a teenager seeing a film version of the story of the three young men in the fiery furnace (Daniel 3). Maybe our God will save us, they said, but even if he doesn't, we won't bow down and worship this load of rubbish of yours. This chapter of Revelation tells a complex tale, in which those who have stood up for what they believe and not worshipped the beast (verse 4) are ultimately vindicated, but not without first paying the price of death for their integrity.

Today is the day we remember St Stephen, the first Christian martyr (witness). His story is told in Acts chapter 7. He was a man full of the Holy Spirit and of wisdom, who testified to the presence of the Spirit of Jesus with courage even when he was vilified and stoned. He was not afraid to challenge those whom he saw as opposing God's truth and God's purposes. He did not 'worship the beast or its image' (verse 4).

What is the 'load of rubbish' that we are tempted to worship instead of the living God? What would giving 'testimony to Jesus' mean in our context?

Pray for those whose lives are in danger because of their testimony to Jesus and to his ways. Try to find the name of one particular person to pray for.

We thank God for the memory of Stephen and for all those who have given courageous witness.

Revealing things as they really are – in fallible human words

The Word of God comes in garments dipped in blood –but it is his own blood, not his victims'. Instead, his effect on those around him comes with the breath of his mouth. These two facts are an important reminder that Revelation throughout subverts the less palatable sides of the imagery. Conquest, for example, is never by force of arms, but by the word of one's testimony. So, words of truth have always had their effect. Here the revelation of things as they really are – the condemnation of millions to lives of misery for the benefit of the few – is a truth that the oppressors have to face up to.

This vision is a reminder to followers of Jesus that God does not allow injustice to remain for ever. The picture of Christ as judge is disturbing, however. Revelation represents one pole of the Christian gospel: the justice of God. Balancing justice and mercy lies in the depths of both Jewish and Christian traditions. Love's ability to 'cover a multitude of sin' (1 Peter 4:8) in a vision of eternal inclusion is always in danger of baptising the status quo of this world's injustice, as the kings, magnates and captains stream into the kingdom on the tide of the love of God. Such sentimentality is challenged by the apocalyptic vision of the book of Revelation.

How have our words had effects on others for good or ill?

Almighty God, to whom all hearts are open, all desires known, and from whom no secrets are hid, cleanse the thoughts of our hearts by the inspiration of your Holy Spirit.

from the Collect for Purity, Book of Common Prayer

December

'I will not cease from mental fight'

The English poet William Blake has inspired generations of people to want to 'build the New Jerusalem' in their own land. He understood this book well and saw that this task required what he called a 'mental fight' – the kind of costly witness carried out by the prophets and those who refused to be marked by the beast. It's not a matter of sitting back and waiting for it to happen, therefore.

There is no temple because the whole of the city is a space pervaded with the glory of God and the Lamb. It's a reminder of the ambivalence towards buildings in the Bible and raises a question about the enormous investment in its buildings by the Christian church down the centuries.

John's vision of a city is communal, a reminder that biblical practice and hope are centred, from first to last, on relationships between humanity and God and humans one with one another. Christianity has too often focused on hope for the individual so that it has lost sight of the central place community and mutual engagement plays in past, present and future expressions of human destiny. Nor is John's an exclusive vision. The light of God's glory is a light for the nations, and the glory of old age is to be brought in.

What do you consider should be the main characteristics of the New Jerusalem? How would your vision differ from John's and why?

Seeing God face to face in a world of plenty

The climax of John's vision in verse 4 has the inhabitants sharing God's character and seeing God face to face (see Matthew 5:8). This is not merely something to be looked forward to in some life after death. Jesus reminded his disciples that the one who sits on the throne of glory is present in the midst of the injustice of the old order (Matthew 25:31-45).

The final chapters of Revelation both console the bereaved and the vulnerable, but also challenge and warn the readers. The vision confronts us with the reality that things, here and now, are profoundly *un*well and that repentance and change of life is required. A profound *dis*ease is present in a world where there is so much plenty, but inadequate provision for the sick and dying. The promise of a new heaven and a new earth involves a vision of judgement on those of us who, without realising it, uphold the culture of Babylon, where money and privilege can buy success, health and wellbeing; where the good life for many people, young and old, is subordinated to the demands of economic accounting and ability to pay.

What would count as 'the healing of the nations' (verse 2) in the contemporary world? What is it that would make for our peace? Can the book of Revelation help us to address that, or is it only a text that can shock us and help us come to our senses?

December

Heeding the wisdom of the eccentrics and non-conformists

In the concluding words of Revelation, we are left in no doubt about the importance that John thought should be attached to his book. This is the book with the most exalted status in the New Testament (verses 6, 18-19), yet it is the one that is least read and most widely feared or misunderstood.

Visionaries are often eccentric. What they see can encourage things that are humanly damaging. They are not immediately to be rejected out of hand, however. The challenge is to learn new habits of mind and behaviour in the face of the other.

Even if we struggle with this book or are uncomfortable with the import of its message, we must not ignore it. Perhaps the problem is that we have tried to understand it when we should have let it stimulate our imaginations to think anew about our world and our role in it. Keeping its words (verse 7) is to allow our outlook on life to be challenged. Its images can, if one allows them to do so, transform action as well as attitudes.

How can you find ways that would enable the challenge of Revelation to be expressed (by pictures, cartoons and the like, for example), which would allow its challenge to be heard afresh by people today?

INTERNATIONAL BIBLE READING ASSOCIATION

A worldwide service of Christian Education
at work in five continents

HEADQUARTERS

1020 Bristol Road
Selly Oak
Birmingham
B29 6LB
Great Britain

www.christianeducation.org.uk
ibra@christianeducation.org.uk

and the following agencies:

AUSTRALIA

UniChurch Books
130 Little Collins Street
Melbourne
VIC 3001

GHANA

IBRA Secretary
Box GP 919
Accra

asempa@ghana.com

INDIA

All India Sunday School Association
Plot No 8, 6th Cross,
Threemurthy Colony
Mahendra Hills
Secunderabad – 500 026
Andhra Pradesh

sundayschoolindia@yahoo.co.in

Fellowship of Professional Workers
Samanvay
Deepthi Chambers
Vijayapuri
Hyderabad – 500 017
Andhra Pradesh

hyd1_cipiardi@sancharnet.in

NEW ZEALAND

Epworth Bookshop
157B Karori Road
Marsden Village
Karori
Wellington 6012

Mailing address:
PO Box 17255
Karori
Wellington 6147

sales@epworthbooks.org.nz

NIGERIA

IBRA Representative
Hinder House
The Cathedral Church of St David
Kudeti
Ibadan
PMB 5298
Ibadan
Oyo State

SOUTH AND CENTRAL AFRICA

IBRA South Africa
6 Roosmaryn Street
Durbanville 7550

biblereading@evmot.com

If you would like to advertise in
Words for Today please contact our
Marketing Department at:

IBRA
1020 Bristol Road
Birmingham
B29 6LB

telephone:
0121 415 2978

email:
marketing@christianeducation.org.uk

Scheme of readings for 2009

READINGS IN LUKE
The coming of the Messiah

THE ECONOMY OF GOD
The economy of grace
The economy of fools

READINGS IN LUKE
Beginnings

CLOTHING
Clothing our nakedness
Robed in honour and glory

READINGS IN GENESIS 1-35
In the beginning
The great flood
God's covenant with Abraham
Abraham, Lot and Isaac, Jacob

READINGS IN LUKE
Confrontation in Jerusalem
The way of the cross
The risen Lord

RESTING PLACES AND SACRED SPACES
The divine imperative to rest
Resting places in the Old Testament
Resting places in the New Testament

THE JESUS WAY
Seeing, touching and tasting/eating
Showing, walking and praying
Living and loving

ROMANS 1-8
Good news for sinners
All have sinned and are now justified
We have peace with God
Life in the Spirit

PETER THE APOSTLE
Peter and Jesus
Peter, a leader

MOODS AND EMOTIONS
From sorrow to joy
From despondency to hope
From anger to creative action
From jealousy to contentment

READINGS IN LUKE
Forerunner and followers
Making people whole

SILENCE
Old Testament silences
New Testament silences

RIVERS OF THE BIBLE

WRITING
Stones, letters and graffiti
Keeping what is Important

OLD AGE
Reflections on old age – God is there
Old age – lived with God

MICAH
What angers God?
What does God require and promise?

RECONCILIATION
Be reconciled to your brother
Called to be reconcilers

WOMEN OF THE NEW TESTAMENT
Women disciples
Women in the early church

READINGS IN LUKE
Living in the kingdom
Stories of the kingdom

TREASURES OF DARKNESS
Are your wonders known in the darkness?
God leads the Israelites in darkness
Darkness in Jesus' life, death and resurrection
Riches hidden in secret places

READINGS IN MATTHEW 1-2
Emmanuel, God is with us

International Bible Reading Association

Help us to continue our work of providing Bible study notes for use by Christians in the UK and throughout the world. The need is as great as it was when IBRA was founded in 1882 by Charles Waters as part of the work of the Sunday School Union.

Please leave a legacy to the International Bible Reading Association.

An easy-to-use leaflet has been prepared to help you provide a legacy. Please write to us at the address below and we will send you this leaflet – and answer any questions you might have about a legacy or other donations. Please help us to strengthen this and the next generation of Christians.

Thank you very much.

International Bible Reading Association
Dept 298, 1020 Bristol Road
Selly Oak
Birmingham
B29 6LB
Great Britain

Tel. 0121 472 7272

Fax 0121 472 7575